*Ti*

# TIME AND CHANCE

Anne Weale

ARROW BOOKS

Arrow Books Limited
20 Vauxhall Bridge Road, London SW1V 2SA

An imprint of Random Century Group

London Melbourne Sydney Auckland
Johannesburg and agencies throughout
the world

First published in Great Britain by Century 1989

Arrow edition 1990

© Anne Weale 1989

Phototypeset by Input Typesetting Ltd, London
Printed and bound in Great Britain by
Courier International Ltd, Tiptree, Essex

ISBN 0 09 9967430 0

*For all my women friends.*

*Without them – their letters, telephone chats, hospitality, advice, jokes, criticisms and encouragement – my life would lack one of its most enjoyable dimensions.*

*And, as always, for my best and dearest friend – Malcolm.*

. . . the race is not to the swift, nor the battle to the strong, neither yet bread to the wise, nor yet riches to men of understanding, nor yet favour to men of skill; but **time and chance** happeneth to them all.

*Ecclesiastes Chapter 9, Verse 11*


I believe in an aristocracy – not an aristocracy of power, based on rank and influence, but an aristocracy of the sensitive, the considerate and the plucky. Its members are to be found in all nations and classes and all through the ages. They represent the true human tradition, the one permanent victory of our race over cruelty and chaos.

E. M. Forster *Two Cheers for Democracy*

# *Prologue*
# *June 1981*

If time were the only measure of life, an old house or even an old tree could claim a greater importance in the scheme of things than a man with his little span of less than a century.

Thickthorn Manor had survived for five hundred years. Like all soundly built houses, it had grown more beautiful with age. Latterly, since the death of its rightful heir, it had not been as well kept up as in former times. But it was still a fine place which, for sale, would merit a full page, in colour, in *Country Life* and *Town & Country*.

Thickthorn Manor had never been sold and never would be. Like its present owner it was nearing the end of its existence.

But while she was to have an easy death from natural causes, the house was due to be destroyed in a manner as horrible as the way of executing heretics when it was built in 1479.


The news that his great-uncle's wife had died in her sleep near the end of her eightieth year was received with jubilation by Theo Boxgrove.

A man of expensive tastes, he needed the money which the niggardly old bitch had denied him for so long, and the house had been wasted on her. Done up by a clever decorator – there were several in his circle – it would be the perfect setting for lavish parties.

After making appropriate noises on the telephone to her manservant, who sounded sincerely upset that the old girl had finally shuffled off, Theo told his current inamorato to open a bottle of champagne.

In the massive oak four-poster bed where, long ago, she had made love, given birth, wept for the loss of her husband and, later, for their only son, the old lady lay at peace.

For some years the many pleasures of her long active life had been reduced to the nightly small glass of whisky approved by her doctor, and the several more generous measures she drank without his approval while enjoying her other indulgence, thrillers supplied by Harrods' library.

An unfinished Dick Francis topped the pile on her night table as she lay with closed eyes and folded hands, her frail body stiffened by the rigor mortis of which she had often read.

Soon the house, which now must pass to her husband's disliked great-nephew, would be filled with his unsavoury friends. At this moment there was only her emaciated corpse and one living person within its ancient walls.

The arsonist was working in the room directly above Lady Boxgrove's bedroom. He was pouring petrol into a condom before attaching it, by thumb tack, to the low attic ceiling.

Shaped like pale shiny gourds when each one was filled with exactly half a pint of liquid – the arsonist's training had made him a man of precision – sixteen of the bulging rubber sheaths already dangled from the ceilings of other attics, their purpose being to assist the fire's progress through the top floor of the secluded manor house.

When it was necessary for him to stand on an antique

8

chair to fasten a condom to a rafter, even though the needlework seat was faded and moth-eaten it was second nature to him to protect it with an old newspaper lying nearby. As he stepped down from the chair he paused to admire the skilful carving of the intertwined ribbons on the crest and splat. It grieved him that during the night many even finer pieces of furniture, valuable paintings and rare tapestries and rugs would be consumed by the flames. Unfortunately there was no way to save them without arousing suspicions that the fire had been started deliberately.

However it wasn't his fault that by tomorrow the house and its treasures would have perished. The blame for that would lie on someone else's conscience, not his. He was merely the instrument of justice.

Very early the following morning, while Theo was still in bed, he received another telephone call concerning his inheritance.

This time it was from the Chief Constable of the county where the late Sir Giles Boxgrove had at one time been Lord Lieutenant.

'I'm sorry to have to tell you there was a serious fire at Thickthorn Manor last night,' he informed the hungover Theo. 'The local brigade and firemen from two other stations did everything possible, but the house was completely gutted.'

'Oh Christ! I can't believe it. How in hell's name did it happen?' Theo demanded.

'That we can't say at the moment. The matter is being investigated. It may have been caused by faulty wiring. I understand it's some time since the Manor's wiring was overhauled.'

'Decades, I shouldn't wonder,' Theo said bitterly. 'The stupid old cow was too mean to keep the place in order. Did she go up with it?'

The Chief Constable knew Mr Boxgrove had already been informed of the old lady's death. He had heard that her heir was the product of a mésalliance made by Sir Giles' nephew. He had also heard other rumours.

In his most repressive tone, he said, 'The late Lady Boxgrove's body was removed from her room by her manservant before the fire reached it. At great personal risk to themselves, he and various other helpers managed to rescue some of the contents of the house. It would be greatly appreciated if you were to come down today to thank them for their sterling efforts.'

At the thought of the splendid house – probably inadequately insured – reduced to a smouldering heap of charred beams and rubble, Theo was grinding his teeth and pounding the mattress with a manicured fist.

His fury disturbed the deep torpor of the bed's other occupant. The youth's shoulder muscles bunched as, lying face down on the black satin sheet, he lifted his head from the pillow to mutter blearily, 'What's up?'

Theo glared at him, cold blue eyes brimming with tears of rage and frustration.


By nine o'clock news of the fire had spread through the nearest village and all those who could came to view what was left of the building most of them saw every year when the church restoration fund fête was held in the Manor garden.

The arsonist was not among those who gazed, appalled, at the wreckage of a monument to the skills of fifteenth century craftsmen.

He had seen the fire at its height, rejoicing in the successful outcome of his careful planning. No matter how satisfying it was to see the result of his handiwork, he knew it would be unwise to linger near it today. His work at the Manor was done; the transgressor suitably punished.

And it might be that, before long, he would be required to perform another act of retribution.

---

## March 1986 – An evening at Annabel's

With not much traffic about – it was more than an hour since the curtain had gone up at most of the West End theatres – the taxi whirled round Berkeley Square, past the gleaming Rolls-Royces in Jack Barclay's showroom on the corner of Brook Street.

At the Piccadilly end of the square it passed the spot where, a long time ago, its passenger had gazed in delighted astonishment at the cascade of water streaming down the plate glass windows of Moyses Stevens, the most breathtaking flower shop she had ever seen.

Now Moyses Stevens had moved to Bruton Street and much else had changed since her arrival in London, not least the young woman herself.

On the west side of the square were the houses surviving from the time when the square was first built early in the eighteenth century. They showed how much Mayfair had lost in the London Blitz and from graceless post-war development. But in summer some of that ugliness would be screened from the handsome west side by the leaves of the mighty plane trees towering over the square's garden.

Like most of London's great private houses, those on the west side had railinged areaways leading down to their basements. At No 44, where the taxi pulled in to the kerb, the area was covered by a green awning and two uniformed doormen were on duty. As soon as the taxi stopped, one of them opened the back door and said good evening to its passenger.

Stepping onto the pavement, the girl smiled and

thanked him before handing the driver the five pound note she had already taken from her small black shoulder bag.

It was a chilly evening. She was wearing a black wool and cashmere coat with a black silk taffeta bow tying back her smoothly brushed hair. From the pearls in the lobes of her ears to the moderate heels of her glacé kid court shoes, there was nothing trendy about her but rather a classic elegance seldom achieved by women before they were thirty.

Her manner was self-possessed, matching her appearance. Seeing her put the change in her purse and turn to the entrance to Annabel's, for twenty-three years the most aristocratic night club in Europe if not the world, no one would have guessed that inwardly she was trembling with nervous excitement.

As she went down the wooden steps with their thick rope handrail, anyone standing at the bottom would, after first noticing her beautiful legs, have taken her to be an habituée of the place.

In fact it was the first time she had turned the corner at the foot of the stairs, seeing ahead of her a series of archways, like a tunnel, parts of it in shadow and other parts glowing with soft light.

Beside an alcove on the left, a man with grey hair, shrewd dark eyes and horn-rimmed spectacles was speaking to a small plump woman standing by a recess on the right. As the girl came into view, they broke off their conversation and turned to her.

'Good evening. I'm meeting Mr Stow-Bedon,' she said to the man.

She guessed he must be Ted Racki, for long the guardian of the club's exclusivity. Peter had told her about him. It would take a very clever imposter to get past Ted, he had said. She wondered if Mr Racki could detect the truth about her, or if his sixth sense about people came into play only when someone pretended to be a

12

member. Most of the women who came here would be wives or girlfriends. Few would be members in their own right.

'Good evening, Miss Lynn. Mr Stow-Bedon is waiting for you in the bar. Would you like to leave your coat with Mabel?'

The cloakroom on the right of the tunnel had two lavatories and two basins with a large pile of blue linen hand towels stacked on the counter beside them. The flowers, Damaris noticed, were not artificial. They were real flowers and they might have been chosen and arranged by Lady Stow-Bedon, Peter's mother and one of her customers. Not that Damaris would have expected to find imitation flowers in a club belonging to a man renowned for his faultless taste.

She knew that Mark Birley, the founder and chairman of Annabel's had named the club after his wife, the former Lady Annabel Vane-Tempest-Stewart, second daughter of the eighth Marquess of Londonderry and now married to Sir James Goldsmith, the international financier. Birley himself was the son of the late Sir Oswald Birley, a distinguished painter, and his club had the reputation of being the only place of its kind where members of the Royal Family and other famous people could dine and dance without fear of being photographed or pried upon.

As it was barely fifteen minutes since Damaris had left her bedroom in Campden Hill Square on the far side of Kensington Gardens, she didn't stay long in the cloakroom. One swift glance in the mirror was enough to confirm that her ivory crêpe de Chine blouse was still neatly tucked into her black silk skirt. It wasn't an outfit to attract envious glances, but nor would it raise any eyebrows.

She found Peter waiting for her where the tunnel opened out into a room with a fire burning behind a club fender and wood panelled walls, painted yellow,

13

hung with a great many pictures, mostly of women and dogs.

At the moment – a quarter to nine – they had the place to themselves. The club opened at eight thirty and, according to Peter, didn't come fully to life until half past ten or eleven. It closed at 3.30 am. However, as Damaris was an early riser and tomorrow was a busy day for her, she wanted to go to bed considerably earlier than most of the people who would be enjoying themselves at Annabel's tonight.

'Are you frozen? I was when I got here,' said Peter, taking her arm and steering her to a sofa piled with cushions which, like the flowers in the cloakroom, had a country house air about them rather than the new, matched, 'decorator' look of cushions in most public places.

'You haven't acclimatised yet,' said Damaris, as they sat down.

She had met him the previous autumn but he had spent most of the winter on expeditions overseas, only recently returning to England. This was the first time she had dined with him. She hoped he had already got the message that she didn't intend to repay his hospitality by letting him spend the night with her.

A waiter in a cream alpaca coat and dark trousers was standing by as Peter said, 'What would you like to drink?'

'A Campari and soda, please.'

'And a gin and tonic for me.' Peter crossed his long legs and settled his shoulders comfortably against the heaped cushions. He was a tall, lean man still in his early thirties but rather more weathered than his contemporaries because from the age of eighteen he had spent most of his time in jungles, deserts and mountains where the sun had burned his skin and bleached the thick straight fair hair which tended to slip in a forelock across his forehead.

14

'Tell me about your day,' he said, with the seemingly genuine interest she found so warming compared with the self-absorption of many men she encountered. The only advantage of their egotism was that men who held forth about themselves were less likely to ask awkward questions.

Damaris had an answer for every question she might be asked about her past, but she felt safer in the present.

*The past is a foreign country: they do things differently there,* she had read in L.P. Hartley's novel after seeing the film *The Go-Between.* She had never read anything more applicable to her own life. In a sense, she had two pasts, both of them foreign countries. One she loathed and would rather die than return to. The other was really someone else's past and hers only by adoption.

She said, 'This morning I took a customer to Syon Lodge to choose urns for her garden in Hampstead. This afternoon I had to supervise the delivery of fifty bags of topsoil which, because there's no back entrance, had to be carried through the hall of a rather chichi house in Chelsea without spoiling the expensive décor. It all went according to plan but it was slightly nerve-racking.'

Self-employed as a garden consultant, Damaris had no fixed hours, regular days off or annual holiday. Her work wasn't only her living, it was her pleasure, her passion, her whole existence. When she did take a day off it was to visit a garden where she might improve her skills and perception. Her dedication left little time or energy for personal relationships except with her customers and the green-fingered housewives who made up her part-time work force.

Until Peter entered her life she had politely refused most invitations from men. Those she had accepted had seldom led to second and third dates. But Peter was different. She liked him better than the others and when he had mentioned Annabel's – of which, apparently, his father had been a founder member – her curiosity about the club had persuaded her to agree to dinner *à deux*.

'How have you spent your day?' she asked, when their drinks arrived.

'At a seminar on survival techniques at the Royal Geographic Society. Interesting – but let's hope I never need to try them out.'

'When are you off to the wilds again?'

'Not until May. Then I'm going to Peru to set up a camp for a dig. I'll be out there for three or four months.'

Presently, the bar still being empty apart from themselves, Damaris got up to look more closely at a painting of two apricot pugs called Margot and Mignonne on the left side of the fire. Near it was a painting of donkeys and, above the fire, a Regency girandole mirror in a gilded frame surmounted by a carved eagle. The convex mirror reflected the curves of the six low arches between this side of the room and the far side where the bar was. The arches and the walls of the central passageway were papered with a design of small indigo flowers and leaves superimposed, in silhouette, on a fainter pattern of crisscross dotted lines.

'There's an interesting story about this wallpaper,' said Peter, while she was trying to decide what the flowers were. 'You know, I expect, that the house above us is John Aspinall's Clermont Club. It was called that after an owner who used to hold extravagant gambling parties, although it was actually built by Lady Isabella Finch, a lady-in-waiting to George II's daughters. When Aspinall bought the house, he got John Fowler of Colefax & Fowler to restore the interior. Fowler found a fragment of eighteenth century paper on one of the walls and liked it so much he had it copied and called it "Berkeley Sprig". It's also in the Gallery at Chequers and Pa's got it in his dressing-room.'

'Do you belong to the Clermont?' Damaris asked.

He shook his head. 'Can't afford to gamble . . . and

anyway it doesn't appeal to me ... never has. Do you like a flutter?'

'I've never tried it and don't intend to,' she answered. 'I work too hard for my money to risk it on games of chance or even small bets on races. This club must be quite expensive, isn't it? Especially when you're not here to use it very often.'

She was curious about Peter's financial status. He was the youngest of three sons and she knew he didn't make money from the expeditions he took part in.

'It's certainly a helluva lot more expensive than when my father first joined. The subscription then was five guineas. One drink can cost more than that now. But as long as my base is a bed-sitter in my parents' house, it's useful to have somewhere like this where I can entertain friends or prop up the bar for an hour if I don't feel like my own company. It's not as much fun as it was about ten years ago. A lot of my friends are married and cutting back to pay school fees.'

At this point two more people arrived; a man with his hair in tight curls which, given his features and colouring, were unlikely to be natural, and a blonde with a hard little mouth, too much cleavage on view, long red nails and a gold ankle chain.

'My father wouldn't like that perm,' Peter murmured, while the newcomers were ordering drinks. 'Pa doesn't belong any more. Doesn't mind showbiz people being a bit flash but can't stand the new money lot. The last time he came, as my guest, the yuppies were here in force ... sent his blood pressure up about ten points. What he doesn't seem to realise is that if places like this depended on old money, they'd rapidly go bankrupt.'

'I suppose they would,' she agreed. Certainly the newcomers were not the sort of people she had expected to find at Annabel's.

Four middle-aged Americans came in, two large dapper men with well-groomed, face-lifted wives who

17

settled themselves on the sofa with its back to the centre arch flanked by two silver bird sconces.

Under cover of their conversation, Damaris said, 'But what I can never understand is why people who have the wit to make lots of money don't have the nous to learn acceptable behaviour. It's not their money your father objects to, I imagine – only their manners.'

The man with the perm had looked very hard at her and Peter and now was staring at the American party. She had the feeling he was celebrity-spotting and would be disappointed if he didn't see someone tonight whose name he could drop tomorrow.

Peter was watching the blonde. He said, in an undertone, 'I wonder where he picked her up. In Shepherd Market perhaps?'

The name made Damaris' insides clench. Until he mentioned it, it hadn't occurred to her how close they were to that seedy area of Mayfair, the haunt of prostitutes.

She remembered the day she had gone there, her first day in London. A schoolgirl, not quite sixteen, she had come to the city from the north, looking for the only person to whom she could turn for help.

Already in shock from being raped the previous afternoon, she had sat in a cheap corner café and watched another dyed blonde accost a man in the street. A few moments later she had recognised the woman as her mother.

Was it possible that, ten years later, in those streets only a short walk from here, Shirley might still be sidling up to men with a false smile and a murmured, 'Anything I can do for you, love?'


The low vaulted ceiling of the dining room was supported by square brass-clad pillars, the golden metal mellowed by more than two decades of daily polishing.

18

The pillars reflected the green glass shades of the table lamps, the pale pink of the damask table cloths and the deep pink cloths on the service tables.

Peter and Damaris were shown to a green banquette at the side of the room by a short, portly, urbane man whom Peter introduced as Louis, the club's manager and one of London's most renowned *maîtres d'hôtel*.

Once again, as she had on arrival, she felt she was being scrutinised but with the utmost discretion. She wondered how many girls Peter had brought here before her and if there was any way in which the manager could tell that, although she had all the external hallmarks of a so-called Sloane Ranger, her real origins were as different from Peter's comfortable upper class background as a bunch of plastic 'daffs' bought at a street market from a green auricula in a Coalport cache-pot.

The club's menu, presented to them on white cards with a vermilion border and *Annabel's* embossed in the same colour at the top, began with a selection of *à la carte* first courses as Maudie had always called them. She wouldn't have approved of 'starter'.

These included Beluga caviar and *prosciutto di San Daniele*. Damaris knew this must be some form of cured ham which she liked but wouldn't ask for because, although she had mastered restaurant French, she wasn't certain about Italian pronunciation. Was the c hard or soft? She made a mental note to look it up tomorrow.

Further down, on a piece of paper attached to the card, came the table d'hôte meal and three house wines, none inexpensive. Below were more *à la carte* choices ranging from a Châteaubriand fillet steak for two people to smoked haddock fishcakes and Annabel's hamburger.

In general the food at the night club seemed to be geared to men's tastes rather than women's, with an American slant in the number of steaks offered, the Caesar salad and the corned beef hash. But as it would usually be a man who picked up the bill here, and

19

already she had seen four Americans, perhaps this wasn't surprising.

Mentally adding the cover charge to the set menu and a bottle of wine, perhaps two, plus coffee and an appropriate tip, Damaris decided that Peter's bill could not be far short of a hundred pounds. By her standards it was a lot of money to spend on an evening out. She would have felt more comfortable had they been sharing the expense. But as this was their first date, and not at an ordinary restaurant, she hadn't liked to suggest it.

'What's your feeling about meat?' Peter asked. 'Are you one of the New Vegetarians, or does a job calling for muscle require something more sustaining than rabbit food?'

'I like fish better than meat, but the rabbit casserole with mushrooms sounds very good,' she said, referring to one of the main courses on the table d'hôte menu.

'I'm told when I get to Peru I'm going to be eating a lot of guinea-pig,' he said, 'but of a much larger type than the ones kept as pets in this country. Are you sure you want rabbit? What about a Dover sole? The fish here is always excellent.'

After dinner, Damaris went to the cloakroom, to retouch her lipstick.

'Give my regards to Mabel,' said Peter, as she left the table.

By this time the club was much busier. Most of the tables were occupied and there were people standing at the bar near the entrance to the dining room. The outer room where she and Peter had sat earlier was crowded now.

As she walked through, she caught snatches of conversation.

'. . . in Scotland as little as six hundred pounds an acre . . .'

'. . . I wish Victor would do more day clothes . . .'

That would be Victor Edelstein, a favourite designer with the ladies who lunched. She had one of his customers among her own; a woman whose idea of a frantic day was a fitting at Victor's in the morning, a gossipy lunch with a girlfriend in Walton Street, followed by an hour with her aromatherapist before resting and changing for a dinner party on the north side of Eaton Square.

It wasn't a life Damaris coveted. She had other aspirations and already was on her way towards their realisation. That she was here tonight was in itself an achievement, given where she had come from. True, the girl with the ankle chain was also here, but with a parvenu, not someone like Peter.

In the Ladies, the woman in black she had seen on arrival was listening to a girl in a red dress. As Damaris locked the door of one of the lavatories, she heard the girl saying, ' . . . so this is my first proper night out since before the baby, which seems a *lifetime* ago. Honestly, Mabel, I had no *idea* that babies were so *incredibly* time-consuming. I never have a *second* to myself. Well, look at the state of my nails.'

The girl was still confiding the trials of motherhood into Mabel's sympathetic ear when Damaris re-emerged. While she was washing her hands, another girl came in.

'Charlotte!'

'Venetia!'

'How *are* you? Where *have* you been? I haven't seen you for *a-a-ages*!'

'I'm amazed that you even recognise me.' The doleful tale of the family nanny, taken ill at the crucial moment, the colicky baby and the critical mother-in-law was begun again for Venetia.

The dance floor was lit from below and, early on, when Peter and Damaris were the only couple on it, had looked like a tropical night sky spangled with stars. The music came from a glass-walled booth at the back where a debonair Jamaican called Cass played Nana Mouskouri singing *Only Love* and other smoochy music.

To the right of the booth, with its shelves of tapes, was a great burst of flowers spilling out of a large brass urn. Like those in the cloakroom and elsewhere, they were real and in fresh condition, bringing a breath of the country to this fashionable night-spot.

To her relief Peter didn't hold her too close when the music was slow and sweet. The man with the perm and the girl with the chain danced in a sexy embrace but Peter's arm circled her lightly and he didn't press her against him.

If he wanted her, and assumed he would have her later, he didn't make it obvious. Nor, when she drank her wine slowly – one glass to his two or three – did he try to increase her intake. If seduction were his objective, he was being very subtle about it. Or perhaps he had weighed her up and knew that a slow approach would relax and disarm her, while an overtly amorous manner would keep him forever at arm's length.

'You wouldn't think it to look at her, but Mabel is getting on for eighty,' said Peter, as they climbed the steps to pavement level. 'My grandfather knew her years ago when she was at Drivers.'

'But she looks about sixty-five. Are you sure she's as old as that?'

'Positive . . . ask Mama if you don't believe me. A taxi, please, Nando.'

In the taxi, Damaris said, 'Mabel was talking about you while I was collecting my coat. She seems to know you quite well.'

'Sometimes, if the club is quiet, I nip in and have a chat. When I first went to Annabel's she used to sit under the stairs leading up to the Clermont. Then they boxed her department in. I hope she gave me a good report.'

'She spoke most approvingly of you. I had the impression you're one of her favourite members.'

In the light from the street-lamps, she saw the crease in his tanned cheek deepen as he smiled.

'And what's your opinion of me . . . now that you know me better?'

Damaris laughed. 'It takes me longer than one evening to make up my mind about people, but you certainly seem very agreeable,' she answered lightly.

He reached out and took her hand which had been lying on her lap. Clasping her fingers in his, he said, 'I should like a better rating than merely "very agreeable". I rate you very highly . . . the most interesting, intelligent, lovely girl it's ever been my pleasure to dine with.'

'I think you're exaggerating, but it's a nice thing to say.' Gently, she withdrew her hand. 'I'm sorry my working hours made it necessary to come away rather earlier than you might have liked to leave. I've enjoyed this evening very much. Thank you, Peter.'

'When can we do it again? Are you doing anything at the weekend? How about lunch in the country on Sunday?'

'I'm afraid I'm busy this weekend and next week is rather full, too.'

This wasn't strictly true. She had no social engagements, but like all self-employed people she could always find work to do. To lunch in the country with Peter would have been a pleasure; but it was one she felt she must deny herself. It wouldn't do to see too much of him. He would not be content with friendship. He would want to make love to her, and she wasn't ready for that yet. Would she ever be?

Would she ever be able to think about sex without

remembering that afternoon in the back bedroom at 13, Laburnum Way when she was fifteen?

Even now, ten years later, sitting in the back of a taxi speeding along Bayswater Road with a man trained from childhood to respect and protect women, she was still haunted by the brutal act which had ended her childhood.

'How about Sunday week?'

'I'm not sure. I'll have to look in my diary.'

He didn't respond to this statement and said nothing more until the taxi drew up outside the house where she lived. Then he sprang out, saying to the driver, 'Wait for me, will you? I'll just see my guest to her door.'

'Right-oh, sir.'

Peter opened the gate and, as they walked up the path, Damaris felt for her latch-key.

'Can I take it that you do want us to meet again?' he asked, when they reached the steps in front of the door.

After a slight hesitation, she said, 'Yes, I do . . . as long as you don't mind my diary always being rather full.'

'I took that for granted,' he said. 'If the Sunday after next is free, keep it for me, will you? I'll call you during the week. Goodnight, Damaris.'

He put one hand on her shoulder and brushed a kiss on her cheek. Then he went back down the path and she put her key in the lock and entered the house. She was waiting to close the door when, at the gate, he looked back, raising his hand in a final farewell. She returned the gesture.

But it wasn't of Peter and his light goodnight kiss that she was thinking as she climbed the stairs to her flat on the top floor, but of Shepherd Market and her mother.

# London: Wednesday, 19 March 1986

**7.00 am** A slow shudder ran through the girl stretched on the bed, her nightdress pushed up to her neck, the sheet and blankets pushed down to her hips.

The man lying beside her, bending his head to her breast, looked up to see her face. Her eyes were closed, but not in ecstasy. He could tell by her tightly closed lips that feeling his mouth, his fingers on the most sensitive parts of her body gave her no pleasure. Rather it was an ordeal she had been enduring in silence, unwilling to admit how much she hated it . . . had always hated it.

Angry with himself for attempting something he already knew was impossible, he swung himself off the bed, his erection thrusting truncheon-stiff against his pyjama trousers.

As he passed the wardrobe, the mirror on the door reflected his handsome dark face and bare olive-skinned torso. It was the face and body of a man who had always attracted girls easily but who had been too preoccupied with his work, his vision, to waste much time gaining other kinds of experience.

As he took his dressing gown from the back of the door, the girl said, 'Joël . . . I'm sorry.'

He shrugged on the robe and pulled it round him, his body throbbing and aching with the excitement aroused by her creamy-white skin, her soft breasts with their shrimp-pink tips.

'It doesn't matter.' His accent was always more pronounced when he was upset. 'Don't worry . . . I shan't try again. That was the last time – ever!'

Without bothering to put on his bedroom slippers he

went out, closing the door very quietly because he wanted to slam it and that would distress her.

He was more angry with himself than with Lucy. It wasn't her fault. He should have listened to his parents. He should never have come to England. He should have stayed where he belonged and married a French girl. Even Marthe with her black moustache and haunches like a sow would have made him happier than he was in this situation.

**7.05 am** For James Muirhead the day began in Louise Picton's bed.

Louise was a career-minded divorcée with whom for three years he had had a convenient, primarily sexual relationship. To call it a friendship would have been an overstatement. There were things he disliked about her and she about him. This was, in a way, an advantage, preventing either of them from becoming seriously involved, a development each knew the other wished to avoid.

On an average of three times a fortnight they had dinner together or went to the theatre, afterwards returning to her place to enjoy some rather brisk sex which was physically satisfactory if not in any other way.

Neither of them was promiscuous. Louise had divorced her husband because he slept around. James had never been interested in casual sex. But he was a virile heterosexual and Louise was far from being the frigid bitch her husband had called her when trying to justify his own barnyard behaviour.

Not long after their first meeting they started sleeping together. Unless, eventually, Louise met someone who changed her mind about marrying again, it seemed likely their relationship would continue for years.

Some people who knew they were lovers wondered why they continued to maintain separate establishments.

Those who had visited both flats realised at once that James could never be at ease for long in Louise's flat, nor she in his.

The king-size divan they were sharing this morning was in a large open-plan living area. Only the bath and lavatory were enclosed spaces in Louise's flat. Most of her furniture was made of chromed steel, mirror glass, black glass and clear glass. She liked Art Deco and the modernist interiors of the Thirties and claimed to have suffered from claustrophobia on the one night they had spent in James' canopied four-poster.

'Aren't you afraid of being thought gay . . . sleeping under a sunburst of pale blue silk?' she had teased him, the following morning.

His grey eyes, normally friendly, had suddenly lost their warmth. She knew she had touched on a raw spot. As by that time he had demonstrated his liking for the female body, and she felt sure he wasn't ambidextrous, she had guessed the bed was a relic of the time he never talked about.

All she knew of his past had been told her by colleagues, not James. He had merely put his cards on the table. He found her attractive. He wanted to sleep with her. That was as far as it went. He was not in the market for any more serious commitment. He was a loner and, at thirty-nine, unlikely to change.

'Hi,' she said drowsily, turning on her back and stretching.

'Hi.' James swung off the bed.

He was forty-two now but still a slim, muscular man as he padded, naked, in the direction of the bathroom.

When he reappeared his brown hair was wet from the shower and he had a towel round his hips. She watched him move into the workspace, as Frank Lloyd Wright had called the kitchen. James wasn't the kind of man who took it for granted that, if there was a woman around, she would deal with the meals and all the other domestic chores.

If he got up first, he fixed breakfast. He never left the bathroom in a mess. Compared with her disaster of a husband, James was a paragon. He wasn't romantic. He never brought her flowers or lover-like presents. For the last two Christmases they had gone skiing with two other architects and their wives. His gifts had been strictly practical, as they were on her birthdays. He was careful to avoid any trace of sentiment, but at the same time he always made sure she had a great orgasm. Which was all she wanted from a man. A presentable escort on call whenever he was needed, and some satisfactory fucking.

James was used to her ways now. In the early days of their liaison she had sensed that he didn't approve of some of her opinions, nor the way she expressed them. He wasn't a male chauvinist sod like Steve – Christ! How she could ever have imagined herself in love with her ex was beyond her comprehension – but some of James' ideas about life and women were as antiquated as the stuff in his flat and the buildings he dealt with professionally.

A bit of a *verray parfit gentil knight* was James – and, at times, rather boring in consequence. But never in bed, thank God. Who had taught him about women's bodies was something Louise never asked. His past was clearly out of bounds. She wasn't curious about it, anyway. It was only when one was in love that one longed to know every detail of the loved one's entire life, she thought sardonically, watching the tall, craggy-featured man who in many ways was still a stranger.

'Breakfast in bed?' he asked her, cocking an eyebrow.

Louise shook her head and reached for her black velours robe. She dressed entirely in black and white to accentuate her natural colouring. Black hair, always cut in the latest style. White skin, always protected by a total sun-block and given a clown-like pallor by her

28

make-up. Eyes the colour of prune juice with heavy lids, dramatically painted.

'I must get up and get organised. I have a full day.' She rose, naked, from the divan.

The boyish lines of her body pleased her more than they did James. She reminded him of a whippet. He preferred a more rounded figure. As he watched her put on her robe and slide her long narrow feet into black and silver mules, he remembered a hot summer morning in France and a girl in a white broderie anglaise peignoir threaded with primrose ribbons, the ruffles at her neck falling open to show the valley between her young honey-coloured breasts.

'So have I.' Dismissing the thought of that day almost eighteen years ago, he concentrated his mind on the work awaiting him at the office.


**7.10 am** Ten minutes after being woken by her alarm clock Damaris Lynn was still in bed, enjoying her small attic bedroom, glad to be alone, not sharing her three-quarter bed with Peter, not obliged to make conversation or organise breakfast for two.

To her, privacy was one of life's greatest luxuries. She had never known it as a child. Now that she had it, she treasured it. Some people dreaded being alone and no doubt for the old and infirm isolation was an added misery. For herself, young and strong, to be able to close the door at the end of a long busy day, to be closeted in solitude and silence – apart from the muted drone of traffic on Bayswater Road – was a benison.

Presently she threw back the duvet and swung her legs to the floor, raking her long brown hair back from her face with her fingers. She was wearing a pair of men's beige and black silk pyjamas from Charvet in Paris which had somehow found their way to a second-hand shop in Camden Town where Damaris looked for clothes from the Twenties and Thirties.

She would have liked to live in that era. Although, if she had, it would have been ten times as difficult to make a life for herself above the station ordained for her at birth. Even in 1976, without Maudie's legacy, it wouldn't have been so easy to escape from the council estate in the north of England where she had grown up.

It was when she arrived in London with nowhere to stay and no one to turn to except the woman who had borne her and who sometimes brought her presents, that Damaris discovered that her mother was a Shepherd Market tart. But for the nest-egg left her by old Maudie Sheringham, she would have had no option but to ask her mother for help, probably ending up in the same line of business.

Unlike many of her contemporaries who seemed to think life was something over which they had little or no control, Damaris was determined to be the mistress of her fate. At twenty-five she was emotionally if not physically inviolate. She had been taken once, against her will, and that was part of the reason why she had no difficulty in resisting men's advances.

But it wasn't only the memory of that afternoon in the back bedroom at 13, Laburnum Way, when she was fifteen, which kept her chaste now. It had made her nervous of men for several years afterwards. Even now she was careful to avoid being alone with some of them; men she knew as well as those she didn't. Rape, as she knew from experience, wasn't a crime committed only by strangers. She had been defiled by a man she had known for years, had never liked but hadn't thought capable of forcing himself on her.

Gradually her horror of him and the male sex in general had subsided into a calmer realisation that what she had undergone hadn't been the action of a normal man. She had seen that she could allow those minutes

30

of pain and revulsion to blight the rest of her life. Or she could be grateful there had been no physical repercussions and steer herself clear of mental hang-ups by putting it firmly out of mind.

Another factor contributing to her resolute celibacy was that she worked very hard. At the beginning she had often gone to bed exhausted; too tired out even to read. Now, when she could have delegated most of the hardest work, taxing her energy was a matter of choice. Also, fortunately for her, it was now much easier to say no to a man than at the height of the permissive era, still in full spate when she first came to London. Now, because of AIDS, promiscuity was going out of fashion. Not, she felt sure, that she would ever have been swayed by what everyone else was doing. People who got to the top were not those who ran with the herd.

In the bathroom she brushed her teeth before bundling her hair inside a plastic cap and stepping into the shower.


**7.35 am** Dressed in a check shirt and needlecord jeans, with her hair tied back with a ribbon at the nape of her neck, and a little light make-up emphasising the green of her irises and the length of her lashes, Damaris went down the three flights of stairs to the hall.

The house was divided into four; the ground floor and first floor being occupied by the owner while the basement, the second floor and her eyrie under the roof were self-contained flats.

Her landlord had already collected the mail from the mat and sorted it and his tenants' newspapers into three neat piles on the hall table. For her there were three letters, *The Times* and *Harpers & Queen*.

Until she was nine years old Damaris had only heard of the *Daily Mirror*. She had been introduced to *The Times*, and much else, by Maudie Sheringham who had

31

lived in one of the better-kept roads on the Woodlands Estate.

It had been the local council's policy to segregate, as far as possible, the most anti-social families in a corner of the estate where, with their untended gardens and undisciplined offspring, they would be less of an annoyance to the more respectable inhabitants.

Damaris – then known by the name her mother had chosen for her – had been part of that shiftless group who were always behind with the rent, who bred like rabbits, whose petty crimes and domestic affrays were regularly reported in the local newspaper and whose social centres were The Thistle, the town's rowdiest pub, the Frenzy disco where two massive bouncers kept order on Saturday nights, and a snooker hall whose habitués were often to be seen going off in a Panda car to help the police with their enquiries.

But even before she had been taken in hand by old Maudie Sheringham, Damaris had felt she didn't belong, that she was different. One of her earliest memories was of being lost in a large shop where the counters, taller than she was, were like the walls of a maze.

She had been starting to wail – more in fear of the clip round the ear she would get when she was found than from fright at being lost – when another slightly older child, standing nearby, said, 'Mummy, that little girl's crying.'

Whereupon a tall lovely person with a gentle voice had turned round and bent over Damaris, saying, 'Oh dear, have you lost your Mummy? Never mind. We'll soon find her for you. What's your name?'

Then she had taken one of Damaris' hands in hers, and her daughter had taken the other, and soon afterwards there had been a loud announcement on the public address system which had brought a flustered Auntie Marlene back into view.

The impression left by that incident had remained

sharp for a long time. It had been, she realised much later, her first contact with people who were not the same as those she lived among. Precisely how they differed and why she felt drawn to them remained unclear until she was older. But a seed of unrest and yearning had been sown in her mind. She had wanted to be like the other child; cleaner, neater, dressed in nicer clothes, with a mother who called her 'darling' instead of 'stupid little bugger' which was what Auntie Marlene had snapped at her for wandering off.

Now, ten years after her escape, life at 13, Laburnum Way seemed like a bad dream. She had been 'born again', not as a Christian but as a different person from the woman she would have grown into if her instinctive but amorphous longings hadn't been encouraged and directed by Maudie.

In retrospect, Damaris realised that Maudie herself had risen from humble beginnings, although not as low as her own. Maudie's father had been a chauffeur, her mother a parlour-maid. She had followed her parents into service and, because of her skill with a needle and a flair for dressing hair, had become first the lady's-maid and eventually the companion and confidante of the Honourable Harriet Wellesbourne, who had lived and died a spinster after losing the man she loved in the First World War.

Damaris was keenly aware how much she owed to the chance of meeting and being helped by Maudie; and to another chance – Mrs Goole from next door saying over the broken back fence to Auntie Marlene, 'There's an old Burt Lancaster film on telly tonight. Burt Lancaster and Rita Hayworth. I always liked 'im.'

The film had been *Separate Tables*. Auntie Marlene hadn't thought much of it. Luckily there had been nothing better to watch on the other channels and Damaris, then aged thirteen, had heard the character played by David Niven say the never-to-be-forgotten words: 'I don't like myself as I am . . . so I've had to invent another person.'

Which was what, two years later, she had done. She had changed her name, her parentage, the circumstances of her upbringing . . . everything. Told repeatedly by Maudie how the upper classes behaved, and aided by her own gift for mimicry and a quick eye and ear for the subtleties of polite behaviour, Damaris had long since lost most of her fear of having her imposture discovered.

'It would never surprise me if your father wasn't one of the gentry, sowing his wild oats,' Maudie had speculated once. 'There's no resemblance between you and your mother's family, that's a certainty. You should try to find out who he was. Not that you could make any claim on him, but at least you'd have the satisfaction of knowing you had decent blood in you. Although that speaks for itself.'

She had taken Damaris' chin in her hand and turned her head this way and that. 'Yes . . . there's good breeding in you, child. You may be obliged to live with that slattern and her brood for the present, but it won't be forever. It's not like it was in my young days. There are opportunities now for anyone blessed with a brain. Work hard at your lessons and you'll go a long way.'

Just how far she had come in the years since that homily, was shown by the contents of the envelopes Damaris opened while waiting for the kettle to boil. In one was a cheque with a pleased note from one of her clients. In another was an invitation to a drinks party at a house in Cadogan Square. In the third was a correspondence card with *from the Countess of Carlyon* printed along the top of it.


**7.45 am** As Laura Denham walked down the stairs, ready to leave the house, she heard footsteps on the path and knew that in a few moments her friend Margaret

Foxley would enter the porch and step on the large coir doormat just as Laura opened the front door.

They had been saying good morning to each other at precisely fifteen minutes to eight every Monday to Friday for a number of years, the only interruptions to this routine being the winter Miss Foxley had flu and the morning after Mrs Denham, Laura's step-mother, died of a heart attack.

'Morning, Laura. You heard the forecast?'

Miss Foxley needn't have asked. Both of them always listened to the seven o'clock news and the weather forecast. It was part of the unvarying pattern of their lives. Now that Mrs Denham was dead they were both on their own with no one to interfere with their orderly habits.

As their ways were so similar, Miss Foxley had once suggested that they could reduce their expenses by sharing a house instead of living two hundred yards from each other with, between them, six bedrooms, four of which were never used. But she hadn't wanted to give up her house, and neither had Laura, so they were still maintaining separate establishments.

'Morning, Margaret. Yes . . . fine until lunchtime, then rain.' Laura took her umbrella from the hallstand, locked the door and followed her friend to the gate which she closed carefully behind her before they set out side by side for Northwood Hills Underground station, a ten-minute walk from the quiet suburban street where they lived.

Both women wore low-heeled, well polished walking shoes, sensible belted raincoats and leather gloves. They carried practical, good quality bags and Miss Foxley's perm was protected from the wind by a neat felt hat. Laura wore a fawn beret. She was still on the right side of forty, Miss Foxley twelve years her senior.

They looked what they were; two unmarried, unloved women, reliable, conscientious, fixed in their habits and increasingly perturbed by the violence and disorder of modern life.

Laura was a senior secretary. Miss Foxley was second in command of one of the most reputable secretarial agencies in London.

They had met and made friends on their morning journeys to work, soon after Mrs Denham had moved from the country to London following the death of her second husband.

Later on, when Laura had told Miss Foxley she wanted to change jobs, the older woman had helped her to find her present post. Now she had it in mind to change jobs again but hesitated to say so, knowing Miss Foxley would be upset and probably put out if Laura announced she was thinking of leaving London.

She dreaded displeasing Miss Foxley, who was her only friend, and felt guilty about deserting her. Yet now that her step-mother was dead and she was at last a free agent, why must she go on living to suit other people and never to please herself?


**8.00 am** Joël Vibrac was pounding along the bank of the Serpentine, one of the many joggers and walkers at exercise in Hyde Park.

He ran to work every morning, wanting to keep his weight down, his muscles toned. Not many of his generation of chefs were as fat as the master-cooks of the past. Mosimann of the Dorchester kept himself in shape. Neither of the Roux brothers was fat. Nico Ladenis was the only one he could think of with the traditional rotundity of chefs and gourmets. Peter Chandler at Paris House was a slim man, as was Raymond Blanc at Le Manoir aux Quat' Saisons, the young chef whom Joël most admired and whom he had hoped to emulate . . . if it hadn't been for Lucy's accident.

Even before the accident she had never been keen on

sex. He had found that out on their honeymoon; and it hadn't been clumsiness or ignorance on his part which had fouled up their three-day stay in one of the twelve double bedrooms at Miller Howe, a small country house hotel renowned for the beauty of its setting and its superb cuisine. He might not have had as much practice as some of his contemporaries, but he knew how to please a girl as well as he knew how to make an *omelette aux fines herbes*. It had been Lucy who was the ignorant one.

She was younger than he; twenty-three to his twenty-eight. They had been married for four years after a whirlwind romance opposed not only by his family but also by Lucy's mother. Mrs Baston was a widow who now shared their flat because her daughter needed more care than the social services could give, or they could afford to pay for privately, except by spending Joël's savings.

Even that would not have provided the devoted attention to Lucy's comfort and welfare given by Gladys Baston. Joël sometimes thought that his mother-in-law did too much for Lucy. A friend who had worked in Canada had told him of seeing, at the Eaton Centre in Toronto, a man in a wheelchair using an escalator. Apparently Toronto was a city where the needs of the disabled had been given more thought than in London or Paris, but Joël couldn't imagine Lucy ever attempting to use an escalator. Not with Mrs Baston fussing over her, treating her as if she were completely paralysed when in fact there were many things which people in her condition could do for themselves.

Whenever he had suggested that Lucy should do more, his mother-in-law had accused him of being unsympathetic not to say callous. She had never liked him. She had wanted her daughter to marry a chartered accountant, not a chef. A man who cooked for his living was not a *parti* in her eyes. She knew nothing of *haute cuisine*, had never heard of men like Jean Troisgros, Paul Bocuse and Michel Guérard who had changed the direction of French gastronomy and been fêted like other great artists. Connoisseurs of food from many nations had made the pilgrimage to the restaurant of the Troisgros brothers. President Giscard d'Estaing had given a luncheon in their honour at the Elysée Palace, an occasion for which they had created one of their most famous dishes, escalope of salmon with sorrel sauce, now to be found on menus all over the world.

But his mother-in-law knew nothing of the esteem in which leading chefs were held, nor the huge salaries they commanded. She considered that Lucy had married beneath her. Mrs Baston even turned up her nose at the food he prepared for them on his days off, complaining that it reeked of garlic.

Ahead of him on the broad path which skirted the lake a girl was jogging towards him, wearing a sweatband to match her apple green track suit. Her body was slim but rounded. The gentle bounce of her breasts reanimated his hunger. As they passed each other he saw that she had a beautiful clear skin. Her cheeks were flushed from exertion in the crisp morning air and her face was lightly dewed with moisture. Their eyes met. He knew that she liked him . . . liked the look of him. He wanted to turn and follow her, as he had followed Lucy the first time he'd seen her.

It had been love at first sight. Something about her had been irresistible to him. But a few weeks after their marriage, as he had realised she was never going to respond to him satisfactorily, he had begun to feel cheated.

He knew that he should have suspected something was wrong when, during their short engagement, she wouldn't allow him to touch her below the waist. And he should have studied Mrs Baston more closely and remembered that girls took after their mothers. He would have seen at a glance that his prospective mother-in-law had never enjoyed sex. Probably it was her fault that Lucy couldn't.

At the Park Lane end of the park he slowed to a brisk walk and continued through the streets of Mayfair to the restaurant where he had worked for the past two years.

It was one of three owned by a syndicate composed of a duke, a theatrical knight, an entrepreneur and a TV personality, with a Swiss manager, Paul Allevard, in charge.

Following the example of the brothers Roux of *Le Gavroche*, Allevard had trained many promising chefs and subsequently helped them to start their own restaurants, thereby making room for more talented young men and women to be apprenticed.

Joël had started as a commis chef at the restaurant in Chelsea. He had then gained further experience in the Belgravia restaurant and was now sous-chef in the Mayfair establishment, waiting for the moment when Allevard considered him ready to graduate to a place of his own.

The system was that a chef with ambitions to become a *patron* would put up what money he could and Allevard would recruit some investors to provide the necessary funds or guarantee a bank loan. The chef concerned always owned at least half the shares and could later buy out his backers and become sole owner of his restaurant.

Had it not been for Lucy's accident, Joël felt sure that by now he would have been established in a suitable place in the provinces, a small country hotel with its own *potager* being what he aspired to. Lucy, formerly a secretary, had been taking a course in hotel management and together they would have become another husband-and-wife partnership like Raymond and Jenny Blanc and Pierre and Annie Koffman. All over England Roux and Allevard-trained chefs were making a name for themselves, contributing to what had been called 'a golden era in British cooking'.

On arriving at the restaurant he had a quick shower and put on his chef's whites and the tall, stiffly starched *toque*. Unlike the chef, he didn't go to the markets first thing every morning. But he seldom left the restaurant until the last order had been cooked so his days were long, another reason Mrs Baston deplored her daughter's choice of husband.

For a time, while he was courting Lucy, he had been irked by the restraints of his profession. Now he was thankful it kept him away from the small flat off Bayswater Road whose only redeeming feature was its nearness to the park.

Born in a small market town in Brittany, near Vannes, Joël disliked big cities and longed for the day when the air he breathed would no longer be tainted by exhaust fumes, and such leisure as he had could be spent in the real countryside, not in an oasis of greenery surrounded by city streets, and the unceasing drone of traffic.

Allevard was in the kitchen, talking to Philippe, the chef. They said good morning to Joël and Allevard added, 'Later I'd like a word with you. When you can spare ten minutes, come to my office, will you?'

Joël's heart leapt. What could Allevard want to discuss with him in private except the long-awaited opportunity?

**9.00 am** When James arrived at the offices of *Clyst, Tacolneston, Muirhead & Hythe*, he was greeted by the secretary he shared with Miles Tacolneston with the news that the senior partner had died of heart failure.

'He died in his seat at the theatre last night,' she told James. 'Mrs Clyst thought he'd nodded off, but when the lights went up for the interval she realised something was wrong. Luckily their son and daughter-in-law were with them and took charge. Poor Mrs Clyst . . . what a shock for her.'

Later Miles Tacolneston said to him, 'A hell of a shock for Margery . . . but not a bad way to bow out for the old boy. He'd have loathed a lingering illness.'

The senior partner, long past the age at which public servants were obliged to retire, had been almost as active in his seventies as in his sixties. Perhaps a little hard of hearing, although he always denied it, and inclined to hold forth on declining standards if not tactfully deflected, but otherwise still a useful member of the partnership he had founded with Miles' father who had retired rather early.

'The big question now,' said Miles, 'is who's going to take on Longwarden? I don't feel I can. I'm already over-extended. Janet is always complaining that she and the children see nothing of me.'

'I doubt if Michael could handle it,' James said thoughtfully, referring to the junior partner. 'Hasn't had enough experience. So that leaves me.'

'But can you fit it in with all your other commitments? And do you want to?' asked Miles. 'It involves an awful lot of driving. Old Maurice didn't mind that. When he was at the cottage he was halfway there. Besides, he'd have taken it on if it had been at Land's End. He'd always wanted to tackle one of the great country houses. He'd worked on plenty of lesser ones but never one in the top league . . . never one of Vanbrugh's places. The day Lord Carlyon rang him up, the old boy was thrilled to bits.'

'Yes, I remember,' said James. 'He came bustling into my office as excited as I've ever seen him. We shall miss him, you know, Miles. He had his trying moments but he was a great enthusiast. And what he didn't know about restoring old buildings wasn't worth knowing.'

'That's probably why Lord Carlyon approached him,' said Miles. 'I shouldn't imagine it was a shot in the dark. No doubt he made some enquiries and heard about the work we've done. Yes, the old chap knew his stuff, but a lot of the firm's reputation rests on your shoulders and mine.'

'Everything rests on us now,' James replied dryly. 'We shall have to start looking for another partner. Meanwhile I think, with a bit of juggling, I can cope with Longwarden. As a matter of fact I should like to. When he told me Carlyon had invited him down for "a preliminary recce" as Maurice put it, it seemed very unlikely that he'd be able to continue scrambling about on scaffolding for much longer. I felt there was little point in his starting something he'd have to hand over in a year or two.'

'By the sound of it, it's a job which is likely to see *you* out, old chap,' said Miles. 'Those vast country seats are like the Forth bridge . . . no sooner put right than in need of some more attention. Shouldn't you ring up Lord Carlyon – tell him what's happened before he reads it in tomorrow's *Times*?'

'Mm . . . you're right. I'd better do that straight away. No, first I'll look through Maurice's notes.'

James left Miles and went up the stairs to the senior partner's office on the floor above, a large book-lined room with a drawing table at one end and a massive desk at the other.

Maurice had had his own secretary, Miss Priesthill, a woman now in her fifties who had been with him for years. She was standing in his office, looking as if she might have shed tears for him. But when James commiserated with her, her response was controlled. She was not much liked by the others, who thought she was stiff and prim. James admired and pitied her, knowing that her life had been devoted to the care of her aged parents. They must have been middle-aged when Miss Priesthill was born, for her mother was approaching her centenary.

42

It occurred to him that, as well as being distressed by her employer's sudden death, she might also be worrying about her future with the firm. Diplomatically he made it clear that her position remained as secure as it had been in Maurice Clyst's lifetime.

When Miss Priesthill had given him the file on Longwarden, he took it down to his own room and quickly glanced through its contents. Maurice had first visited the house last December and made numerous visits since, each one recorded in meticulous detail so that James was left in no doubt about his actions and thoughts.

As he had much else to do that morning James put the notes aside to read later. All he needed to know at the moment was what progress had been made so far. Evidently not much. He was taking over a commission which was still at the discussion stage.

Having briefed himself on the most important points, he rang up Longwarden, explained who he was and asked to speak to Lord Carlyon.


**10.15 am** Joël knocked on the door of Paul Allevard's office.

'Come in.'

He found the restaurant manager on the telephone. He was a small dapper man with a perfectionist's eye for every detail of the service provided by the restaurants he administered. Some of the staff regarded him as an impossibly exacting taskmaster, but he had been understanding and helpful in the difficult period after the accident.

It had happened during a weekend spent with Lucy's friend Susan, in the country. The two girls had gone for a hack, leaving Joël, who didn't know how to ride, relaxing by the Crosbys' large swimming pool.

Where a country lane crossed a main road, Lucy's

mount had been spooked by a fool showing off in a Porsche. There had been a collision with a lorry going the other way. The horse had had to be destroyed and Lucy had been rushed to the nearest casualty department with injuries which had kept her in hospital for over a year and left her immobilised from the waist down.

Allevard gestured for Joël to be seated. A few moments later he said goodbye to the caller and replaced the receiver.

Coming straight to the point, he said, 'The Earl and Countess of Carlyon are looking for a chef. They're a young couple who haven't been married long. The Earl is a professional photographer and the Countess is an American. They live in a large house called Longwarden about two hours' drive from London. I think it's a post which would suit you.'

This wasn't what Joël had expected. He knew, as everyone did, that Albert Roux's first job in this country had been with Lady Astor, an American by birth and England's first woman MP. But the experience of cooking for aristocrats or nouveaux riches in their houses had never been part of his own plan.

'I understand from one of the owners, who asked me if I could suggest anyone suitable for the Earl and Countess of Carlyon, that Longwarden has undergone a long period of neglect but is now to be put to rights,' Allevard went on. 'Between ourselves, Lady Carlyon is an heiress. No doubt it's her father's fortune which is funding the restoration. In view of your wife's state of health, it's an opening which you should consider very seriously, Joël. I know it's not what you had in mind, but we have to adapt to our circumstances. Now that Lucy can no longer be an active partner, I think you must forget about setting up on your own – at least for the time being.'

He was only putting into words what, deep down,

Joël had known all along. Something of the anguish he felt at finally acknowledging the impossibility of an ambition born while he was still in his teens must have shown in his face.

Allevard rose from his chair and opened a cupboard from which he took a bottle of one of the fine wines on the restaurant's list. Half filling two glasses, he placed one within Joël's reach.

'I know it's a great disappointment, but you don't need me to tell you how essential it is, in launching a hotel-restaurant, for the chef to have someone equally committed in charge of the hotel side. It doesn't have to be his wife, but it's difficult to get anyone except a wife to put in the hours involved.'

Joël nodded, unable to speak. For too long he had been in a state of mingled despair and angry frustration. There were times – this morning had been one – when he didn't know how much longer he could stand his predicament; bound to a girl who claimed to care for him but refused him any solace. Even before the accident she had never made love to him. When he had tried to teach her to please him, she had reacted as if he were forcing her into performing some nasty foreign perversion. Now, seeing not only his marriage but his career in ruins, he came close to breaking down and confiding all his troubles to Allevard.

While he was struggling to compose himself, the older man said, 'Lady Carlyon will be in London in a few days' time, I'm told. Why not see her and find out exactly what the job involves? If she appears likely to be a reasonable employer, then you can go to Long-warden to inspect the kitchen and, equally important, the living quarters provided. The Duke told me that, years ago, it used to be one of the finest houses in the country. It may be the present Countess intends to revive that reputation.'

He paused, sipped his wine and continued, 'You could

45

do a lot worse than try it, Joël. We don't want to lose you, but your domestic problems would be eased by a move to the country and opportunities such as this don't occur very often. As the Countess comes from America where salaries are higher than here, she may be prepared to pay you considerably more than you're earning at present.'


**12.45 pm** For lunch, which she ate on a flat roof in Knightsbridge which, by June, had to look like an established garden, Damaris had a hard pear, a carton of yogurt and a hunk of crusty wholemeal bread.

When she looked back at the food she had eaten as a child, most of it out of tins, chips every day of the week, never any properly cooked vegetables; it amazed her that she had grown up with a clear skin, slim body and sound teeth.

Perhaps her unknown father's genes had something to do with it. She didn't know about her mother's teeth, but Auntie Marlene had had false teeth in her twenties and, like her mother before her, had used sweets to shut up her children whenever they whined. Fortunately, Damaris had not been a whiner.

While she ate she re-read the card from the Countess of Carlyon.

Dear Miss Lynn,
I am looking for someone with imagination and flair to take care of the gardens here at Longwarden and your name has been suggested to me. Is it possible for us to meet and discuss the project? You would find it offered plenty of scope for your creative skills. I am often in London and shall be there on Tuesday and Wednesday of next week if either of those days is convenient for you.

Yours sincerely – Jane Carlyon

Replacing the card in her bag, Damaris wondered who

had suggested her to Lady Carlyon. It could have been any one of the titled women whose London gardens were in her care. But would they put her name forward for a post which must inevitably deprive them of her services?

How could she take charge of the gardens at Long-warden – the name of the Countess' house was also printed on the top of the card – and continue her present practice? It wouldn't be possible. The whole basis of her success was that although she could no longer do all the planting and maintenance herself, as she had at the beginning, she still kept a very close eye on all the gardens on her books, and was continually thinking of ways to improve them.

That was how she had met Peter. One evening last September she had been standing in the garden of Sir Robert and Lady Stow-Bedon's house in Chelsea – they were in Scotland – pondering a change in a border when a man had come out of the house and said, 'Hello . . . who are you?' He had turned out to be one of the Stow-Bedons' sons.

During the afternoon she thought about the Countess' offer and wondered if, after being her own boss for so long, she could work under someone else's direction.

How large were the gardens at Longwarden? Who had been in charge of them up to now? Who had laid them out in the first place? How many people were needed to keep them in order? What sort of soil were they on? These and a dozen other questions occurred to her in the odd moments when her mind wasn't fully occupied with the work she already had in hand.

She tried to remember why the name Longwarden rang a faint bell in her memory. Had there been a space in her day she would have gone to Vincent Square, to the library of the Royal Horticultural Society where they would be sure to have some information about Longwarden. Today there was no time for that. Anyway there could be no harm in meeting the Countess next week and finding out what sort of post she was offering.

In Damaris' experience around five in the evening was a good time to catch people on the telephone. She decided to ring up the Countess and make an appointment to see her the following Tuesday.


**5.50 pm** Occasionally Laura had to work after five thirty. When this happened she would telephone Miss Foxley to say she wouldn't be able to meet her at Baker Street station as usual.

It was seldom that her employer kept her at the office later than seven, but even at that time of night she disliked going home by herself, particularly in the winter months. With her friend, Laura felt safe. On her own she was nervous of being attacked by a mugger, accosted by a wino on the scrounge or ogled by an unpleasant man.

It amazed her to see young women going boldly into public houses which she still regarded as men's places and wouldn't have dared to enter. She would have liked sometimes to go to a play in the West End. But Miss Foxley wasn't interested in the theatre and Laura didn't feel equal to going on her own.

Once, during the run of a production she had specially wanted to see, she had mentioned it to her step-mother. Mrs Denham had promptly pointed out all the hazards. How would Laura pass the time between leaving the office and arriving at the theatre? Did she fancy sitting in a Wimpy bar for the best part of two hours? All the nice tea shops would be shut. And what about the journey back, late at night, on the Underground? Every day the papers reported the terrible things which happened in London at night. Rapes, muggings . . . crime was rife. A woman on her own was asking for trouble.

Also, of course, there was the question of who would

keep Mrs Denham company. She couldn't be left on her own, not in her state of health.

So Laura continued to read the critics' opinions of plays in the *Daily Telegraph* – her step-mother culled her view of life from the *Express* and the *News of the World* – but had never yet been to see one.

Since Mrs Denham's death she had taken to spending Sunday afternoons exploring London's museums and art galleries. But for years her only escape from her dull and restricted life had been through books borrowed from Northwood Hills public library.

She did not, like Miss Foxley, enjoy the fantasy world of Mills & Boon romances. Laura sought her vicarious excitement in factual accounts of other people's adventures. When she had worked her way through the travel section – in two decades of nightly reading she had gone through a great many books – she had turned to biography and history. Often she longed for someone with whom to discuss what she read. But there had never been anyone she could talk to in that way and now, she knew, there never would be.

Life wasn't like Miss Foxley's novels in which sooner or later everyone met her dream man. At the age of thirty-nine, after twenty years devoted to the care of an ailing step-parent, Laura had long since resigned herself to permanent spinsterhood.

'Quite an unusual vacancy came in today,' Miss Foxley told her that evening on the way home.

'What was it?' asked Laura, without much interest.

All day she had had a slight headache. She was looking forward to a bath and a glass of sherry. Such self-indulgence had been out of the question in Mrs Denham's lifetime, but now Laura was beginning to pamper herself with a bottle of sherry and a box of chocolates every week. As she no longer had to pay Mrs Tarves, a widow from down the road, to come in and attend to her step-mother during the day, she had some money to spare for inessentials.

'The Countess of Carlyon is looking for a secretary,' said Miss Foxley. 'At least, the work is mainly secretarial but the successful applicant will have some other duties. The snag is she has to live in. Not many people want that – especially not in a house a long way from anywhere. I think we're going to have a problem finding some candidates for the Countess to interview. There aren't many suitable people on our books at the moment. Those who might get it won't want it. Although the pay is very good.'

'Would she take someone with a child?' asked Laura. She knew that many of the women with whom her friend dealt were divorced or single parents. 'I should have thought any single mother would jump at it. A house in the country ... fresh air ... pleasant surroundings ...'

'I didn't ask that, but I shouldn't imagine she would – not at this stage,' said Miss Foxley. 'Not many people want to be bothered with other people's children if they can avoid it. Why should they indeed? I've no patience with all these so-called single parents. Irresponsible nuisances is what I call them.'

Laura had heard her wax indignant on this subject before. A broad vein of moral indignation ran close to the surface of Margaret's character.

Laura didn't disagree with her views. She felt that a lot of people did behave amazingly fecklessly; but they always had and always would. Even responsible people could be tempted from the path of virtue. Perhaps it had never happened to Miss Foxley but it had to Laura and, ever since, she had taken a more sympathetic view of the follies of others. If, years ago, she hadn't pulled herself together at a critical moment, she might now be a single parent herself.

'What are the other duties you mentioned?' she asked, to cut short a familiar diatribe.

'The Countess says she needs someone who can cope with anything, and everything. "A reliable right hand" to use her own expression.' Leaning closer and speaking more confidentially, Miss Foxley went on, 'She's not a member of the aristocracy herself. She told me she's an American. She arrived in England last autumn and now she's doing up the house and needs someone sensible and capable to handle her correspondence and anything else which arises.'

'Do you think I would suit her?' asked Laura, the question surprising her almost as much as her friend.

'*You*?' Miss Foxley echoed, momentarily taken aback. Then, concluding that Laura must be joking, she gave her dry little laugh. 'I'm sure you would suit her admirably. We could find you any number of places if you weren't so comfortably settled with Widdington and Bartlow.'

'I'm not sure I want to stay with W and B forever,' Laura said cautiously. 'Do you really think I would suit the Countess? What's the salary she's offering?'

'Not as much as you're earning, my dear.'

'How much?' Laura persisted.

Miss Foxley began to look displeased. 'I'm afraid that is confidential. I don't think the Countess would like it broadcast.'

Her repressive tone kindled in Laura a spark of the rebellious feeling which, while her step-mother was alive, she had often had to suppress because of Mrs Denham's heart condition. There was nothing wrong with her friend's heart and suddenly Laura resented being spoken to in that voice, as if she were guilty of prying.

'All the applicants will want to know. Why can't I be told?' she said mildly.

'Really, Laura, it isn't like you to be argumentative. Has something upset you at the office today? I thought you weren't looking quite yourself when you came into the station. Is Mr Widdington being difficult? I know how trying he can be . . . but so are all men. You know that, my dear.'

Miss Foxley had suffered from a tyrannical father and a weak-willed, submissive mother who had never stood up to him or supported her daughter when she did. Now her mother was dead and her father was in an old people's home, still trying to bully the staff and his fellow inmates, where his daughter paid him a duty visit every other weekend.

'It's nothing to do with Mr Widdington. He's in one of his good moods this week and anyway I can cope with him,' said Laura. 'But I've felt like a change for some time and this job with the Countess is the first one you've mentioned to me which sounds as if it might be interesting.' With unwonted resolution she added, 'I'd like to apply for it, Margaret.'

This time Miss Foxley's stunned silence lasted considerably longer. At length she said firmly, 'If you really want a change, then of course we'll find you something suitable. You mustn't jump at the first thing which comes along. That would be *most* unwise. You need something in central London . . . something which won't upset your present arrangements.'

'What present arrangements?' asked Laura, foreseeing a battle of wills.

'I don't think you've thought about this carefully,' said Miss Foxley. 'Only last week I had calls from two very good girls whom we placed with a firm which moved from West One to the suburbs. For the staff on that side of London, the removal has been an advantage. But not for two of the secretaries who live on the other side. They now have to spend twice as long on journeys to and from work and also it's more expensive. Short and convenient journeys – such as you have at the moment – are an important consideration.'

'If I got this job with the Countess I shouldn't have to travel at all. It's a living-in post, you said.'

'Which means, I shouldn't be surprised, that you'd find yourself working much longer hours than you do now. The Countess made it clear – as I shall warn all the applicants – that this isn't a five-day week, nine to five position. What she terms "flexible hours" could turn out to mean being at her beck and call at *all* hours,' Miss Foxley said, on a note of foreboding. 'You're a person who's easily put upon, Laura. I shouldn't like to see you exploited *again*.'

'I had a duty to Gwen. I shouldn't be under an obligation to the Countess. It would be quite a different situation.'

At this point they reached Northwood Hills and the conversation was broken off until they had passed through the station and turned away from the shopping centre towards the quieter side streets lined with houses built in the Thirties, many – including their own – with the pebble-dash finish and Tudor-style beams of the period.

Like theirs, the majority of the houses were empty during the day as suburban wives as well as husbands worked to pay off mortgages and hire purchase debts. Both Laura and Miss Foxley were free of those burdens but the expense of upkeep was still a worry.

'I shouldn't have to burn my boats. I could let my house for six months or a year,' said Laura. 'The Middletons, next door but three to me, had no difficulty letting theirs. A Japanese couple took it. They were very quiet, good tenants.'

'I shouldn't fancy having foreigners in my house. Nor should I consider it fair to my neighbours,' Miss Foxley said shortly. 'I wish I had never mentioned this to you, Laura. If I'd had any idea you were in such a strange, restless mood, I shouldn't have told you about it.' After a pause, she added, 'I'm also surprised and hurt that our friendship apparently means so much less to you than to me.'

This was what Laura had dreaded; being made to feel selfish and heartless.

'It means a lot to me too, Margaret, but you know how I've always wanted to live in the country. When I think of being here till I retire, it depresses me terribly. You haven't as long to go to retirement as I have. Then you'll be free to move wherever you fancy. But it's more than twenty years before I retire. It's . . . it's beginning to feel like a life sentence. I must break out of the rut I'm in.'

As she spoke Laura's simmering unrest bubbled up, like milk in a pan, and became, all at once, strong and urgent. She saw that it would have been better to have uprooted herself after Gwen's funeral. Margaret would have accepted it then. But although relieved rather than grieved by her step-mother's death, Laura had needed time to adjust to becoming, at thirty-nine, an independent person.

'Where does the Countess live? How soon can I go for an interview?' she asked, with a sudden fizz of excitement, an emotion she hadn't experienced for a very long time, not since Bernard . . . As she had trained it to do, her mind immediately censored the memories conjured up by the unfamiliar rush of adrenalin.

'That is something I shall have to discuss with Beryl,' said Miss Foxley, referring to the head of the agency. 'You're behaving much too impulsively, Laura. It isn't like you. I'm sure when you've thought it over you'll realise it wouldn't be wise to make such a drastic change without long and careful consideration. There'll be other more suitable jobs if you really feel you need a change. I'll see you tomorrow. Goodnight.'

She left Laura at her gate and continued towards her own house, her umbrage manifest by her stiffly set shoulders and brisk heavy tread.

When she unlocked her front door, Laura was greeted by the welcoming aroma of an oxtail casserole which, thanks to an automatic oven, had been slow-cooking for an hour and a half and would be ready to serve by the time she had changed her clothes and steamed some vegetables to go with it. She found that her headache had gone. She no longer needed a warm bath to relax her. Perhaps instead of sherry she would have a glass of wine, and another with her casserole. Why not?

In her bedroom she took off her grey suit and plain white blouse, hanging the suit on the outside of the wardrobe to be pressed and checked for spots before she put it away. The blouse she would handwash, with her underwear, at bedtime.

Having put on a jumper and skirt, she washed her hands at the basin in the corner of the room and then sat down at the dressing table to comb her hair.

Looking at her reflection, she remembered Margaret saying, 'It isn't like you.'

What *am* I like? thought Laura. Is this dull-looking woman in the mirror the real me? Would I have been someone different if my mother had lived and Daddy hadn't married Gwen?

On the dressing table was a photograph of her father in Royal Air Force uniform with the ribbons of the DFC and DSO underneath his wings. By the end of World War Two he had been a Wing Commander and one of the RAF's most famous pilots.

In 1946, having survived many brushes with death himself, he lost his young wife in childbirth. To the consternation of his friends – Laura had learned this years later – soon afterwards he married the widow of another RAF officer who had been left with two young children to bring up. Eight years later, by then a rep selling fire extinguishers, he had wrapped his car round a tree.

Police evidence at the inquest had shown that he had gone into a skid at a corner, his judgement of his speed probably impaired by the level of alcohol in his bloodstream at the time. It had been, said the Coroner, a regrettable end for a man with a valiant war record.

Laura remembered her father as a split personality; someone funny and loving when they were alone together, but a different, much quieter man in the presence of his second wife and her children. After his death she had heard Gwen telling people that he had gone to pieces after the war, taking to drink because he couldn't adjust to civilian life.

Laura had never believed that. She felt sure it was the loss of her mother and his unhappy second marriage which had driven him to the bottle, if in fact he had drunk as much as her step-mother made out. In Laura's own recollection he had never drunk to excess. If he had been a secret tippler surely the smell of alcohol on his breath would have given him away?

Laura thought it possible he had run out of road deliberately, leaving his widow comfortably provided for by his life insurance. If he had, she didn't blame him for ending a situation he had found intolerable. He couldn't have foreseen that Gwen would become an invalid whose care – her own children being unable, so they claimed, to help her – would fall on his daughter's shoulders.

In retrospect, Laura saw that she shouldn't have let herself be chivvied by Bryan and Joanne into accepting full responsibility for their mother. But she had and at least now she had a clear conscience which was not something they could enjoy – if they ever paused for a moment in their upwardly mobile lives to examine their consciences.

Presently, sipping red wine from the supermarket while the carrots and beans cooked, Laura wondered if Margaret were capable of refusing to allow her to apply for the job with the Countess. There was an adamant streak in her which Laura had noticed on several occasions. She hoped Margaret didn't intend to take an arbitrary line with her when they met in the morning. If she did, Laura wouldn't give in lightly. She had spent more than half her life fitting in with other people, accepting their decisions about what she ought to do. It was time she turned over a new leaf and became more assertive.

While she was eating her solitary meal and worrying about Margaret's attitude, it struck her that a way to avoid an unpleasant clash of wills would be to take the initiative of writing to the Countess herself, and doing it at once – tonight. The only snag was she didn't know her address.

A senior secretary for fifteen years, Laura had long since learnt how to solve such problems. The public library was still open and would be sure to have a copy of *Burke's Peerage*. It would be a simple matter to look up the name and location of the Earls of Carlyon.

Leaving the dishes to be washed up later, she put on her outdoor shoes and her second best raincoat and set out in search of the information she needed.


**8.00 pm** While she was cooking her supper, a bean-sprout omelette, Damaris remembered why the name Longwarden seemed familiar to her.

Somewhere on her bookshelves was a Christmas present from one of her customers, a biography of which so far she had read only the first few pages. Written by Allegra Lomax, who must be the sister-in-law of the Countess who wanted Damaris to work for her, it was a life of the seventh Earl whose interest in plants had taken him, at the turn of the century, to China and the Himalayas in search of new species.

She had been enjoying the book when the need to read others more directly related to her work had forced her to put it aside. The cleaner who, once a week, went through the flat for her, must have tucked it away on the crowded shelves where it had remained forgotten until this evening.

Now, comfortably curled on the sofa with a mug of herb tea at her elbow, Damaris had it beside her on top of a pile of horticultural magazines. Knowing that she ought to be reading the current issue of *The Garden*, she looked again at the photograph of the author on the back of the jacket. Lady Allegra's eyes were the colour of violets, her hair like the leaves of copper beeches in spring.

Damaris wondered what it was like to be born an earl's daughter. It seemed unfair that, as well as that privileged position, she had also been given a dramatically beautiful face and the talent to write a book inspired by and based on her great-grandfather's diaries.

But life was unfair, and as Damaris studied the face of the book's aristocratic author she felt no resentment of her superior advantages, only a profound thankfulness that she had been given the means to break free from her own sordid origins.


**8.30 pm** On her way back from the library, Laura encountered a group of youths engaging in horseplay. Normally she would have crossed the road to avoid them but tonight, mentally composing a letter of application, she walked up to them before she realised they were obstructing the pavement.

To her surprise they made room for her to pass. Automatically Laura's grip on her bag tightened as she wondered if one of them might see her as an easy victim and follow her home to mug her in her own front porch. That had happened to someone in the neighbourhood not long ago.

However a few moments later a quick glance over her shoulder showed the youths moving off in the direction of the pub or the fish and chip shop and soon she was once more preoccupied with her letter.

By nine o'clock it was written and sealed. Although it wouldn't be collected till the following morning, Laura decided to post it tonight, before she could have second thoughts about the wisdom of her action.

The nearest pillar box was past Miss Foxley's house. Through the flowered fibreglass curtains which her friend had chosen for the bay window of her lounge when she'd had it redecorated, Laura could see the radiance of the television screen. Averting her eyes she hurried on to the box and thrust the envelope through the slot, knowing as she did that it might make her friend so angry she would never speak to her again.

Which, if her application were unsuccessful, would result in a very awkward, embarrassing situation.


**10.30 pm** Lucy and Mrs Baston were watching television when Joël returned to the flat.

It seemed to him that they spent more than half their time viewing. At home Papa always switched on TV after supper but soon fell asleep in his chair, whereupon Maman would turn down the sound and, ignoring the flickering screen, get on with her sewing or knitting. Sometimes she read. Madame Vibrac had been a teacher before her marriage to the son of a Breton *pâtissier*.

She herself came from near Paris and had been on holiday on the south coast of Brittany when she met her future husband, not knowing at the time that he wasn't the son of Luc Vibrac, a small town pastry-cook, but a by-blow of the local nobility which was why he was tall and slim and not short and burly like his legal father.

How this had come about had been confided to her when her widowed mother-in-law was dying of cancer. Old Madame Vibrac had wished to unburden herself of a secret kept for fifty years, although it might have been suspected by a few who had noticed the likeness of her son and grandson to the brother of the old man who owned the turreted château a few kilometres out of town.

As a girl the old lady had worked there as one of the laundry-maids. The younger son of the family had been attracted by her sixteen year old prettiness. She had fallen in love with him. When she found herself pregnant, the only way out of her dilemma had been to let her childhood sweetheart, Luc Vibrac, have his way with her.

As she had been a brunette, he would have seen nothing strange in his first-born having black curls and the dark eyes of all his in-laws. Whether, later, he had wondered why his son was six inches taller than anyone in either of their families, and his grandson an equally rangy lad, was something which would never be known.

Old Madame Vibrac had admitted the truth of the matter to the priest for the good of her soul and to Joël's mother for a less commendable reason. She had always felt, quite correctly, that Germaine, who came from a background of local government officials, regarded herself as a cut above the Vibracs.

It had given the old lady immense satisfaction to reveal that, even if on the wrong side of the blanket, Luc was the son of an aristocrat; and that it was through her own youthful indiscretion, not from his mother's side, that Joël came by his distinguished looks and gentlemanly ways.

He had known nothing of all this while he was growing up. His father still didn't. Madame Vibrac saw nothing to be gained by telling her husband, whose blood pressure was already too high, that he was illegitimate.

But when her cherished eldest son had fallen in love with an English girl whom she disliked on sight, she thought it might make him think twice about such an impetuous match if he knew he had blue blood in him and could do better for himself.

To Joël his tenuous connection with the de Tonquedec family was irrelevant. It had surprised him to learn that his prim and proper grandmother had ever been capable of a roll in the hay.

He had never told Lucy, reasoning that if she wouldn't let him make love to her, even when they were engaged, she wouldn't think much of his grandmother who had let two men have her. Also, if Lucy told her mother – to whom she seemed to tell most things – it would be another reason for Gladys Baston to disapprove of him. To be the son of a bastard would be almost as bad as being one himself in Gladys Baston's genteel view of the world.

As he entered the room where they were engrossed in one of the soap operas they followed, both women glanced at him. In Lucy's pale face he read concern that he might still be angry about what had happened that morning. His mother-in-law's expression made it clear that, even if she didn't know the details, she knew he had erred in some way.

A flush tinged Joël's olive skin. It made him angry and embarrassed to wonder if his wife had confided what he had done to her, not only this morning but all the other times when he had tried to persuade her that, just because she couldn't walk, it needn't mean the end of intimate pleasures for either of them.

'Hello Joël. This is nearly over.' Lucy's smile was forced.

As they both knew, the programme had twenty minutes to run. But, even when nothing had happened to disturb the uneasy tenor of their relationship, it had never occurred to her or to her mother to switch off the set and welcome him home.

The fact was he wasn't welcome. To pay the rent – the flat was leased from a man who was working overseas – and the other bills, that was the only use they had for him, he thought bitterly.

'I'll go and make some coffee. Would you like some?' he asked.

'Not at this time of night, thank you.' Mrs Baston's reply conveyed her disapproval of the kind of coffee he made, of drinking it late in the evening, and of husbands who didn't come home at the normal hour. 'You could make us a pot of tea, if you would.'

He went through to the kitchen, wondering how they would react when he told them about the job with the American heiress who was now an English countess.


**10.45 pm** In his tall house in Connaught Square – the lower floors let to a young married couple, both doctors – James Muirhead was comfortably sprawled in what has been called the Rolls-Royce of armchairs, a Deep-seated Titchfield by the London Chairmakers, Lenygon & Morant.

Spread on his lap was a large book, an illustrated life of a man who had been a soldier, a spy, a popular playwright and an inspired designer of palatial mansions at the beginning of the eighteenth century: Sir John Vanbrugh, the architect of Longwarden.

In his telephone call to Lord Carlyon earlier that day, James had discovered that before entrusting the renovation of Longwarden to Clyst, Tacolneston, Muirhead & Hythe, the Earl had satisfied himself that there was another partner capable of handling the job should anything happen to the elderly senior partner.

There had been no need for James to outline his credentials. The Earl seemed to know all about him, and so far as could be judged by a telephone conversation, was himself a brisk, businesslike man with whom it would be easy to deal, although he had said it would be his wife with whom, in the main, James would have to confer.

In his private notes about them, Maurice Clyst had

described the Earl as – *a very fine-looking young man, tall and of splendid physique. Would be too handsome but for a broken nose. Like all aristocrats that I've met – with one notable exception – has pleasant, even genial manner. Shows signs of being deeply in love with his American wife which gives the lie to rumours that it was a marriage of convenience, she being the heiress to many millions of dollars. Lady C. is a beautiful girl with charming manners. They are cousins. She is also a great-grandchild of the so-called Chinese Countess who married the seventh Earl in 1903.*

In the margin alongside these notes, Maurice had added in minuscule writing: *Must read* The Travels of an Edwardian Naturalist, *an account of her great-grandparents' lives by the present Earl's sister, Lady Allegra Lomax.*

James felt it was a book he should read himself, when he had time. For the moment it was the history of the house rather than the activities of its many generations of occupants which interested him.

One of Vanbrugh's most famous buildings was Castle Howard in Yorkshire, an extraordinary achievement for a man who had taken to architecture without any training, although he had had the assistance of Nicholas Hawksmoor who had qualified under Wren and had probably dealt with all the technical aspects.

Blenheim Palace, the gift of a grateful nation to the victorious Duke of Marlborough after he had defeated the supposedly invincible armies of Louis XIV, had been another of Vanbrugh's designs.

Longwarden wasn't as large as Blenheim or Eastbury. It was similar in scale to Seaton Delaval and Grimsthorpe Castle, two more of Vanbrugh's great houses. Studying the photographs of Longwarden, James felt a charge of exhilaration at finding himself responsible for such an important example of England's glorious architectural heritage.

He wished he had someone with whom to share his elation. It was no use ringing up Louise. She was completely uninterested in the conservation of historic buildings. Her idea of a masterpiece was the Centre Pompidou in Paris and Richard Rogers' new building for Lloyds in London, both of which James considered abominations.

There was only one woman who would have understood and shared his excitement. Thinking of her – which he tried not to – his mood changed. Slamming the folio shut, he thrust it aside and sprang up, his body suddenly tense with the futile rage and despair which most of the time he managed to keep under control.


**11.30 pm** Lucy preferred her mother to help her get ready for bed. When Joël entered the bedroom she was lying where he had left her that morning. He knew she was wondering if he would keep his promise never again to make any sexual approaches.

He could see the flicker of apprehension in her eyes when, instead of starting to undress on the far side of the room, he moved into the aisle between the twin beds and sat down on his bed to talk to her.

'I've been offered a job. At least, Allevard has put my name forward for it.'

He saw that his wife's first reaction was relief that it wasn't this morning he wanted to talk about.

It was hard to remember how lovely she had been when he first saw her. Months in hospital, followed by two years in a wheelchair, had drained all the glowing vitality which had first attracted him. Few people looked their best at this time of year, but Lucy was not only pale from being stuck indoors most of the winter but had the drawn look of an invalid. Which she wasn't – or didn't have to be.

'What sort of job?' she asked, without much interest.

Since her involvement in his career had come to an end, she seemed no longer to care about his future.

He told her what Allevard had told him.

'I wouldn't mind leaving here. I'm fed up with this place,' she said. 'But when you tell the Countess you've got a crippled wife she may turn you down. It's no use keeping it quiet. We'd have to take Mother with us. There'd have to be room for her.'

'If the house if enormous, that ought not to be a problem,' he answered. 'I don't know yet what sort of accommodation they're offering. I'll find that out at the interview.' He bent to unlace his shoes, trying to sound casual as he said, 'We can't expect your mother to live with us indefinitely, Lucy. She has a place of her own. She'll want to go back to it one day. I'm sure she must miss her garden.'

'It was Dad who liked gardening, not her. She's thinking about selling *Lingfield*. She doesn't fancy it now, not after other people have lived in it. Besides, what they're paying isn't as much as the interest she'd get if she sold it and invested the money. I'm never going to be able to manage without her helping me, Joël. You'll have to make up your mind to that.'

He reached for her hand which was lying outside the bedclothes and took it gently in his. 'You're too dependent on her, Lucy. You could do more for yourself but she won't let you. What you need are better surroundings . . . gadgets to help you do more things on your own. The bathroom in this place is useless for someone with a handicap.'

'I don't want to be on my own all day while you're working. I need Mum for company as well as for looking after me. You don't realise what it's like. You're only here on Sundays. Without Mum I couldn't stand it.'

'What you need are some more interests,' he said, not for the first time. 'You still have your eyes and your ears and your hands and your brain. There are dozens of things you can do to make life interesting. Watching TV and talking may be enough for your mother. It isn't enough for you. It's not surprising you're bored.'

He had talked to her like this before, many times. Always her thin face stiffened. She refused to listen. Or sometimes she would say mutinously, 'I don't want to join a club and go about with a lot of cripples' or 'What's the point of learning French? I was never any good at it at school.'

Tonight she heard him out in silence, her mouth turned down at the corners, her hand limp in his. Her glum refusal to come to terms with her condition made Joël lose patience with her. When he felt himself wanting to shake her, he stopped talking and moved away.

Later, unable to sleep, tormented by the longing to lie with a willing woman, he wondered how long he could go on like this. Perhaps, in a new environment, Lucy's general attitude might become more positive. But it was no use hoping her attitude to him would change. Perhaps she didn't care if he were unfaithful to her. Perhaps she would be relieved if he found someone else to cater to the needs she found distasteful.

**12.05 am** Lucy Vibrac was dreaming that she was still Lucy Baston, thirteen years old, riding her second pony, Pegasus, in the paddock behind the farmhouse belonging to the parents of her friend Susan Crosby.

As children do, Lucy and Susan had become best friends by force of circumstance rather than because they had things in common and felt drawn to each other.

Susan was one of five children – all the others were boys – whose parents were prosperous yeoman farmers. Mr and Mrs Crosby were a stout, sturdy, friendly couple who enjoyed their busy lives. Being content with their station in life they spoke with a Suffolk accent and Mr Crosby had a laugh which could be heard three fields away. They were proud of their brawny sons and although Susan was a fat child with lank hair and braces on her teeth, they thought she was lovely. Susan received more hugs and kisses in a week than Lucy had in a year. Even her brothers, good-natured lads, never teased her unkindly.

Lucy was an only child. Her father, Arnold Baston, was a senior clerk with an insurance company. All his spare time was devoted to cleaning his car and tending the immaculate garden surrounding his chalet bungalow on a dormitory estate outside Ipswich. Her mother's mission in life was to keep her house equally immaculate and all of them dressed in clothes which, if washable, were never worn more than once before being put in the machine.

Determined that her little girl should never come in contact with the rougher elements attending the local State school, Gladys arranged for Lucy to attend a private school with a nice rust and grey uniform and pupils who came from nice homes. Not all of them quite up to the standard which she and Arnold set themselves — some people who should have known better were surprisingly lax in their domestic standards — but none from working class homes. That was the main thing. Gladys had bettered herself by marrying Arnold and she was going to make sure that Lucy had the opportunity to rise even higher.

Looking to the future, she hoped to see her daughter marry into the executive class, with a large house, a car of her own, a swimming pool and an au pair girl.

At first Arnold took Lucy to school on his way to the office and soon after lunch Gladys caught the bus to town to look round the shops before bringing the child home. Then they discovered there was a car pool operating. If Arnold would ferry in two little girls, their mothers, relieved of the early run, would take it in turns to give Lucy a lift back.

One of the mothers was Mary Crosby. As the Crosbys'

land marched with the Millersmead estate where the Bastons lived, it wasn't long before Susan and Lucy were playing together on Saturday mornings. Mrs Crosby hoped Lucy would make Susan less of a tomboy. Mrs Baston had heard that the Crosbys were highly regarded in the district, even if they were not what you could call refined. Their two elder boys were already at a public school, to be followed by the others when they were old enough. Far-sighted Gladys could see that, if the Crosby boys weren't good enough for Lucy, they might one day have friends who were. Planning her daughter's life took Gladys' mind off the imperfections of her own.

Rather than Lucy taming Susan, it was Susan who was the stronger influence. Given a different best friend, Lucy might never have become an outdoor girl or mad about horses. When small she had liked playing with dolls, endlessly changing their clothes and brushing their nylon hair. By the time she was eight the dolls were entombed in boxes and she was happily sharing the task of grooming Susan's Dartmoor pony and keeping his tack clean.

It was Mrs Crosby who suggested to Gladys that, if Lucy's father would buy a pony for her, they would be pleased to house and feed it.

'Susie has already taught Lucy to ride, but it's not as much fun taking turns on Blackie as it would be if they both had ponies,' was the point she made.

At first Arnold had opposed the idea. Even if they didn't have to pay for the pony's upkeep, Lucy would need riding clothes and there would be other expenses which he could ill afford. It was a matter of pride with him never to have a car more than two years old, and his latest plan for the garden was to build a patio outside the lounge. Also he felt it was time they had a foreign holiday. Not that he wanted to go abroad and he doubted if Gladys did either, but it was what everyone else was doing. Not to have been to Corfu or Torremolinos or Malta was to be out of step. Arnold liked to be in step.

Gladys was nervous of flying and she didn't fancy the food foreigners ate, everything swimming in oil. One of her neighbours had told her that in a Spanish restaurant, she and her husband had unwisely chosen rabbit. It had arrived at the table with its head on; a whole rabbit skinned and split down the middle, served with hunks of bread and a bowl of thick garlic sauce.

'It turned my stomach to look at it,' Mrs Newbold had confided, with a shudder.

Reminding Arnold of other people they knew who had had nasty experiences while abroad, Gladys set out to change his mind about the pony. To put him into a malleable mood – he could be obstinate at times – she allowed him to have intercourse two days sooner than usual.

Sometimes she managed to avoid that unpleasant necessity for as long as three weeks at a time. She had always been highly strung and a good many of her nervous headaches were genuine. But if she made him go without it for too long, Arnold became very irritable. She found that, to maintain a pleasant atmosphere, it was best to let him do it once a week. More often than that and he was like a dog with two tails. She could wind him round her little finger.

Lucy's first pony, Charlie, was a brown Exmoor with a creamy muzzle and underbelly. By the time they were ten, she and Susan had begun to compete in Pony Club gymkhanas. From then on until they left school, they were both horse-mad, thinking and talking of little else. Neither was a good enough rider to win many rosettes and trophies, but they enjoyed themselves. From their parents' point of view it kept them from wanting to go to discos with boys and dressing in the freakish get-ups affected by some of their contemporaries.

It was during this time that Mrs Baston was advised

to have a hysterectomy. One of the perks of Arnold's job being private medical insurance, she was able to have the operation without delay in a comfortable clinic. As soon as she was allowed visitors Lucy saw her every afternoon before going home on the bus, and her husband spent an hour at her bedside after leaving his office.

Kind Mrs Crosby had invited Lucy to stay at the farm while her mother was away, and had also offered to give Arnold his evening meal. He wasn't a man who could cook for himself and neither could Lucy, her mother being a woman who couldn't abide other people making messes in her spotless kitchen.

Lucy would have enjoyed staying with the Crosbys, but her mother felt she should keep her father company. He didn't know how to work the washing machine, and although his shirts were fifty per cent polyester they still needed pressing to look as they should. Their daughter knew how to iron.

Told it might be six months before she felt fully restored and conjugal relations must not be resumed for some weeks Gladys decided to move into the spare room. Not permanently. Just for the time being.

For years she and Arnold had slept on twin divans with buttoned Dralon headboards and machine-washable bedspreads with quilted satin tops surrounded by double flounces of white nylon lace. Although they had never had overnight guests, the spare room was similarly equipped, with a bowl of plastic roses on the kidney-shaped dressing table which had three tiers of nylon lace frills to match the skirts of the bedspread.

Arnold made no objection. He was a considerate man who understood that after her major operation his wife needed time to recover. When Gladys complained that following the disturbed nights in the hospital she wasn't sleeping as well as she had before, it was Arnold who asked the doctor if, as a temporary measure, she could take a mild sleeping pill.

**12.15 am** Lucy often had riding dreams, and sometimes she had strange nightmares from which she would wake up trembling with revulsion at the images conjured by her subconscious mind.

Strangely, she never had nightmares about the accident. All her riding dreams were happy ones, so vivid that, for a moment or two after waking, she would feel her legs were all right; that she could stretch and sit up and her legs would obey her brain instead of lying inert and useless.

When she woke up during the night after Joël had told her about the job in the country, the light of the street lamp filtering through the unlined curtains showed the long sloping shape of his body as he lay with his back to her.

He was a restless sleeper who sometimes rolled onto his back and sometimes lay sprawled, face down, his arms flung above his head. She knew his present position had no significance, but because of what had happened that morning it seemed to symbolise the state of their relationship.

All day she had been haunted by the bitterness in his voice as he snarled, 'Don't worry . . . I shan't try again. That was the last time – ever!'

At first, with her body still cringing from his touch, she had felt relief. But after he had left the flat she had burst into tears and her mother had found her crying when she came in to get her up.

Then of course Mum had wanted to know why she was upset and Lucy had had to pretend she had had a bad night. Not that her mother had believed her. She knew it had something to do with her son-in-law. She couldn't stand Joël. Had never liked him.

71

'You must be out of your mind to drop a nice fellow like Gavin for that Frenchman,' she had stormed, after discovering that Lucy had stopped going out with Gavin, a chartered accountant who had just bought his first Porsche. 'You'll regret it, my girl . . . mark my words.'

Lucy had regretted it – but not for the reason prophesied by her mother: that Joël would never be able to give her all the comforts, indeed the luxuries which were within Gavin's grasp.

It wasn't Joël's fault their marriage was a disaster. It was hers. It would have been just the same with Gavin or any other man. They all wanted something she couldn't give them. She had tried. It was no use. She couldn't.

She had loved Joël at first. She still did – until he started to touch her. Then the affection turned to revulsion. She hated him and all men.

---

# Winterbrook Farm, Near Boston, Massachusetts

On the south-facing lawn in front of the large handsome house built by Thomas Blakewell in 1761, Jane Carlyon stood close to the spot where last spring she had turned around and met the smiling blue gaze of a stranger who was now her husband and the father of the child she was carrying.

It had been a little later in the year, and much earlier in the day, when they had first met each other at the tricentenary celebrations of the arrival in New England of the founding father of one of the oldest and most distinguished families in America.

She had a vivid memory of the way her husband had

looked at her before introducing himself as a cousin from England, leaving her to find out for herself that he was also a peer of the realm, a professional photographer of wild life and – most importantly in view of her reaction to him – a bachelor with a rather wild reputation.

'It's a shame North couldn't come over with you,' said Alison Blakewell, her hostess, coming to join her.

'It would have been nice,' Jane agreed. 'But it was because he was going to be away for a few days that I suddenly thought of spending the weekend with you and Marcus.'

She had come over on Concorde, leaving London at 10.30 am and stepping out of a cab at Bergdorf Goodman on Fifth Avenue at 10.30 am New York time. She had then spent several hours shopping before catching the shuttle to Boston, where Marcus and Alison had met her and driven her from the airport to the historic house where, in August last year, she and North had been married.

'From now on it's going to be a busy year for me,' she told Alison, as they strolled back to the house. 'Up to now I've done very little about changing the way things are run at Longwarden. I wanted to feel my feet and not antagonise anyone by being too much of a new broom. But now Pen has gone to Spain and Mrs Armitage, who's been the cook there for years, is going to marry the milkman, it's time to reorganise a little.'

'Even though you wrote that you liked her, I guess it will be easier not having your mother-in-law with you,' said Alison.

'Not really. In fact I shall miss her. Pen is the antithesis of the difficult mother-in-law,' Jane told her, smiling. 'When I first arrived I think she was frightened of me.'

As the evening breeze disarranged a swathe of her glossy black hair, she lifted a finely boned hand to tuck the strands behind her ear. Her hair and her delicate hands were both legacies from her great-grandmother, the half-Chinese wife of her husband's ancestor, the seventh Earl.

Unlike Alison, who by birth and background belonged to the most exclusive stratum of American society, Jane not only had a dash of Asian blood but was the daughter of a man who had started with nothing and made himself a multi-millionaire, carrying off the daughter of an old money Boston family in the process.

Born in a walk-up apartment on the West Side of Manhattan, before John Graham had made his first million, Jane had spent most of her life travelling around the world with him and Marie-Simone Polignac, the French sculptress who had loved him and lived with him but never replaced Jane's dead mother in her father's heart.

'It's amazing how much you've changed in the short time you've lived in England, Lady Carlyon,' said Alison, using Jane's title in affectionate teasing. 'Having travelled so widely, you were always more cosmopolitan than American, but now I see signs that you're going to become more British than the British. Tell me about your plans for Longwarden.'

'The first major change will be having the Orangery converted into a year-round swimming pool. Pen was worried about a pool being an eyesore in her lovely garden. As the Orangery hasn't been used since North's father had the heating shut off to cut down the fuel bills, it seems the perfect place for it.'

'Shall you leave the gardens as they are?'

'I'm not sure yet. When I get back to London I'm going to talk to a girl I'd like to have take them over. I also have to interview secretaries, and we're going to replace Mrs Armitage with a properly trained chef. Her cooking was fine for everyday family meals, but she wasn't very imaginative and we need someone who can cope with the staff meals as well as ours. During Mrs

Armitage's time there's been only a skeleton staff, but soon we shall have a much larger one.'

'With the baby to plan for as well, it does sound like a busy summer. Don't overdo things, will you?'

Jane laughed. 'That's what Pen says every time she calls me from Spain. She had difficult pregnancies. So far the signs are that I'm going to be luckier. I've never felt better in my life.'

'You look wonderful,' Alison agreed. 'Being pregnant suits some women.'

'It's not only being pregnant . . . it's being happy. I guess at the moment, for me, life is as good as it gets. I only wish it were not such an unhappy time for Allegra and poor little Sarah,' Jane added, her grey eyes clouding as she thought of her sister-in-law and her husband's nineteen year old cousin who had also been brought up at Longwarden.

'That was a terrible thing, Alessandro Risconti being drowned,' said Alison, frowning. 'It was a big news story here and of course the American press picked up his relationship with your sister-in-law. She must be shattered, poor thing. Is she going to stay at Longwarden with you?'

'We don't know. We hope so. It wouldn't be good for her to be by herself in her present state.'

'What's the matter with Sarah? You haven't written about that.'

'She's also lost the man she was in love with. He isn't dead like Andro. Nick has just disappeared. We think he's probably rejoined the Spanish Foreign Legion. He was in the Legion for two years before he came back to Longwarden last October. I liked him. Considering his background, I thought he'd turned out very well.'

'What was his background?'

'He's the illegitimate son of a girl from Longwarden village and a soldier she met at a dance. It was her married sister who raised him, but then died, leaving

75

him to the untender mercies of his foster father. He's a horrible man who used to be a gamekeeper at Longwarden but now works for the syndicate which bought the shooting rights from North's father. Everyone thinks Ted Rivington used to ill-treat Nick. He and Sarah became friends when Nick started helping out in the stables. They've known each other from childhood.'

'If he was being badly treated, why didn't someone do something?' Alison asked.

'That's what I wanted to know. It seems there was no proof. Ted denied it and so did Nick. But when he was nearly eighteen he ran away, leaving Ted with a black eye, which suggests the rumours were true. Now he's disappeared again and Sarah is obviously heartbroken.'

'How did he feel about Sarah?' asked her hostess, as they walked round the side of the house.

'I'm sure he was in love with her and that's why he cut and run . . . because he felt it could never work out.'

'By the sound of it, he was right,' was Alison's comment. 'From what you say Nick is even more ineligible than your father was when he married your mother.'

'But they were very happy together . . . in the few years they had. I don't remember her clearly, but I know Dad never stopped missing her to the last day of his life. He was very fond of Marie-Simone and he knew she wanted to marry him and have his child, but he didn't want another wife. He was such a down to earth man and yet in his heart I believe he felt that his marriage to Mother went beyond "till death us do part",' Jane said reflectively. 'Which is strange, because he also believed that one life is all we have.'

'Have you seen Marie-Simone recently?' asked Alison, as they entered the house.

She had never met John Graham's mistress, but had often heard Jane speak affectionately of her.

'We lost touch for a while but she came to Longwarden for Christmas and I call her or she calls me at least once a week. Next month I may go to see her. *April in Paris . . . chestnuts in blossom . . .*' Jane quoted.

She didn't tell Alison that, during the time she had been out of touch with Marie-Simone, the Frenchwoman had been grappling with a drinking problem brought on by her grief at John Graham's early death in an automobile accident.

Marie-Simone's increasing dependence on drink and pills, and her subsequent cure in a clinic for alcoholics, were secrets which Jane had kept even from her husband.

They were now her only secrets from him, although for some time their marriage had been based on a deliberate deception. Knowing that, at the beginning, North hadn't loved her but had married her for practical reasons, she had made him believe her motive was equally mundane – the desire to have a title and be mistress of a great house.

The truth of the matter was that she had fallen headlong in love with him from the outset, but had tried to delude herself that her reasons were as practical as his, the main one being that the restoration of an historic house in danger of decay had seemed a good use of the fortune her father had left her.

It was only very recently, seeing the abyss of despair in which Allegra had been left by the death of her Italian lover, that Jane had stopped acting a part and admitted to North how much she loved him.

To her incredulous joy, he had confessed to falling deeply in love with her. Since that memorable night of mutual soul-baring, they had been in a state of bliss which had more than made up for the first tense months of their marriage.

Today was the first time they had been apart since declaring their love for each other. As she parted from Alison and went upstairs to take a bath, she found herself missing him already, even though it was barely twelve hours by her body clock since he had kissed her goodbye at Heathrow.

Alison had put her in the bedroom where Jane had slept the night before her wedding, a small private ceremony in the drawing room downstairs. Remembering her nervous misgivings on her last morning as Jane Graham, she smiled to herself as she undressed.

So far the only visible sign of her pregnancy was that her breasts were larger and also more sensitive. She hadn't told North they were tender but he seemed to know it instinctively, fondling them gently, no longer taking her with the repressed savagery of the time when he thought she didn't care for him and was merely paying, with her body, for the title Countess of Carlyon.

She was waiting for the tub to fill when the bedside telephone trilled. After turning off the taps, she hurried to answer it.

'Hello darling. How was your flight?' It was North's deep distinctive voice.

'It was fine and I had a great time shopping in New York. But I'm missing you. How was your day?'

North was spending the weekend at a school for falconers where he was taking photographs for a feature for a newspaper colour supplement. He spent a few minutes talking about it, then said, 'I'm missing you too. I'm having an early night with a book on falconry but even reading in bed is better when there are two of you doing it. Of course it's still early over there. You won't be staying up till the small hours, UK time, will you?'

'There's no point in trying to adjust to American time when I'm over here such a sort while. We're having a lap supper, early, and then Marcus and Alison are watching something on television. I'll be in bed by midnight, your time. Tomorrow Aunt Julia's coming to lunch.'

'That almost makes me glad I'm not with you.'

There was no love lost between North and the matriarchal aunt – the much older sister of Jane's mother – with whom his wife had been living in Boston when he met her.

'I'm glad you said almost. Right now I'd put up with a whole day of Aunt Julia's presence to be in your arms this minute instead of three thousand miles apart.'

'You could have come with me,' he reminded her.

'I know, but I think it's better, when you're working, not to have me tagging along. Have you called Longwarden?'

'Flitton knows where I am if he sees any reason to contact me.' North paused. Evidently he guessed what was on her mind even though they were on different sides of the Atlantic. 'You worry about them too much, sweetie. Neither Allegra nor Sarah is going to be found in the lake because we're away for the weekend.'

In the letters of one of Jane's seventeenth century predecessors, there was a reference to a maidservant who, bereft of her lover, had attempted to drown herself in Longwarden's lake but fortunately had been prevented.

'I guess not . . . but I can't help worrying. I know how desperate I'd feel if I lost you.'

'You're not going to lose me. We're going to grow old together surrounded by our progeny. It isn't good for our firstborn to have you sharing the girls' wretchedness,' he said firmly. 'I'm sorry for them myself. I should have been very glad to have Andro as a brother-in-law – officially or otherwise. But, given time, Allegra will pick up her life and find someone else to share it with. So will Sarah.'

'Maybe . . . but I do believe true love is forever . . . and that it only happens once,' said Jane, thinking of her parents.

'In that case, as you are *my* true love, will you please stop worrying me by worrying too much about them.

79

Give my regards to Marcus and Alison. Tell them it's high time they came over and stayed with us. Goodnight, my love. Sleep tight.'

'Goodnight, darling. Thank you for calling.' She sent him long distance kisses, regretting, as she rang off, that she wasn't in Sussex with him.


When she opened her eyes the next morning it was later than her normal waking time but several hours before anyone in the Blackwell household was likely to be stirring.

All Alison's visitors' rooms were equipped with an electric kettle so that insomniac or early-rising guests could make themselves hot drinks. While waiting for the water to boil, Jane opened one of the parcels bought in New York. She knew it was crazy to start knitting for her baby this soon but she hadn't been able to resist buying the yarn, the pins and the pattern for the cutest little sweater she had noticed in Altman's baby department.

Although, when her father was alive, she had flown around the world doing needlepoint, she had never learned how to knit. But she wanted to make at least a few of her baby's clothes. Sitting up in bed with a book of knitting instructions on one side of her and the pattern on the other, she began slowly to follow the directions.

Some time later, with half an inch of inexpert ribbing on one of the pins, she remembered the letter in her bag and got out of bed to fetch it and read it again.

Written on good quality paper in a clear, well-formed hand, it began

*Dear Lady Carlyon,*
*I understand you are looking for a secretary and should like to offer my*
*services.*

80

This was followed by a curriculum vitae, and in the final paragraph, the reason why Laura Denham (Miss) felt she was a suitable applicant.

*As I am single, a job with elastic hours is not as difficult for me as it might be for someone with family or other commitments. Also, being nearly forty, I enjoy quiet pastimes such as walking and reading rather than wanting to be close to a town as most younger people do. I have always wanted to live in the country but, until very recently, was unable to move from London because I was caring for an invalid who has now died.*

Jane had always like the name Laura and there was something about Miss Denham's handwriting which suggested she would be a likeable person. What she stated in her letter was true; younger secretaries would want a more sophisticated social life than they would find in Longwarden village. Jane had plans to make Longwarden itself a lively, self-sufficient community with entertainment facilities, but that was a dream which it could take years to realise.


On her way home to England, in the airport bookshop at Kennedy, Jane bought a paperback called *Confessions of a Medical Heretic*.

The author was an experienced family physician, Dr Robert S. Mendelsohn. She liked the look of his face on the back cover. But the paragraph which made her buy his book was: *If you're pregnant, you go to the doctor and he treats you as if you're sick. Childbirth is a nine-month disease which must be treated, so you're sold on intravenous fluid bags, fetal monitors, a host of drugs, the totally unnecessary episiotomy, and – the top of the line product – the Caesarean delivery.*

Dr Mendelsohn's message, which made the trans-atlantic flight seem even shorter than three and a half hours, was that ninety per cent of modern medicine was more harmful than beneficial. But he was a positive critic who, having warned his readers of the dangers of meekly submitting to treatments which might not be good for them, then set out what people could do to protect their health. He was adamant that the best place to give birth was at home, describing the birth of a grandchild in his own home to support his contention.

By the time Concorde landed, the book had changed Jane's mind about having her baby in the clinic recommended by the Harley Street gynaecologist who had confirmed her pregnancy and was said to be one of the top men in his field.

She landed at Heathrow, where North was waiting to meet her, determined to have his child in her own bedroom at Longwarden.

---

# *London*

For her first interview with the Countess, Damaris went to Carlyon House in Park Lane.

Her appointment was for two o'clock. After spending the morning planning a garden in the newly gentrified neighbourhood of Fentiman Road SW8, she put her car in the underground park at the north east corner of Hyde Park and, the day being fine, went into the park to have lunch in a deck chair, choosing a spot with a view of the Carlyons' town house. She had been told where it was by the Countess when they talked on the telephone.

As she ate her usual light lunch, she tried to ignore the drone of two streams of traffic – three lanes heading towards Marble Arch, three lanes going south towards the Wellington Arch and the gardens of Buckingham Palace – and to imagine Park Lane as it had been when all the houses were privately owned and it was the most fashionable address in Mayfair.

If I had managed to get to London from the North, thought Damaris, it would have been as a skivvy, toiling all day in the basement and sleeping, exhausted, in a garret up seven flights of back stairs.

Imagining the life she might have led, had she been born towards the end of Queen Victoria's reign, her thoughts drifted to her real beginnings and in particular to the last day of her childhood and brutal introduction to womanhood . . .

'Fer Christ's sake shut yer row, yer little bleeder.'

Not unkindly, sixteen-stone Marlene Clutton stuffed a plastic dummy into the grizzling mouth of her youngest child who was strapped in the battered pushchair bought for the first of her brood.

Six children, innumerable chips, three heaped spoonfuls of sugar in every cup of tea and hours slumped in front of the TV had slowly transformed Marlene from a pretty girl into an ungainly hulk of flaccid flesh.

Taking a final draw on her cigarette and squashing it out in an ashtray, nicked from a pub, which hadn't been emptied for two days and was overflowing with ash and stubs, she buttoned her outsize fun fur of nylon ocelot.

'I'll be gone a coupla hours, Tiff. After I been ter Tesco's I'm going down the charity shop. Then I might 'ave a look round Woollies. When Kev comes in you can see to his tea, can't yer, luv?'

She smiled at her foster-daughter who was standing behind the ironing board, working her way through a pile of clothes from the washing machine.

Marlene was a lazy slattern whose house was a perpetual pigsty and sometimes she lost her temper and lashed out with angry back-handers which, because of her bulk, hurt more than she intended. But in general she was good-humoured and never deliberately cruel like the woman three doors along who punished her children by shutting them in the shed and worse.

Everyone knew she abused them but everyone kept their mouth shut. If you lived in Laburnum Way, you didn't go reporting people in case they got back at you. Most of the families in the street had something they didn't want investigated.

'Yeah . . . I'll look after Kev.'

Tiff – registered soon after birth as Tiffany Sharon Janice, taking her surname, Wigan, from her unmarried mother who shortly afterwards had left her in the care of her aunt – glanced up and returned Marlene's smile.

Three months from her sixteenth birthday, she had no make-up on her face and was dressed like a much younger girl in a plain blouse and pleated skirt bought for her by Maudie Sheringham who didn't approve of the trendy gear and cosmetics worn by the other teenagers on the council estate.

Had she been answering Maudie, Tiff would have said yes not yeah. Maudie couldn't abide what she called slipshod speech. But although Tiff could talk in the way of which Maudie approved, in the house shared by Marlene and Kevin, her common-law husband, it was better to stick to the vernacular. Maudie's manner of speaking and eating would be considered lah-di-dah.

'You're a good little sod,' said Marlene. 'Don't know what I'd do without you, not with Kev and six kids on me 'ands. It's a good thing Shirl did dump you on me, I reckon. If she 'adn't, I'd be a slave. The boys don't never lift a finger.'

Tiff had always run errands and helped with the housework, the only other girl in the family being five year old Diane, now out at play in the street. But as Marlene was the least fastidious of housewives this had not meant doing endless chores. Most of Tiff's time had been spent working with Maudie in her garden, the only one worthy of the name in an area where most of the gardens were actually trampled earth yards. Now the old lady was dead, her house occupied by a couple whose children were rapidly wrecking the grass and its well-tended borders, Tiff filled the gap in her life by trying to make Marlene's house tidier.

She had finished the ironing and was upstairs, curled on her bed, reading a book from the public library, when she heard the back door being opened and closed.

'That you, Diane?' she called.

When there was no reply, she grinned, expecting to hear the slight sounds of the little girl creeping stealthily upstairs until, reaching the narrow landing, she would rush into their shared bedroom in the hope of surprising Tiff. It was a game she had played before and Tiff had reacted with a gasp and a mock-angry exclamation of, 'Bloody 'ell, you didn't 'alf startle me!'

This time she really was startled for it wasn't Diane who suddenly stepped into view but Kevin Nobbold, the father of baby Barry.

'Oh it's you,' she said, sitting up. 'You're back early, int you?'

Kevin nodded. He was a man of few words, most of them coarse. A long distance lorry driver, he was often away overnight. Tiff had heard Marlene telling her best friend Sandra that she suspected Kev of having it off with other women when he was away from home.

'He don't never fuck me no more so it stands to reason he must be getting it down south,' she had said, with a shrug. 'Don't worry me none, I can tell you. I don't want no more bloody kids.'

She had met Kevin through her sister Shirl, to whom he had given a lift on one of her rare visits north. At that time, four years ago, Marlene's now cumbersome body had not lost all trace of shapeliness. Kevin, who had twice fucked her sister in the back of the cab while

85

his lorry was parked outside transport caffs on the M1 had seen in Marlene a refuge from his marital problems.

A good-looking youth before night after night in pubs had blurred his features and given him a beer belly, he had married a forceful girl who thought she could make something of him. She had achieved her other ambitions – the bungalow, the microwave, the video – but had failed to upgrade her husband.

Compared with his shrewish wife and her exacting standards, easy-going Marlene Clutton, with four children by her husband and another by a lodger had offered some welcome relaxation. She didn't care if he put his feet on the furniture or smoked in her front room. With her he could smoke in bed.

Tiff could remember the first time Kevin had slept in the double bed which had its head against the wall between Marlene's room and the small one she shared with Diane. It had been soon after Shirl, Tiff's mother, had returned to her job in London where she worked as a hostess in a night club in the West End.

Tiff had been lying awake, wondering about her father, when through the thin stud-work wall she had heard the bed start to vibrate, followed by muffled sounds which very soon she had realised must be Marlene doing with Kevin what she had used to do with Terry the lodger.

'I'll come down and get your tea,' Tiff said, swinging her feet to the greying pink nylon carpet.

'There's no 'urry. Where's Marl?' Kevin came into her room and sat down on the end of her bed.

'Out . . . but she won't be gone long.' Tiff bent to tie the laces of the gym shoes she had taken off, not for fear of marking the plucked and shabby Welsh blanket which covered her bed, but because she liked to have bare feet when she was reading. 'Whad'yer want? Sausages? Bacon? Pilchards?'

'I'm not 'ungry. I'll 'ave suffing later. What's this

then?' He picked up her book and read out the title. 'The Great Gardens of France ... Christ! That sounds boring. Can't you find nuffing better than that down the library?'

'I like reading about gardens.' She stood up and took the book from him. It was a new one the library had ordered specially for her. She didn't want to return it with any of the pages soiled by his dirty fingers.

Putting it in a plastic bag, she reached up to place it safely on top of the free-standing cupboard which served as a wardrobe. There it was out of Diane's reach.

'Seeing you do that, if I didn't know different I'd think that was a rude book what you didn't want no one to know about,' said Kevin. 'Ever seen a rude book, Tiff?'

She shook her head. There was a note in his voice which, not for the first time, gave her a feeling of unease. Two or three times in recent months she had caught Kevin watching her in a way she hadn't liked. But as she was seldom alone with him it hadn't worried her much.

Between her bed and Diane's there was only a narrow space. As she moved towards the door, Kevin swung up one leg and rested his heel on the child's bed, making a barrier.

'Would you like to?' he asked.

'No, thanks. I'd like to get by.'

He didn't move his leg. 'In a tick ... what's your rush?' He reached out and took her hand. 'You're starting to look like your mum. Quite a looker is Shirl. Pity she in't around to help you get yourself up. Marl's no use for that. Going by old photos she's shown me, she never were much of a dresser even before she got like the back of a bus. Shirl's different. She's got style. So could you 'ave ... with a bit of money spent on you. I don't mind giving you a few quid now and again so's you can get yourself something snazzy to wear.'

As he spoke he pulled on her hand so that, unable to

free it, to stop herself overbalancing she was forced to sit down.

'I've enough clothes already, Kev. Let me go. I've got things to do downstairs.'

She tried not to show her nervousness, feeling that if she stayed calm he would let her go, but if she showed signs of panic it would make matters worse. He might even try to kiss her and she didn't want that to happen. Most of the girls in her class had gone all the way, or so they said. Tiff hadn't even been kissed yet and when she was she wanted it to be with someone like the tall boy she saw at the library, not with a slob like Kevin.

'That blouse what the old bird give you don't do nuffing for you. Makes you look like a kid. What you want is one of them tee shirts what'll show off your tits.' He shifted closer, his other hand going to her waist and then sliding upwards to find the soft shape of her breast.

Tiff recoiled from his touch with a shocked, angry gasp. She tried to push him away but he only laughed. A moment later he had both arms round her and was pressing his mouth over hers, forcing his hot wet tongue between her resisting lips.

It was the most repulsive sensation she had ever experienced. She thought she was going to suffocate or be sick. Nothing she had read about kissing had prepared her for the prickly roughness of his unshaven cheeks, the stifling pressure of his mouth and, worst of all, his slug-like, snake-like tongue probing the corners of her mouth, threatening to choke her.

At first she thought that would be all: one long slobbering horrible kiss forced on her as a sick joke.

Even when he lifted his head and she saw how red he had gone – even the whites of his eyes were red and there was sweat on his face – she couldn't believe he meant her any more harm.

He said, in a queer hoarse voice, 'Don't go making a fuss or you'll 'ave Diane coming in, letting on to Marl.

88

You wouldn't want her to know you been leading me on like.'

Before she could take this in, he put his hand over her mouth and pushed her head onto the bed while he felt for her briefs and dragged them roughly down her legs.

It all happened so quickly, while she was still shocked from the kiss, that he had them off before she began to struggle. Belatedly starting to defend herself, she pounded at him with clenched fists, squirming, kicking, snarling with rage and fear inside the hard gag of the hand clamped over her jaw.

But even the strength of panic was no match for the strength of lust. Ignoring her muffled cries, he kept her pinned down while he unzipped his jeans. Then he was between her thighs, ramming what felt like a broom handle into her cringing body, making her groan with pain as he did it again and again, the cruel stabs growing faster and faster until, when she thought she must die from the agony of it, his body went into a violent convulsion and sagged on top of her, a dead weight as still and heavy as if he had died.

Perhaps it was only moments but it seemed a long time that she lay crushed beneath him, her body torn, her mind dazed by what had happened. She had thought of rape as something which happened in dark isolated places, not in daylight, at home, at the hands of someone you knew.

At last Kevin heaved himself off her and rose from the bed. With a shudder of disgust she saw his now semi-limp cock dangling in front of her eyes, smeared with her blood, dripping a viscous white slime like snot from a child's nose.

Sickened, defiled, betrayed, she whimpered and looked away.

She was still there, still in shock, when he came back

from the bathroom, his jeans zipped, his face its normal colour.

'You'd better go and clean yourself up while there's no one around,' he told her. 'If you know what's good for you, you won't say nothing to Marl. If you're anything like your mum, you'll be begging for it soon. She can't get enough of it, Shirl can't. Here you are . . . buy yourself a lipstick . . . earrings . . . whatever you fancy.'

He threw some money onto the bed by her feet and turned away, closing the door. She heard him thumping heavy-footed down the stairs.

The next morning it was pouring. Tiff put on some extra clothes which wouldn't be noticed under her raincoat. Taking out her school books and shoving them under the bed, she packed as much as she could in her school bag. Instead of catching the bus which went past the huge comprehensive school where she had been among the brighter of its one thousand pupils, she got on a different bus and went to the station. With the money Kevin had given her and the funds no one knew she had, she was able to buy a single ticket to London.

She hoped that when she arrived her mother would help her. If Shirl couldn't or wouldn't, and tried to make her come back, she would have to manage on her own.

As the train left the town where she had lived all her life she looked at the dismal view of back-to-back Victorian dwellings and, further along, acres of modern but scarcely less ugly council houses, and she hoped she would never set eyes on the place again.

It was a long way to London and everyone else in the carriage had something to read. Tiff gazed out of the window, trying to concentrate on the future but unable to stop herself thinking about what had happened yesterday.

While her body still hurt, not only between her legs

where Kevin had smashed his way into her, but everywhere he had used force to hold her down, it was impossible to forget it. Taking her turn in the scruffy bathroom this morning, she had seen that four bruises had begun to show on one side of her face with another on the opposite cheekbone. They marked where his fingers and thumb had dug in while he was keeping her quiet.

If she had been able to scream, would it have made much difference? Raucous rows between husbands and wives, the shrieks of children having tantrums or being clouted, pop music blaring, teenagers shouting defiance, mothers nagging at the tops of their voices, the thunderous revving of motorbikes – noise was the norm in Laburnum Way. Her screams might not have been noticed, or been deliberately ignored.

It wasn't Kevin's unspecified threat which had kept her from telling Marlene what he had done. He knew and so did Tiff that even with a willing fifteen year old it would have been an offence. If she had gone, in the state she was in when he'd finished with her, to the nearest police station, he would be in detention now, charged with the rape of a minor.

She would have liked to see him punished. But not, she had decided reluctantly, if it meant Marlene and Barry being punished as well. Not only did Marlene need the housekeeping money Kevin gave her, but she wouldn't be able to face the whispers and sniggers when it was known that her youngest kid's dad was a rapist.

By the time the train arrived at Euston she had already decided that, even if it cost a lot, it would be worth taking a taxi to the club where her mother worked rather than finding her way there by the Underground or on foot.

People were queuing for taxis in the station forecourt. When her turn came she said to the driver, 'I want to go to the Blue Grotto Club in Shepherd Market, please.'

He stared at her for a moment. Perhaps the marks on

her face were more noticeable now. Then he said, 'Right you are,' and she climbed into the back and put her school bag on the seat beside her.

Twice while they were held up by the traffic lights Tiff saw the driver looking at her in his mirror. The meter had clocked one pound fifty when he reached back to open the glass screen between his seat and hers.

'Come down from up north, have you, love?'

'Yes.'

'Who told you about the Blue Grotto?'

'I know someone who works there.'

'I see.' He slowed and steered through a gap between two parked vehicles which she would have thought was too narrow for the taxi to get through. 'Doubt if you'll find it open, this time of day. Most of the clubs don't start up until the evening. You may have to hang about . . . unless you know where your friend lives.'

'No, I don't.' Were all London taxi drivers as nosey and chatty?

He didn't say any more until they arrived at a building with the name *Blue Grotto* on a board and an arrow indicating the club was in the basement.

The fare was now over two pounds. Tiff gave the driver a fiver. While he was sorting out change, he said, 'First time you've been in London, is it?'

'Yes.'

'I've a daughter your age . . . sixteen last week she was.'

'I'm older than I look . . . seventeen.'

She didn't think he believed her. Instead of handing her the change he was scribbling on a piece of paper.

'In case your friend don't show up, or you don't like the look of the place, here's where you can get a bed for the night,' he said as he finished writing. 'It's a hostel . . . run by nuns. They won't turn you away if you're stuck. London's not a nice place for a girl your age on her own. If you want somewhere safe you go here, love.' He handed over the paper and with it her change.

'Thank you.' Unable to smile at him, she put the money in her pocket and turned away.

As the taxi moved off she saw that the door at the front of the steps leading down into a railinged area was shut, the window beside it barred outside and shuttered inside. The club *was* closed.

Not sure what to do next, Tiff looked about for a café where she could have a cup of tea and something to eat. Not far from the club she found a small corner snack-bar. There was no one inside except the woman behind the counter.

'Yes, love?'

'A cup of tea and an egg and tomato sandwich, please.'

The sandwiches were ready-made, wrapped in cling film. The woman put one on a plate and dropped a tea-bag into a thick white cup, filling it with boiling water from a machine. She put a spoon on the saucer. 'Help yourself to milk and sugar. That'll be one pound fifty.'

'One pound fifty?' Tiff exclaimed. Where she came from tea and a sandwich would have cost half that.

The woman who hadn't looked closely at her before now eyed her with more attention. 'The scones is cheaper. Fifty pee including the butter.'

Tiff looked at the scones piled under a plastic dome. They were small, not more than four mouthfuls even eaten the way Maudie had taught her.

*'You aren't loading a cement-mixer, child. Small bites and eat with your back teeth and your mouth closed. That's better. That's a good girl.'*

'No, I'll have the sandwich,' she said, putting down the two pound notes the driver had given her.

The tin, buried in Maudie's garden which, when the old lady was dying, she had told Tiff to dig up, telling no one she had it, had been filled with £20 notes. So many of them, rolled tightly together, that Tiff had been awed by the thought of possessing so much money. But what she had spent already today made her realise how quickly a £20 note could be reduced to a few coins.

'West End prices is always more,' said the woman, as she closed the till. 'From out of London, are you?'

Tiff nodded, taking her tea to a Formica shelf with some stools under it where she could look out of the window and avoid being drawn into another conversation. She had been told that people in the south were more standoffish, less disposed to be friendly than northerners. It didn't seem to apply to the Londoners she had met so far.

The sandwich consisted of two rounds of sliced brown bread enclosing a thin layer of filling and cut in half diagonally. She had eaten one half and was sipping the tea and idly watching a man standing in the street, when a woman came up and spoke to him. At first glance Tiff didn't know her. The last time she'd seen her mother Shirl's hair had been its natural colour. Now she was blonde. She was wearing a white sweater, a white leather mini, black lace tights and four-inch heels. She looks like a tart, thought Tiff, the instant before she recognised her.

When she did, she jumped up from the stool and, too relieved by this stroke of luck to care about the pain it caused her, rushed out of the snack-bar.

'Shirl . . . hey, Shirl,' she called out, as the pair began to walk away.

Her mother stopped and looked round. The man, whom Tiff had seen without noting anything about him except that he was old and bald, also stopped.

Perhaps because Tiff had grown taller in the two years since Shirl's last visit, her mother took a minute to recognise her.

'Bloody hell! Where did you spring from, for Christ's sake?' she asked, not looking pleased.

94

'I came down by train this morning. I was going to wait until the club opened,' Tiff began, her impulse to fling her arms round her quelled by Shirl's expression.

Shirl glanced at the man, 'I won't be long, dear. It's three doors along . . . the first floor. I won't keep you a tick.' Turning back to Tiff, she said briskly, 'I can't talk to you now. I'm busy. Get yourself a cuppa in the caff.' Thrusting some money at her, she hurried after the man, her buttocks outlined by the tight white leather.

When Tiff returned to the café, the woman said, 'If you'll take a tip from me, love, you won't go leaving your bag about . . . not in London. It's all right with only me here, but if we'd been busy you might not have seen it again. Quick as lightning, thieves are – and there's a lot of them around. I'm just warning you, seeing as you're new here.'

The thought that her bag, with the tin inside it, could have been stolen while she was out in the street made Tiff's stomach turn over. She went back to finish her tea. She was upset by her mother's reaction to seeing her. Not only that but by the growing suspicion that Shirl was now 'on the game' as people called it.

The idea of her mother being willing to allow a stranger to do to her what Kevin had done to Tiff yesterday, even if not as brutally, made her want to retch. Suddenly she knew that with Shirl she wouldn't find a refuge but only another and possibly worse trap than the squalid house she had left.

If she wanted to make a new life for herself, fulfil Maudie's hopes for her, she would have to start somewhere else. Not in this part of London with a mother who had taken to prostitution.

Re-wrapping the other half of the sandwich, she put it in her bag and took the plate and cup and saucer back to the counter. She knew the woman had seen her speaking to Shirl. She said, 'I've got to go. If that lady

95

comes in and asks for me, would you tell her I couldn't wait, please?'

'Go back to where you come from, that's my advice, love. You don't want to get mixed up with the girls what work around here. I know them all by sight. I've been here for years. Quite nice girls, some of 'em, when I first seen 'em. Youngsters like you, up from the country. God alone knows where they end up. They don't none of them make old bones, you can be sure of that. There used to be one called Penny – '

Tiff didn't wait to hear any more. She said, 'Goodbye,' and left, hurrying as fast as she could in the opposite direction from the house where her mother was busy with the man with the bald head.


The nun had ginger hair showing under the starched white band to which her veil was attached. She wore a pair of bifocals through which her calm, pale grey eyes studied Tiff's face.

'Those are nasty bruises.'

Tiff flushed, not sure how much of the truth to confide.

'What made you come to London without a job or a place to stay?' the nun asked.

'I thought I could stay with . . . a friend while I looked for a job. But when I found out what she was doing, I didn't want to stay with her. A man I met told me to come here.'

'That was good advice. You should be grateful to him. But could you not go home to your family?'

Tiff shook her head. 'My foster mother is all right, but the man who lives with her now . . .' She put her hand up to her face, touching her cheek with her fingertips. 'I'm better off here. If you can give me a bed for a few nights, I'll soon find work. I've some money saved up. I can pay.'

'How old are you?'

'Seventeen.' It made her uncomfortable to tell lies to a nun, but if she told the truth they might have to report her to the police, and the police might try to send her back.

'And what is your name?'

Tiff hesitated, but only for a fraction of a second. She had chosen a name for her new self a long time ago.

'Damaris . . . Damaris Lynn.'

'That's a very pretty name. Perhaps you were named after the Athenian lady whom Saint Paul converted to Christianity. Have you read about her in the Bible?'

'I've never read the Bible.'

'Dear me, that's a great pity. It's full of interesting stories. Do you like reading, Damaris?'


As she sat in the sun in Hyde Park, lost in thoughts of the past, a spaniel puppy came bouncing across the grass towards Damaris. She petted him for a few moments until his owner recalled him, then looked at her watch. It was time to make tracks for Carlyon House and her appointment with the Countess.

As she walked towards the nearest park gate, she wondered why all those long-dormant memories should have surfaced today. In the intervening years she had sometimes wished she could trace the taxi driver and tell him how vital a part he had played in her life. If he hadn't written down the address of the hostel, then run by dear Sister Joseph, Tiff might not have left the snack-bar and found her way to that sanctuary for runaway girls. Damaris Lynn might never have come into existence, or not without many more difficulties than she had actually experienced because of that help given to her at a crucial hour of her life.

As she made her way to the east side of Park Lane, she wondered if, not far away, the snack-bar was still in business and Shirl was still approaching men with that false professional smile, or if she had now sunk even lower, or was dead.

Dismissing Shirl from her mind, Damaris mounted the steps to the front door of Carlyon House and tugged the old-fashioned bell pull.

She was admitted by a man whose function wasn't clear to her. Did footmen wear boiler suits nowadays? He looked more like a handyman.

The interior of the building was unexpectedly impersonal; luxurious in the way of a very grand public place rather than a private house. Passing the imposing main staircase, he led her to what must originally have been the back stairs used by the servants. Damaris found herself climbing to the top of the house.

The third surprise was the Countess herself. A beautiful girl with black hair and friendly grey eyes, she was about the same age as Damaris – possibly a little younger – and she spoke with a trace of an American accent.

'This floor is the only part of the house we occupy now,' she explained, when they had shaken hands and she was leading her visitor into an exotically furnished sitting room. 'The rest of the building is leased. The contrast between downstairs and up here is striking, isn't it?'

Her gesture encompassed a décor reminiscent of a seraglio, an effect heightened by the presence of blackamoors in the small hall and a particularly fine, vividly costumed Venetian blackamoor in this room.

'This is really my sister-in-law's flat which the rest of us use as a *pied-à-terre*,' she explained. 'Have you, by any chance, read her book *The Travels of an Edwardian Naturalist*, Miss Lynn?'

'I was given it for Christmas.'

'Then you already know something about Longwarden. You might also like to have a look through these photographs while I make us some coffee.'

The young Countess handed her a large green folder before disappearing. The collection of prints in the folder had been taken by a professional photographer. There were about twenty views of what, to a layman's eyes, was a typical English country house garden. Not much of the house was to be seen, but enough to indicate that it was one of the larger stately homes with an extensive park surrounding the pleasure gardens.

To Damaris' more knowledgeable eye the photographs also revealed that, like so many great gardens during the twentieth century, the one at Longwarden had gradually been modified as the number of gardeners dwindled. Lately, she guessed, keeping it up had become a struggle. It was still a beautiful garden but it had the look of a place where for many seasons past money and labour had been in short supply. It was not a forsaken garden – that would have been an irresistible temptation to her – but rather one which had stopped developing, probably about ten years ago. Some of the prints made her long to introduce new vitality to the scene they presented. She could see at once that much needed to be done, especially in the old walled kitchen garden of which only part seemed to be in use.

'These are excellent photographs. Who took them, Lady Carlyon?' she asked, when the Countess returned.

'My husband. He's a professional photographer. Jungles and deserts are more in his line than gardens, but he took those pictures for his mother who was, in effect, the head gardener. She was a widow for years and the garden was her occupation, but now she has married again and gone abroad, which is why we need someone to take over.'

'Your mother-in-law had help presumably?' said Damaris. 'She couldn't have managed a garden of this size single-handed.'

'She had two very old men who've worked at Longwarden all their lives and are still doing the best they can,' Lady Carlyon explained. 'But they can't hold the fort for much longer. Things are getting out of hand already.'

'How did you hear about me?'

'From my mother-in-law . . . Mrs Ashford, as she is now. A year or two ago you designed a garden for the Chelsea Flower Show which she felt was very well thought out. You also wrote a piece for *The Garden* which she cut out for future reference. In fact before she left England she hunted out various articles about you, Miss Lynn. You've made quite a name for yourself.'

'I've had a lot of luck,' said Damaris. 'The first person who employed me as a freelance garden designer happened to be a friend of Mrs Betty Kenward who writes the social diary in *Harpers & Queen*. Soon after I'd redesigned her garden, my first employer gave an al fresco party. Mrs Kenward wrote some approving remarks about it and mentioned my name. She's tremendously influential. From then on I never looked back.'

The Countess smiled at her. 'My father, who was a very successful man, said that no one could get on without luck, but luck itself was no use without talent and hard work. Obviously you deserved the plug Mrs Kenward gave you. I have the impression you've worked mainly in London. Is that correct? Or have you also done country gardens?'

'Only one weekend-cottage garden. I've no experience of very large gardens like yours,' Damaris told her frankly, replacing the photographs in their folder.

'Would you like to take on a large garden . . . try your hand at it?'

'Very much, but it doesn't seem practicable. I can't drop my London commitments. It wouldn't be fair to the people I work for, or the ones I employ.'

'Of course not. I understand that. But could you, I wonder, tackle the job in the way that our architect will be dealing with the structural renovations? He's in

100

partnership in London but he'll give us two days a week, sometimes more, sometimes less, depending how much time is necessary. Would that be a workable compromise?'

'I'm not sure. I'd have to look at the gardens, discuss your ideas about them and look into the difficulty or otherwise of building up a work force.'

'How soon could you come? Next weekend? We'd be delighted to put you up and I'm sure you'd enjoy seeing the gardens even if, in the end, you decided against taking them over.'

'I'm sure I should. That's very kind of you, Lady Carlyon. I'd be delighted to come.'

'Good. We'll expect you for dinner on Friday. I've had some little maps printed showing people how to find us. I'm told that getting out of London on a Friday evening can take forever, but once you're on the M4 it's an easy run and the last part is lovely, especially at this time of year.'

She handed Damaris a card with the route from the motorway exit to Longwarden village, and from there to the house, clearly marked.

---

# *April*

'I shouldn't have told you,' Sarah Lomax said bitterly. 'I ought to have kept it to myself. It's my business . . . my decision. But you gave me your word, Allegra . . . you promised you wouldn't tell anyone,' she reminded her cousin.

'And I shan't,' Allegra retorted. 'But, having told me, you can't expect me to stand by and say nothing while you go ahead with this utterly mad . . . *insane* plan to ride at Badminton – regardless of the fact that you're going to be fifteen weeks pregnant. I've heard of girls in the pudding club doing some crazy things to dislodge an unwanted baby. I've done a few of them myself. But nothing to match this.'

The cousins were in Sarah's bed-sitter in the top of the stone arch which was the entrance to Longwarden's stable yard. This was a part of the great house where Allegra hardly ever came. Like her brother, the ninth Earl, she wasn't a horsey person. But naturally she took an interest in Sarah's achievements as what the popular press called 'the golden girl of three day eventing'.

Six months ago, after making horse trials history by riding her Arab gelding, Bedouin Star, to first place and a gold medal in the horse trials at Burghley, Sarah had been a golden girl. Her long blonde hair neatly plaited, with a few curly tendrils escaping round her glowing, happy face, she had been seen on television looking a worthy idol of the thousands of Pony Club members who day-dreamed of emulating her. At this moment, white-faced and drawn after a bout of morning sickness, she bore little resemblance to the radiant young achiever of last September, thought her cousin.

But Allegra didn't allow her love and compassion to show. Her manner was briskly down to earth as she went on, 'You'll not only lose the baby but you'll probably do it in public . . . and possibly even on TV! Is that really what you want? To make a spectacle of yourself? Perhaps to wreck your insides? A miscarriage is a nasty experience, Sarah. There's a lot of pain . . . a lot of blood. Christ! I can see it now . . . you lying on the ground with your white britches turning red, and all your fans gawping in horror. It's not on . . . definitely not on.'

'It won't be like that,' Sarah said stubbornly. 'I'm not going to lose the baby. It says in the books that it's all right to go on doing anything you're used to, and that includes sports.'

'Tennis, swimming . . . those sort of sports. Not riding

hell for leather round a cross country course with huge fences and other tricky jumps,' Allegra said impatiently. 'You'll lose the baby . . . and you'll throw away any chance of being picked to ride for Britain in the 1988 Olympics,' she added, with deliberate harshness.

It was now more than a week since Sarah had come to her room and confided her secret: she was pregnant by Nick Dean.

Allegra had been surprised but not shocked. Her own wild past had made her unshockable. In her time she had committed every folly except one; unlike many of her contemporaries she had steered clear of drugs.

When her nineteen year old cousin had blurted out, 'I think I'm pregnant,' Allegra hadn't hesitated before advising her what to do. At Sarah's age – and particularly when the father of the child had disappeared – there was only one thing to be done.

What *had* shocked Allegra, and worried her even more now after days of unavailing argument, was Sarah's refusal to consider a discreet abortion. She was prepared to chance a spontaneous abortion brought on by the physical stresses of training for and riding in Britain's most testing three day event at Badminton; but she wouldn't even consider the infinitely more sensible course of having the unwanted foetus safely removed by Allegra's gynaecologist.

'Don't go on at me, Allegra. You've said it all ten times already. You're wasting your breath,' said Sarah. 'I'm sorry now that I involved you in this. It was a moment of weakness brought on by Aunt Pen's wedding. That wasn't a good day for either of us,' she added more gently.

She knew that her own trouble, bad as it was, was nothing compared with the tragedy which had struck her cousin. Somewhere in the world Nick was alive. She might never see him again but even that was more bearable than Allegra's burden. She had to live with the certainty of *never* seeing her lover again.

A famous painter of portraits and a wonderfully vital and attractive personality, Alessandro Risconti – known to them all as Andro – had been drowned off the coast of Barbados where he and Allegra had spent several weeks escaping from the weather in Europe. What had made it an even worse shock for Allegra was that she had come back to England to attend a friend's wedding, leaving Andro to spend a few more days painting in the West Indies. She had heard about the accident in London.

'No, it was a good day for Mother but a rotten day for you and me,' Allegra answered bleakly. 'And another rotten day for me will be watching you tackling that horribly tough, gruelling cross country course at Badminton in a fortnight's time,' she added. 'It would be so easy for you to pull out. It happens all the time. A horse goes lame or gets some infection and has to be withdrawn at the last moment. If you announce that Beddo has something wrong with him, the only person who will know it isn't true is Kate.'

Kate Hastings was the new groom who had replaced Sammy O'Brien the ageing Irishman who, after working at Longwarden since before Sarah was born, had surprised them by leaving to live with a widow he had met while in hospital for the removal of gall-stones.

'Something may go wrong in reality,' was Sarah's weary reply. She didn't need to be reminded how often months of training had to be written off because of a last-minute injury.

Her cousin was tempted to say, 'I hope to God it does' but decided to hold her tongue. It was true. She had argued long enough. There was nothing more to be said; no way of turning the younger girl from her crazy determination to ride at Badminton in front of several hundred thousand enthusiasts on the spot and several

104

million armchair spectators. She was going to do it if it killed her – as it might.

Bedouin Star, in training since soon after Christmas, was now at a high pitch of fitness. Sarah, although she put on a show of normality for the rest of the family, was obviously badly pulled down by the morning sickness which had been the second sign that Nick Dean, himself the by-blow of an anonymous soldier, had fathered another unwanted bastard.

However, worried as she was, Allegra saw nothing to be gained by breaking faith with her cousin and telling her brother and sister-in-law what was going on. Nothing they could say would carry any more weight than the arguments she herself had marshalled. North would undoubtedly lose his temper with Sarah, but what would that achieve?

The only remaining possibility was that, if nothing went wrong providentially, perhaps it could be made to go wrong. The trouble with that idea was that, not being a horsewoman herself and having no horsey cronies, Allegra didn't know how to go about nobbling the Arab badly enough to put him out of action for Badminton but not so badly as to do permanent damage. And who could she ask without arousing suspicion? Not Kate. Not Sammy. Not Daniel Langden, Sarah's vet, or Rob Wareham who shod the horses.

'I must go back to work,' said Sarah, getting up.

When Allegra had knocked on her door, she had just finished being sick and was making a cup of tea. Fortunately the bouts of nausea occurred at a time of the morning when she could slip away from the stables and, as Jane would say, throw up her breakfast without Kate catching on.

Allegra followed her down the winding stone staircase to ground level and left the yard by the archway from which a drive led round the side of the house to join the main drive.

There had been a time when each morning she had spent at least half an hour deliberating on what to wear from her extensive and somewhat eccentric wardrobe. Dressing had been a joy to her, an act of creation to which she had given as much thought and care as other people gave to cooking or arranging flowers.

Nowadays she threw on whatever garments came to hand, brushed her dark reddish-brown hair and did little or nothing to dramatise the hyacinth-blue eyes which were her most striking feature. Even without make-up she was a beautiful woman. Like her brother North she was tall and naturally graceful. Years ago, at a dinner party, someone had put forward the premise that all human beings bore a marked resemblance to a dog, their host being an obvious Airedale and his wife a Welsh collie.

When it came to deciding which breed Allegra resembled there had been unanimous agreement that she had the style and hauteur of an Afghan hound; and in those days with her thick mane of hair often flowing loose down her back, and her liking for scarves and shawls, anyone seeing her striding through Mayfair or – when she was in funds – springing in and out of taxis to and from Belgravia and Chelsea, would have been struck by her likeness to the long-haired, long-legged aristocrats of the dog world.

Walking aimlessly along the drive, she wished that like Sarah she had some work she must do. Kate couldn't manage to care for the horses single-handed. No matter how wretched she felt, either mentally or physically, Sarah had certain tasks which must be performed or the animals she loved would suffer.

Like Kate, most of the people at Longwarden worked because they were paid to and would be taken to task if they neglected their duties. But Allegra had only her own will-power to drive her. She had been a wage-slave when younger but now, in her twenty-ninth year, she was a woman of independent means. Not only had her first book, a biography of her great-grandparents, best-sold on both sides of the Atlantic, but Andro had left her the fortune he had amassed as the most sought-after portrait painter of the decade.

Unless she chose to do so, she need never work again. But she wanted to work, *longed* to work. The trouble was she couldn't find a subject. For her second book she had been going to write the life of a Victorian field marshal but that idea had been vetoed as too uncommercial by her American publisher, Elliott Lincoln.

In its place he had proposed a book about the man she loved and Allegra had jumped at the suggestion. Most of the work on the text had been done while she and Andro were in Barbados. Since then she had been unable to bring herself to finish it and had agreed with Elliott that it should be left until she could think about Andro with less emotion. She wondered if that would ever be the case.

She found herself at a loose end at the very time when, more than ever before, she needed the distraction and panacea of concentrating on matters unconnected with her own life. Without work, she was a lost soul wandering in a wilderness of despair.

In a strange twisted way, Sarah's trouble had been good for her, giving her something else to think and worry about instead of being totally immersed in her own tragedy.

'Where are you off to?'

Deeply preoccupied, Allegra had been only vaguely aware of the approach of the car which now drew up alongside her, driven by her brother.

'Nowhere in particular. Just walking.'

'I'm going to the village. Want to come?'

She shook her head. She had not been beyond the grounds since taking refuge at Longwarden and she wasn't ready to face the outside world yet. The tabloid press had made a big story of Andro's death and his liaison with her. Elsewhere a nine day's wonder, quickly replaced by a fresher and juicier scandal, in Longwarden village it would still be a subject for gossip and speculation. Allegra had no wish to be the cynosure of curious stares.

'No thanks. I'm just stretching my legs before another stint in the library.'

In an effort to find a subject for her third book, and to give herself something to do, she was reading her way through the handsomely bound volumes of the Dictionary of National Biography bought for his library by their great-grandfather, the seventh Earl, to which Allegra herself had added the later volumes which brought the great work up to date.

'Okay . . . see you later.'

With a smile and a wave North drove on, leaving her to ponder the vagaries of fate or chance which, since this time last year, had transformed both their lives, giving him marriage and love, in that order, while for her love had come first but marriage and children were forever out of reach.

Not that she had wanted either until recently. Now she would give her soul to have Andro's child growing inside her. It seemed one of life's cruellest ironies that Sarah, who needed a baby like a hole in the head, should be pregnant while Allegra, who longed for one, was not. If only she had stopped taking her contraceptive pills earlier, she might have something to live for . . . a future less desolate than the great desert of time which stretched ahead of her now.

But even if she had never taken the pills, she might not have conceived. In spite of her gynaecologist's assurance that the abortion she had had ten years ago could have had no effect on her fertility, at the back of her mind she had always had the feeling it might have. The rational side of her brain told her that was superstitious nonsense implanted by Nanny and Mother, both of them brain-washed into believing that sex outside marriage was sinful and abortion the worst sin of all.

But the doubt remained in her subconscious, as annoyingly ineradicable as a lot of other nanny-lore and mother-lore put into her head before she was old enough to select the principles she wanted to live by and discard the ones she disagreed with.

Watching her brother's car disappear down the drive, she wondered how he would react to Sarah's bombshell. Jane would be sympathetic. But North was likely to blow his top, thought Allegra, remembering the cataclysmic results on the rare occasions when her brother lost his temper.

Unlike their father, the eighth Earl, a man of chronic ill-humour, North was seldom annoyed. At the moment with a beautiful, rich bride, no more financial problems and his first child on the way, he was visibly happier than at any time in his life.

But very soon he was going to be seriously enraged. Which was why it was polite not to break the news to him directly. The best approach was through Jane. He wouldn't rant and storm at her. Especially not now she was pregnant.

North would never be an uxorious husband. He wasn't that type of man. But Allegra had noticed that lately he was more demonstrative in public than in the first months of his marriage. When, last spring in New York, North had told his sister he intended to marry Jane, although they had only just met, he had given the impression that it was his American cousin's money which was her chief attraction. Now it was clear to all of them that he was deeply in love with her. The fifty million dollar fortune left to Jane by her father, although it was badly needed to put the estate to rights, was not her principal hold on North. Not often, but once or twice

Allegra had seen him looking at her sister-in-law with the authentic glow of a lasting passion in his eyes.

Allegra had recognised the expression because, not so long ago, a man had looked at her like that.

Now, for her, love was over. With luck, for her brother and Jane it would last many years. She could only hope that being in love with his wife would make North more sympathetic to the less happy outcome of someone else's love affair.

'Miss Lynn? This is Jane Carlyon. I wonder if you would mind if we changed our arrangements slightly?'

'Of course not, Lady Carlyon.'

'I've invited a Frenchman – a chef at a London restaurant – to come down and cook some meals for us. He doesn't have a car and he wants to bring quite a lot of equipment with him. Would it be a great imposition to ask you to give him a lift on Saturday morning?'

'Not at all. I'd be pleased to bring him.'

'How kind of you. Thank you so much. As a matter of fact I think you'll enjoy the drive more on Saturday, when the roads are quieter, than during the Friday exodus. I'll give you his name and address.'

Before the Countess' call, Damaris had been thinking about what to wear at the weekend. Often in summer she would spend Saturday and Sunday visiting gardens open to the public, putting up for the night at a pub or a modest hotel. For such expeditions it was unnecessary to pack much. Putting together clothes for the weekend at Longwarden called for more careful thought. Lady Carlyon had mentioned that they lived 'very informally' but what did that mean in the context of a house such as Longwarden?

Although her work had brought her into contact with both the old and the new rich, Damaris wasn't at all sure what to expect this weekend. Life at Longwarden

110

had been anything but informal during the period described in the book by Allegra Lomax. For decade after decade large and luxurious house parties had characterised the way of life of the present Earl's predecessors. Did he and his American wife carry on the tradition? Or did they prefer a quieter life?

Would she be their only guest or would there be others? Not that it made any difference; she wasn't afraid of meeting people or answering the more personal questions which might arise in a partly professional, partly social situation. The official story of her life wasn't something she had invented, on which she could be caught out. The background she had adopted was a real one, described to her by Maudie, not once but many times.


In Damaris' mind 'French chef' called up an image of a short, stout, sallow-faced man with pale pudgy hands, softened by frequent washing, and a volatile temperament.

It was a surprise to see that the man waiting in the entrance to the block of flats was younger, taller and altogether different from the stereotype she had expected. Asked to guess his occupation, she would have opted for something sporting. As he lifted two laden grips and came out to meet the car, his movements were limber, even graceful.

She stopped the car and jumped out, smiling at him across the roof before walking round to his side.

'Good morning. I take it you're Monsieur Vibrac? I'm Damaris Lynn. How d'you do?' She offered her hand.

The Frenchman had already set down the grip in his right hand. 'How do you do? It's very kind of you to give me a lift.' His clasp was firm, his palm and fingers warm but not moist.

'Not at all. I'll unlock the back.'

His baggage stowed, they took their seats. The space

111

in front of the passenger seat was rather cramped for his long legs in light summer trousers. His shoes looked expensive, pale grey glacé kid with matching socks, if not silk a good imitation. Under a terracotta sweater he was wearing an open-necked linen shirt in a paler tone of the same colour. Damaris wasn't sure what to make of the overall effect. It could be a French way of dressing. Or he could be a bit of a dandy, or a homosexual.

'If you'd like some more leg room the seat will adjust a bit. The lever is under the front of it.'

'Thank you.' He located the lever and slid himself backwards.

As he fastened his seat belt she noticed he was wearing a wedding ring. If he was married it seemed strange the Countess hadn't invited young Madame Vibrac to accompany him. Presumably if the Carlyons decided to take him on, his wife would be going there with him. Perhaps she was working this weekend.

'Wouldn't your wife have liked to come with you?' she asked.

He said 'No,' and left it at that.

Separated? she wondered. In that case would he continue to wear a ring? Possibly. The French had different ways, different customs of which she knew little.

'This weekend is a busman's holiday for you, I gather?' In case he didn't understand the expression – there hadn't been time to judge how well he spoke English – she added, 'I hear you'll be doing some cooking during your visit.'

'I am cooking dinner tonight and lunch tomorrow,' he agreed. 'And you, Miss Lynn? What reason takes you to Longwarden?'

'I'm a garden consultant. The Countess would like me to supervise changes she wants to make.'

'I see. Are you interested in vegetables or only in flowers?'

'Extremely interested in vegetables, although I've

112

never been asked to design and plant a kitchen garden. Whether there's already a good one at Longwarden, I don't know yet.'

'I hope so,' said the Frenchman. 'Excellent vegetables – as fresh as possible and not too large – are very important to my work.'

'There are so many styles of cooking now. *Nouvelle . . . naturelle . . . minceur*. Which is yours?'

'In the restaurant where I work now it's mainly *nouvelle cuisine*. My own style is flexible,' he told her. 'Sometimes I like to cook in the classic manner, sometimes in the bourgeois style. *Nouvelle cuisine* is popular with some businessmen at lunch. They worry about their weight and they don't pay from their own pockets. But in the evening when many diners are celebrating a special occasion they want to see more for their money. Do you agree?'

'Absolutely. To be honest I think *nouvelle cuisine* is often a huge confidence trick. Not in all restaurants perhaps, but I've been to two or three where the food was exquisitely arranged on the plate but to anyone with a healthy appetite it didn't amount to more than a couple of mouthfuls.'

He laughed. 'I know what you mean. Unfortunately it is a style which does lend itself to what I think you call a travesty – yes? – of the original conception.'

'Your English is perfect. How long have you been over here?'

'Several years. I am from Brittany. Do you know that part of France?'

'I don't know France at all. It's rather a shaming admission but I've been too busy building up my business to have time to travel. When I do get around to going abroad, the first place on my list is the Château de Villandry. I want to see the gardens there, especially the *potager*.'

'Villandry is in the Touraine which is called the

garden of France. They tell me the part of the country where we are going today is also very beautiful. Have you seen it before?'

'I've never been through the village of Longwarden but I've done a good deal of exploring in Oxfordshire and Gloucestershire. It's the part of England I'd choose to live in if I could. I certainly don't plan to stay in London forever, but at the moment it's where I earn my bread and butter. Working for the Countess will only be on a consultancy basis. I shan't be there full-time. Will it be the first time you've cooked for a family rather than a restaurant?'

'Yes and I don't know how it will suit me in that respect. But I'll enjoy the country. I don't care for London very much. I was born in a small market town where everyone knows everyone and there's a sense of community. In London I only know the people I work with. The people who live in the other flats have nothing to do with each other. Some of them don't even say good morning or good evening.'

Damaris nodded. 'Big cities can be lonely places . . . but I wonder if, in a rural part of England, you may find it difficult to get the ingredients you need? Does Longwarden have a home farm which supplies it with dairy produce and meat, do you know?'

'I asked that when I saw the Countess. They used to have their own farm but not any more. It seems the place has been neglected for a long time and now she is going to make changes and improvements. I didn't expect her to be so young . . . or so beautiful. Did you?'

'I didn't know what to expect, but I liked her very much. I think she would be a considerate person to work for. It will be interesting to see what Lord Carlyon is like. Did you know he's a professional photographer?'

'Yes – which is good. When people work they understand other people's problems better than if they had nothing to do but enjoy themselves.'

'I don't think there are many idle aristocrats about today,' she answered. 'Most of the stately homes have to be run as a business to survive.'

By this time they had reached the M4 and were zipping along the westbound side of the motorway which led, ultimately, to south Wales. The traffic on it was much lighter than it would have been the previous evening, during the main outflow of motorists heading for the country, and there were fewer lorries than on a weekday. As they continued to discuss the ménage at Longwarden, Damaris was able to glance at her passenger now and then.

The first time she did this she caught him looking her over in a way which seemed to confirm that his marriage hadn't worked out – or else that he didn't let it stop him eyeing the field if not actually playing it.

But as he looked slightly embarrassed at being caught out, she concluded that looking might be as far as he went. Sitting straight in his seat, his dark hair almost brushing the roof of the car, his arms folded over his chest, he wasn't giving the body signals of a man who regarded every woman he met as a potential bed-partner.

'Berkshire is very built up but once we get west of Reading the countryside opens out,' she told him. 'I like this time of year, don't you? Next month is even better. In one of my gardening books by a marvellous old man called Mr E. A. Bowles he writes that if he had three wishes, one of them would be to have time stopped on a fine May morning.'

'I'd go along with that – but for me it would be even better if it were also the first day of the asparagus season. I like very much the slim green asparagus which the English prefer to the white Continental asparagus. I wonder if they grow it at Longwarden?'

'I'll find that out this afternoon when I go round the

garden with the Countess. How many people is she having to dinner tonight?'

'Twelve people tonight and eight for lunch tomorrow. I don't know how well-equipped the kitchen will be so, as you see, I've brought quite a lot of things with me.'

The connection between gardening and cooking kept the conversation flowing until they reached the motor-way exit shown on the Countess' map-card. From there on it lapsed into occasional remarks as Damaris looked out for signs and turnings and the Frenchman gazed more attentively at the scenery leading to their destination.

'It's very picturesque,' he said, as they passed through a village with a tithe-barn, a Norman church, a timbered inn called *The Plough* and cottages of golden stone, some roofed with stone tiles, others with thatch. 'This is England as I imagined it before I came here.'

The remark reminded her briefly of the drab industrial town where she had grown up. It might have been on another planet it bore so little relation to this countryside of woods, water-mills, turreted dovecotes and ancient manor houses.

Presently, approaching an old bridge, she pulled in to the side of the quiet minor road.

'We've made better time than I expected. We're going to be early. Shall we sit in the sun for a few minutes? You won't see much of it this afternoon, I imagine.'

She had brought a flask of coffee with her. They sat on the sun-warmed stone parapet, watching the stream below flowing lazily through the water-meadows.

'It's so peaceful here,' he said, looking towards a cop-pice with bluebells growing under the trees.

She murmured agreement, thinking that peace wasn't something most men in his age group appreciated. She had an instinctive feeling that he wasn't happy. Also it struck her that he was the first unknown man with whom

116

she felt perfectly at ease, even though earlier on she had seen him looking at her body.

To her surprise she found herself wondering if it were true that Frenchmen were better lovers than the English. Or was it merely a myth?

On the Saturday morning after her interview with the Countess, Laura received a letter offering her the job.

Her excitement was tempered by the thought of telling Miss Foxley what she had done. Knowing she was sure to be displeased Laura dialled the other woman's number and asked if it were convenient for her to come round.

'Certainly, Laura.' Her friend sounded surprised. 'It's a little early but I'll put the kettle on for coffee.'

When, a few minutes later, she opened her front door, she was wearing the royal blue nylon overall in which on Saturdays she spray-polished every surface which could be shone.

Laura couldn't see why a house occupied only by one tidy middle-aged woman should need such regular cleaning, but Miss Foxley liked everything 'just so'. A squashed cushion, a crumb on the carpet, a fallen petal were never seen in her house, or never for more than seconds.

'There's a special offer on a new disinfectant today,' she told Laura, when they met. She always did her weekend shopping first thing in the morning before the shops became busy.

'I don't think I need any,' said Laura. She had started to quake on the short walk between their houses. Now she felt like a naughty schoolgirl about to admit a heinous misdeed to the headmistress.

'Let me take you coat.' It was put on a hanger and concealed in the hall cupboard. It was not Miss Foxley's

117

way to drape a coat over the banisters or cast it on a chair.

Her lounge had the unlived in look of a room setting in a furniture showroom. Not for Miss Foxley the mugs and biscuit tins of some people's mid-morning breaks. Bone china cups with apostle spoons in the saucers were waiting on a tray with an embroidered cloth on it, and the sweet biscuits were arranged on a plate with a paper doily, another of the little touches of refinement which she liked to maintain in an age when standards were dropping all the time.

'You look worried, Laura,' she said, as they sat down. 'Is anything the matter?'

'No ... in fact something rather exciting has happened,' Laura took the Countess' letter from her bag and unfolded it. 'This came this morning.' She handed it over for Margaret to read for herself.

As Miss Foxley saw the die-stamped address at the top of the thick cream laid paper, her eyebrows arched and then, as she scanned the lines, fell back into place and contracted, deepening the grooves between them.

She read through the letter twice.


At Longwarden Jane was speaking on the house telephone to her butler.

'I want to be at the door to welcome Miss Lynn, Flitton. Let me know as soon as you hear from the lodge, will you?'

'Very good, m'Lady.'

'Thank you, Flitton.' She replaced the receiver and crossed out a note on the index card she used as an aide-memoire. Now she was free until mid-morning and, as the rest of the day would be a busy one, she decided to take an hour off from her duties as a châtelaine and go for a walk with the dogs.

One of her first innovations at Longwarden had been

to have the two lodge houses by the main gate spruced up, both outside and inside.

For years only one had been lived in, its occupant being Ted Rivington, the last of Longwarden's game-keepers and the unwilling foster father of Nick Dean.

As he was now an employee of the syndicate which held shooting rights on the estate, and also a slovenly tenant who for years had neglected to keep his cottage in good order, Jane had had no compunction in telling him he would have to move to a smaller one-bedroom cottage, which she had repaired and made liveable, by an entrance to the park which was no longer used.

Now both lodge cottages looked as they had in the generations when the Earls of Carlyon were among the richest men in England and their property was kept in impeccable order.

The cottage where Nick had grown up, and from which he had run away at the age of eighteen to enlist in the Spanish Foreign Legion, was now the house of an electrician who was going to work full-time at Long-warden and whose wife had agreed to be a gate-keeper.

In Rivington's time sometimes the gates had been closed, sometimes they had stood open; the former being an inconvenience particularly for women drivers who had to get out of their cars, perhaps in the rain, and wrestle with what felt like a ton of wrought-iron; the latter allowing anyone who chose to enter the grounds.

Jane had had the great gates remote-controlled so that they could be opened from inside the lodges. At present the second cottage was still empty but she hoped to install another couple, one of whom would share the duties of lodge-keeping so that all the comings and goings by way of the main gate would be seen and recorded.

For a long time Longwarden and its contents had had little or no protection and although it was very difficult to make the house totally secure she felt it was time a good deal more care was taken.

She knew that the fifty million dollar fortune she had inherited from her father had been mentioned in several gossip columns and, although kidnapping was almost unknown in England, she could not help worrying a little about her baby's safety. At the same time she didn't want to emulate some millionaires and surround herself with guard dogs and body-guards.

To be aware of someone shadowing her every time she went for a walk on her husband's land would take away much of the joy of having private meadows and woods in which to wander.

'I am at a loss for words, Laura,' said Miss Foxley, folding the Countess' letter and returning it to its envelope.

What did that mean? Laura wondered.

Miss Foxley recovered her power to express herself in speech. 'That you – that you, of all people, in whom I had the utmost confidence – should behave in this underhand way is quite beyond my comprehension. To say I am shocked is an understatement. I wouldn't have believed it of you, Laura. Even though your mother told me, more than once, that you had what she called a difficult streak, I never – '

'She wasn't my *mother*, Margaret. She was my step-mother.' Years of exasperation at her friend's repeated use of the misnomer lay behind Laura's interruption. 'It's not the same thing.'

'Whether you like it or not, she was your real mother. She brought you up . . . cared for you . . . tried to do her best for you,' Miss Foxley said piously.

'She made use of me. There was never any affection between us. It's no use pretending there was.'

'I hardly think it becomes you to speak of being made

120

use of when you yourself have made use of confidential information in this unscrupulous way.' Miss Foxley put the envelope on the coffee table as if it contained something of such an unpleasant nature that even to hold it offended her. 'What Beryl will have to say to this, I don't like to think.'

'Why must you tell her? Lady Carlyon didn't ask me how I heard about the job. Perhaps she felt it wasn't important as long as I had the right qualifications and acceptable references. I expect when you go to work on Monday there'll be a note from her saying the post has been filled. As for the agency's fee . . . if you'd let me apply through the agency, as I wanted to, you would have had the fee. If you like I'll pay it myself.'

'If you really believe that a moral lapse of this magnitude can be put right by the payment of money, I'm afraid that your outlook and mine differ far more than I had realised,' Miss Foxley said coldly.

'I'm sure they do,' Laura retorted, surprising herself.

In spite of her guilty feelings earlier, now her misdeed had been admitted – and was it really so heinous? – Margaret's pompous tone was making her feel more defiant than contrite.

'I thought that when you more or less told me I couldn't apply,' she went on. 'I've had over twenty years of being told what I can and can't do and from now on I'm going to make my own decisions.'

'In that case there is no more to be said. I must say I'm very grieved – very grieved indeed – by your attitude. That a friendship which I at least valued should come to an end in this way . . .' Miss Foxley shook out a clean cotton handkerchief and put it to her nose.

'I value our friendship too. Why should this end it?' said Laura. Yet even as she spoke, she knew in her heart that the relationship between them had never been a real friendship but rather a close acquaintance which, if it ended, would leave no gap in her own life.

If she were honest, there was no one and nothing from her past – except her memories of her father – which she wanted to take into her future. She was on the brink of a new life and if she could cut herself free from her drab existence in Northwood Hills, so much the better.

'Because you have betrayed my faith in you,' said Miss Foxley, in a muffled voice.

'Oh really Margaret, what a drama about nothing . . . or nothing very much. I only went behind your back because you were so obstructive, so certain you knew what was best for me. The truth is you were being selfish. You didn't want me to leave you. If you were a true friend, as you claim, you would want what was best for me, even if it didn't suit you.'

As Miss Foxley had never heard Laura speak in such a firm and forceful tone before, she could not have looked more astonished had part of the ceiling caved in.

'I can't think what has come over you,' she exclaimed, in a stunned voice.

'Nothing has come over me. I was always like this inside. I never let it show,' said Laura. 'If you're not going to pour out the coffee, shall I do it?' She felt in need of a cup. A glass of sherry would have been even better but she felt she had given Miss Foxley enough shocks for one morning. She would have a drink when she got home.

However as she stretched out her arm to pick up the coffee pot, Miss Foxley made a noise which sounded alarmingly like a smothered sob and, jumping up, rushed from the room.

It was Laura's turn to be startled. It seemed so unlike Margaret to cry. But perhaps she also had depths she had never revealed before. Until now her only strong emotions had seemed to be anger and dislike, both of which she displayed quite frequently although they were usually directed at other people, not Laura.

For her to weep was unheard of and Laura began to

feel worried and guilty again. She wondered if she should go after her ... apologise for the accusation of selfishness ... assure her she hadn't meant to hurt her ... perhaps had expressed herself too strongly.

On second thought it seemed best to wait a little. Perhaps a few tears in the privacy of her bedroom were what Margaret needed. Left to herself, she might presently reappear in a calmer mood.

Laura filled one of the cups. Her hand was shaking and she felt stirred up inside. She had always hated having scenes and had usually managed to avoid them.

Alone in Miss Foxley's immaculate lounge, drinking Camp coffee, Laura saw that her worst fault – the trait which had made her life such a dull one – was that she had always preferred to be upset herself than to upset other people. Mrs Denham had seen that weakness in her and played on it, and it might be that Margaret thought she could do the same thing.

But this time I'll stick to my guns. I'll be strong, Laura thought determinedly.

She reached for the Countess' letter and put it in her pocket.

'We had better be moving,' said Damaris, reluctant to leave so pleasant a spot but also keenly looking forward to seeing Longwarden and its gardens.

Half an hour later they were at their destination, or rather outside the impressive gateway to Lord Carlyon's domain.

Joël was about to get out and go to the lodge when, as if they were being drawn back by invisible hands, the gates swung slowly open.

The drive was a long one. Their first glimpse of the house made them both give startled exclamations. They had known it would be a large house but not that it would be a palace of golden stone of such august beauty that Damaris felt a catch in her throat at the sight of it.

'I hadn't realised it would be so magnificent,' Joël murmured. 'This is, in effect, a *château*. I had imagined a large *manoir*.'

'I wonder how much of it's occupied, and how much closed up?' said Damaris, also wondering whether to drive up to the steps ascending to a very grand portico or whether to follow the branch of the drive leading round to the side of the building.

Her uncertainty was resolved when a young woman appeared between the innermost pair of columns supporting the portico. As they recognised her as the Countess, she waved and ran down the steps to meet them.

'Good morning. I hope you had no difficulty in finding the way,' she said, bending down to smile at them through the driver's window.

'Good morning. None at all, thank you. From the motorway to here is a lovely run,' said Damaris, climbing out and shaking hands.

Then Joël came round from the other side of the car and Lady Carlyon said, '*Bonjour*, Monsieur Vibrac,' and asked him something in French, to which, having bowed over her hand, Joël replied in his own language.

No doubt the Countess assumed that Damaris also spoke French. However although, in addition to restaurant French, she had learnt the meaning of most of the words and phrases she was likely to hear in conversation, she could only guess what they were saying to each other.

'If you give your keys to Flitton, Miss Lynn, he will drive your car round to the stables and attend to your baggage,' said the Countess, as a man in a charcoal suit, white shirt and plain tie came down the steps at a dignified pace.

Thanks to Maudie's meticulous training in how to

behave in every eventuality, Damaris knew better than
to offer her hand to this personage. She smiled at him,
said good morning and added, 'My keys are in the
ignition. My bag is the green and tan one. Everything
else belongs to Monsieur Vibrac.'

'Perhaps I should also go to the stables,' said Joël,
clearly uncertain of his standing.

'There is plenty of time for your preparations for
tonight. First come and have coffee on the terrace with
Miss Lynn and me,' said the Countess.

'Excuse me, m'Lady, it would be a help if Monsieur
Vibrac would tell me which is his personal luggage and
which his culinary equipment,' said the butler.

This done, he took charge of the car and the Countess
led the other two up the steps trodden – as Damaris
knew from reading the sister-in-law's book – by kings
and princes, prime ministers, ambassadors and a host
of other distinguished people.


'This is called The Setting Sun Room,' said the Countess, when she showed Damaris where she was to sleep.
'But not because it faces west. The name comes from
that painting.' She nodded at a large canvas on the wall
facing the doorway.

'It's a design by Boucher for a tapestry to be made at
the Gobelins factory. Originally it belonged to Madame
de Pompadour. It came here when my husband's great
great-grandfather bought it at a sale in France in 1855.
He may have bought The Rising Sun as well but, if so,
it's disappeared. It could be somewhere in the house,
rolled up or even folded. Longwarden is full of forgotten
treasures.'

Damaris had expected to be put up in considerable
comfort, but the size and magnificence of the bedroom
assigned to her was far beyond her expectations.

'I do hope you'll be comfortable,' said the Countess,

a trifle anxiously. 'I've only been here a short time and the visitors' bedrooms aren't yet as I want them to be. But at least you'll find the mattress comfortable and there's an electric blanket instead of the copper and earthenware hot water bottles which were used here until fairly recently. Lunch is at one, on the terrace where we had coffee. Afterwards I'll show you the garden.'

A good deal of the garden, surrounded by a vast park, was visible from the two tall windows framed by curtains of deep blue silk which had faded almost to white at the edges exposed to the light. Not only faded but frayed, Damaris noted, looking more closely at the places where the silk was starting to disintegrate.

Although she could have spent a long time gazing at the view, it seemed more important to find out where all her things had been put. Maudie Sheringham's reminiscences had prepared her for having her suitcase unpacked for her and she had also known better than to rush out and buy a new pair of bedroom slippers to replace the black espadrilles which she kept under her bed in London.

Only upstarts worried about what the servants might think, Maudie had told her. The aristocracy and gentry didn't care what anyone thought. She had once unpacked for a Duchess who slept in a man's flannel night-shirt and red bed-socks and whose comb had lost half its teeth.

So Damaris had brought the espadrilles, with their trodden down backs, and her Charvet pyjamas. The first she found with her other shoes on the rails at the bottom of the massive free-standing wardrobe. The pyjamas and her underwear were in the sliding trays in the side section of the wardrobe.

Adjoining the bedroom was a bathroom much larger than her bedroom at the flat. The bath, far longer and deeper than modern baths, was boxed in by mahogany

126

panelling, as was the lavatory, its lid being in the centre of a wide polished seat with a pot of massed lilies of the valley on one side and a stack of magazines on the other.

The wash basin was a grey marble affair with a new tablet of Pears' transparent brown soap in the hollow on the right of the solid brass taps and white huckaback linen hand towels folded over the rail at the side.

The selection of terry towels on the main towel rail included a face cloth, she noticed. She guessed that was one of the young American's innovations. Something Damaris had learnt from Peter's traveller's tales was that, throughout North America, hotel bathrooms were equipped with face cloths, relieving people in transit of the need to carry a wet one in their baggage.

She had brought her own, wrapped in a plastic bag inside her wash bag. Now, neatly folded, it lay beside the basin. Her toothbrush and cosmetics had also been put out for her. Whoever had unpacked evidently knew that women of her generation usually did their faces by a basin rather than at a dressing table.

How large a staff did it take to run this huge house? she wondered, as she washed her hands. More to the point, how and where was she going to recruit enough people to keep the gardens in order?

Cross that bridge when you come to it. You haven't got the job yet, she reminded herself.


Joël's case had not been unpacked for him. His room was in the wing being converted into modern staff quarters.

As he arranged his belongings, he found himself looking forward to the journey back to London late tomorrow afternoon. She was easy to talk to, the garden girl . . . and very attractive. He remembered a country inn they had passed on the way along. It had looked a nice place to spend a relaxing weekend. The sort of place he had once hoped to own.

He imagined staying there – with her. How would she be in bed? Not like Lucy, he'd bet on that. Even though Damaris Lynn's manner had been no more than friendly, there was something about her which convinced him she would be a warm and willing partner. Was there a man in her life? She hadn't said anything to suggest it. But there must be someone. No girl of her age, with her looks, would be living alone.

Continuing to fantasise about her, he worked himself up to a pitch from which the only release was to go into the shower and do what he had done as a schoolboy, before he had his first girl. It made him angry to be reduced to this expedient, but what else was there? He was not a promiscuous man. It was his nature, once married and settled down, to be a faithful husband. But he hadn't bargained for a wife who had never, voluntarily, touched this part of him; who refused to admit that even now they could still have a workable sex life. Not good, but better than nothing.

His thoughts returned to Damaris. Closing his eyes, he visualised her being in the shower cabinet with him . . . or, better still, lying on a bed in that roadside inn, her arms held up to embrace him, her slim legs spread to receive him.


'I'm very keen,' said the Countess, at lunch, 'on providing satisfying work for local teenagers. For a long time they've been going off to the nearest town to be wage-slaves in boring jobs. I'd like to reverse that trend and encourage them to stay here, doing the work which their grandfathers and grandmothers did but for better pay and with reasonable hours. My husband is sceptical about it, but I'm determined to try. What do you think, Miss Lynn?'

'My views are biased by my personal feelings,' said Damaris. 'Given a choice between gardening in the rain

128

and re-stocking supermarket shelves in the dry, I'd choose gardening every time. Why are you sceptical, Lord Carlyon?'

The Earl looked up from his salad. His eyes were as blue as delphiniums. He was even taller than Joël with hair and eyebrows as dark as the Frenchman's. But other than being, in different ways, tall, dark and handsome, they were markedly dissimilar men.

North – as the Countess called him – was a man who emanated self-assurance. With his looks, his position, his professional success and his beautiful wife, it would have been surprising if he hadn't.

Joël Vibrac, although he must be an exceptionally able chef to have been summoned here, did not share Lord Carlyon's air of confidence. Damaris had felt him to be a far more vulnerable personality. He was having his lunch somewhere else.

'I hope that my wife is right and we can achieve her objectives,' said the Earl, in reply to her question. 'Like you, I rate job-satisfaction very highly. I can't imagine anything worse than being in a dead-end job, longing for knocking off time. But there are all sorts of pressures to prevent people doing work which they might find more rewarding than being on a check-out till or re-stocking shelves all day. In my opinion those jobs must be tedious beyond endurance, but they're thought to be less demeaning than working as a maid or a waiter. Why do you suppose so many hotels in this country are staffed by foreigners?'

'Because they come from poorer countries and are prepared to put up with inconvenient hours of hotel work, I should imagine,' said Damaris.

'That's part of it,' he agreed, 'but it's also because, as a nation, we resent serving other people. It's a hangover from the days when some people in service were abused and exploited. On the whole *my* forbears were fair and considerate employers, yet most people in the village would rather find jobs in Melchester than come to work here.'

'I'm not so sure,' said his wife. 'I'm going to have a talk with the headmaster of the secondary school and see what he thinks. He should know much more about the hopes and ambitions of the village teenagers than you do, darling. You don't have anything to do with them. Do you have young people working for you in London, Miss Lynn?'

'No, my work force is made up of married women who don't want to work full time because of their domestic commitments. They're all conscientious people who can be relied on to do what's required of them without someone breathing down their necks.'

The Countess nodded. 'Like our team of cleaners. Unfortunately, now that more of the house is being used, we haven't nearly enough helpers. Which is why I'm testing the ground to see whether, if we had a crêche to offer them, we might get some much younger women to join our cleaning brigade.'

She saw her husband raise a sardonic eyebrow.

'You may be right. All my ideas may fall flat,' she admitted, with her lovely smile. 'But it's worth a try, don't you think.'

The Earl's rather hard face softened. 'Try it by all means, sweetie.'

Watching the look they exchanged, Damaris felt an outsider catching a glimpse of a private world from which she was excluded, not because of her background, but because it seemed very unlikely that she would ever experience the love which Jane Carlyon clearly felt for her husband and he for her.


After lunch the Countess took Damaris on a tour of the garden.

'This is the laburnum walk which I haven't seen at

its best yet because I didn't arrive here until last September,' said the Countess, as they entered a long tunnel of giant metal hoops from which, in a few weeks' time, would cascade the yellow flowers of the many laburnums planted between the hoops and trained to grow over them.

'Do you know when it was planted?' Damaris asked, beset by a host of unwelcome memories.

If Laburnum Way had taken its name from trees like these, she had no memory of them. Probably they had been vandalised long before her time. But the name of the street where she had grown up had left her with an ineradicable dislike of the tree and its bright yellow flowers. She could never bring herself to use it in her garden plans and disliked the idea of having a profusion of laburnums in a garden which, in all other respects delighted her with its beauty and its possibilities.

'I don't know, but my sister-in-law may. When she was writing her book, she found that as well as being a diarist, her great-grandfather also kept notes of everything he planted and when. The laburnum walk may have been his wife's idea. It was she who invented the butterfly ballroom, and the bamboo forest was planted to remind her of China. Flora was half-Chinese, you know. My black hair is a legacy from her. My husband and I are distant cousins, but I am the only descendant who looks a little like her. That's how I met North last year. It was at a sort of clan gathering in America and he noticed my resemblance to his great-grandmother as a young woman and introduced himself.'

'I should think he might have done that anyway,' said Damaris, smiling.

Simply dressed in a cotton shirt and blue denim skirt, with very little if any make-up enhancing her large grey eyes and curling lips, the Countess was a natural beauty who must have attracted numerous men when she was single.

131

Presently, after they had been strolling and chatting for about half an hour, Lady Carlyon glanced at her watch and said, 'Will you excuse me now? I have several things to do and I expect you'd like to wander about on your own for a while. There'll be tea on the terrace at four-thirty.'

For dinner that evening Damaris had chosen to wear a printed crêpe de Chine frock made in the Forties and bought from a King's Road antique market.

The frock had a distinctive pattern of small lemon and pale green flowers on a navy ground. Although not expensive when new, now its fabric and finish were superior to many of today's 'designer' clothes and even at about ten times its original price it had still been cheaper than a new dress.

As she was ready too early to go downstairs, she felt there could be no objection to her exploring some of the corridors she had seen on the way to her room, all of them hung with paintings and furnished with chairs, chests and busts.

She had wandered some way from her room and was looking at an arrangement of large tropical butterflies in a glass case when the door near it opened and a tall woman appeared.

Almost immediately Damaris knew who she was. Not that she looked the same as she had in the glamorous photograph on the back of *The Travels of an Edwardian Naturalist*. In the flesh, she looked older and more haggard. But even with dark shadows under them, the extraordinary amethyst eyes were unmistakable, as was the copper beech hair and the striking bone structure.

At the sight of a stranger in the corridor, the Earl's sister frowned. For a moment she seemed on the point of retreating into the room behind her. Then, with a reluctant 'Good evening', she closed the door behind her and walked briskly away.

'Good evening,' Damaris murmured, a little belatedly.

Had Lady Allegra looked displeased because it was not the done thing for guests to explore their hosts' house, even one as large as this?

Some yards along the passage, the other woman checked her stride. Turning, she said, 'I've seen that dress before.' She eyed it for a few seconds. 'Was it in Bonham's costume sale last summer?'

Damaris shook her head. 'I bought it at Antiquarius in Chelsea.'

The other woman retraced her steps. 'I remember it now. It was on Adrienne Hutter's stand. I was tempted by it myself. Seeing how good it looks on you, I wish I had succumbed.' She held out her hand. 'I'm Allegra Lomax and you must be the gardening consultant my mother recommended to my sister-in-law.'

'Damaris Lynn . . . how do you do?'

'I think the lace collar was put on by the first owner, don't you?' said Lady Allegra, looking at the fichu of hand-made lace attached to the frock's V neckline. 'She probably hadn't enough clothing coupons to buy herself more than one dress and tried to make it look different adding the collar. According to my mother food and clothes rationing went on for years after the war. God knows why. Clothes weren't rationed in France. I suppose some killjoy Minister in the post-war Socialist government thought it would be a good thing to keep women dowdy and downcast for another five years.'

'Perhaps I should try it without the collar,' said Damaris. 'But although I bought it last year, so far I've only worn it a couple of times.'

'Do you always buy old clothes?'

'Not always . . . quite a lot.'

'I almost never buy new things. Half my wardrobe comes from trunks in the attics and the other half is

133

from market stalls and the Gallery of Antique Costumes and Textiles,' said Lady Allegra.

At the moment she was wearing a pair of cavalry twill jodhpurs cut in the old-fashioned way and a boy's striped rugger shirt. Why wasn't she dressing for dinner? Damaris wondered.

'Are you lost, or just pottering about till drinks time?' the other woman asked.

'Pottering. I was ready too early.'

After a glance at her watch, the Earl's sister said, 'You're all right to go down now. I've opted out of the dinner party. They've invited one of my *bêtes noires*. A man called Michael Marchington. I shouldn't think Jane will have put you next to him but, if she has, watch out. He's the world champion groper. He wouldn't be asked except that he has a sweet wife whom everyone likes and their parties are always rather good.'

Damaris smiled. 'Thanks for the warning.'

'I'll probably see you tomorrow.'

With a friendly nod, Lady Allegra went on her way.


'What do you think of Damaris Lynn?' Jane asked her husband, when he came to her bedroom that night after undressing in his room.

'I had very little conversation with her.'

'You must have formed some impression. Don't you think she's attractive? I do.'

'Marchington obviously thought so, but he didn't seem to be making much headway,' North replied, getting into bed.

Jane was still at the dressing table, removing her make-up. 'No, she wasn't interested, was she? Perhaps she recognised him as a womaniser or perhaps she's already spoken for. From what I saw and overheard, she handled him very adroitly. I expect she's had lots of practice at repulsing men gracefully.'

134

'Not necessarily. That Marchington made a set at her means nothing. He paws the ground at the sight of any female under forty. I doubt if she'd have that effect on anyone else. I think she's rather a cold piece.'

'Cold? What a strange thing to say. When we went round the garden together, I was struck by her warmth and enthusiasm.' Jane anticipated her husband's comment and forestalled it by adding, 'Yes, I know – people usually are enthusiastic about earning money but I don't think it was only that. I felt her excitement was sincere. She fell on some of the plants as if they were long-lost friends, and she's extraordinarily knowledgeable. She recognised plants which right now are no more than cut-back stumps.'

'So she should. It's her job. When I said she looked cold, I meant from a man's point of view. The only time I saw her sparkle was when she was talking to you and the other women. Whether that's an indication of her sexual preference, or – '

'I'm sure she isn't a lesbian,' Jane said positively. 'But I don't want her here if you don't like her. Talk to her some more tomorrow, darling.'


Having had a shower that morning and again before dinner, Damaris finished the day with a warm, scented bath which she hoped would relax her after the testing dinner party.

None of the possible pitfalls she had foreseen had materialised. As far as she knew she hadn't made any faux pas. The only questions they had asked had all been related to gardening problems. Most of the other guests had been far more interested in scrounging some free advice than in probing her past.

But having got through the dinner without making any boners didn't mean she had landed the job. It might be that, in spite of the recommendation from the Earl's mother, she was only one of a short list of garden consultants who were being invited here for an in-depth vetting.

I want this job. I want it badly, she thought, drying herself on one of the many thick towels folded over hot rails. As she got into bed, she wondered if Joël were still awake, wondering and worrying about the Carlyons' reactions to his cooking.

Damaris had set her alarm clock to wake her before first light.

Having foreseen that to go into the garden at an early hour might not be as simple a matter as from an ordinary house, she had consulted the butler and been shown where and how to get out without setting off the alarm system.

To have the great garden to herself at sunrise on a spring morning was to come closer to bliss than ever before in her life. White and blue anemones, *Muscari viridis* the scented greenish form of grape hyacinth, naturalised daffodils and fritillaries . . . everywhere she looked something lovely was growing. Presently, burying her face in a cluster of the green-eyed clear yellow flowers of a deliciously scented polyanthus, she felt a powerful longing to give up her work in London and devote herself to this glorious place, but she knew that was wishful thinking, at least for the present.

After about an hour of wandering for pleasure, she took out her mini-recorder and began to add to the mental and scribbled notes made yesterday. Then, reluctantly, she returned to her room, there to sit down at the writing table to combine the two sets of notes into an assessment of the gardens in its present form and to make her proposals for its future.

At that moment Sarah Lomax was crouching beside the

lavatory pan in her bathroom, waiting to finish being sick so that she could get back to the stables.

She had known she was pregnant when, a fortnight after Nick's disappearance, her period didn't start on time. It had been no use hoping it was late. Her insides had always functioned like clockwork. Also the night Nick had made love to her had been at the very time when she was most likely to conceive.

She hadn't known that when she begged him to take her. Such a mundane consideration hadn't even occurred to her. She had thought of nothing but how much she loved him, and how passionately she wanted him to be her first and only lover.

The next morning he had gone. Apart from one telephone message from somewhere abroad – taken by someone else – in which he had said he would write, there had been no further word from him.

The morning sickness had started exactly six weeks after their night together. On the day it began she had woken up feeling normal, attended to the horses as usual, eaten a substantial breakfast and, half an hour later, fled to her private quarters above the stable-yard arch, there to be convulsively sick. By now it had become a routine; an unpleasant ten minutes from which she would quickly recover after a cup of tea.

Jane appeared to be sailing through her first weeks with no problems at all. Not that, having announced her condition, she had continued to talk about it. She had scarcely mentioned it again, perhaps out of consideration for Allegra who now had nothing to look forward to.

When the final surge of nausea was spent, Sarah rinsed her mouth at the handbasin. The mirror above it reflected a face which was thinner than it had been at Christmas. Her last summer's tan long gone, she could barely recognise herself as the radiantly smiling nineteen year old whose photograph had appeared on the cover of *Eventing* after her triumph at Burghley.

She felt years, not a few months, older. And looked it. Unhappiness, worry and being sick every morning had made her lose weight, sharpening the shape of her face and her resemblance to her dead father, Ranulf Lomax, the younger brother of North's father.

For contestants and followers of the sport of three-day eventing, the most important English horse trials of the year were those which were due to take place very soon at Badminton, the Duke of Beaufort's estate in Gloucestershire.

The previous autumn, soon after Jane's arrival in England, Sarah and her favourite horse, Bedouin Star, had had a sensational success at the almost equally prestigious horse trials at Burghley. If they did well at Badminton she had an excellent chance of being picked for the equestrian team to represent Britain in the 1988 Olympics.

But would they do well? And even if they did, how would the selectors react when it came out that she was pregnant? She wouldn't be able to ride any more this year after Badminton.

In a way that worried her less than breaking the news to North. Although both her father and her uncle had been killed in riding accidents, Sarah had never been afraid of the hazards of the hunting field or the cross country phase of horse trials. But she was nervous, very nervous of her cousin's reaction when he found out what she had done. She knew he wouldn't give a damn what the world thought. It was what he would think, and say, about Nick which worried her; and the pressure she was sure he would put on her to have the baby aborted.

That had been Allegra's advice: get rid of it.

But whatever it cost her in public humiliation and lost opportunities, Sarah had known from the first that she couldn't get rid of Nick's child. Not deliberately. In fact she didn't really want to risk losing it by riding at Badminton, but how could she let Beddo down? She had to let him have his chance. Fortunately the dates of the trials didn't coincide with the time when she would have been menstruating and that, according to a book she had bought in Melchester, was when the risk of a miscarriage was highest.

It was half past nine before Damaris had finished typing a copy of her report on the paper she had brought with her. By then, although she had had several cups of tea made with the electric kettle and other equipment provided on a side table, she was hungry for something more substantial than the biscuits in the air-tight tin.

Her hostess had told her that, at weekends, visitors to Longwarden could have breakfast at any time they liked between eight and eleven. Finding the way to the room where breakfast was served wasn't a problem because the American girl had had some cards printed showing the way from the visitors' bedrooms to the principal rooms on the ground floor.

When she arrived the only people there were the Carlyons, both of whom had finished eating and were reading newspapers.

'Good morning, Miss Lynn.' The Countess put aside one of the Sunday colour supplements. 'You were out very early. I saw you from my window. I hope that wasn't because you hadn't slept well.'

After explaining the reason for her early outing, Damaris said, 'I would have come down much earlier but I wanted to type out my thoughts about the garden. You may not have time to read them today, but I thought you would like to have them as soon as possible.' She handed the Countess the large buff envelope containing the report.

'I'll read them at once,' said the Countess. Having seen the length of the report, she added, 'You have been working hard! I didn't expect such a detailed reaction

139

as soon as this. Before I read it, I'll make a copy for my husband. Shall I make one for you as well? I expect you took a carbon but a photo-copy is better, don't you think?'

'My wife is a great believer in modern technology,' said the Earl, when she had left them. 'She has introduced us to gadgets no one here had even heard of, but they don't include a microwave oven.' He waved a hand at the sideboard. 'You'll find various things keeping hot in the old-fashioned way. While you're looking under the covers, let me pour you some coffee or tea.'

'Thank you, but I'd rather have that later . . . after some orange juice,' said Damaris, seeing a large jug of it. 'Please . . . do go on reading your paper.'

However much he might wish to re-immerse himself, the Earl was determinedly polite and poured the orange juice for her which he then took to the table where he drew out the chair next to his.

'Are you always as quick as this in addressing yourself to the problems put to you, Miss Lynn?' he asked, when she was seated beside him with a bowl of muesli in front of her.

She had the feeling he might think her reactions were too quick to be well thought out.

'In general, yes. I like rapid responses to my problems and I try to deal quickly and efficiently with other people's,' she answered. 'But as you'll see when you read my report I've suggested waiting a year before making any changes to the garden as a whole. I'd prefer to watch it through its full seasonal cycle before doing anything to it. Meanwhile there are two aspects which do need immediate attention. One is planting the orangery to make an attractive setting for the new swimming pool. The second equally urgent priority is the kitchen garden. That needs a lot doing to it if Monsieur Vibrac or whoever you appoint as your chef is to have an adequate supply of vegetables and soft fruit this summer.'

'You drove down with Vibrac, I hear.'

'Yes, and we're going back together this afternoon.'

'D'you find him a conversable chap?'

'Very, although our chief topic – vegetables – might not be considered riveting by most people. He's the first chef I've met. I found him extremely interesting.'

'He certainly makes first-rate croissants. I think I might have another,' said the Earl, getting up.

Damaris watched him unwrap the napkin lining a basket standing on one of the several hot plates. She thought him well-matched with his wife, although the damage to his nose, which had a broken bridge, stopped him from being as handsome as his wife was beautiful.

At that moment Lady Carlyon returned with three sets of copies protected by plastic pockets.

'Seeing you strolling in the garden early reminded me of my first morning here,' she said to Damaris. 'I went out to explore and met my mother-in-law who, as I think I mentioned, last month got married again and is starting a garden from scratch in the backwoods of Spain.'

'That should be an interesting challenge, but presumably it's much easier to get gardeners in Spain than it is here.'

The Countess shook her head. 'Apparently not. Household and outdoor help is as difficult to come by there as it is in England, at least in the areas where there are lots of foreigners. My mother-in-law and her husband aren't on the coast where most of the foreigners congregate, but they're not far inland. However, having grappled with the gardens here with only her two old henchmen, Mr Hazell and Mr Craskett, I doubt if she'll have problems with her new garden. She's being helped by a book called *The Dry Garden* by Beth Chatto whose stand at this year's Chelsea Show is something she says I must see. Would you agree?'

'Absolutely. Mrs Chatto is one of the great garden influencers of our time,' said Damaris. 'But the man who has influenced me most is, or rather was, an American although he worked mainly in this country.'

'You don't mean Lanning Roper, do you?' Jane asked.

'Yes. Did you know him?'

'No, but he worked on the garden at Winterbrook Farm, near Boston, Massachusetts, where North and I were married. I was there last month, staying with cousins of my mother, and they were telling me about him. But he died in 1983 and his best work, they said, was done in the Sixties and Seventies. Were you a pupil of his?'

'No, I never met him but the woman who taught me to garden used to cut out the articles he wrote for *The Sunday Times* and later I read all his pieces for *Country Life*. Although he wasn't an Englishman, he had an extraordinary understanding of English gardens.'

'My cousins were saying that, had he been alive today, he would have been the best person to advise us on the gardens here. Well, isn't that great . . . you being a disciple of his,' the Countess said, in a pleased tone.

Her manner led Damaris to hope that, even before she read the notes, Lady Carlyon had more or less made up her mind to appoint her as their adviser.

But when the Earl said, 'No doubt Mr Roper influenced a great many people,' she felt that he had reservations about her, and his might be the casting vote.


'Have they offered you the job? Or are they going to write to you?' asked Damaris, as soon as she and Joël were alone in the car, setting out on the drive back to London.

'They will write,' said the Frenchman. 'The Countess

142

seemed very pleased but she says she has not yet had time to talk to her husband. I've been told she is very rich, but I don't think she is a wife *qui porte la culotte* . . . wears the trousers. What did you think of the food? Did you enjoy it? Did the other guests seem to like it?'

'I thought it was all delicious and so did everyone else. They not only ate it with relish, they talked about it,' she told him. 'The lamb we had last night was wonderful, and so was the chicken at lunch today.'

'Thank you . . . you're very kind. The *selle d'agneau* I borrowed from Fredy Girardet who some people think is the best chef in Europe. The chicken *en persillade* is a method of my own. But tell me, how did you get on? Must you also wait for a letter?'

'Yes . . . and like you I feel that a lot depends on Lord Carlyon's opinion. But I watched him eating at both meals and I'm sure the job's yours – if you want it. What are the kitchens like? Do they need a lot of modernisation?'

'They are not as bad as I expected, and yes, I should like to work here,' he said, as they came to the great gates, already open in readiness for their departure. 'But I am not optimistic. You see, I have a disadvantage. My wife is unable to walk and we have her mother living with us to look after her. They may not like that.'

'I see. I wondered why your wife hadn't come with you. How badly is she disabled? Can she get about in a wheelchair?'

'Yes, and to live in the country would be better for her than London. But from their point of view it's not good to have an invalid around. I'm sure they would prefer their chef to have a healthy wife who could make herself useful in some way.'

Damaris was inclined to agree with him, but she said, 'The Countess struck me as very kind and sympathetic. I don't think she would turn you down for that reason.

143

I'm not so sure about the Earl. Is your wife ill, or is her condition the result of an accident?'

'She fell off a horse. She used to be very keen on riding. Myself, I have never liked horses. Did you meet the Earl's cousin, the one who's a famous rider?'

'Perhaps she's away. I didn't see any sign of her. I did meet Lord Carlyon's sister, Lady Allegra, but only by chance. She wasn't at dinner or lunch.'

'She eats in her room when there are guests,' Joël explained. 'The reason was explained to me. It's not many weeks since her lover was drowned in the sea. They say she is heart-broken.'

So that was the reason the sister looked startlingly haggard. Damaris felt a twinge of pity. She wondered who the lover had been. Obviously someone exceptional to have captured the beautiful writer's heart in the first place and to leave her shattered by his death. The gods, having showered her with gifts, were making her pay for them now, poor thing.

'How depressing these city streets look,' said Joël, as they entered the suburbs. 'Last night, when I'd finished my work, I went outside and breathed in the good country air. You can't smell the earth in London . . . only the fumes from the traffic.'

She wondered if it was not only London which depressed him, but the return to a ménage composed of a crippled wife and a mother-in-law whose help he needed but whose presence might be an aggravation. However much he loved his wife, it must be terribly hard for a young energetic man to live with a girl for whom all physical activity was now severely restricted.

When she stopped the car at the spot where she had picked him up, she half expected him to invite her in to meet his wife. But he didn't. Perhaps he felt she wouldn't be happy about his spending several hours in the company of another young woman. Perhaps her disability had made her jealous. It would be understandable.

144

'Thank you very much, Miss Lynn. Taking all this down by car was much easier for me than a train journey,' he said, unloading his gear. 'I hope we shall meet again . . . at Longwarden. In the meantime, if you have a friend you would like to bring to the restaurant where I am working now, it would give me great pleasure for you to be my guests for dinner . . . a small return for your kindness to me this weekend.'

As he spoke, he took a bill-fold from his hip pocket and handed her a card with the name of the restaurant and its telephone number. 'When you ring up, don't forget to say you are my guest so that I can make sure you and your friend have one of our best tables. You will come . . . perhaps one night next week?'

'Thank you . . . that's very nice of you. After this weekend's experience of *haute cuisine* I'd love to try some more of it.' And return Peter's hospitality at the same time, she thought.

'Good. In that case I won't say goodbye but only *au revoir*.' He held out his hand. 'It's been a great pleasure to meet you and, if all goes well, I hope to have many more conversations with you.'

'I hope so too. I'd really like the chance to turn that neglected kitchen garden into a *jardin potager* worthy of your culinary skills,' she replied, smiling.

Was there a hint of something more than friendliness in his eyes as he held her hand for perhaps longer than was necessary? Normally, if a man who was married showed even the mildest tendency to become amorous, Damaris was quick to nip it in the bud. But it was difficult to do that with a man who had just invited her to dine at his expense – not that he would be charged anything like the cost to the restaurant's patrons – and anyway she might be mistaken. It might be that French handclasps always lasted longer than English ones and that the warmth in his eyes as he looked at her signified nothing more than a Gallic liking for the female sex as a whole. It seemed best, for the time being, to give him the benefit of the doubt.

Half an hour before dinner, North and Jane strolled in the garden, their hands loosely linked.

'So you're happy about taking on Joël Vibrac?' she said, when her husband had agreed he couldn't fault the two meals the Frenchman had cooked for them.

'By all means. But, if he's married, doesn't it rather depend on his wife's reaction to living here? It'll be a big change from London for her. Why didn't she come with him this weekend, I wonder?'

Jane had already debated telling him what Joël had told her about his wife. It worried her not to be straight with North, but she was almost certain that he wouldn't approve of engaging a chef with an invalid wife. It wasn't that he was a hard man who didn't care about other people's difficulties. At the same time his sympathies were not engaged by every hard luck story.

'His wife wasn't brought up in London. He told me he's sure she'll like it here.' Rather guiltily dropping that subject, she said, 'Now that you've read her report, what's your feeling about Damaris?' she asked.

'I'm in favour,' he answered. 'Mother was impressed by her and I'm impressed by that report. I like her sense of priorities. To concentrate on the orangery and the kitchen garden, keeping the rest in good order while she sees what's what, shows very sound judgement. What we need here is someone imaginative but not over-innovative.'

'Have you changed your mind about her coldness?' Jane had noticed him talking to Damaris before and after lunch.

'Not altogether, but I've questioned her about her staff relations in London and there doesn't seem to be a problem in that sphere which is the main thing. And you like her, don't you?'

'Very much.'

'*Courage and stamina have always been essential qualities for success in three-day eventing. This year, here at Badminton, the Duke of Beaufort's great estate in Gloucestershire – or Avon, to give it its official name – those attributes are about to be tested even more severely than usual*,' were the commentator's opening words, as Sarah's family settled down to watch the television coverage of the most important and formidable horse trials of the year.

Last year, Jane remembered, her mother-in-law had been here to watch the cross country phase of the trials. When, to their astonishment and horror, Sarah had fallen off, they had clasped each other's hands, their shared apprehension breaking down reserves which might have kept them at arm's length for months.

'*Days of heavy rain have made the going very wet and heavy . . . in places a quagmire*,' continued the commentator. '*It's a treacherous course on which even the best riders may come to grief. However Colonel Frank Weldon, who is celebrating his twenty-first year as Badminton's course designer, has taken the decision to go ahead and only four riders have withdrawn their horses.*

'*One of the few riders here who won't have been worried by the wet weather we've been having is twenty-one year old Rachel Hunt riding Piglet II, whose previous successes have usually been in conditions not unlike those we're seeing today. At Boekelo two years ago he was the only horse to finish a very muddy course inside the optimum time, and at last year's Gatcombe trials, in torrential rain, he clocked up the fastest cross-country round and won his section.*

'*Even younger than Rachel is Sarah Lomax. She's riding Bedouin Star with whom she won a gold medal at Burghley in September. As many viewers will remember, that triumph fol-*

147

*lowed a seemingly disastrous fall, and Sarah and Beddo, as she
calls him, are one of the most promising partnerships the sport
has seen since Lucinda Green's early successes. But whether
Sarah's Arab takes kindly to the conditions here today remains
to be seen.*

*'Virginia Leng riding Night Cap is the first to go. She was,
of course, last year's winner, with a good chance of achieving a
double.'*

Allegra got up from her chair and went to the drinks
table where she poured a strong gin and tonic.

'Anything I can get for you two?' she asked, over her
shoulder.

Jane shook her head. North rose from the sofa he was
sharing with her. 'I'll have a beer, but I'll get it.'

An innovation in the library was a concealed refriger-
ator so that they could have cold drinks without always
ringing for Flitton.

Allegra returned to her chair, wishing she had chosen
to watch the horse trials on the set in her room. It was
difficult to hide her extreme anxiety from the others.
The appalling conditions at Badminton must increase
the horrendous risk her cousin was taking.

*'Normally,'* the commentator continued, *'the only hope of
winning the Whitbread Trophy has been to achieve high marks
in the dressage test and go clear and fast on the cross country
course. But I think it's unlikely that anyone is going to get round
without some penalties today and what sort of times they will
make is, at this stage, anyone's guess. The overnight leader is
Bruce Davidson with J J Babu who was a runner-up at Badminton four years ago. Last night Lucinda Green had doubts about
running her big gelding Shannagh, who hates this sort of soft
going, but she's decided to go ahead and in any contest calling
for grit, determination and experience Lucinda always stands a
good chance.'*

A few minutes later he was commiserating with Ginny
Leng who had been thrown off-balance when her horse
jumped very steeply off the Jetty in the middle of the

lake. Her momentary loss of control was long enough for Night Cap to slip out beside the Boathouse.

When Sarah set out on the course it seemed likely the camera would stay with her most of the way, as it had with Rachel Hunt, the first rider to come in clear of jumping penalties. But before Sarah had reached the trickiest jumps, a drama between the first two fences became the focus of attention.

'What the hell is a car doing on the course?' Allegra exclaimed, furious at losing sight of her cousin.

'God knows! Some slip-up in the stewarding presumably,' said her brother.

The commentator said, *'We don't know quite how that happened but it seems there's no serious harm done. Dylan II, ridden by Polly Schwerdt, was in collision with a car – something I personally have never seen happen before.'*

'Oh dear, are we going to lose the whole of Sarah's round?' Jane said, frowning, her sympathy for Dylan II and his rider tempered by her desire to see how Sarah was faring at the lake.

*'It seems that in spite of a bruised chest, Dylan is keen to go on,'* the commentator continued. *'What a game little horse he is . . . only 15 hands and 16 years old. This is his fifth crack at Badminton . . . now back to the lake where Sarah Lomax has decided to take the alternative slower route. A wise decision perhaps, in view of the number of refusals there've been here, but a bit surprising all the same. This girl doesn't usually err on the side of caution. She and Bedouin Star have grown up together and have total confidence in each other. I would have thought she would always go for the fast route but it seems I was wrong.'*

'He's right: she doesn't seem to be riding as flat out as she did at Burghley, but I suppose that's the state of the course,' said Jane, a few minutes later, when the camera was still with Sarah.

'No, she doesn't,' North agreed, 'but the ground is already badly poached and Beddo may not care for it. I feel sorry for Beaufort. The whole place is going to be

149

one hell of a mess by the time it's all over. It'll look like a First World War battlefield.'

'She did so well in the dressage. It'll be a shame if she drops back on this,' said Jane.

Allegra was thankful that her cousin was playing safe – if putting a horse at any of those dauntingly difficult obstacles could be called that. It was amazing that Sarah's condition didn't show. Jane's was beginning to. Her slender waist had thickened and her breasts were noticeably fuller. Sarah showed no sign of being pregnant. Today she was wearing a loose sweater but yesterday, for the dressage, she had had to appear in the close-fitting black tailcoat and top hat which were *de rigueur* for that phase of the trials. If her tummy had been as rounded as Jane's it would have been obvious to everyone.

The camera covering the fourth fence came into action. Lucinda Green was in trouble at the Chevrons. There, it was only a run out but at the Stockholm Fence she took a serious fall, being thrown head first into the ditch. With typical courage she re-mounted, only to have another fall at the lake. Somehow she managed to stay on until she was outside the penalty zone.

'That girl has more guts than anyone I've ever seen,' said North. 'It's high time she was made a Dame – except that it's such a bloody awful title that she probably wouldn't want it.'

Soon after Mrs Green finished the course, the commentator said, '*After that very brave performance, Lucinda has just been given the sad news that Walkabout, ridden by her husband David Green, has died after a suspected heart attack on the steeplechase phase.*'

'Why the hell didn't they cancel?' Allegra exclaimed angrily. She was terrified that there was still time for Sarah to be the next major casualty. 'It's ridiculous to go ahead in these conditions.'

She swallowed the last of her drink and jumped up to

refill her glass, causing Jane to shoot a meaning glance at North behind her sister-in-law's back.

'*I've just heard that Sarah Lomax has completed the course,*' said the commentator, '*but her time will put her out of the running for the trophy, I'm afraid. She's definitely not on her usual form today and even if she does well in tomorrow's show jumping, I doubt if she'll make the first four.*'

The last rider to go was Ian Stark, only just recovered from a bad attack of shingles. He had the advantage of all the other riders' experiences on the course, but the disadvantage of the worst going. Towards the end it was clear that his horse, Sir Wattie, was tiring, but he continued to jump well and he and Stark finished with the fourth fastest time.

The commentator wound up the coverage by announcing that Stark, Rachel Hunt, Rodney Powell and Ginny Leng had retained the first four positions, with Mark Todd on Any Chance taking fifth place when Davidson had a fence down, and Sarah Lomax coming seventh.

'Not what she hoped for, but not bad, all things considered,' said North, as the programme ended and he switched off the set.

And you don't know half of it, thought Allegra.

She went up to her room, relieved that Sarah had survived the two most dangerous phases of the trials, but still worried that between now and tomorrow the stress and exertion of riding that gruelling course might bring on a painful and humiliating miscarriage.

Allegra knew that she wouldn't feel at ease until Sarah was safely back at Longwarden. Even then there was North to be confronted.


In view of what had happened to her father's mistress, Marie-Simone Polignac, after his sudden death, Jane was increasingly worried that Allegra might also become hooked on alcohol.

'It can't be good for Allegra to knock back such huge gin and tonics,' she said to North, after her sister-in-law had left the library.

'Probably not, but she wouldn't take kindly to either of us telling her that,' he said dryly. 'I'd rather she drank than took pills. Those things are really dangerous.'

'Alcohol isn't harmless – especially not for women,' said Jane. 'We have smaller livers than men.'

'I don't suppose Allegra will go on punishing her liver indefinitely. She has to have some sort of crutch at the moment. Don't worry about her. She'll pull herself together eventually. She could do with some interesting work to get her teeth into.'

'Yes, but neither Claudia or Ellen, nor the man in New York, have come up with any appealing suggestions and her own mind is in no state to generate bright ideas. I do worry about her. I can't help it. I'm fond of her and I hate to see her damaging her health and her looks. Drinking like this will begin to show pretty soon.'

North shrugged. 'There's nothing we can do about it, sweetie. My sister has never been influenced by anyone. She rejects advice on principle . . . always has.'

'From her father and mother . . . but perhaps not from you. She admires you more than she lets on.'

Jane also knew that he cared for his sister more than his apparent indifference to her drinking suggested. They were a lot alike, North and Allegra; both a law unto themselves with a hint of arrogance in their manner which could be unnerving to anyone with less self-assurance. But behind the devil-may-care façades they presented to the world, both were capable of deep feeling and unexpected sensitivity. North's capacity for tenderness still filled Jane with wonder and joy. She had no doubt that Allegra, too, had shown a side of herself to Alessandro Risconti which no one else would ever see.

He had been the great love of her life, but for such a short space of time that Jane sometimes felt it might have been better if they had never met.

Would she have wanted to meet North if the price of a few months in paradise had been years in a hell of loneliness? It was a question impossible to answer. To Jane now, a life without North was unimaginable and she felt sure that no other man could ever have made her as happy and fulfilled as he had.

He said, 'My dear girl, I've just advised you not to worry about her. Has it made you stop worrying? No. Nor would my advice to Allegra stop her hitting the bottle. Even people who *ask* for advice hardly ever take it. It's a waste of breath. Whether Allegra sinks or swims depends on her own nature and her own will-power.' He drew in his long, outstretched legs and stood up. 'We've been sitting about long enough. Let's go for a walk.'

From her window, a short time later, Allegra watched them crossing the park. They were holding hands. The sight of them filled her with misery. For her it was over, that special companionship which made even something as mundane as going for a walk a wonderful experience.

Her telephone rang. Glad of any distraction from her thoughts, she flung herself into a chair and reached for the receiver.

'Hello?'

'Allegra . . . it's Sarah. Did you watch?'

'Of course . . . how are you feeling?'

'Tired but okay. What did the others say? Were they disappointed we didn't do better?'

'No – relieved that you did so well. When Lucinda Green has problems, everyone's in trouble.'

'Yes . . . and wasn't it tragic about Walkabout? I feel so sad for them both. It was a horrible thing to happen.'

To Allegra, the death of a horse, although upsetting to those immediately concerned, did not rate as a tragedy. She said, 'Never mind Walkabout. Are you sure you're all right? If you've got any sense, you'll go to bed as soon as possible.'

'I'm going to. The reason I'm ringing is to ask if you'd mind dropping a hint to the others. More than a hint . . . telling them. I'm not trying to chicken out, but I've been thinking it over and it might be better for everyone if you could prepare the ground. It'll give North time to cool down before I get back. Otherwise there'll be a huge row which will upset Jane and be the last straw for me. By the time I get home, I'm going to be pretty worn out . . .'

Allegra heard her cousin's voice quaver and guessed that she was close to exhaustion already.

'Of course I'll tell them. Leave it to me.'

'You're a brick . . . you really are. I'm going to tell Kate on the way home. I've no idea how she'll take it. She may want to leave when she finds out we shan't be – ' Sarah stopped in mid-sentence, perhaps deciding it was wiser not to be too specific on the telephone. 'Anyway I'll see you tomorrow . . . and thanks again for your help.'

'Any time. Good luck and take care.' As Allegra rang off, her mind was already at work on how best to tackle North.


'Who would have thought anyone would win the trophy with 20.4 time penalties on the cross country,' said Kate, as she drove the trailer away from the devastation left by spectators and vehicles after probably the muddiest Badminton since its inception.

After more rain on Saturday night, the condition of the ground had forced the organisers to make most of Sunday's spectators leave their cars in and beyond Badminton village, giving them a long walk through the estate to the showjumping ground. The area round the stands had looked like a ploughed field, the mud almost knee-high in parts.

The championship had been won by Ian Stark and Sir Wattie who had damaged a tendon at the Flight Butt at Burghley in 1984 and been laid off for a year. The long rest and his present triumph encouraged Sarah to hope that Beddo and she would not lose their chance of being chosen for the next Olympics because they were going to be laid off for the rest of this year.

For the first part of the drive home she and Kate discussed Pomeroy, Rodney Powell's horse, who, some people were forecasting, might be next year's winner.

Then, bracing herself, Sarah broached the subject uppermost in her mind.

'Kate . . . I'm afraid I've got some rather bad news for you,' she began.

Her groom flashed a startled glance at her, then returned her attention to the road, her hands no longer relaxed and easy on the wheel but gripping it tightly.

'You're not satisfied with me, is that it?'

'No, no . . . nothing like that. How could I be dissatisfied with someone who works as hard and efficiently as you do? You're terrific . . . surely you know that?'

Kate didn't answer for a moment. Then she said, 'I'm not everyone's cup of tea. I'm not sociable. Sometimes I put people's backs up.'

'Do you? I haven't noticed it. I feel we get on very well . . . don't you?'

The older girl nodded. 'So what's this bad news?'

'I'm not going to be able to compete any more for a while. I – I'm expecting a baby.'

The groom received this in silence, thinking about it for a full minute before she said, 'So that's why you played safe on the cross country yesterday. I wondered what was the matter. It was a pretty mad thing to do, wasn't it? You don't show at all yet, but you must be quite far along. Nick left Longwarden in January.'

'I'm more or less level with Jane, but luckily it doesn't show yet and this month, thank God, I haven't been sick every morning as I was in March and February.'

Kate nodded. 'I knew something was wrong. You looked ghastly for weeks. I put it down to being upset about Nick going off. Tell me to mind my own business if I'm stepping out of line, but have you heard from him at all?'

'No . . . not a line,' Sarah said bleakly.

'Can I ask you something very personal?' Kate said diffidently. 'I don't want to pry but I can't help being curious. Why have you decided to stay pregnant? I take it no one else knows yet?' she added. 'If they had, they would have tried to stop you coming to Badminton.'

'Allegra knows and by now she'll have told North and Jane. Otherwise you're the first person I've told. As for why I'm going ahead . . . I love Nick. I always shall. But I may never see him again. How could I deliberately get rid of the only thing I have left of him?'

After thinking about that for a while, Kate said, 'I should like to have children but I never shall.'

'Do you mean you can't?' asked Sarah. She had often wondered what lay behind the other girl's reserved and sometimes abrupt manner, but Kate had never talked about her personal background and Sarah had never probed.

'I don't know. I should think I'm technically capable of it. I'm healthy. My insides function as they should. I'm not abnormal in that way.' Kate paused. 'But I don't like men. Marriage is out for me. So I shan't ever have a baby.'

It was Sarah's turn to be silent.

Before she had decided what comment to make on Kate's statement, her groom said, 'I've wanted to tell you for some time. It makes me uneasy not to have things understood. But I'm very happy at Longwarden and I was afraid it would put you off me . . . make you feel threatened. A lot of people feel uncomfortable with people like me, but there's really no need to. We're just the same as everyone else except we would prefer to have our closest relationship with another woman rather than a man. I haven't met the right person for me yet . . . and maybe I never will.'

'Have you always known that you were . . . different?' asked Sarah.

'Not really, no. I suppose, looking back, there were signs. I was never interested in boys. But I wasn't interested in girls, either. I liked horses better than people. I still do. I didn't really get the message about myself until a young vet I knew and liked made a pass at me. It was quite a gentlemanly pass and I saw it coming and didn't back off. I thought it was time I found out what all the fuss was about. I didn't expect the first time to be much good. It turned out rather better than I expected. He was a nice guy who knew how to turn women on – if they could be turned on. The affair went on for several weeks before I finally admitted to myself why I had to pull out. I didn't tell him the real reason. How could I? He would have felt . . . contaminated.' After a slight pause, she added, 'As you'd taken me into your confidence, it seemed a good moment to get something off my chest. You'd better think about it for a few days. It's not something you can decide about in a split second when it's come at you out of the blue.'

'Decide about?' Sarah said perplexedly. 'What is there to decide?'

'Whether to keep me on or look for a replacement.'

'Of course I want to keep you on . . . if you don't mind the hiatus of the next six or seven months. It may be even longer before I'm back to normal.'

'Doesn't matter to me,' said Kate. 'I like the job whether the horses are working or not. I expect you'll be back on form by the time we need to start training for next year's Badminton. Your condition is temporary. Mine isn't. It's permanent. I'm a lesbian.'

Underlying the flat statement was a note of defiance. It sounded to Sarah as if, although Kate had acknowledged her nature, she wasn't at ease with it.

'For all we know Dan may be a shoe fetishist and Rob and Emily may go in for bondage,' said Sarah. 'I couldn't care less what they do in private. That's their business.'

As she spoke, she realised that Kate might conclude from this that she regarded female homosexuality as a form of perversion. Actually she had never closely examined her attitude to women who preferred lovers of their own sex. It was something which had never impinged directly on her before, and she didn't want to think about it now. She didn't want to face any problems but the ones she already had.


Allegra found Jane writing letters in the room she had chosen to be what she called her workroom. It adjoined what was going to be her secretary's office.

Allegra knew that her sister-in-law was concerned about her. Sometimes she felt she ought not to be here, her presence a blight on Jane's happiness. But where else was she to go now her life had been turned upside down? The flat in London was impossible. She hadn't the energy to travel. This house was her only refuge.

'If you're not too busy, there's something I'd like to discuss with you,' she said, bracing herself.

'You make me sound more like a wage-slave than a pregnant housewife,' Jane said smiling. 'Go ahead . . . what's on your mind?'

Grateful for the unwitting cue, Allegra said, 'Somebody else here is pregnant. There's going to be more than one baby born at Longwarden this year.'

For a moment or two Jane looked baffled. 'Do you mean that you –?'

'Oh God – no! Not me. If it were me there'd be no problem. No, it's Sarah who's got herself knocked up.'

Predictably Jane looked appalled. 'That's terrible . . . I can't believe it. Is she sure? Has she seen a doctor?'

'No, but she's missed two periods. There isn't any doubt about it.'

'When did she tell you? How could you let her go to Badminton if you knew she was pregnant?'

'I couldn't stop her, Jane. I've known since the night of Mother's wedding but she made me swear not to let on. My immediate reaction was the usual one . . . a discreet abortion . . . no one any the wiser.'

Her sister-in-law said nothing but her slight grimace showed how she felt about abortions. A natural response, thought Allegra. How else would someone like Jane feel? Safely married, in love with the father of her child, surrounded by comfort and beauty, how could she ever fully understand the panic of having an unwanted foetus in one's womb? No one could who hadn't experienced it.

'But Sarah wouldn't hear of it,' she went on. 'Nick's disappearance hasn't changed the way she feels about him. She's not going to get rid of his baby. If North tries to make her, either she'll disappear herself – or she might do something even worse,' she added seriously.

Jane looked shocked. 'North wouldn't do that, Allegra.'

'He's going to go up like a rocket. That's why I've come to you first. Somehow you've got to stop him losing his temper with her.'

'I'll be the one he castigates,' Jane said soberly. 'It was I who encouraged their friendship. North warned me, more than once, that it could lead to trouble. But I felt Nick could be trusted . . . that he'd never do anything to hurt Sarah. I could have sworn that he loved

159

her. To disappear, leaving her pregnant . . . how could he? That's a terrible thing to do.'

'He wouldn't have known she was pregnant. From what I can make out, it can't have been going on long before he took off. In fact I've a strong suspicion they may have made love only once.'

'But how could he be such an idiot?' Jane exclaimed. 'How could he be so irresponsible?'

Allegra shrugged. 'How could she? It isn't only the dimwits who lose their heads in the heat of the moment, you know. People do it all the time. A lot of legitimate babies are accidents . . . probably half. I'm more surprised at her than at him. With her knowledge of stallions at stud, Sarah must have known what a chance she was taking. But I got knocked up at her age so who am I to talk? In my case it happened because I'd had too much to drink.'

Jane's reaction was sympathetic rather than shocked. 'Poor you . . . how miserable for you.'

Perhaps, from all she's heard about my misspent youth, she assumed I was likely to have had at least one abortion, thought Allegra.

She said, 'Yes, it was pretty unpleasant . . . but better than having an unwanted baby by a man I didn't much like the next time I met him, cold sober. At least Sarah's baby will be a love-child, not the result of ten minutes' drunken lust.'

'I must say it's quite a shock,' said Jane, leaning back in the painted Hepplewhite armchair she had chosen to go with a Regency satinwood writing table. 'Oh dear, what a scandal there'll be when this news gets out. It's the sort of story the tabloids revel in, isn't it?'

'Mm . . . they'll have a field day,' Allegra agreed, with the bitterness of someone who has suffered from the attentions of the popular press. 'What will hurt Sarah most is if they find out there's only one person who could be the father and start dredging up Nick's origins. I'm afraid, with one thing and another, it's going to be a tough year for her, poor kid. So I hope you can reason with North. She can do without a tirade from him when she gets back.'


So far the only difference being pregnant had made to Jane's life was that about four o'clock she would be overcome with tiredness. If she tried to resist it she would feel drowsy for the rest of the day. If she had half an hour's nap she woke up refreshed and alert.

Today, woken by kisses, she had found North lying beside her, his black hair still damp from the shower, smelling of soap and toothpaste.

Now, wearing the Paisley silk dresssing gown she had given him for Christmas, he was eating a cookie and looking out of the window at the drifts of daffodils and narcissi in the long grass. His height, his broad-shouldered frame and his naturally energetic temperament allowed him to indulge a schoolboyish pleasure in what the English called biscuits, and in the home-made cakes which were Mrs Armitage's speciality.

Reluctant to spoil his mood, Jane looked at her husband's strong profile and hoped that his pleasant expression was not going to harden into the wrathful glare which could make him look so intimidating.

She said, 'Darling, I'm afraid something's happened which isn't going to please you, but I hope you won't be too annoyed about it.'

At once breaking off his idle contemplation of the garden, North turned his head to smile at her. His eyes were the vivid blue of the minute flowers of a herb which, when she arrived at Longwarden, had been growing between the flags on the south terrace. Her mother-in-law had told her it was called speedwell.

'What is it?' he asked, obviously expecting to hear something comparatively trivial.

161

Jane drew a deep breath. 'It's Sarah. She needs our help, North. She needs all the loving support we can give her. You see . . . she's going to have a baby.'

Her husband's mouth, which only a short time ago had teased hers with soft nibbling kisses, now tightened into a hard line. But he didn't say 'What did I tell you?' as she had dreaded. He said nothing, controlling his anger with a visible effort until, such was its force, he sprang up and paced the room, his hands clenched into fists and thrust into the pockets of his robe, pulling the dark silk taut over his powerful shoulders.

Jane watched him stride back and forth, regretting that, against his wishes, she had helped to bring about this disastrous turn of events.

At last North came to a halt. 'How far along is she?'

'About sixteen weeks.'

'Then there's no time to waste. She must have it terminated immediately.'

'That was Allegra's advice. But Sarah refuses to consider it.'

'She has no option,' he said brusquely. 'My God, if I could get my hands on that young rat I'd make him sorry he ever came back here.'

Seeing the furious blaze in his eyes, Jane let some moments elapse before she said quietly, 'She's determined to have the baby, North. Nothing any of us can say will alter her decision. Allegra thinks, and I agree, that if we try to coerce her she may crack under the strain.'

'Crack? In what way?'

'She's only twenty. The man she loves has run out on her. She's having to break off what amounts to her career. Sooner or later she's going to be hassled by the press. That's a lot for a young girl to take. She could have a breakdown. She might even get to the point of feeling life wasn't worth living. People do.'

'Not if their name is Lomax,' he said with conviction.

'Her grandfather won the VC. Her father was a steeple-chase jockey. Sarah's already proved her guts. She's not the type to go under when the going gets tough.'

He returned to the window seat. 'Anyway we can avoid all that aggro by doing the sensible thing . . . the only thing in the circumstances.'

'She won't. She's made up her mind. You won't budge her, darling. The only thing you might do is to drive her away from Longwarden.'

'She has nowhere to go. Mother would have her, I suppose, but she couldn't take the horses to Spain and she wouldn't go without them. She *has* to stay here – and if you and Allegra between you have failed to make her see sense, then I'd better talk to her.'

'What makes you think you can influence her? It will only upset her . . . and it won't do any good,' Jane assured him. 'If Allegra was pregnant she'd go ahead and have the baby. Would you try to make her get rid of it?'

'That would be an entirely different situation,' said her husband. 'Allegra is almost thirty and she hasn't been left in the lurch. If Andro hadn't been drowned, I've no doubt that sooner or later they would have married. Also Allegra can afford to bring up a child. It might have been a good thing if Andro had left her pregnant. In Sarah's case it's a disaster – but one which can still be averted.'

'You're not allowing for the fact that some women – *many* women – believe that abortions are wrong except in very special circumstances. I do myself. If I were told that our baby had something terribly wrong with him, then for his sake I'd have to have one. But not for any other reason. Not because it wasn't convenient . . . or to avoid a scandal. Ask yourself *why* you think Sarah should get rid of this baby, North.'

'That's easily answered: a child needs two parents.'

'Ideally, yes. But – '

'And in practice,' he interrupted. 'All these so-called one-parent families we hear about now aren't really families. They're makeshifts. Nine times out of ten they work at someone else's expense. Taxpayers cough up the money which should be provided by the father, or female relations rally round and do the mother's job for her. Nick Dean is a case in point. His mother dumped him on her sister. She should never have had him. It would have saved us all a great deal of trouble.'

'Considering your own peccadilloes, you take a very stern view of other people's mistakes,' said Jane, remembering how when they first met he had admitted that, during his time at Harvard, he had seduced the youngest of Aunt Julia's daughters.

'I never left anyone pregnant,' he answered curtly. 'If she has this byblow of Dean's, it will upset Sarah's whole life. How many men want to take on another man's bastard? Ted Rivington certainly didn't. He had the boy foisted on him and later he knocked him about – or so they say. Unwanted children always have a hard time. If not physically then in other ways. When the time comes for Sarah to marry, she'll be much better off unencumbered by a child from this stupid affair.'

'I hope you won't call it a stupid affair in her hearing. Whatever Nick felt about her, she was – and still is – in love with him. Maybe she always will be.'

North bit off a pithy retort. After a moment he said, 'Calf love. She'll grow out of it. She's not sufficiently mature to have a child, Jane. She still has a lot of growing up to do on her own account. And there's another aspect which she obviously hasn't considered. Since her gold medal at Burghley, Sarah's become the idol of thousands of Pony Club riders. That's a responsibility not to be taken lightly. What sort of example is she setting if she chucks this year's events to have a baby by a man who's disappeared? When people like us behave badly it has far more impact than when the proles do.'

This, Jane had to concede, was a side of it she hadn't considered. When she and her sister-in-law had discussed the unpleasant publicity which inevitably lay ahead of Sarah, they had been thinking only of its effect on her, not about the reactions of her teenage admirers.

Not being able to argue with him on that score, she could only say, 'Yes, I'm afraid you're right – but if you throw *noblesse oblige* at her, she's likely to throw your own past right back at you. From what I've heard, both you and Allegra were regularly in the gossip columns at one time.'

'A long time ago. I doubt if it impinged on Sarah. She was reading *Horse & Hound* not Nigel Dempster and Co,' he said dryly. 'Anyway the fact that we set a poor example is no reason for her to. You said I should ask myself why I believe she should have an abortion. Now give me one good reason why you think she shouldn't.'

Her response was slower than his had been. 'Because the easy way out of a dilemma is hardly ever the right one,' she said, frowning. 'You say if she has the baby it could upset her whole life. An abortion could do that too. It's hard for men to understand women's feelings about these things. I feel a mother already, but can you honestly say that you feel a father?'

To his credit he didn't dismiss the question with a glib answer. He gave it some moments' thought. 'Not really, no,' he agreed. 'But nor do I think you can compare your feelings with Sarah's. You wanted to start a baby. Her pregnancy was an accident. In a world where war and famine kill thousands of children every day, and we don't have nightmares about it, it's sentimental nonsense for a girl in her situation to have scruples about getting rid of a small blob of matter which has barely begun to look human.'

'You've been reading my baby book.' As soon as an

ultrasound scan had given early confirmation that she was pregnant, Jane had bought a book which explained the whole process of gestation. She wanted to know what to expect at every stage of her child's development and now was eagerly awaiting the first butterfly flutters of movement.

'Yes, I've read the first couple of chapters. Why not? It's my seed you've got in there,' said North, with the first loving look since they had begun this discussion.

She stepped forward to put her arms round him. 'Before you tell Sarah what you think, listen to her, will you . . . please? No matter what any of *us* think, it has to be *her* decision. It wouldn't be right to make her do something that she feels very strongly is wrong.'

'I've no intention of browbeating her. I happen to be very fond of her.'

'I know, but you can be pretty forceful and right now she's rather fragile emotionally. Not hearing a word from Nick has been a terrible let-down.'

'Considering the way he's behaved, I should have thought she'd be cured of her crush on him.'

'It was never a schoolgirl crush, North. She cared for Nick very deeply and she's been in hell since he left. Don't forget she's already taken some nasty knocks from life. Even if Sarah doesn't remember her, it's not a comfortable feeling to know that your mother deserted you. I'm sure the loss of her father, whom she adored, must have hurt her very much. The "golden girl" image is really quite superficial. Being able to compete with men in a tough sport doesn't mean she's not vulnerable as a person.'

'Don't worry. I shan't upset her.' His arms tightened round her slender body. 'I wish you didn't have to cope with all these extra problems. You have enough on your plate re-organising the household without having to deal with Allegra's and Sarah's crises. I should have liked this to be a time without any troubles for you.'

She lifted her cheek from his shoulder and smiled up into his eyes. 'I can cope with anything as long as there are no more misunderstandings between us.'

Damaris sat on a sofa covered with claret-covered velvet, looking at a painting of a French country road and listening to the conversations of the other people in the small bar of the restaurant where Joël was a chef.

The two businessmen in the corner were discussing cars. There was also a man with a girl who could have been his daughter if she hadn't been flirting with him. Damaris wondered if he had paid for the dress and the jewellery she was wearing; and if the pleasure of being expensively dressed and dining in places like this was worth the price of being undressed by his middle-aged, manicured hands. The thought sent a shiver through her.

Unlike the girl who was showing a lot of silky young skin, tonight Damaris was wearing a skirt of midnight blue velvet with a matching satin belt and a shirt of cream jacquard silk. None of her few evening clothes was overtly sexy. She wished to look nice, to have style, but not to allure.

Before Maudie Sheringham died she had given Damaris the address of a solicitor, warning her never to lose it and, when she was twenty-one, to be sure and write to him.

The outcome had been a second legacy of small *objets d'art* and adornments given to Maudie during her years as a lady's-maid to the Honourable Harriet Welles-bourne. Having no use for them herself and fearing they might be stolen, Maudie had kept them in a metal deed box at a bank. After Damaris had satisfied the solicitor that she was Maudie's legatee, the box had been sent to a branch of the bank in London where she found that her new possessions included a sprig of holly with purpurin berries in a rock crystal pot made by the Russian court jeweller, Peter Carl Fabergé, and a long rope of carved jade beads, two of which she had had made into earrings.

She was wearing the beads in a loose double loop tonight, with her long hair put up in a coil at the back of her head and speared by two beautiful haircombs of translucent golden horn which had also been part of Maudie's unexpected bequest.


*'Faites marcher deux timbales de foies de volaille – deux.'*
   *'Entendu.'*

Behind the scenes at the restaurant the pace was beginning to quicken.

*'Rôtisseur, une noisette de veau à la hongroise – une.'*
   *'Oui.'*

In the servery the kitchen clerk known as the *aboyeur* – the link-man between the waiters and the chefs de parti, his name meaning the barker – was shouting out the orders, each one being loudly acknowledged by the chef concerned.

*'Pâtissier, une mille-feuilles aux fraises – une.'*
   *'Entendu.'*

Joël was also in the servery, checking the dishes as they came through from the kitchens to make sure each one was perfect before it was taken away to be presented at table by a chef de rang or demi-chef, the traditional names for a waiter and a junior station waiter.

At this restaurant the commis waiters, the most junior of all, still wore short café jackets with white bow ties and long white aprons. The wine waiter, or sommelier, wore a black apron and a chain and cellar key.

Few of the restaurant's patrons, many of them over-weight businessmen dining at their companies' expense, had any real appreciation of the expertise needed by a station waiter to attend to five or six tables seating at least twenty diners, every one of whom might have ordered a different dish. Charles Ritz, son of the legendary hotelier Cesar Ritz, had coined the phrase 'table radar' to describe a waiter's ability to anticipate his patrons' needs without being over-attentive.

Even fewer of the diners understood how the exemplary quality of what they were eating had been achieved. They had been drawn to the restaurant by its reputation but lacked the knowledge to judge whether its reputation was deserved. Most of them would have been more impressed by the spectacle of flaming brandy than by their noisettes being garnished with *châtaignes*, small wild chestnuts with a more subtle flavour than the large cultivated sort.

In general the young ambitious chefs were men of greater discernment than the people they served.

Joël had explained to Allevard why he wanted to entertain Miss Lynn and a friend at the restaurant and the manager had agreed. But the waiter who came to tell Joël that one of his guests had arrived, and was having a glass of sherry while she waited in the bar, was plainly curious about the connection between them.

Joël was equally curious to find out who Damaris had invited to come with her. He expected a man but, for reasons he chose not to examine, would have preferred a girl. Had her weekend at Longwarden had a successful outcome, as his had? That he would find out later.


A thick lock of his straw-fair hair was beginning to slip forward in a cow-lick when Peter came into the bar.

'Am I late?'

'No, I was early.'

As he sat down beside her, Damaris wondered why she had felt no leap of the heart, no secret frisson of desire when he came, smiling, to join her.

'How are your preparations for Peru going?' she asked.

'I'm not taking a lot of personal gear. It's a country where you've only got to take your eyes off your belongings for half a second and they disappear. So I've pared my kit to the barest minimum. It's all in one medium-sized grip with a padlocked zip.'

Soon after the bar waiter had brought Peter a gin and tonic and another sherry for Damaris, the head waiter appeared, bade them both a cordial good evening and offered them each a *carte* in a glossy folder.

'Monsieur Vibrac suggests that when you have decided what you would like to eat, Miss Lynn, you allow him to select the wines to enhance your choice.'

'Who is Monsieur Vibrac, and what is it we're celebrating?' asked Peter, when they were alone again.

On the telephone Damaris had said only that her career had taken a new and exciting direction and she would like him to celebrate this with her.

She explained about her appointment as garden consultant to the Carlyons and tonight's dinner being a return for giving another candidate for a post there a lift to Longwarden and back.

Peter grimaced. 'I should loathe being a chef. Can't think of anything I'd hate more than being stuck in a kitchen all day and half the night. The top chaps get very highly paid, so one hears, but I think it must be a hellish life.'

'No more hellish than being in the City, stuck in front of a computer for twelve hours a day.'

'That wouldn't suit me either . . . or you. We're both outdoor people.'

'You more so than I. You enjoy roughing it. I'm only an outdoor person from nine to five. After that I like my creature comforts. Sleeping under canvas and having cold showers doesn't appeal to me at all.'

'You might like it more than you think. Tell me about this weekend at Longwarden.'

'Yes, I will, but first I think we should make our decisions,' she said, starting to scan the menu.

Their table in the restaurant proved to be one of the best in the room; a comfortable corner banquette giving them both a good view of their fellow diners from a more secluded position than the tables in the centre.

As the table was pushed back in place and their napkins were shaken out and spread on their laps, Damaris wondered if Joël would appear later on. She had once been taken to *Le Gavroche* and had seen the famed Albert Roux moving from table to table, chatting to regular patrons. But perhaps that was only done by the great master chefs.

While she ate her hot oysters and Peter his *coquilles Saint Jacques* she began to tell him about her weekend and how excited she was by the Longwarden project.

'It sounds all right in a fine summer, but have you thought about next winter . . . driving all that way in bad weather?' Peter asked. 'That won't be much fun for you.'

'I'll worry about that when the time comes,' Damaris said cheerfully, sipping the very good Chablis which accompanied their first course.

It was followed by a *mignonette* of lamb with parsley and mushrooms for her, a *noisette* of venison for him, a selection of perfectly cooked vegetables and a bottle of Côtes du Rhône.

'I've never been here before and I gather you haven't either,' said Peter.

Damaris shook her head. As she had during dinner at Annabel's, she sensed his curiosity about the other men in her life. He had told her the majority of girls didn't want to know about someone like himself who was here today and gone tomorrow. To which she had replied that for her, friends who came and went were an advantage as her career didn't allow her to run too intensive a social life.

'If you're going to take on all this extra work at Long-warden, shouldn't you have a holiday this year?' said Peter. 'Why not fly out to Peru and spend a couple of weeks with me as your guide? There are decent hotels in Cuzco and once I've got the camp organised I needn't be there all the time.'

She shook her head. 'I can't possibly spare the time for a jaunt to South America. Anyway, going to Long-warden will be a holiday for me. It's the most heavenly place.' She told him some more about the gardens, what she had seen of the house and also the people she had met at the Carlyons' dinner and lunch parties. 'What I should love to do is go down there for the whole summer but I have too many commitments here,' she ended regretfully.

'What would happen if you were put out of action for some reason? Have you no one to hold the fort if you were laid up with flu or a broken arm or whatever?'

'There is one of my team who could take over in an emergency but I don't think she'd want to do it for long. She has the type of husband who expects his wife to make him her principal interest.'

'D'you disapprove?' Peter asked.

'Not if she doesn't mind . . . which apparently she doesn't. I think people ought to live in whatever way happens to suit them. I should disapprove if she wanted to work full-time for me and her husband was obstructive. No one has the right to restrict someone else, do you think? When I advertised for part-timers, I had a deluge of letters . . . proving that a lot of women want some independence but not the struggle to cope with two jobs at once.'

'I agree with your point about not restricting other people,' said Peter. 'That, basically, is the reason I'm still a bachelor. I like the idea of marriage but not the settling down bit, which is what most women seem to expect after marriage. What I really need is a wife who wouldn't mind waving me goodbye and getting on with her own thing until I reappeared. As I'd also like to have children, and she would be lumbered with full responsibility for them when I was away, that narrows the field even further.'

'It does sound rather a tall order,' said Damaris. 'But I expect you'll find her some day. Anything one really wants, one generally gets, don't you think?'

'I hope so.'

She knew he was watching her and sensed that the look in his eyes might be more intense than she wanted it to be.

She picked up her glass. 'Meanwhile, here's to successful endeavours in Peru and at Longwarden,' she said lightly.

When the restaurant's cheese board was wheeled to their table Peter's eyes gleamed with a different light at the sight of three English, eight French and one Italian cheese, all at the point of perfection.

With the arrival of the pudding trolley Damaris couldn't resist some more of the chocolate *Marquise* Joël had made for Jane Carlyon's lunch party. On her recommendation, this was also Peter's choice.

They were having coffee when she saw Joël coming towards them, looking handsome and very French in a crisply laundered white tunic with a double row of buttons and a long white apron with its strings tied at the front. It was an outfit which emphasised, even more than the clothes in which she had first seen him, that whatever his cooking might do to other people's figures, his own body was lean and muscular. She wondered how he contrived to look immaculate after spending most of the day in a hot kitchen. Perhaps he had changed into a clean uniform before appearing before the restaurant's patrons.

'Good evening.' At first, he ignored her companion,

looking only at her. Instead of shaking her hand, he bowed and kissed it.

As she looked at the dark head bending over her hand, Damaris was aware that by coming to her table and greeting her in this way Joël had made her, if only momentarily, the cynosure of the room. She had never before had her hand kissed and the gesture and the attention made her normal poise slip for a moment. She felt herself starting to blush.

'Good evening. I was hoping to see you.' As he straightened, releasing her hand, she added, 'This is my friend Peter Stow-Bedon. Peter, this is Monsieur Vibrac, our very kind host.'

Peter had already risen. The two men shook hands. Although they were much the same height, the contrast in their colouring was striking. Both epitomised the looks associated with their nationalities. Watching them, Damaris had the feeling that, in spite of their polite exchange of greetings, both were masking the traditional dislike of the Frenchman for the Englishman and vice versa.

It could be that she was mistaken. Peter's manner was pleasant enough as, after saying how do you do, he added, 'I consider myself very lucky to be chosen to share the splendid meal we've just had. I've certainly never had a better one outside France.'

'Thank you. I'm glad you enjoyed it,' Joël said formally. He turned to Damaris. 'You permit that I join you for a moment?'

'Please . . .'

Although the table was laid for two tonight, the banquette was built to seat three and, with the addition of a chair on its outer side, the table could accommodate four.

Damaris was sitting in the centre of the banquette with Peter on her left. Joël slipped into the place on her right.

'This is my last week here. The manager has agreed to release me at short notice. This time next week I shall be the chef at Longwarden,' he told her. 'And you? Shall I see you there?'

'Yes, I found favour as well. I've been telling Peter what a marvellous place Longwarden is. I'm sure we're both going to get a lot of satisfaction from working there.'

'I think so – yes. The quality of life will be better.'

'Particularly the food,' she said, smiling. 'I shall give up eating except on my two days at Longwarden. As Peter says, our dinner tonight has been superb. It was most kind of you to invite us.'

'*De rien* . . . it's a small return for your kindness to me. I am glad if you have enjoyed your evening here.'

A few moments later he left them, his glossy dark hair curling into ducks' tails just above the collar of his tunic, Damaris noticed, as she watched him walking away. She also noticed that, as he passed the table where the elderly man and the young girl were sitting, while the man was having a cigar lit with a match by a waiter, the girl flashed her eyes at the young Frenchman.

Had he seen and returned the signal, Damaris wondered, as he disappeared from view.

'I visualised Monsieur Vibrac as middle-aged and paunchy,' said Peter.

'So did I, before I met him. He looks more like an athlete than a chef, doesn't he?'

'Don't be swept off your feet by all that hand-kissing, will you?' Peter said lightly.

'Monsieur Vibrac is married,' she answered.

'That's no guarantee that he won't make a pass at you,' he said dryly. 'The Frogs are notoriously unfaithful. Sexual fidelity isn't important to them. They have a much more pragmatic attitude to marriage than the English and the Americans.'

'I'm sure that's a myth which you don't really believe,'

she said, smiling. 'Monsieur Vibrac's only interest in me is as a provider of perfect vegetables.'

'I doubt that. If he isn't interested in you as a woman, why was he hostile to me?'

'Was he? I didn't notice any signs of hostility,' she said untruthfully, having sensed a mutual antipathy from the moment they shook hands.

'You were distracted by all the Gallic gallantry, but Englishmen can do all that too, you know.'

Regardless of who might be watching, he captured her hand and lifted it to his lips. Not content with kissing the back of it, he then pressed his mouth to the inside of her wrist.

This time she survived the caress with her composure intact.

'I never doubted it,' she said calmly, withdrawing her hand.

Peter didn't try to retain it but she guessed, from the look in his eyes, that tonight when he took her home it wasn't her cheek he would kiss.

---

# *May*

To Laura's surprise it was Lady Carlyon herself who met the coach when it stopped in the square of a market town not far from the M4 motorway.

'Good morning, Miss Denham. Welcome back to the country,' the Countess said, smiling, as Laura emerged from the coach.

They shook hands. The Countess was casually dressed in an outdoor sweater with trousers. A silk handkerchief was knotted round her slim neck and silver hoop earrings gleamed against the dark fall of her hair. She appeared to be wearing no make-up. Her skin was as clear and satiny as a child's.

She made Laura, who had put on her raincoat and beret before the coach stopped, feel dull and middle-aged.

'My car isn't far.' Lady Carlyon seized one of Laura's two suitcases as the driver unloaded them. 'Is this all your luggage? You haven't brought very much.'

After Laura had thanked and tipped the driver, Lady Carlyon led the way to where she had left her car, a Japanese hatch-back with plenty of room for the cases.

'I expect you're feeling a bit tired after getting your house in London ready for your tenants,' she said, as they set off. 'Or are you a very neat person whose things are always in order? You look as if you might be.'

'I suppose I am,' Laura answered. 'It's not difficult to be tidy when you live alone.'

'Not if you're tidy by nature. Some people seem to be born to chaos. I'm not obsessively neat but I can't stand total muddle,' said the younger woman.

Once outside the town she drove fast but with care. She didn't make Laura feel nervous as Bernard had when he put his foot down. Once, driving at eighty, he had told her that speed was an aphrodisiac which made women feel sexy. He had enjoyed trying to shock her, and usually succeeded.

Closing her mind to those humiliating memories called up by being in a car on a country road for the first time since that long-ago infatuation, Laura made herself concentrate on the spring countryside.

At the same time Lady Carlyon pushed a cassette into a slot on the dashboard. After a brief pause some orchestral music began, relieving them both of the need to make polite conversation; although from time to time the Countess did point out interesting features of the landscape.

177

It was about half an hour later that they came to a junction of by-roads.

'That's our wall,' said the Countess, indicating a high stone wall bordering the lane they were about to enter. 'Longwarden village is on the left and our main gates are to the right about half a mile further on. I expect you're longing for a cup of coffee, aren't you? Did you have any breakfast?'

'Yes, thank you, I had a good breakfast. But a cup of coffee would be nice.'

'You shall have one as soon as we arrive. Your rooms include a little pantry where you can make yourself hot drinks and snacks. Main meals for you and Mr Muirhead, our architect, and Miss Lynn, who's in charge of the gardens, will be served in a room called the Cabinet. My husband and I have breakfast in our own quarters but quite often we'll join you for lunch and sometimes for dinner. You see, we're trying to run Longwarden as a community within which people can also have privacy when they feel like it. We no longer have – or want – the huge staff who used to run the house. So a good deal of stream-lining is necessary, particularly where meals are concerned. To be honest it's all rather experimental at present. We may change these arrangements if we find others which work better.'


The photographs of the rooms set aside for her secretary which the Countess had shown her in London had not prepared Laura for the luxurious elegance of the reality. The bedroom where she was unpacking was four or five times as spacious as the largest bedroom in her own house, and the attention to detail made her feel more like a guest than an employee.

One of her suitcases contained only clothes and these were soon put away in the more than adequate storage space. Laura had brought some clothes hangers but need

178

not have done so as the wardrobe was equipped with twice as many hangers as she could ever use, ranging from polished wooden hangers for coats and suits to prettily padded hangers for delicate blouses.

Clearly the Countess was a perfectionist. Laura felt sure it must be at her instigation that all these ultra-thoughtful touches had been provided. She couldn't believe a housekeeper would go to such lengths off her own bat, not for a fellow employee.

In the second suitcase she had packed a few treasured possessions such as the photographs of her parents. She had also brought the last birthday present her father had given her.

Mrs Denham and Bryan and Joanne had thought it a poor sort of present; a small, old yellow box hand-painted with curling blue ribbons and tiny posies.

Now, holding it on the palm of her hand – it weighed barely an ounce – Laura remembered, with a pang, the private smile she had exchanged with her father. He had known she would love it and she had, although it was not until later, when they were alone, that he had told her its secret.

The box was so light because it was made from dried orange peel. It was a rarity, a collector's piece. Robert Denham had been shown it by the owner of a country antique shop opposite the pub where he had stopped for lunch while trying to sell fire extinguishers to reluctant farmers.

'It's the sort of thing your mother liked,' he had told Laura. 'Actually it cost rather more than the bracelet Joanne had for her birthday. But we'd better keep that to ourselves, chick.'

She put the box on the table beside the bed, next to a small white vase holding a bunch of spring flowers. It struck her suddenly that the box belonged in this room in a way it never had in London. In that house, furnished and decorated in a style chosen by her step-mother, it had always looked out of place.

Perhaps, if my box looks right here, I shall fit in too, she thought hopefully. I don't feel I do at the moment. But perhaps I may . . . given time.


About thirty miles north of Benidorm – arguably the most ugly, overcrowded, noisy resort at the western end of the Mediterranean – the town of Jávea had escaped most of the worst horrors inflicted on once lovely Spanish fishing villages by the package tour industry.

Along the sea front at Jávea there still remained some of the villas built by well-to-do Spaniards long before their country became a mecca for sun-seekers from northern Europe. The most popular bathing place at Jávea was the Arenal, a wide crescent of sand backed by an esplanade and beach bars with, behind them, a large colony of medium-rise holiday apartments. Jávea had resisted the high-rise which had ruined Benidorm.

Tucked out of sight behind the harbour at Jávea, under the towering ochre cliffs of a great promontory, there was also the *playa del pope*, the priest's beach.

Here there was no sand to lie on. The cobbled strand shelved into water too deep for small children. Sometimes there were strong breakers which churned the wet shingle, discouraging poor swimmers from venturing in.

But there were many days when the sea was calm, the colour of a peacock's neck feathers. Early in the morning, before the one beach bar had opened, its deserted terrace offered a perfect setting for a champagne breakfast *à deux*.

On such a morning, a woman who had been swimming not far from the beach came out of the water and turned to look for her companion. The beach was in sunlight but close to the cliffs of the cape the sea was in shadow, making the water there look deep and mysterious. When she could see no sign of him, she felt a stab of anxiety. He had said it was impossible to drown while wearing a snorkel mask, but suppose . . .

At that moment she spotted him and was annoyed with herself for being so quickly alarmed. How beautifully he swam; his brown arms rising and falling in powerful strokes which even when he was not wearing flippers propelled him through the water with a speed and grace she loved to watch.

Moving easily over the pebbles, her feet protected by plastic sandals, the woman who had once been the eighth Countess of Carlyon returned to the terrace where they had left their clothes, a picnic basket and a cool box.

Although there was no one about, it was instinctive with her to put a towel round her shoulders before peeling down the top of her plain black one-piece and putting on the bra of a two-piece. For long a deeply shy woman, recently Pen had come out of her shell, but not to the extent of baring her bosom in public.

Her wet bathing suit was spread out to dry on the wall of the terrace, and she was unpacking the basket, by the time her companion joined her.

'Sorry darling . . . have I kept you waiting?'

'Not at all. Was the water clear?'

'Very clear today.' Towelling his thick dark hair, now rather more grey at the temples than when her son had engaged him as a butler at Longwarden, he began to describe the fish he had seen.

With a disastrous marriage and ten years of widowhood behind her, Pen had been deeply dismayed to find herself, this time last spring, falling in love with him.

It was not until early this year, when they had both come to Spain on holiday and he had been introduced to her at a party as Colonel Piers Ashford, that a closer relationship between them had begun to seem possible.

Now, after two months of marriage, she still couldn't

quite believe that happiness was hers at last. And such happiness! Not only mental rapport but physical harmony. For the first time in her life she was experiencing sexual fulfilment. It made her feel ten years younger and immeasurably more confident.

Unlike many men of his age, Piers had kept the thirty inch waist of his Sandhurst years and was wearing a brief bathing slip bought on their honeymoon journey through France in March. The sun was already quite hot and he didn't bother to change before opening a bottle of champagne and filling two glasses.

'Many happy returns of the day, my love.' His tone and his look made it more than a casual endearment.

Smiling into each other's eyes, they touched glasses and sampled the chilled Freixenet.

'Who would have thought that being fifty-one would be something to celebrate,' Pen said happily.

Piers put his arm round her waist. 'As the Frogs say, *entre deux âges* . . . not young but not old . . . in your prime.'

There being no one about they kissed. His skin was still cool from the sea and his lips cold from the champagne. When he drew back after kissing her, she saw that where, moments before, his body had been inert, now it strained against the brief slip in visible, vigorous evidence of the effect she had on him.

He glanced downwards. 'You see? What more proof do you need? Not only are you in your prime but you rejuvenate me. Damn . . . there's somebody coming. I'd better cover up.' He reached for a towel to wrap round himself.

Fortunately the elderly man who was approaching wasn't someone they knew. With a polite '*Guten morgen*,' he passed by and was soon plunging into the sea, leaving them to picnic undisturbed.

Later, on the way back to their converted farmhouse, they called at the *Correos* in Benissa to collect mail from their post office box. With a birthday card from Pen's niece was a letter which, when she started to read it in the car, made her give a startled exclamation.

As her husband took his eyes off the road to glance at her, he saw that her happy expression had been replaced by a look of deep anxiety.

'Something wrong?' he asked, annoyed at having her birthday blighted in any way.

'Yes, I'm afraid there is. This is from Sarah. She's going to have a baby.'


Later in the day Jane called Pen and they discussed the news from Sarah.

'How did North take it?' Pen asked.

'Angrily at first. He still doesn't approve of her having the baby, but he seems to have accepted the situation. What does Piers think about it?'

'He's furious with Nick. He thought very highly of him until this happened. He can't understand a boy who knows all about the problems of illegitimacy leaving a girl in the same boat as his mother. But I suppose they were both carried away and forgot about taking precautions.'

For most of Pen's adult life the forces which drove people to abandon prudence had been a mystery to her. Passion had been a closed book. Now she understood very well how, in the right man's arms, a woman could forget everything but her longing for the ultimate closeness.


Laura had been at Longwarden for a week when she went to the Cabinet for lunch – the Carlyons were both out that day – and found someone else there before her: a man of about her own age who had taken his place at the table where he was doing *The Times* crossword.

As she entered the room, he rose and came to shake hands.

'I'm James Muirhead. How do you do?'

He was younger and much better looking than she had expected the architect in charge of the fabric to be. His attractiveness made her shy.

'How do you do, Mr Muirhead. I'm Laura Denham . . . Lady Carlyon's new secretary. I only arrived here last week. You know Longwarden well, I imagine.'

'On the contrary,' he answered. 'I'm a newcomer too. It was my firm's senior partner whom Lord Carlyon engaged to look after the repairs to the exterior and the structure. Unfortunately he died recently. I've had to step into his shoes. Where would you like to sit?'

The round table was laid for four people. Laura concluded the others would be Sarah Lomax and Damaris Lynn. She felt sure Mr Muirhead would prefer to have them on either side of him.

'I'll sit here,' she said, moving towards the remaining chair.

He drew it out for her. 'Do you live locally, Miss Denham?'

'Thank you. No, I've come from London.' As he returned to his place, she added diffidently, 'I'm enjoying looking out of the windows and seeing trees instead of houses. I – I feel as if I'm on holiday.'

'I feel the same when I'm down here. To look around one and see nothing unsightly is a rather rare pleasure these days. Longwarden is very soothing.'

The arrival of Miss Lynn made him rise to his feet again and also made it unnecessary for Laura to think of another remark. Talking to men, except in relation to work, was something she was not used to and she was afraid of being a bore.

*

That afternoon, in a tall house in Harley Street, a door opened, momentarily silencing the soft gargling sound of Arabic undertones from the other end of the waiting room.

Glancing up from a copy of *Country Life*, Jane saw a plump girl in black robes coming in with an older woman. They spoke to the three women waiting and after a brief conversation there was a swish of silk draperies as they departed, leaving behind them a blend of expensive scents and some magazines on the floor where the two children with them, a small dark-eyed boy and girl, had been looking at the pictures.

Jane had seen their car waiting outside; a vast limousine with a liveried driver and another Arab in attendance.

There was now no one else waiting to see Mr Crossmichael, the gynaecologist who had confirmed her pregnancy. At that time the mere fact of being pregnant had been all that mattered to her. She had been beginning to worry that starting a baby might not be as easy as she had thought. In the joy of finding that she *was* pregnant, she had gone along with all that had been suggested to her. But now she had other ideas and it was these she wanted to discuss with the consultant.

When the door opened again it was the middle-aged nurse whom Jane remembered from last time. She wore a blue uniform dress with a white cap and cuffs and the consultant called her Sister.

'Good afternoon, Lady Carlyon. Would you come through, please?'

As Jane rose from her chair and replaced *Country Life* on the table, Sister caught sight of the magazines left on the floor. With an exclamation of annoyance, she gathered them up and placed them alongside the others.

After rolling her eyes heavenwards, she said in a confidential tone, 'Money to burn but no idea how to behave! I hope the children weren't annoying you. They

185

let them do as they like, you know.' Her mouth pursed with disapproval. 'No discipline. That's the trouble.'

Jane followed her along the corridor to the spacious consulting room where Mr Crossmichael was waiting to shake her hand.

'How are you, Lady Carlyon? How are things going?'

The consultant was in his late forties; a well-built, well-tailored man who kept himself fit by skiing, sailing and playing golf, so he had told her at their first meeting.

'I'm fine, thank you . . . never felt better,' she said, with a smile, as he ushered her to the chair in front of his desk.

'Good . . . splendid . . . now let me see' – he took a sheet of notes from the expensive blotting pad – 'your baby is due on October the nineteenth.'

'Or thereabouts,' said Jane. 'First babies are often unpunctual, I gather.'

'In the past, yes, but nowadays we have ways of helping things along if they're running late. I think most of my patients feel that nine months is quite long enough without having to hang about even longer. Women are busy people. A lot of them have careers to get back to, or other important commitments. If we've told you your EDD – estimated delivery date – is the nineteenth, I think you can rely on that being the big day. Unless, of course, your baby is one of the impatient ones and decides to arrive a bit early,' he added, with a chuckle.

'I see. Do the majority of your patients have an induced labour?' Jane asked.

'They do indeed – for a number of very good reasons. I take the view that elective induction – that is, an induction which has been decided on beforehand rather than one which is necessary for medical reasons – is the best thing for everyone concerned. Let me explain.'

He pushed back his chair, crossed his legs and also folded his arms, all three movements suggesting that he had plenty of time to discuss every aspect in detail.

'In the first place I think it's best for the mother and baby. It relieves the mother, and' – with another chuckle – 'the father, of the anxiety of wondering if her labour will start in the middle of the night or at some other inconvenient time. You wouldn't want your waters to break at a dinner party, would you? It has happened.'

A white petal fell from the flower arrangement on his desk. Looking faintly put out, the consultant leaned forward to pick it from the flawless green leather surface and drop it into his wastepaper basket.

'It's also much better for the baby not to be overdue,' he continued. 'The placenta from which, as you know, the baby receives oxygen and nourishment doesn't always function as well towards the end of a pregnancy. Like all our organs, the placenta ages. Sometimes an elderly placenta ceases to perform as efficiently as it did in its youth and the baby is then better off outside the uterus.'

He paused, giving her time to ask a question if she wished to. When Jane didn't speak, he went on, 'Thirdly, and this actually I regard as the least important factor, elective induction does allow the staff of a hospital to organise themselves better and to give all their patients the maximum attention and care. It stands to reason, doesn't it, that we are all more on our toes – particularly when problems arise – at, say, three o'clock in the afternoon than three o'clock in the morning after dealing with an unexpected rush of deliveries?'

'I suppose it does,' Jane agreed. 'Although from what I can make out most babies, left to themselves, seem to prefer night arrivals.'

'Ah, now quite often that is because the labour has been allowed to drag on a good deal longer than is wise. In Victorian times, and even more recently, women were often in labour for very long periods, poor things. By the time they gave birth they were exhausted. Not so today. We can not only start labour off, we can also accelerate it. In fact, given the most advanced obstetrical care, a woman can sail through her pregnancy confident that she will be able to have her baby on a given day and with complete pain relief.'

'That sounds marvellous,' said Jane. 'But the thing is that I should like to have my baby with as little medical intervention as possible, and I also want to have it at home . . . at Longwarden.'

The faint flicker of displeasure which had crossed his face before briefly reappeared.

'Is it Lord Carlyon's wish that your child should be born there?' he asked.

'No, it's mine. My husband is prepared to go along with anything I want, and I very much want to give birth in my own bed, surrounded by familiar things and with North on call if I need him.'

'But of course you shall have your husband with you, if that's what you want,' he said instantly. 'I have no objection to fathers being present. We usually suggest that they wait outside for a few minutes during certain procedures but at all other times they're most welcome to help and encourage their wives through the less active stages of labour. You needn't have any worries about your husband being excluded from the proceedings.'

'I haven't. If my husband wanted to be with me, the most dragon-like Chief Nursing Officer wouldn't be able to keep him out,' Jane said cheerfully. 'But in fact at the moment he doesn't particularly want to see his child born. He feels that it's women's work and men – except obstetricians – are out of place.'

'A very sensible view,' said Mr Crossmichael, nodding. 'To be perfectly frank with you, having brought their wives to the hospital, it's much better for husbands to go back to work or whatever until the whole thing is over. This idea of a father assisting at the birth of his baby is a very recent one. Traditionally, in our culture, men have never had anything to do with it except in a professional capacity. I certainly wasn't around when our four children were born and I don't think most men, if they're honest, want to see their wives in labour. Even without the pain women used to have before epidural anaesthesia, giving birth is never elegant.'

'Do you do a lot of epidurals?'

'We give epidurals in all first labours except when the patient's blood pressure is raised. The anaesthetic is very similar to the one your dentist gives you and the beauty of it is that although it deadens all pain – to the extent that even Caesarean sections can be done with an epidural – the patient remains fully conscious and able to watch what is happening.'

'But if she is numb from the waist down, presumably watching is all she can do?' said Jane. 'How can she help if she has no feeling? And doesn't the anaesthetic affect the baby?'

'It sometimes makes the baby a little drowsy but that's nothing to worry about. The mother can still take an active part in the birth because she will see her contractions starting on the monitor screen. She can still do the relaxation and breathing she's learned at her ante-natal classes.'

'To be perfectly frank, Mr Crossmichael,' Jane said, repeating his own phrase, 'I don't at all like the idea of being wired up to a monitor, or being induced, or having an epidural. If something goes wrong during my pregnancy, or if at the end some complication crops up, then of course I'll be willing to go into hospital and have all the technological help that's available. But right now I'm feeling great and I want an old-fashioned birth at home in my bedroom. One thing I particularly don't want is an episiotomy, and from what you've been saying I feel all your patients may have one.'

'They do indeed,' he said blandly. 'Perhaps you've been told something about episiotomies which has alarmed you unnecessarily. It consists of a short neat snick in the perineum – between the vagina and the rectum – to give the baby's head more room and avoid the possibility of tearing. After the birth the cut is sutured – and I make a point of doing that myself, not leaving it to a midwife or medical student – with the result that the patient has a small neat scar instead of a larger more ragged one. Talk to any of my senior colleagues at London's teaching hospitals and they'll all tell you the same thing, as will most American obstetricians.'

'But I read recently that when midwives delivered most babies there were very few episiotomies and not a great deal of tearing, either. The book said that episiotomies had only become standard practice since doctors – predominantly male – took over the management of childbirth.'

'Which book was that?' he asked.

Aware that she wasn't being tactful, but feeling that these were issues which must be tackled forthrightly, Jane told him.

'Ah yes, that writer,' he said, with a smile which was noticeably cooler than the one she had received on arrival. 'Not a qualified obstetrician but widely read and extremely influential. The first thing most young women do, once they know they are pregnant, is to buy a book by an "expert" and make that their bible. That's fine. That's understandable. Intelligent women want to know what's happening to them and a book contains far more information than a gynaecologist can give in half a dozen consultations. The trouble is many of the books – and there are dozens to choose from – give rather too much information, a lot of it more alarming than reassuring.'

'The only thing I've found alarming is the way that having a baby has become a hospital experience rather than a home one,' said Jane. 'You haven't said what you think about my child being born at Longwarden, Mr Crossmichael.'

'I have to admit I'm not happy about it. Even the Princess of – '

'In that case I won't waste any more of your time. I know how busy you must be,' Jane said, rising to her feet.

The consultant, obviously accustomed to more conformable patients, was visibly disconcerted by her decisiveness.

'My dear Lady Carlyon, I didn't mean to suggest that under no circumstances would I deliver you at Longwarden. I am merely advising you against it.'

'Perhaps your advice is wise and I'm foolish not to be guided by it, Mr Crossmichael. However I think in the circumstances it would be better for me to look for a doctor who shares my preference for home confinements.'

He came out from behind the desk. 'If you can find one,' he said dryly. 'Even at GP level, there are not many doctors who will attend a home confinement.'

'There must be midwives who will.'

'I don't think your husband would be very happy about that.'

He came with her to the street door, chatting as affably as if the consultation had gone smoothly. She had the feeling he was reluctant to lose her; or rather to lose Lady Carlyon, the American millionaire's daughter. She had liked him the first time they met but today she found him too suave, more like a merchant banker than a medical man. What it boiled down to was that she didn't trust him to deliver her baby in the manner she wanted rather than the way which suited him best.

She and North were spending the night at Carlyon House and going to the theatre together. At the junction with Wigmore Street she turned in the direction of the park intending to walk a couple of blocks and then cut through St Christopher's Place, an alley of chic little shops. From the other end it was not far to the Davies

Street antique market, in happier times one of Allegra's favourite haunts, where Jane hoped to find one or two pretty baubles to add to her Christmas present drawer. It might, to most people, seem a strange time of year to be thinking of Christmas, but in November and December she would be busy with the baby.

Going over her talk with Mr Crossmichael, she wondered if North *would* disapprove of his child being delivered by a midwife. The consultant's tone had implied that they were far below doctors on the professional scale. Yet surely because they were women, many of whom had had babies themselves, they must understand childbirth in a way a man never could.

Privately she had been astonished when the consultant had told her that he had been absent from his wife's four confinements. She could understand a layman being reluctant to take part, particularly one who knew himself to be squeamish. But how could a man to whom birth was an everyday occurrence not want to be there when his own wife was in labour? What else could he give his mind to, when she was going through one of life's major experiences? Although, by the sound of it, giving birth under his aegis would be more like having an operation than doing something normal and natural.

*Giving birth is never elegant*, he had said. Neither is sex, thought Jane. But perhaps Mr Crossmichael and his wife aren't as comfortable with their bodies as we are. Maybe they don't take showers together or lie around naked as North and I do. Maybe the Crossmichaels only do it in the dark. The fact that they have four children doesn't make them passionate lovers. All those Victorian wives who lay back and thought of England had a succession of pregnancies but never, so we're told, an orgasm. But how does anyone know?

'Everything okay?' asked North, when he arrived at the flat to find her relaxing in the bathtub.

'Yes, fine . . . how was your day?'

She had decided not to tell him what had happened until she had made alternative arrangements.

'Interesting . . . tell you about it as soon as I've organised a drink. Can I bring you something?'

'A diet tonic with ice and lemon, please.'

'I'll be right back.' He swooped over the bath to brush a light kiss on her lips.

Jane liked staying at the flat with him. There was a special feeling about being on their own together in the heart of a great city. As her sister-in-law hadn't been to the flat since her return from Barbados in February – it had been here, while unpacking, that she had found Andro's farewell letter to her – yesterday Jane had asked her secretary to telephone Fortnums and have them deliver various provisions including the lemons for drinks.

North came back with two tall glasses. One he handed to her. The other he put on a shelf.

'Just going to strip off,' he said, before disappearing again.

Jane wondered how much gin or vodka he had sloshed into his glass. Doubly health conscious since her pregnancy started, she sometimes thought that Allegra wasn't the only member of the family who drank more than was good for them. But maybe alcohol was a less harmful crutch than the chemicals doled out by doctors. I guess I'm not very pro the medical profession right now, she thought, sipping her tonic.

When North came back, she said, 'Remind me to call Marie-Simone before we go out. She was out when I tried last night.'

Ever since the discovery that a combination of pills and liquor had made an addict of the woman who, in everything but name was her father's widow, Jane had been keeping in close touch.

North nodded and lowered himself into the towelling-cushioned steamer chair which had started its life on the deck of some long-scrapped liner. He stretched his long legs, reached for his drink and said, 'Would you mind if I was away for three weeks in August?'

She felt a little sinking of the heart at the prospect of three weeks without him, but said cheerfully, 'Not at all if something interesting has come up.'

'I've been offered a place on a balloon trip over the Pyrenees. The object of the exercise is to research mountain airflow.'

'What fun! Of course you must go.'

How dangerous was it? she wondered.

'The guy I had lunch with today is a lecturer in meteorology. He was ballooning in the Himalayas last winter and may do it again next winter. Now that is something I'd give my eye teeth to do,' North said enthusiastically.

'Yes . . . the roof of the world . . . who wouldn't?' Jane agreed. And perhaps, a few months ago, she would have meant it and looked forward to going with him, if not in the actual balloon, at least to the expedition's base camp.

Now her spirit of adventure had been quenched by the primaeval instinct to protect the new life inside her, and as North was in a sense her protector, she would rather have had him close by, both before and after the birth. But she knew the man she had married, although he was taking a far greater interest in his heritage than ever before, wasn't ready to give up the adventurous, footloose life he had led before they met. She must never try to restrain him or make him feel guilty for leaving her. He was giving her a free hand and she must give him the same freedom, even if sometimes it made her anxious for his safety.


Damaris sat by the stream which fed Longwarden's lake,

eating the picnic lunch Joël had prepared specially for her.

Probably, because of this early heat-wave, whoever was lunching at the house today would also eat out of doors, under the white sunbrellas on the south terrace. But although she enjoyed talking to her employers, they were not always present and she preferred her own company to that of the mousy secretary and the horsey cousin, neither of whom ever had much to say for themselves.

For a middle-aged woman Miss Denham was abnormally shy and, except when someone spoke to her, Sarah Lomax ate in silence, leaving the table before the coffee and sometimes before the pudding. For an active, athletic girl she had a remarkably poor appetite, picking at Joël's creations as if they were greasy spoon fare.

Once or twice Damaris had tried to get through to her by asking about her horses. Sarah had answered politely but with none of the enthusiasm with which experts usually talked about their pet subject. Perhaps she had found the questions fatuous, or perhaps she reserved her animation for other horsey people and found Miss Denham and Damaris too boring to bother to simulate interest in them.

She had a girl working for her, Kate Somebody. One would have thought they would have had lunch together. But apparently Kate was a vegan, living on pulses and grains which she cooked for herself. Possibly that was the reason Sarah never seemed hungry. It could be that Kate was trying to convert her to strict vegetarianism, making her feel guilty about eating the eggs, cheese and cream which Joël used in his cuisine.

The Carlyons preferred chicken and fish to red meat and a few things, such as chickens' livers, were banned from their table, Joël had told Damaris. Otherwise he was free to cook what he pleased and so far Lady Carlyon hadn't made any changes to the menus he had suggested to her.

He was obviously enjoying his new post, taking particular delight in the perfection of the vegetables which were not cut or dug until shortly before he needed them. How his wife and mother-in-law were settling in he hadn't mentioned. Nor had Damaris seen them yet.

She had come to the country very early this morning. Yesterday London had been unbearable; the temperature soaring into the upper eighties and the parks full of people making the most of what the pessimists said might be the year's only hot spell.

So today, having nothing to keep her in town for the next forty-eight hours, she had set out before it was light, breakfasting on cold toast, an apple and coffee from a flask in a lay-by on the motorway where she had watched the mist on the fields evaporate as the sun rose above the hedgerows.

Now she was having another packed meal, one rather more elaborate than her makeshift breakfast. Going to the kitchen to see Joël had been the first thing she had done on arriving at Longwarden. He had offered her some more coffee – made from freshly ground beans – and had a cup with her, sitting on a bench in the herb garden.

She had already been told by Lady Carlyon that whenever she had time to spend more than one day at Longwarden there would be a room ready for her. After coffee with Joël, Damaris had gone to the secretary's office to tell her that, if it were convenient, she would like to stay overnight and possibly tomorrow night as well.

'I'll tell Lady Carlyon as soon as I see her, Miss Lynn.' Miss Denham had made a note on her pad.

In her office she didn't seem shy but super-efficient. It was only in social contexts that she lost her confidence, poor woman.

Sitting on the grass in the sun, watching a twig being swirled lazily lakewards, Damaris wondered why she thought of Miss Denham in that way. Doubtlessly she was paid well for a job which would be jumped at by many secretaries whose working conditions and duties were drab and dull by comparison.

It must be because she's unmarried and always will be that I feel sorry for her, she thought. Which is illogical because she is probably a great deal happier than a lot of married women. Why do most people still think, if only subconsciously, that a woman without a man in her life is deprived?

Even I do, and God knows I've seen what a rotten state marriage can be and what sods some men are. Yet in spite of all that I don't want to live and die a spinster like Laura Denham. It suits me now. I prefer it for the time being. But I'd hate to think I'd never have a shared orgasm, never have a child, never find out what love is . . .

Her lunch finished, she rose and wandered towards the lake. By now it was very hot. Even in a short-sleeved shirt and shorts she felt overdressed.

Presently, there being no one about, she took off her shirt and turned up the legs of her knee-length shorts. At this hottest time of day it wouldn't do to stroll about in her bra for too long, but this side of the lake was well-shaded and after ten minutes or so she would take cover.

Though the lake was covered with weed in places where there was no current, in others the water was invitingly clear. She was irresistibly tempted to take a dip.

After a moment's hesitation while her commonsense told her it would take several days' sunshine to raise the temperature of the water even at the lake's edges, she bent to unfasten her sandals and then shed the rest of her clothes.

Being naked in the sun felt wonderful. Leaving her

garments scattered on the long grass, she looked for a place without rushes or plants to impede her way into the water.

At first, where it was shallow, it didn't feel cold to her feet and legs. But as it rose above her knees she knew her commonsense had been right. In spite of the heat-wave it was much too early in the year for lake-swimming. However, having got to this point, she was not going to chicken out without a least a quick plunge to boast of at dinner tonight. Bracing herself, she waded resolutely on until she could throw herself forward.

In a glade in the wood which bordered the lake at its western corner, a man stopped munching a sandwich. The loud splash and the muffled cry had surprised him. As he continued to listen, his sharp ears recognised the noises following the first splash as the sound made by someone swimming with rapid overarm strokes.

He finished the sandwich. Then he took a box of matches from his pocket and set light to the paper in which his food had been wrapped. He watched the small flame of the match flare into a larger flame, turning the paper first brown and then black, consuming it.

When nothing was left but ash, he got to his feet and disappeared into the wood.

Damaris was goose-fleshed when she came out of the water, but once back on land she began to feel marvel-lously invigorated.

Drying herself with her cotton shirt which itself would soon dry when draped on a nearby bush, she then put on her spotted micro-briefs but not the light matching bra. Luckily her hair was up today, plaited and pinned in a coil at the back of her head. Although it was wet and dripping gently down her neck, it wasn't impossibly uncomfortable. As soon as she lay down the drips would fall into the grass.

With her shorts spread under her bare back, she stretched out luxuriously. She felt good . . . very good . . . her whole body toned and energised by the shock of the icy-feeling water, a vigorous swim and now the deep relaxation of lying in the sun with no sound to disturb her peace but the muffled call of a cuckoo deep in the woods.

The air was so fresh here compared with London. No dust, no fumes, only the scent of warm meadow-grass, leaf-mould and wild flowers; what a perfumer would call 'green notes'.

On a fine day this place is paradise, she thought. How pleased Maudie would be to know that I'm here, a part of it, someone they treat with respect. Wherever you are, Maudie darling, I hope you know that I've made it. I've achieved all and more than your hopes for me.

Not that she really believed, as Maudie had wanted her to, that there was a life after death, and a virtuous life here on earth would be rewarded in heaven. Yet, in spite of her lack of belief, sometimes it pleased Damaris to think of Maudie happily working in a great garden in the sky, and to talk to her as if her spirit were still in existence somewhere.

She was thinking about the old lady when there was a whirring of wings and she lifted her head in time to see two largish birds flying away from the wood, as if something there had alarmed them.

I should know more about birds, she thought lazily, letting her head fall. The two which were crossing the lake were not among the species she recognised.

The sun was hot on her eyelids and on the tips of her breasts. Soon she would have to move or her unprotected skin would burn. Tomorrow, if the heat-wave held, she would bring a towel and some sun-cream.

The next disturbance was some small creature alighting on her waist. It tickled. Without looking she brushed it away, leaving her hand on her body, aware that the afternoon heat was beginning to generate another kind of heat inside her.

Her fingertips stroked her warm skin, feeling its chamois-soft texture and the outlines of her ribs. Slowly her hand moved higher, covering her breast, her thumb lightly brushing the nipple, bringing it into full bud, making her quiver and sigh with anticipatory pleasure.

A few moments later, her mind less alert than her senses, she heard the soft swishing behind her without immediately registering that it was the sound of someone walking through long grass.

'You're not supposed to do that, you know.'

Startling Damaris out of her trance of sensuous enjoyment, the man's voice shattered the peace of the hot afternoon as effectively as an aircraft breaking the sound barrier.

Her eyes flew open. Half-dazzled by the bright sunlight, she saw first his blue-jeaned legs.

Even now, so many years later, the sight of grubby blue jeans could still make her shudder inwardly. That this pair of jeans was clean did not, in the first instant, strike her. She saw Levis and muscular thighs with a bulge where they met and the old buried fear of male strength and male brutality came flooding back.

As she scrambled up, grabbing her shorts and clutching them against her, the man said, 'They say you should never sunbathe at this time of day. Before ten and after three, that's when they advise you to do it.'

She glared at him, ready to run, ready to scream her lungs out.

'Who are you? What are you doing here?'

'I work here. This is my lunch break.' He seemed to realise she was more than merely startled. He backed off, no longer grinning. 'There's no need to be scared. Nobody's going to prosecute you for having a swim. I don't say they encourage trespassers, but in your case his Lordship would most likely be more impressed by your guts than annoyed with you for sneaking in here.'

'I'm not a trespasser,' she retorted. 'Lord Carlyon knows that I'm here. I haven't seen you before,' she added suspiciously.

He wasn't one of those people you met and forgot minutes later. He was too solidly built, too firm of feature, to leave an ephemeral impression on anyone who had encountered him.

'You haven't,' he agreed. 'I work in the carpentry shop.'

Her panic had died down, but she still wasn't comfortable with him. 'If you don't mind I'd like to dress.'

He nodded. 'I'll be on my way. Sorry if I gave you a fright. It wasn't intended. I heard someone swimming and came to see who it was.'

He turned on his heel and she had a view of broad shoulders and a hard sexy backside before he went into the wood.


Allegra lay on her bed, listening to one of the tapes Andro had sent her while he was in America and she in London. Tears trickled from her closed eyes as his deep, slightly accented voice told her what he had been doing since recording the previous tape a few days earlier.

'*That's all for now, my darling. You know, don't you, that I miss you every day and every night? I can't help wishing we lived in an earlier time when women didn't have careers and you would have been content to travel with me and spend your time shopping and so on. Yes, I know that's selfish of me. You also have a gift which mustn't be wasted. Goodbye now. Take care of yourself, bellissima. It won't be long before we're together again.*'

As the recording ended, Allegra turned on her side

201

and buried her face in the pillow, racked by deep shuddering sobs.

It tortured her to listen to the tapes yet she couldn't resist playing them again and again.


Drying her shampooed hair before dinner, Damaris cringed at the thought that, if he had wished, instead of approaching and speaking, the carpenter could have stood by and watched her pleasure herself.

As it was he had seen enough to cause her acute embarrassment should they ever meet again. Now that she had her wits about her, she knew that his opening remark, *You ought not to do that, you know*, hadn't been a reference to sun-bathing. He had seen her stroking herself. Probably, if she *had* been a trespasser, he would have continued to mock her. He might even have offered to finish what he had interrupted.


'What would please me,' said Joël to Damaris, 'is if we could grow the small purple winter artichoke. Have you ever tried them? No?'

He touched the tips of finger and thumb to his lips and blew a kiss into the air.

'They're perfection! In the south of France they're in season in winter and spring. Sometimes we had a consignment flown to the restaurant. They're so tender that when they're cooked you can eat them whole, not only the base of the leaf as you do with an English artichoke. Or you can shred the raw hearts and put them in a salad. Could they be grown in a greenhouse, do you think?'

'I don't know, but I can find out. Is there anything else you long for?'

They were walking round the vegetable plots which, when she had recruited more helpers, she was going to expand. In times past, indeed right up to the outbreak of World War Two in 1939, Longwarden's kitchen garden had filled every foot of soil within the high serpentine walls which still sheltered it.

However the abundance of produce needed to feed a large staff had long since been reduced in proportion to the steady reduction of the household.

'What else do I long for?' said Joël. He stopped beside the old well and sat down on its weathered cover. 'That is, as they say, a good question. Unfortunately what I want most I cannot have . . . ever.' As she sat down beside him, he went on, 'I wanted to have my own restaurant . . . my own small hotel in the country. But now that my wife is disabled that dream has become an impossibility. I can never become a *patron*.'

It was the first time he had spoken of the difficulties of his private life. She wasn't sure that she wanted to become his confidante. She liked Joël and found him interesting on his subject. But she thought it was a mistake for people who worked together or for the same employer to become involved in each others' private lives. It was better to stick to impersonal topics.

At the same time she felt sorry for him and didn't want to seem unsympathetic. It couldn't help his situation to be in a foreign country, far away from his family. She had the impression that the French were more family-minded than the English, giving and receiving support from their relations in times of trouble.

'How is your wife liking the move to the country?' she asked.

'I hope she will be happier here. My mother-in-law is the problem. We couldn't manage without her but at the same time she makes matters worse by discouraging Lucy from doing many things she could do. It's possible Lucy could help in the stables in small ways. There must be pieces of equipment she could clean and polish.

I don't know much about horses but she does. That was how she was injured . . . in a riding accident.'

'Yes, you told me. Why not speak to Miss Lomax about it? Does your wife life flowers? Would she be interested in doing a few odd jobs for me? How mobile is she?'

'She could be much more mobile but getting about in a wheelchair is like any other exercise: you have to do it regularly to build up the necessary muscles. Lucy is out of condition because of having everything done for her by her mother. Even when they went to the park, my mother-in-law would push her instead of letting her wheel herself and develop her shoulder and arm muscles. I find it very difficult to reason with my mother-in-law. She is a most obstinate woman.'

He went on about her at some length and Damaris, reluctantly listening to resentments which obviously he had been bottling up for a long time, thought it sounded a most unhappy ménage.

When the outpouring came to an end and he sat with his shoulders hunched and a look of deep depression on his handsome face, she said kindly, 'Things will improve now that you're somewhere with more scope for Lucy to do things, Joël. With ramps at strategic points, there's no reason why she shouldn't have the run of the grounds. I'm sure Lady Carlyon wouldn't mind. I know she's making arrangements for housebound people in the village to be brought here for tea on fine afternoons in the summer. She certainly wouldn't object to your wife enjoying the garden.'

Before he could reply, she added, 'I must go. I have to change. See you tomorrow.'

Having made her escape, she felt a little guilty about the excuse to leave him. She didn't really need to hurry away and indeed had no intention of going up to change yet.

Examining her reasons for the somewhat abrupt getaway, she found two; a general reluctance to be involved in other people's troubles and a particular unease about letting Joël cry on her shoulder.

'Watch out for that amorous Frog,' Peter had warned her, not entirely in fun, before he left for Peru.

She didn't think there was anything remotely amorous in Joël's present attitude to her. But if one of his troubles was that he was going short of sex, and if she allowed him to make a habit of telling her his other troubles, she could find herself having to cope with *all* his problems.

Even if it never got to that stage, merely to be seen chatting to him too often could be a mistake. Although they were both paid for their services, they were on a different footing; he a member of the staff, she a visiting consultant. It might be that among the Carlyon's social circle she would meet the man she would one day marry, the man who could give her the life she wanted, the garden she wanted. For that reason it was important to keep a delicate balance in her relationships with the staff at Longwarden, the same balance kept by the Countess herself who was unfailingly polite, kind and interested but with whom they would never be familiar, never intimate.

Presently, strolling along the broad grass walk between the massive yew hedges which must be among the most ancient features of the garden but whose dark bulk she did not admire, Damaris turned and walked backwards for a few paces, the better to study the long view behind her.

When two powerful hands suddenly clamped on her upper arms and a voice said, 'I hope you don't back your car facing forward,' she almost jumped out of her skin.

With a gasp she pulled free and whirled round.

'Oh . . . what a start you gave me!' she exclaimed crossly, irritability added to shock on seeing who – not for the first time – had caught her unawares.

He must have come through the archway leading to the lake path. Why hadn't he spoken instead of deliberately giving her a fright?

'I seem to be making a habit of it, don't I?' he said unrepentantly. 'I know who you are this time. Miss Damaris Lynn . . . the gardening expert. My name's Sam Warstock. Pleased to meet you.' He offered one of the hands whose strength she had already felt.

Damaris, far from pleased to meet him again, was tempted to ignore his hand and bid him a frigid good evening. Then, feeling that a snub would have only one effect, to make him even more objectionable, she put out her hand and said stiffly, 'How do you do.'

The hand which closed over hers had a warm, dry grip which, had they met in different circumstances, she would have noted with approval. She couldn't stand feeble handshakes from men or women.

As things were, the physical contact served only to increase her embarrassment at the memory of their first encounter.

'Talking about habits,' he said, still holding her hand, 'if you're going to make a regular thing of swimming in the lake this summer, you could do with a couple of planks to dive from. It's easier diving into cold water than walking in. If his Lordship has no objection, I'll get it fixed up for you.'

He had a slight regional accent she couldn't place. It wasn't local.

Withdrawing her hand, she said, 'That won't be necessary. The lake is far too cold and the pool in the Orangery will be finished quite soon.'

'Oh, you'll be using that, will you? I didn't know you were a friend of the family.'

'I'm not . . . but we have mutual friends.' It could be true. Peter's mother and Lord Carlyon's mother could have been at school together or come out together.

He said, 'I'm not too keen on swimming pools myself.

I don't like the chemicals they put in them. They make my eyes smart. I prefer a lake, or the sea.'

Damaris didn't like the way he was looking at her. He wouldn't have that glint in his eyes if he were talking to Sarah Lomax.

Changing her mind about snubbing him, she said, 'You only get very strong chlorine in public pools. It isn't necessary in private pools used by people who bath regularly and who don't let their children pee in them.'

The moment she had said it, she regretted it. But it had the effect she'd intended. His mocking expression gave place to a look of annoyance.

'Oh, you're one of those, are you?' he said. 'One of the "them and us" brigade. Well, as you've already deduced, I'm what you would call an oik. I daresay my neck and my arse are as clean as yours, but that doesn't make any difference. I'm still one of the great unwashed . . . the proles . . . the plebs.' He took a pace towards her. 'Shall I tell you what I think you are? A stuck up, po-faced bitch. Now if you want to complain to his Lordship that I've insulted you, go ahead. Feel free. Because although I'm an oik, I'm also too much of a gentleman to say anything derogatory about you.' He gave her a contemptuous grin. 'You wouldn't expect a carpenter to know a long word like that, would you? Anyone who works with his hands has to be thick, in your book.'

At first dumbfounded by the ire she had unleashed, Damaris rallied. 'That isn't true,' she said hotly. 'I work with my hands.'

To her astonishment he grabbed one of her wrists and inspected her nails and palm. 'Doesn't look like a working gardener's hand to me.' He released his hold. 'I hope you know how to handle the people who have to work for you. Maybe wherever you've come from, jobs are short. Not so around here. It's the serfs who are scarce in these parts. Take a haughty tone with the local people and you could find yourself with some soil under those nice clean nails.'

He brushed past her and strode down the yew walk, leaving her glowering at his back and nursing the wrist which had felt the hard pressure of his fingers.

Creaming her hands, as she did every night, Damaris had a vivid memory of Sam Warstock holding her wrist in a grip of which by tomorrow she might have a visible reminder.

This afternoon in the yew walk was the first time a man had touched her roughly since that other afternoon when Kevin's brutal handling had left her with bruises everywhere.

For a few minutes after the carpenter had walked away from her she had felt an upsurge of the blind and bitter hatred she had once felt towards all men. Twice he had reminded her of the worst day of her life. First by the lake where her first glimpse of him had been of blue-denimed legs and a partial erection restrained by the tightness of his jeans; and again today when, for a few seconds, he had used his superior strength on her.

That she had provoked his anger she couldn't deny. Yet she ought to have known by the look of the man that he wasn't the sort to let anyone insult him and get away with it. It was a wonder he hadn't lashed back even more forcefully. He could, if he'd wanted, have been very scathing about what he'd seen by the lake.

Massaging the lanolin-rich cream into her fingers as if she were easing on a new pair of gloves, Damaris wondered how many hours she had spent on the nightly ritual which was only part of the care which so far had kept her hands from bearing the marks of her occupation. It wasn't easy for a gardener to have soft hands and unbroken nails but it was possible. Sam Warstock was not the first person to remark on the condition of her hands. Several women gardeners had asked how she managed it when their own hands were permanently marked. The answer, as she had explained, was always to wear gloves or a barrier cream, and twice a week to sleep in gloves over an extra thick buttering of Lancôme's *Nutrix Mains*.

Tonight she had applied only enough to be completely absorbed after five minutes' massage. As she climbed into bed, she wondered how the carpenter would react if he knew that it wasn't only her hands which had misled him. Little did he guess that for more than half her life *she* had belonged to the great unwashed.

Where had he picked up that expression? Read it perhaps. Clearly he had more intelligence than she had given him credit for. She had categorised him as working class beefcake, not strictly handsome above the neck but very well-built below it.

It was stupid of me to antagonise him. I may need him to make something for me, she thought, as she climbed into the silk-draped *bâteau lit* which was only one of the fine antiques in the room she had been given on this visit.

She found herself wondering if the carpenter lived at Longwarden or came to work daily from the village. He might be a married man. The way he had looked at her didn't prove he was single. He looked about thirty, old enough to be the father of several children if he had married young.

Why am I thinking about him? she asked herself, realising that he had been in her mind ever since she came up to bed.

Not ready to sleep, she read an article about the cabbage root fly in the current issue of *The Garden* and another about tender perennials. Then she put out the light and lay down.

For a few minutes she thought about her brief from

Lady Carlyon and the number of helpers she would need to recruit.

'*It's the serfs who are scarce around here.*' Sam Warstock's caustic tone echoed in her mind. An intrusive memory of his scornful face pushed aside the calm thoughts she wanted to think before sleeping.


The idea that it might be possible for her to adopt Sarah's baby came to Allegra in the small hours of the morning.

She was not sleeping well but refused to take pills, having seen too many people hooked on them and preferring to poison her system with traditional rather than modern chemicals.

Before Sarah's announcement that she was pregnant, Allegra knew she had been drinking too much. Now she had it under control and had stopped drinking in her room. When she couldn't sleep, she drank maté, a South American tea sent to her by Elliott Lincoln, her American publisher who, during one of his frequent transatlantic telephone calls, had told her it was the stimulant recommended by Dorothea Brande.

Allegra had never heard of her, whereupon Elliott had said mysteriously that rather than explain who she was and perhaps put Allegra off her, he would send her a copy of Dorothea Brande's book which, in his opinion, was required reading for all writers.

The book, *Becoming a Writer*, and the maté, had come – like all Elliott's offerings – by an express courier service. The book was a first edition, published in 1934, explaining methods of harnessing the unconscious mind. So far they hadn't worked for Allegra but she liked the maté and brewed it at times when she didn't feel justified in having a glass of wine or a gin and tonic. Such as now, at three in the morning with the rest of the household asleep and four hours to go to daylight.

Theoretically, of course, a stimulant was the worst possible thing to take for insomnia, but in practice she found that after reading and sipping maté for an hour or so she would become drowsy and sleep for the rest of the night.

Perhaps it was the maté which had stimulated her brain into seeing that if she couldn't have the child she wanted – Andro's child – the next best thing might be to take over Sarah's baby and bring it up as her own. Had she thought of it sooner – and had her cousin been agreeable – it should have been possible to organise matters in such a way that no one need ever have known it wasn't Allegra's child. But that would have involved both of them disappearing for five or six months and Sarah would never agree to being parted from the horses for so long.

Jane's mail was steadily increasing. Nearly all the letters were direct or indirect appeals for money.

She had known this would happen as soon as it became known that she was a very rich woman. Begging letters, of one sort or another, were among the penalties of wealth and her father had been similarly inundated. As he had, she left it to her secretary to sort the mail into two baskets; one containing the appeals which would be answered with a courteous but firm refusal and the other for the letters which Jane might wish to reply to personally.

Today there were only two letters in the second basket; an invitation from a duchess to sit on her charity committee and a request for an interview from an American freelance journalist.

After dictating replies, Jane said, 'Some time today would you ring up Mrs Monro and ask them to send me a sample of chintz called *Polyanthus* which is in this month's *World of Interiors*, please, Laura? You don't mind if I use your first name, do you?'

'Not in the least,' said Laura, rather pleased at this advance in their relationship.

'Laura is such a pretty name,' said the Countess. 'It's on my list of possible names for the baby. Laura and Lomax sound good together. On the other hand some of my husband's ancestresses had names that I like very much. One of the eighteenth century daughters was called Celestria. However, there's a long time to go before that decision has to be made.'

It seemed to Laura that her employer's expression clouded and she spent a few moments doodling on her note-pad before saying, 'I'm going to tell you something in confidence, Laura. It can't be kept quiet for much longer but at present only the family knows that Sarah is having a baby about the same time as I am.'

Laura was startled and yet, in a way, not surprised. She had felt there was something strange in Sarah's demeanour, a look which didn't belong in the eyes of a girl of her age.

'You're going to hear garbled versions sooner or later, so you may as well hear the truth of the matter from me,' Lady Carlyon continued. 'The father of Sarah's baby is a young man she has known since childhood. In his teens he worked as a groom here. When he was eighteen he left and joined the Spanish Foreign Legion. He came back last autumn and was here until early this year. Sarah fell in love with him. I believe it was mutual. But Nick obviously realised he wasn't a suitable husband for her – no money, no prospects, not the right social background – so one night he left, perhaps to rejoin the Foreign Legion. He doesn't know that she's pregnant and she doesn't know where he is. It's a very unhappy situation.'

'A tragic situation,' Laura said quietly. 'I've felt for

212

some time that Miss Lomax was unhappy. This explains it.'

'It's also a situation which is going to get worse when the popular press find out . . . as eventually they must,' said the Countess. 'The time will come when we'll be besieged by reporters and photographers from the tabloids. We had a taste of that treatment when my mother-in-law married Colonel Piers Ashford who was butler here before Flitton. Several newspapers tried to muscle in on their wedding but we managed to frustrate them. When Sarah becomes visibly pregnant, they'll use every trick in the book to get photographs of her. It's the sort of scandal they love: an earl's cousin left in the lurch by a gamekeeper's foster-son. You can imagine what they'll make of that.'

Laura nodded. She remembered one or two sensational stories read out to her by Mrs Denham. It wasn't only the semi-literate members of the population who revelled in lubricious revelations. People like her step-mother also enjoyed steamy exposés. She could imagine the relish, disguised as shocked disapproval, with which Mrs Denham would have pored over the details of this brewing scandal.

'If Lord Carlyon's mother is living abroad, wouldn't it be possible for Miss Lomax to go and stay with her until the baby is born?' she suggested.

'That thought had occurred to me, too, but it wouldn't work out. Even if Sarah could be persuaded to leave the horses, Colonel and Mrs Ashford are newly-weds who wouldn't really want to have a third person around all the time – although they would never admit that if the suggestion were put to them. But in any case they're coming back here from the end of next month until midway through September. Apart from those factors, the crux of the matter is that Sarah isn't planning to have her baby adopted. She wants to keep it. So to disappear for some months wouldn't really help at all.'

'I see,' said Laura. 'At least she has more privacy here than in an ordinary house where she wouldn't be able to step outside the door without having a long-range lens focused on her.'

'Yes, she has some degree of protection here. But if you remember, the press managed to photograph the Princess of Wales in a bikini during her first pregnancy, and in the grounds of Highgrove giving Prince Charles a hug, so no one is really safe from their intrusions. Anyway, now you know what lies ahead of us. By the way, there's no need to be formal in private. You're welcome to use my first name. I'm going to the Orangery now to see how the pool is progressing. I'll see you later.'

At lunch that day, the Earl said, 'It seems we have an arsonist in the village or somewhere in this area. I was chatting to Police Sergeant Lacock this morning. He told me the fire which burnt down the old wooden shack on the road to Longwarden St Michael a couple of days ago was no accident. It was started deliberately.'

'Definitely not with a view to claiming insurance on it,' Jane said dryly. 'The last time I drove that way I remember thinking that shack looked on the point of collapse. Why would anyone set fire to it?'

'Presumably for kicks,' said her husband.

They were eating fruit salad. Laura passed the cream jug to Sarah who handed it on without taking any.

She looked rather pale, Laura thought, with a curiously rigid expression. Perhaps she was feeling queasy as some people did in the early months of pregnancy.

It was her cousin's mention of Sergeant Lacock which had made Sarah's face stiffen.

She knew it had been the police sergeant who had broken the news to Mrs Osgood, formerly a cleaner at

214

Longwarden, that her son Tark had been found dead, apparently killed by a patch of black ice which had sent his motorbike into a fatal skid on the same night Nick had disappeared.

Even an indirect reminder of that night was painful to Sarah. It brought back the horror of Tark's brutal attack on her, the bliss of falling asleep in Nick's arms, the anguish of reading his farewell note the next morning and – as if she had not already been through enough – the terror of suspecting that he might have had something to do with Tark's death.

Fear, joy, despair and dread; in the space of less than twelve hours she had known such extremes of feeling that even now, many months later, she still felt emotionally wrung out.

'Sarah . . . wait a minute.'

Catching up with the younger girl as she walked back to the stables, Jane said, 'I think I may have found the ideal person to deliver the babies.'

She had already told Sarah about her talk with Mr Crossmichael.

'Who is it?' Sarah asked.

'Mrs Seaton . . . a middle-aged midwife who trained before modern technology took over, so she knows all the lost arts like how to "guard" the perineum to prevent it tearing. She was working with a group of community midwives in another part of the country but her husband has been moved to Melchester and they've bought a house six miles from here. She's been thinking of retiring, mainly because hospital births are the norm in this county. But maybe the three of us can change that state of affairs. Mrs Seaton is coming to tea with me this afternoon. Would you like to join us?'

'Why don't you talk to her first and bring me in later. You may not like her when you meet her.'

'I liked the sound of her on the telephone.'

'How did you find her?'

'I rang various organisations which help women to have the kind of births they want, and the secretary of one of them knew about Mrs Seaton moving here and gave me her number. I'm told that she's one of the most experienced midwives in the country and all the mothers of babies she's delivered are her friends for life.'

When Mrs Seaton was shown into her sitting room, Jane was instantly reminded of the Duchess of Devonshire's description of a Chatsworth librarian as one of those lucky people whose face was arranged in a smile even in repose.

'I thought as I came up the drive what a wonderful place this must be for children to grow up,' said the midwife, after shaking hands.

Neither overawed nor unctuous, she exuded cheerful commonsense, and within minutes of meeting her Jane was convinced that here was the ideal person to assist at her own and Sarah's confinement.

Presently, when they had had tea and talked about Jane's pregnancy and her birth plan, she explained about Sarah's baby and used the house telephone to ask the younger girl to join them.

Later they both saw Mrs Seaton to her car and watched her drive away.

'I like her,' said Sarah. 'She looks as if nothing would ruffle her.'

'She's had three babies herself – one in hospital and two at home,' said Jane. 'They were all straightforward births but she said the second and third were much more enjoyable than the first one. I'm sure we're in good hands with her.'

\*

In the third week of May, Jane and Damaris went to the Chelsea Flower Show together.

After looking at the extraordinary corkscrew-stemmed bay trees in the gold medal Fabergé garden, and the *Sunday Times* literary garden based on Jane Eyre's description of the garden at Lowood orphanage, they were walking round Christie's eighteenth century garden when Jane felt a movement inside her; the first fluttering sign that she was sharing her body with someone else.

She stopped short, her hands automatically going to her belly. But the movement wasn't repeated and everyone else, including Damaris, was too preoccupied to notice the smile which lit up her face.


Having told her family and Kate she was pregnant, Sarah knew her next duty was to tell Sammy, the old Irish groom who had been her closest companion for much of her life.

In his youth a jockey's valet, Sammy had come to Longwarden when Sarah's father was making a name for himself as an amateur jump jockey. After Ranulf Lomax had been killed, Sammy had stayed on to help groom her uncle's hunters and to see that the five year old orphan grew up a competent horsewoman.

Until she fell in love with Nick Dean, Sammy had been the person she had loved best in the world. Now, having found an affectionate companion to share his old age, he had retired and left Longwarden. But the bond between him and Sarah was still a close one. They talked on the telephone every week, discussing not only horse trials and the condition of her horses but also the racing results.

She went to see him on a Sunday, arriving at Eileen Slane's bungalow half an hour before lunch.

'You look tired, my dear,' said Mrs Slane, when Sarah stepped into the widow's mauve-carpeted hall with its plastic flowers and Boots prints of *Flatford Mill* and *The Hay Wain*. 'I expect it's a reaction to the strain of competing at Badminton.'

'Probably. How are you, Mrs Slane?'

'Very well, thank you. Sammy was a bit poorly during the week but he's feeling better today and looking forward to seeing you. He's in the garden.'

'What was the matter with him?' asked Sarah.

'I don't know. He felt under the weather. I'd like him to go to the doctor for another check-up but you know how stubborn he is. Perhaps you can persuade him.'

'Not if you can't,' said Sarah. 'Are you seriously worried about him?'

'No, no . . . I wouldn't say that. We all have our up and down days . . . especially at our age. It may have been Nature's way of making him take it easy. He'd been working too hard in the garden. He overdoes it, you know . . . but that's the way men are. Fetch him in for a drink before lunch while I put the vegetables on.'

Following her into the kitchen, Sarah could smell roasting meat but she no longer reacted to cooking smells with nausea.

Going outside by the glazed back door, she found Sammy behind the beech hedge planted by Eileen's husband to screen the small vegetable plot.

'Hello, Sammy. How are you?'

He straightened his back, his high colour deepened by bending. As long as she could remember his skin had been netted with veins caused by being out in all weathers and a liking for whiskey.

He seemed surprised to see her. 'I didn't hear the car. Are you early or am I behind?'

'It's twenty to one. Eileen says lunch won't be long.'

'I'll have to finish here later.' He massaged the small of his back. 'Did I tell you she bought me one of those video recorders so I could make a tape of you riding at Badminton? I've run it through several times already.

218

After lunch we'll watch it together. You weren't going as well as you did at Burghley, you know. I'm not saying you didn't do well, but you could have done better. I should have been there to advise you. This girl you've got now may be useful, up to a point, but she's not the help to you that I was.'

'Nobody could be that, Sammy, but Kate's not to blame. It was my fault I didn't do better. I was off form, that's all.'

He looked searchingly at her. 'You've a peaky look about you. Are you still moping for that spalpeen?'

She had never told him she loved Nick but Sammy must have guessed it. Last October, not long after Nick's return from the Spanish Foreign Legion, Sammy had collapsed and been whipped into hospital for the removal of gallstones. That was why Nick had stayed at Longwarden for longer than he had intended.

Ignoring the question, she said, 'There's always a feeling of tiredness and anticlimax after a major event – especially if one didn't do as well as one hoped. You've been below par yourself, I hear.'

'Not at all . . . Eileen fusses too much. I'm as right as ninepence, so I am.' Dismissing the subject of his health, he began to talk about the runners in the previous day's handicap chase at Sedgefield.

Eileen was an excellent cook of the kind of food Sammy liked – well-done roast beef, crisply browned Yorkshire pudding, new potatoes, spring cabbage and Bisto-thickened gravy.

After giving them both large helpings of the first course, she brought in an apple tart and a bowl of whipped cream.

Watching the cream being ladled onto the generous wedge of tart which her hostess had cut for her, Sarah couldn't help wondering if it did Sammy good to be fed like this every day.

When she offered to help with the dishes, her hostess

said firmly, 'No, no . . . you're only here for a few hours. You two go into the lounge and watch the video of Badminton. It won't take me long to wash up and then I'll make us some coffee.'

'She's a wonderful woman is Eileen,' said Sammy, a few minutes later, when he and Sarah were alone in the bungalow's mauve and gold lounge.

It had picture windows at both ends but the one facing the street was screened by a spotless curtain of embroidered white nylon to prevent passersby seeing in.

'Yes, you're very lucky to have met her,' Sarah agreed. 'Sammy, I've seen the tape North made. Rather than seeing it again, I'd like to talk to you . . . to explain the reason why I didn't do as well as you hoped.'

'I know the reason,' he said. 'You weren't giving it all you've got. If I didn't know you, I'd have said you were nervous. There was nothing wrong with Beddo, I'm sure of that. It was you who was holding back . . . taking the long way round . . . riding like a worried novice.'

'I was worried,' she admitted.

Sammy looked amazed. 'What for?'

'I was afraid of coming off.'

'Now that I'll never believe. You're no more afraid of a tumble than your father was. Brave to a fault, the pair of you. Don't try to make me believe you've lost your nerve, Sarah Lomax.'

'I didn't say that . . . I haven't. It was a temporary thing. The next time I ride I'll be all right. But that won't be until next year.' Her mouth had gone dry and she swallowed. 'I'm taking the rest of the year off. I'm going to have a baby, Sammy.'

'I don't believe it,' he said, after a long stunned pause.

'I'm afraid it's true,' she said quietly. 'It's due in

October. I'm already four months' pregnant. That was the reason I rode carefully.'

He looked at her blankly, still astounded. 'I don't believe it,' he repeated.

'Until it begins to show, you and Eileen will be the only people who know apart from the family . . . and Kate,' said Sarah. 'Don't be angry with me, Sammy. I know it's a shock and a terrible embarrassment for everyone. But there are worse things than a scandal. If I'd broken my neck, like Daddy and Uncle Edward, this would seem much less awful. You'd rather have me pregnant than dead, wouldn't you?'

His face began to change colour. In the garden, before lunch, it was stooping which had made him redden. This time it was rage. She had seen it once or twice before; the deepening flush turning from red to purple as his Irish temper built up to the point of explosion.

'How could you let him touch you? Were you out of your mind? Were you tipsy?' he demanded angrily.

'Don't shout at me, Sammy. You'll upset Eileen if you work yourself into a fury.'

'You must have had too much to drink at that bloody ball. In your right mind you'd never have let that lout lay his dirty hands on you. How could you demean yourself . . . you a lady and him a nobody? Good God! What'll his Lordship have to say?'

'He already knows,' said Sarah. 'My baby and his will be born about the same time. He and Jane have been kind . . . very supportive.'

'Well, don't expect kindness from me,' Sammy blazed at her. 'You're a disgrace to your name, so you are. I'll tell you what it is: it's your mam's bad blood coming out. She was no better than she should be and now you're going the same way. God knows how many men she'd had before poor Mr Ranulf. A high class tart, that's what she was . . . and now, as soon as my back's turned, her daughter's at it.'

'That's not true, Sammy. I loved Nick. I wanted to marry him.'

'Which his Lordship would never have allowed, as you very well know. Can you see him giving his blessing to your marriage to a guttersnipe like Nick! If you had to disgrace yourself, could you not have picked one of your own kind? Someone who could have made an honest woman of you and given the child a decent name. What's to become of you now?'

He stamped out of the room, banging the door behind him.


'Where's Sammy?' asked Mrs Slane, coming in with the coffee tray and finding Sarah alone and the television screen blank.

'He's gone to his room. I've upset him,' Sarah said huskily. She had been crying.

'And he's upset you, by the look of it,' said the widow, putting the tray down. 'He hasn't been telling you off about Badminton, has he?'

'No, it's nothing to do with that . . . or only indirectly. I've given him a bad shock. You see . . . I'm expecting a baby . . . Nick's baby. Sammy's furious about it.' Sarah's voice quavered and her eyes filled with tears.

For a few moments Mrs Slane was as flabbergasted as Sammy. But not only did she recover herself more quickly, her reaction was very different from his.

'Oh, my poor child . . . don't cry.' She sat down on the sofa and put her arm round Sarah's shoulders. 'No wonder you look run down. What are your family thinking of to allow you to ride at Badminton in your condition? It's a wonder you haven't miscarried. You should be taking things easy. How far along are you?'

'T-twenty-one w-weeks,' Sarah sobbed, unmanned by the little widow's unexpected sympathy.

'You were four months gone and in the saddle for

three days! It's a miracle you haven't lost it. Is that why you did it . . . in the hope that you would miscarry?'

Sarah shook her head, struggling to regain self-control. When she could speak, she said, 'I didn't want to lose the baby but I had to ride . . . for Beddo's sake. My cousin Allegra was the only one who knew. Kate suspected but she wasn't sure.' She blew her nose and wiped the tears from her cheeks. 'You d–don't seem as horrified as Sammy,' she said unsteadily.

'Men look at life differently, don't they? I could see how you felt about Nick that time the two of you came here. When young people are in love, these things happen,' said Mrs Slane.

'More often to the good girls than the bad girls, I shouldn't be surprised,' she added dryly. 'I wasn't flighty as a young thing but it happened to me. Shall I ever forget the panic when I missed my period? And I was engaged to my husband at the time so it was only a question of putting the wedding day forward. But in those days, you see, people had long engagements while they saved up to get married. I had to admit to my parents that I'd been doing what nice girls weren't sup-posed to do, and they weren't pleased, I can tell you. I haven't told Sammy about it. He's a bit old-fashioned in some ways. Whatever he said to make you cry, I'm sure he didn't mean it, my dear. He flies off the handle sometimes.'

Having poured out some coffee for Sarah, she said she would take a cup to Sammy in his room and see if he were calming down.

Remembering his occasional rages in the past – none of them directed at her until today – Sarah thought it might be several days before he adjusted to the shock she had given him.

She wasn't surprised when Mrs Slane came back and said, 'I've tried to make him look at the situation more calmly but he's still up in arms, I'm afraid. The fact is, my dear, he was always jealous of Nick. You've been like his own child to Sammy, and fathers often are upset when their little girls grow up and prefer the company of younger men.'

'But Sammy used to like Nick . . . he felt sorry for him for being ill-treated by Ted Rivington.'

'That was before Nick came back from the Foreign Legion. Now I come to think of it, after you and Nick visited us on the day after Boxing Day, Sammy told me he thought Nick was getting above himself. Does Nick know about the baby? Are you in touch with him?'

'No, he's gone . . . I don't know where. I doubt if I'll ever see him again. He loved me – or said he did – but he felt he wasn't good enough for me.'

'I'm sure he'd come back if he knew the trouble you're in. But perhaps it's better that he doesn't. I liked him, myself, very much, but he seemed a restless young man with no definite plans for the future . . . too young and footloose to marry and settle down yet.'

By half past three Sammy had not reappeared and Sarah felt she ought to be starting back.

After going again to his room, Mrs Slane reported that now the door was locked and snores could be heard from within.

'He keeps a bottle of whiskey in there. I could smell it on his breath before. I expect he's had one or two more and now he'll sleep through till this evening. I hope he wakes up with a headache. If he doesn't he'll certainly have one when I've given him a piece of my mind. Don't let this silly tantrum upset you, Miss Sarah. Drive carefully, won't you? Sammy would never forgive himself if you had an accident on the way home. He loves you dearly, you know. He'll come round in a day or two.'

Sarah felt sure he would but nevertheless it was hurtful to leave without saying goodbye and there were tears in her eyes many times on the way home.

Every day of the week that followed she hoped for a call from Sammy. When, by Sunday, she hadn't heard from him, she rang his number.

It was Mrs Slane who answered. 'I don't think he'll come to the phone,' she said, when Sarah asked to speak to him. 'He's barely on speaking terms with me at the moment. In fact it's our first real row. I'm quite out of patience with him.'

'Oh dear . . . I'm so sorry,' said Sarah. 'I don't want to be a bone of contention between you.'

'Don't worry about it, my dear. It'll blow over sooner or later. How are you feeling?'

But Sarah couldn't help worrying that it might not blow over. How terrible if Sammy and Eileen fell out because of her. Mrs Slane was a strong-minded woman. She would put up for a while with Sammy's black mood, but not indefinitely. And if she told him to leave, what would become of him? He had nowhere else to go. Long-warden had been his home for more than twenty years but he would never come back if, after a week to think about it, he still felt that Sarah had disgraced herself beyond forgiveness.

She didn't tell anyone else about their estrangement but brooded about it in secret, confiding her unhappy thoughts only to Beddo, now turned out to grass and enjoying all that horses liked best; nights of deep sleep in the open and days of leisurely grazing.

If he was puzzled at being suddenly freed from the discipline of training, and by his owner's low spirits, which he undoubtedly sensed, the Arab gelding had no means of satisfying his curiosity. That he knew all was not well was demonstrated by gentle nudges and soft exhalations from his chamois-soft nostrils, his way of showing he was aware she was unhappy. The fact that he was always there at the gate of his paddock, his pricked ears having heard her coming long before he

225

saw her, was the one unfailing comfort in a world which had suddenly become full of uncertainties.

The next time Damaris went to Longwarden she was able to show Lady Carlyon a detailed plan for the kitchen garden.

'What it needs is a focal point here,' she said, tapping the central space with the blunt end of her pencil. 'I have a small file of suggestions.' She opened a folder containing pictures of *treillage* temples, rose-draped arches and various other garden features.

The Countess looked through them. 'Before we design anything new, I think we should check what's in storage. It would be silly to start from scratch if there's something suitable in existence. Let's have a look right away, shall we? I love poking about in the attics and the barns. Dealers would drool if they saw what we have lying about here. It would stock half a dozen antique markets. I'll just let Laura know where I'm going to be for the next half an hour or so.' She picked up the house telephone.

Ten minutes later, after leading the way through parts of the house and its out-buildings where Damaris had never been before, she crossed an internal courtyard and opened a wicket in one of a pair of huge doors which, when opened, would admit a pantechnicon.

From outside Damaris had heard the high-pitched whine of a power-driven saw. Following the Countess inside, inhaling the mingled scents of wood, glue and linseed oil, she realised that this must be Longwarden's carpentry shop.

Two men and a youth in light blue overalls paused in their work as the two women entered. The power blade was switched off.

'Good afternoon.'

Jane Carlyon's greeting was addressed to them all and they all responded.

'Is Mr Warstock about?' she asked the man nearest to her.

'Yes, ma'am. He's in the office.' He jerked a thumb in the direction of a walled-in corner of the building's interior.

The Countess made her way there, making a friendly remark to the other man as she passed him.

At the mention of Sam Warstock's name, Damaris' insides had clenched. She had known she was bound to encounter him again sooner or later, but she hadn't expected another brush with him today. He would have to behave himself in the presence of his employer but even so she shrank from meeting him.

Above waist level, the internal walls of the office were glazed, revealing a workmanlike layout of shelving and cupboards surrounding an old roll-top desk and a smoker's bow chair in which he was sitting with his back to them. He was on the telephone.

'Sam Warstock is our new foreman,' the Countess murmured to Damaris, as they waited outside for him to finish his call. 'He's young for the job but exceptionally well qualified. I like him very much. He has a great sense of humour and he's extremely intelligent. I'm sure you'll find him most helpful any time you need him.'

At that moment one of the carpenters tapped on the glass to attract the foreman's attention to his visitors. As he saw who was waiting, he said something to the person he had been speaking to, placed the receiver on the desk and hurried to open the door.

'I'm sorry, m'Lady.' He didn't glance at Damaris. She might not have been there.

'Don't apologise. Finish your call. We're in no hurry.'

'It won't take a minute. Please come in.'

As well as the desk chair, there was a high-backed Windsor chair which he offered to the Countess before moving his own chair to a position beside it, showing that he was aware of another presence even if he hadn't glanced at Damaris yet.

'Thank you.' Lady Carlyon sat down and crossed her legs.

Today she was wearing trousers, as was Damaris. Unlike the other carpenters in their uniform overalls, the foreman had on clean blue jeans and a white tee shirt which clung to the powerful structure of his shoulders and torso. As he replaced the receiver, after quickly concluding the call which had evidently been an order to a wholesale ironmonger, a well-developed muscle bulged slightly where the sleeve of his shirt gave place to the smooth, sun-tanned skin of his upper arm. From elbow to wrist, his arm had a light covering of dark hair.

As she had already told Damaris who he was, the Countess said, 'This is Miss Lynn who is in charge of the garden, Sam.'

For the second time he offered his hand and said, 'Pleased to meet you.'

This time Damaris mustered a smile to accompany a friendly, 'Hello.'

'Miss Lynn is re-planting the kitchen garden to make it more productive and also more attractive,' Lady Carlyon told him. 'She needs some kind of centrepiece. Have a look through this file of ideas. You may have seen something suitable on your checks through the storerooms. If not – '

She broke off as the house telephone started to ring.

'Excuse me.' Sam Warstock lifted the receiver. 'Carpentry shop. Warstock speaking.' He listened for a few moments. 'It's your secretary, m'Lady.'

'Oh dear . . .' Frowning slightly, Jane took the receiver from him. 'I have to leave you,' she told them, a few moments later. 'Someone has called to see me. I shall have to offer them tea. What a nuisance but it can't be helped. Never mind: I'm sure, between you, you can sort something out.'

The foreman opened the door for her. After he had closed it again, it seemed to Damaris that the office had suddenly become a much more confined space than when Jane Carlyon had been with them.

Sam Warstock sat down in the chair vacated by his employer and began to study the photographs in the file.

'Has the Countess said which she prefers of these ideas you've put up?' he asked, after going through the file a second time.

'I think what she was going to say when the telephone rang was that if there's nothing in storage for us to use, we shall have to design and build something. In that case she may take advice from Mr Muirhead. You must know him, don't you?'

He nodded. 'Not a bad bloke. I haven't much time for architects, as a rule. Not the modern ones. Ought to be shot, the lot of 'em, if you ask me. But Muirhead's okay. He likes stone the way I like wood. Ever heard him talking about stone?'

She shook her head.

'It's his pet subject. Try to get him on it some time. You'll hear some fascinating stuff. But maybe it wouldn't interest you.'

He added this final comment without any change of expression but she felt it was more than a simple statement of possibility. It was intended as a dig at her.

'I'm sure it would interest me very much,' she said evenly. 'People with passionate enthusiasms are nearly always worth listening to.'

There was a tap on the door and he called out, 'Come in, Billy.'

A boy in his middle teens entered, carrying a tray on which was a mug of tea, a cup of tea and a plate of pastries.

'You've forgotten to bring any sugar. Do you take sugar, Miss Lynn?'

'No, I don't.' She smiled at the boy. 'Thank you for bringing a cup for me, Billy.'

He blushed. 'That's okay, miss.'

As he turned to go, the foreman said, 'Hang on a minute, lad.' To her, he said, 'We have our tea on the strong side. Do you want some more milk in yours?'

'I don't mind strong tea,' she said untruthfully.

At the flat she drank only China tea or herbal teas. She knew that the taste of strong Indian tea would remind her of times she preferred to forget, but to weaken it with milk would make no difference.

'Have a cake,' said Sam, when the boy had gone back to the tea break taking place at the far end of the carpentry shop.

'Not for me, thanks.'

'Watching your weight?'

The question reminded her – not that any reminder was needed – that he had seen her stripped and knew how much flesh there was on her.

'I haven't a sweet tooth.'

'I have. I like all the things they tell you not to eat. Pork pies. Bangers and mash. Mars bars. Crisps. Fish and chips.'

Again she had the feeling that although he seemed only to be listing his favourite junk foods, he was also taking the mickey.

'They don't appear to have done you any harm so far.' She noticed there was no ash tray to be seen, and no smell of cigarettes in the office. 'But you don't smoke, I gather.'

'Not likely! Fags are a menace in a carpentry shop. Some of the lads smoke off duty, but nothing while they're working. The first one I catch having a drag will be out on his ear. A fag-end left lying around here and this place could go up like a bonfire with petrol on it.'

He chose one of the pastries. 'We had better cakes with our tea when Mrs Armitage was doing the cooking. This French bloke's okay on some things but he can't make a decent cake. This sort of stuff is all right for old ladies at bridge parties, but the lads don't go for it much. Two bites and it's gone. We like something we can get our teeth into. Fruit cake . . . a nice chunk of parkin . . . old-fashioned stuff like that.'

'I expect the chef could make them if you asked him.'

'I doubt it. The Frogs don't go in for proper cake. It's the same with biscuits. Theirs aren't a patch on ours. Cheeses are what they're good at . . . cheeses and fancy meats . . . *charcuterie* . . . is that how you pronounce it?'

She sensed an undercurrent of mockery in everything he said to her.

Determined not to let him rile her, she said, 'I don't speak French. I've never been to France. Have you?'

Her answer seemed to surprise him. 'Yes . . . I've been there a few times. A mate of mine had a motorbike. He gave me a lift on the back of it. You don't need to speak the lingo to have a good time there. Where do you go for your holidays?'

She thought she would make it clear that she wasn't the dilettante he seemed to think her. 'Being self-employed, I haven't been able to take a lot of time off. When I do take a short break, it's generally to look at gardens. There are foreign gardens I'd like to see when I can.' She finished her tea and replaced the cup on the saucer.

'Like some more?' he said.

'No thanks.' She didn't want to prolong their tête-à-téte. 'What about this centrepiece? Are there any possibilities?'

'There's a metal effort . . . sort of a mini-bandstand. You could grow climbers up it. It's a bit fancy for my taste. Late Victorian, I should think, by the style of it. Or there's a stack of pieces which may be a Gothic summerhouse. Without putting them together it's hard to tell what they are. When I've finished my tea, I'll show you.'

He took another of the criticised pastries, clearly not intending to hurry himself.

Finding silence uncomfortable, Damaris asked, 'Where did you work before you came here?'

His manners were noticeably less crude than those of the men she had grown up with. He swallowed the food in his mouth before he answered her.

'Nearer London . . . for a small firm making top quality repro furniture. Breakfront bookcases . . . "Chippendale" chairs . . . that sort of thing. They were doing very well. The prospects were good. But the work was a bit monotonous. I like more variety. Here, every day something different comes up. Today, for instance, we're re-runging two broken ladders, repairing a couple of doors and replacing a wormy leg on a chair. I don't have to spend too much time on ordering and paper-work. Most of the day I'm doing the practical work I prefer.'

As his mug was still half-full of tea and it looked as if he might polish off all four pastries, Damaris resigned herself to several more minutes' conversation.

She said, 'Talking of paper-work, I've spent several evenings reading the planting notes made by the fifth and seventh earls, both of whom were very keen botanists. There must be some interesting records to do with the carpentry shop, aren't there?'

'Yes, the clerks of the works in the old days kept log-books of all the work done here. But all the valuable records – like invoices from famous cabinet-makers – are kept in the muniments room in the house.'

Reluctantly, Damaris acknowledged that the Countess was probably right in describing him as very intelligent.

Not because she was interested but for something to say, she asked, 'Do you live here or in the village?'

'Here . . . they've made me a flat out of what used to be two sculleries. They're converting all the unused parts into staff flats . . . good ones . . . well planned and well equipped. By the end of next year, the staff will have a gym and a pool and satellite TV. They won't need to go outside for their entertainment. It'll all be laid on for them here.'

'That's fine for the older, married staff but the young ones, like my trainee gardeners, will still want to spend their evenings where other young people congregate. There won't be enough of them here to give them an adequate choice of boyfriends and girlfriends.'

'From what Billy tells me, there's not much of a selection at the Saturday night disco in the village. According to him, the girls who go there are scrubbers and the boys are dropouts and rowdies. The ones with some brains in their heads have to make their own entertainments. Apart from the evening classes up at the school, and the cycling club, there isn't a lot going for them, but the Countess has plans to change that. She'll do it if anyone can. She's a live wire that girl.'

Indoctrinated by Maudie, Damaris disapproved of a carpenter, even a foreman, referring to Jane Carlyon as 'that girl'. At the same time she couldn't fault his courtesy while their employer had been with them.

'Yes, I'm sure Lady Carlyon will do a great deal of good,' she agreed. 'It's very stimulating to work for someone with such open, imaginative ideas.' She glanced at her watch. 'I think we should get on with looking for this centrepiece, don't you?'

'Yes, ma'am . . . right away, ma'am.'

The infuriating gleam of mockery showed in his hazel eyes as he jumped up and took a bunch of keys from a hook. He knew what she had been thinking and he didn't give a damn for her opinion. In his, he was as good as anyone. He might mind his manners with the Countess,

233

but he certainly wouldn't with Damaris – as he had already proved in the yew walk.

Had she been on her own, she would have had nothing but pleasure from exploring the stores they toured. None of the architectural salvage warehouses she had sometimes visited in quest of features for gardens could compare with the amazing assortment of discards in storage at Longwarden.

Even with Sam's disturbing presence at her elbow, there were moments when she forgot her unease and pounced with delight on a box of leather overshoes worn by the horses which in earlier times had drawn rollers and then cylinder mowers over acres of velvet lawn. Elsewhere another box contained porcelain plant labels, many of them broken, impressed with the crest from the Carlyon coat of arms.

'Oh, look . . . a clay watering pot . . . probably seventeenth century . . . This would have been used for damping the herbs they used to scatter on the floors,' she told Sam excitedly, momentarily forgetting his antipathy.

He glanced briefly at the pot. 'You should smile more often, Miss Lynn. It suits you better than your haughty look.'

His own smile and his narrowed eyes made her suddenly sharply aware how isolated they were. If he came closer . . . touched her . . . what could she do about it?

She replaced the pot on its shelf, alongside a row of early metal watering cans which looked as if they had stood there, gathering dust and cobwebs, since long before she was born.

'Where is the Gothic summerhouse you mentioned?'

'On the floor above . . . up those stairs.'

He indicated a rickety-looking stairway, hardly more than a ladder with a handrail.

Glad she wasn't wearing a skirt, she climbed the narrow treads and came out into a large loft with exposed rafters, one gable having a window and the other a pair of doors with, she guessed, a pulley outside them. Most of the things stored up here were too large to have come up the stairs.

Partially hidden behind a stack of other junk, the ogee-arched windows and panels of trellis did look as if they might make up into a pretty gazebo from which to admire the mixed beds of flowers and vegetables.

'It would take forever to get them out from behind there,' she said, peering through a gap at a panel inset with a quatrefoil opening.

'It's not a five minute job, what with clearing a way to those doors and lowering the stuff to ground level,' said Sam. 'But I reckon a couple of evenings should do it. I'll get Billy to give me a hand. He's an obliging kid and stronger than he looks. If you show me where you want it to go, and assuming there's nothing missing, we could probably get it fixed up by some time next week. Would that suit you?'

'That would be splendid. Of course there's no guarantee it will look right when it's up, but I've always liked the Gothic style.'

'So have I.' His wide mouth curled at one corner. 'That's one thing we have in common.'

Damaris made no comment. 'I must run. I have a lot to attend to in the short time I'm here.'

'You ought to be here all the time. Why aren't you?' he asked.

'I have commitments in London.'

'I couldn't stand living in London. Compared with here it's a hellhole.'

'I agree, but it's where my business is. I can't let down the people I work for, or the women who work for me.'

'Couldn't you sell the business?'

'Possibly . . . if I wanted to. I don't know that I do yet. Longwarden is lovely now but there's the winter to consider,' she answered, remembering Peter's warning.

'I know where I'd rather be, come Christmas time. Perhaps you go home for Christmas.'

She shook her head. 'I have no family home.'

'That makes two of us. Nor have I. Something else we have in common.'

Having already indicated that she wanted to leave, but being unable to return to the stairway until he did, or stood aside, Damaris said, 'You'll have to excuse me. I really must get on.'

'Okay.' He turned away.

Reminded by his broad shoulders and narrow hips of her first sight of his back view, she wondered if she would ever be able to forget that humiliating introduction.

Going down the stairway, he paused, his head still above the level of the floorboards. 'There ought to be extinguishers in all these stores. The fire chief would do his nut if he saw the stuff stacked in here. If it caught, it'd burn like a bush fire.'

'Yes, but it's not very likely.'

'All the same, I'll have a word with the Earl. There was a fire in the village last night. Someone put a match to a shed at the back of a derelict cottage. It could have been done by kids or there could be someone around who's looking for things to burn. They could have a right rave-up up here.' He continued down the stairs.

In the walled yard outside the store, he showed her a door which would save her going back the way they had come. He opened it for her.

'Thanks. I'll see you next week.'

It was not until she was on her way back to London that she wondered how word of a minor fire in the village could have reached his ears so quickly. Then she realised that Billy or one of the two other men might live near the derelict house.

# June

At 13 Laburnum Way, Marlene Clutton was having a fag and a sit-down after a tiring trip to the shops when her friend, Sandra burst into the house by way of the back door.

'Whatever's up, Sandra?' asked Marlene, having heard the hurried clicking of high heels on the concrete path at the side of her end-of-row house and caught a glimpse of Sandra's expression as she passed the window which overlooked number thirteen's neglected back yard.

'You're never going to guess who I've seen up the surgery, Marl. I can't hardly believe it myself . . . but I'm sure it were her . . . I'm sure it were Tiff.'

'Our Tiff? Up the surgery? Never! Don't be daft, Sandra. Why would she come back now . . . after all these years?'

'She weren't there herself . . . not sitting there. There were a photograph of her in one of the books. Any day but Monday I'd have slipped it in with my shopping and brought it to show you. But you know what the waiting room's like on a Monday – packed all the morning. Someone would have seen. You'll have to go up there yourself. I'll come with you. I've forgotten what the book was called but I remember the cover.'

'It's a long way from 'ere to the surgery, Sandra. I'm knackered already without trailing up there,' said Marlene.

Sixty cigarettes a day and her weight, now twenty pounds more than when her niece had run away from home, made her increasingly breathless. Almost any exertion brought on long bouts of coughing. She went out as little as possible and spent most of her time watching television or films from the video library. Kevin had bought the video to be able to watch blue movies and what some people called video nasties. Marlene didn't go for them herself. The one she had seen out of curiosity had turned her stomach. But she couldn't stop Kevin watching them and so far he hadn't tried any of that rough stuff on her.

'I don't suppose it is Tiff,' she said. 'It's just someone like her.'

'I don't think so. I'm sure it's Tiff. It's her eyes . . . her eyebrows . . . her nose. She's changed a bit, that's only natural. It's a long time since she ran off. But she never did look like other girls, if you remember. There was always something about her that was different to the rest of them.'

'She didn't wear no make-up, that's all,' said her aunt. 'Have a bit of sense, Sandra. What would Tiff be doing in a book? If she'd gone into films or modelling someone round here would have recognised her before now. Anyway, she didn't have the looks. You could never call her a pretty girl . . . not with that nose and chin.'

'Barbra Streisand's got a funny nose. It didn't stop her being a star. I thought Tiff – if it is her – looked smashing. But she isn't a model. The bit underneath the picture said she had her own business – giving advice about gardens. Now don't tell me that's not possible. You know the hours she spent with that old girl what used to live in the next road. Always in there the kid was. I tell you it *is* Tiff, Marlene. I won't say I'd stake my life on it, but I'm ninety-nine per cent sure.'

'Bloody 'ell! It *is* Tiff. Well I'm buggered,' said Marlene half an hour later, after Sandra had succeeded in dragging her up to the waiting room of the group medical practice which served their part of the town.

The picture of Tiff was in an old, tattered copy of a magazine called *Working Woman*. It showed her on her knees by a flower bed, sitting back on her heels to smile at the camera. She was wearing a shirt and trousers with a small scarf knotted round her long neck and gold hoop earrings.

Marlene remembered Tiff's neck because she herself had no neck at all to speak of, not even when she was young and slim. It had meant that she'd never been able to wear the dangling drop earrings she'd always fancied herself in. On her they didn't dangle but trailed on her shoulders. It was the same with hair. She looked a right berk with long hair.

'I'm going to tear this out,' she said decisively.

The sound of two pages being ripped from the magazine made everyone look at her, a few with disapproval, most with bored indifference. Marlene put the pages in her bag and she and Sandra left.

'Are you going to get in touch with her?' asked Sandra, as they walked back to Laburnum Way.

'I don't know. I'll see what Kev says.'

Marlene had sometimes wondered if Kev knew more about Tiff's sudden disappearance than he had let on. More than once in the days when Marlene and he still went out together she had seen him eyeing young girls. She wouldn't put it past him to have tried more than looking with Tiff. Something must have upset her. Why else would she have run off like that?

Marlene hadn't voiced her suspicions. Kev wouldn't never admit it if he had had a go at Tiff, she thought. There was no point in having a row about it. They had enough fights as it was.

A few days after Tiff's disappearance Marlene had had a letter from her sister in London. Shirley had written that Tiff had turned up unexpectedly but had disappeared again before Shirl could find out what the hell the kid was doing in London. Would Marlene ring her as soon as possible.

As the telephones in the boxes near Laburnum Way were more or less permanently unusable, being re-vandalized within hours of being replaced or repaired, Marlene had had to go to the town centre to find one which worked. It had been a waste of time and money really. There was nothing she could tell her sister except that Tiff had run away, and Shirl had no further news of her.

The following week, a school attendance official called to see Marlene.

'Didn't it occur to you to report your niece's disappearance, Mrs Clutton?'

'I couldn't see no point. I mean, what are the police going to do about it? There's hundreds of kids go missing. They don't never find them . . . not unless they get murdered.'

The disapproving official was followed, a few days later, by a female police sergeant who not only questioned Marlene more closely but also had the bloody cheek to ask people round about if they could suggest any reason why Mrs Clutton's niece had left home so suddenly.

However after a while the police stopped making enquiries, the gossip died down and Tiff was forgotten by everyone except Marlene and little Diane who sometimes said, 'When's Tiff coming back?'


Jane was opening a parcel from Marie-Simone in Paris.

In it she found three books, including *Birth Without Violence* by Frédérick Leboyer, a Frenchman with radical ideas on the conduct of childbirth, and photocopies of several French magazine articles about Dr Michel Odent, the director of a maternity unit at Pithiviers and another enlightened obstetrician.

The Frenchwoman had also sent several canisters of orange-flower water which Jane wanted to refresh her during labour but hadn't been able to find on sale in London.

When she returned to her flat that night, Damaris re-read the postcard from Peru which had arrived in the morning.

On the back of a picture of a llama standing in the ruins of Machupicchu, Peter had written – *Hangovers at this altitude are death so resting my liver. In absence of camp doctor, was called to deal with 'a broken leg' seven miles up a mountain. Arrived to find that, with leg attached by skin only, patient had bled to death. Locals don't know about tourniquets. They tend to want aspirin for decapitation and field hospital for splinter. Hope that Frog is keeping his distance. Writing. Love. P.*

Barney Dunbar was in financial trouble.

The younger brother of Claudia Dunbar, co-director of Brentwood & Dunbar, the London publishers, he had been in debt since his schooldays, his condition worsening from the moment he acquired his first credit card.

He worked in academic publishing but wasn't well-paid. To maintain his image of a well-heeled young man about town, he had to supplement his income by any means which came to hand. So far all his sidelines had been legal.

Barney had a good eye for quality. On country weekends he would visit local antique shops, sometimes picking up things he could sell to dealers in London for a decent profit. For that reason he ran an estate car rather than the sleek sports car he would have preferred to drive. As well as searching for antiques, he also looked out for repro and modern furniture which, after it had been hand-painted or stencilled by one of his ex-girlfriends, he could sell to interior decorators.

He was also a stringer for more than one newspaper columnist, supplying them with snippets of gossip or rumours to be followed up. He kept this activity secret and none of his well-connected friends suspected that what he saw and heard in their houses was often relayed to the gossip-mongers.

He had once been approached to push drugs but although the money was tempting he considered the risks too high. When his grandmother died, as her heir he would have no more problems. He knew, because she had told him, that she was leaving everything to him. She was a jolly old stick and he didn't want her to die. But being already nearly eighty, she couldn't go on forever. By the time he was thirty he ought to be comfortably off. No more homilies from his bank manager. No more letters from creditors. No more worries.

Early in June, Barney spent a weekend with his grandmother, hoping to scrounge some money from her. Usually, if he exerted himself to be an affectionate grandson, she would cough up the necessary to straighten him out for the time being.

Normally June was a high-living month for him as for all committed free-loaders, if they were young, male and reasonably personable. Last year, thanks to good tips for the Derby and Ascot, he had ended the month in the black. This year, hoping to repeat that happy situation, he had gone down badly on the Derby and was now seriously in the red. To make matters worse, his grandmother was not in one of her generous moods. Her housekeeper was in hospital and might not be able to work again. The old girl was worried about it and worry made her short-tempered, even with him.

On Sunday morning, while Mrs Dunbar was at church, Barney had appointments with dealers. Afterwards, as his grandmother was going out to lunch, he decided to look up Sarah Lomax.

They had met at the Longwarden ball in December. The invitation had come via his sister, who had published a book by the Earl of Carlyon's sister. It had been one of the best dances Barney had ever attended, but when he had tried to make a date with Lord Carlyon's young cousin, one of the prettiest girls he had ever laid eyes on, she had turned him down on the grounds that he was a town mouse and she was a country mouse.

In fact, at that time, he had been rather heavily involved with someone else so he had accepted her refusal with a good grace. But now the affair with Caro had come to an end and there was a space in his love life which he wouldn't mind filling with the delicious Sarah. If he hadn't known it beforehand, he would never have guessed she was a horsey girl. The dance had been a fancy dress affair and she had been a Twenties flapper in a blue dress with sequins on it. Instead of looking tough and muscular, she had looked adorably cuddly. He looked forward to seeing her again. If he turned up there about noon, she would have to ask him to lunch. Unless she was out, of course. He would have to take a chance on that. Barney didn't believe in ringing up people beforehand. Experience had taught him it was better to arrive on their doorsteps. On the telephone, they could make excuses. Presenting oneself in person put them at a disadvantage.

When he arrived at the main gates, they were closed. He had to get out of the car and knock on the door of the lodge house.

'Good morning,' he said to the woman who opened it. 'I've come to see Miss Lomax. Would someone open the gates for me, please?'

There was a child howling somewhere in the background and a smell of burnt food. The woman looked harassed.

'Yes, sir.' She pressed one of several buttons on a control panel which included a telephone.

As he walked back to the car he guessed that the usual drill with unexpected visitors was for her to ring up the house before admitting them. Perhaps he had been lucky to catch her in the middle of a domestic *crise*.

When Longwarden came into view – it had been dark when he arrived last time, only the lighted windows indicating its scale and magnificence – he decided not to drive up to the front door where he would be received by the butler, but to go round to the stable block in the hope of finding Sarah there.

However it was another girl he saw when he drove through the massive archway leading into the stable yard.

'Hello . . . is Sarah about?' he asked, smiling.

The girl didn't smile back. 'Who are you?'

'Barney Dunbar . . . a friend of hers. I don't think we've met. Who are you?'

'Kate Hastings . . . I work for Sarah. Is she expecting you?'

'No, but I said I'd drop in next time I was staying with my grandmother. I haven't been down since the Carlyons gave a dance to celebrate their marriage and Sarah's gold medal. Were you here then?'

She shook her head. 'Sarah may be out. I'll find out for you.'

At that moment Sarah herself came out of a doorway, stopping short at the sight of him.

He crossed the yard towards her. 'Hello there. Remember me? Barney Dunbar . . . Claudia's brother. I'm spending the weekend with my grandmother but she has a lunch date today and you're the only other person I know in these parts. I was hoping you'd take pity on me and come out for lunch.'

'Oh . . . hello, Barney. How are you?'

Although, unlike the unfriendly groom, Sarah did give

him a smile, he sensed that he wasn't welcome. Her manner was that of someone caught on the wrong foot and unsure how to deal with a situation.

'I'm fine, but bored with my own company. How about an introduction to your horses, especially the one you rode at Burghley and Badminton?'

In April, he had intended to watch Badminton on TV and telephone her afterwards, but then he had an invitation to spend the weekend with people who weren't interested in sporting events and so he had missed it. But he'd read a report of the horse trials in *Country Life* and knew she had not done as well as she had at Burghley.

'I'm afraid I'm rather busy today, Barney. What a pity you didn't ring up. You could have saved yourself the drive.'

'That's disappointing. Why are you so busy? Is there something big on this week?'

She had changed since December, he noticed. She had put on weight. Her boobs had enlarged, which was fine – the bigger the better for his taste – but she seemed to have lost her slim waist. Good lord, she was really quite tubby. What the hell had happened to her figure?

'It's a busy time of year,' she answered.

She had suddenly flushed a deep red and he felt strong vibes of discomfiture coming from her.

'Oh come on, you can't send me packing now that I'm here. If there's work to be done, let me help. I'm just what you need – an extra pair of hands.'

'But not hands which are used to working with horses. I didn't think you were even interested in them.' She began to walk towards his car, rather too obviously anxious to speed him on his way. When she saw that the back of the car had several pieces of furniture in it, she said, 'What's all that?'

He didn't advertise the fact that he was a part-time runner. 'Oh, just one or two things Granny's given me for my flat. Look, you have to eat and it needn't take more than an hour to have lunch with me. There are several nice looking pubs within a few miles of here. I hate eating on my own.'

'I'm sorry, Barney. I can't. My sister-in-law has guests today. She's expecting me to meet them.'

It wouldn't have been beyond him to propose himself as an extra guest. But not only was he piqued by her manifest lack of interest in him, but he found her much less attractive than he had six months earlier. If she went on putting on flab, she would soon lose her looks altogether. Perhaps this was the reason she hadn't done well at Badminton. She was getting out of condition. None of the top class eventers he had seen carried any surplus flesh, but Sarah was now overweight to the point of looking almost as tubby as Georgina, a girl at the office who was pregnant.

He looked at her body more closely. Bloody hell, *she* was pregnant! That wasn't a soft spare tyre she had round her middle. It was the solid swelling of a bun in the oven; the very same shape that Georgina was.

He glanced quickly at her left hand. No ring ergo no husband. What was one to make of that?

'Where are you competing next?' he asked.

'I – I'm not sure. Two of my horses are out of action at the moment.'

Barney noticed the slight hesitation, an almost infallible sign of someone who was normally truthful being forced to tell a lie.

'That's hard luck . . . but an occupational hazard, I gather.' He didn't know much about eventing, but he did know that the horses underwent rigorous veterinary inspections and weren't allowed to compete if they had the least thing wrong with them.

However he was pretty sure there was nothing wrong with Sarah's horses. It was she who was out of action.

It was on the tip of his tongue to say, 'When's the

happy event?' and startle her into confirming that she had been knocked up. But some instinct made him hold his tongue.

He glanced at his watch. A quarter to one. If she had really been going to have lunch with the Carlyons' guests, she wouldn't be here, wearing stable kit. By now she'd be in the house, tidied up, drinking sherry.

He said, 'Well, you'll want to go and get changed so I'd better take myself off for a solitary pint and a sandwich. I hope it isn't too long before the horses are fit again. Next time I come down I'll give you a ring in advance.'

'Yes, do,' she said politely.

Hypocritical little bitch. You don't care if you never set eyes on me again, Barney thought irritably. But he smiled and wished her luck for the rest of the season, as if he hadn't noticed anything, before climbing into his car and driving away.


'D'you think he noticed?' asked Kate, coming out of the tack room after hearing the car leave.

Sarah looked down at her distended middle. In winter it would have been easier to disguise her increasing girth with baggy sweaters. Yesterday it had been cool enough to wear a loose shirt outside her jeans. Today it was hot. She was wearing a tee shirt and shorts.

'He would have to be incredibly unobservant not to have noticed, don't you think?'

'Most men aren't observant,' said Kate. 'They're too full of themselves to study other people the way we do. He struck me as deeply pleased with himself.'

Sarah nodded. 'I think he is, but I'm pretty sure he did notice. Whether he'll talk about it remains to be seen. Men gossip less than women, don't you think?'

'No, I don't,' Kate said acidly. 'They don't ring round their friends the way women do, but they spread the word in other ways. Whether he'll broadcast the news about you depends on whether he knows people who would be interested. Who is he anyway?'

Sarah explained, and went on, 'I can't see why anyone he knows should be interested in me. He moves in literary circles. Most of the people he mixes with will never have heard of me. He may tell his sister, but I don't think she would pass it on in case it got back to Allegra that she had gossiped.'


In *The Partridge* at Longwarden St Michael, one of the outlying villages which presumably was part of North Carlyon's estate, or had belonged to his forbears, Barney looked at the bar lunch menu and ordered moussaka. While the barmaid put it in the microwave, he drank some lager and wondered how best to use his knowledge that Sarah Lomax was in the family way.

It hadn't taken him long to realise that he was on to something much more important than a paragraph of innuendo in one of the gossip columns.

The tabloids could build something like this into a major scandal. A headline such as EARL'S COUSIN COMES A CROPPER followed by a spicy exposé of sexy goings-on behind the scenes at the great country house horse trials was the sort of thing their readers lapped up.


Barney's lunch, during the week, usually consisted of a sandwich fetched from the local takeaway by the secretary he shared with two other junior editors. Not for him the epicurean revelries of London's best restaurants enjoyed by literary agents and the top brass of the mass market publishing houses.

According to Claudia even they were tending to cut down on long boozy lunches from which they returned to their desks in an alcoholic haze. The new breed of women publishers had led the way in replacing the traditional lavish publishing lunch with much shorter discussions fuelled by Perrier and rabbit food. Not only were most women publishers watching their weight but they had a lot more to cope with than their male counterparts; domestic responsibilities as well as career problems.

'We haven't time for four course, three hour lunches,' his sister had told him austerely. 'I personally would prefer to cut out lunches altogether and have authors and agents come to the office for any discussions which can't be handled by letter or telephone.'

Barney hadn't argued with her but privately he thought that publishing must have been a lot more fun in the days when it had been 'an occupation for gentlemen', before it had been infiltrated by all these ambitious, sternly self-disciplined females.

On the Monday after his weekend with his grandmother, he had another pub lunch, but this time not by himself. During the morning he had rung up a man he knew slightly, a staff reporter on one of the tabloids.

When they were settled in a corner of the bar with beer and hamburgers, he said, 'Tell me, how much would your News Editor pay for a lead to a first class story? Something really juicy.'

'That depends,' said his contact. 'To answer that, I'd have to know more about it.'

Barney had expected this response and had spent a lot of time preparing a reply which would whet the reporter's appetite for scandal without giving away too much. He didn't trust any of these press bastards. If they had any scruples they wouldn't be doing what they did. This guy would think nothing of stealing a march on Barney if he could.

He said, 'This could be the best story you've had this year. I'll give you the bare bones and then, if you think he'd be interested, I'd like to meet your boss and talk business before filling in the details.'

'May I speak to Miss Denham, please?'

'Speaking.'

'Laura, this is Margaret Foxley. I'm afraid I have some bad news. There's been a fire at your house.'

'Oh no! I can't believe it.'

Laura's exclamation of dismay caused Jane, who was in her secretary's office, to raise interrogative eyebrows.

'I thought you would want to be told,' Miss Foxley continued. 'I've just heard the news from my neighbour. She rang me up here at the office a few minutes ago. She happened to be passing your house as the fire engine arrived.'

'Does she know what happened to my tenants? Were they in the house when it caught fire? Did they get out of it all right?'

'Yes, yes . . . no one was hurt. The front of the house wasn't burnt. The firemen came very quickly.'

'Are you sure? They weren't injured at all? Not even minor burns?' Laura asked anxiously.

'Quite sure,' Miss Foxley assured her. 'The silly woman was standing outside in the garden telling my neighbour how it happened while the firemen were inside. It was entirely her fault. She admitted that. I should think you could sue her for criminal negligence.'

'Oh goodness, I wouldn't do that,' Laura exclaimed. 'Anyone can have an accident. I expect she feels terrible about it. Hold on a moment, please, will you?'

She put her hand over the mouthpiece to explain to Jane what had happened before saying, 'Thank you for letting me know, Margaret. I'll ring up Mrs Washwood and hear the full story from her. Whatever damage has been done I'm sure the insurance will cover it. That neither she nor her husband were hurt is really all that matters.'

'I must say you take it very calmly,' said Miss Foxley, her own tone indignant. 'I should be extremely annoyed at having *my* house badly damaged by such carelessness. It appears that your Mrs Washwood left a pan of oil on the cooker when she went to answer the telephone. She then had a long conversation with her married daughter who rings her up daily – what they can find to talk about I cannot imagine! – and it wasn't until she smelt smoke that she realised the pan had caught fire. Your kitchen is a ruin, my neighbour tells me. After the firemen had left she went in to see the damage. The last time she saw such havoc was during the Blitz, she said.'

'Oh dear . . . well, it can't be helped. These things happen. It might have been worse,' Laura replied philosophically.

She was quite surprised to find how little she minded. Now that she knew Mrs Washwood had escaped injury, she found that she wasn't upset. The damage to the house seemed unimportant. Nothing she valued was there. She had left some winter clothes in the cupboard in the third bedroom, but even if they had been destroyed it wouldn't have worried her.

'If I were you, I should reserve judgement until you have seen for yourself just how extensive the damage is,' Miss Foxley said shortly. 'I did warn you, if you remember, that letting a house is very rarely plain sailing. I've never known anyone yet who hasn't regretted it.'

She enlarged on this theme at some length, giving Laura the feeling that she wasn't entirely displeased that her warning had been fulfilled.

'I'm sure you must be busy, Margaret, so I won't keep you any longer,' she said, when Miss Foxley paused for breath. 'Thank you very much for passing the news on. I'll get in touch with Mrs Washwood right away. Goodbye for the present.'

As she replaced the receiver someone knocked on the door and was bidden to enter by Jane.

It was James Muirhead. Before he could say what he wanted, Jane said to him, 'Poor Miss Denham has just been told there's been a fire at her house in London.'

'I'm sorry to hear that, Miss Denham. How bad was it? Do you know yet?'

'Not too bad. Only the kitchen is completely burnt out . . . and I suppose the room above it will have been damaged. Still it's an awful nuisance, especially for my tenants who will have to cope with all the mess.'

'Are you going to inspect the damage? If so, may I give you a lift?' He looked at his watch. 'Four-fifteen now. I'm leaving here about five.'

'It's very kind of you to offer, but I hadn't thought of going up,' Laura began.

'You haven't had a chance to think of anything,' Jane intervened. 'Of course you must go, Laura. If you see the damage for yourself, you'll worry about it much less than if you only have other people's reports to go on. It's lucky Mr Muirhead is here today. Have another cup of tea to restore you, and then go and pack an overnight case. Tomorrow you'll need to have talks with the insurance people. I shan't expect you back until the evening – or even the day after tomorrow if you find there are complications.'

As she spoke, she refilled Laura's cup for her.

'I'm sure I shan't need to be away as long as that,' said Laura, more concerned about her duties at Longwarden than about the contretemps in London. 'I'll be back by lunchtime at the latest.'

'See how it goes,' Jane advised. 'There may be some shopping you want to do while you're there. There's nothing of any great urgency requiring your attention here tomorrow.'

Laura didn't possess an overnight case. Her father had had one, she remembered, but after his death Gwen

252

Denham had sold his suits to a second-hand dealer and his unsaleable possessions had gone to a charity shop.

Laura had been shocked about the suits and had shown it. Whereupon she had been told sharply that her father's extravagance – the suits had been made to measure by a good tailor – had cost Gwen and her children many things they would have liked, and from now on there would be no more preferential treatment and spoiling for Laura. She would have to learn to take a back seat for a change.

Not wishing to take one of the larger suitcases to London, she ventured to ask Mr Flitton if he knew of a soft-topped case or a holdall she could borrow.

'Certainly, Miss Denham,' said the butler. 'Would you care to come along to the luggage room and choose for yourself?'

On the way to the luggage room she explained why she needed a case.

'Dear me, that's very unfortunate. I hope your insurance cover will ensure that you're not out of pocket by the time it's been put to rights,' he said sympathetically. 'Are your tenants young people?'

'No, they're a middle-aged couple. The wife was having a chat with her grown-up daughter when it happened.'

'No doubt her husband will have something to say when he comes home to find his dinner has gone up in flames – literally,' was the butler's dry comment.

'I'm sure he will. I'm afraid he may be very nasty to her. He struck me as an overbearing even bullying sort of man,' said Laura. 'He will probably never let her forget it.'

'Perhaps she should count herself lucky that she isn't responsible for anything worse than the ruination of your kitchen. It would have been more understandable had she been a young woman harassed by a crying baby or the demands of several children. For someone of mature years to behave so carelessly . . .' Mr Flitton clicked his tongue disapprovingly.

The luggage room and its contents astonished Laura. It was stacked with all manner of cabin trunks, wardrobe trunks, Gladstone bags, hat boxes, smaller round leather boxes made to hold stiffly starched collars, bags for transporting guns, golf clubs and fishing rods, baskets for animals to travel in, a stout wooden tuck box such as boys took to boarding school and many more items whose purpose she wouldn't have known had the butler not explained it.

'Perhaps this would do,' he suggested, removing the canvas storage cover from a blue leather soft-topped case.

'It looks new,' said Laura doubtfully.

'This isn't new, Miss Denham. I would venture to say it's at least half a century old . . . a relic of the thirties.'

The keys were attached to the handle. He unlocked and opened the case, revealing an interior lined with pale blue moiré silk and fitted with many pockets and wide loops for holding things in place.

'Yes, a pre-war lady's dressing-case of very good quality. Nowadays you would only find this at Asprey's or Cartier. It might have been as much as five guineas when it was new. Now four or five hundred pounds would be nearer the mark.'

'Good gracious! As much as that? In that case it's much too valuable for me to borrow. Something might happen to damage it,' Laura said, shaking her head.

'I'm sure *you* are not a careless person, Miss Denham,' he said, with an approving glance at her neat appearance. 'There must be at least a dozen cases of this type stored here. I've no doubt her Ladyship will readily give her permission for you to borrow this one.'

As she felt sure this was true, and she didn't want to keep Mr Muirhead waiting, Laura stifled her scruples and took the case to her room. It didn't take her long to fill it with the few things she would need. Then she put on her outdoor clothes and went in search of her employer.

'**DM** – I wonder whose monogram that was?' said Jane Carlyon, after Laura had said apologetically that she hoped she hadn't been presumptuous in taking her permission for granted. 'No, of course I don't mind, Laura. I would have offered you one of my cases if you'd mentioned that you needed one. My small case would have been lighter for you to carry. Whoever **DM** was, I don't suppose *she* ever carried a suitcase. How would they survive in the modern world, those women who never even grappled with their own suspenders?' She saw that Laura was puzzled. 'Their maids put on their stockings for them. Unimaginable, isn't it? I shouldn't have liked that at all.'

She came to see Laura off and to say goodbye to Mr Muirhead until his next visit.

The architect's car was larger than the one Lady Carlyon referred to as her runabout. Until they came to the motorway it seemed to Laura that he was a less speedy driver than the energetic American girl.

However, once on the motorway the big solid car surged forward, beginning to sweep past other vehicles although, had there been no other traffic on the road, Laura wouldn't have guessed they were travelling at a high speed.

Content to sit in silence but feeling she ought to make an attempt at conversation and having the idea that cars were a favourite topic among men, she said, 'What a very comfortable car this is. I'm afraid I don't know much about them. Is it an English make?'

'Swedish . . . a Volvo,' he told her. 'My third Volvo. They wear well and they have an excellent safety record. Ask any fireman stationed near an accident black spot and he'll tell you that more people are got out of Volvos in one piece than from any other make of car. Talking of firemen, where is your house, Miss Denham? This side of London or the other?'

'On the northern side . . . Northwood Hills, between Ruislip and Watford. If you could drop me at or near Baker Street station there's a very good train service and my house is quite close to Northwood Hills Underground station.'

'I'll drop you outside your door. If you like I'll come in and take a look at the damage . . . give you my opinion of what the repairs are likely to cost you. It would only be a very rough estimate, of course.'

'It's very kind of you, but I couldn't possibly put you to that trouble. Northwood Hills is miles out of your way and – '

'It's no trouble. I have nothing in particular to do this evening. I shouldn't dream of dropping you at Baker Street with a case to carry. No arguments please,' he said firmly.

Laura thought how kind he was to put himself out for her.

'I suppose how to reduce fire risks in buildings is part of an architect's training,' she said.

'It's an important aspect of designing new buildings. In my view there isn't enough consultation with fire experts while buildings are still on the drawing board. As I don't deal with new buildings, I'm only concerned with reducing the danger of fire in existing properties.'

Laura said, 'The small case you put in the boot for me is borrowed from the luggage room at Longwarden. While I was there with Mr Flitton, he was saying how worried he is that some of the workmen may be careless about their cigarette ends. He told me he can't sleep at night unless he has personally inspected everywhere they've been working to check that they haven't left any smouldering stubs about.'

'I'm not surprised it worries him. A lot of bad fires have been started by discarded butts. Smoking causes millions of pounds of damage every year. Ideally, workmen shouldn't smoke on the job. But as it's difficult to stop them, the best we can do is to have plenty of sand buckets around and checks at the end of the day's work. Next to smoking comes arson. In fact arson may have overtaken smoking as the prime cause of fires. Unfortunately in recent years it's been what one could call a growth industry.'

'It's hard to understand how anyone could start a fire deliberately. It's such a *wicked* thing to do.'

'There are a lot of wicked people about, Miss Denham. Possibly more wicked people than good ones.'

'Oh, do you think so? I don't. I'm sure there are far more good people than bad in the world.' This was a subject she had argued with Miss Foxley and on which she could speak with confidence and conviction. 'Think how much life has improved in this country alone over the centuries. That could only have been achieved by good people working for the good of everyone.'

He took his eyes off the road for a moment to smile at her. 'I doubt if you've ever done anything wrong in your life, have you?'

His smile, and its effect on her, took her aback for a moment. She had seen him smile and laugh at the lunch table while chatting to Miss Lynn and Miss Lomax, but he had never smiled directly at Laura before. The gentle raillery of his question took her back to the time when her father had sometimes teased her, but always in a loving way.

'I don't think I've ever done anything illegal,' she answered. 'And perhaps I've never done anything *actively* wrong, but I certainly had some very unchristian thoughts about my previous employer when he was in his difficult moods.'

Mr Muirhead laughed. 'We all have those, except saints. Who was your last employer?'

\*

257

In the largest bedroom at *Las Golondrinas*, the Spanish farmhouse Piers Ashford had bought years ago when his first wife was alive and which had stood empty and neglected until he had brought Pen to live here, she was starting to pack.

Her feelings about returning to Longwarden were mixed. Many of the women she had met in Spain envied her the chance to leave it before the temperatures rose into the eighties and swarms of tourists descended on the coastal resorts, crowding the markets and restaurants and, on the *urbanizaciónes*, disturbing the all-year residents with their late and often drunken revelries.

It seemed that, if they could afford to, most expatriates went somewhere else for July and August. Those who had to stay complained that by mid-September they would be exhausted after having the house full of visitors who expected to be fed, taken shopping, taken to the beach and generally given a good time.

A few people enjoyed the heat of high summer. Ian Dalbeattie, a widower with whom Piers sometimes went snorkelling, liked the hottest months best. But he had spent his life in hot climates and when he went to the beach he swam out to deep water where the creatures he encountered lived in a silence broken only by the occasional drone of a pleasure cruiser or a power boat towing a water-skier.

When, at a recent dinner party, someone had remarked that the beach at Calpe in August was their idea of hell, he had retorted brusquely that if they bought a small boat they would find there were still plenty of coves they could have to themselves and, a few kilometres inland, peaceful places to walk.

'In the cooler months – yes. But one can't go for walks in August, old man. Too bloody hot,' said another man, causing Dalbeattie's bristling grey eyebrows to twitch disapprovingly at the use of that adjective in mixed company.

Although he looked a fit seventy, he was over eighty with attitudes fixed in his forties when the world had been a different place. Women, even if they found him intimidating, liked his old-fashioned courtesies. But, lacking Piers' ability to get on with most sorts of people, he wasn't liked by many men.

When Dalbeattie had first come to Spain, more than twenty years ago, modern tourism had been in its infancy. The comparatively small numbers of foreigners who had retired there because, apart from the good climate, the cost of living was low and there were still maids and gardeners to be found, had nearly all come from similar backgrounds and found each other congenial.

Many of them had been empire-builders; people who, after a lifetime of tropical postings with minions to wait on them, couldn't face growing old in Britain where servants were another dying breed and pensions didn't go as far as in Spain.

'You'd have liked it much better in those days,' Ian Dalbeattie had told Pen, the first time he had come to tea at *Las Golondrinas*.

'There were none of these eyesore developments which have ruined most of the coast, and no burglaries then – not in Franco's day! One didn't have to lock up one's house every time one went shopping, or lock the car when one went swimming. There were no big supermarkets and local shops didn't have all the imported stuff they stock nowadays. French cheese wasn't standard at dinner parties when my wife and I first came here. People sometimes brought cheese back from England, or from trips to France. It was a special treat – and enjoyed all the more for that reason.'

He had reminisced at some length, sitting on the Ashfords' *naya* overlooking the garden of wild mountain plants which Pen was beginning to create on the thin stony soil.

'You're looking rather glum, darling. What's the matter?' asked Piers, coming into their bedroom to find his wife standing beside the bed on which, a short time earlier, he had placed a large heavy leather suitcase, a relic of the days when travellers overseas did not expect to handle their baggage themselves.

'I was thinking about Ian Dalbeattie . . . how lonely he must be.'

'I daresay he is at times, but at least he's still in good health and can afford to run a car and send to London for the books he wants. He's happier here than he would be on his own in England, shut indoors much of the time.'

'I suppose so, but it must be awful being alone after a long happy marriage. I've only had you for a few months but I can't bear to contemplate being on my own again.'

Her husband came to where she was standing and put his arms round her. 'Nor can I,' he said softly. 'But I don't think it's something we need worry about yet. One can never take life or health for granted, but in the normal course of events you and I have a good many years of shared happiness ahead of us, my love. We don't smoke. Neither of us is overweight. We get plenty of exercise. With any luck we'll still be going strong in our eighties like Ian.'

'I hope so . . . I like the idea of spending the next thirty years with you.' Pen slipped her arms round his neck.

For some moments they stood lovingly embraced, smiling into each other's eyes. But their kiss although tender didn't lead to other kisses. He had already made love to her, first thing that morning. Now they had much to do in preparation for an early departure tomorrow.

As they had on their southbound honeymoon journey in March, they planned to motor slowly through France, spending at least six nights in country hotels.

When they drew apart, Pen to go to her clothes cupboards and Piers to his chest of drawers, she said over her shoulder, 'It's a pity we couldn't have had longer here before going back. We've barely had time to settle in. I must admit I'm rather loath to uproot myself so soon.'

'So am I in a way,' he agreed. 'But from what we're told it sounds as if it can be pretty disagreeable here in the high season. Unfortunately Spain doesn't attract the more discriminating tourists any more. According to Tom it's the dregs of Toulouse and Marseille who pour down here to fill up the camping sites, some of them paying for their hols with a few break-ins while they're here.'

Tom, the best man at their wedding, had lived in this part of Spain since leaving the Army. He had once been Piers' second in command and the two men were still close friends. But Pen found she had little in common with Marguerite Kilmartin. The lack of rapport between them was the only small flaw in her otherwise total contentment with her new life.

Whenever they were alone together, she found Marguerite a bore. A lot of the expats were bores but the others could be avoided. Marguerite couldn't. There was nothing for it but to show polite interest when she talked endlessly about her grandchildren, repeating their *mots* and showing the latest photographs of them.

Pen was interested, naturally, in the arrival of her own first grandchild but she didn't expect it to become her principal topic of conversation. She had her own life to lead now, and her son and her sweet daughter-in-law, though both dear to her, were on the circumference of it, no longer central figures.

'I think Tom made a mistake buying a newly-built "villa" on an *urbanización*,' she said, folding a silk shirt. 'Without exception, all the villas I've been into have been not only quite hideous but not very comfortable

261

either. Converted farmhouses, or small town houses like the Wimbornes' place are what most of the discriminating residents seem to have settled for.'

'If I had foreseen the way things would go I'd have bought one of the larger town houses which would have been going for a song then. There's a splendid old place for sale in Benissa, I hear. Quite imposing from the outside and positively palatial inside. There would be no need to worry about break-ins with a place like that, right in the heart of the town. I've no doubt there is plenty of crime in Madrid and Barcelona, but it doesn't seem to have spread to the smaller provincial towns yet.'

'But would it have much of a garden? I thought even the larger Spanish houses only had courtyards, not proper gardens?'

Piers smiled. 'You couldn't live without a proper garden, could you, my flower?'

Of all his endearments, this was the one she liked best, perhaps partly because she thought it was hers alone, not one he had used with his first wife. Pen wasn't jealous of Camilla Ashford. Already, in their short time together, Piers had amply demonstrated that his second marriage was as much a love match as his first, not merely a late-in-life marriage of convenience for the sake of having someone to talk to, which was what led some widowers and widows into partnership. She knew that he loved her passionately and saw her as beautiful and desirable even if to everyone else she looked a rather thin middle-aged woman with hair now more than half grey and wrinkles which would deepen more rapidly in this dry, dusty climate.

'I could bear it more easily now that I have you,' she told him. 'Probably a really large courtyard could be made into a charming garden, but, given a choice, I'd sooner have what we have here. I don't think we'll be broken into while we're away. This house is a long way off the main road and there are no other foreigners' houses along our lane. I can't see why a burglar should be tempted to come up here. Even if they do, the absence of a television aerial will suggest that there isn't anything worth stealing inside. What worries me more than the possibility of a break-in is whether the plants we've put in will survive the long drought.'

'The mountain plants definitely will. Whether the cardoons you brought from Longwarden will be flourishing remains to be seen.'

'I do hope so.'

The six foot tall, sometimes more, *Cynara cardunculus*, with its spectacular silver leaves and blue thistle-like heads was one of her favourite plants, both in borders and for flower arrangements.

'They grow wild in the *garigue* in France so I don't see why they shouldn't survive,' she said hopefully.

Piers looked at his watch. 'With any luck, this time tomorrow we'll have finished our first day's run and be holed up in some quiet French hostelry with a bottle of wine to restore us and a splendid dinner ahead of us.'

She looked up from her packing and smiled, knowing that he was remembering their journey south in March when, at the end of each day's run, they had made love as eagerly as honeymooners in their twenties.

Africa, where she had spent her first honeymoon, was forever associated in her mind with all manner of physical discomforts, from the red dust in which they were covered after each day's safari to the soreness inside her after Edward Carlyon's nightly penetrations of her dry vagina.

How different her memories of France! Delicious food. Double beds. Early nights with a man she adored who made love with a gentle ardour which left her feeling like a plant which had somehow managed to survive in all the wrong conditions but had now been transplanted to the right ones.

*

263

When Laura began to recognise familiar landmarks and realised they were nearly there, it surprised her to realise how easily and pleasantly the conversation had flowed for the last hour of the journey. They had talked almost non-stop, exchanging views on all manner of things. She couldn't remember talking at such length since . . . when? Not for years. Not since she was a child on one of the rare and treasured occasions when she had had her father to herself.

'It's the house with the silver birch in the garden,' she said, pointing it out as James Muirhead drove slowly along the street which had been her home for so many long dull empty years.

Although she had only been away for a short time, she felt as if she were returning after a much longer absence; as if it were months not weeks since she and Miss Foxley had walked sedately down the hill every morning to catch the 8.15.

Seen from the road, the house didn't look as if something traumatic had happened there just a few hours ago. The garden wasn't as well-kept as it had been when she left, and the brass fittings on the front door bore the tarnish of several weeks' neglect, but otherwise no one would have guessed that behind the peaceful façade lay a scene of recent destruction.

'Typical of its period. In another hundred years' time, if not before, these Thirties semi-detached will be having their internal details put back with as much enthusiasm as late Vic artisans' cottages are receiving now,' said James Muirhead, pausing to look at the exterior before he opened the gate for her.

Had she been on her own, long before now Laura would have had butterflies in her stomach at the thought of confronting Mr Washwood. His car was parked in the space between the garage and the double gates.

With Mr Muirhead to support her, she felt less apprehensive although still not looking forward to another meeting with a man she hadn't liked the first time she met him. If it hadn't been for his wife being so taken with the house, and so upset at having to leave her previous home, Laura wouldn't have agreed to let it to them.

'I thought you said he struck you as a bit of a bully? He seemed an inoffensive sort of chap to me,' said James Muirhead, as he opened the front passenger door of his car.

'His attitude was quite different today. I hardly recognised him as the same man. Perhaps he only puts on that unpleasant manner when there are no other men present,' said Laura. As he took his place behind the wheel, she added, 'There's a bed and breakfast place near here which I've heard is very clean and nice. If you could drop me there, I needn't delay you any more. I can't tell you how grateful I am for being brought right to the door and having you with me in there.'

'It's been a pleasure,' he said. 'But this bed and breakfast place sounds a bit dreary. Why not come into central London and have dinner with me? There's a small private hotel not far from my house. It's the sort of place where members of the Women's Institute stay when they come up to London for that annual rally or whatever that they hold at the Albert Hall. If you spend the night there you'll be close to the shops in the morning.'

Laura had thought that, after booking a room at the b & b place, she would walk back here to see Margaret and perhaps be invited to supper. Whatever their differences at the time of Laura's departure, Margaret would want to hear Laura's impression of the damage, and how the interview with the Washwoods had gone off.

But now that Mr Muirhead had asked her to have dinner with him, the prospect of an evening with Miss Foxley seemed even less attractive than it had before.

Could he really want her to dine with him? Was he just being kind because he felt sorry for her? Even if she hadn't bored him yet, wasn't it more than likely that she would if they spent a whole evening together?

Misinterpreting her hesitation, he said, 'But I was forgetting . . . you must have any number of friends in this area you want to look up.'

'Oh no, I hardly know anyone,' Laura replied. 'You see, I was out at work all day and in the evenings I had to keep my step-mother company. We didn't mix very much. She preferred watching television and I enjoyed reading. I – I'd like to have dinner with you.'

'Good. Let's be on our way then. I don't know about you, but I'm ready for a gin and tonic.'

'Whereabouts do you live, Mr Muirhead?' she asked, as the car moved off.

'In Connaught village. It isn't really a village, but Connaught Square is remarkably quiet considering that Edgware Road and Bayswater Road are only a stone's throw away. Connaught Street is very much like the high street in any small country town. We have a fishmonger, a newsagent, a florist, a chemist . . . all we lack is a baker and a post office. My house in the square was left to me by my grandmother. She was an amazing old girl.'

As they reached the end of the road he asked Laura which way to turn.

'You were talking about your grandmother,' she reminded him, when they were on the main road which would take them to the West End.

'Oh yes . . . Granny Blanche she was called, to distinguish her from Granny Mary, my mother's mother. Apart from being the same age, they couldn't have been less alike. Granny Mary lived in the country and devoted herself to good works and gardening. Granny Blanche never left London and spent her days playing the stock market – very successfully. When Capital Gains Tax

266

was announced, she said she might as well die as the Chancellor had taken all the fun out of her life. Three months later she did . . . leaving her house to me, her French furniture to my sisters and most of her money to the couple who had looked after her, on condition they went on caring for her three white Pekinese.'

'I should think they were delighted to, weren't they?'

Laura wondered if he and his sisters had been annoyed that the old lady had left her money outside the family. Perhaps they were generous-minded people who felt the legacy had been deserved and were satisfied with what they had received.

Bryan and Joanne had been furious when they found out that their mother hadn't left the house to them because it had never belonged to her. It was Laura's property, left to her by her father with the provision that his second wife should have the use of it for life or until she remarried.

Robert Denham couldn't have foreseen that a house which had cost him £7,000 in 1969 would now fetch over £100,000. But perhaps he had guessed that generosity would not be one of the primary characteristics of his step-children when they grew up. Laura felt certain that if the house had been Mrs Denham's to dispose of it would have gone to her children who would certainly not have allowed Laura to continue living in it, or felt she deserved a share of the proceeds when they sold it.

'Yes, they were – and we were equally delighted not to have had the spoilt little brutes left in our care,' he answered. 'Fortunately the Larkhills put some of the money into a house in the country because, even though it was sensibly invested, the rest of the capital isn't now the handsome nest-egg it seemed at the time. The French furniture has appreciated in value and of course my house has rocketed. My grandmother would be astounded if she knew what the houses in the square are fetching today.'

'It's amazing to me how many people seem able to afford the huge sums which houses in London fetch now,' said Laura. 'I know houses in the best areas are always expensive, but surely never as exorbitant as they are at present?'

They continued to discuss property values until he said, 'Here we are and for once there's no problem parking.' With the expertise of experience he tucked the car into a space she would have thought was too small for it.

Surrounded by Georgian houses overlooking the grass and trees of a garden enclosed by black railings, the square was like scores of others in all parts of central London. Laura had often walked through similar squares, admiring the elegant proportions of the houses and wishing it had been her destiny to live with tall windows with shutters inside them instead of with imitation leaded lights.

'We'll have a drink first and then on the way to *Knoodles* we'll book you in at the hotel,' said James Muirhead, locking the car.

From the moment she stepped inside his house everything she looked at was so beautiful that, even more than before, she was embarrassed by the ugliness of her house which he wasn't to know didn't represent her own taste.

Here were no garish patterns, no ill-chosen ornaments, no prints of well-known masterpieces in plastic imitations of antique gilt frames. The flowers were real, fresh or dried, the pictures originals in simple frames, the cushions larger and softer than her step-mother's hard little scatter cushions. Instead of the unread, matched set of Dickens in shiny leather-type bindings which filled one shelf of the fitment housing the TV in the lounge at Northwood Hills, in James Muirhead's first floor drawing room there were hundreds of books, some of them stacked on tables and stools because there was no space left on the packed bookshelves.

'What a lovely room,' Laura exclaimed.

She wondered if he or his wife had chosen the striped cotton, like old-fashioned mattress ticking, which loose-covered several chairs, and the pale honey-coloured material of the long full curtains held back by tasselled cords.

'Thank you. Let me take your coat.' He helped her to remove it, putting it over the back of a chair and asking, 'What would you like to drink?'

Before she could reply the telephone rang.

'Excuse me.' He went to answer it. 'Hello?' After listening for several moments, he said, 'She's here with me now. I'll put her on. It's Lady Carlyon, Miss Denham.'

'I've been worried about you. I hoped Mr Muirhead would give you his moral support,' said the Countess when she heard Laura's voice. 'Is the damage very bad?'

While Laura was telling her about it, James Muirhead, now standing by a drinks table, lifted a bottle of gin and raised his eyebrows enquiringly. She nodded but signalled with her finger and thumb that she would like a small measure.

'Lady Carlyon said she was worried about me,' she told him, when the call was over. 'She's such a warm person . . . always so kind and considerate. It's not surprising everyone likes her.'

'Yes, Lord Carlyon is a lucky chap.' He handed her a glass with ice and a slice of lemon in it. 'I hope nothing goes wrong for them. At the moment they seem to have everything life has to offer. Let's hope the gods don't get jealous and lob out some nasty comeuppance.'

She thought it a strange remark to come from a man. While he was ringing the restaurant to book a table, she wondered if it had been prompted by whatever circumstance had put an end to his marriage. Whether it had been death or divorce wasn't known and naturally no one would ask him.

'Would it be advisable to ring the hotel as well?' she asked, as he replaced the receiver.

He nodded and looked up the number. Some minutes later, when the first hotel and another he knew of had proved to be full up, he said wryly, 'Perhaps I've done you a disservice bringing you into the centre.'

'The more expensive hotels may not be as full,' said Laura. 'I should think one night in London might be considered a necessary expense by my insurers.'

When two more telephone calls had failed to produce a room for her, he said, 'This is becoming a bore. Look, I have a comfortable spare bed. Why not stay here?'

Laura couldn't think of anything she would like more than to spend a night in this beautiful house, but she felt it would be far too much of an imposition.

'Perhaps it would worry you,' he said. 'The young think nothing of putting up with friends of the opposite sex, but you may feel it's not your style. Don't be afraid to say so. I shan't be offended. It just seems to me the simplest solution to the problem.'

The propriety of staying the night hadn't struck her. She was nervous of men she didn't know in places where she could be attacked, but it wouldn't have occurred to her that someone like Mr Muirhead would make advances to her. Even when she was young she hadn't been attractive to men, and now that she was middle-aged . . .

'It wouldn't worry me,' she said, 'but it's such a nuisance for you . . . making up a bed and so on.'

He grinned. 'I'll let you do that – and cook your own breakfast. That's settled then. You'll stay here. I expect you'd like to wash before we go out. I'll nip down and fetch your case and then show you your room.'

While he was gone she wandered about the drawing room, looking at all the interesting things it contained.

She couldn't quite believe she was here, drinking gin, about to be taken out to dinner and later to spend the night in one of the houses she had often longed to see inside. Who would have thought that from the disaster of the fire would come the realisation of a day-dream?

It wasn't long before Mr Muirhead reappeared and showed her where she was to sleep. His spare room was furnished with twin beds and had its own bathroom where she washed her face and hands and, on impulse, changed her blouse for the clean one she had packed to wear tomorrow.

All her blouses were white or cream with tie-necks or revers and real mother-of-pearl buttons she sewed on herself with silk because with machine-sewn buttons the thread soon worked itself loose. Her blouses weren't smart: that wasn't their purpose. She dressed to look neat and efficient. But now, as she combed her hair, she couldn't help wishing she had something dressier to wear. Not that Mr Muirhead was likely to notice what she wore, but a nice dress and a piece of jewellery – a string of pearls or a brooch – would have boosted her confidence. The last time she had eaten in a restaurant at night was with Bernard, years ago. She hoped the place she was going to with Mr Muirhead wasn't too smart and sophisticated. But no, he was much too thoughtful to take her somewhere where she would feel out of place, as she often had with Bernard. Of course she had been younger then, more easily awed by haughty head waiters who seemed to guess that she didn't know what half the dishes on the menu were and hadn't the courage to ask.

I was more like a girl of seventeen than a woman of twenty-seven, she thought with a sigh for the total inexperience of life and men which had made her such easy game when a practised womaniser had made a determined set at her.

When she went down to the drawing room, she found

that Mr Muirhead had also changed from the country tweeds and one of the Tattersall-checked shirts he wore on his visits to Longwarden. But he hadn't put on a city suit. He was casually dressed in a pink shirt under a dark brick-red cotton top of the kind people wore for jogging. His trousers were silvery-grey corduroy and in place of brown brogues he had a pair of slip-on shoes similar to the ones Lady Carlyon wore with trousers.

Holding Laura's coat for her, he said, 'I hope you like pasta. As you'd expect, most of the dishes at *Knoodles* are pasta-based. I eat there about once a fortnight and the same at our local French place. Most weekends I have a meal with my tenants or they come and eat with me. The rest of the time I cook for myself. There's a very good branch of Safeways not far up Edgware Road, or sometimes, if I'm feeling extravagant, I go to the Marble Arch branch of Marks and Sparks and buy one of their ready-made meals. Foodwise, do you find life a lot easier at Longwarden? Or was cooking something you enjoyed?'

'I've enjoyed it more since I've been on my own,' said Laura, as they went down the stairs. 'My step-mother had digestive problems and had to have food which wasn't very interesting to cook. Since she died I've been able to experiment and I think I could like cooking very much. But of course the food at Longwarden is wonderful and it is a great luxury having delicious food served three times a day without any effort on my part.'

At one end of the square was Connaught Street with the village-y atmosphere he had described to her. At the far end she could see the tall trees of another square and about halfway down on the right was a pub with chairs and tables set on the pavement outside it. Although they had had their ground floors altered to accommodate businesses, above the shop fronts the buildings lining the street retained the façades of Regency houses with small graceful wrought-iron balconies outside some of the windows.

*Knoodles* was very small with shop-type plate glass windows on either side of the door. As Laura mounted the steps and saw the people at the window tables glancing at the newcomers, she was surprised to find that she didn't feel the flutter of nervousness she had always experienced when entering a restaurant with Bernard.

Perhaps the gin and tonic had had a calming effect, or perhaps it was merely that, being older and wiser, she knew now that most people were far too preoccupied with their own problems and shortcomings to look critically at her.

The staff here were friendly youngsters. After they had looked at the menu, Mr Muirhead said, 'It's rather elbow-to-elbow here but when I'm alone I find that an advantage. One can tune in to one's neighbours' conversations. It's extraordinary the things some people say in public places. I've heard them confiding details I wouldn't discuss with a close friend in private.'

'I find that very strange too,' she agreed. 'Sometimes, at the office where I worked before, I would go to the cloakroom and find the young girls discussing the most amazing things.'

The memory of a particular conversation brought a tinge of pink to her cheeks even in retrospect. At the time it had made her blush scarlet, embarrassment making her sound like a real old vinegar bottle as she told the girls they weren't being paid to spend their time gossiping.

'Perhaps you and I are both a bit old-fashioned,' he said, smiling at her. 'But I think it would be rather stuffy to go on using each other's surnames. Would you mind if I called you Laura?'

'Not at all. Please do . . . James.' She felt her blush deepen a tinge and wondered if he could see it in the soft light from the candles. She hoped not.

With their *tagliatelle verde* and salad, they drank red wine. By the time they had had a sweet and coffee the bottle was empty. Laura hoped she hadn't drunk too much. Two glasses was her usual limit and tonight she had had at least three on top of the gin.

'Do you feel like a short stroll?' he asked, while the bill was being made out.

Instead of answering his question, she said, 'I hope you will let me share the bill, James.'

'Certainly not. This isn't one of the smart joints where three shrimps, an artistic radish and some slivers of carrot marinaded in absinthe cost an arm and a leg.'

She saw that he was not to be argued with and made a mental note to find some way to return his kindness.

'You suggested a stroll . . . is it all right to walk about here at night?' she asked, as they left the warmth of the restaurant for the cooler air outside.

'I've never seen anything to put me off stretching my legs after supper.' He put his hand on her arm to steer her across the road. 'I did hear a rumour that someone had been mugged in the grounds of some blocks of flats, but in general it's a quiet neighbourhood – apart from the occasional drunk roaring noisily home in the small hours.'

'It seems to me we see less of that husband of yours here than we did in London,' Mrs Baston said fretfully, turning off the sound of a commercial break. 'What's he up to at this time of night? He can't be cooking at this hour.'

'There's a lot to do besides the actual cooking, Mum, and you know he doesn't like watching television,' said Lucy.

'It's what most people do in the evenings,' said her mother, reaching for a chocolate.

'Not so much in the summer. It's light till after nine now. Maybe Joël went for a jog.'

'He can't be jogging at this hour. His place is with you . . . keeping you company. He neglects you, that's the fact of the matter. You shouldn't stand for it, Lucy. You should tell him.'

'Oh Mum . . . don't start going on. Joël has a lot to put up with. Let him do what he likes in his free time. He's a young active man. He needs exercise. I can't go for walks with him . . . I can't do anything with him,' she added glumly.

'That isn't your fault, is it? He married you for better or worse. It's his *duty* to spend time with you. If you ask me – ' Mrs Baston paused. Perhaps it would be better not to say what was in her mind until tomorrow when there would be no possibility of being interrupted by her son-in-law.

'Well, go on,' Lucy prompted.

Gladys wiped the corners of her mouth with the tip of her little finger. 'I don't want to upset you, dear, but I think he may be spending too much of his time with that Lynn girl. If you want me to be honest, I wouldn't put it past her to be setting her cap at him.'

'Whatever makes you think that?'

'I overheard two of the cleaning ladies discussing it when I was in the house a few days ago. They stopped talking the minute I came round the corner. I could see they were embarrassed in case I'd heard what they were saying. Well, I had. They'd been agreeing what a lot of time Mr Vibrac spent in the kitchen garden with Miss Lynn.'

'I expect he does,' Lucy said calmly. 'He's mad about vegetables, you know that. I should think he's chatting about vegetables, not chatting her up.'

'I should hope not,' said Mrs Baston. 'He's a married man. He has no business to be chatting up anyone. But how do we know what her principles are? She may not have any. She may fancy him and see no reason why she shouldn't have him. Girls do have affairs with other people's husbands.'

'Why should she pick on Joël? I expect she's got plenty of boyfriends in London without making eyes at him. The show's on again now, Mum.' They were watching a weekly comedy show.

'I don't think much of it tonight,' said Mrs Baston, who had the remote control on the arm of her chair. 'I think it's more important to talk about this. Why should she make eyes at him, you ask. For a start he's a Frenchman, a novelty. Frenchmen have a reputation for being hot-blooded, haven't they? She may fancy that. She looks an over-sexed girl.'

'I don't know what makes you say that. I like her. I think she's quite nice.'

'You won't like her when she's taken your husband away from you,' her mother said ominously. 'You're in a very vulnerable position, Lucy. An invalid wife hasn't the hold on her husband that a normal wife has, and I'm not speaking just of the intimate side of married life. She can't keep an eye on him the same. It stands to reason a man whose wife's in a wheelchair has a lot more opportunities to get up to things he shouldn't.'

'So what do you think I should do? Ask Joël if he's seeing too much of her? If he isn't – if it's perfectly innocent – it might put the idea in his head.'

'You should try to keep him with you more. Ask him where he's been and what he's been doing when he comes in. Don't take it for granted he's been working or jogging. Ask him.'

'I don't see what good that will do. If he's got something to hide, I'll be forcing him to tell lies. Personally I don't think Damaris Lynn is interested in Jöel, but if she is and it's mutual there's nothing I can do about it. If you want the truth, I think it's inevitable that Joël is going to have a woman on the side sooner or later. I've

276

accepted that. There's a lot of things I have to accept. Now will you put the sound on, please. It's not as funny as last week but it's better than talking about things which only depress me.'

Lucy spoke with unusual firmness and her mother did as she was asked. But although they appeared to be watching the action of the screen, neither of them was paying attention.

Mrs Baston was wishing they had never come to the country, not because of her suspicions about her son-in-law but because she didn't like it at Longwarden. It was too isolated. She had never lived so far from the shops . . . such few shops as there were in the village. The nearest shops you could call shops were twelve miles away in Melchester and the bus service there and back was terrible.

But it was more than the isolation of Longwarden which was getting her down; it was the thought of continuing to care for Lucy for years on end. It wasn't right, thought Gladys, that at her time of life she should be burdened with all this nursing. It was too much; she wasn't sure how much longer she could stand it.

In the past Joël had accused her of doing too much for her daughter. Perhaps he was right. Perhaps she had. At first she'd been glad to help them. It had been her duty as a mother and nothing had been too much trouble for her. Everyone she knew told her what a tower of strength she had been, and Lucy herself had been more grateful, more appreciative.

Now she seemed to take it all for granted and Gladys was beginning to feel put upon. If they hadn't had her to call on, they would have had to manage somehow. As things were they seemed to assume that she was at their beck and call forever.

Unaware of her mother's smouldering resentment, Lucy was wondering how much truth, if any, there was in the gossip she had overheard.

Was it true that she had accepted Joël's infidelity as inevitable? How could she tell what she would feel until it happened?

What did worry her was the idea, raised by her mother, that he might not stop at having a discreet affair. Under pressure from the other woman he might decide to leave her.

Without Joël, what would her future hold? Nothing. As long as she was his wife – even if only in name – she had a place in the world, something to cling to. If he left her, she might as well be dead.

It took James and Laura about ten minutes to walk round by Bayswater Road, where taxis and other traffic still shuttled busily past the railinged acres of Hyde Park, and back to the door of his house through the other end of the square. On her own she wouldn't have liked it, but with him she felt safe.

'What time do you usually go to bed?' he asked, unlocking the door.

The ground floor shutters were closed now, she noticed, with light showing through the chinks. One or both of the young married doctors who occupied his ground floor must be in. She wouldn't be surprised if the rent he charged them was far below what he could ask for the flat. Remarks he had made during dinner had reinforced her impression that he was a good man, one who cared about people, not like Bernard who hadn't cared for anyone but himself.

'Quite early, but usually I read until half past ten or eleven,' she answered, as he stood aside to let her enter the house first. 'What about you?'

'I don't need a lot of sleep. Usually I sit up till midnight, reading or listening to music. If I were you I shouldn't turn in too early tonight or you may lie awake worrying about the fire. Let's have a nightcap, shall we, and I'll play you my new record. That's if it wouldn't bore you. Not everyone shares my taste for classical guitar music.'

'I'd like that very much,' said Laura, 'but as I've already had rather a lot of alcohol for me, may I make myself a cup of tea?'

'I'll make the tea while you make your bed up,' he said. 'You'll find plenty of bed linen on the shelves in the cupboard and there's an electric blanket under the mattress cover. Switch it to four, then the bed will be warm when you go up. You needn't worry about the mattress not being aired. My Portuguese home help airs both beds every week when she cleans the place for me.'

Upstairs Laura hung up her coat and found the neat stacks of top sheets, fitted bottom sheets and pillowcases. There were two sets for each bed and she chose the grey-and-white stripes with ruffles round the edges of the pillow-slips. The other set had apricot sprigs, both sets tying in with the bedroom's peach and grey décor.

His choice or his wife's? she wondered. Or a scheme worked out by them both, before whatever had happened to remove her and leave him alone. Somehow she couldn't believe that his marriage had ended in divorce. Yet hadn't her father married unwisely the second time? Good intelligent men did make terrible mistakes, choosing women who made them unhappy and even, in some cases, were unfaithful to them.

She had just finished making the bed when James came up to ask how she liked her tea. Going downstairs with him, Laura found that his kitchen was very different from the one which was now a charred wreck at the back of her house.

Mrs Denham had had the kitchen modernised with fitted units faced with laminated plastic, practical but not cosy. James' kitchen had a pine dresser, a red Aga and paintings of cats on the walls.

'I think it's a poor sort of kitchen which doesn't have

279

a geranium on the window-sill and a cat asleep on a chair,' he said, with a smile. 'But I can't have a cat at the moment as I'm not always here to feed it.'

Before he put on his record, he looked along a shelf housing oversize books to find one which he said would enhance her enjoyment of the music.

Sitting in a lamp-lit wing chair in his tranquil drawing room with a cup of weak tea beside her and a book of superb colour photographs of Spain spread on her lap, Laura felt even happier than she had earlier. Nice as the restaurant was, it had become a little crowded and noisy by the time they left. Here in this lovely room, with the music beginning and James settling himself comfortably in a large armchair, was the quiet companionship she had always longed for. Of course it was only for this one evening and would never happen again, but even a taste of heaven was better than nothing.

The telephone rang. James frowned and stretched out his arm.

'Hello?' he said, a touch brusquely. 'Oh Louise . . . hold on a minute, will you? I'll speak on the other phone.'

As he rose to leave the room, Laura asked, 'Would you like me to replace this receiver when you've picked up the other one?'

'No, don't disturb yourself. I shan't be long. Sorry for the interruption.'

He went away, leaving her to wonder who Louise was. One of the sisters he had mentioned, perhaps.


The next morning Sarah had a call from a women's magazine which wanted to do an illustrated feature about her.

When she told them she had two horses laid up and was going on holiday, they wanted to make arrangements to come down and take photographs as soon as

280

she came back. In the end she had to tell them that she didn't like publicity and, not being sponsored, was in a position to avoid it.

'What about your fans, Miss Lomax? Don't you think you owe them something?' the woman from the magazine asked rather huffily.

'Not really . . . no,' said Sarah. 'I'm not like an actress or a pop singer. I don't depend on fans to keep me going. I'm flattered that you think your readers would be interested in me, but I do find that being interviewed and photographed is awfully time consuming and quite honestly I'd rather be doing other things.'

After her call to Longwarden, Cheryl Clitheroe, deputy features editor on *Her World* dialled the number of the national newspaper where she had worked as a fashion page assistant until six months ago.

When the switchboard put her through to the extension she wanted, she said, 'Ronnie? It's Cheryl. I've just talked to Sarah Lomax. She doesn't want to know about being featured in the magazine. She claims not to like publicity, but she didn't seem to mind it last year after she won her gold medal. I thought she sounded embarrassed and nervous . . . that she has got something to hide. If I were you I'd go down there and snout about. If she is preggers, someone will know.'

'Thanks, Cheryl. Thanks a lot.'

'Any time. Best of luck.'

As she replaced the receiver, she felt a slight twinge of conscience. For the year their affair had lasted Ronnie had given her a good time, and what were old friends for if not to do each other favours? But had it been right to help him in his enquiries about the Lomax girl?

In what was still largely a man's world, women had to stick together, too. Maybe she shouldn't have agreed to test the young eventer's reaction to a proposed interview. If the rumour Ronnie was working on turned out to be true, his paper would crucify the girl, and not only her but the guy responsible for her condition. God help his wife, if he were married. Everyone involved in the scandal would have all their secrets exposed to public view. There was no one better at dishing the dirt than Ronnie, once he got his teeth into a story.

After Cheryl's call, Ronnie left his desk and took the lift to the newspaper library. There he was given a large manila envelope, containing every story the paper had run about Longwarden and the Lomax family as far back as the Second World War. All the pre-war files had been burned in the Blitz.

The most recent clippings included stories about the previous Countess' marriage to her butler who had turned out to be an ex-Army officer; the present Earl's marriage to an American heiress; a description of the no-expense-spared ball given by them in December, and several short filler paragraphs about a cleaner at Longwarden, Mavis Osgood. It seemed that Mrs Osgood had been shop-lifting in a big way. The police had found stolen goods to the value of £5,000 hidden in her house in Longwarden village. She would have been sent to prison but for the fact that her only son had been killed in a motorcycle crash shortly before her arrest. For that reason the magistrates had let her off with a fine and two years' probation.

Wonder where she is now? Ronnie thought. It seemed a reasonable assumption that the woman would not have continued to live in the village once she had been exposed as a professional thief. Shouldn't take long to find out, was his next thought. The police will have her on their data base. Wherever she is, she's probably short of cash. It shouldn't cost much to get her to spill all she knows about Sarah's love life.

*

Laura stood in a cubicle on Selfridges fashion floor, gazing doubtfully at her reflection in the fitting room mirror.

In place of her discreet white blouse she was wearing a bright red one, the shoulders fitted with large pads. It was very much like a blouse she had seen in *Knoodles* last night. The fact that its wearer had been considerably older than herself, but had not looked like mutton dressed as lamb, had encouraged Laura to think that perhaps she too could aspire to a little more dash, at least outside working hours.

However, although a very similar blouse had looked well on the older woman, setting off her crisp steel-grey hair and olive complexion, the bright colour did nothing for Laura. Nor did she feel at ease with the wide self-confident shoulders.

'I'm afraid it's not me,' she replied, when a sales-woman looked round the curtain and asked her, 'How is it?'

'Oh dear . . . are you sure? I think it looks very good on you. What it needs is a matching lipstick and some nice gold ear-rings. It's a very fashionable colour. Joan Collins was wearing a blouse just like that on *Dynasty* the other night.'

'In that case it's definitely not me,' Laura said dryly.

'Why not try it in the blue? That could be a better colour for you . . . not as hard as the red. Let me see if we've got it in your size.'

Before Laura could refuse, the saleswoman whisked away to return with a selection of blouses.

But Laura, for long too biddable for her own good, was becoming a little less so. Having looked at the blouses in turn, she said firmly, 'No, thank you, I don't really like any of them and' – with a glance at her watch – 'I'm running out of shopping time.'

This was a white lie. James was working at home this morning. After lunch he was going to run her to the coach station on the way to his office. She would have to get a taxi at the other end but she ought to be back at Longwarden in good time for the evening meal. Meanwhile she had two more hours in Oxford Street where she hoped to find something to liven up the dullness of her wardrobe.

Leaving the fashion floor by the central escalator brought her down to the book department where she browsed for about half an hour before choosing a hardback for James and some paperbacks for herself, an assistant having assured her that her friend could change it if he didn't like the book she had chosen for him.

By the time she walked back to Connaught Square she had bought herself a pair of ear-rings and a slightly more vivid lipstick – not as bright as the red silk blouse – but the clothes she had wanted had eluded her.

'What! No parcels to speak of?' said James, when he opened the door. 'I expected to see you laden like a beast of burden. After a morning in London my sisters are always bowed down.'

Smiling, she shook her head. 'I couldn't find what I wanted.'

'That's disappointing. What were you looking for?'

'I'm not really sure . . . something different . . . a little smarter. I felt I should know it when I saw it, but I didn't see it.'

'I like the ear-rings.'

She had put them on in the shop, twists of gilt rather larger than the pearl studs she usually wore.

'How observant of you to notice,' she said, blushing under his scrutiny.

'I've been trained to notice details. A study of buildings leads to a study of people . . . at least in appearance, not necessarily in depth. I'm no great student of human nature but I notice people's looks and clothes. You're always extremely neat and well-groomed – the antithesis of the woman who follows the current craze for looking crumpled and wind-blown. Sometimes, looking at my sisters' glossy magazines, I wonder how women can let themselves be conned into spending large sums of money on hairstyles which make them look as if they've been out in a gale. However, my teenage nieces tell me I'm out of touch,' he added dryly.

Laura laughed. 'That makes two of us. I don't care for those wild hairstyles either. Not everyone young goes in for them. Lady Carlyon has beautiful hair, and so do Miss Lomax and Miss Lynn.'

'They are all girls of strong character and discriminating taste,' he said. 'Generally speaking it's the less intelligent woman who's the most susceptible to being conned by the poufters in the smart salons.'

He had come up the staircase behind her and as, on reaching the first floor landing, she glanced at him, she thought he looked faintly embarrassed by his last remark. Did he think he had shocked her? Did she seem prudish to him?

'I'm not sure it's lack of intelligence which makes people follow fashion,' Laura said thoughtfully, as they entered the drawing room. 'Don't you think that a lot of people aren't very sure of themselves and being fashionable boosts their confidence? The younger they are the more they need to be like everyone else . . . to conform to whatever is "trendy".'

'I can see you take a kinder view of human foibles than I do. My . . . I used often to be told that I was intolerant and it may be that I'm getting worse as I get older. I must watch it. Let me give you a glass of sherry.'

'Thank you.'

It could be that she had misheard, thought Laura as she sat down. Perhaps he hadn't said 'My' before 'I'. But she felt almost certain he had and that it had been 'my wife' who had chided him for his intolerance.

As well as vacuuming and dusting, his Portuguese weekly woman, who was still at work upstairs, had put

285

potatoes in the oven and made a salad for their lunch. The smoked trout and the Brie to follow it had been fetched by James from the supermarket. As he was going to drive he drank non-alcoholic beer but insisted on Laura having a glass of white wine.

It wasn't until just before they left for the coach station that she gave him the book.

'This is just a small token of how grateful I am for your kindness,' she told him shyly. 'If it isn't a book which appeals to you, Selfridges say they will change it.'

'My dear girl ... this is quite unnecessary ... but how very nice of you, and how well-chosen. I wanted to read this when I read the reviews a couple of weeks ago, but I haven't been into a bookshop since then and I might have jibbed at the price and decided to wait for the paperback. Much as I deplore your extravagance, I'm delighted with it. Thank you.'

All the way back on the coach, 'My dear girl' and the warm look in his eyes interfered with her concentration on one of the paperbacks. In the end she gave up trying to read and sat gazing out of the window, reliving all that had happened since this time yesterday.


The first time Damaris saw him he was sitting astride a motor-bike outside the gate of the house where she lived.

She didn't take any notice of him until he said, ''Allo, Tiffany. You're looking good.'

To hear herself called by that name after so long was a terrible shock.

'Don't you recognise me?' he said. 'I've changed more than you 'ave I s'pose. I were still a kid when you left. I'm Gary ... your cousin Gary.'

Damaris recovered herself. 'I'm afraid you've made a mistake. My name isn't Tiffany and I've never seen you before,' she said with freezing hauteur.

For a moment he looked disconcerted. Clearly he hadn't expected her voice to have lost all trace of his own strong accent.

Then, in the same way that she had hurriedly pulled herself together a few seconds earlier, he dismissed the momentary doubt with a laugh and a confident, 'Come off it! Pull the other one. Okay, you've changed your name and you talk lah-di-dah now but you can't fool me, Tiff. I'd have known you anywhere.'

His certainty made her feel sick. She recognised him now, seeing in this cocky young man of twenty the traces of a younger face. Of all her cousins he had been the one she liked least. A real life Artful Dodger was Gary Clutton. Even at ten he had looked at the world with a shrewd and sly eye to the main-chance. If he were running true to form, by now he was probably either the master-mind of a gang of football hooligans or pushing drugs to school kids. She couldn't imagine how he had managed to find her but she knew already why he had come looking for her. It could only be because he intended to put the pressure on. What she had always dreaded had happened at last. Her past had caught up with her.

'I'm afraid you're mistaken,' Damaris repeated coldly. 'I have no idea what you're talking about.'

She walked past her cousin and entered the garden, closing the gate behind her without giving him another glance. But as she felt for her key her hand was shaking and she fumbled her first attempt to fit it in the lock.

Once inside the house, she leaned against the closed door feeling her heart pounding with nervous reaction. How had the little swine found her? How much would he try to squeeze out of her? What would he threaten her with? Exposure, obviously. But exposure to whom? How long had he known where she lived? How long had be been watching her come and go? For all she knew he might have been shadowing her on her journeys about London for some time. The West End was full of motor cyclists dodging their way through the traffic jams, providing an express delivery service for urgent packages. In their leathers and boots and crash helmets they all looked alike to her. She might have noticed a car following her, but not a dark-visored figure on a motorbike.

Having climbed the stairs to her flat, she took a cautious peep from the window overlooking the street. He was still there, smoking a cigarette. What if he came to the door and rang not her bell but her landlord's? Did he *know* she had changed her name or had that been a guess? If he did know, did he also know what her new name was? Might he use it to inveigle his way into the house?

Perhaps the best thing to do would be to ring the police now; to take them into her confidence. 'I need your help. Ten years ago I ran away from home because I was being molested by my foster-mother's common law husband. Now one of my cousins has turned up and I think he's going to try some blackmail. Can you make him leave me alone? I haven't done anything wrong. I just don't want people to know the sort of background I come from.'

If she told them that, would they help her? Or would they say, 'Sorry, miss, there's nothing we can do until a crime has been committed.'

Even if they were prepared to help and send Gary packing, he might shop her out of spite. There had always been a vicious streak in his nature. The year before she ran away he had been involved in a case brought by the RSPCA against four boys accused of killing nestlings by dropping lighted matches into their gaping beaks.

The two eldest boys had been sent to Borstal for what the magistrate had described as 'one of the most

288

despicable crimes ever to come before this court'. A third boy and Gary had claimed to be reluctant spectators, too scared of being victimised themselves to protest at the cruelty. They had been given the benefit of the doubt. In Tiff's mind and those of most people who knew him well, it was more likely to have been Gary who had thought of torturing the birds and the others who had gone along with it. He had certainly inflicted physical and mental cruelties on his siblings from time to time.

He had never tried bullying his cousin because she was bigger then he was. At ten he had been undersized; a thin, pale-faced boy with a naturally shifty expression over which he could, when he chose, superimpose a look of angelic innocence.

Now he looked to be as tall as she, with a shock of dirty-looking hair coiling greasily onto the collar of his jacket, and pustules of acne disfiguring a face which would not have been pleasing even without the spots.

As she watched him from the top floor, Damaris saw him throw away his cigarette and put on his helmet. A few moments later, after some unnecessary revving which could have been intended for her to hear or might merely be showing off, he rode away.

His departure didn't make her mind easier. She had no doubt he would be back. Or he might reappear somewhere else, at a time and place where he could cause her serious embarrassment.

What she was most afraid of was that he would seek out her mother and, if Shirl were still on the game, use her as his principal threat. Damaris felt that her clients might not care very much that she came from what in social workers' jargon was now called a disadvantaged background. But would they want the keys of their houses to be in the hands of the daughter of a prostitute?

*

'You might talk to me sometimes, Joël. You hardly say a word to me these days,' Lucy said plaintively.

He had gone out at first light to run in the park. Now, having showered, he was dressing to go to the house and cook breakfast for the family.

'It's a bit early in the morning for sparkling conversation, don't you think? We never did have much to say to each other at this hour.'

'I suppose not. But we talked at other times of day. I thought when we came here I'd see more of you, but it's not working out that way.'

'I'm not in a nine to five job, Lucy. In some ways being a chef in private service is more demanding than working in a busy restaurant. There it's team work. Here it's just me and two half-trained assistants. It'll ease up as time goes on. The first few months in a job are always the hardest. I've got to go now. See you later.'

He bent over the bed to brush a light kiss on her cheek. A few moments later she heard the outer door bang.


'Mr Muirhead will be here tomorrow.'

The Countess' casual remark, as she looked at her desk diary made Laura's heart leap in a most foolish way.

She didn't want to admit how much she was looking forward to seeing James again. The days which, before she went to London, had passed in an even succession, all of them equally pleasant, were now days to be crossed off, figuratively, on the calendar; each one bringing her closer to the day of James' next visit.

After the night spent at Connaught Square, she had tried to convince herself that her response to his kindness was no more than ordinary gratitude and pleasure at finding him so easy to get on with. Deep down, however, she had known that at some point in the time she had spent with him she had begun to fall in love.

But she wasn't yet headlong in love. If she had any sense, she told herself firmly, she never would be. Because however kind he might be to her, the chances of a man like James Muirhead losing his heart to Laura Denham were so slight as to be non-existent.

The thing to do was to nip her tender feelings in the bud. If she didn't, the only outcome would be a great deal of pain. Having suffered before, she had no wish to be hurt a second time.

Nevertheless, whatever commonsense dictated, it wasn't easy to quash the pleasurable excitement which welled up inside her, unbidden, as soon as she woke up next morning and knew that in a few hours the Volvo would be turning in at the main gates.


Deliberately, Laura delayed her arrival in the dining room so that there was little likelihood of finding herself alone with James.

Both he and Lord Carlyon rose as she entered the room, the lastcomer. James left his place to pull out the vacant chair for her.

'Hello. How are you?' he said, smiling.

'Very well, thank you. And you?' she asked with formal politeness, seating herself and repeating her thanks as he pushed in the chair.

'I'm fine.' He went back to his chair on the other side of Damaris Lynn.

On Laura's left was Miss Lomax who paused to say hello to her before continuing to talk to the Earl about her horses.

At the end of the meal Laura was the first to leave the table. She had had no direct conversation with James and had avoided looking at him. She returned to her office, pleased with herself for her self-discipline.

Lady Carlyon was out that afternoon and Laura had finished what she had to do by three. She decided to go for a walk, leaving the answering machine to deal with any incoming calls to the Countess' private line.

She was setting off across the park when a halloo from behind made her turn. With dismay she saw James loping after her.

'If you're going for a walk, may I join you?' he asked, catching up with her. 'I've had too little exercise this week . . . been stuck in the office interviewing applicants for the junior partnership.'

Laura was torn between despair and delight. 'Has there been anyone promising?' she asked, as they moved on.

He had already told her the circumstances which had led to his coming to Longwarden and to his firm needing fresh blood.

'No . . . a pretty dud lot unfortunately; or perhaps it would be fairer to say not much use to a firm like ours. We're looking for a young Quinlan Terry and most of the chaps who've applied have been disciples of Richard Rogers.'

'I'm afraid I haven't heard of either of them, but I gather they represent different schools of architectural thought?'

'And how!' was James' smiling comment. 'Quinlan Terry is a classicist who takes his inspiration from the past and for years was almost a lone voice crying in the wilderness of modernism. Rogers designed the Pompidou Centre and the rows between those who approve of it and those who regard it as a desecration of Paris are still reverberating. Have you seen photographs of it?'

'Not that I remember.'

'I'll bring some to show you next week . . . if they would interest you?' he added.

If she were honest, a fortnight ago they would not have. She had taken pleasure in old buildings but that had been the extent of her interest in architecture. It had only recently become a closed book she would like to open. Since the night she had spent in Connaught Square.

'Yes, very much,' she said politely. 'Have you been to Paris and seen it . . . this Pompidou place?'

He nodded. 'In fairness to Rogers, it has to be said that it's livened up a part of the city which was very run down. As a building I find it a monstrosity. After he won the competition to design the Centre Pompidou complex in 1974, Rogers set up home in Paris. He found an apartment in the Place des Vosges which is one of the city's most beautiful and historic squares. In France, if a building is listed, the interior as well as the exterior is protected. But somehow Rogers was able to turn the inside of the flat into the kind of modernist environment he likes . . . an open-tread metal staircase, blown-up portraits of Chairman Mao, bright yellow bean bags to sit on. I think it's sheer vandalism to do that to an ancient building.'

'Do you know him? Did you go to the flat? Having seen your house, I can't imagine you being at ease on a bean bag,' said Laura, amused by the thought.

'Who could be . . . except children and teenagers. No, I've chatted to Rogers once or twice but I couldn't claim to know him and I never saw the flat for myself . . . only photographs of it in the glossies. But I have seen – and been appalled by – his high-tech building for Lloyds in the City.'

He continued to talk about architecture and the opposing factions within the profession until they came to the obelisk, commemorating the Longwarden staff who had died in the two world wars, which had been Laura's first objective. Here she would usually sit down on the base of the monument and spend a few minutes admiring the view of the house and the lake before walking on to another of the park's vantage points.

She knew that today, if she were sensible, she would pretend the obelisk had been her final objective from which she must return to the house to get on with her work. James wasn't to know how extremely flexible her hours were so that on fine afternoons she was free to enjoy the good weather and, if necessary, work in the evening.

Finding herself, like James and his radical colleagues, split by opposing forces, in her case the conflict between her head and her heart, she put off making a choice by seating herself on the ledge near the base of the stone plinth.

'You were very quiet at lunch today. Not that you ever say much, but you seemed even quieter than usual,' James remarked, sitting beside her.

In a way it pleased her that he had taken note of her behaviour, but her sensible self found his observation embarrassing.

'The conversation was never in danger of flagging. I prefer listening to talking.'

'So I've noticed. But today you seemed rather . . . distraite. You aren't having difficulties with your insurers, are you?'

'None at all. They've been very helpful.'

'So they should be. It's a profitable business. But sometimes one hears of some companies being a bit difficult. By the way, I've finished your book. I read it at a couple of sittings and found it first-rate. I shall read it again after an interval. It's the sort of book one returns to.'

'I'm glad you enjoyed it.' She looked at her watch. 'I must get back to work. I didn't come out for a long break.'

He checked his own watch. 'I'd better be getting back myself. I have an appointment with one of the contractors at four. I'd much rather go for a stroll in the woods but duty calls.' He looked in the direction of the beechwood to the west of the war memorial. '*The woods are lovely, dark and deep. But I have promises to keep, And miles to go before I sleep.* Do you know that poem?'

Laura nodded. 'Robert Frost. There's another poem of his I like. *Two roads diverged in a wood, and I – I took the one less travelled by, And that has made all the difference.*'

'It was my grandmother who got me going on poetry,' he said. 'She was a great believer in learning by rote . . . multiplication tables, historical dates, poetry. When my sisters and I stayed with her in the holidays she would keep us quiet by offering pocket money supplements for learning something off by heart. The first poem I remember being paid for was – "*Is anybody there?" said the Traveller, Knocking on the moonlit door.* I sometimes recite them when I'm driving, as a memory test. Most of them are still there, filed away at the back of the brain. Not Robert Frost. He came later.'

It wasn't fair, Laura thought. How many men liked poetry? Ten in a thousand? Every new thing she learned about him made it harder to stick to her resolve.

'I rather like T. S. Eliot,' she said. 'I don't find his poems easy. Some are beyond me. But then comes one marvellous line . . . *I have measured out my life with coffee spoons.* That's true of so many people.'

Of me. Of my life, she was thinking.

James said, 'I was put off Eliot at school, as one is put off so many things. If you find him good, I must try him again.'

They walked back towards the house until, approaching the point where their ways would separate, he said, 'I'm thinking of staying overnight at a riverside inn a few miles from here. I'm told they have excellent food. If I can get a room at short notice, would you have dinner with me?'

More than anything in her life she wanted to say 'I'd love to.' If he had said 'a pub' or 'a country inn', she might have succumbed to that longing. But a riverside inn had been the setting for an episode in her past which she bitterly regretted and didn't want to be reminded of.

She said, 'It's kind of you to suggest it, but I have things to do for the Countess this evening. I hope you find the food at the inn is as good as it's reported to be. Goodbye.'


'Miss Lomax? You won't know me but I'm a mate of Nick Dean's. He asked me to get in touch with you.'

Sarah drew in a sharp startled breath. For some moments she couldn't speak. After all this time . . . more than six months . . . it was such a shock. Such a wonderful, marvellous shock.

'Miss Lomax? Are you there?' The voice had a slight Midlands accent.

'Yes, I'm here. How is he? *Where* is he?'

'I don't want to say too much on the telephone. It would be better to meet.'

'Where are you speaking from?'

'I'm at Melchester . . . not far from you. Could you drive over here? I'm on my way to Bristol but I promised Nick I'd stop off and see you.'

'Yes . . . yes, I'll come right away. I'll be there in about half an hour. Where shall I meet you?' she asked.

'I'm in a call box in Market Square, outside a pub called *The Unicorn*. It'll be open by the time you get here. I'll be in the bar. I know what you look like. I've seen a photograph of you.'

'I'll get there as soon as I can. You don't know what this means to me. I've been so worried about him. Goodbye for now.'

Scarcely waiting for his reply, she replaced the receiver, intending quickly to change her stable clothes. Then she remembered the night of Nick's return to Longwarden after hitching rides on lorries through

France, ravenous with hunger because he had run out of money. Probably his friend would be similarly travel-stained and weary. It might put him more at his ease if she went as she was.

The small car which had been her aunt's runabout now belonged to Sarah. Very soon she was pipping the horn for the gates to be opened for her. A few moments later another driver was blasting his horn at her for coming out onto the road without checking both directions.

Mouthing 'Sorry' as he drove past glaring, Sarah realised that she mustn't let her feverish excitement make her careless. Had this been a busy main road she might have caused an accident.

For the rest of the way to Melchester she drove with particular care, allowing only part of her mind to consider the implications of Nick's friend's statement that he didn't want to say too much on the telephone.

Ever since Nick's disappearance it had worried her that he might have been involved in the death of Tark Osgood whom he had caught trying to rape her in the small hours of that unforgettably horrible, wonderful night.

Tark's death had been attributed to the high level of alcohol in his bloodstream and possibly black ice on the road where the accident had happened. But there had been unexplained aspects of the accident which had led her to wonder if the injuries caused by the crash had disguised other injuries inflicted by Nick who had some-how arranged the accident to cover up manslaughter – or murder.

Whatever had happened that night made no difference to her feelings. She loved him and always would.

Arriving in Melchester, she found a space in a car park near the town centre and hurried to her rendezvous at *The Unicorn*. It was the first time she had been outside the estate since Badminton and since her condition had begun to show. That she might run into someone she knew didn't worry her. It didn't even occur to her. The only thought in her mind was that very soon she would know where Nick was, how he was.

There were several men in the pub's lounge, most of them at the bar but one sitting by himself at a table in the corner. At the sight of her he stood up and came towards her.

She had expected him to be about Nick's age but he was older, between thirty and thirty-five. If he had travelled far and hard, it didn't show in his face or appearance. He was wearing a sports shirt and a pair of light linen-look trousers of the kind sold in chain stores and worn by thousands of men in warm weather. His hair was brushed forward across the top of his forehead, perhaps to camouflage a prematurely receding hairline.

'Miss Lomax?' He held out his hand. 'Pleased to meet you. I'm Ken. Is it okay to call you Sarah?'

'Of course,' she said, smiling.

'What can I get you to drink?'

'Oh . . . anything. Coke . . . bitter lemon . . . whatever they have.'

'Nothing stronger? You wouldn't like a gin and tonic?'

'No, thanks.'

'Shan't be long.' He gestured for her to sit down while he went to the bar.

He didn't have any baggage with him, she noticed. Perhaps he had left it at the station. There was a plastic carrier bag, with something in it, on the table by his glass of beer. Perhaps he had done some shopping while he was waiting for her.

When he came back, he said, 'Are you having a soft drink because you're driving or because you're expecting?'

She blushed. 'I never did drink very much and not at all now.'

He sat down at right angles to her. 'Very wise.' He put his hand into the carrier. 'Do you smoke?'

She shook her head.

'In that case I won't either.' He withdrew his hand and picked up the pint mug of beer.

'I don't mind if you want to smoke.'

'I put one out just before you came in. I'm trying to cut down.' He lifted the mug to his lips.

'When were you with Nick . . . and where?' Sarah asked, impatient to come to the point of their meeting.

There was something about this man Ken that she didn't much like. He wasn't the sort of person she would have expected Nick to be friendly with, but she knew that in his two years in the Spanish Foreign Legion he had mixed with all kinds of people; an American who was AWOL from the US Marines, an English wife-beater, a German who had boasted of escaping from prison but had not revealed why he was there. Ken had a sharp look about him which made her feel that, even if he had never done anything criminal, he wasn't a person she would trust very far. But his morals weren't her concern. She only wanted to know all he could tell her about Nick.

In Spain . . . a couple of weeks ago,' he said, as he put the mug down. 'When I told you I was a mate of his I didn't mean we'd known each other a long time. I ran into him on the Costa del Sol. I was in a bar where there was a bit of a bust-up. Nothing to do with me. I was an innocent bystander, but if Nick hadn't of stepped in I might have got my face split open by a broken bottle. He's a big, macho guy, your feller, isn't he?'

She remembered the savage beating Nick would have given Tark if she hadn't intervened. The attempted rape had made him insane with rage.

'Yes,' she said, with an inward shudder.

'It's his kid you're expecting, I take it?'

Sarah's chin lifted. 'Of course.'

'Yes, sure . . . sorry I asked,' he said quickly. 'When's it due?'

'In October. What was Nick doing on the Costa del Sol?'


Gary Clutton watched Tiff park her car in a street in the posh part of London between Buckingham Palace and Sloane Square.

He kept out of sight while she put a coin in the meter before unloading a tray of plants from the back of her car. His presence concealed by a van whose driver was making a delivery, he stayed out of sight while she rang a doorbell and carried the plants into a house. Then Gary found a place to park his bike and strolled back to the house she had entered and pressed the bell button.

The door was opened by a middle-aged woman who looked surprised to see a leathered and helmeted figure on the doorstep.

'Special delivery for Miss Damaris Lynn,' he said, reading the name off the large envelope he was holding.

He had found out what the drill was by chatting up genuine messengers in a square off Oxford Street where a lot of them parked their bikes while taking a break for a snack lunch.

'Miss Lynn is busy in the garden. I'll see she gets it,' said the woman.

He shook his head. 'Sorry, I can't hand it over except to her. Got to get her signature on my delivery slip.'

'You'd better come in. Make sure you wipe your feet well, young man,' she instructed.

Gary did as she told him, thinking: This stupid old cow must be out of her tiny mind letting me into the house without identification. I could be the neighbourhood rapist for all she knows. Jesus! These silly bleeders ask to get done over.

However the woman did keep an eye on him as they

300

walked down a long narrow hall, past the foot of a staircase and down another length of hall to a glazed door leading to the garden.

The glass had no bars to protect it, he noticed, but maybe the door was wired to set off an alarm if anyone tampered with it.

'You'll find Miss Lynn down there,' said the woman, pointing to the far end of the long narrow garden where he could see outdoor furniture stacked in a summerhouse and also a small greenhouse.

As he walked along the brick path, Gary took off his helmet and put it under his arm. The sound of his booted footsteps on the bricks alerted Tiff to his arrival and she came to the door of the greenhouse.

He grinned at her. "'Allo, Tiff . . . oh sorry, I forgot . . . it's Damaris now, in't it?'

He pronounced the name with the accent on the second syllable.


The sight of Gary swaggering towards her made Damaris feel cold and sick. But at least, having seen him before, she didn't have to pretend not to recognise him.

'What are you doing here?' she asked, with icy displeasure.

'The old bird thinks I'm a messenger,' he said, with a flourish of the envelope. 'I thought you might not be keen on me telling 'er you and me is cousins . . . more like brother and sister really, wouldn't you say?'

With a calm she was far from feeling, Damaris said, 'I'm prepared to believe that I bear an uncanny resemblance to this person called Tiffany. But if you refuse to accept that I'm not your cousin – which I think must be patently obvious to anyone but a half-wit – you could find yourself in big trouble. You may not realise it but to enter a private house by false pretences is a serious offence. I could call the police.'

'You could ... but you won't,' he said impudently. ''Cos I can prove that we're cousins.'

She raised her eyebrows. 'Oh, really? How can you prove it?'

'I've got a picture of us together. I'll show you.' He lowered the zipper on his jacket to take something from an inside pocket. ''Ere you are ... Mum, you and me took together when Sandra won a camera.'

Damaris remembered the occasion. Auntie Marlene's friend Sandra, from next door, had liked entering competitions. She had never won a major prize – a weekend for two in Paris or a fitted kitchen – but she had been lucky with minor prizes. When the camera had arrived, with two complimentary cartridges of film, she had snapped everyone she knew.

When Gary handed over the print of his mother with one arm round him and the other round fourteen year old Tiff, it gave Damaris a curious pang to see herself as she had been all those years ago.

Giving it back, she said coolly, 'All that proves, I'm afraid, is that the child in this snap bears a very slight likeness to me. At that age I was at boarding school. I'll see you out, Mr ... Dutton did you say?'

Gary's manner became less amiable. 'Clutton ... as you bloody well know, and you never went to no boarding school ... you was at Sheffield Road comprehensive.'

She saw that the moment had come when denials were not enough. She had to do something more forceful. Stepping to one side she walked past him and made for the house.

He followed her. 'Where are you off to?'

'To call the police,' she said briskly. 'I've had enough of this nonsense.'

He caught hold of her arm, forcing her to a halt. 'You

302

do that and you'll regret it,' he told her. 'They can't pin nothing on me but I know enough about you to really dump you in the shit. I won't – not if you treat me right. I'm glad you've done well for yourself. I don't blame you for scarpering and not letting on where you was. I shan't let on that I've found you. I know you don't want Mum and Kev and Auntie Shirl coming round scrounging and showing you up. I wouldn't meself, in your place.'

'If you don't let go of my arm, I'll start shouting for help,' she snapped at him.

But she felt that her fury didn't carry conviction. He was sure of his ground and equally sure she wasn't going to call the police.

To her surprise, he released her. 'Okay, I'm going. You're busy . . . we can't talk now. Tell you what, let's meet in the pub round the corner from your place. The *Grenadier*. I'll be there about eight. See you later. 'Ere, you'd better have this or the old biddy might smell a rat.'

He gave her the envelope and tramped off towards the house, leaving her frantically trying to decide what to do.

Before he reached the garden door, Mrs Morley, the owners' housekeeper, appeared to escort him through the house. Had she been watching them talking? Damaris wondered. Had she seen Gary grab her arm? Would she want to know why?

She hadn't been back in the greenhouse for long when Mrs Morley brought her a cup of coffee and a biscuit.

'Did you know that young man . . . the messenger, Miss Lynn?' she asked.

'No, but he thought he knew me,' Damaris answered. 'His behaviour was most odd. I think I shall ring up his firm and report that he seemed very strange and unbalanced. Did you ask to see his identification before you let him in?'

'I didn't.' The housekeeper looked slightly flustered. 'If someone I wasn't expecting claimed to be from the Gas Board or a telephone engineer I should have done so, but as he asked for you by name and had a package addressed to you, it didn't seem necessary.'

Damaris nodded. 'Thank you for the coffee, Mrs Morley.' She wanted to be left alone to grapple with her dilemma.

Presently, seeing that the envelope Gary had pushed into her hand contained something, wondering what it was, she opened it. The magazine she drew out had a girl with huge breasts on the cover. Inside were more pictures of girls. They all had three things in common; enormous breasts, brainless faces and a willingness to pose in any position however demeaning. Turning the pages, Damaris felt more and more revolted. How could anyone make a living like this? Didn't they know or care what kind of creeps gloated over these pictures? Didn't it occur to them that they helped to titillate the desires of men like Kev who then went and worked off their lust on girls like herself? She felt it degraded all women that some of them were prepared to appear in seedy publications of this sort.

Flinging it from her in disgust, and then cramming it back into the envelope in case Mrs Morley should come back to fetch the cup and saucer, she went on with what she had been doing before Gary's intrusion. But while her hands performed accustomed movements, her thoughts whirled in frightened confusion, searching for some escape from a situation which had suddenly grown from an unlikely possibility into a threatening reality.


Sarah drove back to Longwarden oppressed by a sense of anticlimax. Apart from confirming that Nick was alive and well – which she had never seriously doubted – her talk with Ken, whose surname she still didn't know, hadn't relieved her mind of any of its deepest worries.

She still had no address to write to, no understanding of why Nick hadn't written or telephoned her. According to Ken, Nick had been passing through Marbella after spending some time in the Spanish town of Ronda where there was a big Legion garrison. When they had said goodbye, Nick had been on his way to Marseille with the idea of joining the French Foreign Legion.

Although it had warmed her to hear Ken speak admiringly of Nick's fluent Spanish and his expertise on a sail-board, there were many questions he hadn't been able to answer for her.


Driving back to London after the job in Melchester with Ronnie, Colin Bardolph who, a fortnight ago, had been working out his notice on a provincial evening paper preparatory to starting his first job on a national, was listening to Ronnie playing back his conversation with the Lomax girl.

Colin's job had been to photograph her without being aware of it. The photographs had to show that she was pregnant.

Unaccustomed to snapping people without their knowledge, he hadn't liked the assignment. He liked it even less now that he was hearing the result of Ronnie's talk with her.

She had a nice voice. Not one of those loud, drawling, affectedly plummy voices he had sometimes heard when photographing Tory bun fights and agricultural shows in the county he had left. Voices like that put your back up, made everyone a Commie. Her voice was soft and clear, except when it turned a bit husky when she was telling Ronnie about her boyfriend. Once or twice during the playback she sounded near to tears.

When it finished and Ronnie switched off the miniature recorder on which he had taped his questions and her answers, Colin said, 'It's a bit of a rotten trick really . . . pretending you'd met her boyfriend, don't you think?'

'Tit for tat, laddie. You want to talk to Terry about the time he was sent to get pictures of the Countess marrying the butler. Ask him about the tricks this kid's family played on him and the other photographers.'

'What sort of tricks?' asked Colin.

Ronnie told him.

'Yeah, but that's not the same thing, is it?' was Colin's comment. 'I mean, that was all in good fun. This is different. This girl's in a bad way. Having a baby by a bloke who's scarpered isn't funny. I feel dead sorry for her. Don't you?'

Ronnie lit a cigarette. 'You start feeling sorry for people, you won't last five minutes in this game, old son. Detachment, that's what you need. Same as doctors and nurses. They don't get involved with patients and neither should we. My job is to get a story and that's what I do. Sometimes it's bloody nearly impossible. There was no way you and I were going to get inside Longwarden so I had to think of a scheme to get Sarah out, so that you could take pictures of her, and also get her to talk to me. Okay, so it involved a spot of play-acting but if the Earl starts complaining we can say: Look who's talking.'

'You must draw a line somewhere, don't you?' said Colin.

'Where I draw the line is at losing my job,' Ronnie answered. 'If I don't get the story, some other bastard will, you can be sure of that. There are plenty more where you came from, laddie. If you're wise you won't forget it. Anyway, when you boil it all down, if Sarah wanted to keep her name out of the papers she shouldn't have let Nick get her knickers off. Don't let a pretty face fool you. She says he's the father but who knows? She may take after her cousin, Lady Allegra. I should think she's lost count of the men she's had. Huntin', shootin', fishin', and fuckin' – that's what the upper crust like, and not necessarily in that order.'

Damaris stopped the car beside a skip and tossed the envelope containing the girlie magazine on top of a pile of builders' refuse.

Having decided what to do – although not with any great confidence that it was the best course of action – she had a great many arrangements to make.

Returning to her flat, she dialled the number of the woman who had been her first assistant.

'Eve? This is Damaris. Look, I know it's a lot to ask, and terribly short notice too, but I wonder if you'd be prepared to take over the reins for three or four weeks? The thing is that I've had an unexpected invitation to join a house-party abroad. As you know I've had almost no time off since I started the business and I suddenly feel rather desperately in need of a break. You would? That's angelic of you. Naturally I'll make it worth your while. When am I leaving? Well, I warned you it was very short notice . . . I'd like to take off tonight.'

They talked for about ten minutes, discussing details.

Finally, Damaris said, 'I don't want anyone to know where I am. If anyone asks – anyone at all – tell them you don't know, will you? It will be true. Where I'm going doesn't have a telephone and there's no point in giving you the address because mail takes forever to get there apparently. I'm literally going to disappear into the blue. You'll have to expect me when you see me. I'm sure you'll cope splendidly.'

Replacing the receiver after they had said goodbye, she felt guilty at telling white lies to someone who trusted her, but what other recourse did she have? The only way to be certain that no one could, even unwittingly, give her away was not to tell anyone where she was going.

Next she went downstairs and told her landlord a similar story.

'Do you the world of good, m'dear. Everyone needs a long break at least once a year. Weekends are all very well but they don't give the system time to wind down properly. What about your mail?'

'I'm not expecting anything important. Just hold it for me would you, please? Oh, by the way, the other day I noticed a youth on a motor-bike hanging about outside the gate. He may have turned off the main road to have a quiet smoke, but as noise doesn't usually bother those ton-up boys I thought it an odd place to find one. Perhaps I'm being over-suspicious but I didn't like the look of him.'

'Can't be too careful these days, m'dear,' said her landlord. 'If I see him hanging about again, I'll get the police to find out what he's up to.'


''Ave you seen the paper, Sharon?' asked Mrs Weedon, unloading her wire mesh basket at the checkout counter in the village supermarket.

The blonde at the till shook her head. 'Dad takes it to work. Likes to read it in his lunch hour. He brings it home after work, but I don't usually bother to look at it.'

'You'll want to read it tonight. It's all about Sarah Lomax having a baby by Nick Dean. Admitted it straight out, she has. There's pictures of them an' all. Only one of him but two or three of her. You'd think she'd want to keep it quiet, wouldn't you? I'm surprised she hasn't got rid of it . . . a girl in her position. But no – bold as brass she is.'

'Well, I'm buggered,' Sharon exclaimed.

She remembered giving Nick the come on one night

in the pub, but he hadn't been interested. Now she knew why. He'd been having it off with the horse-riding girl.

By mid-morning the news was spreading rapidly. The blacksmith's wife, Emily Wareham, heard it when she went to the paper shop to pay their monthly bill for *The Telegraph* and *The World of Interiors*.

Rob Wareham was an ex-public school boy who had chosen to devote his life to one of the ancient crafts. He and Emily had been the first outsiders to know about Sarah's baby. She had introduced Nick to them when he first came back to Longwarden and later he had confided to Emily that he was in love with Sarah but felt himself to be hopelessly unacceptable to her family.

When Emily entered the shop, a more than usually animated discussion was going on at the counter. When she grasped what it was about, she was appalled. The tabloid carrying the story was a paper she knew by sight from the rack outside the shop door. Sometimes, on a Sunday morning, pages of it littered the pavement outside the fish and chip shop where they had been cast by people who were either too sloshed or too lazy to put them in the shop's bins. It was a publication which, normally, she wouldn't have had in the house. But this morning she bought one of the two remaining copies and hurried home to read it and show it to Rob.

'What I can't understand,' she said bewilderedly, 'is where they got all this information, if not from Sarah. Is it legal to put things in quotation marks if the person concerned hasn't said them?'

'I shouldn't think this rag cares too much about legality. Beating their rivals in the circulation stakes is all that matters to them. Damages after libel suits are counted as part of their overheads probably,' said Rob. 'But this interview with Sarah does sound straight from the horse's mouth and the photographs of her in Melchester are obviously authentic. What the devil was she doing over there?'

'I can't imagine,' said Emily. 'She said she was going to stay inside the grounds all summer. It's not like being confined to an ordinary house and garden. I wonder if they know about this at Longwarden? I shouldn't think anyone there takes this rag, would you? Apart from that awful Mrs Osgood, the cleaners are all too intelligent to read this rubbish.'

'Rubbish it may be, but this issue is going to be read by pretty well everyone in the village who can get hold of a copy,' Rob said, with a wry grimace. 'There are more revelations to come tomorrow, I see.'

'I think I ought to ring Sarah and warn her about it,' said Emily. 'I just can't believe that she ever spoke to this horrible man Ronnie Wirral. What utter shits they must be, the people who write these exposés. Don't they care about the pain they cause?'

'Obviously not or they wouldn't work for the press barons who own the muck-rakers. Why not speak to Kate about it? She and Sarah are pretty close now. She should know why Sarah was in Melchester and if – inconceivable as it seems – she did talk to Ronnie Wirral.' Rob went back to work in the forge.

Longwarden had several telephone numbers, not all of them listed. Emily dialled the number which would ring a bell in the stable yard and bring either Sarah or Kate to the telephone in the tack room.

As she listened to the ringing tone, she looked again at the photograph of Sarah with the columns supporting the domed roof of Melchester's eighteenth century butter cross visible in the background and her friend's clearly pregnant figure in the foreground. In one corner of the picture was an inset enlargement of Sarah's face, showing a look of intense unhappiness. It was captioned: *Worrying about the whereabouts of her baby's father?*

'Hello?' It was the groom's abrupt voice, not Sarah's.

'Kate, this is Emily. Does Sarah already know that she's national news? If one can call this moronic muck-sheet a newspaper.'

'National news? What are you talking about?'

Emily explained.

'Oh Christ . . . that bloody swine. I'd like to cut his balls off,' Kate said venomously.

'You mean Sarah *did* talk to Ronnie Wirral? What in God's name possessed her?'

'He tricked her, called himself Ken. He made out he was a friend of Nick's . . . had a message for her from him. She met him in a pub in Melchester. It upset her more than it helped her, but she never dreamt – nor did I – that he wasn't who he said he was. If you've got a copy of the paper, could you possibly bring it for us to see . . . right away? Or shall I come down and fetch it?'


Half an hour later Jane told North what had happened.

'Sarah has seen it and she's falling apart. I think she could have a miscarriage, she's so distraught. Kate and Emily are with her.'

'Where is the paper?' said North.

Jane produced it from behind her back where she had been holding it while she explained the situation.

As he scanned the double-page spread which was the paper's main feature, his already frowning face became a taut mask of anger, the muscles of his jaw knotting under the sun-tanned skin, the mouth which could kiss so tenderly compressing into a hard line.

But the explosion she expected didn't come. He said, 'Where is Sarah?'

'In her room. If they haven't been able to calm her, we may have to call the doctor. She's been so brave up to now, but this disgusting trap they laid for her has broken her up, poor little thing.'

'The doctor will only stuff her full of sedatives. I'll calm her,' said North.

Jane followed him through the great house, half-running to keep up with his long, impatient strides. He went up the spiral stone stairs in the archway ahead of her, taking them three at a time with the elastic springs of a man whose physique at thirty-one was as good as it had been at twenty.

When they entered Sarah's bedsitter, Jane still behind her husband, his cousin was huddled on the bed, muffling her sobs in the pillow with the other two trying to soothe her. Kate was on her knees by the bed, with one hand on Sarah's heaving back. Emily was sitting by her legs. They both turned worried faces towards North as he paused in the doorway.

'I'll take over now, girls,' he said.

As they got out of the way, he moved to the bedside and, as if Sarah were a small child, lifted her from her face-down position and settled her in his arms. Jane had a brief glimpse of her face, awash with tears, her eyelids tight slits of misery, before it was hidden again in the shelter of North's broad shoulder.

'It's all right . . . it's going to be all right. Take it easy. Don't worry about it . . .'

He spoke in the firm, soothing tone which calmed horses after a fright and children after a nightmare. When Kate and Emily had gone quietly away, Jane remained by the door, watching North pull Sarah back from the edge of a complete breakdown.

She hadn't realised before how much he cared for his cousin. He wasn't a man who showed his feelings in public. But a deeply protective affection was clearly visible now in the way he held Sarah to him, his long powerful hands moving gently over her hair and her shoulders as he went on repeating words of comfort.

He was going to be a wonderful father, Jane thought, watching his dark head bent over his cousin's fair one.

312

It couldn't have been more than five minutes later that he made Sarah lie down and told her to go to sleep. Which, to Jane's surprise, she did.

'She's exhausted,' he said, covering his cousin with what Jane was learning to call a rug. 'She may not sleep long. Stay with her, will you? I'm going to speak to my lawyer and find out if we can stop them printing any more of that trash.'


'Have you heard about Allegra's cousin?' Ellen Brentwood asked Claudia Dunbar.

'What about her?'

'She's expecting a baby . . . was pregnant when she rode at Badminton. The father, who used to be a groom at Longwarden, has walked out on her.'

'I don't believe it,' said Claudia. 'Where on earth did you hear that wild rumour?'

'I read it in my daily's paper. She knows we publish Allegra and she brought it for me to see.' Having hung up her mack, Ellen opened her briefcase. 'Here you are. See for yourself.' She handed the tabloid to her partner.

Claudia read the story in silence. Finally she said, 'It's unbelievable!'

'What is? That she's going ahead with it, or that she talked to Ronnie Whatsisname about it?'

'Both! I find the whole thing incredible . . . having the baby *and* talking to him.

'So do I,' agreed Ellen. 'And I bet Allegra does too. If ever there was a case for a pregnancy being terminated, this must be it. I saw Nick Dean at the dance wearing that stunning uniform and looking very square-jawed and macho. But I didn't have any conversation with him. Did you?'

'Not a lot. I got the impression he hasn't a lot to say for himself, or perhaps it was just that he felt a fish out of water. It was pretty obvious how Sarah felt about him. She's too young to hide her feelings. But I shouldn't have thought she was sufficiently naïve to get herself knocked up. God, what a mess! I wonder how the Carlyons are taking it?'

'With considerably less agitation than most of us would, I should imagine,' said Ellen. 'People like that don't get fussed by this sort of scandal nearly as much as the rest of us. Why should they? Nobody's going to look down their noses at them. I shouldn't think North Carlyon could care less what anyone thinks. Allegra obviously doesn't.'

'No, that's true. But you wouldn't catch Allegra having an unwanted baby . . . or telling all to the gutter press. What was your daily's reaction to this lot?' asked Claudia, handing the paper back.

'Fascination at the licentious goings on of the upper classes. She remembers when Allegra's affairs were being catalogued. "A very naughty girl in her day, that Lady Allegra", she said to me. But not in a critical tone. I think she rather admires her. With Sarah, she's sympathetic . . . reckons that Nick seduced her. "If she'd known what it was all about, she'd have been on the pill, Mrs Brentwood",' said Ellen, imitating her daily's voice. 'No doubt she's right.'

'Maybe, but whatever happened, it's not going to help her career to be out of action for the rest of this year. And they say that once women have had babies they never compete with the same dash in sports which could break their necks. There's the subconscious thought: Who will look after the baby if anything happens to me?'


By lunchtime Sarah had pulled herself together and was calm enough to join in a family conference at the lunch table, although she ate next to nothing, Jane noticed.

'It doesn't look as if we have grounds to sue,' said North.

He had come to the table from another telephone talk with his lawyer who, following North's earlier call, had been looking into the matter.

'This man Wirral's extensive use of direct quotes indicates that he had a tape recorder planted somewhere while Sarah was talking to him. It may have been under the table or even in his pocket.

'It must have been in the plastic bag on the table,' said Sarah. 'He offered me a cigarette and put his hand in the bag as if to take out a packet. He must have been switching it on. I should have smelt a rat. But I had no reason to suspect that he wasn't who he said he was.'

'Surely it can't be legal to go round taping conversations without the knowledge and permission of the person whose voice is being recorded?' said Allegra.

'It isn't,' North agreed. 'But the point about this situation is that so far nothing has been published which isn't true. We may deplore the methods Wirral used to get the story but it isn't libellous in the sense of being grossly untrue. One can argue that it is damaging. Even an unflattering interview can be judged libellous. But I'm advised that to take it to court will only make matters worse.'

'How could they be worse?' Sarah said bitterly.

'If we sued Wirral and his editor, the case would be covered by other papers . . . the ones which are read by intelligent people. His paper caters for the half-wits. The stories they run are all nine day wonders, forgotten as soon as some new scandal erupts.'

'Are you saying we should let them get away with it?' Allegra asked indignantly. 'Even if we don't sue, surely there is something we can do? Complain to the Press Council, for instance.'

'Yes, we can do that,' said North. 'Not that rebukes from the Council carry much weight with the gutter press, but I'll certainly write a letter to them. I also intend to confront Muirmill, who owns the paper and point out that if he condones this sort of thing, it makes him persona non grata in the circles he aspires to move in. I don't have a lot of influence, but I know people who do and who can probably make sure he never gets the peerage he's after. He can let his hacks loose on some people with impunity, but not on everyone.'

Piers and Pen spent their last night in France in Combourg in northern Brittany; a place with the same number of inhabitants as Longwarden but with many more shops in its main street, at one end of which stood its great house, a fortified château open to visitors.

This building loomed over the Place Châteaubriand where two hotels, each with the branches of an ancient wistaria twining across its façade, faced each other across a square with a statue of the French writer and diplomat at its centre.

The Hôtel du Château was recommended by their Michelin for good food at moderate prices, and the food at the Hôtel du Lac was commended by their Logis. As it also overlooked the lake, they decided to try the latter and were soon installed in a bedroom where, after uncorking a bottle of wine, Piers spent some time at the window, studying the lake's bird life through his field glasses while Pen lay on the bed watching French television.

At dinner, the food was not memorable. Perhaps the present chef was not the one who had cooked for the guidebook's inspector.

That evening Claudia Dunbar rang her brother.

After talking about other matters, she said, 'Have you heard about Sarah Lomax, Barney?'

There was now, in his bank account, the full amount

316

the paper had agreed to pay him. He had never been so much in credit before.

'I hardly ever look at the sports pages. Has she won something big?'

'She's having a baby by Nick Dean. He was dressed as a foreign legionnaire at the Longwarden dance. You must have seen him.'

Barney had thought about how he should react when the subject came up.

'They're married?' he said, in a surprised voice. 'When did that happen?'

'They're not married and he's disappeared.'

'Good Lord! The rotten sod.'

'And not only him,' said Claudia. 'There's another sod somewhere in all this. Or maybe a sodess.'

'What do you mean?'

She told him about the exposé in the tabloid. 'I talked to Allegra this afternoon. Ronnie Wirral set a trap for Sarah but there's no way he could have found out she was pregnant in the first place unless someone tipped him off. Allegra's determined to find out who that person was. If and when she does, there'll be hell to pay. Between them, she and her brother have a lot of clout. Whoever did it will wish very much that they hadn't.'

Climbing into bed, Pen and her husband discovered that their combined weight made it sag in the middle.

'Sorry, darling . . . 'fraid I picked the wrong place,' said Piers. 'We'd have done better over the road.'

'Possibly . . . possibly not.' She felt for his hand and squeezed it. 'We both decided on this one.'

As far as she was concerned, one mediocre dinner and a night on a hammocky mattress were unimportant compared with their safe arrival at their destination.

She was sorry their journey was almost over. Travelling with Piers, staying at places where no one knew

317

them, their exact whereabouts unknown to those who did know them, gave her a special pleasure. She liked being alone with him. At Longwarden they would not be alone, or not to the same extent as they were in Spain. There she had only one role: his wife. Tomorrow she would be forced to resume other roles: mother, mother-in-law, aunt. The past, and her place in the past, would cling to her in a way it didn't in Spain. There she had no past. People, when they found out that she and Piers hadn't been married for long, didn't ask about her life before she became Mrs Ashford. It was easy to live in the present, ignoring the troubled past. At Longwarden that was impossible. There, past and present were inextricably interwoven.

In his bedroom, the arsonist read the details of the Earl's cousin's public disgrace.

The evidence that the Lomax family were unfit for their high position was building up. The Earl's sister was known to have led an immoral life, culminating in a liaison with an Italian artist who had already received his punishment for loose living.

Now the younger girl's lax behaviour was common gossip. The fact that she had previously enjoyed the admiration and esteem of large numbers of easily-influenced adolescent girls made her fall from grace the more culpable. Given a splendid opportunity to set a good example, she had failed in her duty, adding her name to the long list of privileged people who shamed themselves and led others into evil ways.

Also there was the matter of the Countess' money; a great fortune which could have been used to benefit the less fortunate but instead was being spent on extravagant self-indulgences such as an indoor swimming pool and food prepared by a French chef.

The arsonist could see the time coming when, not for the first time, it would be his duty to punish the ungodly.


'What a day!' said Jane, with a sigh, as she dropped the two pillows she used when reading in bed onto the floor. 'The only bright spot has been Damaris' decision to give us her undivided attention for a month.'

'What made her change her mind? I thought she told you it was impossible to spend more than two days a week here,' said North, leaning sideways to switch off the lamp on his side of the wide bed.

'She did, but I think she's fallen in love with our garden and finds it harder and harder to tear herself away from it. She seems to think her second in command can cope for a month, perhaps longer,' said Jane, turning out her light.

'Is it the garden she's in love with . . . or could it be the chef?' said North, as his wife took off her white lawn nightdress before lying down beside him.

Startled, Jane turned her head to peer at him. The bedroom wasn't in darkness. He had opened the curtains before he got into bed and bright summer moonlight was pouring through the tall windows.

'Whatever makes you say that?'

'I happened to come round a corner and catch Vibrac watching her working in the kitchen garden. The look on his face made it obvious he fancies her. It may be mutual.'

'Oh dear – I hope not!' said Jane. 'That's a problem I didn't foresee. But the first time she came here, you said you thought she looked cold.'

'I may have been wrong. That he lusts after her isn't too surprising. With his wife in a wheelchair, he's probably not getting enough sex at home.'

'No, probably not, but it would be pretty stupid to have an affair with Damaris – right under his wife's nose. Oh! . . . oh North . . . quickly . . . feel this.' She reached for his hand and brought it to her belly where a burst of activity more vigorous than any she had felt before had begun. 'Goodness . . . what *is* it doing?' she said, with a gurgle of laughter. 'Can you feel all these physical jerks?'

'Mm . . . like a jumping bean. Can you sleep with that going on?'

'No, but it won't last long. It's funny: it always seems to come to life when I'm relaxed.'

Intent on their child's lively movements, they forgot what they had been discussing a few moments earlier.


Unable to sleep, Sarah wondered if it were possible that the paper might be read by someone abroad, someone who knew Nick or recognised him from the photograph the paper had used.

Somehow they had got hold of a picture of him in Spanish Foreign Legion uniform. It could only have been taken at the Christmas dance by the photographer sent down by *Harpers & Queen*. Among the pictures printed in a subsequent issue of the magazine, there hadn't been one of Nick, but the photographer must have taken one and by some means, possibly bribery, the paper had got their hands on it.

Sarah knew that Aunt Pen and Piers were able to buy *The Times* in the small Spanish town near their *finca*. No doubt the popular tabloids were on sale in the tourist resorts.

If Nick had returned to Spain, there was a chance he might see or hear about the exposé. If he did, would it bring him back to her?


'Poor girl, I expect she is dreading my arrival,' said Pen,

as she and Piers sat on the deck of the ferry taking them from Cherbourg to Portsmouth.

'Who? Oh, the gardening consultant . . . Damaris Something.'

'Damaris Lynn. Wouldn't you be, if you were in her shoes? She probably visualises me as a female version of North at his most autocratic and expects severe disapproval of all the changes she's planning.'

'I should think Jane has disabused her of the idea that you're a dragon,' said her husband. 'As for disapproving . . . well, I'm sure you won't show it but I think you're bound to feel a pang over some of the changes. Surely that's inevitable?'

'I don't think so,' said Pen, firmly shaking her head. 'Now that I have my own garden, I shan't mind what has been done or is to be done at Longwarden. I no longer feel possessive about it.'

'In that case it should be a beautiful friendship,' he said, smiling. 'The instant rapport of two people with a common passion.'

'I hope so.' Her expression clouded. 'I'm rather dreading meeting Allegra and Sarah. What does one say to people who must still be so deeply unhappy?'

He put his arm round her shoulders and gave her a comforting hug. 'Unhappiness is part of life, darling. We've both had our share of it. Very few people escape it entirely. Because the two girls are having a bad time at present, you mustn't feel guilty that you're not.'

'I know . . . that would be foolish. But it does seem so terribly unfair that, after so many ups and downs, Allegra should find the right man only to lose him. And poor Sarah's had so much bad luck. A gold medal at Burghley last autumn isn't much of a counterbalance to losing one's father and being deserted by one's mother and lover. I hope to heaven that, having decided to have it, she doesn't lose this baby.'

'My dear, why should that happen? She's young and healthy. She'll have the best possible care.'

'I know, but somehow I have a horrid premonition that something else is going to go wrong before this year is out. Bad things always seem to go in threes. First Nick disappeared, leaving Sarah pregnant. Then Andro was drowned in Barbados. What is the third thing going to be?'

'Pen, that's nonsense, and you know it. Trouble doesn't come in threes, fives or any other sequence. It just happens, entirely at random.'

'That's what my commonsense tells me. But somehow, deep down in the superstitious part of me, I still have this uneasy feeling. I didn't tell you before because I knew you'd pooh-pooh it, but one night last week I had a dream about one of the babies being stillborn. I don't know which one.'

'I should certainly have pooh-poohed it,' said Piers, in the sternest, most critical tone he had ever used to her. 'You know as well as I do that dreams have no significance. You were probably thinking about the girls' babies before you went to sleep, and possibly about your own difficult pregnancies, and your subconscious mind came up with a nightmare on the subject. To take it as some kind of portent is ridiculous.'

'I know,' she said meekly. 'You're right.'

She wished now she hadn't told him. She ought to have kept it to herself as she had the morning after the dream. To blurt it out now had been foolish, would make him think less of her.

# July

With the birds beginning their dawn chorus soon after four and the sun coming up before five, now that she was living at Longwarden Damaris was able to get in a good two hours' work before breakfast at half past seven.

She loved the first hours of the day before her assistants arrived. Four part-timers, all married women, had joined the two aged men who had worked for Lord Carlyon's mother.

Since his illness the previous autumn when Ménière's disease had been diagnosed, old Henry Hazell had had several falls during dizzy spells and now had to be fetched and returned to his cottage in the village by car. He could still do light jobs in the potting shed, but spent a lot of his time sitting on the bench outside it, reminiscing with Mr Craskett. With their rambling tales of the past, they were really more hindrance than help but Damaris agreed with the Countess that as they had worked at Longwarden since leaving school, it would be cruel to make them feel anything but welcome.

This summer, when the school year ended, three teenagers would be joining Damaris' team, and already one boy, keen to start, was coming after school and at weekends to help her re-lay the kitchen garden. Nigel came from a background similar to her own. But his headmaster spoke well of him and there was something about him which Damaris liked, even though at times he reminded her of her cousins.

Although she told herself there was no possibility of his tracking her to Longwarden, her cousin Gary was still a weight on her mind.

Early one morning, she was on her knees planting out

Feuille de Chêne in one of the new lettuce beds, when she sensed a presence behind her. For a horrible instant she expected to turn and find Gary's unpleasant face smirking at her.

But when she twisted round, it wasn't her cousin who stood there but a tall slender woman in jeans and a cotton shirt with a sweater tied round her shoulders.

'Good morning. You must be Miss Lynn. I'm Penelope Ashford.'

As Damaris scrambled to her feet, the Earl's mother came closer and held out a sunburned hand.

'I'm delighted to meet you at last. My daughter-in-law has written to me about your plans for the garden and I must say I'm *most* impressed by what you've done here already. Where did you find that delightful Gothic summerhouse?'

Her enthusiasm, clearly sincere, relieved Damaris of all anxiety that the former Countess might not take kindly to the changes being made to what had been her domain.

Very soon, encouraged by Mrs Ashford's interested questions, she found herself confiding her plan to establish a colony of manure worms to make compost from kitchen waste.

'I've already made friends with Damaris. She was hard at work in the kitchen garden when I went for an early look round,' said Pen, when she joined her husband and children for breakfast. 'I like her very much.'

'So do I . . . we all do,' said Jane. 'Oh, it *is* nice to have you both back. We've missed you.'

Her mother-in-law was sitting beside her and with a spontaneous gesture of affection, she put her hand on Pen's arm and gave it a loving squeeze.

'Although you're so happy in Spain, I'm sure you're both going to enjoy making the dairies into your summer

324

house. We've had them cleared out and cleaned and the partition walls taken down in what will be your drawing room. All you have to do is decide on the decorations and choose the furniture you want. As you know there's enough in store here to furnish half a dozen houses.'

On their second night at Longwarden, in the recently redecorated bedroom where she had slept alone for most of her first marriage and throughout her years as a widow, Piers Ashford said to his wife, 'Tomorrow we'll make a start on fixing up the dairies. I must admit that having had you to myself for three months, I'm rather keen to move in there as soon as possible. I know we have your sitting room next door to use when we want to be alone, but it's not quite the same as a separate place of our own.'

'I know what you mean and I feel the same,' said Pen. Brushing her hair, she moved to the open window where one morning, more than a year ago, she had looked down at Piers – then working as Flitton's predecessor – and known that she was in love with him. 'What a lovely night . . . almost as warm as at home. How strange that after living here for so long, and there for only a short time, I feel so much more at home at *Las Golondrinas*. But it's going to be fun poking about in the junk rooms, looking for things we like. We may find some pieces we can take back to Spain. I'm sure North wouldn't mind. As Jane says, there's a huge amount of surplus furniture stacked up in the north-facing rooms.'

'I know. I used to air those rooms from time to time,' he reminded her. 'I have the feeling Flitton doesn't much like waiting on someone who used to do his job. He's very efficient but appears to have no sense of humour, Jane tells me.'

'I should certainly never have fallen in love with *him*,' said Pen. 'Have you noticed his mouth? He has no

lips . . . like a snake. Do you think he's a homosexual . . .
a repressed one, perhaps?'

'Can't say I've given it much thought. How do you
think the girls look?'

'They're both doing their best to be cheerful for our
arrival but I think Allegra looks ghastly. As for Sarah,
my heart bleeds for her, poor child. Can there be anything more miserable than having a baby without the
love and support of its father?'

Although perhaps it's no worse than being married to
its father but not being loved by him, or loving him, she
thought, remembering her own pregnancies years ago.

'She could have no family . . . no home,' said Piers.
'Even that wretched business with the tabloids last
month would have been a lot worse if she'd lived anywhere but here.'

Pen nodded. 'But although she claims to feel well, I
don't think she looks it. At least not compared with Jane
who absolutely *glows* with health. I do wonder if they
are wise to insist on having their babies here. If anything
should go wrong . . .'

'I'm sure nothing will go wrong and even if it did,
this is not the depths of the jungle with the nearest
hospital two days' journey away. By the way, North tells
me he's thinking of learning to fly a helicopter and
having a landing pad made on one of the paddocks . . .'


All week Laura was haunted by the rebuffed, puzzled
look she had seen on James Muirhead's face after she
had refused his invitation to dine with him.

She knew she had done the right thing, the sensible
thing. He wouldn't ask her again. The coolness of her
refusal, with no expression of regret that she was otherwise occupied, must have altered his friendly feelings
towards her. She could almost be said to have snubbed

him, and what man likes to be snubbed – least of all by a middle-aged spinster?

Her sense of having been ungracious grew stronger as the week went on. When the day of his next visit came, it wouldn't have surprised her if he had chosen to ignore her.

But when she arrived at the lunch table, James being the only man there, he rose to pull out a chair and gave no sign of being offended.

Towards the end of the meal he even turned to her and said, 'I've been having another go at T. S. Eliot. Like you I find him very obscure in places, but it's worth ploughing through the heavy stuff to get at the nuggets. By the way, I've brought those pictures of the Centre Pompidou.'

Hearing this last remark, Lady Carlyon said, 'Don't tell me you approve of that dreadful building, Mr Muirhead? I should have thought you would hate it.'

'I do: I think it's a shocker. Miss Denham hasn't seen it – or not that she recalls.'

'I hear from a friend in Paris that now French opinion is split over a seventy-foot high glass pyramid designed by a Chinese-American to be built in front of the Louvre,' said the Countess.

'It may turn out to be less horrific than it sounds,' he said. 'The architect, Ieoh Ming Pei, was chosen by Jacqueline Kennedy, as she then was, to design the Kennedy Library, the family memorial to her husband. He was also the architect of the new wing of the National Gallery in Washington. Do you know those buildings, Lady Carlyon?'

It seemed that the Countess knew them only from photographs, having spent most of her life travelling outside the United States with her father. She had walked on the Great Wall of China and stayed in hotels which had once been the palaces of Indian maharajahs.

327

She was unimpressed by the buildings of her own century.

Her conversation made Laura aware how narrow her own life had been. She had never even crossed the Channel. What a dull nonentity she must seem compared with this beautiful, sophisticated girl who had been all over the world and could speak several languages.

I'm almost forty. Is it too late to make something of myself? Laura wondered.


'Elliott! It's great to see you.'

Informed by Flitton that her publisher's car had arrived at the main gates, Allegra had rushed from her room to be there when it drew up in front of Longwarden's palatial entrance.

'It's wonderful to be here.' Taking the hand she offered him, Elliott Lincoln put his other hand on her shoulder and bent forward to kiss her lightly on both cheeks.

Elliott was far too diplomatic to ask how she was although he did give her a searching look as he said, 'I hope your brother and sister-in-law don't mind my inviting myself here, but as I was prevented from coming to the ball they gave last year I felt it was permissible to propose myself.'

'They're looking forward to meeting you . . . and I'm looking forward to an orgy of shop talk and book world gossip.'

Today, for Elliott's benefit, Allegra had dressed with care. He had never seen her looking anything but elegant and this morning, the weather being chilly with rain forecast later, she had put on a favourite Missoni close-fitting top and full skirt, knitted from very fine wool in a subtle combination of colours, the pattern probably inspired by an old piece of Florentine embroidery.

A silk scarf pinned by a brooch, tights chosen to

tone with her shoes, ringed and manicured fingers, ten minutes spent painting her eyes – for the first time since her mother's wedding day, she had gone to town on her appearance. Elliott was not the sort of man who would sympathise with 'letting go' whatever the circumstances.

He himself was not in the town clothes in which she was accustomed to seeing him. Before leaving London, where he had been for two days, he had changed into what he considered suitable for a country house visit. To Allegra's eye the effect was a little too immaculate, a little too much as if he had stepped out of an advertisement for single malt whisky or bespoke sporting guns.

She had thought he was driving himself down, but the car he had come in was a Daimler with a driver at present engaged in removing the luggage from the boot.

'I've arranged for Carson to stay at the pub in the village,' he told her.

Flitton was coming down the steps. After Allegra had introduced him, they left the butler and Carson to deal with the four large cases which Elliott was taking round the European capitals and she took him into the house.

'How extravagant you are . . . paying for a driver to kick his heels in the village for forty-eight hours,' she remarked.

'I always have Carson drive me when I need to go outside London. I dislike driving on the left and the work I've done on the way here will more than cover the expense. There is no point in saving money only to waste time, Allegra. Time is the most valuable thing we have. Too few people realise that.'

'How flattering that you think I merit so much time. Or is Longwarden the attraction?' she asked, to tease him.

She had a feeling that, when he returned to America, Elliott would enjoy dropping references to Longwarden into his conversation.

'A private visit to one of England's finest houses must

give any discerning person a great deal of pleasure,' he said smoothly. 'But it's you, not your brother's house, I've come to see. There are several ideas for books I want to discuss with you.'

'I'll show you your room later on. Let's go to the library and have some champagne to celebrate your arrival. North and Jane are in London today. They'll be back about four.'

Allegra had asked Flitton to have champagne ready for her guest's arrival because she felt it would help her make the effort to be animated. She wasn't ready to see people yet – would she ever be? – but Elliott's manner of proposing himself had made it impossible to put him off.

Predictably, he was delighted by the library.

'What a magnificent room!' His gaze ranged over the furlongs of closely packed shelves rising up the walls to a gallery reached by a spiral staircase at each corner.

Allegra nodded. 'My favourite room. As you can see from the design of the balustrade, the gallery was a Regency addition.'

'The pattern shows particularly well where the gallery passes the windows – and what splendid windows.' Elliott's admiring eyes took in the tall expanses of glass in the end walls and the three in the wall which faced the great stone chimneypiece of a much earlier date than the gallery. He noticed the shelves where books in bright modern dust jackets were stored within easy reach of the shabby leather Chesterfields, Victorian club chairs and more graceful earlier chairs which formed a large group round the hearth. 'Ah, these are the recent additions.'

'My great-grandparents always took off the wrappers and threw them away,' said Allegra. 'Some older people still do that but I think it's a pity. I like colourful jackets, especially as modern bindings are mostly rather drab. I told Flitton there was no need to open the bottle for us. Will you do it, Elliott?'

'With pleasure.' He dealt deftly with the caged cork and filled the two flutes placed on a silver salver beside the ice bucket. As he handed one of them to her, he said, 'Let's drink to books . . . and the making of them.'

Allegra lifted her glass. 'To books.' She swallowed two mouthfuls of wine in rapid succession, hoping to feel a quick lift.

Instead, the taste of champagne evoked a vivid recollection of the last time she had drunk it in the library; on Christmas Night at the present-giving ceremony when Nick Dean had helped her brother to hand out the many parcels encircling the base of the glittering Christmas tree.

She remembered her present to Andro, an ivory netsuke, and his to her, a necklace of antique cameos which he had put on and fastened for her – and some hours later removed while making love to her.

The happiness of those memories of their first and last Christmas together, and the anguish of living without him, shattered her self-control like a sharp stone striking a windscreen. Her hand shook. Her eyes filled with tears. She felt her lips starting to tremble and sobs rising in her chest. Not even at her mother's wedding – a day of refined torture for her – had she felt the great rush of emotion which overwhelmed her now.

In a smaller room, with more warning, she might have been able to mumble an excuse to slip away. Here, trapped by the size of the library, she could only turn away to hide her face.

To break down in front of Elliott of all people . . . she could imagine his embarrassment.

'My poor girl . . .' He took the glass from her unsteady hand, replaced it with a large linen handkerchief and took her firmly in his arms. 'Go ahead: cry. You'll feel a lot better for it.'

*

331

'Oh my God! What an exhibition. Poor Elliott . . . what must you be thinking?' Allegra said shakily, lifting a ravaged face from his shoulder.

'That I'm glad I was here when you needed someone to lean on.' He took his damp handkerchief from her and, holding her chin, gently wiped her wet cheeks.

She knew she must look a wreck, eye make-up everywhere. But, exhausted by the storm of tears, she felt too limp to care. She could only be grateful that Elliott had taken it so calmly, as if weeping women were a commonplace in his life which she was very sure they were not. But he had been a husband and still was a loving father. Because of his urbane professional persona, one tended to forget that.

They were still standing where she had burst into tears. Now he said, 'Come and sit down,' and steered her to the nearest sofa.

'It's good that you can cry,' he said. 'Better for you than bottling it up.'

'But better for others if I do it in private. It won't happen again, I promise you. It's never happened in public before.'

'This isn't "in public". You were alone with a friend. I am your friend as well as your publisher, I hope?'

'Need you ask? I can't think of anyone else I would allow to see me in this state.'

Elliott collected some more cushions to pile behind her. 'I'm a little tired of seeing women trying not to smile in case it will bring on a wrinkle. New York is full of women who make a fetish of their looks and torture themselves trying to stay young. You are more beautiful now, as you are at this moment, than any of the faces I see in the fashionable restaurants. I mean that sincerely.'

She could see that he did and was touched and a little surprised. Perhaps Elliott was a deeper, more complex man than she had realised. She had put him down as a very successful businessman, probably a bit of a woman-

332

iser, generous, kind, particularly when it was in his interests to be so, but not deeply sympathetic to other people's misfortunes.

He topped up her glass, bringing it and his own to the sofa where he sat down beside her.

'I wonder if this is the best place for you to be at this time?' he said. 'Maybe somewhere which has no distressing associations would be better. Here almost every room must hold painful reminders.'

She nodded. 'But where could I go?' she answered, with a long sigh.

'No, I guess you're right ... it's not something you can escape from ... it has to be lived through ... survived. The only thing which does seem to help is work. However little you may feel like it, you must get started on something.'

It had taken Piers and Pen half an hour to get at the *faux* bamboo writing table they had spotted half hidden away at the back of a higgledy-piggledy collection of desks, washstands, chest of drawers, *étagères* and other unwanted pieces of furniture.

Pen had always liked *faux* bamboo and had suggested to her husband that, if they could find enough, it would be more suitable for the converted dairies than anything grander.

So far the day's search had yielded two pairs of chairs and an odd one, a double bed, a screen, a standing embroidery frame, some hanging shelves and a cheval glass. They had also come across various other things they liked; a blue and white Staffordshire footbath which Pen meant to fill with flowers, a black basalt bust of Piers' hero, the Iron Duke, and a handsome pine chimneypiece decorated with swags of carved fruit.

When they had disinterred the writing table from its corner and carried it along the bare-boarded attic corri-

333

dor to the room where they were assembling their finds, Piers looked at his watch and said, 'I think we must call it a day now and go and get cleaned up for drinks with Allegra's American.'

'Oh lord, I didn't realise how late it was. I could do with a long leisurely soak after all this rummaging, but there won't be time,' said Pen, looking at her grimy hands, unwashed since before lunch which they had eaten *à deux* in her sitting room.

On the way downstairs she said, 'I must remember to ask Jane if she's come across any old curtains or bolts of chintz in her explorations. If we can re-use old curtains, they will dictate our choice of colours for the walls. Today has been fun, hasn't it?'

'Yes, it has . . . but are you feeling tired now?' he asked. 'You don't have to meet this chap tonight if you don't feel like it. I'm sure they won't mind if we make our excuses.'

'I think it's Jane who may be tired after running round London. A quick bath and a glass of sherry and I shall be fine,' said Pen. 'Today has been a picnic compared with the hours I used to work in the garden.'

'You used to work far too hard,' said Piers, opening the door at the foot of the west attic staircase through which they re-entered the part of the house where the floorboards were polished and spread with mellow old rugs. 'The Lynn girl is making improvements, but nothing that you wouldn't have done with more help and more money.'

The remark was typical of his loving understanding of her feelings. For although she liked Damaris Lynn and was glad that suggesting her to Jane was turning out so successfully, Pen would have been less than human if she hadn't felt some regret that her own gift as a gardener had always been hampered by lack of money. Nearly all her best ideas for the garden had had to remain pipe-dreams and it was a little galling – but only

334

a little – to see her successor enjoying complete *carte blanche* and therefore achieving wonders which had always been beyond Pen's scope.

Disliking herself for feeling any resentment, she said, 'There was nothing to stop me hunting out the Gothic summerhouse and re-laying the paths with those left-over bricks from the stable yard. Her improvements aren't all dependent on a bigger budget.'

'My dear, it took you all your time to keep the kitchen garden going at all. It's entirely thanks to you that the whole place didn't become a wilderness,' Piers said firmly.


'We've brought you a present, Allegra,' said Jane, as Flitton wheeled in a very large cardboard carton on the rubber-wheeled trolley used for replenishing the log baskets.

Her sister-in-law had introduced Elliott and the four of them were having drinks in the library before dinner.

'Good heavens: what on earth is it?' Allegra exclaimed.

'Try a guess.'

'I have no idea. The size of it baffles me.'

'Perhaps its weight will give a clue,' suggested Elliott. 'May I lift it up, Lady Carlyon?'

'By all means . . . and please call me Jane.'

He put his arms round the box and lifted it easily. 'It's something light. I would think there's a good deal of packing material in there and the object itself is con-siderably smaller than the box. I would guess a portable TV.'

'I already have one,' said Allegra.

'It's not a TV,' said North. 'But Elliott's guess is getting warm. What's inside there does have a television connection.'

'A video?' Allegra suggested, although she couldn't

think why they should buy her a video when they already had one she could use if the need arose.

Jane shook her head. 'I'll give you a clue . . . it's a three-in-one thing.'

Allegra continued to look mystified while Elliott rose from his chair and went to the telephone table where he scribbled something on the note-pad, tore off the top sheet and showed it to North who nodded and said, 'Spot on.'

'A brilliant idea – I wish I had thought of it first,' said Elliott. 'But I doubt if Allegra will guess what it is. It's outside her present ken.'

'How can it be outside my ken if it's within yours?' she asked.

'I'm an American,' he said cryptically.

'We shall have to let her open it,' said her brother, after a few more moments. 'I'll slit the tapes.' He produced a pocket knife and ran the blade along the plastic tape sealing the flaps of the carton.

Elliott had been correct in thinking it contained a considerable amount of packing material. At first, when her brother disinterred a long black plastic object, Allegra was still no wiser about the nature of the present. But the next thing he lifted out was a keyboard like that on her typewriter but with many extra keys, and then from the bottom of the box came what looked like a small TV set.

'A computer!' she exclaimed.

'A word processor,' said Jane. 'We thought that, while you're between books, it would be a good time for you to learn how to use one.'

'An excellent time,' Elliott agreed. 'Once you have got the hang of it, you'll wonder how you ever got along with a typewriter, Allegra. Almost all our authors have been using word processors for some time but I gather that British writers are lagging a little in harnessing modern technology. Does this model you've chosen have an author-friendly program, Jane?'

'Yes, we didn't buy it without doing some research. This isn't the most expensive or sophisticated word processor available but we think it's a good one to learn on. I've also bought one for my secretary who already knows how to use it.'

At this point the Ashfords joined them, and presently Flitton appeared.

'Dinner is served, m'Lady.'


'It was an inspired idea to give Allegra a word processor,' Elliott said to his hostess, as they strolled in the garden before lunch the next day.

'I'm glad you approve. I felt, and North agreed, it might give her something to grapple with at a time when she desperately needs to be occupied. You knew Andro Risconti, didn't you?'

'I met him a couple of times, first in London and then in New York before Christmas.'

'He and Allegra were so much in love,' Jane said sadly. 'So right for each other in every way. I'm afraid it will take a long time for her to get over it . . . if she ever does. They say time heals all wounds, but is it true? There must be some wounds too deep ever to heal.'

She was thinking, as she spoke, of her father's death and how much she still missed him even though she had North to love now.

'She will recover eventually,' Elliott said confidently. 'How long it will take, who can say? But she's a young and beautiful woman. However deeply she loved Risconti, she can't spend the rest of her life in mourning for him.'

'Andro certainly wouldn't have wanted that,' Jane answered.

Watching her compatriot as he read the words on the

sun dial – *Horas non numero sed serenas* (I count only the sunny hours) – she wondered if, in a few years' time, Elliott Lincoln might be the person who would replace Andro in her sister-in-law's heart. No, not replace . . . no one could ever replace the charismatic Italian painter. But if Allegra went on writing and Elliott continued to publish her, it might be that gradually a closer bond would develop.

As the day approached when she would have been at Longwarden for three months, Laura began to worry that the Countess might not want to keep her.

She knew – or felt reasonably sure – that no one could have performed her duties more conscientiously. What worried her was that Lady Carlyon might find her a bore and prefer to have someone more congenial, even if less efficient, as her personal assistant.

No hints had been dropped to warn her that the Countess found her, in some ways, unsatisfactory. Even so Laura couldn't help feeling apprehensive. From her own point of view the post at Longwarden was perfect for her. She enjoyed every aspect of it. Had she not met James and foolishly fallen in love with him, she would have been completely happy.

Two days before the probationary period came to an end, after dealing with the morning mail, Lady Carlyon said, 'How do you feel about staying on permanently, Laura? I'm sure you've been thinking about it but' – she gave Laura her glowing smile – 'you play your cards close to your chest, as they say, and I'm not sure if you feel as satisfied as I do. I think we work well together but I don't want to press you to stay if you're secretly restless here.'

Laura's relief was so great that her voice shook slightly as she said, 'Oh no, I'm not restless at all! I love it here.

338

I'd like to stay on very much. But I felt that perhaps you might prefer someone younger and livelier.'

The Countess laughed and shook her head. 'What I need is someone efficient, sensible, reliable and flexible,' she said. 'You have all those qualities *par excellence*. Good: that's settled. You are here to stay and I hope that will be for a long time.'

As she had the first time they met, today Laura arrived for lunch to find James alone in the room, pondering a crossword clue. She had hoped to find him by himself.

He said good morning – he was not, unlike her previous employer, a man who insisted on saying good afternoon the moment it was past midday – and pulled out the chair beside him.

'Thank you. I should be glad of your advice,' said Laura. They would not be alone for long. 'I am now on the permanent staff here which means that I could sell my house. But would that be a wise thing to do? In your opinion is the rise in the price of houses going to continue?'

'I don't think even an experienced estate agent could advise you on that with any certainty,' he said cautiously. 'I'm afraid my opinion is no more informed than the next man's. One thing I do know: no boom goes on forever. On the other hand this one may still have some way to go before something happens to end it.'

'Have house prices fallen back much in our lifetime?' asked Laura. 'I haven't taken much interest in property until recently, but it seems to me they've been rising as long as I can remember.'

'There have been falls from time to time, although never to compare with the rises. I think if your house were mine I'd be inclined to hang on to it. I certainly shouldn't think of selling my house if, for example, I were offered an interesting five-year contract to work in America.'

'Might that happen?' she asked.

'No, no – I was speaking theoretically. Most people only sell houses in order to buy another house somewhere else. That isn't your situation, so you'd be faced with the problem of what to do with the money; in other words how to invest it. Have you any investments at the moment? Is it a subject which interests you?'

'No, none . . . and I don't know the first thing about it,' she admitted.

'In that case, I should keep the house. It was bad luck having a fire so soon after letting it, but I shouldn't let that influence you too much.'

At this point Lord Carlyon joined them, followed a few moments later by his wife and the others. Conversation became general.


'The last time I asked you to have dinner with me, it was on the spur of the moment and you were working that evening,' said James, having come to Laura's office and found her alone. 'Are you free on the twenty-ninth?'

She felt a flutter of excitement that, having been turned down once, he should try again. Perhaps he had thought her excuse last time was genuine.

As the date he was asking about was a fortnight ahead, this time it was more difficult to fabricate a reason for saying no.

'I – I'll have to look in the Countess' book,' she said, playing for time.

James followed her to the other desk and watched as she opened the large leather-bound Smythson's diary. As yet nothing was entered in the space for the twenty-ninth, a Friday.

'There's nothing down at the moment, but I can't say something won't come up.'

'I'm sure Lady Carlyon doesn't expect you to make your social life entirely contingent on her activities. That would be unreasonable,' he said. 'Why not ask her today if you can have that weekend off? That is, if you'd like to see *Heat Wave* with me? I've been given two very good seats by a satisfied client. As you know the show's booked up for months and I'm told there's such a demand the touts are asking a hundred pounds a ticket.'

'Good heavens! Are they really?' Laura was terribly tempted. The show had had rave reviews confirmed by a personal report from Jane Carlyon who had seen it in the week it opened. 'Wouldn't one of your sisters like to see it?' she suggested.

'They both have seats booked for September. The question is, would *you* like to see it?' he asked, watching her with a rather quizzical expression.

How could she deny it, thought Laura. Without being openly ungracious, which she had no wish to be, there was nothing she could do but accept.

'I'd love to see it – providing it doesn't conflict with a busy weekend here.'

'I'm sure it won't. Ah, here's Lady Carlyon now. We can ask her. I've been given tickets for *Heat Wave* on the twenty-ninth, Lady Carlyon. Laura would like to see it but wants to be sure you won't need her here that weekend.'

'Never mind what's happening here. You must see it, Laura. It's a wonderful show. You'll love it,' said the Countess, without hesitation. 'Have the weekend off. It'll be the first proper break you've had since you came here.'

'I was away overnight when my kitchen was burnt,' Laura reminded her.

'And have been at my beck and call every day since then. The time you take off is minimal. You're a workaholic.'

341

'Hardly that,' said Laura. 'Some days there isn't enough to keep me busy.'

'Only because you're so efficient and do everything in half the time it would take anyone else. There's nothing in the book that weekend and I'm going to make sure it stays that way. We've been rather too sociable lately. It's time for a breathing space. So I don't want to see you from Friday to Monday – inclusive. That's not a suggestion, it's a very firm instruction.'

After which smiling statement she asked her secretary for a file and took it away with her, leaving Laura once more alone with James.

She felt some embarrassment at her employer's insistence that she must take a long weekend off in case he should feel obliged to suggest they spent more time together than one evening at the theatre.

This, greatly to her chagrin, was exactly what happened as soon as Jane had left the room.

He said, 'In that case I'll organise something for Saturday and Sunday.'

'Oh no, no – that isn't necessary. I can find plenty to do without bothering you,' she protested.

'You won't be bothering me, Laura. I'll be glad of your company.' His expression became quizzical again. 'Or was that intended to be an oblique brush-off because you don't really want more than one night of my company?'

'You know it wasn't. I just don't want to impose on you . . . or be imposed on you by Lady Carlyon.'

'It doesn't arise. I find you very good company . . . the kind of quiet, thoughtful, undemanding company which is a pleasure, not a strain. I hoped it was the same for you.'

'It is,' she admitted.

'Then why can't we spend the whole or most of that weekend together. What about going to the coast? Do you like the sea?'

'What little I've seen of it – yes.'

'A lot depends on the weather. If it's fine we'll go to the coast. If the weather is poor there are sure to be some exhibitions we'd both enjoy.'

'A parcel for you, Mrs Ashford,' said Flitton, finding her sitting with Jane on the south terrace. 'Do you wish to open it here, or would you prefer to have it taken to your sitting room?'

'Leave it here, please.' When he had gone, Pen said, 'These must be the things of my mother's which my sister-in-law said she would send me. I can't think what they can be. Poor Barbara. How thankful she must feel to have her house to herself after fifteen years of being bossed about by Mother. Not that Barbara was ever the doormat that I was as a girl. Even so it can't be much fun having one's ma-in-law breathing down one's neck all the time. Rest assured I shall never inflict that fate on you.'

'Being the antithesis of a martinet, how could you?' Jane answered, smiling.

She had heard what a ruthless bully North's maternal grandmother had been, pushing Pen into a disastrous first marriage to satisfy her own social ambitions.

Old Lady Standish had died in her sleep the night before the Ashfords left Spain. When the news had been telephoned to North from Scotland, where his grandmother had lived in old age with her second son and his wife, deliberately he had not rung *Las Golondrinas* until he knew that Piers and Pen would have set out for France.

'Ma would probably feel obliged to fly back for the funeral. I'll have to go, but I see no reason why she should miss the trip through France to stand at the grave of someone who inflicted so much misery on her,' he had said to Jane.

343

She had agreed with him. By the time her mother-in-law arrived at Longwarden, the small family funeral was over.

The parcel was fastened with sticky tape which Pen cut through with Jane's sewing scissors. Inside the brown wrapping paper was a stout cardboard box with the faded label of a shop in Edinburgh on it. Pen took off the lid and opened the leaves of old tissue paper enfolding the contents.

'Your wedding dress?' Jane asked, as Pen lifted out a mass of once-white taffeta and tulle to which long storage had given a parchment tinge.

'No, I gave that away to a jumble sale years ago. This is my coming out dress. I had no idea Mother had kept it. Foof! What a reek of mothballs,' exclaimed Pen, pulling a face.

As she shook out the voluminous skirt, the last remaining fragments of camphor scattered on the flagstones.

'I suppose, to her, it represented something she had longed for herself and achieved, vicariously, through me – up to a point. She would have liked me to be the Deb of the Year, instead of which I was the Disaster of the Year . . . the one who spent most of her time skulking in the Ladies. Oh, Jane, being a beauty yourself, you can't imagine the wretchedness of a plain girl's coming out year.'

'But were you really a plain girl . . . or merely one with no confidence in herself?' asked Jane. 'Maybe that dress was the fashion the year you came out, but all those lace frills aren't your style.'

'No, I felt ludicrous in it . . . a beanpole got up like a wedding cake. I don't know why Barbara bothered to send this to me. It'll go the same way as the wedding dress . . . to the next jumble sale.'

'No, no . . . it's an interesting period piece. Who was it made by?' asked Jane.

'Norman Hartnell. He had made the Queen's wedding

dress and I suppose Mother hoped he could transform her ugly duckling into a swan. I remember thinking he was more like a farmer than a couturier. He had a very high colour which gave him a bucolic look.'

'Then it definitely should be preserved with the other two coming out dresses . . . Flora's and Diana's,' said Jane. Diana had been Flora's daughter-in-law. 'Is there anything else in the box?'

Pen tossed the dress on a chair. 'I don't think so . . . oh, yes, there is. An album.' She sat down and opened a large leather-bound album. 'Oh Lord, my life in photographs from birth to . . . when?' She turned to the end of the album but the last page was blank. She had to turn back several pages to find the last photograph. 'North's christening.'

'May I see that?' Jane asked eagerly.

Pen joined her in the shade of the awning over the swing couch. She liked to sit in the sun, not caring if it deepened the lines which an outdoor life had long since imprinted on her fine dry skin. Jane, whose skin was still flawless, never exposed it to the sun without a total sunblock on her face and high protection creams on the rest of her.

After looking at the pictures of North in the hand-made lace christening robe which before long his child would wear, they went through the album together.

It was years since Pen had seen these photographs and she was startled to discover that she had been much less plain than she had always thought.

'With a different hairstyle and the clothes which girls wear today, I could have been not bad looking,' she exclaimed in surprise.

'You could have been lovely,' said Jane.

Before showing the album to her husband, Pen cut out and tore up the pages of pictures of her wedding to Edward Carlyon. It pained her to be reminded how, unable to stand up to her forceful mother, she had wasted years of her life in an unhappy marriage.

Yet if she hadn't married Edward, she would not be Piers' wife today. North and Allegra wouldn't exist and the future of Longwarden would still be in jeopardy because, even with a wife more to his liking, Edward would probably have wasted his inheritance and if his son had been someone else, would Jane have met and loved him?

How strange life was; some of its worst follies turning out well in the end, and every action affecting so many other lives.


One day Mrs Ashford invited Damaris to have supper with her and her husband in their private sitting room.

Damaris had already heard from Joël that the Carlyons were going to a dance at another large country house, and they were with the Ashfords when she presented herself at the appointed hour.

The Countess was wearing one of the most beautiful dresses Damaris had ever seen; a floating cloud of grey chiffon matching her eyes and concealing her vanished waistline.

Her hair was up, displaying her long elegant neck, round the base of which was an extraordinary necklace composed of pairs of grasshoppers, holding large baroque pearls between their front and back feet.

Because of the hair combs left to her by Maudie, Damaris recognised the material the grasshoppers were carved from as horn. Their golden translucency accentuated the exquisite skin Jane Carlyon had inherited from her Chinese ancestress.

A few minutes after Damaris' arrival, the Earl said it was time for them to leave.

Watching the warmly affectionate way the Countess and her mother-in-law kissed each other goodnight,

Damaris felt a pang of envy for people who went through life sustained by loving relationships.

Would there ever be an older woman who would say of her, as Mrs Ashford did when the younger couple had gone, 'Doesn't my daughter-in-law look ravishing tonight?' even if, in her own case, it would be a fond exaggeration rather than, as in this case, a statement of fact.

'Yes . . . breathtaking,' she agreed.

They were drinking sherry and Mrs Ashford was describing her garden in Spain when she was interrupted by the telephone.

Her husband got up to answer it. 'It's for you, Miss Lynn.'

'For me? Are you sure?'

Who could be ringing her here? Nobody local. And no one in London knew she was here. She was supposed to be abroad.

Oh my God! Can it be Gary? Can he have found out where I am?

As she made no move to get up, being momentarily petrified with horror at the possibility that it was her cousin who was calling, Mrs Ashford said, 'It may be private. You can take it in my bedroom next door, Damaris,' and, rising, led the way to the connecting door.

'T-thank you.' Trying to mask her apprehension, Damaris walked through the door which the older woman had opened for her.

'It's on the far side of the bed.'

Mrs Ashford closed the door, leaving Damaris to walk round the large four-poster with as much dread in her heart as if the telephone were a coiled snake, possibly venomous, which she was forced to pick up.

Her mouth was dry as she said, 'Damaris Lynn speaking,' and heard the click of Mr Ashford replacing the receiver in the other room.

'Damaris, it's Peter. I couldn't get a reply from your flat so I thought I'd try Longwarden.'

Relief flooded through her.

'Hello? Are you there, Damaris?'

'Yes, I'm here . . . struck dumb with surprise! How extravagant . . . ringing from Peru.'

'I'm not in Peru. I'm in London. Flew in this morning. My mother's been ill . . . still is, but over the worst, they hope. Pa thought it was touch and go and wired me to jump on a plane, which I was thinking of doing anyway . . . for another reason. When are you coming back to London?'

'I'm not. I'm staying here for a bit. There's so much to do at the moment. Two days a week isn't enough.'

'Oh hell! I was hoping to see you. Can't you take tomorrow off?'

'I'm afraid that's impossible, Peter. I've got things organised for tomorrow which can't be put off.'

'What about tomorrow night? Pa and Ma were going to see *Heat Wave*. He booked the seats months ago. They'll be wasted if we don't use them. He doesn't want to go by himself or with anyone but Ma. It was planned as a wedding anniversary celebration. He'd rather wait until she's better. Do come, dear girl. If you don't fancy the drive, I'll come and fetch you. You can't say you don't want to see it. Everyone does.'

Damaris couldn't deny she wanted to see the show, preferably with its present cast. It was only the thought that Gary might still be in London which made her hesitate. But even if he were there, what were the chances of running into him? Practically nil. She needn't spend the night at the flat. She could drive back to Longwarden afterwards. Late at night it would be a fast run.

'There's no need for that. I don't mind the drive,' she said. 'All right – I'll see you tomorrow. Is your mother

348

at home or in hospital? I'd like to bring her some flowers, if she's well enough to enjoy them.'

'Of course – cut as many as you like,' said Jane, the following day, when Damaris asked her permission to take some of the garden's exquisite old roses to someone who was ill.

After further thought, Damaris had decided that, as Peter might fuss over her driving back after midnight, she would spend the night in a modest hotel she knew of, telling him that her bedroom at the flat was in the process of being redecorated.

As the applause died down and the house lights went up, Peter and Damaris rose to go to the bar where he had ordered drinks for the first interval. Everyone in their row was getting up. As Damaris was following him towards the aisle on his side of the auditorium she scanned the rows behind to see if there was anyone she knew.

The only face she recognised was the last one she would have expected to see. Sam Warstock was sitting about ten rows back, looking over the shoulder of a girl who was reading something aloud from the programme.

On reaching the aisle Peter stood aside for Damaris to go first. As Sam was still intent on the programme notes, Damaris was able to have a good look at them both. Sam was wearing a suit and tie and the girl had on a plain dress with a single string of pearls and a brooch on her shoulder. She had a light fringe and straight hair cut on the level with her chin. There was nothing flashy or sexy about her. The way they were sitting, their upper arms pressed together from elbow to shoulder suggested that they were on terms of considerable intimacy.

Perhaps, as people sometimes did, he sensed he was being watched. His head turned towards the slow procession in the aisle, his gaze passing from face to face until it reached Damaris and was arrested.

She could have looked away before he saw her, pretended not to have noticed him. But she didn't. She smiled at him.

Whereupon, to her surprise, Sam half-rose from his seat and smiled back at her.

His movement made the girl with him look up. Seen full face it was immediately obvious why they had been sharing the arm-rest in the manner of people at ease with each other's bodies. Although her features were more delicate, the likeness was very marked. She must be his sister.

Damaris looked away. It was now her turn to be conscious that they were looking at her. No doubt the girl was asking him who she was. What would he tell her? she wondered. Nothing flattering, that was for sure. Yet his smile had seemed friendly.

'Who was that?' Peter murmured in her ear, after they had passed the end of Sam's row.

'He works at Longwarden.'

In the bar Peter was spotted by some friends of his parents. After the introductions, Mrs Westerhope said to Damaris, 'Are you involved in Peter's expeditions, Miss Lynn?'

Damaris shook her head. 'I'm a gardening consultant. I met Peter through looking after his parents' garden in London.'

Mrs Westerhope's eyes lit up in a way Damaris had come to recognise as the sign that a free consultation was about to be sought.

Sipping her wine and listening to the older woman's horticultural problems, she permitted herself an occasional glance round the bar to see if Sam and his sister had come in. She was slightly puzzled by the way he had risen from his seat, an unexpected courtesy.

She would have credited him with enough savoir-faire to stand up if the Carlyons appeared while he was seated, but that he should rise for her didn't tally with his previous behaviour. His sister, too, was not as she would have imagined her. If Damaris had been asked to guess what her occupation was – she looked some years younger than Sam, perhaps twenty-four or five – she would have suggested a job at Sotheby's or possibly with one of the up-market estate agencies such as Knight Frank & Rutley.

As soon as the first bell went, Peter said they had better get back to their seats.

'Sorry about that,' he said, when they had parted from the older couple. 'Was she being a tremendous bore? She's one of Ma's fund-raising cronies.'

'Not at all. We were talking about the viburnum beetle.'

Re-entering the auditorium, she saw that Sam and his sister were still in their seats. Perhaps they would go to the bar in the second interval.


'Would you like another drink?' asked Peter, when the lights went up for the second interval.

'Yes, please.'

This time the seats where Sam and his sister had been sitting were empty. They must have headed for the bar as soon as the curtain fell.

Not having left an order for this interval, Peter had to wait his turn to be served at the crowded bar. Half expecting to see Sam's sister also waiting for him to emerge from the scrum, Damaris found she wasn't there. Perhaps she was in the Ladies. But among the throng at the bar there was no sign of him either. The theatre had more than one bar. They must have gone to a different one.

'I was afraid we might be lumbered with the Wester-hopes again . . . or the chap from Longwarden,' said Peter, when he rejoined her. 'I'd rather have you to myself. What did you think of the last act?'

They discussed the play and the actors. Damaris wondered if Sam had gone to another bar to avoid her. Perhaps they would meet afterwards, on the way out, but she was inclined to doubt that. Peter would be intent on getting a taxi and Sam and the girl might be in a hurry to queue for a bus to the suburbs or to join the post-theatre rush for the nearest Underground.

At the end when, after many curtain calls, it fell for the last time, Peter said, 'I booked a table for ten-fifteen. It's not far from here. Shall we walk?'

'By all means.' As he helped her to put on her jacket, she saw Sam and his sister short-cutting along an empty row to one of the side exits.

When the girl reached the door a man was holding it open for her. Before he followed her out of sight, Sam turned and looked across the rows of emptied seats to where Damaris was buttoning her jacket. He raised a hand in farewell then turned away. Whether he saw her answering wave she couldn't tell.

'What does that chap do at Longwarden?' Peter asked.

'He's the head carpenter.'

'That seems the least crowded way out. Let's go that way ourselves.'

But when they came out into the street the other two were not to be seen among the bobbing heads of the dispersing audience. Although it was a fine night, the air seemed chilly after the heat in the theatre.

Seeing her involuntary shiver, Peter said, 'Are you cold?' He reached for her hand, tucking her arm through his and hugging it to his ribs.

'Not really. Where are we going?'

'A new place. I've heard it's good. Not top notch like that place you took me to, though. How is the French chap getting on? The chef?'

'I gather the Carlyons are delighted with him. He certainly cooks like an angel.'

They crossed the road and walked past a packed fast food place. Glancing at the young couples sitting at the window tables, Damaris wondered if Sam and his sister were in there. For a reason she didn't analyse, she didn't particularly want to be seen by him walking arm in arm with Peter.


When they had finished eating and the waiter had brought a tall pot of coffee to their secluded booth in a corner of the restaurant, Peter said, 'You've changed. There's something different about you but I can't decide what it is.'

'You're imagining it,' she said, smiling.

He shook his head. 'I don't think so. It worries me.'

'Worries you? Why? Do you mean you think I look ill?'

Surely he couldn't detect that while he had been away she had spent several days in acute fear of exposure and still wasn't easy in her mind . . . could never be easy again while the risk of Gary reappearing existed.

'Not ill . . . blooming,' said Peter. 'You look wonderful.'

'That's living at Longwarden,' she said. 'It's so beautiful there . . . so peaceful. To me it's paradise.'

'And is there an Adam in your Eden?'

She had been folding the shiny brown paper slipcase from a wafer of thin black chocolate into a miniature spill. Raising her eyes to his, she said, 'If you mean have I fallen for Joël Vibrac, no I haven't. I have only lost my heart to Longwarden. If you saw it you'd understand why.'

'Why don't I do that ... go down with you tomorrow ... put up at a country pub ... come back the following day? The Carlyons wouldn't object to your showing me this paradise, would they?'

'They might think it rather strange. It's the place where I work. It isn't usual to invite friends to see round one's workplace.'

'I'd like to be more than a friend ... I'd like to be your husband,' he said. 'No, wait a minute. Don't say anything yet. Hear me out first. As soon as I got to Peru, I realised how mad it was to go away for months without telling you my feelings. D'you remember I said on the phone last night that I was thinking of coming back anyway, apart from Ma's illness? That's what I meant ... I had to come back and tell you I love you ... have loved you for quite some time. How you feel about me, I've no idea. You seem to like me ... in spite of the negative signals whenever I've shown signs of wanting to make love to you. I've never been held at arm's length before. Surprisingly, I haven't minded. That's what made me realise I was serious about you. I kept on wanting to see you again in spite of being ninety-nine per cent sure that the evening would end on your doorstep.'

There was a considerable pause in which Damaris fiddled with the little piece of paper and searched for the right words to express her reaction to a proposal she had feared might come one day but had not expected tonight.

It was he who ended the pause. 'It's clear that you're going to say no, but could you enlarge on that a bit? I mean, why have you gone on seeing me if there's something about me which outweighs whatever you do like?'

'I like everything about you, Peter, but I only want friendship ... not love. Unfortunately that seems to be impossible between men and women. I suppose it was stupid and wrong of me to continue seeing you. I never meant to hurt you.'

'Why don't you want love?' he asked. 'Has it gone wrong for you in the past? Is that why you're afraid of it?'

'Not afraid . . . immune. I seem to lack the capacity to love anyone. My dreams are of gardens, not men. I like you enormously . . . can see how attractive you are . . . but all I feel is friendliness. I'm sorry.'

Peter took the spoon from his saucer and examined it minutely. Then he put it back and smiled at her. 'Don't worry about it. You can't help not being in love with me. But I don't believe you're immune. It'll strike you sooner or later. Meanwhile I'll settle for the status quo.'

'Peter, that's impossible now. We have to stop seeing each other. To go on can only make you unhappier and me uncomfortable.'

'Why? I'm not going to start looking lovelorn. Why kill off a good friendship? Let's wipe the last five minutes off the tape and go back to where we were.'


At Longwarden Jane was sitting at her dressing table.

'James is taking Laura to see *Heat Wave* next weekend,' she said, brushing her hair.

'A lucky break for her.' North was already in bed, flicking through *Time*.

Jane put down her hairbrush and opened the drawer in which she kept her scents. 'What do you mean . . . a lucky break?'

'Presumably whoever he booked the seat for can't go,' said her husband.

She selected a spray and slipped the straps of her nightie off the ends of her shoulders, letting the loose garment slide to the tops of her thighs.

'I hadn't thought of that,' she said, spraying puffs of scent onto her neck and breasts. 'I assumed Laura was the person the ticket was bought for.'

'Not very likely, do you think? People are pulling all

kinds of strings to get in, including paying through the nose for black market tickets. Your secretary isn't the kind of woman who gets taken to it . . . except as a last resort.' He looked up from the magazine, saw his wife's naked back, and the front of her torso reflected in the triple mirrors, and leapt from the bed with such unexpected energy and speed that she gave a startled exclamation as he bounded across the room.

'Mmmmm . . .' He wrapped an arm round her, sniffing his way along the top of her shoulder to the curve of her neck as eagerly as a hound picking up the scent of a fox, his free hand fondling her satiny breasts.

'You are the kind of girl who gets taken to *Heat Wave* . . . and to bed afterwards,' he murmured, against her throat. 'Your secretary has never been to bed with a man in her life. She's the archetypal spinster. If Muirhead is taking her out, it can only be out of kindness.'

'Do you think so?' Jane leaned against him, watching his caresses through the looking-glass.

'Sure of it.'


In her room in another part of the house Laura had let fall the book she was reading – *Four Centuries of English Architecture* – and was wondering what James had meant by describing her company as 'undemanding'.

Had he meant that he didn't think she would set her cap at him? Had it been a hint to her not to do so, in case she should be thinking of it? 'Quiet, thoughtful, undemanding' – what sort of person did that description bring to mind? By itself 'thoughtful' sounded quite complimentary. In conjunction with 'quiet' and 'undemanding' the impression seemed one of great dullness. Which was what she was – dull. How could it be otherwise when she had led such a dull life? Reading about exciting places wasn't the same as going to them. All her adventures had been second-hand. Everything she knew which was interesting had been culled from someone else's experience.

Yet hadn't he also said, *I find you very good company* and gone on to say something else about her companionship being a pleasure and not a strain.

What sort of women did he find a strain? she wondered. Perhaps, if they went to the coast, she would ask him.

Not wanting to read any more – the book was rather heavy going but she wanted to be able to listen and respond more knowledgeably when James talked about his profession – she turned out the light and lay thinking about their forthcoming weekend.

What ought she to wear for the theatre? Very good seats, he had said. How much did people dress up? She would have to ask Jane.


In her room over the archway, Sarah could feel the baby moving.

Was it a boy or a girl? Would it be brown-haired like Nick, or fair like herself?

She hoped it would be a boy and take after its father; a boy with all Nick's best qualities but no chip on his shoulder about his origins. What did origins matter? It was what people did with their lives which was important. Why couldn't Nick have seen that?

Sometimes, lying awake in the dark or, if there was a moon and a clear sky, in the dim light coming through her bedsitter's half round windows, she would remember the night he had shared this bed with her.

Would that hour of bliss in his arms be all she would ever know of love and happiness?

At that time she had been sleeping in the house while Nick occupied this room. By leaving her room and padding through the silent house, determined to make him make love to her, had she ruined both their lives?

If the impulse which had driven her to go to him had happened the night before or the night after, everything would have turned out differently. Because she had acted on the same night that Tark Osgood had chosen for his attempted burglary, the outcome had been a disaster for all of them. By the next morning Tark had been dead, Nick had gone and she had conceived.

If she had stayed in her room, it wouldn't have stopped Nick leaving. He had planned to go, anyway. But Tark would have been alive and the child she could feel inside her would never have come into existence.

Having made the wrong decision that night, had she been right to insist on having the baby?

Allegra and North didn't think so. What did Aunt Pen think about it? Sarah hadn't dared to ask her, and she knew the kind letter her aunt had written to her on learning she was pregnant might not represent her private feelings. When Aunt Pen was young becoming an unmarried mother had been a disgrace. Perhaps in her heart she and Piers thought it still was. Sammy did. He was still refusing to have anything to do with her.

His implacable attitude made Sarah's eyes fill with tears but she wouldn't allow herself to turn over and sob into her pillow. It might be bad for the baby to give way to the misery she often felt at being cut off from the old man who had been like a grandfather to her.

Jane believed that pre-natal influences might be very important; that a pregnant woman's moods and the things she did might affect the being in her womb. She had confided to Sarah, but not told anyone else, that she was setting aside an hour every day to play music and read poetry to her baby.

'You may think me silly,' she had said, 'but I'm prepared to go along with the theories that babies can hear sounds from the outside world. It certainly can't do him or her any harm and – who knows? – it may do some good.'

Instead of weeping, Sarah blinked back her tears and began to murmur aloud the words of the Bedouin legend about the creation of the first Arab horse. For she wanted her child to love horses as much as she did. Loving horses was so much safer than loving people.

'*Then Allah took a handful of the South Wind and He breathed thereon, creating the horse and saying, "Thy name shall be Arabian, and virtue bound into the hair of thy forelock, and plunder on thy back. I have preferred thee above all beasts of burden . . ."*'

Four miles away, on the other side of the village, firemen were busy dousing the smouldering timbers of an old barn used to store sacks of fertiliser.

Two thirds had been on fire when they arrived. What they had managed to save would have to be pulled down and the whole thing rebuilt.

The farmer on whose land it stood and who had dialled 999 on seeing the flames from his landing on the way to bed, said to the Station Officer in charge, 'Deliberate was it, d'you reckon?'

The other man nodded, his mouth grim. This was the fifth recent fire which they didn't think was accidental and each had been more ambitious than the one before.

Already most of the buildings in the area which could be set alight without danger to people or animals had gone up. What would be the next target? The responsibility of the fire service was confined to dealing with the fires and going through the wreckage afterwards for clues to what had caused them. After that it was up to the police to continue the investigations. So far they weren't making any progress.

At the edge of the wood at the top of the ten-acre field sloping down to the road and, near it, the now ruined barn, the arsonist watched the men in yellow helmets moving about in the glare from the spotlights.

He was watching them through slits in a leg from a pair of black tights pulled over his head and down to his neck so that no one below would catch a glimpse of a face.

It had been a good blaze while it lasted, better than the one before which he hadn't been able to watch, but had enjoyed hearing described by those who had seen it.

He had already decided what to burn next. If he timed it right, when it was discovered they'd need to send out more than two pumps. They'd have to get help from another fire station. A biggie, the next one would be. A real biggie . . .


At breakfast in their bedroom the following morning Jane remembered last night's unfinished conversation about Laura.

'I wonder if you are right in thinking that James couldn't possibly be interested in Laura?' she said thoughtfully. 'She might not appeal to you, darling, but that doesn't mean she's unattractive to all men. If she played up her assets a bit more, I think she could look rather good. She reminds me of your mother when I first met her. Pen underrated herself and so does Laura.'

'Does she? I wouldn't know. I've never looked at her closely. She never has much to say for herself when I'm around. A very dull stick, I should have said.'

'Next time you see her, look more closely. She has a perfectly good figure camouflaged by dull, matronly clothes. Look at her legs. I'm surprised you haven't already.'

'I prefer to look at your legs, sweetie. The rest of your sex are no longer of interest to me . . . or only of academic interest. Are you planning to transform Miss

Denham in the way you transformed my mother? If you do, you may lose her.'

'That would be a disaster. She's a marvel . . . as good as my father's secretary but less of a dragon. The reverse of a dragon, in fact. Laura can be very brisk and business-like when she's talking to people on the telephone or organizing something for me, but in her private persona she seems extraordinarily timid. She hasn't said much about it, but I think this invalid person whom she had to look after for years kept her in a state of subjection.'

Seeing that North wasn't greatly interested in her secretary's psychological problems, she dropped the subject and said, 'Mm . . . I feel marvellous this morning . . . all my hormones the right way up.'

In the act of helping himself to another of the freshly made croissants which came up from the kitchen as perfect as if they had been baked in the best *boulangerie* in Paris, North's blue eyes answered her smile with a look which told her without words that he felt the same way.

'It does say in your book that however hard the chap inside you gets bumped, the only effect will be to make him bob about like a cork in a glass of water,' he remarked.

'He must have thought he was in the Bay of Biscay last night.' Jane ate a piece of apple before adding, 'North, you won't set your heart on a son, will you? I'll give you a son before long, but maybe not this first time.'

He reached across the table for her hand. 'Dear girl, all I want is for you to be safely delivered of a healthy child,' he said seriously. 'Boy or girl, what does it matter?'

'It matters as long as Longwarden and your title can only pass to male heirs. I'm sure you would rather they were inherited by your son than by some distant offshoot in Australia or wherever.'

'I suppose so, but it isn't of primary importance to me. I shan't look down in the mouth if our first child is a girl. I don't doubt my father would have done, but he and I never saw eye to eye on anything. He never really liked women . . . thought them a necessary evil. My attitude is quite different. I thought I proved that last night.'

'You did.' A month short of their first wedding anniversary, he could still make her blush a little when he looked at her in a certain way, reminding her of the abandonment of her response to his love-making.

North smiled at the faint blush of colour tingeing her golden cheeks. 'I had better go and get dressed or you'll tempt me back into bed and too much bobbing might make Tiddleywinks sea-sick.'

He drank the last of his coffee, tossed his napkin on the cloth and came round the table to plant a kiss on her forehead.

' 'Bye, sweetie. See you at lunch.'

It was the first time he had given the being inside her a nickname. On present signs, he was going to be a very good father, not like his own despotic parent.

Gently stroking her belly, she wondered about Tiddleywinks' sex. She could have found out if she'd wanted but she felt it was more fun to wait until the great day.

'You know Laura, your hair looks much nicer now that your perm has all but grown out,' Jane said to her secretary a few days later. 'Have you always had perms? Have you ever tried letting it follow its natural inclination?'

'Not since I left school,' said Laura. 'It was always rather untidy hair. I had a perm for my first job.'

That had been Mrs Denham's decision rather than Laura's own wish. Mrs Denham had belonged to the generation and group of women who had permanent waves all their lives and, with slight variations from decade to decade, much the same hairstyle.

'Perhaps it was only untidy because you were still growing up. How you wear your hair is your affair but I think the smoother style suits you better than the tighter curls and waves you had when you arrived,' said Jane.

'I went through a phase as a child of longing to have curly hair,' she went on. 'Then my friend, Marie-Simone, who as you might guess is French, made me see that curls aren't becoming to Asian women. They look best with their hair long and straight or coiled up in elegant chignons decorated with flowers. As I am one-eighth Chinese – did you realise that Countess Flora whose portraits are all over the house was my great-grandmother – I have Asian hair. I know I don't look good with curls because I've tried on curly wigs.'

Laura had noticed the resemblance between Jane Carlyon and the so-called Chinese countess. She was conscious of some surprise that her employer should draw attention to her Asian antecedents. Later she realised that this was an attitude inculcated by her step-mother who had looked down on everyone but the English. She hadn't thought well of the Welsh, the Scots and the Irish but at least they were white. To Mrs Denham, a Chinese ancestress – although not as bad as a black one – would have been a skeleton to be kept firmly locked in a closet.

'Perhaps you're right,' she said. 'Perhaps I should try doing my hair differently. I've been meaning to ask your advice about what to wear to go to the theatre with James . . . Mr Muirhead.' Not liking to admit she had never been to a West End theatre, she said, 'I'm rather out of touch with what people are wearing at the theatre now.'

'Anything and everything. Some people overdress and others don't dress at all and even turn up looking scruffy. I think a silk shirt and black skirt or a short dinner dress is best, except at a gala first night. If you feel you haven't anything suitable, why not have a look in that shop in the Market Place in Melchester? I have to go there tomorrow. I was going to suggest you came with me. It will be a change of scene and, from what I've seen in their window, that shop has some attractive clothes.'

'I'd like to come. How kind of you,' said Laura, thinking how fortunate she was to have such a considerate employer. 'In fact, if you have the time, I'd be grateful if you'd help me choose something. I'd like to buy something a little more fashionable than usual but I don't want to go too far.'

Privately Jane thought that the likelihood of her secretary going overboard in any sphere was so slight as to be non-existent. She would always need urging, not restraining.

'I'd love to come and help you choose,' she said. 'Whoever does the buying for that shop has excellent taste and would probably tell you what did or didn't suit you. But she may not be there all the time and some sales assistants are useless. They say *everything* looks wonderful.'

Laura looked over her shoulder at the pile of large and small carriers on the back seat of the car.

She and Jane were returning from their visit to Melchester where Laura had bought not only a dress for the theatre but shoes, tights, a thing for her hair, an outfit of summery separates and even some new underwear.

Egged on by Jane, she had spent more money on clothes than ever before in her life. But why not? She could afford it. She had no one else to spend money on and nothing in particular to save for – except a rainy day.

'Are you feeling pleased with yourself?' Jane asked, seeing the backward glance.

'I'm feeling very extravagant.' As she spoke, Laura wondered if the word had any meaning for Jane who was reputed to be a millionairess many times over.

Yet she didn't behave like someone to whom money was no object. After they had bought the main items, she had taken Laura into Boots and other shops selling inexpensive but fashionable jewellery and had pointed out earrings and beads and a wide plastic bracelet which she thought were a necessary finishing touch to the separates.

Jane's summer bag, Laura had noticed, had a discreet gilt plaque attached to the lining, with the name *Hermès* incised on it. It could only be seen by someone sitting alongside her when she opened the bag and it was the bag's interior finish as much as the unobtrusive label which told Laura it had been expensive. Yet when Jane had picked up a cheap straw satchel in Boots and slung it over her shoulder for Laura to judge the effect, on her it had looked as good as the *Hermès* bag.

The American was one of those people who gave clothes style rather than taking style from them, Laura thought wistfully, wishing she had the same flair.

'I think everything you've bought will earn its keep in your wardrobe,' said Jane. 'That's sensible spending – not extravagance. What *I* considered extravagant was the dress that other woman bought for a wedding tomorrow. Can you imagine running around to find a dress twenty-four hours beforehand? And then choosing something which is ten years too young for her, needs a rushed alteration and can *only* be worn for a wedding or a hot day at Ascot. I'm sure she'll regret the money she splurged on that – but do the very same thing next time a big occasion crops up in her life. Some women never learn!'

Laura murmured agreement, although with a certain sympathy for the hot, flustered, overweight customer who several times had emerged from a fitting room to posture in front of the mirrored wall in the shop in dresses which did nothing for her. Her large hips and bosom had made Laura feel, by comparison, slim and shapely. She wondered what James would think of her new clothes – if he noticed them.

As well as buying clothes in Melchester, while Jane was dealing with her errands Laura had been to the library and found among the hotel guides one listing bed and breakfast establishments in London and the provinces. There was one very close to Connaught Square, although not the one he had mentioned. Later that day she booked a room for three nights, confirming the booking by letter with a deposit.

The next time she saw him James arranged to meet her at Victoria Coach Station, but he made no mention of where she was going to stay. Was he expecting her to stay with him again? Much as she would have liked to, she felt it wasn't the thing to do – except when there was no alternative, like last time.

On every fine evening, and even in light rain, Damaris was to be found working in the garden after supper. There was always so much to be done and, besides, her work was her joy.

One evening, having changed her clothes to go into the house for drinks with some of the Carlyons' neighbours who were themselves keen gardeners, after her meal she went up to her room to write an article she hoped would be published in *The Garden*.

But it wasn't long before the scents of the summer evening drifting through her open window lured her outside and presently her leisurely stroll – something she rarely had time for – brought her to the kitchen garden.

The long regimented beds laid out in an era long past

and never altered, and the old dilapidated fruit cages had gone now; replaced by small, closely planted beds, where flowers, herbs and vegetables were beginning to mingle in colourful profusion among a network of brick paths.

Old cottage clove pinks grew in the triangles formed by the stakes for sugar peas. Borage, which Mr Craskett and Mr Hazell called beebread, was in bright blue flower round the gooseberries she was training as standards. The pink plumes of a clump of astilbe called Ostrich Feather gave height to a circle of cabbages, and parsley grew beside foxgloves as it always had in cottagers' gardens and, before that, in monastery gardens.

Presently, to her dismay, she saw the Frenchman approaching. She would rather have been on her own. But she smiled and said, 'Hello, Joël . . . what a beautiful evening.'

Together they walked round the path which followed the walls, looking at the fruit trees.

As Damaris bent to inhale the scent of white lilies growing in a pot, the neckline of her cotton shirt fell open above the second button, giving Joël a glimpse of the tops of her breasts and a white net bra of the kind which was more for decoration than support.

Already partially aroused merely by being in her company, he felt a surge of desire as he looked at the smooth swelling flesh and imagined himself releasing the clip of the bra and holding those soft but firm globes gently in his palms.

It seemed more like years than months since he had last touched his wife. Now it wasn't Lucy's body which tormented him. The woman he wanted was Damaris and he felt sure she wanted him, even though so far she had given no sign of it. She was not the sort of girl who would. Whatever she felt, however passionately she longed for him, she would never show it out of respect for his marriage.

How was she to know how empty his marriage was? If she guessed he wasn't happy – and surely she must? – she was far too refined and feminine even to hint that she could remedy his loneliness. The first move was his prerogative, but so far he had never quite brought himself to the point of advancing their relationship beyond its present limit.

She had finished smelling the lilies and had turned away, bending lower to examine the leaves of a shrub. She looked at plants the way mothers looked at their children. He wished she would look at him, touch him in that loving fashion.

Her posture and the cut of the skirt she was wearing outlined the shape of her hips and bottom. He looked at the taut material and in his mind's eye he saw her naked, kneeling on a bed, waiting for him to take her from behind. Lucy had never allowed any of the variations he had attempted to teach her. Damaris would. He was sure of it. One had only to look at her mouth to know that although some people called her stand-offish, the coolness of her manner masked a nature far warmer and more amorous than Lucy's.

'Damaris . . .'

She straightened but didn't glance at him. 'Mm?' Her interrogative murmur indicated that she was paying some attention to him but not as much as he wanted.

His body throbbing with a need he could no longer control, he took a step towards her.

When Damaris felt Joël's hands close on her waist, her mind was on the success of planting rings of white alyssum round the boles of the oldest apple trees and growing white sweet peas up their trunks.

As Joël turned her to face him he muttered something in French. The next instant he was embracing her.

It was too unexpected for her to react immediately. For the second time in her life a man had caught her off-guard. But, apart from the shock, everything else was different and so, at first, was her response.

Emotionally if not physically, she had still been a child when Kevin had grabbed her. He had smelt of stale sweat, tobacco and dirty hair. He had plunged his tongue into her mouth.

Now she was a woman and Joël was a man she liked and also found attractive. His hair, clothes and body were clean; fresh as the flower she had sniffed a few moments before. And his tongue wasn't raping her mouth, making her gag. His lips were nuzzling her neck, under her ear. She could breathe. She was out of doors. There was no need to panic.

'Joël . . . please . . . let me go.' She put her hands on his chest and attempted to push him away.

His arms tightened round her, drawing her more closely against him. He stopped kissing her neck and raised his head. Dark eyes, burning with hunger, peered blindly into hers.

Damaris began to feel frightened. This wasn't the Joël she knew. This was a man who soon would be out of control; a mindless zombie driven by the same urge which had made Kevin attack her. Already, on a level with her hip bones, she could feel his body stiffening and thrusting against her. She had to break free at once, before it was too late.

'Have you gone mad? *Let me go!*' This time she used her full strength to escape the encircling arms.

Perhaps surprised by her violence, he slackened his hold long enough for her to get away. She didn't pause to see if he would come to his senses and apologise. She ran.

'*Attendez!* Wait . . . come back.'

Hearing his hoarse command, she glanced over her shoulder. He was starting to come after her.

Knowing that he ran every day and could easily overtake her, she cursed the hampering straightness of her linen skirt. In the trousers she usually wore she would have stood a chance.

'Damaris . . . stop . . . listen to me.'

He was catching her up. Would anyone hear if she screamed? Panic had taken over now. Memories of that last day in the back bedroom at Laburnum Way were vivid in her mind. She felt certain that Joël, if he caught her, would fling her down there and then. Anywhere would do for a man in the grip of that madness.

Which way to go when – if! – she reached the gate? Right or left? Now she knew what it felt like to be a rabbit with a dog at its heels.

Joël was gaining, was close behind her when she reached the gate and tore through it, turning right in the direction of the house.

Her relief at the sight of Sam Warstock strolling towards her, hands in pockets, was like waking up from the nightmares which had made her shiver and sweat for months after running away.

Unable to stop in her tracks, she slowed down as soon as she could but not before Sam had registered that she and Joël had not been running for exercise. His eyebrows shot up.

'What's the hurry?'

Breathing fast, trying not to pant, she said, 'Hello . . . Sam. Wh-where are you going?'

'Nowhere special . . . just walking.' He gave her a thoughtful look before turning to stare at Joël who glowered back with undisguised hostility.

There was a long tense silence broken only by the muted calling of ring doves and the thump-thump of Damaris' heart, although perhaps only she could hear its agitated pounding.

Suddenly, when it seemed they might stand there indefinitely, nobody speaking, Joël said something under his breath and walked quickly away.

'What was that all about?' asked Sam. 'Don't tell me. Let me guess. You gave the poor sod the green light and then changed your mind.'

'I did no such thing,' she said indignantly. 'He . . . he suddenly grabbed me.'

'Without provocation? Come off it. You led him on.'

'I didn't . . . I did *not*, damn you.' The second denial burst out as she saw the sceptical lift of his mobile left eyebrow.

'Never knew a guy to make a pass without some encouragement,' he said dryly.

'Well you do now,' she retorted. And then, to her chagrin, she felt her lips start to tremble and tears flood her angry eyes. 'Bloody men! How I loathe the lot of you.'

'Oh yes? You could have fooled me. I thought you fancied the chef. You spend enough time talking to him.'

'Not from choice, I assure you. I would much rather be on my own. He . . . he's taken to following me.'

Her voice broke. She shut her eyes but the tears squeezed between her closed lids as she tried, with one inadequate paper tissue, to hide the fact that she was crying. If she hadn't been afraid that Joël might be lying in wait for her, she would have rushed away.

'You'd better have this. It might not look it but it's clean.'

A large unironed khaki handkerchief was put into her hand. Thankfully Damaris buried her face in it, striving to suppress the deep sobs which were welling up in her chest like bubbles of pond-gas.

Sam was the last person she would have wished to witness this breakdown of her normal control, although it was his accusation on top of Joël's behaviour which had taken her past the point of being able to hide her feelings.

'Damaris . . . please don't cry. I didn't mean to annoy you.'

It was the Frenchman's voice, speaking from close by, which stopped her silent sobs and made her lift a tear-blotched face from the concealing handkerchief.

At first Sam looked as taken aback as she was by Joël's reappearance, his returning footsteps soundless on the grass walk where they were standing.

Then he said curtly, 'I think you've caused enough trouble for one night, Vibrac. Get lost.'

'I have to speak to Damaris . . . to explain . . .' the chef said, his face darkly flushed.

'Like hell you will,' Sam said fiercely. 'I didn't see what happened but she didn't come tearing round the corner like a bat out of hell because you were paying her compliments. So beat it before I give you something to explain to your wife.'

With his right hand folded into a formidable fist, he patted it with his left palm as if he would like nothing better than to bring it into forceful contact with the other man's chin.

Joël looked nervous but stood his ground. 'This is not your business.'

'I'm making it my business. If you want to go home with a black eye . . .' Sam took a threatening step forward.

At this point Damaris intervened. 'Please don't hit him. He doesn't deserve it.'

Sam glared at her. 'A moment ago you told me it wasn't your fault he made a pass at you.'

'It wasn't . . . but I . . . perhaps I overreacted.' She turned to the other man. 'Please do as he says . . . go away. I don't want to talk about it.'

'Very well . . . if that is what *you* wish.' For the second

372

time Joël walked away, his shoulders hunched, his head down.

Damaris blew her nose on Sam's handkerchief. 'I'll give this back to you tomorrow.'

He looked consideringly at her. 'What you need is a cup of tea and/or a stiff whisky. If you feel you can trust yourself with a member of the sex you loathe, I'll put the kettle on at my place.' When she hesitated, he added, 'You don't want to go through the house looking like a wet weekend, do you? Someone might want to know what's been going on. You can wash your face in my bathroom. Come on.'

Clearly expecting her to follow, he set off along the walk in the same direction Joël had taken.

Not without some misgivings, but worried about what she looked like and of exciting the curiosity of anyone she met on the way to her room, Damaris decided to go with him.

Considering that he had started by blaming her for the incident, Sam's threatening attitude to Joël had surprised and, in a way, pleased her. She couldn't understand why being defended by him should warm her, but it did.

Presently, in his small tidy bathroom, she looked at her reflection in the mirror-faced cabinet on the wall behind the hand basin. Her lashes were sticking together in spiky clumps. Although tears had disproved the maker's claim that her mascara was waterproof, washing failed to remove all trace of the smudges under her eyes. She looked in the cabinet to see if Sam kept any kind of cream which would be a more effective remover.

He didn't. Apart from his toothbrush and paste – the same brand she used – a bag of disposable razor blades and some first aid bits and pieces, the shelves were bare. No hair stuff. No deodorant. No aftershave. He didn't even keep pain killers or Alka Seltzer. A plain soap and water man, Sam. She had already noticed there wasn't any shampoo on the ledge behind the bath taps, only a large Special Offer bottle of supermarket shower gel with which, presumably, he also washed his hair. Remembering, with a shudder, the disgusting condition of the communal brushes and combs in the bathroom of her childhood home, Damaris looked approvingly at the clean-as-new comb Sam kept on the bottom shelf of his cabinet.

By the time she returned to his living room, he had made tea in an old-fashioned brown pot.

Damaris shook her head when he offered her some Scotch. 'No thanks. A cup of tea is all I need.'

He did not put the milk in first, she noticed, slightly surprised.

'You know, I would have said you were a girl who could cope with almost any situation . . . certainly with randy Frogs,' he said, as he put a cup of tea and the milk jug on the table beside the chair she had chosen. 'So how come it was panic stations with Vibrac?'

When she didn't answer, he went on, 'You say you overreacted, but if he really scared you, he may be a psycho who needs watching.'

'I'm sure he's not. He's just very unhappy. He detests his mother-in-law and his wife's disability must make life very difficult for him.'

'Knowing that, don't you think it would have been wiser to keep him at arm's length?' said Sam.

'How can you cold-shoulder someone who wants to talk? I have tried to discourage his confidences but what would you do if, say, Laura Denham kept appearing and talking to you?'

'It's not likely she'd make a grab at me. That's always on the cards when a man starts following a woman around . . . particularly a girl as attractive as you are. Be honest: you know you turn people on. You'd have to be stupid not to know it.'

Did 'people' include himself? Had she been a fool to

come here? Was he hoping to succeed where Joël had failed, she wondered uneasily.

'If I do it isn't intentional. The last thing I want is . . . what happened in the kitchen garden. I try to make that very clear.'

'You certainly succeeded with me,' he said. 'I got the message that anything more than a respectful touching of the forelock would be stamped on very smartly.'

'That wasn't the message intended. I only meant to convey that – ' She paused, torn by indecision. Then, on an impulse she knew she might regret, she went on, 'If you must know, some years ago I was . . . attacked by a man. It's rather put me off your sex. That's why I panicked this evening. I thought Joël had gone berserk like . . . like the other man.'

'I see. That explains a lot,' Sam said quietly. 'I'm sorry. It must be hard to get over a thing like that.'

Did he understand it had been a rape? she wondered. Perhaps he thought it had only been an attempted rape or a mugging. She wasn't going to spell it out for him. Already she felt it had been a mistake to say anything. Why had she told him, of all people, something she had never confided to anyone, not even Sister Joseph?

'What are all these?' she asked, getting up and crossing the room to look at a group of unusual small paintings.

She had seen thematic collections of paintings before. Usually the theme was sailing ships, or hunting scenes, or dogs. Sam's chosen theme was volcanoes, painted in gouache.

'Do you like them?' he asked, coming to stand close behind her. 'They're the forerunners of picture post-cards. When young men went on the Grand Tour, they bought these for about the same price we would pay for a view of the pier or the Tower of London. I paid more than that, but not much more. But they're getting expensive now. That's the first one I bought. Mount Etna in eruption at night.'

He pointed to the painting showing a soaring fountain of flame lighting up a night sky while cascades of white-hot lava poured down the sides of the mountain towards dimly seen village rooftops.

'The first and the best, don't you think?'

'It's very striking,' she agreed, but she couldn't say she liked the picture. It depicted too vividly the horror about to engulf the houses in the path of the lava.

'It must be a fantastic sight . . . a big volcano blowing its top.'

When she glanced at him, Sam was gazing at the painting with a curious intensity as if, in his mind, he were there, standing at a safe distance, watching the earth's molten core boil over with an awesome display of pyrotechnics.

'I should hate to live near a volcano . . . or on the San Andreas fault,' she said. Her eye was caught by a curious gadget on top of the bookcase standing beneath the pictures. 'What's this?'

'A bandage winder . . . said to have been invented by Florence Nightingale during the Crimean War.' He picked up the object next to it which expanded like a telescope although it was clearly not one. 'This is a wooden stethoscope. It's probably early Victorian but the doctor who gave it to me said his grandfather had used it up to the First World War.'

'And that?' she asked, with a nod at the third thing on top of the bookcase.

'That's a diabolo.' He picked up the two wooden globes joined by a central stem. 'It's a game. You had to balance this on a string attached to sticks. It was a craze – like hoola hoops or Rubik's Cube – from about 1910 to 1914. This one is what they called a singing diabolo. Feel it. It's a lovely bit of turning.'

She took it, feeling the smoothness and symmetry of

the polished wood, understanding the tactile pleasure it gave him.

'It's beautifully made. Have you tried using it?'

'No, but if you'd like to try it, I can soon make a pair of sticks for it.'

'It might get damaged. I shouldn't like to risk it.' As she handed it back their fingers brushed. She found herself wondering if there was a girl whose skin he stroked with those long square-tipped fingers.

'Was the diabolo given to you?' she asked, going back to her cup of tea.

'I found it in a junk shop. What did you think of *Heat Wave*?'

'Enjoyed it enormously. Didn't you?'

He nodded, then startled her by asking, 'The guy you were with . . . have you got something serious going with him?'

'No . . . he's just a friend.'

'You didn't spend the night with him?'

She was even more taken aback. 'What an extraordinary question!'

'Not really. You weren't at your London number. I concluded you were sleeping at his place.'

'What makes you think I wasn't at my flat?'

'I rang up . . . twice. Once at midnight and again at one thirty. There was no reply.'

'You rang me up? Why?'

'For the usual reason. I wanted to talk to you.'

'What about?'

'Whether I tell you that depends on your answer to my question. Were you with him?'

'Certainly not. We had dinner together after the show and then I stayed at an hotel – by myself. I hadn't expected to be in London that week and my flat was having things done to it.'

'You say "certainly not" as if I'd accused you of something outrageous. There's no reason why you shouldn't have a close relationship with a man. You must have had plenty of approaches. Are you waiting for the Duke of Right?'

It surprised her that he knew that joke. She said, 'I've answered your question. Now I'd like the answer to mine. Do you make a habit of ringing people in the small hours of the morning?'

'No, but I couldn't sleep . . . for thinking about you . . . and the reason why I hadn't liked seeing you with the guy with the jet-setter's tan.'

Although the way he was watching her was deeply disturbing, Damaris found herself unable to look away. 'Peter isn't a jet-setter. He's been in Peru . . . working there.'

'Okay, so he's not a rich parasite . . . I still don't like him. Do I have to spell out why not?'

She couldn't believe what he seemed to be saying. And yet, as she tried and failed to wrench her gaze free from his, she was finally forced to admit to herself that underneath the antipathy there had always been a powerful attraction.

'Yes, you do,' she said breathlessly. 'I'm not at all clear what you're talking about.'

'I think you are, but I'll say it anyway.' He sat forward in his chair, his elbows on his spread knees, his hands loosely clasped between them. 'I want you for myself. I've fallen for you.'

'I – I thought you disliked me . . . detested me.'

'That's what I thought . . . at first. I was wrong. You're the first girl who's ever kept me awake at night. I'm becoming a chronic insomniac because of you. I lie awake wondering what's come over me . . . and wishing it hadn't. Unless, in spite of the odds against it, the same thing has come over you. It couldn't possibly be that you feel the way I do, could it?'

She wanted to say no, it couldn't. She wanted to lie, to deny it. But she found that it wasn't possible. Something strange *had* come over her, but unlike him she had only just recognised it for what it was. Peter had seen the change in her and thought she had fallen for Joël. But all the time it had been Sam she wanted . . . wanted and feared.

There was a long pause which he ended by saying, 'It's not like you to be lost for words. All you have to say is yes or no.'

'I . . . it's not as simple as that.'

'Why not? You haven't got a husband lurking in the background, have you?'

'No . . . nothing like that.'

'But there's something, hm? Some complication. Okay, we'll get to that later. First things first.'

In a single supple movement he rose, crossed the space between their chairs and, taking her by both hands, drew her to her feet and, slowly and gently, close to him.

'You don't want to run away from me, do you?' he asked.

She found that she didn't – not yet. 'No,' she agreed.

With one arm round her waist and his other hand tilting her chin, Sam brushed a soft fleeting kiss first on one cheek and then the other. He kissed her between the eyebrows and on the tip of her nose. Finally his lips found her mouth, still with the same light pressure. There was infinite tenderness but no sign of passion in his kiss.

'I love you,' he murmured, his hand now deep in her hair.

'Oh Sam . . .' she whispered, not wholly relaxed but not as tense as she had expected to be.

Was this the first step on the path to being a normal woman? Was Sam the man who would make her past seem unimportant? She wasn't sure yet. But having got to this point, she knew there was no going back.

\*

The sun was shining when Laura got up on the Saturday morning of her weekend away. She put on her new separates; the first trousers she had ever worn, with a tee shirt and overshirt. Then she added the details prescribed by Jane, ear-studs, a striped cotton handkerchief knotted at one side of her neck, a belt of plaited leather slotted through the loops of the trousers.

Although she had had several dress rehearsals in the privacy of her room at Longwarden, she went down to breakfast, which was served in the small hotel's cheerfully-decorated basement, feeling uncomfortably conspicuous.

However, nobody took any notice of her beyond saying good morning and by the time she returned to her room she was starting to feel more at ease. James had said he would pick her up at nine to avoid the build-up of coast-bound traffic later in the morning.

She was waiting for him under the white-columned Victorian portico when his car came round the corner. Having stopped, he jumped out to open the passenger door for her.

'You're looking very nice,' he said. 'I haven't seen you in trousers before, have I?'

'I never wear them when I'm working. I don't think Lady Carlyon would mind, but they wouldn't have done at my last post so I only wear them at weekends,' she said, stretching the truth because she didn't want him to know that everything she had on was new, bought for this weekend.

Even her bra was new, an under-wired style with delicate embroidery on the otherwise transparent cups. This had not, of course, been bought for James' benefit but simply because she had never had a pretty bra before. Not even for the nights with Bernard.

He had laughed about her underwear, she remembered. Convent school issue, he had called it. The next time she had spent a night with him he had brought her some red satin garments trimmed with black lace and

380

forced her to model them for him. They had seemed to her the sort of things a strip-teaser or a tart might wear and she wondered where he had got them, but she hadn't asked. She had been too deeply embarrassed.

The second night had been almost as painful and even more disappointing than the first. Soon afterwards she had thought she was pregnant and, bowed down with guilt and shame, had put an end to an affair she knew she should never have begun.

Why am I thinking of that now? she wondered.

'Did you have a good time?' asked Jane, when she entered her secretary's office on Monday morning.

'A wonderful time,' said Laura.

Which was true – up to a point.

Going to the theatre on Friday and to the coast on Saturday had been perfect. But Sunday had fallen flat. She wasn't sure why.

When James had come to her hotel, he had looked as if he hadn't slept well and although it might not have been noticed by anyone else, she had sensed a change in his manner.

Before lunch they had walked in the park and looked at the paintings hung by artists and dealers on the railings along Bayswater Road. After lunch he had taken her to see the Summer Exhibition at the Royal Academy where, in the gallery devoted to architectural drawings and models, his firm was exhibiting plans for the conversion into flats of a mansion in Hampshire and the restoration of a Dockland pub.

Afterwards he had taken her back to the coach station at Victoria, saying goodbye with a handshake instead of the kiss on the cheek he had given her the night before.

Even though it had been only a friendly peck, she felt now that the kiss was an impulse he had regretted and had tried, on Sunday, to expunge from their relationship.

When, at Victoria, she had repeated her thanks for a marvellous weekend, he said that he had enjoyed it too. But his tone had been polite rather than enthusiastic and he hadn't said anything about spending another weekend together.

---

## *August*

*Dear Elliott,*
*Just as I think I've got this machine under control, it disobeys me or, to be more accurate, I give it the wrong command. However I'm making progress and losing my fear of erasing something by mistake.*

As someone knocked on her door, Allegra stopped lightly stroking the keys of her computer and turned away from the monitor screen to call, 'Come in.'

It was Flitton.

'I'm sorry to disturb you, Lady Allegra, but a crate from France has arrived for you by carrier and I thought you might wish to know about it at once. Shall I have it brought up?'

'I can't think what it can be. I'm not expecting anything from France. Do you know what it contains?'

'The carrier's invoice says a modern work of art, m'Lady.'

Allegra flinched, but it was an inward flinching of the heart and mind rather than a physical reaction. Every morning, within seconds of waking, the thought of Andro came like a cloud across the sun. But there were times in the day when, although it was always there, she wasn't consciously aware of the pain of living without him.

Experimenting with the computer called for a level of concentration which excluded all other thoughts. Today, for the past two hours before starting a letter to Elliott, she had been trying to master the mailshot facility. Not because she was ever likely to use it but simply as a mental exercise.

The arrival of a work of art, which must have to do with Andro, abruptly ended her state of forgetfulness and brought the pain back with a rush.

'Where is the crate at the moment?'

'In the hall by the lift, m'Lady.'

The lift had been installed by Flora Carlyon, the seventh Countess, when she had had part of the house made into a convalescent home for wounded and shell-shocked soldiers during the First World War.

'Yes, have it brought up here, would you?'

When he had gone, Allegra returned her attention to the monitor screen on which a flickering blob of light marked the place where she had broken off the letter to New York. She felt too disturbed to continue it.

She was remembering the day when a crate had been carried upstairs to her flat at Carlyon House. It had contained a magnificent Venetian blackamoor, the climactic gift in Andro's extraordinary long-distance courtship.

Could this work of art from France be another gift he had arranged for her?


With permission from his employers, Sam had built a simple diving board at the deepest part of the lake and cleared the area of weeds. Weather permitting, he swam there every morning and again after work.

Today being the start of a hot spell forecast to last several days, he and Damaris had arranged to meet there at noon, swim together and then find a glade in the woods where they could eat packed lunches.

Sam had asked for and collected both lunchboxes. Not that fetching her box would have involved Damaris in

383

an embarrassing encounter with Joël. The boxes, which had to be ordered by nine o'clock by everyone who wanted to eat out of doors, were set out in one of the sculleries.

The day after the episode in the kitchen garden she had received a note in which Joël apologised for what had happened. Since then he had avoided her and she had been too preoccupied with her new relationship with Sam to give much thought to the Frenchman's state of mind.

Sam was ready to swim before she was and while she was pinning up her hair she watched him standing at the end of the board, his fists on his hips, his head turned up to the cloudless sky.

When he lifted an arm to scratch the back of his neck, the skin of his shoulders had the same silky sheen as the coats of Sarah Lomax's horses, and the same play of muscle under the smooth suntanned flesh.

Without clothes his body looked even more fit and powerful than when he was dressed. With such a physique, he must have a sex drive at least as strong as the urge which had driven Joël to embrace her. Yet, presumably because of her distressed reaction to that incident, so far Sam had kept his feelings rigidly in check. At the end of their evening walks he would kiss her before saying goodnight, but his kisses were always gentle rather than ardent.

At first she had been grateful for his restraint. But now she was beginning to feel a certain impatience, to want him to hold her closer and kiss her with slightly more passion.

There was a splash as he dived. She could see him swimming under the water while circular ripples spread from his point of entry.

Perhaps he was waiting for her to indicate that she was ready to take things a stage or two further. Perhaps, after lunch, she would do that.

*

384

When the crate was brought to Allegra's room it was accompanied by one of the carpenters who prised it open for her.

'Shall I unpack it for you?' he asked, as a mass of spongy plastic pieces was revealed when the lid was removed.

'If you would, please.' Inside the pockets of her trousers her hands were clenched into fists as she waited tensely to see what was hidden by the packing.

The carpenter had brought a binliner with him. He stuffed fistfuls of plastic inside it.

'It feel like a sculpture . . . a bust,' he said presently, delving into the crate. 'It's wrapped in a cloth.'

A few moments later he lifted it out. 'Where would you like me to put it?'

She looked around for an empty space and moved a stack of magazines from the table at one end of her sofa.

'Oh here, please. Don't bother about the cloth. I can take that off.'

It wasn't until he had gone that she fetched scissors from her desk and snipped the large stitches holding the wrapping in place. Then she pulled it away from the object it had concealed.

The carpenter had guessed correctly. It was a head of Alessandro Risconti.


'There was another fire last night.' Sam put his clenched hand to his mouth to eject the stone of a greengage which he then flung into the bushes at the edge of the clearing.

'Where?' Damaris hadn't quite finished the *pâté de forestier* which, with a carton of salad, had been the first course of their picnic.

'The pavilion at Longwarden sports ground. Burnt to the ground with everything in it which last night was more than usual because of the fête at the weekend.'

Damaris had seen the pavilion, a flat-roofed green-painted building, standing on short concrete piers but otherwise built of wood, which was the headquarters for the village's football and cricket teams and also an out-of-general-earshot rehearsal hall for the local pop group.

'Do they think it was another case of arson? Or was it an accident this time?'

'The word is that it was arson.'

'But that building is . . . was in full view of a row of houses and close to a fairly busy road. How could it have been set alight without someone seeing something suspicious? What time did the fire start?'

'Twelve forty-five . . . so I'm told. Not many people about at that time of night.'

'No, but with so many outbreaks of fire in this area recently, one would think the police would be keeping a pretty close watch on all the places which might appeal to a fire-freak.'

'Easier said than done,' said Sam. 'There are too many burnable places and too few police. I doubt if they've got a clue yet. It's not an easy crime to solve and the fire-freak, whoever he is, obviously knows what he's doing. It could take them months to catch him . . . if they ever do.'


Cast in a silver-grey metal the colour of his thick curly hair, the bust of Andro captured with shocking realism the physical presence of the man; the curious amalgam of patrician and peasant breeding which had given him the neck of a gladiator and the brows and nose of a senator.

Slowly, as she had so many times before, Allegra ran the tips of her fingers over his head. The sculptor had captured perfectly the texture of the coarse springy curls, but this time they didn't yield to her touch, nor did the finely-moulded lips part to nibble her fingertips.

'Oh my love . . . my darling . . .'

Vainly she pressed her mouth to the cold lifeless metal, aching to feel again the warmth and vigour of his kisses. How could he be dead? How could that surging life force have ceased to exist? Why, when people who found life a bore and bored everyone around them lived to be even more tedious in their old age, had a man like this been cut down? It was so unfair, such a waste.

With a groan of mingled pain and rage, she sank to her knees by the table and wept for all the lost years, all the lost happiness.

'I never liked green eyes until I saw yours,' said Sam. 'Not that they're all that common. The only other green eyes I've seen were light green . . . a bit sub-human. Yours are darker and warmer . . . the same colour as the lake on a day like today.'

Damaris was lying on her back on the grass, her hands clasped under her head, her long shorts turned up the better to brown her thighs.

Sam had been stretched out beside her, stripped to the waist. But a moment ago he had rolled onto his stomach and now, propped on his elbows, was leaning over her, his head shading her face.

'Do you remember the first time we saw each other?'

'How could I forget it? I was never more embarrassed in my life.'

'I don't know why. You looked beautiful . . . lying in the sun . . . almost naked.'

'But I – ' She stopped short. Was it possible he hadn't realised what he had interrupted? Even now, several months later, her face still burned at the memory of that shame-making first encounter.

Sam stroked her hot cheek with his knuckles.

'You were angry and obviously scared of me. If we'd been introduced by the Countess – as we were later on

387

– we might have got to this point quite a lot sooner.' He leaned closer, closing his eyes as he bent to kiss her.

Damaris closed her eyes too, feeling his lips alight on her cheekbone as delicately as one of the many butterflies fluttering at the margins of the lake and in the sunlit glades of the surrounding woods.

It took him some time to work his way down to her mouth. Even before he reached it she was aware of the first stirrings of the sensations she had been feeling the first time he saw her. Induced by Sam they were different . . . better . . . more exciting. As their lips met, she freed a hand from beneath her head and put one arm round his neck.


The envelope was taped to the back of the cube of polished dark stone on which the head of Risconti was poised.

Until she opened the envelope and drew out the letter inside Allegra had given no thought to who had sculpted the bust or sent it to her. For a moment the address in Paris and the signature *Marie-Simone* meant nothing to her. Then she remembered Jane's French friend who had come to Longwarden for Christmas and of whom Allegra had been fleetingly jealous because she and Andro had spent a good deal of time together in the sculpture gallery and going round the house looking at paintings.

*Dear Allegra* the Frenchwoman had written

*I know what it is to lose the man you love. Jane's father was everything to me. I sculpted John many times and although it hurt me to look at those likenesses after his death, it was also a comfort, as I hope this likeness of Andro will be to you. Although it has been done from memory and a few sketches, I feel it is one of my best pieces of work. He had a magnificent head.*

*From my own experience – and there were times when I was in a hell which only those who have been through it can understand – the grief you feel now will get better as time goes on. You cannot imagine it at present, but one day you will find, with surprise, that life has gradually become worth living again.*

*Until that time comes, you have my deepest sympathy. But if either of us had known how our love for these two men would end, would we have chosen to forego the happiness they gave us in order to escape the misery which followed? I don't think so.*

Sam gave a smothered groan and rolled away from her.

Her trance of pleasure brought to an abrupt conclusion, Damaris opened her eyes only to be dazzled by the sunlight from which he was no longer screening her.

'What is it? What's the matter?' she asked, peering at his back view through slitted eyelids.

He sat up, shaking his head as if to clear it. 'This isn't the time or the place . . . there could be other people about.'

He had already unbuttoned the cotton shirt which was all she was wearing on her top half. Before pulling away, he had started to unfasten the belt of her shorts. She had known he was loosening the buckle and for the first time today felt a twinge of panic. But now that he'd stopped she was conscious of disappointment.

It was no longer Sam she feared. He had already proved himself a different species from Kevin. All that frightened her now was that, because of that experience, she might only be capable of a limited response.

'Anyway it's time we were getting back to work.' He got to his feet and began to gather up their things.

As her pregnancy advanced, Sarah found herself starting to be out of breath after climbing the stairs to her room and grooming the horses.

When she reported this to Mrs Seaton, the midwife said, 'Nothing to worry about. You'll find it will go off next month when the baby "engages" and your bulge drops a bit. Then your breathing will be easier but you'll want to spend a penny more often. Are you having any trouble with heartburn?'

Sarah shook her head. 'Apart from the breathlessness, I'm fine.'

She didn't mention the nights when she woke up, went to the lavatory and couldn't get back to sleep again. Then, alone in her single bed, plagued by doubts and anxieties which loomed larger than during the day, she longed to be like Jane who spent her nights close to North and who, if she had a bad dream, had only to reach out her hand to feel his reassuring presence.


Sam and Damaris had dinner at a riverside pub, driving there and back in her car because Sam's transport was a second-hand motorbike and he didn't have a spare helmet.

'Anyway I can't see you on the back of a bike,' he had told her. 'I'll have to trade it in for something more comfortable.'

The implication troubled her. Although he had said he loved her several times since his first declaration, she hadn't yet admitted in so many words that she loved him.

Was this indeed love, or merely a belated first love, not strong enough to last long? How lasting were his feelings for her? What did loving a woman mean to him? Marriage – an affair?

These quandaries preoccupied her as she drove back to Longwarden. Beside her, in the passenger seat, Sam also was deep in his own thoughts.

The parking place for her car was in a barn formerly used to store fodder for horses in the days when every loose box in the stables had been occupied. To return to his quarters from the barn, Sam had to go one way, she another.

'It's not late. Do you feel like a nightcap?' he asked, as she locked the car, an unnecessary precaution here continued from force of habit.

She knew that if she said yes, she would be agreeing to stay with him until morning. For a moment or two she hesitated.

He was standing with his back to the moonlight streaming through the high open doors of the barn. In silhouette, he looked very tough, very macho.

Trying to sound casual with a dry mouth and tight throat, she said huskily, 'Yes . . . why not?'


In her bathroom, Jane was massaging herself with vitamin E oil in the hope of avoiding stretch marks.

But she wasn't thinking of her own child as, having finished her tummy, she began to apply the oil to the tops of her thighs. She was wondering if it would be possible to find out if Nick Dean *had* re-enlisted in the Spanish Foreign Legion. Although North and Allegra didn't agree, her own feeling was that Nick ought to know Sarah was pregnant.

It was possible that, as an unwanted child himself, and an abused one if the rumours about Ted Rivington's treatment of him were true, Nick was incapable of loving the baby he didn't know he had fathered.

Yet somehow she couldn't believe that. She had felt last winter, and still did, that Nick had been deeply and painfully in love with Sarah and had disappeared only because he could see no shared future for them.


Sam's hand, as he poured the brandy, had been as steady as hers when she pricked out a delicate seedling.

But now Damaris' fingers were shaking as she lifted the glass to her lips.

'You're afraid again . . . why?' he asked quietly, coming to join her on the sofa. 'There's no need to be. Surely you know that?'

'Yes . . . it's not you . . . it's me I'm afraid of.'

'Darling, you're talking in riddles.'

'I know . . . but it's hard to explain. Oh, Sam . . . let's not talk about it . . .' She swallowed the brandy at a gulp. 'Just take me to bed, would you, please?'

'I was planning to,' he said, smiling, putting his own glass aside, the spirit in it still untouched.

He took her in his arms and kissed her; not, at first, on her mouth but on her temples and eyelids and then, slowly, slowly down her cheek and along her jawline, first to her chin and then back to the lobe of her ear. Her eyes closed, she felt him take it between his teeth, gently nibbling and tugging. She began to relax.

'Your skin tastes of honey . . . or maybe it's apples . . . I don't know . . . something delicious,' he murmured, nuzzling the place behind her lobe. Then his lips glided warmly down her neck, to the base of her throat.

Her head tilting slowly back as his warm mouth circled her neck, she thought: As long as it's like this it's fine. Gentle. Slow. Not impatient.

Sam kissed her under her chin, and then on her chin, and then, at last, full on her mouth. Pleasure began to flow through her, but still, underneath, lurked the fear that, suddenly, all this might change to the thrusting tongue, the groping hands.

But it didn't. A long time later, after many kisses, he scooped her up in his arms and carried her through to his bedroom.

The curtains were open, summer moonlight streaming through the windows.

'I put on clean sheets . . . hoping you'd stay with me tonight.'

He set her on her feet and began to undress her. First her blouse. Then her full cotton skirt. With the button and zipper unfastened, it slid down her thighs to the floor.

Sam started kissing her shoulders, stroking her waist. 'Mm . . . your skin is lovely . . . like touching a perfect veneer.' He let his fingertips glide down one side of her spine and go back up the other.

Damaris found herself smiling. She turned to him, filled with tenderness. Taking his face between her hands, she said, 'Oh Sam . . . only you could compare a woman to wood' – and kissed him.

'Was it silly? I s'pose it was. I'm not very good with words.'

'You don't need to be. The way you touch me is wonderful.'

Afraid that she might have hurt him, wanting to please him, she reached behind her to undo the clip of her bra.

'Oh God! My beautiful girl!'

He sank down on the side of the bed and drew her onto his lap.


Exhausted by bliss, she bestirred herself.

'But Sam . . . you haven't . . .'

His head was pillowed on her thigh. Without moving, he said, 'I know . . . but we have all night. Relax . . . have a rest . . . I can wait.'

Her eyes filled with tears of gratitude for his self-control, his generosity.

'But I don't want you to wait. I want you to take me . . . now!'


He sensed that something was wrong and lifted his head to peer at her.

'You're crying . . . I've hurt you,' he whispered.

'No, no . . . you could never hurt me. I'm crying for happiness. Women do . . . didn't you know? No, don't go away. Stay with me.' She wrapped her arms tightly round him.


Allegra was dialling the number of the hotel where, six months earlier, she had contemplated slashing her wrists. Whether, when it came to the point, she would have done it was something she would never know. At the critical moment the hotel's assistant manager, a woman whose husband had been murdered by IRA terrorists, had intervened.

When the number answered, Allegra said, 'May I speak to Mrs Macroom, please? My name is Allegra Lomax.'

A few moments later, a pleasant voice said, 'Good evening, Lady Allegra. This is a nice surprise. How are you?'

'I'm well. And you?'

'Very well, thank you. Very busy. We've got a big sales conference going on here at the moment. But I've just come off-duty so you've picked a good time to call.'

'When are you coming to stay with me?'

Allegra had invited Pamela Macroom to visit Long-warden after the widow had helped her through those ghastly first days following Andro's death. She knew she should have repeated the invitation sooner. Pamela wasn't the kind of person who would propose herself on the strength of a suggestion made when Allegra was saying goodbye to her.

It turned out that Mrs Macroom could take a long weekend early in September. Having read Allegra's book, she was obviously delighted at the prospect of seeing for herself the background to the biography.

After they had rung off, Allegra remembered the older

woman's suggestion that she should write a story for children based on the adventures she and North had enjoyed with their great-grandmother.

Since Elliott's visit, she had tried to whip up enthusiasm for one of the several ideas he had mooted. But none of them really interested her. Nothing did.

Now, knowing that tonight was going to be one of the bad nights when she would lie awake for hours, she decided to write down all she could remember of the journeys they had made as children with Flora Carlyon.

Sitting down in front of the computer, which she had left switched on after writing a letter of thanks to Marie-Simone, she touched the keys which would bring a blank page onto the screen.

*When I was nine, Granny Flora took me to Venice* . . .

Safely back in the past, before love, before joy, before pain, she began to relive the time when bliss was a dish of cassata at the Caffè Florian.


The day before their first wedding anniversary, North came back from ballooning over the Pyrenees. He was as tanned as a gypsy and eager to repeat the experience as soon as possible.

'You must try it, sweetie,' he told Jane. 'It's a fantastic sensation.'

She had missed him deeply but refrained from saying so because it might make him feel he should have missed her more. Clearly, for him, their three weeks apart had flown by.

'I'm glad you're mad about balloons. I'm getting more and more like one,' she said cheerfully.

'You're lovely. Let's go to bed.'

He swept her upstairs and made love to her with so much tender enthusiasm that the doubt at the back of her mind that he could still find her desirable was swiftly banished.

# September

Gary Clutton stuck a cigarette between his lips and tossed the empty pack aside.

As he flicked his lighter, a voice said, 'The proper place for rubbish is a rubbish bin, young man. Kindly pick up that packet and all these cigarette ends you've scattered around you. I object to litter outside my gate. What are you doing here? Are you waiting for someone?'

For some moments he gaped in astonishment at the woman who had dared to reprimand him. The last time he had heard that tone of voice had been at the juvenile court in his home town.

Small, wizened, with dabs of rouge on her seamed cheeks and a gaze as bright and beady as the glass-eyed stare of the pre-war silver fox slung round her narrow shoulders, the old lady rapped the pavement with the tip of her umbrella.

'I asked you a question, young man. I should like a reply,' she told him imperiously.

In Gary's experience, the old were afraid of the young. Not long ago, up north, seeing some old josser glaring at him in the furtive way they did, he had said to him, '. . . and up yours, Granpa', which was no more than what the stupid old sod had been thinking about him. Talk about shit-scared! The old feller had fucking nearly had a heart attack.

But this little old biddy from the house next door to where Tiff lived wasn't scared of him. She looked capable, if he talked back to her, of giving him a swipe with her brolly.

In the normal way his reaction would have been to

tell her to piss off. But seeing that she was going shopping, he decided to play up to the old cow.

'Okay, Granny, keep your hair on. I didn't mean no 'arm.' He got off his bike, picked up the discarded packet and booted a couple of fag ends from the pavement into the gutter. 'There . . .'ow's that?' he asked her, smiling.

'You won't live to my age if you continue to smoke,' she said. 'Wasting money *and* ruining your health is very foolish. I should give it up if I were you.'

Apparently forgetting she had wanted to know why he was there, she turned away, trotting with short steps in the direction of the main road.

Gary watched her, calculating that at the rate she walked it was going to be at least half an hour, probably longer, before she came back. Plenty of time to be in, out and away with whatever loot might be in there. Sure to be something worth nicking in a house that size. Unlike the one next door, which was split into flats, the old girl was the only person he had seen coming out of her gate. Lived on her own, by the look of it.

If he could do himself a bit of good it would make up for the time wasted waiting for Tiff to show up again. He hadn't been able to keep a close watch on her place because he wasn't in London regular, but several times since she'd failed to meet him at the pub, he had sat here hoping to catch her coming or going. He had also made some further efforts to track down his mum's sister Shirl, but that had been another waste of time.

While smoking his last cigarette, he had made up his mind to forget about putting the screws on Tiff. He was certain she *was* his cousin, but she wasn't the type who scared easy and hanging around, waiting for her, was too much sodding trouble. There were easier ways to make a few quid. Much easier ways.

The old lady had turned the corner and was out of sight. There was no one else about. Gary took his keys out of the ignition. He would chance having his helmet and gauntlets nicked. Unless the place was a lot more difficult to break into than he expected it to be, he wouldn't be gone long.

Five minutes later, in the antique shop where, one by one, she was selling off her treasures because she had no one to leave them to and needed the money to keep her eight cats in comfort now and after she had gone to her Maker, Mrs Lavinia Massingham said, 'I wonder if you would allow me to use your telephone? I think I ought to have a word with the police about a young man who is loitering outside my house. I've a feeling he's up to no good.'

Driving her shiny black Porsche 924, which every man who admired it always assumed must have been a present from a man, Louise Picton looked for a parking space in the streets close to James Muirhead's house.

Had it been a part of London where expensive cars were likely to have their coachwork scored with a sharp instrument by a resentful have-not, she would have come in a taxi. But Connaught village was a neighbourhood where Rolls-Royces and Ferraris stood at the kerb's edge unharmed – at least for the present.

That this would continue, Louise was inclined to doubt. Although she had no wish to encumber her life with a living-in male, she was increasingly aware of the dangers of being on her own. She was not of a nervous temperament but she wasn't as relaxed as she had been, ten years ago, going about London at night. There were too few police cars and too many muggers and rapists.

Not to mention too much rubbish, she thought, with a fastidious frown at a stack of full bin bags awaiting removal from the pavement.

If I were Maggie Thatcher, everyone on social security

would have to do some street cleaning, she thought crossly, locking the car. But as she walked towards the Square, her high heels shortening her steps, she knew that her irritation was caused as much by sexual frustration as by London's untidiness compared with the continental cities she had visited the week before.

It was more than six weeks now since she and James had spent a night together. They had talked on the telephone but each time she had been the one to make the call, and each time he had been unable to meet her for dinner or to go to the theatre. Suddenly his life seemed to have become twice as busy as it had ever been before, and Louise wasn't convinced that this was solely attributable to the death of old Maurice Clyst, the former head of James' firm.

Which was why she was paying an unexpected call on him. Face to face, she would know whether she was right in suspecting that their convenient affair had, on his side, begun to cool off.

When she arrived at his house, she could see he was at home by the lights in the first floor living room – the drawing room as he always called it.

On the doorstep she checked her make-up in the mirror on the flap of her evening bag. Under her black wool coat – she would have preferred to wear Blackglama mink but that would be asking for trouble not only from the yobs but also from the anti-fur lot – she was dressed for a fashionable dinner party although she had not been to one.

When James opened the door he looked surprised and, in the first fraction of a second, not pleased.

'Hallo. Have I called at an inconvenient moment?' she asked, smiling.

'Not at all,' he said politely, standing back to admit her.

'I've been dining with friends down the road but it was a bit of a bore so I came away early and thought

I'd pop in for five minutes on my way home in case you felt neglected. If you called my office last week' – she knew he hadn't: it had been her first question to her secretary – 'they'll have told you I was abroad.'

'Oh really? Where have you been?' he asked, following her up the staircase.

She told him about her trip, making it sound much more fun than in fact it had been.

In the drawing room she undid her coat and he helped her remove it.

'New dress. Like it?' she asked, twirling to show it off.

The dress was made of silk velvet, as soft as a black kitten's fur, with a low neckline for which she had bought a bra which made the most of her cleavage.

'Very slinky,' said James, taking in the thigh-high side slit, the black diamond-patterned tights and the four-inch heels.

But he didn't sound or look switched on.

'What can I give you to drink?'

'Soda with a drop of Campari, please. I mean a drop literally, James. I came in the car so I've got to watch it. Can't afford to lose my licence.'

She hoped he would say, Why not drive home in the morning? Do you realise how long it is since we last went to bed together?

But he didn't. He said only, 'Pale pink soda coming up,' and moved across the room to the drinks cupboard.

While he was fixing her drink, Louise arranged herself in the chair with the most flattering light, in a pose she had tried out at home in front of a mirror, her legs crossed so that the slit in her dress fell open exposing maximum thigh.

'Tell me what you've been doing. Anything exciting?' she asked.

'Not really. The Longwarden job is occupying a lot of my time.'

He brought her a tall glass with ice and a sliver of

lemon floating at the brim. Then he retired to the chair where he had been reading, a glass of whisky and water at his elbow.

'Why was your dinner boring? I didn't know you had friends in this part of town.'

'When I said down the road I actually meant across the park . . . Montpelier Square. Why was it boring? I'm not sure. You know how it is with dinner parties. Sometimes they gel and sometimes they don't. Anyway I made the excuse of an early appointment tomorrow thinking that, if you were at home, I'd have a nightcap here. We haven't seen much of each other lately.'

'No, we haven't.'

James drank some whisky and looked at the toe of his shoe, not at her.

Louise said, 'My neighbour at dinner was telling me about a new restaurant he thought rather good. Shall we try it out? Have you a night free next week?'

'I don't think I have, actually. I've rather a lot on my plate at the moment.'

'Really? I wouldn't have guessed it from your reading matter,' she said dryly.

The book he had laid on the arm of his chair was a biography, nothing to do with architecture.

'James, let's not beat about the bush. Are you really busy or is that a polite excuse? I would rather know where I stand. If you want to end our arrangement, you have only to say so. I'm not going to throw a tantrum. I'm not that sort of woman.'

He looked at her. 'I know you aren't. Well, yes, since you ask, I think it might be better if we called it a day. We shall, I hope, always be friends, but – '

'But no longer lovers,' she put in. 'I agree. I've been thinking along the same lines and, to be honest, that's why I came round tonight. To put my cards on the table. I was very loath to hurt your feelings but, happily, now I don't have to.' She sipped her drink and gave him a brilliant smile. 'So we can end our relationship without rows or recriminations and wish each other well.'

He looked surprised and relieved. Obviously he hadn't expected to be able to end it so easily. And, if he knew the truth, what she really wanted to do was to swear and scream and throw things at him.

It required all her willpower to keep those feelings battened down and say calmly, 'I imagine your reason is the same as mine . . . you've met someone else. Someone at Longwarden, perhaps?'

It was a shot in the dark, but his reaction told her she had hit the mark.

'There is someone I like there – yes.'

'Is it serious this time?' she asked.

He frowned. 'I think you know my situation, Louise.'

'Yes, I do. You've never talked about it, but other people have. To be frank, I thought you probably used it as an excuse not to get too involved. But if this time it goes beyond sex, presumably – '

He cut her short. 'Sex has no part in it.'

She raised her eyebrows. 'Really? That sounds most unlike you. I take it you mean not yet. Is she keeping you guessing? How very trying. If you've been held at arm's length since the last time we did it, you must be getting rather edgy.'

Suddenly she wanted him more than ever before. She put down her drink and crossed the space between their chairs. Going down on her knees beside his, she put her hand on him. 'Our affair was fun while it lasted. As a farewell gesture, shall I – ?'

Grabbing her wrist, he snatched her hand away. Louise laughed and put her other hand on him. He pulled that away, but not before she had felt his involuntary reaction.

'Oh, come on,' she said. 'Don't be prudish. We've

know each other too long. You want it. I'll give it to you. It's the least I can do.'

'For God's sake, Louise, behave yourself.' His fingers bit into her wrists.

'You do want it, don't you? I know you do. I remember the first time you had me. I'd thought you looked rather austere but – my God! – not between the sheets. You were *ravenous* – as you are now.' She rubbed her breasts against his knees, amused by his furious scowl as, against his will, his body responded to hers.

She had a feeling that tonight was going to be something special; so good that he might change his mind about the bitch at Longwarden, whoever she was.

'You're making a fool of yourself,' he said curtly. 'What was between us is over.'

'Tomorrow – yes. I agree. But tonight let's have a last fling. You feel in the mood. So do I. What are we waiting for?'

She opened her mouth and ran the tip of her tongue around the edges of her lips, watching a rush of blood darken his cheeks.

'One last time,' she said softly. 'Why not? You know you want to.'

'I do *not* want to,' he grated, the bulge in his trousers belying his angry denial.

She knew she had only to persist and he would capitulate.

She pouted. 'You're hurting me, James.'

His fingers slackened a little but he didn't let go of her wrists.


In the night, unable to sleep, James was filled with the same self-loathing he had felt on a previous occasion: the time he and Louise had copulated in the bed in which he lay now – Belinda's bed.

He remembered Louise's remark the following morning.

'Aren't you afraid of being taken for a poofter, sleeping in a bed like this?' she had asked, looking up at the sunburst of pale blue silk which had taken Belinda hours of pinning and unpinning to get right.

When every fold was perfect, she had applied a silk-covered disc to the centre on which she had already embroidered a posy of forget-me-nots and, in minuscule letters, her initials and the year.

Belinda Kendal, later to become Belinda Muirhead.

Thinking of her, it sickened him that the demands of his body could drive him to actions which he regretted immediately his need was satisfied. Not that there was any real satisfaction in having sex with a woman one didn't love. He didn't even like Louise. She was merely the owner of a body which he knew to be clean, wholesome and available when he needed it.

He despised himself for that, too; making use of a woman for whom he felt no affection. Some men did it all the time, without scruple. But he had grown up loving women, his mother, his sisters, his grandmothers. From boyhood, he had liked and respected the opposite sex and, outwardly, had gone through the motions of liking and respecting Louise.

But inwardly his attitude to her had been that of other men towards a call girl. He had taken her, enjoyed her and secretly despised her for opening her legs and performing other intimate services for a man who cared nothing for her and meant nothing to her.

After a while he got up and went down to the kitchen where he poured himself a glass of water and found some aspirins which he took to the drawing room, intending to close his mind to useless remorse by reading.

The book he had been reading earlier was on the table by his chair but he had not found it gripping. Looking along the shelves for a paperback thriller he had bought for a skiing holiday but never read, he passed the book Laura had given him.

How disgusted she would be if she knew what had happened in here a few hours earlier. It would be beyond her comprehension. More than likely she was still a virgin. How could a woman who had been chaste all her life feel anything but revulsion at an act of animal lust?

He found the thriller and started to read it. But after a couple of pages it failed to distract him from his headache and his thoughts. He drank some more water and leaned back, closing his eyes.

In his mind's eye he saw a stream and two children with fishing nets on the end of canes and jam jars with string handles in which to put their catch of sticklebacks.

The boy was himself, aged ten. The girl, also wearing shorts and a tee shirt, with her hair held back by a tortoiseshell slide, was Belinda then eight.

They had known each other all their lives. He had bossed her about and looked after her as if she were a younger sister. Once, to his subsequent chagrin, he had slapped her for disobeying him, whereupon she had made a fist and punched him in the eye.

But that had been when they were pre-adolescent. Once they were both in their teens there had been no more quarrels, no more scraps. Often as they must have exasperated their elders, they had seldom upset each other. There had been arguments but never rows; times of restless uncertainty but, deep down, no real doubts that although for a while their paths might take different directions, eventually they would converge, leading to a shared future.

At half past four in the morning, seventeen years after the day she had kissed him goodbye, James sat in the room filled with Belinda's treasures, the muscles at the point of his jaw clenched as he remembered her.

*

'James . . . can you lend me two pounds?'

Her hazel eyes bright with excitement, her clear skin glowing from the cold of a winter's day, Belinda burst into the barber's where he was having his hair cut.

'I expect so. What's it for?'

Except in its details, he knew the answer in advance. Having already spent her pocket money in one of the town's antique shops, now she had seen something else she couldn't resist.

During the holidays, he frequently had to lend her money from his own more generous allowance. His father was a consultant, hers was a schoolmaster, now retired.

'Mr Colburn has just shown me the most divine thing you ever saw . . . a little box made from orange peel. It's so pretty . . . I *must* have it, James. Are you sure you can spare – ?'

'Yes, of course. But two pounds seems an awful lot to pay for something made out of orange peel.'

'You would never guess that was what it was made from. I thought it was tôle or Vernis Martin.'

At sixteen she was as knowledgeable as many of the dealers with whom she hobnobbed. Given a free choice, she would have chosen to be a dealer herself. But she was clever and, having had the advantage of extra tuition from her father, there was little doubt that she would follow in his footsteps and be accepted by one of the colleges at Cambridge. Only James knew that she didn't really want to go to university, but longed to open a junk shop or have a stand at antique fairs. But that would have disappointed her parents whom she adored.

'If they hadn't had the guts to have me in spite of the old wives' tales about late pregnancies, think what I would have missed,' she had once said to James.

On the bus going back to the village where they both lived, she confessed that the box had cost not two pounds but five.

'Don't let on, will you? The Old Folks would have blue fits.'

It was what she often called her parents, but in a most loving way. They were much older than his parents, having married late in life. Mr Kendal had been in his middle fifties when Belinda was born and his wife well into her forties.

'I'll tell them myself, but not yet. I'm going to sell some of my other bits and pieces to pay for it. I won't keep you waiting more than a week for your two pounds,' she promised him.

'There's no hurry. I'm flush this month. I wish Mum hadn't persuaded Dad not to let me have a car,' said James, fidgeted by the slowness of the bus's roundabout route. He had passed the driving test but the car he had hoped to be given for his eighteenth birthday would not be forthcoming until he reached twenty.

'She's terrified of you speeding – which, if you're honest, you probably would,' said Belinda. 'You wouldn't be flush if you had a car of your own. You'd be permanently broke . . . scrounging from me instead of the other way round. You do like the box, don't you?'

'It's very pretty, but you know your trouble. You can never hide your feelings. I bet old Colburn saw you were mad about it and put the price up.'

'He doesn't do that sort of thing. The price was on a tag inside it. Five pounds is the trade price. Mr Colburn is a dealer of the old school. He thinks it's awful the way the new breed of dealers pick a number and double it. He's going to retire before long because he won't stock Victorian stuff and it's getting so hard to find earlier things. He says I should spend every penny I have on anything which takes my fancy because I've got a good eye and every penny I spend now will be worth a pound in years to come.'

'I can't see that box ever being worth five hundred pounds.'

'Nor can I, actually, but I do know that if Mr Colburn buys something really choice, he doesn't put it in the shop. It goes into his private store to support him in his old age. What shall we do this afternoon?'

'We could go for a walk with the dogs . . . round by Wood Farm and the ford. It may be pouring tomorrow.'

'Okay, I'll come round after lunch.'


*'James!'*

Having unwrapped the small parcel of tissue paper and cotton wool, Belinda's reaction was a gasp of rapturous astonishment.

'Where *did* you find it? I've been longing for one since forever but I've only seen three. Two were madly expensive and the one which wasn't was damaged.'

She held in on the palm of her hand: a piece of ivory, no more than three inches long, carved in the shape of a pea-pod.

He had spotted it on a stall on a street market. It had been in a glass-topped box filled with odds and ends of jewellery and silver. It might have caught his eye, but he wouldn't have know what it was if Belinda hadn't once shown him a photograph in a book and told him it was one of the two things she longed to add to her collection of antique needlework tools. The other was a thimble made of mother of pearl and he would have liked to give her both but had only succeeded in finding the pea-pod needle-case.

'It isn't your main present,' he said. 'I'm bringing that to the party tonight.'

It was the morning of her eighteenth birthday which this year, very conveniently, fell on a Saturday. But even if it had not, he would have come down from London for her party.

By a rare stroke of luck the price of the pea-pod had

been only a pound, but he had spent much more than that on a fan he thought she would like.

'It couldn't be nicer than this,' she said. 'This is my heart's desire . . . or one of them. Isn't the carving marvellous? You can *feel* the peas inside the pod. I must show it to Mummy.'

Then, realising that she hadn't actually said thank you, although to him her joyful reaction was thanks enough, she said, 'Thank you *very* much, James.'

And she followed that by standing on tiptoe to brush a soft kiss on his cheek.

There had been a time, not long ago, when the kiss would have been a smacker accompanied by an uninhibited hug. But he'd noticed that since he had left home she had been much less demonstrative, although whenever he came back they still spent most of their time together.

For his part he felt a strong impulse to grab her and kiss her properly. But he knew that both his and her parents trusted him to behave himself with her and, even if they hadn't, his sexual feelings about her were restrained by a wish to protect her and keep her friendship. The thought of other guys making determined passes at her – as he did at girls in London – made him angry; especially the thought that she might respond to them in the same way that a couple of girls had to him.

The fact that, in one of their talks about Life and their plans for it, she had told him she didn't intend to sleep with anyone until she was seriously in love wasn't totally reassuring. He was pretty certain she had little or no experience even of petting and didn't yet know how easy it was for feelings to get out of hand.

What he wanted was for her to stay as she was until, in a few years' time, he had finished sowing his wild oats as Granny Blanche called it and was ready to settle down.

At the moment, even if he wanted to marry her now,

their parents would never allow it. They would say she was far too young.

'Why are you looking at me in that funny way?' Belinda asked.

He realised that by staring at her he had made her blush. Suddenly he was almost sure that she had a crush on him and that was why, in spite of their almost sibling relationship, she had spasms of shyness with him.

To test his theory, he said, 'I was thinking how pretty you are,' in the tone of voice and with the look which seemed to work on girls in London.

That made her blush even more. 'Thank you,' she murmured.

Then she gave him a glowing look which made his heart give a great lurch. Suddenly two or three years seemed an eternity to wait.


The weekend his car was in dock and he went home by train, he was expecting his mother to meet him at the station. His father drove a BMW and his mother had a small blue Daihatsu for shopping and attending the meetings of the various committees she served on.

But it was Belinda who was waiting for him as he walked down the platform. It was some time since he'd seen her and he hadn't known that she was going to be at home this weekend. He quickened his pace and waved, feeling pleasure course through him like the warming effect of whisky on a cold day.

'Hello, James. How are you?'

As he handed over his ticket and passed the barrier she offered him her cheek.

At twenty-one she had the self-possession one would expect of a girl who had taken a brilliant degree and was poised on the brink of what was expected to be an equally brilliant career.

Putting his lips to her smooth cheek, he caught a faint

fragrance of lilies of the valley and was pleased that she was still wearing *Diorissimo*, the scent he had given her two Christmases ago.

'I'm well . . . and you look wonderful.'

'Thank you.' These days she didn't blush but took compliments in her graceful stride. 'Your mother has a bit of a cold so I volunteered to come for her and have a look round my old haunts beforehand. Just as well I did or I might have missed something rather fabulous. You can help me put it together when we get home.'

'What is it this time?' he asked. 'Something to keep or something for Sotheby's?'

From time to time her unerring eye for quality enabled her to make not inconsiderable amounts of money by picking up something, if not for a song, for far less than its market value.

'This is to keep,' she said, as they left the station building.

'What in God's name is all that?' said James, seeing his mother's car surmounted by an enormous bundle wrapped in plastic and lashed to the roof-rack.

'My marriage-bed,' she said casually.

'Your what?'

'The bed I'm going to sleep in with my husband. It's all there, bar the mattress which will have to be specially made for it. I'm going to have to get an overdraft from the bank to pay for it, but I shouldn't think that will be a problem. Mr Colburn took a hundred on account and I promised the balance before the end of the month.'

James checked that the load was secure before getting into the car and pushing the passenger seat as far back as it would go to accommodate his long legs. He had forgotten that one of the items on the list of her heart's desires was a four-poster bed.

'So you've finally found it,' he said, as he fastened his seat belt.

'Yes . . . at long last. Now all I have to do is to put

411

it in order, by which time I hope the man who is going to sleep in it will have proposed to me.'

He felt suddenly icy cold. 'When and where did you pick him out?'

She gave him a mischievous look. 'Not in an antique shop.'

'Have I met him?'

He had been to Cambridge several times while she was there and had met some of the male undergraduates whom she described as friends although they were all visibly panting for her.

Belinda nodded, most of her attention on backing and turning the car in a rather tight space. That accomplished, she said, 'I'd hoped he would have asked me by now but he hasn't.'

James felt hot with rage at the thought that one of those swine, none of whom had been remotely worthy of her, might be stringing her along. It was hard to imagine anyone not having serious intentions towards her, but there were some bastards about.

'Being a man, you know how their minds work. Give me your advice,' she said. 'What is the best way of bringing a man to the point . . . assuming one has reason to believe that he's seriously interested?'

He didn't want to discuss it or think about it. He couldn't believe it had happened. She hadn't been in love with anyone the last time he saw her. She had talked of nothing but the career options which were open to her. How could it have happened so quickly, and just at the very time when he felt he could show his own feelings without upsetting her parents? She was still very young, but not impossibly young and already she had fulfilled a large part of their hopes for her by achieving such a good degree.

'What makes you think he is serious? That he makes love to you doesn't prove anything,' he said acidly.

'There's nothing like that between us. I wish there

were. I'm aching for it. It's virtually unheard of to be *virgo intacto* at my age. But what's one to do when the only man one wants to go to bed with doesn't try even a mild pass? At first I used to seethe with jealousy while he chased other girls. Not that he ever talked about them to me, but I heard about his affairs from other people. Now all that's stopped, thank heaven, but he still isn't breathing his fiery breath in my direction. Do tell me what to do, James.'

'If he hasn't made any approaches, what gives you the idea he's interested?'

'He doesn't talk only about himself . . . he wants to know what I think. He asks questions and listens to my answers. That's always a good sign. We don't go about together on a regular basis, but when we do we always have a terrific time. He's more fun than anyone I know and there are little hints that he wouldn't mind bedding me.'

'What sort of hints?' He didn't want to hear: at the same time he couldn't help asking. Like a slow-starting fire, an outbreak of jealous anger had begun to build up inside him and would eventually reach flash point when he wouldn't be able to contain it. It was just as well he wasn't driving. The people on the pedestrian crossing ahead would have had to jump for their lives.

'An occasional rather burning look . . . and sometimes very nice presents . . . thoughtful presents . . . you know what I mean. What I want you to tell me is how to bring him to the boil . . . short of saying straight out that I'm mad about him.'

'I have no idea,' he said curtly. 'Why not ask your girlfriends or your mother. It's more in their line than mine.'

'That's not very helpful. They don't even know he exists. They probably guess there's someone I'm in love with, but I've never talked to them about him. I've only confided in you because I'm so desperate. It's not only that I want him madly, there's a practical problem looming up.'

'What d'you mean?'

'As soon as I've made up my mind about this job in London I've been offered, I'll have to start thinking where to live. You know what a hassle that is. It seems pretty silly to go through it if sooner or later I'm going to be living with him.'

'He's going to be working in London as well, I presume?'

'Mm . . . it's already organised and there's more than enough room for two in his bachelor pad.'

'In that case,' James said reluctantly, grudging any advice which might advance her relationship with his rival, 'I can only suggest that you say what you've just said to me. Tell him you're worried about finding somewhere civilised to live in London. If that doesn't bring him to the point, I can't think what else would.'

'I could make a pass at him,' said Belinda. 'I've thought about it several times but at the last moment I always lose my nerve. Perhaps I'll try your idea. It might work.'

For the rest of the journey she talked of other matters. In the past if he had been upset or angry she would have sensed it at once and asked what was troubling him. Today, her head full of thoughts of the other guy, she had lost her sensitivity to James' feelings. Nor could he empathise with her. Far from wanting her to be happy even if it cost him his own happiness – which was supposed to be the sign of true, unselfish love – he was convinced that no one else could love her as much as he did.

She was his. She had always been his. How could he stand by and let her throw herself away on some fool who hadn't even the nous to guess how she felt about him?

At her parents' house he helped her unload the parts

414

of the four-poster bed from the roof-rack. Then Mrs
Kendal offered him tea which he accepted, first tele-
phoning his mother to explain where he was and that
he would be home shortly.

'If you've nothing better to do tomorrow morning,
would you help me put the bed together?' Belinda asked,
while they were having tea in her father's study.

Fifteen years earlier, when the Church Commissioners
had built a small, more up to date house for a new Vicar
and his young family, the Kendals had bought the old
Vicarage so that Mrs Kendal would have enough garden
to grow all her vegetables and keep some livestock.

In the opinion of the Muirheads, she was a health
crank who wouldn't eat shop-bought meat because she
said it was full of the poisons farms put on their pastures
and the hormones and antibiotics they injected into their
stock.

More than once in their growing-up years James had
comforted a red-eyed, grief-stricken Belinda after the
death of a bullock she had known since it was a long-
lashed, still playful calf.

That, taken to the slaughter-house by Mr Kendal, its
end would have been less distressing than that of a farm-
bred animal herded onto a truck and treated like the
victims of a pogrom had not been a comfort to Belinda
in the days immediately following the animal's departure. For several years during her teens she had become
a vegetarian but now ate meat if it were served to her
but never from choice.

James had thought, when he first caught sight of her
at the station, of taking her out to dinner that night. In
the light of her revelation, he had changed his mind.

'Yes, I'll give you a hand,' he agreed.

The last thing he wanted was to put up a bed in
which she was hoping to give someone else the delight of
making love to her. At the same time he couldn't let her
struggle with the bed on her own. Like her mother,

Belinda was a gifted needlewoman who could run up curtains, make canvas work covers for stools and re-cover lampshades. But when it came to restoring old furniture she had often turned to him for help with the processes involving the traditionally male skills with a saw, hammer and power-drill.

'You'll find Belinda upstairs, dear,' said Mrs Kendal, when he arrived at The Old Vicarage the following morning.

Normally he would have sprung up the staircase three at a time, but a restless night had given him a headache and he felt as if the bottom had dropped out of his world and nothing would ever be right again.

The house, which was mid-Victorian, had four large rooms on the first floor and attics above.

The Kendals slept in one of the two large front bed-rooms and Belinda had the other. With his help with the painting and papering, she had several times altered its décor and had an eye for colour as good as her eye for antiques.

Her door was closed. He knocked.

'Come in, James.'

She had already moved her single bed and cleared the area where the four-poster would stand while she made new hangings for it. She was wearing a pair of old jeans and a white tee shirt which showed the shape of her breasts. She looked bright-eyed and energetic. Clearly she had slept as well as he had slept badly, perhaps with the bonus of an erotic dream about Mr Wonderful, he thought savagely.

What had tortured him during the night had been her remark in the car: *I'm aching for it . . . but what's one to do when the only man one wants to go to bed with doesn't make even a mild pass?*

416

'You look a bit hungover,' she said. 'Did you go out last night?'

'Nope. Stayed home. Watched TV. Listened to Dad's usual tirade about the decline of the NHS.'

'Have you had breakfast?'

He shook his head. 'I overslept. By the time I got up Mum had gone to her hair appointment. They're going out to dinner tonight. I could have fixed myself something but I wasn't hungry. I expect your mother will produce something good for elevenses. She always does. I'll hang on till then.'

'I'll fix you something now,' said Belinda. 'Going without breakfast is bad for people – especially someone of your size. Come on down and I'll make you a nice hunk of cheese on toast. Perhaps you're getting a cold. You look rotten, poor love.'

Her sympathy – that of an affectionate sister – for a condition she had caused, didn't make him feel better.

'I'm okay. Don't fuss,' he said crossly. 'I don't want anything now. Let's get the bed up.'

It took them most of the morning to erect the four-poster which he had to admit was probably worth the price she had paid for it.

'Will you have lunch with us, James?' asked Mrs Kendal, when she brought their elevenses on a tray.

As he had foreseen, there was a selection of goodies from her Saturday morning cooking session on a plate, and the appetising smell of freshly baked bread pervaded the whole house.

'Thank you, yes, if I may?' He thought he was probably mad to prolong the torture of being with Belinda, but it was a bitter-sweet pain and this might be the last time he had her to himself.

So far she hadn't mentioned the subject which must be foremost in her mind. As they ate their elevenses on the windowseat built round the large bay window and scattered with cushions she had made from fragments of a torn and threadbare antique French carpet, she gazed out at the garden, her thoughts clearly miles away.

He had thought her pretty at eighteen but now she was more than that. She had never suffered from puppy fat but her face had had a certain roundness which since then had disappeared, leaving her cheeks slightly hollowed and emphasising the lovely moulding of her features. She was beautiful now; so beautiful that it wrung his heart to look at her.

Suddenly she turned her head and looked at him. 'You know, James, I'm really worried about this whole London business. Most of my friends would give their eyeteeth for the job I've landed, but it doesn't thrill me a bit. Nor does the idea of sharing a flat with two or three other girls which seems to be the only way I can afford to live in central London. If Cambridge taught me anything it's that communal life doesn't really suit me. I'm not a loner, not a bit. What I'd like is to share with just one other person . . . someone who has the same tastes . . . someone like you.'

He wanted to shake her for her insensitivity in bringing up the subject again. But then hadn't she always turned to him with her worries? How was she to know that this was a problem he couldn't discuss with detachment because it involved him.

'If you do what I suggested yesterday, you may find yourself sharing with someone who's even more on your wave-length than I am,' he said brusquely.

Belinda unfolded herself from the position in which she had been curled. She put her mug back on the tray.

'Unfortunately, something seems to have gone wrong with our wave-length. We're not tuned in to the same frequency. I *have* done what you suggested and it hasn't got through. Think about it. Think about it hard. I'm going out for some fresh air.'

She got up and walked out of the room.

\*

'Good morning. Are we on fire?' Mr Kendal asked, minutes later, having emerged from his study to be almost bowled over by James leaping down the stairs.

'No, sir . . . sorry . . . good morning . . . can't stop now . . .'

James shot past him and rushed from the house. Which way had she gone? Where would he find her?

Belinda was sitting on the swing under the towering horse chestnut in whose branches there was a treehouse built long before their time but still usable. She wasn't swinging. Her hands were in the pockets of an old wind-cheater and she was staring at her track shoes. She didn't look up as he approached.

He said, 'If you're really not keen on this job, how would you feel about keeping house for me? It would leave you plenty of time to do all the things you like doing. Between us I think we could manage until my salary gets better.'

She glanced up at him. 'Is that intended to be a proposal of marriage?'

'Definitely. Not a very good one, perhaps, but –'

'Not very good? *Abysmal!* Pathetic . . . ludicrous. I shouldn't think any girl, ever, could have had a worse one.' She jumped to her feet. 'But the answer is yes . . . *yes* . . . YES!!!'

Her joyous shout rang round the garden.


The following afternoon, her parents having gone to lunch with friends in a distant village, James and Belinda looked at the cracks in the ceiling plaster through the empty frame for the four-poster's canopy.

They were lying on the floor inside and below the bed's lower framework. Beneath them were cushions and a rumpled eiderdown.

Belinda lifted her head from his naked shoulder. She

419

turned over to rest her slim arms and bare breasts on his chest.

'I forgive you everything,' she said, smiling. 'You may make an awful hash of telling a girl you love her, but you certainly know how to make love. For my first time that was amazing. Is there time to do it again?'

'Better not. Your parents might come back early. They wouldn't approve, even though we are engaged now.' He touched her cheek with his knuckles. 'You would make a good lover of anyone. You're so beautiful, Belinda. I can't believe that you're mine . . . mine for the rest of my life.'

'I've always been yours. I knew that ages ago. It was misery for me when you started having girlfriends. I've spent hours of my life alternately moping and fuming at the thought of you doing this with them instead of with me.' She sat up and ran her hand slowly down the centre of his body. 'Do you realise that, in spite of the most intense curiosity, today is the first time I've seen one of these fascinating things in close-up. I've had them nudging me at dances but that's all. Have you read the *Kama Sutra*?'

He shook his head. 'Have you?'

'Naturally. Those who can, do. Those who can't, read about it. Now at last I can try out all the arts of love I've learnt from Vatsyayana and Co.'

With gentle fingers and soft lips she began to practise on him.



'. . . for better for worse, for richer for poorer, in sickness and in health, from this day forward until death us do part.'

As the Vicar read the vows and James repeated them, he was no longer shaking with nerves as he had been a short time earlier – albeit not visibly – while he and his best man stood by the chancel steps waiting for the bride to arrive.

The wedding had got out of hand. He and Belinda had wanted an informal wedding in the presence of their closest relations. Their mothers and James' sisters had had other ideas and somehow the wedding had blossomed from a small, quiet affair into an elaborate morning dress ceremony with three bridesmaids and a page, three hundred guests and a reception at a nearby country club.

Some elements of the simple wedding they would have preferred had been retained. Belinda was wearing an Edwardian lace wedding dress she had bought at a jumble sale for £3 and lovingly laundered and repaired. Her mother had made and iced the wedding cake. The flowers decorating the church were from gardens in the village and their arrangements had been supervised by the chairman of the WI who was also one of the county's leading flower arrangers.

'And thereto I plight thee my troth.'

As he completed his vows, James was no longer aware of his family in one of the front pews and of all the friends and relations his mother had said must be invited or they would be deeply offended.

He was only aware of the Vicar in his starched surplice and of the exquisite girl to whom, with passionate sincerity, he had just pledged himself for life.

As she had come up the aisle on her father's arm, there had been a concerted murmur of admiration for the vision of radiant young love gliding serenely past the dazzled congregation in a dress which had first been worn more than sixty years ago.

James had not been allowed to see it before, but he knew that Belinda had found out to whom it had belonged and looked up the date of her marriage. He had also heard his sisters saying that only someone with a long neck and a tiny waist could wear it. Belinda had both. To his eyes the bridal dress with its throat-hugging collar and lace trim looked as if it might have been made for her.

She wasn't wearing a veil. His mother had offered her the Limerick veil worn by his sisters for their weddings. But Belinda had tactfully refused it. Her hair was piled high on her head in a cottage-loaf style in keeping with the period of the dress and round the top-knot she wore a circlet of flowers.

Nor had she carried a bouquet. In her hand had been the spangled silk fan he had given her when she was eighteen, but now this was in the care of the eldest bridesmaid and Belinda was wearing the ring they had chosen, a plain gold band inscribed on the inside with their initials and the date.


The next day they flew to Toulouse where they picked up a rented car and drove north-east along the Tarn, on roads striped with the shadows of plane trees, to the village where an architect James knew had a holiday house he had offered them for their honeymoon.

It was basically a stone-built tower, once used as a *pigeonnier*, to which had been added some rooms and a stream-fed swimming pool.

It was the perfect place to begin their marriage. They slept in a high wooden bed under a duvet which, when she had opened the shutters, Belinda would hang out of the window to air in the morning sun.

Then, hand in hand, they would stroll the half mile to the village baker's shop to buy flaky croissants and bread, both still warm from an old-fashioned brick oven.

After breakfast they would go for more vigorous walks, exploring the countryside and picnicking on local cheeses and *charcuterie*. James would take a small ruck-sack in which to carry the food and wine and each day they tried something different; rabbit pâté and Chabichou cheese with a bottle of fruity red Bergerac; a poultry terrine with a dry white Montravel; partridge pâté with a full-bodied Pecharmant.

On hot afternoons they would swim in the bracing stream water and then lie naked in the sun, sometimes making love out of doors. The place was completely secluded, nobody came there.

In the evenings, taking the car, they would drive to eating places recommended by the owner of La Pigeonnerie, most of them the dining rooms of small family-run hotels, serving the cuisine of the region to critical locals.

The one delicacy Belinda would not try was *foie gras*. The only time, in ten days, that he saw her frown was when she came across it on a menu and was reminded of how the birds' livers were fattened which she thought revoltingly cruel. But her scruples didn't rule out the other goose dish, *confits d'oie*, with black truffles; and having tried it, she bought a bottle of Eau de Noix, a liquer made from walnuts in the shell, to take home for her parents.

Now and then they spent some time reading, and on their walks they talked of their plans for the future. A weekend cottage in the country. In a few years' time, the first of two babies. Perhaps, one day far ahead, a summer place somewhere in France.

But for the most part their honeymoon was a feast of sensual delights; sun-bathing, wonderful food, wine, birdsong, the sound of the stream and, above all, the ultimate ecstasy which they shared at any hour of the day or night.

'If only it lasted longer. It's so lovely . . . but so fleeting,' Belinda said drowsily.

It was noon on their last but one day, and so hot that she had closed the shutters but not in their upright position which excluded almost all light. They were the type of shutter which could be pushed out at the bottom,

423

forming a downward slope and leaving an open space to admit light and air.

'Perhaps it's a provision of nature,' she added. 'If that wonderful bit at the end, that feeling of utter bliss, were to last five minutes, or ten, people might enjoy it less. Rather the way a second helping of pudding, however delicious, is never as good as the first.'

James, who had been sprawled on his back in an attitude of exhaustion, suddenly revived. Rolling onto his side, he raised himself on one elbow and looked at the lightly tanned body which was now as familiar as his own.

'You are my favourite pudding and as far as I'm concerned every helping is better than the last. How about another?'

She shifted closer. 'Help yourself.'

He dropped a light kiss on her mouth before drawing back. 'I was bluffing. I haven't the strength . . . at least not immediately. Perhaps after lunch. But that's no reason why you shouldn't – ' He paused as she deflected his hand from its destination. 'No? Why not? Women are inexhaustible.'

'At the moment I'm hungry for other things,' Belinda said, sitting up. 'Let's go down and have lunch. We can come back later . . . revitalised.'

As she would have climbed off the bed, James caught her round the waist, his hands sliding upwards to fondle her warm, firm breasts.

'I'm revitalised already.'

'Satyr!' She wriggled free, but with a backward glance to check that he wasn't serious.

If he had been, he knew, she would have stayed in his arms. She was as generous with her body as she was in every way. It had not been a deficiency of sexuality which had made it possible for her to resist the blandishments of other men. Clearly she had been speaking the truth when she told him she had seen no point in sex without love.

It made him regret his own past experiments which, lacking any deep feeling, seemed in retrospect not much better than sex with a prostitute. He had liked the girls he had had and they had seemed to like him, but what they had done together had borne as little relationship to making love with Belinda as – in the jargon of his family – plastic cheese to ripe Camembert.


James woke with a crick in his neck having fallen asleep in the chair where he'd spent half the night remembering his life before the watershed.

Long before rock and reggae and heavy metal, there had been a popular song which the disc jockeys of the day had played ad nauseam. He remembered only one line. *Into each life some rain must fall but too much is falling in mine* . . .

What had happened to him had been more like a dam-burst. One day everything had been fine and then, like a great wall of water, catastrophe had burst upon him, so sudden and shocking as to be unbelievable. He had survived it . . . somehow.

But on mornings like this, after a bad night, he still wished he hadn't.


Watching the telecast of the horse trials at Burghley, Sarah felt like an outcast.

What made it worse was that the commentator, although he referred frequently to outstanding perform-ances at previous Burghleys, never once mentioned last year's winners – Beddo and herself. It made her feel like a pariah who, after being subjected to an ignominious trial by the tabloids, now was being deliberately ignored by everyone whose opinion mattered to her.

In the days following the trials, she found it desperately hurtful that none of the riders whom she had thought were her friends rang up to regale her with bits of insiders' chit-chat. Surely they must have some inkling of how much she had missed being there?

But the worse hurt of all was receiving no call from Sammy. He had refused to speak to her too many times for her to try again. But she had hoped against hope that memories of last year's triumph would make him relent and telephone her.

Damaris woke in Sam's bed where she had slept, more soundly than ever before, since the night he had asked her back to his place for a nightcap.

Fortunately the quarters he occupied had been designed to accommodate a married couple. So their nights together, whether asleep or making love, had not been cramped by the narrowness of a single bed.

This morning he had woken first and got up without disturbing her. It was the sound of the shower which had woken her. The bathroom window was next to the bedroom window and when the water was full on it sounded like sudden rain.

Unless he had already soaped himself, in a moment he would turn it off and there would be an interval while he covered his body with lather and then ran the water again, adjusting it from hot to cold. She knew this because one morning she had taken a shower with him. Then he would wrap himself in an old striped bath robe, roughly dry his wet hair, and make a pot of tea which he would bring to the bedroom.

They didn't have breakfast together because she was keeping to her routine of working in the garden before breakfasting in the house. So far nobody knew she was no longer sleeping there.

Every morning, when first she woke, it still took her by

surprise that, literally overnight, her world had changed. Thanks to Sam. Wonderful Sam who, by his amazing tenderness and understanding, had dispelled all her fears and nightmares and replaced them with a memory she would keep and treasure as long as she lived.

She still hadn't told him the full story of what had happened to her and she never would. It would only hurt and enrage him. Anyway it no longer mattered. In Sam's arms she had experienced all the feelings she had once thought were ruined for her. She was not an emotional cripple. She was all right. Better than all right.

She was sitting up, combing her hair, when Sam appeared with the tray.

'Hello. How are you this morning?'

She smiled at him. 'Fine. How are you?'

'Pretty good.' His eyes told her he felt, as she did, on top of the world.

'I'm going to ring my assistant in London today . . . see if I can persuade her to run things for another month,' she said, while he poured out the tea.

'Do you think she'll agree?'

'I hope so. Reverting to two days a week doesn't fill me with enthusiasm.'

'We would only have one night together. Not enough . . . not nearly enough. I want you with me every night.'

'Do you think the Carlyons would mind if they knew what was going on between us?'

'Why should they? It's not their business. We're not frightening the horses.'

She knew the source of this allusion and was no longer surprised that he did. She was becoming accustomed to the breadth and depth of Sam's knowledge. Quite often he made some remark which was over her head. Except in relation to plants, this never happened in reverse.

The future of their relationship was something he

hadn't mentioned. She felt that, like her, for the time being he was content to live in the blissful present.

'Pen, are you sure you wouldn't like to put off going back to Spain until after the babies are born?' Piers asked, descending the step-ladder.

He had been hanging their drawing room curtains made from rolls of cotton put away long ago and forgotten until he and his wife had unearthed them.

'If Jane's baby turns up late – as first babies often do – that would mean staying on till nearly the end of October. I'd rather go back at the end of this month as we planned.'

For Pen, the overriding consideration was that, although he would never say so, she knew Piers was looking forward to resuming his daily snorkeling sessions.

By the end of September the beaches in Spain would no longer be intolerably crowded but the sea would still be lukewarm. It would cool down during November, she had been told, but with luck they would be able to continue swimming until Christmas and, in a mild winter, after it.

For her own part, much as she had enjoyed their return to Longwarden and the fun of doing up the dairies, she was eager to see how the garden at *Las Golondrinas* had fared in their absence.

'There's nothing to stop us flying back for a week in November, after the babies have arrived,' she added.

'Yes, we could do that – why not?' He tested the cords which opened and closed the curtains. 'How do they look? Are you pleased with them?'

The curtains had been made by a woman in the village who, having no room to work on them in her own small house, had sewn them at Longwarden. During the making up they had been seen by a visiting textiles conservator who had become very excited by the colour, indigo on white, and the pattern, engravings of scenes from the Fables of the French poet, Jean de La Fontaine.

Apparently the material, although not marked on its edges, had probably been manufactured by Christophe Oberkamf who, in the late eighteenth century, had made chintzes for Madame de Pompadour at his factory at Jouy-en-Josas, not far from Versailles. It was he who had developed the copper-plate printed *toiles de Jouy* which had become all the rage throughout fashionable Europe.

Most of them had been printed with a reddish-pink dye made by fermenting the roots of the madder plant. Some had been dyed with indigo, not much of this surviving because it was prone to fading. According to the conservator, the fabric which Pen and Piers had found was a very rare 'document' which should have been handed over to a museum.

She had made Pen feel guilty of unwitting vandalism. Jane, however, had said firmly that the cotton had been bought for Longwarden – possibly by her great-grandmother in France between the wars – and this was where it belonged. Jane was never in the least intimidated by the increasing number of 'experts' who came to the house to advise and sometimes to criticise.

'I think they look marvellous. Don't you?' Pen had always loved blue and white and, when they came back next summer, hoped to have a profusion of both blue and white delphiniums growing in their small private garden at the back of the dairies. 'I should never have guessed, if that woman hadn't told us, that the *toiles* were all boiled in cow dung to fix the dyes. There are three or four metres left over. Should I send them to her for her archives or have them made up into cushions for the striped sofa?'

One of the things she particularly enjoyed about her second marriage was that neither of them made decisions without discussing their ideas with the other. Edward Carlyon had either laid down the law or taken no interest at all. Piers was interested in everything.

Deprived in her first marriage of the pleasure most young couples took in setting up house together, she had experienced it twice in her second marriage, first in Spain and now here.

Not that they had much time left in which to enjoy the results of their summer labours. In fact their house-warming lunch party was fixed for the day before their departure for France.

---

# October

Nine days before the baby was due, Sarah received an agitated telephone call.

'Miss Sarah? It's Eileen Slane. I don't like to upset you, my dear, but I think you'd want to be told. It's Sammy . . . he's ill . . . a heart attack. He's been asking for you.'

'I'll come right away,' said Sarah. 'Where is he? At home or in hospital?'

After being taken ill in a shop, the old Irishman was now in the intensive care unit of the local hospital which was where Mrs Slane was ringing from.

'You'll have to get someone to bring you. You can't drive so near your time. I'm not sure you ought to come, but they think he may not pull through. They haven't said that . . . not straight out . . . but it's what they think, I can tell. You've been like a daughter to him . . . he's worried about being so hard on you. I wouldn't like him to die with a weight on his mind.'

As she listened to a distressed and disjointed account of Sammy's collapse and the anxious wait for the ambulance, Sarah's mind was working on the quickest way to reach the hospital.

Mrs Slane might be right in thinking it wasn't advisable for her to drive herself. But she couldn't ask Kate to take her because she was needed here. Allegra had gone to London. Jane was equally pregnant. North was away.

Which meant she would have to chance it.

Within half an hour of Mrs Slane's telephone call she had scribbled notes to Kate and Jane – who might make a fuss if told her intention beforehand – packed an overnight case and was on her way.

'You shouldn't have come,' Sammy whispered. 'Eileen had no business to tell you.'

'Well, I'm in the right place if all this rushing around makes the baby come early,' said Sarah, trying to sound cheerful.

The hospital staff had not wanted to let her see him. It seemed they had very strict rules about who was allowed to visit seriously ill patients. Sarah, not being related by blood or marriage, didn't qualify as a suitable visitor even though she had come a long way and Sammy had been asking for her. It was only when Eileen Slane had made a fuss and insisted on speaking to one of the senior doctors that permission had been given.

'I was hard on you, child. I said things I'd no right to say.' Sammy's voice was a weak thread of sound which she had to bend close to catch.

'Never mind that, Sammy dear. Just put your mind to getting better. I want you to be at the christening. I want you to be a godfather.'

'I'd like that . . . I'd like it fine . . . but I don't think I'm going to make it.'

'You thought you were going to die last time, and

then look what happened. You met Eileen,' Sarah said smiling.

But he did look terribly ill, far worse than last year when she had driven him to hospital, Sammy convinced he had cancer and was going to die on the operating table. That crisis had had a happy outcome. This one, judging by his appearance, might not.

Impelled by a fear that these few minutes at his bedside might be the last time she talked to him, she said, 'Did I ever tell you how much I love you, Sammy? I don't think I ever did. I assumed that you knew it.'

It was an effort for him to speak. 'And I love you, mavourneen.'

There was a great lump in her throat and she was trying hard to batten down her emotions when a hand touched her shoulder.

'Your time is up, Miss Lomax. Mr O'Brien needs to rest.'

Reluctantly Sarah rose, then bent to kiss Sammy's cheek. 'I'll be back later,' she murmured.

In case she should be tempted to linger, the staff nurse took her firmly by the elbow and drew her away from the bed.

In the waiting area along the corridor Eileen was talking to another woman. She broke off the conversation when she saw Sarah coming.

'How does he look to you? What do you think?' she asked anxiously.

'He's having the best possible care. I'm sure they'll pull him through,' Sarah said, trying to sound optimistic.

Inwardly she doubted if they would and she wondered if being in hospital, surrounded by machinery and strangers, was the best possible care for an old man in his last hours. Wouldn't he be more comfortable in his own bed with the people he loved taking care of him?

*

'Jane? It's Sarah.'

'Oh Sarah . . . thank goodness you've rung. We've been on pins about you. Where are you? How is Sammy?'

'Not good . . . very poorly indeed. It's touch and go, I'm afraid. Whatever happens I shall stay with Eileen tonight and possibly longer.'

'Has she any family to rally round her if he doesn't recover?'

'No, but I'm here and she isn't the type to fall apart. She's a very sensible, good-in-a-crisis sort of person.'

'It's a pity North isn't home. He'd have come with you. Does it seem a good hospital?'

'I suppose so. How does one tell? They have all the latest equipment and everywhere's spotlessly clean. It isn't what you'd call cosy. If Sammy is going to die, I think he'd be just as well off in his own bed instead of wired up to machines, but maybe they'll pull him through.'

'How are you feeling?'

'I'm fine. Don't worry about me. I'm upset about Sammy, naturally, but whatever happens we've made our peace. That's a comfort . . . for him and for me. I'll ring you again this evening . . . or if there's no news I'll call Kate and talk to her. Anyway I'll keep in touch.'


Sammy died late that afternoon. Mrs Slane and Sarah weren't with him. As neither of them had had any food since breakfast, they had gone across the road to a café for a cup of tea and something to eat. When they came back, his body had already been removed to the hospital mortuary.

Sarah was shocked and annoyed by the dispatch with which this had been done, but they were told that the bed had been urgently needed for another patient and she realised that for her to protest could only add to Mrs Slane's quiet distress.

'Perhaps it's for the best,' said Eileen, wiping her eyes in the taxi which took them back to her bungalow. 'He would have hated being an invalid. I'm so glad that he made it up with you, my dear. It's a shame that it took a heart attack to make him see how foolish he'd been. He was an obstinate man, but we were nice company for each other. I shall miss him very much.'

They spent the evening talking about him, often close to tears but comforted by the other's presence.

In the early hours of the following morning Sarah awoke from a nightmare about Sammy's body being carted off to the hospital incinerator because she had not been there to sign the form for funeral arrangements. Her attempt to stop the trolley by stepping in front of it resulted in the porter banging it against her stomach, making her cry out, 'Be careful! I'm having a baby.'

Within seconds of waking, she realised that the painful jolt of the trolley had been a real sensation. She was having a contraction.


'Did you have a poor night, dear?' asked Mrs Slane, coming into the kitchen shortly before eight o'clock to find Sarah there before her.

'I slept well at first. Then I woke up and couldn't get back to sleep. How did you sleep?'

'Quite well in the circumstances, thank you. What would you like for your breakfast? A poached egg on toast? Or there's bacon, if you prefer.'

'I'll have toast . . . nothing else. I'm not hungry.'

'Toast isn't very nourishing. Could you fancy a boiled egg? You should have something.'

Before Sarah could reply, she felt the beginning of another contraction.

Mrs Slane had started bustling about and she didn't

notice that Sarah hadn't replied because she needed to concentrate on her breathing for the thirty seconds the contraction lasted.

When it was over, she said, as calmly as she could, 'I'm afraid I'm not going to be a lot of help to you today. I'm in the first stage of labour.'

'You're not? Oh dear! I was afraid this might happen. It's coming all that way yesterday and being upset about Sammy.'

'Perhaps it's a false alarm. I could be having Braxton Hicks contractions . . . a false labour,' Sarah added, thinking that someone of Mrs Slane's generation was more likely to understand that term than the medical one.

'When did the pains start?'

'About four o'clock.'

'You've been in labour four hours! You should have woken me. We'd better telephone the surgery's emergency number and get someone to come and look at you. First babies don't come in a hurry . . . not as a rule. There could be time to get you home in an ambulance.'

'I hadn't thought of that,' said Sarah. 'But I don't much fancy having the baby delivered by an ambulance driver in a lay-by. If there's any risk of that I'd rather stay here.' She saw Eileen Slane looking taken aback and apprehensive. 'I don't mean in your house . . . the maternity wing at the hospital must have some beds for emergencies. I didn't want to have the baby in hospital but it looks as if I'll have to.'

'Yes, perhaps that would be the best. Anyway the first thing is to get a doctor to you.'

Half an hour later a district nurse arrived at the bungalow.

'You've got yourself in a bit of a pickle, haven't you?' she said cheerfully, preparing to test Sarah's blood pressure. 'What made you come all this way so near your time?'

Sarah explained.

'I see. Well, don't worry, dear, we'll look after you.'

Sarah went to the hospital sooner than she really wanted to because she could tell it was worrying Mrs Slane to have her wandering about the bungalow.

The widow had enough on her mind already without the additional anxiety of keeping an eye on a girl in labour. It seemed best for Sarah to leave her in peace, and indeed she wasn't sorry to get away from the bungalow and the obstetrical reminiscences of a neighbour who, having heard about Sammy, had called to condole. No sooner had she been introduced to Sarah than she had started to regale her with the details of her own complicated deliveries.

When her admission to the hospital had been arranged on the telephone by the district nurse, Sarah had hoped she might have a private room both before and after the birth. However she had been told that although the labour rooms were private, her post-natal care would be in a ward with other mothers. She could only hope that neither they nor the staff would recognise her as the girl who had been the subject of a scandal during the summer. In the taxi taking her to the hospital, she wished she had given a false name.

On arrival she was taken in charge by a friendly young midwife who, in the admission room, first filled in a form and then did the routine checks.

'Right: that's that. Now let's get you prepped. We don't give mothers a full shave . . . only a mini-shave.'

'Can I opt out of it altogether?' asked Sarah. Her own midwife, Mrs Seaton, had agreed with Jane that being shaved was not only unnecessary but resulted in maddening itching while the hair was growing back.

The nurse smiled and shook her head. 'It's a precaution in case you need suturing afterwards.'

'I'm hoping I won't.'

'Perhaps you won't, but it's best to be on the safe side. It won't take a minute and I'll stop if your next pain comes on.'

Practice had made the nurse deft and quick with the razor but even so Sarah disliked lying on her back with her legs splayed, like a trapped beetle.

'There . . . all done, but stay where you are while I pop in a suppository to clear your bowel.'

'I don't think I need one,' said Sarah. 'I went to the lavatory this morning and I only had a very light breakfast.'

'Don't worry: this isn't like the old-fashioned soap and water enema. You'll have plenty of time to get to the loo, and then you won't have to worry about wanting to go in the delivery room.'

The nurse split open a plastic casing and expertly inserted a bullet-shaped pellet into Sarah's rectum.

'Have you anyone coming to be with you?' She knew from Sarah's details that she came from a different part of the country and had nobody local to support her. 'Have you let your family know what's happened?'

'No, I haven't. There's no one who's free to come and it would only worry them. I'll let them know when it's over. I don't mind being on my own . . . anyway I'm not, am I?' Determinedly cheerful, Sarah smiled and patted her swollen body.

At that moment another contraction started. It felt like two large hard hands gripping and squeezing the underside of her belly, tighter . . . tighter . . . *tighter*.

When it was over she thought it might have felt fiercer than the others because she had been lying down. Somehow it didn't seem the right position to be in. She was glad to hoist herself upright and lower her feet to the floor.

After the suppository had worked, she was taken to have a shower and given a hospital gown and a large

437

terry robe. As it was a warm day and the maternity wing had glass-walled south-facing corridors, the temperature in the building made the robe seem unnecessary.

The labour room was painted a cheerful pale yellow with two large prints on the walls and a small vase of real flowers on a corner bracket.

'Aren't they lovely? The Lady Mayoress sends us all her bouquets,' said the nurse.

'Do I need to lie down yet?' asked Sarah, not wanting to climb on the bed.

'Yes, please. I'm going to ask Doctor to look at you now. He may want your waters broken.'

Another contraction was starting and Sarah stayed standing up and concentrated on her breathing.

In the middle of it, a man in a white coat walked in, giving an abrupt instruction to someone in the passage as he entered. The nurse who was timing the contraction, handed him Sarah's notes attached to a clipboard.

By the time he had read them, Sarah was able to say, 'Good morning,' and smile at him.

She didn't get a smile back. 'Not very wise of you to leave home so near your time, Miss Lomax,' he said, with a frown. 'You're lucky we have a bed for you.'

While the nurse helped her onto it, pulled up her gown and arranged her legs in the splayed position, Sarah explained the circumstances. The doctor made no comment. He gave the impression of being either tired or put out and her spirits sank at the thought of having him in charge of her delivery.

Perhaps because his fingers were larger, his examination of her cervix felt rougher and more uncomfortable than when the nurse had checked its state of dilation. She had an instinctive feeling that, even if she had not left home in a hurry and forgotten her birth plan, this cross-looking man was unlikely to approve of women having a voice in the conduct of their deliveries. Everything about him from his ungentle hands to the deep groove between his eyebrows suggested a dictatorial and unrelaxed personality.

'Doctor, it's very important to me to avoid an episiotomy if it's at all possible,' she said anxiously.

He looked at the nurse and smirked. 'You'll have to watch your step, Nurse. This patient has been taking advice from the experts. Which of them is your favourite guru, Miss Lomax?'

'No one in particular. I've read several books about childbirth. Don't you think women should read about what's likely to happen to them?'

'I suppose it does no harm providing they realise that the pet theories of unqualified feminists aren't as reliable as the knowledge, based on experience, of qualified obstetricians. If an episiotomy is necessary, you will have one. If it isn't, you won't.'

He gave brisk instructions to the midwife and left the room.

'He's the senior consultant. You don't want to put his back up,' she warned Sarah, when he had gone.

'Why should it put his back up to make a reasonable request? He didn't even ask why I made it,' said Sarah. 'May I get up now?'

The nurse shook her head. 'You're not making very much progress if you started at four this morning. We're going to help things along with an ARM – that's short for artificial rupture of the membranes. Breaking the waters nearly always speeds things up. If the first stage goes on too long, you'll be tired before the really hard work starts.'

Presently, left on her own, Sarah began to wish she had taken a chance on going back to Longwarden by ambulance. As matters had turned out, she would have been there by now, safely back in her own home with a midwife she knew and no arbitrary males in attendance unless things went seriously wrong.

When the next contraction came it didn't seem noticeably different from the one before. She wished she had brought something to read. With nothing to do and no one to talk to, the intervals seemed very long.

Jane had said that she visualised contractions being like great ocean breakers with, between them, pauses for floating and resting in calm water before the next roller surged in.

In Sarah's mind giving birth was more like the cross country phase of horse trials, but miles longer and with many more obstacles. Before leaving Longwarden yesterday, she had looked forward to the birth with the same mixture of confidence, excitement and tension as she had felt before riding at Burghley last autumn. Now, being here instead of where she had planned to be, she felt all the apprehension of a rider tackling a course she hadn't walked beforehand.

Another contraction came and went and still no one looked in to see how she was getting on. She climbed awkwardly off the high bed and, going to the window, opened the vertical louvres which had been almost closed. The room overlooked a passageway between two parts of the building. There was nothing to be seen but a wall with some frosted glass windows.

Accustomed to the long green views from almost every window at Longwarden, and to high ceilings and rooms filled with paintings and objects, she began to find that – even with its two prints and the Mayoress' flowers – the labour room was claustrophobically small and impersonal. Shut away by herself, she was beginning to feel as if she had been admitted to some kind of penal institution where she had none of the rights of a normal person.

She remembered that on the way here from the admissions room they had passed through two pairs of fire doors on either side of a waiting area. She had noticed some magazines there. Perhaps she could borrow a couple.

There was no one about in the passage but, halfway along it, feeling absurdly guilty at venturing out without permission, she was stopped in her tracks by a howl from one of the other labour rooms.

Anywhere else, Sarah would have thought the noise had been made by an animal. Here it could only come from a woman in pain. It was followed by another loud cry and then another and another. Whoever was in there sounded as if they were in agony.

Shocked and alarmed, Sarah clutched her quiescent belly. Was she going to be howling with pain in an hour or two's time? Was the woman in there on her own with no one to help her? Perhaps she was crying out for help.

At that moment a door opened and a nurse stepped into the corridor, giving Sarah a glimpse of the scene within; a girl with sweat-bedraggled hair having it stroked from her forehead by a worried-looking man.

'What are you doing wandering about?' said the nurse, in a tone of reproof.

'I was going to get something to read from the waiting room. I – I was stopped by the screams.'

The nurse looked at her more kindly. 'Don't let it worry you, dear. She's the kind who would yell blue murder if she stubbed her toe. She's not really in a bad way. You'd better go back to your room. Mr Poulton won't like it if he finds you're not where you should be.'

'But I don't like being shut away when there's nothing much happening,' said Sarah.

Then she felt the first twinge of another contraction beginning and instinctively moved to the wall, spreading her hands against it, starting the slow quiet breathing which would help her over this next 'fence' on the first stretch of the strenuous course ahead of her.

'What is this patient doing here?'

The brusque voice was the senior consultant's and it came from the threshold of another room.

The nurse, looking worried, said, 'I was just asking her to go back to her room, Mr Poulton.' She put her arm round Sarah's waist. 'Come along, dear.'

Sarah felt a wave of irritation at being disturbed at a moment when she had no energy, physical or mental, to spare for anything but the sensation engulfing her body. It required all her concentration and she wanted to stay where she was until it was over.

'In a minute . . . wait a minute.' She slid her palms over the painted surface of the wall until her forearms were flat and she could rest her head on her wrists. In this position her belly hung down like a ripe melon. Ignoring the nurse and the doctor, she rode out the pain.


'I'm worried about Sarah, Laura.'

Jane entered her secretary's office with an anxious frown on her usually serene face.

'I've been talking to a friend of the woman who is, in effect, Sammy O'Brien's widow. Mrs Slane was busy with the undertaker and this neighbour of hers seems to feel she is much too distraught to be with Sarah at the hospital.'

After explaining as much as she knew about Sarah's admission, Jane went on, 'Yesterday, on the telephone, Sarah told me Mrs Slane was a sensible woman, but that was before Sammy died. She seems now to have gone to pieces. The shock, I suppose. I don't at all like the idea of Sarah being on her own. Perhaps I should go to her . . . get Flitton to drive me . . . or Damaris.'

'No, I don't think you should,' said Laura, with the firmness she sometimes showed when speaking to people on Jane's behalf. 'Lord Carlyon would be most annoyed if I let you go there yourself. I would offer to go but I don't think my presence would be very reassuring. The best person to support Sarah is your sister-in-law . . . if we can get in touch with her.'

'I agree, but I don't think we can. When Allegra rang up yesterday to say she was going to stay the night with Claudia Dunbar her plan was to spend today shopping. I was delighted to hear it. It's the first time she's shown any interest in shopping since Andro died. But when I contacted Claudia right after calling Mrs Slane, she said Allegra had told her she was going to see some old man she used to be friendly with. She did mention his name but Claudia can't remember it.'

'Do you think it would be worth leaving a message with the caretaker at Carlyon House?' Laura suggested.

'Anything is worth trying, but I shouldn't expect her to go there. The flat has too many painful associations for her. Try Stanley's number, would you? If he's there, I'll speak to him myself.'

While Laura dialled the caretaker's number, Jane paced to the window and back, regretting that Pen and Piers were no longer at Longwarden. They would have been the ideal people to handle this emergency.

The trouble was Sarah had very few friends. Her horses took the place of human friends. She had quite a close relationship with Rob and Emily Wareham and Jane felt sure that Emily would have gone to her aid like a shot had she not been nursing her own new baby, born at the end of August.


In a respite between contractions, Sarah shifted and squirmed in a futile effort to find a more comfortable position.

With the tube from a drip bag held in place on her left hand by sticky tape and two straps fastened quite tightly above and below her navel, she had very little freedom of movement.

One of the straps held a pressure gauge which was

recording her contractions. The other held a transducer to record the baby's heartbeats. Both were connected to the monitor alongside the bed.

It was clear now that transfusions by intravenous drip and electronic fetal monitoring were standard practice in this hospital. To avoid having them attached to her, she would have had to make a fuss and that, as she had discovered, wasn't easy to do during labour. The long act of giving birth seemed to sap one's normal resistance to coercion.

At the moment the solution in the drip-bag was dextroglucose – or so they had told her. She couldn't read the label and she didn't entirely trust the nurses to tell her the truth. They were kind but they weren't on her side. Following hospital regulations and keeping on the right side of the doctors was what mattered most to them. What the doctors decreed was law. If, in Mr Poulton's opinion, the right place for a woman in labour was flat on her back, unable to turn on her side because of the gadgets attached to her, that was where she had to be.

I need someone, Sarah thought helplessly. Kate would do, but it's Nick I really want. Oh Nick, why aren't you here? Why am I having your baby all by myself. It isn't right. It isn't fair.

The student nurse who was sitting with her gave a murmur of dismay as the monitor started to make a noise.

'Why is it doing that?' Sarah asked.

'It's the alarm. Something's wrong . . . but it may only be the machine. They do go wrong sometimes. I'll get someone to look at it.'

She hurried out, leaving Sarah to wonder, with mounting panic, if the baby's heart had stopped beating.

She remembered that ARM was said to increase the danger of pressure on the umbilical cord. Was the cord

444

round the baby's neck? Was he in distress? She was filled with remorse for thinking only of herself.

'Oh come on . . . come on . . . where are you?' she exclaimed aloud, praying for the door to open and someone to come to the rescue. Even the dour Mr Poulton.

By lunchtime Jane was a little easier in her mind. Although it had not been possible to speak to Sarah, she had talked to the Chief Nursing Officer at the hospital and been reassured that Sarah was in good hands and her labour was progressing normally.

Jane had lunch with Laura and Damaris, on the south terrace. They were getting on better, she noticed. There had been a time when Laura had been content to sit and listen while other people did the talking. Now she not only had more to say for herself but she looked far more attractive than when she had arrived at Longwarden.

Not that she would ever be a beauty like Damaris Lynn. Jane had thought Damaris lovely the first time they met, but since she had left her London business in the hands of her assistant and spent all her time at Longwarden she had acquired an extra sparkle. Clearly country life suited her. Or was it something else which was making her green eyes shine and her mouth curl up at the corners? Could it be that her glow came from that well-known enhancer of women's looks – a satisfactory love affair?

If so, who was the man in her life? Not Joël Vibrac, Jane hoped. It wouldn't be surprising if he had fallen for Damaris. With a difficult mother-in-law and a wife not only disabled but also extremely dejected, it would be an exceptional husband who didn't look longingly at their energetic and vital garden consultant.

Jane had tried to befriend Lucy Vibrac and help her make the best of her necessarily restricted life. But Lucy had a chip on her shoulder which Jane thought had probably been there before her accident. Neither she nor her mother were likeable. Mrs Baston's every word and gesture set Jane's teeth on edge, and she didn't really take to Lucy although she felt deeply sorry for her.

After the cold cherry soup and salad, Damaris asked them to excuse her. Watching her walk away, Jane envied her narrow waist and limber stride. She was finding the last few weeks of her pregnancy slightly wearisome, especially in his hot weather. It seemed a very long time since her own waist had been slender and she knew that now, when she walked, it was with a ponderous waddle quite different from her normal walk.

She wished that, like Sarah, she was within a few hours of being relieved of the bulk she had carted around for so long.

'Don't worry about her. I'm sure she'll be all right,' said Laura, thinking that she was still uneasy about the younger girl.

'As a matter of fact I was wishing my time had come,' said Jane, smiling. 'I feel such an elephant. Never mind: not much longer.'

It seemed to her that a slightly wistful expression crossed her secretary's face. She wondered if Laura longed for a child and feared she might never have one. Jane suspected her of having a *tendresse* for James Muirhead. But since the weekend he had taken her to the theatre in London, they had not, as far as Jane knew, seen any more of each other. Perhaps North's assessment of James' interest had been nearer the mark than her own.

Studying her secretary more closely, it seemed to Jane that although Laura had gained in looks and confidence, she had also lost something. Perhaps her tranquillity. She had seemed at first like a nun; calm, self-effacing, unaffected by worldly influences. But not any more. Now she struck Jane as a woman who ought by rights to have a husband and a teenage family. A woman whom life had passed by and who knew it and regretted it.

Sarah knew she must be at the difficult stage called transition when she felt first hot and then cold and her legs started shaking.

Although she'd had nothing to eat since the toast in Mrs Slane's kitchen, she also felt sick – sick, tired and bitterly angry at going through all this by herself.

It took two people to make a baby, so why did she have to endure this ordeal alone? Why wasn't Nick here to help her? If he had been, she could have stood it. Without him she felt abandoned to uncaring strangers.

The people who came and went wore masks when they looked at her now, but the only part of her they were interested in was between her legs. They looked at the monitor more often than they did at her face, and they didn't include her in their murmured discussions. When they did speak to her, they addressed her as Mother, never by name. She felt that she wasn't a person any more. She had become a pod, her only function being to do as they told her.

It was nearly seven o'clock in the evening when Allegra arrived at the hospital.

'I don't know how long I'll be. Possibly an hour,' she said to the driver of the car which had brought her from London.

From Reception in the main block she was directed to the maternity wing. After weeks in seclusion, two days in London had tired her. The journey by road with the frequent hold-ups of the suburb-bound rush hour had not been restful. She longed for the peace of her room and a stiff gin and tonic.

At the next desk, she said, 'Good evening. I've come

to see my cousin, Sarah Lomax, who was admitted this morning.'

'It's fathers only in the evening and visiting finishes in five minutes.'

'This baby's father is abroad and I've had to come down from London. I'm sure you can bend the rules a little in this case,' she said, smiling her most winning smile at the po-faced porter behind the desk.

'I doubt it but I'll ask for you. Lomax, did you say?' He looked at a list on a clipboard before picking up a receiver and pressing a button. 'There's a lady here to see Miss Sarah Lomax. Yes, I've told her that, but she says she's come from London. Ask Sister if she can make an exception, will you?'

Guessing that it would be a few minutes before permission came through, Allegra glanced round the reception area and thought how ugly it was with its mottled brick walls, built-in planters filled with shiny-leaved cheese plants and orange plastic chairs. Presumably they were supposed to look cheerful.

'I'm sorry, miss. You can't see your cousin this evening. You'll have to come back tomorrow. Morning visiting starts at eleven.'

'What is her room number?'

'She's in Dunlop Ward on the third floor. The lift's over there.'

'Thank you.' Allegra made for it.

'Here . . . you can't go up now. Tomorrow, I said.'

Ignoring his protests, she entered the open lift. Ten seconds later she stepped into a wide corridor with more cheese plants. Nearby was a smaller waiting area with a counter but no one behind it. At that moment a bell rang. Soon afterwards a man, followed by others, came through the double swing doors beyond the desk. Husbands, obediently leaving on the dot of seven, she thought, as they passed her. Did they mind being chucked out so early? Or were they secretly glad to be having a brief return to bachelor freedom before their wives and babies came home and the broken nights began? Some of the older men would have other children to look after. For them, their wives' time in hospital would mean less free time.

Not all the husbands had gone when Allegra entered the ward. Two or three still lingered at bedsides. Scanning the twenty-four beds, at first she couldn't see Sarah. Then, right at the far end, she saw her cousin's blonde head and hurried towards her.

Sarah was not asleep. But although her eyes were open she was taking no interest in what was going on around her. Neither sitting up nor lying down but slumped against a bank of pillows, her arms lying lax at her sides, she looked exhausted.

There was no cot beside her bed as there was by most of the others. For a ghastly moment Allegra wondered if the child had been stillborn. But surely, if that were the case, they couldn't be so unfeeling as to put her in here with mothers of healthy children?

'*Allegra!*'

For an instant Sarah's face brightened with a look of incredulous delight. Then her mouth turned down at the corners and began to tremble. She turned her face towards the wall.

'Oh, Allegra . . . it's been awful . . . *awful!*' she said, her voice breaking.

With two brisk jerks Allegra drew the curtains which formed a screen round the bed. Then she sat on the edge of the bed and took Sarah's hands in hers.

'Poor darling, I'm sorry you had to go through it all on your own. But I didn't hear what had happened until late this afternoon. I got here as fast as I could. Now, tell me all about it.'

But before Sarah, her face still working, could regain enough control to answer, the curtains were opened and they were joined by a middle-aged woman in a dark blue dress and white cap.

'Now what is going on here?' she demanded. 'If you are the person who enquired a few minutes ago about seeing Miss Lomax, you were asked to come back tomorrow.'

'I think my cousin needs me here now,' Allegra said calmly. 'I've rushed down from London to see her and I've no intention of waiting until tomorrow to find out why she's upset. While she's telling me, perhaps you'd be good enough to organise a private room for her. I don't understand why she isn't in one already.'

'There are no private rooms in this hospital. We have some amenity beds but they're all occupied at the moment. Miss Lomax was lucky that we were able to admit her at all,' said the ward sister stiffly. 'What she needs is rest. She'll feel much better tomorrow. In the circumstances, I'll allow you five minutes together. But after that you must leave.' She withdrew, closing the curtains after her.

'Reminds me of the mistresses at school. Quite kind-hearted at rock bottom but a stickler for rules and regs,' said Allegra. 'I thought in maternity wards it would be a lot more relaxed. But it seems Jane was right. She sends you her love, by the way. She's been frantically worried about you. If she hadn't known North would blow his top, she'd have come here herself as soon as she heard what was happening. Did you have a very bad time? Where is the baby?'

'I only saw him for a few minutes. Then they took him away to be cleaned up. He was covered with white stuff, like yoghurt, and his poor little face looked all squashed. It was a forceps delivery. I didn't know anything about it. They made me have an injection. They said it had gone on too long.'

Sarah began to cry and Allegra put her arms round her and wondered if it would be possible to take mother and baby back to Longwarden tonight. She decided it wouldn't.

It was actually about fifteen minutes before a nurse came to remind her she had to leave and by then Sarah was calmer.

'Could you go and see Mrs Slane for me . . . tell her I'm all right. She may have rung up. You could sleep there . . . in the bed I had.'

'I'd rather stay at an hotel. But I'll go and see her. I hate to leave you so soon but I think I'll have to. There's no point in putting their backs up while you're in their hands. Tomorrow, if there aren't any private clinics where you can have peace and quiet, perhaps I can whisk you home in the car I came down in. It depends how you feel in the morning.'

Only three or four times in her life had Allegra pulled family strings. As she left the ward, she felt this was a situation – an individual versus an institution – in which the use of such pull as she had was justified.

On being told where Sister's office was, she tapped on the door and walked in.

'I'm so sorry . . . I didn't introduce myself.' She offered her card. 'It was good of you to let me spend a little time with my cousin. You can imagine how worried her family has been since we heard that rushing down here to visit an old man who used to work for her father – he died in this hospital yesterday – had brought on the baby. I should like to see the child, if I may? My brother and his wife – who is also about to give birth – will want to know that he's all right.'

As Allegra had foreseen, the ward sister was impressed. 'He's a fine boy . . . nearly eight pounds. You have no need to worry on that score, Lady Allegra. There was nothing about his birth which need cause your family concern. It was a forceps delivery, but that was to be expected. The baby is large and Miss Lomax has a small pelvis and was also very tense and nervous.'

'Hardly surprising, in the circumstances. Why isn't the baby with her? She tells me she's hardly seen him.'

'The new babies are kept in the nursery for the first three nights. Their crying can be very disturbing to mothers needing rest. He'll be brought down every four hours for his feed. You'll see him when you come tomorrow.'

'I'd prefer to see him now . . . before I telephone my family,' Allegra said firmly.

'Very well . . . if you insist.'

Allegra smiled, certain that no amount of insistence would have gained her the entrée to the nursery if she hadn't been the daughter of a peer.

On his first day out of the womb, Sarah's son was not an appealing little creature. In her opinion, none of the babies were. But the infant labelled Lomax was even uglier than most. His looks reminded her of a boxer who had taken a lot of beatings and had just lost his latest fight. His eyelids were puffy, his nose squashed, his tiny ears folded forward. The white stuff mentioned by Sarah had been washed off and his shock of dark hair stood on end like the hair of the red-coated, staring-eyed golliwog Allegra had loved as a small child.

She was only allowed to look at him through the nursery window and had to take their word for it that he had no defects other than his strange and unprepossessing appearance. For the offspring of two exceptionally good-looking people, he was singularly hideous, she thought. Perhaps he was going to take after Nick's unknown father.

On leaving the hospital Allegra booked a room at the town's best hotel and put a call through to Longwarden.

Her report to Jane was diplomatically guarded. She saw no point in upsetting her sister-in-law by giving the full facts, so she concentrated on the baby's weight.

452

'It's a good thing he has turned up early. By the week after next he might have been even larger,' she said. 'May I leave you to relay the news to Kate and Mother and the Warehams?'

'Of course, I'll call Pen right away,' said Jane. 'She'll be thrilled to hear she's a great-aunt. Has Sarah decided what to call him?'

'Not as far as I know. We had so little time together. I'll ring you again after I've seen her tomorrow. Goodnight, Jane.'

After changing into the silk shirt she had worn to dine with Claudia and the Brentwoods the night before, Allegra went down for a restorative drink and a meal in the hotel's restaurant before going to see Mrs Slane.


'I'm going to call him Thomas,' Sarah said, the next day. 'Thomas Nicholas Lomax.'

The baby, still bearing a marked resemblance to a battered boxer, was now in a cot by her bed, as were all the other mothers' infants. Friends and relations were allowed during morning visiting hours and some had brought children with them. Allegra found the ward noisy and also excessively hot.

'It's like an oven in here. Aren't you boiled?' she asked her cousin.

'Yes, it's unbearably close to anyone used to fresh air. The woman in the next bed, who's been in here before, says it's kept at this temperature for the babies. New babies are easily chilled. But in this heat they get dehydrated so they have to be given water with glucose in it, which isn't a good idea if one wants to breastfeed. Thomas doesn't seem hungry yet and I hate the idea of being supervised. I'm sure I could manage much better if only they'd leave me alone with him.'

'I've already made enquiries about getting you moved,' said Allegra. 'There's a private clinic about ten miles away but if you're going to go there you might just as easily go home, if you're up to it. How are you feeling today?'

'I didn't want to take one of the sleeping pills they lob out at night but I was too strung up to sleep. So I'm tired and my tail end feels hellish, but otherwise I'm okay. That bloody man Poulton cut me when I was unconscious and the stitches feel like huge thorns. I'm dreading going to the loo.'

When visiting was over, Allegra asked to speak to the consultant in charge.

'I'd like to take my cousin home,' she told him. 'She and my sister-in-law intended to give birth at Long-warden and Sarah will have every care. Is there any reason why she shouldn't be discharged?'

'It would be extremely unwise . . . and against my advice.'

'Why? Is Sarah ill? What's the matter with her? Apart from the pain from her stitches, that is. How long will that last? Days? Weeks? My cousin is a professional horsewoman. It's important for her to get back in the saddle as soon as possible . . . that's why she particularly asked not to be cut.'

'She would be in much more discomfort from a bad tear than from an episiotomy,' the consultant replied repressively. 'If Miss Lomax discharges herself against my advice, she will have to sign a statement accepting full responsibility for any ill effects to herself or the child.'

'Well, I know that *I* couldn't stand the heat in that ward, or the lack of privacy and space. I think she'll be much better off in her own home where she and Thomas can be together all the time and not be governed by a timetable,' said Allegra. 'It would be insincere to thank you for your help, Mr Poulton, because, frankly, I think the whole thing has been badly mismanaged. Sarah had already been through one harrowing experience – the

454

death of someone she loved in your intensive care unit – and she needed all the support and kindness she could get. Some of the nurses were kind, up to a point. But she obviously found you very daunting and unhelpful. I think you should examine your attitudes and consider the possibility that you have allowed self-importance to override your concern for your patients' feelings. Good morning.'


In half an hour's rapid shopping in one of the town's department stores, Allegra assembled the necessities for the journey; a blanket, half a dozen pillows and pillow-cases, a carrycot, wrappings and nappies for Thomas and a large coolbox.

While Barlow, her driver, took these back to the Daimler, she dashed into Marks & Spencer where she bought sandwiches, fruit, two litres of spring water and two bottles of champagne.

Not for the first time, since she had stopped being hard up, she was grateful for the ability to spend money without a second thought when, as now, it was necessary.

Before leaving town, with Sarah stretched on the back seat, Thomas in his cot on the floor, and Allegra in front with Barlow, they made a very brief stop at Eileen Slane's bungalow for the widow to peep at the baby.

Then they set out for Longwarden.


'Isn't he the sweetest thing?' said Jane, as she and her sister-in-law left Sarah and Thomas in the care of Mrs Seaton.

'With those cauliflower ears and that fright wig? You've got to be joking,' said Allegra. 'I wouldn't say so to Sarah but I think he's the most peculiar little object.'

'I hope you're equally tactful when my even more peculiar little object makes its bow,' Jane said laughing. In a more serious tone, she went on, 'I was worried when you called to say you were bringing her back so soon. But she looks in pretty good shape considering it's barely twenty-four hours since she had him.'

'I dosed her with Granny Flora's favourite medicine – champagne. And had several glasses myself.'

Allegra would never admit it, but the decision to remove Sarah from the hospital had worried her even more. Although Sarah had wanted to come home, she wouldn't have discharged herself from the hospital without her cousin's support. If she had started to haemorrhage, or something had gone wrong with Thomas, it would have been Allegra's fault. She was glad the journey was over and mother and baby were now in the experienced hands of Jane's quiet, friendly midwife.

In her sister-in-law's sitting room, she fixed herself a drink and sank onto the comfortable sofa where, this time tomorrow, her brother would be relaxing and telling his wife about his short visit to Dudhwa National Park to photograph tigers under the guidance of India's distinguished naturalist, Billy Arjan Singh.

Allegra felt almost as tired as if she had been to India and back. Apart from the strain of today, it had taken a lot of willpower to make herself go to the flat for the first time since Andro's death. Although as it had turned out, she had barely entered the building before Stanley had given her the message to telephone home immediately.

After more than twenty-four hours of behaving like a drowsy dormouse, Thomas Nicholas Lomax finally bestirred himself. He was in Sarah's arms when he opened his still puffy eyelids and peered at the world with the wandering unfocused gaze of the day-old infant.

After a while he turned his head towards her and started to make little movements with his tiny pink mouth. They were alone in the room, the nurse having gone to speak to Jane about something.

Sarah unbuttoned the front of her Laura Ashley nightie and slipped the frilled strap off her shoulder. His shock of hair tickled her bare skin as she settled him against her breast and hoped he knew more about what to do next than she did. One tiny arm waved in the air, the hand like a miniature starfish. Suddenly, looking at him, she remembered Bedouin Star as a newborn foal nuzzling his dam in exactly the same way as this funny little baby of hers was instinctively seeking nourishment. The strong love she had felt for the foal, and still felt for her favourite horse, welled up for the child she was holding.

Everything she had been through, even the pain she was feeling now from the stitches, ceased to matter. It had all been worth it.

When the midwife returned and saw what had happened in her absence, she said, 'Isn't that splendid? He's feeding . . . not just sucking . . . although he'll enjoy that too. You can tell when a baby is swallowing by the movement of the jawbone here . . . just under his ear. I had a feeling it wouldn't take the two of you long to get the hang of it. I said to Lady Carlyon: anyone with a way with horses is sure to be good with babies. And I was right, wasn't I?'

At the wheel of her car, Sam took his eyes off the road to glance at Damaris. Two days ago he had asked her to marry him and she had accepted.

'What's the joke?' he asked.

'I was smiling at my own absurdity. Until I met you I didn't believe in marrying for love. I was prepared to marry almost anyone who had the sort of house and

457

land where I could create my dream garden. He didn't have to be rich as long as he had a minimum of five acres and a house which wouldn't spoil my grand design. Can you believe that anyone could be so dotty?'

'The way you feel about gardening, it doesn't sound all that dotty to me,' Sam replied. 'How do you know that in a few years' time, when we're used to each other, settling down as people do, you won't start hankering after those five acres?'

'Because I know now that, at the end of the day – however much I've enjoyed the day – I want to sit by the fire with someone I love, not someone I never cared for even at the beginning. I still want a garden of my own but it doesn't have to be as large as the original conception. A quarter of an acre will do . . . less if necessary . . . whatever we can afford.'

He gave her a loving look. 'Maybe one day I'll be able to give you your five acres.'

She smiled. 'Not unless you start doing the pools. The sort of set-up I had in mind would cost at least two hundred thousand to buy, and that's in one of the cheaper parts of the country. Anyway, working at Longwarden has purged me of grandiose ambitions.'

'*Better a dinner of herbs where love is, than a stalled ox and hatred therewith*,' Sam said, surprising her.

It sounded like part of a poem she ought to know; one of the gaps in her education which always gave her a small stab of vexation like finding a run in her tights or a spot which would have to be dry-cleaned.

'Who wrote that? I can't remember.'

'It's from Proverbs. I used to work with an old boy who was always quoting the Bible. Most of it went in one ear and out the other but that bit stuck.'

'Perhaps, if we work hard and spend sensibly, we'll be able to have a stalled ox as well as love. If not, a dinner of herbs with you sounds good to me.'

They were on their way to see his sister. As they

crossed the Thames, she began to feel nervous. Sam's background was nothing like as bad as her own, she was certain of that. But it might be that his sister had married down rather than up and there would be some similarities between Chapel Street, Battersea and Laburnum Way; reminders of a past of which he knew nothing and, she hoped, never would.

'We're nearly there. I'll grab this space in case there's nowhere to park outside John and Polly's house.'

As Sam backed the car into the space, Damaris' heart sank at the sight of dingy net curtains, peeling paintwork and all the signs of a street inhabited by people who were not only poor but shiftless as well.

Oh God! I don't want to know, she thought. I've had this and got away from it. I don't want to come back, even as an outsider.

But Sam loved his sister and Damaris loved him. There was nothing for it but to brace herself for several hours' intense discomfort. It surprised her that he seemed quite unconcerned by the squalid air of the district where his sister lived. Damaris would have cringed had she had to take him to her childhood home and introduce her relations. Sam, who was under the impression that she came from a much higher social stratum than his own, gave no sign of being worried about her possible reactions.

She began to see why when they turned into another street. Here the houses were much better kept. In fact it looked as if gentrification was going on.

'Is this Chapel Street?' she asked hopefully.

'Yes, this is where they live. As I thought, there's no room to park but as soon as there is I'll go and fetch the car.'

Although the houses here was almost identical to the ones in the other street, they showed what a difference good paintwork, clean windows and well-kept window boxes or plants on the interior sills could make.

Within seconds of Sam ringing the bell at number twenty-four, the door was opened by a young woman Damaris recognised as the girl who had been at the theatre with him.

'This is Polly,' he said.

'Hello. I've been longing to meet you,' his sister said warmly. 'I've suspected for ages that Sam had finally met his fate but he's been very secretive about you.'

'I didn't think she liked me,' said Sam, as the girls shook hands.

'You aren't everyone's cup of tea,' his sister agreed teasingly, as she turned to exchange a hug and a kiss on the cheek with him.

'Come into the sitting room, Damaris. I expect you're longing for a cup of coffee or possibly something stronger? It's a bit nerve-racking meeting one's future in-laws for the first time, or it was for me.'

'Where's John?' Sam asked, as she led the way down the narrow hall to the room which to earlier generations of occupants would have been known as the front room and reserved for special occasions.

'He's taken the children to the park. He'll be back in about an hour,' said Polly. 'As Sam may have told you, Damaris, we have a toddler of two and a baby of eight months. Unfortunately, they're both cutting teeth at the moment and it makes them grumpy, poor sweets. Hopefully, after a morning in the fresh air – or what passes for fresh air in London – they'll be ready for naps after lunch and we can talk in peace. I adore my own tots but I was never very enthusiastic about other people's before I was married.'

By this time she had ushered her guest into the sitting room which, as Damaris saw at a glance, was utterly unlike her preconception of it. Indeed both Polly and her house were so different from her expectations that she was confused and puzzled.

'I'll go and make the coffee. You know where the

drinks are, Sam, if you two would like a gin and tonic or whatever.' Polly left them alone together.

'Would you like something?' he asked.

She shook her head. 'What a pretty room.'

Sam glanced round the small sitting room with its rag-rolled walls, chintz loose-covers, tray-tables and gilded Regency overmantel.

'Polly worked for a couple of posh decorators before she started having babies. She still freelances for one of them. That table's her work,' he said, pointing to the dull-green tray standing on faux bamboo legs and embellished with ribbon-tied posies which Damaris had already noticed.

'It's charming,' she said.

So that was the explanation of Polly's taste. She had picked it up from the people she worked for, and not only their taste in decorating but also the way they dressed and spoke and behaved. It looked as if, instead of being a pain, she might be exactly the sort of sister-in-law Damaris would have chosen; someone who, like herself, was bright enough to adopt new ways of living but less likely than, say, Allegra Lomax to suspect, from some minor mistake, that Damaris' background wouldn't bear investigation.

'What does John do for a living?' she asked.

'He's got a white-collar job . . . something in the City. Sounds deadly boring to me but he seems to like it. This was his bachelor pad and a bit of a dump before Polly got to work on it. When the children are older they're going to move out to the country. John's bought a house which needs a lot of doing up and that's where they'll live in a few years' time. Polly doesn't like London. It was okay when she was single and looking for Mr Right but now she wants cleaner air and better walks. She's a country girl at heart. I should think the coffee'll be ready by now. I'll bring the tray through for her.'

His absence gave Damaris a chance to look at the

room more closely. Asked to guess which interior decorators Polly had worked for, she would have said Colefax & Fowler and Charles Hammond, although there were other firms which would do up a room in this modified country house style.

It sounded as if her husband was a bit of a Yuppie, determined to get to the top. If so he had picked the right wife. Polly would know how to spend his money to advantage rather than frittering it on status symbols which would brand them as newly rich.

'Sam tells me you painted this table, Polly,' she said, when the others returned. 'I looked at one in Charles Hammond's last Sale, but even reduced it was four or five hundred pounds which was more than I could afford.'

'I don't work for them but I can assure you that the cost price was miles below that. Decorators twitter on about the exorbitant cost of labour to their customers, but a lot of it's done by cottage workers like me and the rates they pay us aren't *that* high,' said Polly. 'I make some useful pin money but it's peanuts compared with the profit they make on my work. To be fair they do have horrendous overheads, but even so the price of a pair of good curtains now is just crazy. Any woman who's at all handy can save herself thousands – literally! – by doing it herself. But first one has to learn how professionals tackle things. Which is why all these DIY classes in paint finishes and so on are mushrooming.'

'Couldn't you make more money by selling direct to the customer?' Damaris suggested.

'I've thought of that, but there are complications. For the time being it suits me to continue as a cottage worker. Until Mousey, the baby, starts school, I'm going to be a full-time mum. By that time we'll be in the country and then I'll start my own business.'

'What's Mousey's real name?' asked Damaris.

'My son is Frederick – Freddy – and the baby is

Martha. We couldn't make up our minds about a girl's name so we called her Mousey *pro tem* and it's stuck.'

They were having a second cup of coffee when Sam noticed a space among the vehicles lining the street and went off to fetch Damaris' car.

'Luckily we have a lock-up where John can keep our car out of the way of the local vandals,' said Polly. 'During the week he goes to work on a bike unless it's pouring. Then he buses. Would you like to see the rest of the house?'

'I'd love to.'

The bedroom Polly shared with her husband was dominated by a French bed with a cane headboard and footboard.

'It's much too large for this room but I have a passion for cane and I found this in a dealer's back yard, the woodwork all treacle varnish and the caning rotting away. It cost me ten pounds and now that I've painted the wood this soft blue-grey and replaced the caning I think it looks lovely . . . and will look even better when we move and have a larger bedroom.'

'How clever you are,' said Damaris. 'Isn't caning difficult?'

'Not really. I'm looking out for some chairs to cane. I've seen you before, you know. At the theatre. I was with Sam and you were with a man who looked as if he'd just come back from the tropics. Perhaps you don't remember.'

'I remember very well.'

'Were you interested in him at that stage? He was interested in you. When he saw you with that brown-faced man it made him as cross as two cats.'

'Really? What did he say about me?'

'I forget his exact words but when I asked who you were he was rather offhand about you. Something told me he liked you but had been getting the cold shoulder or even a complete brush-off. Which wasn't surprising in the circumstances.'

'What do you mean? What circumstances?' asked Damaris, forgetting her interest in the appointments of the bedroom in her much greater interest in what Sam had told his sister about her.

'A carpenter, even the foreman in charge of the carpentry shop at Longwarden, can't be the sort of man you expected to marry, surely? Aren't your parents going to take a pretty dim view of him?'

'My parents are dead.'

'That removes one complication, but won't your other relations and your friends be surprised and disapproving?'

'I have no relations. I'm quite alone in the world. As for my friends, I'm sure as soon as they meet Sam they'll realise that his being a carpenter is irrelevant. He's a marvellous *man* – that's what matters.'

'Yes, he is and he's had a pretty raw deal all his life so I couldn't be happier that at last he's found someone who loves him and values him,' said Polly. 'He was always my favourite brother, but –'

The doorbell announced Sam's return and his sister excused herself to go and let him in.

Longing to know why she felt he had had a raw deal, but guessing that she wouldn't pursue the subject until they had another tête-à-tête, Damaris followed her downstairs to get her bag and ask if she might wash her hands in the pretty peach and white bathroom Polly had already shown her.


The reason why Polly had been at the theatre with Sam was explained to Damaris by her host shortly before lunch.

He had been introduced to her on his return from the park and she had made the right remarks about his two offspring, both of whom were a great deal more taking than the runny-nosed, urine-scented, dummy-sucking babies of Laburnum Way.

After some general conversation, Polly had gone to the kitchen to attend to the final preparations for lunch and now Sam was in the adjoining dining room, talking to his sister and keeping Freddy and Mousey out of her hair while Damaris and John Condover continued to chat in the sitting room.

He was very much what she had expected from Sam's description of him; a self-made man in the making, on the way up from lower middle-class origins, considerably superior to her own, and with the same slightly artificial diction as Mrs Thatcher and Edward Heath.

Whereas his wife's voice sounded natural and Damaris knew that her own did – although in fact it was the result of elocution lessons and a natural gift for mimicry – John's voice was rather too plummy.

'Let me give you a glass of sherry. No doubt the cook would like one too,' he said. 'Sam may prefer a beer. I'll ask him. Excuse me for a moment.'

While he was gone Damaris wondered if he looked down on his brother-in-law, regarding him as an inferior because he worked with his hands.

When a drink for everyone had been organised, John settled himself in a comfortable chair and said, 'My wife has seen you before . . . one night at the theatre some time ago. We should both have been there but I had a really fierce cold and wasn't fit to go out. So Sam, who had been going to babysit for us, went in my place. I remember Polly coming back and saying that the gardening consultant from Longwarden had been sitting a few rows in front of them.'

'So she was telling me earlier. But Sam and I were not on good terms at that stage. We got off to a bad start.'

'So did Polly and I. She thought me a total non-starter . . . as her grandparents still do. I shall never win their approval,' he said, with a shrug.

'Why not?' asked Damaris.

'Hasn't Sam told you? My father was an undertaker. Not the sort of person a baronet wants to be related to, even remotely. The old boy hasn't cut Polly off, the way he did Sam, but he still makes it clear that I'm persona non grata. If it weren't for the fact that Polly and her grandmother are so fond of each other, I'd oblige him by staying away. As it is I swallow my pride and we spend a weekend there about once a month.'

Sam came into the room with the baby on one arm and Freddy holding his other hand. 'Polly wants us at the table.'

'Right: I'll pop Mousey in her chair and get her bibbed up. Fetch the bibs, would you, Freddy.' John took charge of his daughter and followed his son to the other room.

'What's the matter?' Sam asked, seeing something in Damaris' expression which told him all was not well.

She drained her glass. 'Nothing. Shall I bring this through?'

'In a minute.' He took it from her and put it aside before taking her in his arms.

With his mouth on hers, she forgot everything but the joy of being held in strong arms and kissed as if they had been apart for far longer than a few minutes.

When he released her, she said, 'Now you have lipstick on you and mine must be smudged. Let me give you a tissue.'

She found one in her bag and handed it to him before checking the state of her own lips in the mirror of her powder-case.

Sam wiped his mouth with one hand and pushed the door to with the other.

'What was John saying when I came in? You had a funny look on your face.'

466

'He was telling me that he and Polly visit your grandparents about once a month. He said something about your grandfather cutting you off . . . what did he mean?'

'We have nothing to do with each other,' he said curtly. 'The old bastard can't stand me and he doesn't care for John either. But John puts up with him and I told him to go to hell years ago. We shan't be seeing him at all. Come on: lunch is almost ready.'

He picked up her glass and John's and steered her to the next room. Plainly this was a subject he didn't wish to discuss and wished John hadn't mentioned. Had she misheard the word 'baronet'? Had it been some kind of joke?

Feeling mystified and uneasy, and in no mood for lunch, Damaris entered the part of the house she had not yet seen.


When Polly came downstairs after taking Freddy up for his nap – the baby was already asleep in her carrycot in the sitting room – Sam had just eaten the last spoonful of his third helping of a large lemon meringue pie.

'Eeh . . . you're a grand cook, lass,' he said, patting his muscular midriff. 'No wonder our John's getting ploomp.'

'You're right. I am putting it on. Polly feeds me too well. If I didn't bike to the office and back, I'd be seriously overweight,' John agreed.

'It was delicious, Polly. Now why don't you put your feet up while I do the washing up,' Damaris suggested.

'Certainly not. My dishwasher will handle all that,' said Polly.

'Oh, do you have one?' Damaris had thought the kitchen too small to accommodate a dishwasher as well as the essential washing machine and dryer.

'The best on the market,' said Polly, giving her husband a hug from behind his chair. 'And Sam is an excellent wiper-upper, you'll be pleased to hear.'

'None better,' her brother agreed, starting to clear the table.

It was when he had put on a Lancashire voice to compliment his sister on her cooking, that Damaris had suddenly realised that during lunch Sam had dropped his customary accent and had been speaking without any regional inflections in his voice.

Had it been a deliberate effort to match the way the rest of them spoke? Or was it his real voice? In that case, the voice he used at Longwarden was a false one.

As soon as she was alone with his sister, she said, in a voice kept low so as not to disturb the sleeping baby, 'Polly, before lunch you said that Sam had had a raw deal. What exactly did you mean by that?'

After a considerable pause, Polly said, 'Do you mean Sam hasn't talked to you about his schooldays and his rows with Grandfather?'

'He told me you lost your parents when you were small and were brought up by your father's parents. Other than that, he's said nothing. I assumed that, as in my own case, there was nothing very interesting to tell.'

'You knew about me. Did he mention Hugh, our older brother?'

'No, he didn't. Where does Hugh live?'

'Hugh is dead. He was killed in a car smash two years ago.'

'Perhaps that's why Sam hasn't mentioned him . . . because it still upsets him.'

'They weren't close. When they were boys, Hugh used Sam as his scapegoat. Hugh was Grandfather's blue-eyed boy and Sam was the one he blamed and punished and never had a good word for. If it hadn't been for Granny loving him, and trying to make it up to him, Sam's life would have been a misery. I sometimes think

Grandfather isn't quite sane. The way he treated Sam was abominable . . . and all because Sam looks like our mother and Grandfather didn't want his son to marry her. He doesn't approve of John, either.'

'John mentioned that before lunch. He said it was because his father was an undertaker.'

'Which is a perfectly respectable, useful thing to be,' said Polly. 'But you see my grandparents are both in their late seventies and they can't come to terms with the way life has changed since their youth when people were born above or below the salt and those below were never accepted as equals by those above. To Grandfather an undertaker is as unacceptable as a terrorist or a drug-pusher would be to us. Well, I don't need to tell you how hide-bound some old people are. You say you have no relations but you must have come across people who haven't adjusted their ideas to the realities of modern life.'

'I suppose I have – yes.'

'Not being on the receiving end of their snobbishness, you may not have noticed it,' said Polly.

'John said something about your grandfather being a baronet.'

'Is that something else Sam hasn't mentioned?'

Damaris nodded. 'I was under the impression he came from a humble background.'

'And loved him regardless. Good for you . . . just what he needs: someone who fell for him before he had any of the things he'll inherit when Grandfather dies. Sam says he won't accept them, but he may now he has you. Although *I* shouldn't want the house . . . low ceilings and never much sun. As for the garden . . . well, you might be able to make something of it. I hope Sam won't be angry with me for telling you all this.'

A sound from the cot made her get up to peer at her daughter.

'Dreaming,' she said, coming back to her chair.

'Anyway, as I've started you may as well hear the whole story. Now that I have children myself, it makes my blood boil even more than it did at the time. Sam was sent away to school at eight! Can you imagine the awfulness of being pushed out of the nest at eight years old? I think it's outright brutality. Not that the nest was a cosy one as far as he was concerned. He probably got fewer whacks at his prep school than he did at home. Grandfather was a great believer in "spare the rod" with Sam.'

'He sounds a monster,' said Damaris. 'Didn't your grandmother have any influence on him?'

'Precious little. Most wives of her generation didn't, I think. Or perhaps it was that despotic men deliberately chose submissive wives who wouldn't stand up to them. Apart from being sent away early, Sam was also sent to different schools. Hugh went to Marlborough like all the Warstocks before him, but Sam was pushed off to one of the minor public schools. Grandfather claimed that he couldn't afford the fees for them both to go to Marlborough, but everyone knew it was favouritism.'

'I should think Sam didn't mind where he went as long as it was away from his grandfather.'

'You would think so, wouldn't you, but in fact he loathed school as well. Perhaps my grandfather warned them he was a bad boy and they took his word for it. You won't believe this, but at prep school he was kept in shorts, as a punishment, right to the end of his last term. Normally the boys went into long trousers at eleven but Sam had bare knees in winter for another two years. Apart from the physical discomfort, can you imagine the humiliation? Especially for a boy who was taller than average.'

'What sort of crimes was he committing?'

'Nothing that a more sensible headmaster would have taken too seriously. One of the things he told me about was being caught in possession of condoms. Another boy had pinched a packet from his father – or possibly from a shop – and several of them were trying the things on when a master pounced on them, hoping to catch them smoking which was strictly forbidden. Sam, as usual, was accused of being the ring-leader of the debauch. As he didn't deny it and the other boy didn't own up, he got the caning and the withholding of privileges. Then he got another beating at home when the Head wrote and told Grandfather.'

The thought of the schoolboy Sam, who had already lost his parents, being beaten twice for such a trivial offence made Damaris furious.

'Surely he must have done something worse than that to be kept in short pants for so long?'

'He was caught fighting quite a lot . . . that was considered serious, especially when someone lost a tooth. But the worst thing which happened in his time was actually done by another boy who was expelled for it.'

'What did he do?'

'Burnt down the cricket pavilion. Sam was accused of being involved and everyone thought he was the culprit, but for once he had watertight proof that he wasn't. Because the fire brigade had been called, and they knew it was arson, there was a police investigation. Actually I think it wasn't really arson so much as a schoolboy prank which got out of hand. Anyway the chief culprit panicked and confessed and if any other boys were involved they kept their mouths shut and got away with it. If Sam had been one of them, I'm sure he'd have told me, but he swore he had nothing to do with it.'

'Did things improve at his next school?'

'Not much. He was often in trouble for fighting and always at the bottom of the class.'

'What about games? Surely he was good at those?'

His sister shook her head. 'Sam doesn't have the team spirit which is the very essence of the public school ethos. He likes doing things by himself. The only thing he was good at was woodwork and I think that was mainly because it was taught by a retired cabinetmaker, not a proper schoolmaster. But of course being good with your hands isn't considered as important as academic success or prowess at games. A talent for making things may have been encouraged at Lord Linley's school but it certainly wasn't at Sam's, or not by anyone other than the old boy who taught him carpentry.'

As this point they were interrupted by Sam coming in with coffee, accompanied by John who asked if they would like a liqueur.

'Not for me, thank you,' said Damaris, relieved to see only two cups on the tray. Evidently the men were having their coffee elsewhere.

'We're talking about cars and computers which I know would bore you, so we'll stay in the other room,' said John.

'I thought there was a definite tinge of M C Piggery in that remark, didn't you?' said Polly, after the door closed behind them. But her tone held no real rancour.

'So the next thing that happened,' she went on, picking up her story, 'was that having sat for his O levels and achieved the most abysmal grades in every subject, Sam had a tremendous row with Grandfather and ran away from home. Poor Granny was frantic with worry until she had a letter to say he was living in digs and working as a fork-lift driver in a timberyard. "Good riddance to bad rubbish" was Grandfather's reaction to that, but at that time of course he had all his hopes pinned on Hugh. Now Hugh is dead he's changing his tune. He knows that I see Sam regularly and he's made some overtures through me. But Sam doesn't want to know. He's had lunch in London with Granny a couple of times, but he won't have anything to do with Grandfather and I don't blame him. Do you?'

The discovery that Sam had also been through the experience of running away from home – although

472

clearly his grandfather's house, like 13, Laburnum Way, had never been a real home – made Damaris' heart swell with longing to give him all the tender care which, apart from the love of his sister, he had missed as a child.

At the same time she saw very clearly that if, at some time in the future, he changed his mind about taking up his inheritance, her own background ruled her out as a suitable wife.

For Sam Warstock, carpenter – yes. For Sir Samuel Warstock Bart – no. Thank God she had never taken him into her confidence.

'No, I don't blame him at all. I think your grandfather's treatment of him was unforgivable,' she said.

'You haven't heard the worst yet. When Sam had been at the woodyard for about three months there was a serious fire there. As he was the newest employee and not liked by some of his workmates because he didn't drop his aitches and slurp his tea – which is why ever since he's put on a Norfolk accent – the police checked him out very thoroughly. First they got in touch with his school and heard about the cricket pavilion and talked to the local police. Then they contacted Grandfather who you'd think would, if nothing else, have wanted to avoid a scandal involving the family name. But instead of telling them they were barking up the wrong tree, he actually agreed that Sam might be capable of arson.'

'How do you know? Did your grandmother hear him saying that?'

'Yes – and was so distraught at the thought of Sam going to prison that the poor old thing sent him money to flee the country. She believed it, you see. She thought he *had* done it. Even Hugh did. I knew it wasn't possible because of the way Sam loves wood. You must have seen him sniffing a piece of it, haven't you? He likes to smell it, to stroke it . . . he would never destroy it.'

473

'No, of course not,' Damaris agreed. 'Did they catch the person responsible.'

'I'm not sure. The job at the yard was only to tide him over until he could find what he wanted. But the police were obviously satisfied that he didn't do it. When he told them he was leaving they didn't want to keep tabs on him. After he'd moved to his new job, the only way he would have heard the outcome of the case was by going back there. He wasn't sufficiently interested.'

It was on the tip of Damaris' tongue to say: He seems fated to be on the spot when someone is setting fire to things. There's an arsonist at work in the Longwarden area.

But some instinct made her refrain from voicing this thought.


'You and Polly had a long chat-session this afternoon. I gather you liked her?' said Sam, on the way back to Damaris' flat where they were spending the night.

'Very much . . . and John . . . and the babies. Although I was nervous beforehand, as soon as I met her I began to enjoy it. Now I'm looking forward to the next time.'

'They liked you too,' said Sam. 'They both told me what a lucky chap I am to have found a girl with brains, beauty and a sense of humour.'

After a pause, she said, 'When are you going to take me to see your grandparents?'

'Never,' he answered abruptly. 'I know John and Polly go there, but I never shall. I can't stand the sight of my grandfather and my grandmother's getting too old to travel. Polly's been talking, I suppose. How much has she told you?'

'Enough to make me realise that some of my ideas about you are miles off course. Why didn't you tell me that yourself?'

'I liked the feeling that you cared about me regardless of my social shortcomings. It seemed a harmless deception. The other way round is the con trick . . . pretending to be in the Almanach de Gotha in order to sponge on gullible Yanks.'

Damaris felt her insides clench. Although she had never heard of the almanac he referred to, what he meant was plain enough. Pretending to be a sow's ear was all right. Masquerading as a silk purse wasn't.

'You aren't cross with me, are you?' he said. 'I didn't mean any harm, darling. I was going to own up eventually. Sometimes I thought you suspected.'

'No, never – why should I?'

'You can't be very observant. Sometimes, when we were together, I found myself slipping up . . . saying and doing things which weren't really in character.'

Perhaps, being a fake myself, I didn't recognise them, she thought.

'Did you? I didn't notice. You were such an unknown quantity that nothing would have surprised me.'

At the flat he took her to bed. Afterwards, while he dozed in her arms, Damaris gazed at the ceiling, trying to come to terms with the situation.

If she made a clean breast of her own deception, she felt certain he would stand by her. How could he not? Probably he wouldn't give a damn what her mother was.

But other people would. If, in spite of his present scruples, eventually he decided to take his proper place in society and it ever came to light that his wife had a streetwalker in her family, they would both be cold-shouldered. Few people were as bigoted as his grandfather, but equally few were so broad-minded that they wouldn't mind having a tart's daughter at their dinner tables.

Some eccentricities and even scandals were surmountable; but this wasn't one of them. She could be a falling down drunk, or even a taker of drugs, and people would pity and forgive her – as long as she was one of them. But once her real background was known she would never be accepted.

At breakfast next morning, Sam said, 'How soon can we get married? How long does it take to get a special licence?'

She smiled at him. 'I've no idea, but isn't that rather rushing things? We've only just got together.'

'I want to make it official. I want to say "This is my wife".'

Trying to stave off the moment when she would have to tell him there wasn't going to be a marriage, she said, 'Don't you think a trial run might be a good idea . . . just to make sure?'

He frowned. 'No, I don't. What for? We're not too young to know our own minds. This isn't just sex . . . it's love. I want to be your husband, not your boyfriend . . . to live with you, not just to sleep with you.'

His declaration touched her so deeply she felt her eyes fill with tears. Blinking them back, she said huskily, 'That's sweet, Sam . . . terribly sweet. But I do think you're being rather impetuous. There are all sorts of things to think out.'

'What things? I can't think of any.'

Nor could she; or none that she could confide to him. Frantically racking her brains for feasible reasons, she said, 'For a start I have to sort out my working life. Then we'd have to talk to the Carlyons . . . see what they thought about it.'

'Why should they object, for God's sake?'

'Because if – for some reason – one of us wanted to leave, it would mean losing both of us . . . or, if they were dissatisfied with one of us, giving both of us the sack.'

Sam demolished that argument by saying, 'As long as we're living under their roof I'd rather they did know about us. There's something a bit underhand about sleeping together by stealth as we do at the moment. Okay, so it's none of their business if you choose to sleep in my bed, not in your own, but I'd rather be open about it.' He paused, looking at her thoughtfully. 'If you don't want to be married right away, let's announce our engagement.'

'I – I think engagements are pointless except as a breathing space when there's going to be a big wedding with hundreds of guests and six bridesmaids. Sam . . . please . . . don't press me on this. I'm not ready to jump into marriage . . . I'm not even sure I think it's necessary to marry . . . not unless one has children . . . and do I want children, I ask myself?'

This might be a hurdle he couldn't get over. He was very fond of his sister's children, she had noticed.

'I'm not sure that I do either,' Sam said, with a shrug.

'But you have things to hand on . . . a title . . . a house.'

'The title means nothing to me. The house won't be left to me, it will go to Freddy.'

'To an undertaker's grandson? Not in your brother-in-law's opinion. According to him – and your sister – your grandfather would never do that. Freddy isn't a Warstock. You are.'

'There are other Warstocks about . . . distant cousins. Anyway, all that's irrelevant. I'm not in Carlyon's position.'

Damaris looked at her watch. 'We were up late. I must go and change.'

She was going to have lunch with her assistant to discuss reversing the arrangement whereby she had planned to spend two days a week at Longwarden and the rest of the time in London. Now she wanted to live in the country and come to London once a week or, better still, once a fortnight. It might even be that, with her husband's consent, Eve was ready now to take over altogether.

'Okay . . . we'll talk later,' said Sam. 'But I'll tell you now it's all or nothing for me, Damaris. I want you for keeps and I want the whole world to know it . . . and for you to feel the same way.'

She wanted, with all her heart, to tell him she did. She felt exactly the same way. But with Shirl and Gary rattling their bones in her closet how could she?


Sarah was sitting in a bath of heavily salted warm water, the treatment prescribed by Mrs Seaton to help heal the episiotomy.

Every day the midwife inspected the wound to make sure there was no infection. The first time she looked at it Sarah had seen her lips tighten.

'Who stitched you up, Miss Lomax?'

'I don't know . . . not the senior doctor . . . one of his assistants. It seemed to take ages. How long do you think it will be before I can ride?'

'It's hard to say. Some people heal more quickly than others. Not for some weeks, I'm afraid. It can be several months before the scar tissue feels comfortable but the arnica tablets and the ointment should help to speed things up.'

Mrs Seaton took a broad view of medicine and saw no reason not to use homoeopathic treatments which in her experience were effective. Sarah felt certain that, had Thomas been delivered by this good-humoured, sensible woman, it wouldn't be necessary now to sit on a rubber cushion while nursing him.

She had hoped to be back in the saddle quite soon after his birth. But now, even if she could endure the pain, it seemed likely that riding too soon would delay the healing.

Convinced in her own mind that neither the cut nor the forceps had been really necessary, she felt she had been routinely and pointlessly mutilated. Partly, of course, it had been her own fault for allowing the labour room atmosphere to make her surrender control of the situation. But far from home and with no one to back her up that had been almost inevitable. It would have taken a very strong-minded primagravida to stand her ground in those circumstances.

Mrs Seaton seemed to know what was in her mind. Yesterday, applying the ointment and a clean dressing to Sarah's rear end, she had said, 'Don't dwell on the fact that Thomas' birth wasn't a very happy experience for you, my dear. Put that behind you now and just be glad you've got a lovely healthy little son. The jaundice is nothing to worry about. A lot of new babies have it.'

Since his arrival at Longwarden Thomas had developed what looked like a sun tan but was in fact neonatal jaundice, but only the commonplace and harmless physiological form of it caused, Mrs Seaton had explained, by substance called bilrubin with which his little liver was unable to cope fast enough.

It was probably the jaundice which made him such a sleepy baby who usually had to be woken up for his feeds. But once woken he enjoyed his meals and Sarah had been startled to find how much sensuous pleasure it gave her to nurse him. It reminded her of the night Nick had made love to her.

She wondered if it was wrong and unnatural to feel the same pleasure now as she had that night. She knew she would have to be careful, as a single parent, not to become over-emotional about Thomas. She must never suffocate him with love. He would have difficulties enough without the added burden of a possessive mother.

*

Driving to her lunch date with Eve, Damaris tried to think about her dilemma coolly and rationally.

Sam was an intelligent man. He was going to apply his mind to her extraordinary volte-face and it shouldn't take him long to work out that the cause of it must have to do with her discovery that marrying him would not be the mésalliance it would have seemed to the world yesterday.

When he had thought about that for a bit, he would know that the only reason a woman would mind finding out that her lover was a great deal more eligible than she had supposed would be if she had something disreputable about her. Having arrived at that conclusion, he would then demand to know what it was. He would insist on an answer. Having got it, being Sam, he would dismiss it as unimportant. Which it wasn't.

She had two options. She could tell him, agree to marry him and take the risk that her blackmailing cousin would never reappear.

Or she could walk out of Sam's life, covering her tracks so carefully that he would never find her. She had already changed her identity once. She could do it again. It would never be difficult for a professional gardener to make a living.

But why the hell should she? Why should she let a double-dyed shit like Gary spoil things for her? Not only for her but for Sam. She loved Sam and she owed him the deepest gratitude for his skill in repairing the damage done to her by Kevin. Which was worse: to repay him by running out on him, or to take a chance that, even if Gary couldn't squeeze any money out of them, he would still take a perverse pleasure in exposing her?

She got back to Campden Hill Square soon after three o'clock. Sam was reading when she opened the door which led directly into her living room.

He jumped up, coming towards her with arms outstretched. 'I've missed you.' He kissed her at some length before asking, 'How did it go?'

'Fine. Eve's keen and her husband wasn't as obstructive as I thought he might be. He isn't a hundred per cent enthusiastic, but he seems to accept that if she wants to do the lion's share of running the business he shouldn't stand in her way.'

'That's great.'

'Sam . . . there's something I've got to tell you. Something about me. Until yesterday it wasn't important, but now it is. I'm afraid it's going to come as a shock to you – as much of a shock as what Polly told me about you, but rather more unpleasant. In fact, *very* unpleasant.'

'Whatever it is, I'm glad you've decided to tell me instead of pretending you aren't ready for marriage. The only explanation I've been able to think of while you've been out is that you already have a husband and had lied to me saying you hadn't.'

'No, I've never been married . . . and nor has my mother.'

'Well, that's not uncommon. A lot of people are born out of wedlock. Who cares?'

'It's worse than that.' She disengaged herself from his arms and moved away. 'I have no idea who my father was and nor has she. My mother is a prostitute, Sam . . . a cheap whore. At least she was the last time I saw her. Unless she's died of VD or drugs or AIDS, I expect she still is.'

As she had anticipated, his first reaction was incredulity. It was his second reaction she dreaded; the expression, however fleeting, however quickly controlled, which would betray his involuntary shock and disgust.

'I see,' Sam said, after a moment. 'That explains a lot which has puzzled me. The man who put you off men . . . was he one of her customers?'

She shook her head. 'She didn't bring me up. I was dumped on her sister. Eventually, like you, I ran away. Everything you know about me – even my name – it's all false.'

He reached out and took her by the shoulders, pulling her towards him.

*'What's in a name? that which we call a rose by any other name would smell as sweet; so Juliet would, were she not Juliet called, retain that dear perfection which she owes without that title. Juliet, doff thy name, and for that name which is no part of thee take all myself.'* He smiled at her. 'I learned that by writing it out twenty times as a punishment. It's actually one of Juliet's speeches about Romeo. There's another bit of that scene I remember. *The brightness of her cheek would shame those stars as daylight doth a lamp . . . See how she leans her cheek upon her hand. O, that I were a glove upon that hand that I might touch that cheek.'*

He lifted one hand from her shoulder to stroke her face. 'I love you. I don't care who your parents were . . . are. If they gave you a rotten start in life, what you've made of it only proves what a fine, special person you are. If we're both runaways that's something else we have in common.'

'Oh Sam . . .'

Limp with relief, she leaned against him, burying her face in his shoulder.

Then she stiffened and raised her face to his. 'But there's something else I haven't told you . . . the worst thing of all. I'm being blackmailed.'

'By your mother?'

'No . . . by one of my aunt's sons.'

Sam drew her towards the sofa and made her sit down.

'I'm going to make a cup of tea and then I think you'd better tell me the whole thing from the beginning.'

*

Towards the end of her pregnancy Jane had begun to record her baby's movements on a simple chart. The most active time was the evening. Or perhaps it was merely that she noticed the movements more when she was relaxing. In the mornings, when she was busy, the baby was quiet. His evening activities reassured her that all was well inside her uterus, particularly after she had passed her expected delivery date.

She was in the garden when her waters broke.

The sudden gush of warm fluid took her by surprise. Every morning, since the baby had failed to arrive on its EDD, one of her first thoughts on waking had been: Will today be the day?

But with plenty of other things to think about, afterwards she had forgotten about it for hours at a time. When liquid began to pour down the insides of her thighs, she thought for a moment she had lost control of her bladder.

Then, as she realised what was happening, she was filled with excitement. It was beginning . . . had begun! At last the mysterious being inside her was ready to be born.

A lot of the water was soaked up by what she called her clown's pants, a pair of loose trousers on braces worn with a cotton sweatshirt. But some of it trickled down her calves and into her shoes and she thought what a good thing it was that this had happened out of doors where no mopping up was necessary and the only damage was to her garden loafers.

When the flow seemed to have stopped, she headed for the house. On the way she met Kate.

'Hi! I'm on my way to ring the midwife. The baby has started,' she announced joyfully.

'Oh . . . that's wonderful,' said the other girl, looking rather startled at the sight of Jane's wet trousers. 'Are you all right? Shall I come with you?'

'No, thanks . . . I'm fine. The waters breaking is only

the beginning. It will probably be hours before anything more happens.'

But as she continued on her way to the house, Jane realised that the slight ache down in her back which she had had all morning and ignored, taking it for ordinary backache, must have been the first sign that today, or possibly tomorrow, would be the long awaited day.

She met no one else on her way to her room. In the bathroom, she took off her clothes and shoes, washed the amniotic fluid from her legs and, wrapped in a bath robe specially made to accommodate her bulge, sat down to dial Mrs Seaton's number.

'I'll come up right away,' said her midwife, when she heard what had happened. 'I'll be there in about twenty minutes.'

Jane replaced the receiver and put both hands on her belly. By this time tomorrow the huge bulge would have deflated and her firstborn would be in her arms or in the cradle by her bed.

'I can't wait to see you,' she said, wondering how long it would be before she felt the first proper contraction.

Nothing else had happened and she had changed into a loose soft robe and had just made a pot of tea when the midwife arrived.

'Any more progress?' she asked, as she came in.

Jane shook her head. 'Not so far . . . *oh!*'

Her exclamation was caused by a sudden quite strong sensation of being gripped and held tightly round the lower part of the bulge and in the small of her back. It didn't last long and then the pressure was released and she let out the breath which surprise had made her hold while the brief contraction lasted.

Mrs Seaton looked at her watch. 'Four-seventeen.' Then she looked at the teatray. 'I wouldn't mind a cup of tea myself.'

'I'll get you a cup and saucer.' Jane went to the cupboard where the tea things were kept. 'Has my offspring picked a bad day from your point of view? Were you hoping to go out this evening?'

'Don't worry . . . you haven't upset any plans. How are you feeling?'

'Delighted to have something happening at long last. Being pregnant was beginning to feel like a permanent way of life.'

The midwife sat down on the window seat. 'In a minute I'll listen in and see what he or she's up to.'

The next contraction came as Jane was about to pour the midwife a second cup of tea. As the tightening sensation began she put down the teapot in case this time the feeling was strong enough to make her hand wobble. In fact it was much the same as the previous contraction.

'Eight minutes,' said Mrs Seaton. 'Early days yet.'

Her examination revealed that Jane's cervix was already dilated to three centimetres and the baby's heart was beating well.

After the third contraction the midwife said, 'Nothing much is going to happen for some time yet so this would be a good time for your husband or someone else to keep you company while I nip along to see how Mrs Bisley and her baby are getting on. Then I'll come back and concentrate on you. Are you happy about that?'

'Yes, that's fine. Give my regards to Mrs Bisley.'

Jane knew that the Bisley baby had been born in Melchester cottage hospital two days earlier but was now at home in a bungalow on the outskirts of Longwarden village.

'Is Lord Carlyon in the house?' the midwife asked.

'Maybe not in the house, but not far away. I'll put out a call for him. There's no need for you to wait until he shows up. I'm not worried about being alone for a short time at this stage,' Jane assured her.

But after the midwife had left her, she decided not to call North yet. She would need his support later on. Right now she was fine on her own.

The contractions continued to come at eight minute intervals. Between them she sat by the window doing needlepoint until, while she was threading her needle with a fresh strand of yarn, she felt the pressure building up to a much stronger contraction than the one before. Also this one lasted longer. She timed it. A full thirty seconds which sounded like no time at all but felt like minutes while she was in the grip of it.

When it was over, she got up and walked about, hoping North would come in soon. She was beginning to need the comfort of his presence.

She wondered how the baby was feeling.


When the telephone rang, Damaris wondered if it might be Eve calling to say that, under pressure from her husband, she was having second thoughts about taking charge of the business.

But when she picked up the receiver she found it was her landlord who wanted to speak to her.

'If you're not busy, come down and have a glass of sherry,' he suggested.

'I wonder what he wants to talk about?' she said to Sam, after accepting the invitation. 'He sounds as if there's more on his mind than being sociable.'

'Perhaps he doesn't approve of your having overnight guests of the opposite sex.'

'I can't believe it's that,' she answered. 'He's not a snoopy man and anyway it's really no business of his whom I have here – unless someone moved in permanently, in which case I suppose he would be entitled to adjust the rent. I certainly can't sublet without his consent, but as I pay six months in advance the question of what to do about the flat doesn't arise yet. A great deal depends on how Eve gets on in the next few months.'

'Do you want to take me down and introduce me as your future husband?' said Sam.

She shook her head. 'Next time perhaps. I shan't be long . . . half an hour at the most.'

Sam was reading a book he had found on her shelves when Damaris re-entered her sitting room. She closed the door and leaned against it.

'We don't have to worry about my detestable cousin any more . . . or at least not for quite some time. He's in prison.'

Sam's eyebrows shot up. 'How do you know that?'

'Before I moved out of here in June, I told Mr Selborne, my landlord, that I'd seen a scruffy-looking biker hanging about in the street. He kept a look out but never saw him, but the old lady next door did. One day when she was going shopping she spoke to Gary and then, in case he planned to break in while she was out, she rang the police. Her instinct was right. He did break in and they caught him coming out with some of her silver and jewellery on him. She had to give evidence in court and told Mr Selborne all about it. As Gary had two other breaking-and-enterings on his record, this time the magistrate didn't go easy on him.'

'Good,' said Sam. 'Prison sounds the best place for him. Pity they can't keep him locked up permanently. Anyway, by the time he gets out you'll be my wife and if he ever reappears – which is highly unlikely – he'll have me to deal with.'

'Yes, it's good that he's out of the way for a year or two, but not so good that I now have a cousin who as well as being a blackmailer is also a convicted house-breaker.'

Sam crossed the room and put his hands flat on the door on either side of her head. 'He's disrupted your life enough. Forget about him. I love you. You love me. That's all that matters.'

He leaned closer to kiss her.

*

Margaret Seaton watched Lord Carlyon come back from the bathroom with a wash cloth wrung out in cold water which he used to refresh his wife's face.

She was sitting astride a low chair with a pillow over the backrest for her to lean on. Her hair was tied back in a plait and she was wearing a loose white tee shirt and long socks. Nothing else. Her long firm thighs and her bottom were still golden brown from exposing her body to the sun as often as possible throughout the summer.

It was some time since Mrs Seaton had drawn the curtains against the melancholy dusk of an autumn evening. The bedroom was lit by a single silk-shaded lamp and by the light of the fire which from time to time she built up to keep the temperature high and the flames bright.

Otherwise, up to this point, her presence had been largely superfluous, for her patient's tall, black-haired husband was proving himself a calm and competent attendant.

He would have made a good doctor, better than some she had met, thought Mrs Seaton. To be given the confidence to cope, that was what women needed more than anything; and this young man had that gift. She could see he was a natural leader, one who would instinctively take charge instead of, like most people, waiting to be told what to do.

'The music's stopped!' said the Countess. As it started again, she said sharply, 'No, no – not that. I want the Tchaikovsky again.'

Margaret Seaton had known the American girl long enough to recognise the sharp impatience in her voice as foreign to her normal nature. It was the irritability typical of the transition from the long first stage of labour to the final stage which was usually much shorter.

*

Jane had always loved Tchaikovsky's only concerto for the violin. She had listened to it innumerable times during her pregnancy and now it was the perfect music to accompany her labour.

To have it played over and over again might be driving North and the midwife mad but tonight their feelings were less important than hers. Tonight the only people who mattered were herself and the baby and anything which helped them must be tolerated by their two helpers.

After North had wiped her face and given her iced water to sip, she resumed her resting position, soothed by the lyrical theme of the concerto's first movement.

After a lull, when nothing much seemed to be happening, she felt a powerful contraction quite different from any before. Some had been almost more painful than she could bear. At one point she had become alarmed and confused, forgetting her breathing until North had helped her to recover the rhythm.

'Not long now . . . loosen up . . . open up.' He was behind her, lifting her off the low chair and holding her firmly supported in a half-kneeling position while the midwife checked the dilation of the cervix.

'Nearly there, dear. You're doing fine.'

When Jane groaned it was not from pain but with effort. An overwhelming urge to bear down had come upon her. She felt all her tissues expanding to let the child through.

It was something like a tremendous orgasm; wave after rolling wave of an amazing sensation beyond anything she had imagined.

'There . . . look . . . you can see the head.'

The midwife tilted a mirror and, with a shout of excitement, Jane saw the top of her baby's wet skull starting to push through the opening. She put her hand down to touch it and a few convulsive moments later the whole head was through and was turning as first one shoulder and then the other appeared, followed by a slithery rush as the rest of the body emerged trailing a long slimy spiral of purplish-blue cord very much like a pulsating telephone cord.

'It's a boy. Well done . . . clever girl.' North's voice, close to her ear, was thick with emotion.

Sitting on the sheeted floor, leaning against the warm wall of her husband's body, with the midwife kneeling in front of them, Jane reached out to receive her crumpled, blood-smeared son.

As she cuddled him close there were tears in her eyes but she was beaming like the Cheshire Cat.


Long after the midwife had gone home and Allegra and Sarah had drunk a champagne toast by the cradle of Simon John Caspar Lomax, Viscount Hawksmere, Jane and North continued to gaze in delighted wonder at the child they had made.

Far from wanting to rest and sleep, Jane had never felt more wide awake.

'I feel like an actress after a brilliant first night,' she said, between mouthfuls of scrambled egg, a supplement to the light supper she had eaten earlier. 'And so hungry!'

In fact it was the early hours of the morning after her son's birthday before her exalted state of mind gave place to happy exhaustion and she was able to sleep.

## November

Laura had never liked November with its drifts of dead leaves and misty dark mornings and evenings. A dismal month even here, she thought, looking out at the rain-swept park from the window of her office.

She had just come downstairs from her employer's sitting room where they had dealt with the post. It was a week since the birth of the Carlyons' son and the Countess was still devoting most of her time to him. She had engaged a nanny – a cheerful Scots girl called Morag – but it wasn't her intention to leave him entirely in her care.

This morning she had handed Simon to Laura who had held him gingerly at first and then, when he showed no inclination to howl at finding himself in the inexpert grasp of a stranger, had begun to enjoy the experience.

Now, remembering how it had felt to have him in her arms, she was swept by a sense of desolation. If she had been a woman with exceptional gifts and burning ambitions, she wouldn't have minded missing out on love and marriage. But for someone like herself – an ordinary woman with no singular talents – loving a man and bearing his children were the best things life had to offer. Even Jane Carlyon – beautiful, rich, widely travelled – had confided that the night of Simon's birth had changed the world for her.

'Good morning.'

The sound of James' voice made her jump. She had known she would meet him at lunchtime, but she hadn't expected to see him before then.

'Laura . . . what is it? You're crying,' he exclaimed, advancing towards her.

'No . . . n-not really,' she stammered, making a dive for the drawer where she kept a box of tissues.

James intercepted her.

'But you are! Something's wrong. Tell me,' he commanded, putting one arm round her waist, his other hand tipping her chin up.

'It's nothing . . . nothing, I assure you. I . . . I was depressed by the weather.' She tried to break free but couldn't.

'I'm sure it was something more than that. Can't

you tell me . . . perhaps I can help,' he said, looking concernedly down at her.

His sympathy was more than she could bear. Didn't he know that *he* was the cause of her unhappiness. How did he expect her to feel at having his friendship withdrawn without any explanation? He had avoided her ever since their weekend together.

'It's nothing. Please don't make a fuss. Everyone feels "down" at times. You must yourself.'

'Very often . . . especially lately.'

Laura put up her hand to wipe away the few tears she had so unwisely permitted to run down her cheeks in her fit of unwonted self-pity.

'Why lately?' she asked.

'Because I miss you,' he said heavily.

'Miss me?'

'Talking to you . . . spending time with you.'

'Then why have you stopped?'

'I should never have started it,' he said. 'I should never have begun a friendship. But I was lonely and so were you and I – I couldn't bring myself to tell you there was no future in it . . . not the kind of future you would wish for.'

'What do you mean? Why is there no future in it?'

'Because the right future for you is marriage and a home of your own. I can never give you that.'

She said dully, 'You're married already.'

'Yes . . . I'm afraid so.'

Laura gave a small stifled moan. 'I should have asked you if you were. I persuaded myself that if you weren't free you would have said so. You should have told me. You should have been straight with me.'

'I know.'

'I don't understand this,' she said. 'Where is your wife? Did she leave you?'

'Not in the sense you mean. She walked out of the house one morning and she never came back. She . . .

she was struck by a car and her brain was damaged. Her body is well but her mind is almost inert. She has to be fed and cared for like a small child. I go to see her every month, but she doesn't know me. There's no hope of recovery.'

He spoke in a flat even tone, his face devoid of expression. Then, suddenly, he swung away, saying in an agonised rasp, 'She was the most beautiful girl you ever saw and she was having a baby. All this summer seeing Lady Carlyon and Sarah reminded me of Belinda . . . the way she was then. Now . . . now she's what people call a vegetable.'

His shoulders heaved. She heard a strange tearing sound and realised, with shock and pity, that it was a sob.

'Oh my love . . . my poor love,' she exclaimed, slipping her arms quickly round him, pressing her cheek to his back.

She had never dreamt that such an appalling tragedy was the cause of the sadness she had sometimes seen in his eyes.

She felt him struggling to control the surge of emotion which speaking of it had released, drawing in deep unsteady breaths, trying to replace the battens on feelings he tried to keep hidden.

When she felt him regaining control, she said, 'How could you think I would turn away from you, James? Do I seem so narrow-minded?'

He took one of her hands from his chest and pressed his lips to the back of it. 'No, not at all . . . but you're made for marriage, Laura . . . not for any other relationship.'

He released himself from her embrace and turned to face her. 'There's still time for you to have children . . . if I were free. But even now, loving you, I can't divorce Belinda. I'm not a deeply religious man but I can't bring myself to break the vow I made her . . . "for better for worse, in sickness and in health . . . till death us do part". I know most people would say that, in the circumstances, I shouldn't feel bound by that promise. But I do. Loving you hasn't changed that. Does that make any sense to you?'

'Yes, it does,' she said quietly. 'My father lost my mother when I was born. He married again for my sake but it was a terrible mistake because he didn't love my step-mother. Even if they had got on, he wouldn't have forgotten my mother. She was part of him as your wife is part of you. I understand how you feel. I expect in your heart you still hope for a miracle to happen . . . for her to recover.'

'For a long time, yes – I did hope that. But then I knew it was impossible and I hoped she would die. Not to release me but to release her,' he said. 'If we have souls . . . if there is an after-life . . . hers is trapped in her body which they are keeping alive. Each time I go there . . . see her . . . I find it terrible to see her being kept alive when she isn't alive. But as long as she's there, I must go. I can't put her out of my mind . . . out of my life.'

The Ashfords flew in from Spain the afternoon before both babies were to be christened in the private chapel.

Marie-Simone had already arrived from Paris, and Marcus and Alison Blakewell had come over from Boston. Alison was to be Simon's godmother and Marcus one of his godfathers. He would also have two English sponsors, both friends from North's schooldays whom Jane had met and liked. One was a barrister, the other a banker.

'They may not do much for his soul but they'll be good chaps to turn to for secular advice.' North wasn't really in favour of christenings, considering it a nonsense to make promises in the name of infants who might grow

494

up to be non-believers like himself. But he was prepared to go along with Jane's feeling that christenings were a social and family tradition which ought to be kept up even if, for many people, they no longer had a religious significance.

Sarah had asked Rob and Emily Wareham to be Thomas' godparents and North to be his second male sponsor.

The morning after the christening there was to be a quiet wedding in the chapel; the second one that year.

When Sam and Damaris had told Jane they were getting married, it had been their intention to have a civil ceremony at Melchester Registry Office. Now, at Jane and North's invitation, they were being married at Longwarden and, like the Ashfords before them, having a lunch party there before setting off on their honeymoon, ten days in New York.

Alone with Jane and Simon, the night before his christening, Pen said, 'Piers and I have been talking about Christmas. We wondered if this year it might be a good plan for you to spend it with us. Our house is quite habitable now. You wouldn't be uncomfortable. The reason we suggest it – and naturally you'll want to discuss it with North before deciding – is that Christmas at Longwarden is bound to be rather a grim time for Allegra and Sarah. It can't fail to stir up painful memories for them both. In Spain there'll be fewer reminders of the two who are missing. How does the idea strike you?'

'As a matter of fact I've been wondering and worrying about Christmas for exactly that reason,' said Jane. 'I've toyed with one or two alternatives but somehow it didn't occur to me that we might come to you. I think it's an excellent idea, if you're sure you have room for five adults and two babies.'

'Ample room and everyone tells us the weather is usually glorious. It's not all uncommon for people to have champagne breakfasts on their terraces on Christmas morning. One or two hardy souls even go for a dip in the sea.'

'I'll discuss it with North tonight.'


In the kitchen Joël was putting the finishing touches to the wedding cake the Countess had asked him to make.

The christening cake had been made some time ago and he had spent many evenings designing the decoration and perfecting the technique required to recreate his sketches with icing sugar, not a medium he had used much before.

The news that Damaris was to be married had come as a shock and a blow to him. Even if he could never have her himself, he couldn't bear to think of her belonging to Sam. He was plainly unworthy of her in every way . . . a common carpenter, even if he had been put in charge of the other carpenters, not even an *ébéniste* who might one day be famous and respected like the great cabinetmakers of the past. Joël still fumed with resentment for the way Sam had interfered on that unfortunate occasion when he had lost his head.


'It's a deliberate slight . . . that's what it is.'

When Mrs Baston was aggrieved, her voice rose to a pitch which went through her daughter's head like the whine of a chainsaw.

'That's silly talk, Mum. Why should we be invited? It's going to be a small quiet wedding with only a few people there.'

'The girl who works in the stables is going. Those two old men from the village have been invited. Not to ask you and Joël . . . it's an insult if you ask me. Especially

496

with all the extra work Joël has had to do for the christening party let alone this sudden wedding.'

'He's enjoyed it,' said Lucy. 'He likes catering for special occasions. The christening cake's been a challenge. Tomorrow morning Lord Carlyon's going to take photographs of the cake and the buffet table. Joël didn't ask him; he offered. I expect Lady C put him up to it. She'd know Joël would like to have pictures of it.'

'You'd think she'd know that he'd like his wife to be invited,' said Mrs Baston tartly. 'Why that Hastings girl should have preference I can't understand.'

'She's not going to the wedding . . . only the christening. The only people at the wedding will be Lord and Lady C, Lady Allegra and Miss Sarah, Mr and Mrs Ashford and the bridegroom's sister and her husband.'

'I wonder why none of her relatives are coming?' said Mrs Baston. 'Don't approve of him, I shouldn't wonder. It wouldn't surprise me if she had got herself pregnant. That's the usual reason people get married in a hurry. I've always thought she looked no better than she should be, in spite of her hoity-toity manner.'

'She's too sophisticated to have to get married,' said Lucy. 'For some reason you've got your knife into her. It's not long since you thought she had her eye on Joël . . . or he fancied her.'

Her mother scowled at her. 'I still think it's very peculiar we haven't had an invite to the christening party. That's not a small affair. They've asked everyone . . . even the midwife.'

Mrs Baston had been astonished by a Countess having her baby delivered at home by a midwife instead of in some exclusive private clinic with a Harley Street consultant in attendance. But then none of the family behaved in the way she felt aristocrats should behave.

However, even though she didn't approve of them, it didn't lessen her fury at being left out of tomorrow's celebrations. It would have been a chance to dress up . . . something to put in her letters to one or two people she would have liked to impress.

The night before her wedding Damaris woke up in Sam's bed and found herself alone. She wanted to pee and assumed that was what he was doing, but after waiting for some time to hear the lavatory being flushed, she turned over and saw, through the open curtains, that no light was shining from the bathroom next door.

Throwing back the bedclothes, she sat up, put her feet into her old espadrilles and reached for her wrapper. Perhaps Sam couldn't sleep . . . perhaps he was having eleventh hour jitters, although it didn't seem like him.

To her surprise and puzzlement he was not in the sitting room or in the galley-sized kitchen. It was 3.17 am. Where could he be at this hour?

While she thought about it, Damaris went to the lavatory and then went back to the kitchen to half fill the kettle. Then she went to the outer door and found it unlocked. Opening it, she saw that it was a dry bright night with an almost full moon still riding high in the sky. Sam must have gone for a walk. Which suggested that he was really jittery about tomorrow. And yet last night he had seemed completely calm and confident that they were doing the right thing.

They had gone out to dinner. Coming back, he had suggested that she ought to sleep in the house because it was said to be bad luck for the groom to see the bride before the wedding. She had laughed and told him she wasn't superstitious and might not sleep well on her own now she had become used to having him curled round behind her. Now she wondered if he had wanted her to sleep in the room where her wedding clothes were hanging up, waiting to be put on at ten o'clock tomorrow . . . today.

She was pouring a second cup of tea when she heard

him open and close the outer door. He would have seen from the chinks of light showing round the edges of the living room curtains that she was up. He didn't look surprised to find her curled up on the sofa. Nor did he look pleased to find her waiting for him.

'What are you doing up?' he asked brusquely.

'I had to go to the loo and then I began to wonder if my bridegroom had got cold feet and done a bolt,' she said, smiling.

'Couldn't sleep so I went for a walk. The garden looks good by moonlight.'

'Like a cup of tea?'

He shook his head. 'I'm going back to bed. I'll sleep now.'

She decided to skip the second cupful of tea. 'I'll come with you.'

As they got into bed, she asked, 'Why couldn't you sleep? Second thoughts?'

Sam put out the light. 'Definitely not. Are you having them?'

'No.'

'Good.'

She was lying on her back and he hooked an arm round her and turned her to lie with her spine against his chest and his thighs under hers. He kissed the nape of her neck, his nose cold from the outside air. 'G'night.'

Within a few minutes his breathing told her he had gone to sleep.

She wondered if he had lied about having no doubts about the rightness of marrying her tomorrow. Was he more perturbed by her unsavoury past than he let on? What other reason could there be for a man to go for a long walk in the small hours of the morning before his wedding?


'Be specially nice to her, North,' said Jane, after telling

him that Damaris was ready to be taken to the chapel. 'It must be a funny feeling, having no one of your own at your wedding.'

North took her hand and placed it on the left side of his chest.

*'What needest thou thy tribes' black tents who hast the red pavilion of my heart?'*

'Dearly beloved, we are gathered together here in the sight of God, and in the face of this Congregation . . .'

The last wedding Laura had attended had been that of Mrs Denham's daughter, Joanne. It had cost far more than Mrs Denham could afford, but mother and daughter had both been determined to put on an impressive show with all the male principals in hired morning dress, six bridesmaids, a three course lunch in the banquet room of an hotel which specialised in wedding receptions, an elaborate tiered cake and a honeymoon in the bridal suite of the Imperial Hotel at Torquay.

Laura had felt it was madness to get into debt for the sake of a few hours' ostentatious display but hadn't expressed that view, knowing it would be disregarded.

How long ago it seemed, that life of submission and secret unhappiness. Not that she was happy now – and never could be while James was unhappy – but at least she was living with people she admired and respected in a beautiful place instead of a spiritual prison.

Unlike Joanne who had been married in yards of nylon lace with a diamanté tiara holding her veil and a bouquet of wired white lilies and asparagus fern, Damaris Lynn had entered the chapel in the simplest and plainest of cream gabardine suits worn over a cream silk tee shirt. A single string of matched creamy pearls circled the base of her neck with larger pearls in her ears and, at the back of her head, a large bow of shot silk ribbon which repeated the dark and light browns of her long glossy hair.

She had not carried any flowers and stood now, composed and elegant, by the side of Sam Warstock who, in his well-cut grey suit, looked unexpectedly different from his workmanlike everyday self.

As the service proceeded and she listened to them committing themselves to each other for the rest of their lives, Laura thought of the vows James had made and by which he still felt bound as long as his wife was alive.

Not many people took their marriage vows as seriously as that nowadays. People parted for reasons far more trivial than an irreversible injury to one partner's brain. Some would say it was foolish for James to ruin his own life; that his wife would not want such a sacrifice. But perhaps those people weren't capable of loving as deeply as he had loved the girl he married.

That sort of love is a once in a lifetime thing, thought Laura. He is the love of my life but she was the love of his. He's fond of me and he needs someone, but that's a far cry from love. Can I be satisfied with that? Can I persuade him to take me on the only terms open to us? Will it work? Will I be comfortable as his mistress . . . girlfriend . . . whatever I would become if we went on spending weekends together?

At present James was adamantly opposed to an irregular relationship. He seemed to have put her on a pedestal, regarding her as being too pure, too fine for anything but marriage. She hadn't yet told him about Bernard.

Standing beside Piers Ashford, Allegra watched Sam slide the ring along Damaris' finger and, holding it there, repeat after the vicar, 'With this ring I thee wed, with my body I thee worship, and with all my worldly goods I thee endow.'

Does it hurt less? she asked herself. Has six months made any difference? Is life slightly more worth living? Perhaps . . . a little . . . not much. It's like losing a leg or an eye, or being permanently crippled like Joël Vibrac's wife. People adjust, they have to, but life is never, ever the same again. When love has gone, the world is a different place. I hope it lasts longer for these two than it did for me.

Between the service and the lunch party Sarah slipped upstairs to feed Thomas who was being minded by Morag.

No longer jaundiced, and starting to shed the shock of dark hair, he was a contented baby who seemed to have survived unscathed by his traumatic arrival.

She lifted him out of his cot and, supporting his wobbly head, held him against her shoulder as she carried him to the windowseat.

He spent most of his time in the stables with her and Kate, lying in an old-fashioned high pram, protected by a cat-net from the stableyard tabbies.

'Did Miss Lynn look nice?' asked Morag.

'Lovely,' said Sarah. She described what Damaris was wearing.

'I think a dress is more feminine. A suit's too businesslike . . . all right for a registry office but not for a church wedding,' said Morag. 'Is she going away in it? Cream will show every mark.'

'I don't know,' said Sarah.

She liked Morag but at this moment she longed to be alone with Thomas. Watching other people get married was and always would be a painful reminder that she had lost the man she wanted to marry and, unless he came back to her one day, would never turn a radiant face to her wedding guests as Damaris had a short time ago.

*

502

'. . . the worst fire yet. Whoever's behind these outbreaks is getting more ambitious. The insurers will have to pay out a lot of money for last night's blaze. Perhaps they'll bring in some investigators who will make more headway than the police have so far.'

The Earl was speaking to his mother's husband. Damaris, standing nearby, heard what he said because of a momentary hiatus in her conversation with Kate.

'Do I gather there's been another fire?' she asked Kate, who today was wearing a printed silk shirt dress in place of her unisex working clothes.

'Yes . . . a weekend cottage belonging to people from London has been burnt down. I'm told by one of the cleaners that the owner is a well-known TV actor. I've forgotten his name but he's in one of the soap operas she watches. He and his boyfriend bought it a couple of years ago. If it was burnt deliberately, as everyone seems to think, perhaps someone's working off a grudge against incomers . . . or against homosexuals,' said Kate.

'Could be,' said Damaris. 'When did it happen? Yesterday evening?'

'No, in the small hours of this morning. About three, I think. The cottage stands by itself so the flames had got a good hold before the fire engines arrived.'

Damaris looked across the room at Sam. Everyone was drinking champagne and waiting for lunch to be announced. He was laughing, looking incredibly dashing in a pink and white striped shirt with a white carnation in his buttonhole.

'How far is the cottage from here?' she asked.

'Very close. It used to be part of the estate . . . one of the bits sold off by Sarah's uncle. Where are you staying in New York?'

Her eyes on Sam, Damaris told her.


'North thinks Christmas with you is a great idea and

Allegra jumped at it. I think she's been dreading Christmas here.'

The wedding celebrations were over and Jane and her mother-in-law were having tea by themselves.

'How can she not?' said Pen. 'I know how I'd feel at facing Christmas without Piers – although this time last year I never dreamed that a few months later I'd be married to him. For me this whole year has been an *annus mirablis*.'

'For me too,' Jane agreed.

'Have you talked about Christmas to Sarah?'

'She'd like to come but feels she can't leave Kate to cope single-handed. They've both been invited to have Christmas lunch with Rob and Emily Wareham and to go there on Boxing Day. So if Sarah does stay behind she won't be lonely.'

'Actually for her to come to Spain might not be such a good idea,' said Pen. 'As he speaks the language fluently, it's the most likely place for Nick Dean to be, isn't it? That would be upsetting for her. Unlike Allegra who, one day, will be able to put the past behind her, Sarah has no hope of doing that. Every time she looks at her baby, she must feel a pang, poor little soul. I feel desperately sorry for her, don't you?'

'Yes, and to make matters worse she's still in pain from that wretched episiotomy. I'm furious about it. I'm sure it was totally unnecessary. If I could give birth to a bigger baby without tearing, why did Sarah need to be cut? I was back to normal almost immediately, but Sarah's had weeks of misery. It's agony for her to ride, Kate says. Not that she'll admit it but Kate can see that it hurts her.'

'I remember hurting too,' said Pen. 'But in those days I took it for granted that whatever was done to me must be necessary and right. I'm much more sceptical now ... and more confident about standing up for myself. That's mostly Piers' doing ... and yours. We've been invited to a rather splendid party next week. I'm going to wear the dress you bullied me into wearing for the dance last December. I shan't have to pluck up my courage to put it on this time.'

Sam and Damaris were dropped off at Heathrow by his sister and brother-in-law on their way back to London.

When, the airport formalities accomplished, they were waiting for their flight to be called, Damaris said, 'Did you hear about the cottage which was burned down last night?'

'I'm surprised I didn't see it going up while I was out last night,' said Sam. 'Usually a big blaze like that shows up in the sky for miles around. If I'd walked right round the house I expect I might have done, but I stayed on the west side. Anyway, I was pretty deep in thought.'

'What about?'

'Yesterday morning I had a letter – forwarded by Polly – from my grandmother. She wants to meet you. My grandfather's seeking a *rapprochement*, it seems. Polly thinks I should accept the olive branch. I don't. But I don't have only myself to consider any more. What do you think?'

'I think it's something only you can decide, Sam. I should find it hard to be civil to anyone who had treated you badly, but I feel quite sorry for your grandmother.'

She wanted to accept his explanation of his absence during the night, yet it seemed odd that Polly hadn't mentioned the letter during the drive from Longwarden. If she had forwarded it to him, wouldn't she have wanted to know what his grandmother had said in it?

It was a terrible thing, in the first hours of marriage, to consider the possibility that one's husband might be an arsonist, Damaris thought miserably.

She wished she had the courage to ask him point blank. But how could she? If he were innocent, he would be terribly wounded by her suspicions. All she could do was to try to put last night's fire out of her mind and hope that by the time they returned the arsonist would have been caught, proving her doubts completely groundless.

Towards the end of the month the weather worsened and Mrs Baston's litany of complaints lengthened. It became more than Lucy could bear on top of everything else.

'Oh, Mum, for God's sake stop whining. If you hate it here that much why not walk out? I would if I could, but I can't. I'm trapped in this chair for the rest of my life . . . and a bloody rotten life it's been so far,' she added bitterly.

'I'll put up with a lot, my girl, but I won't stand being spoken to like that,' said Mrs Baston, putting on her aggrieved face. 'After all I've done for you, the least you –'

Lucy's self-control snapped. 'You've messed up my life . . . that's what you've done. Even before I was crippled, you'd messed it up,' she burst out.

'*Oh!* What a wicked thing to say to your mother who's done so much for you. When I think of the sacrifices I made to send you to a nice school and dress you nicely and give you a pony and everything . . . I don't know how you can be so cruel and ungrateful.'

'You didn't do all that for me . . . you did it for yourself,' Lucy said savagely. 'And if you had done it for me, it wouldn't have made up for what *he* did. You've always pretended not to know about that, haven't you . . . made out what a good man he was. But I think he did things to me because you wouldn't let him near you.'

'I don't know what you're talking about . . . who you're talking about.'

'Yes, you do . . . I'm talking about your husband and

my father who used to sneak into my bed when you wouldn't have him in yours.'

Mrs Baston's mouth opened but no sound came out. For once in her life she was dumbstruck. Her expression reminded Lucy of a goldfish in a tank, the same popping eyes, the same gaping lips.

When she recovered her voice, it was an outraged squeak. 'May God forgive you. You're a wicked, *wicked* girl to say such a vile, terrible thing about a man who idolised you and worked himself into his grave to give you everything you wanted.'

'I'd rather have had a father who spent all his money on drink and never gave me a farthing . . . and a mother who didn't pretend to have sick headaches and stuff herself with sleeping pills to avoid having to put up with what I had to go through.'

After the years of silence and secrecy, now that she had finally spoken the unspeakable, Lucy didn't regret her outburst. She felt an extraordinary sense of relief. It was in the open at last, the thing which had ruined her teens and blighted her marriage to Joël.

'I was glad when he dropped dead,' she said. 'I'd been praying for two years that he'd be killed in the car or get cancer or something. I knew it would be useless telling you. You wouldn't have stopped him . . . you wouldn't have believed me.'

'I don't believe you now. I think you've gone mad,' said her mother. 'It's a pack of filthy lies, that's what it is. Arnold would never –'

'Not much he wouldn't,' said Lucy. 'He started when you were in hospital. I wanted to stay with the Crosbys but you wouldn't let me. You said I must look after him. You gave him the chance and he took it. He came to my room the very first night you were gone.'

'I won't listen to this . . . I won't listen.' With tightly closed eyes, her mother shook her head from side to side.

'You will listen,' said Lucy relentlessly. 'It's time you

507

knew what I went through. You ought to be thanking your stars I didn't tell someone else . . . Mrs Crosby or one of the teachers. That's what I ought to have done, but I was too scared. I didn't know what would happen . . . if they'd send him to prison for life . . . or if you'd commit suicide. He put that idea in my head. "Your mother's very highly strung. It wouldn't do to upset her".'

'I'm sorry to disturb you, m'Lord, but Mr Vibrac would like a work with you. I suggested he should wait until tomorrow but he's most insistent that he must speak to you tonight.'

North raised his eyebrows. 'Then you'd better wheel him in, Flitton.'

The butler said, 'He would like to see you privately, m'Lord.'

North glanced enquiringly at Jane whose expression and shrug indicated that she had no more idea why the chef must speak to him than he had.

'It appears that whatever is worrying him is not a matter with which he wishes to bother her Ladyship,' the butler added.

'Curiouser and curiouser,' North murmured. 'Very well, I'll come and see him. Shan't be long, darling.'

Jane watched him stride from the room with her usually smooth forehead wrinkled in perplexity. What could have happened in the kitchen or in the young Frenchman's ménage to make him want to see North rather than herself? He must really have dug his heels in to overcome Flitton's objections to disturbing them.

Could it be that either his wife or his mother-in-law were not happy at Longwarden and were demanding to leave? But if something like that had blown up, it was her province, not North's.

'Oh dear, don't say our splendid culinary arrange-

508

ments are about to break down,' she murmured to William, Pen's old cat, who had curled himself up next to her.

Vibrac, when North first saw him, was sitting on a chair in the Great Hall with his head in his hands in an attitude of deep despondency.

It took a cough from Flitton to alert him to their presence whereupon he gave a nervous start and jumped to his feet.

'Good evening, Vibrac. What's the problem?' North saw at a glance that the Frenchman was in a state of deep agitation although he was trying to control it. 'Thank you, Flitton,' he added, seeing that the answer to his question would not be forthcoming until the butler had gone.

Vibrac waited until he was sure Flitton was out of earshot before he said, in a low voice, 'Something very bad has happened . . . something I could not tell you in front of her Ladyship.'

'If it's as bad as that you'd better have something to steady your own nerves,' said North.

'No, sir . . . thank you, but no. I've already had some brandy. I must not drink any more. When the police come they –'

'You've sent for the police?' North asked sharply.

'No, sir . . . m'Lord . . . not yet. I wanted to speak to you first . . . to ask you what I should do. You see, when I went back tonight I found that my wife was . . . dead. Also her mother . . . both dead.'

'*Both* of them?' North said, aghast.

The younger man nodded. 'Both. My wife killed with terrible violence . . . blood everywhere . . . and the old bitch dead on her bed from pills and much whisky.'

'Are you saying that your mother-in-law has murdered your wife and then committed suicide?'

From what little he had seen of the two women it seemed so wildly improbable that into North's mind there came a more believable alternative; that the murderer wasn't that big-busted middle-aged woman but the young man who stood before him, visibly shaking.

'It was not done by someone else. There has been no robbery . . . no sign of any disturbance except the blood . . . so much blood.' Vibrac shuddered at the recollection. 'I have never liked my *belle-mère* but I didn't think her capable of this. To kill her own daughter . . . to strike her so many times. *C'est incroyable!*'

He burst into tears.


'You've been ages. I was on the point of coming to find out what was going on,' said Jane, when North reappeared. 'What's the matter? Why are you looking so grim?'

He came to where she was sitting at one end of an enormous sofa. 'I'm afraid we have a bit of a catastrophe on our hands, Jane. You must try not to let it upset you. It's because he was afraid of distressing you that Vibrac asked to see me.'

'What sort of catastrophe?' she asked anxiously as he took her hands in his. 'Does Joël want to leave?'

It was some time since she had dropped the formal Monsieur Vibrac and started to use the chef's first name.

'I'm afraid it's rather worse than that, darling. At the moment I only know what he's told me and what he says he thinks happened . . . which may or may not be correct. It seems that this afternoon his wife and her mother had a row . . . a very serious row.'

'Oh God . . . Lucy's killed herself. Is that it?' she whispered.

'She is dead – yes. What made you jump to that conclusion?'

'Something about her has worried me ever since I met

her . . . a look in her eyes . . . very difficult to explain. Oh, poor girl . . . poor unhappy girl . . . and poor Joël. I must see him, North . . . try to comfort him. He won't get any sympathy from Mrs Baston. They can't stand each other. I saw that at once.'

She attempted to rise but North tightened his hold on her hands and made her stay where she was. 'You can talk to him later. Not now. The police are coming and they'll want to question him. I haven't told you everything. I'm afraid it's a lot more . . . complex than a straightforward suicide. Lucy's mother is also dead.'

'*No!*' Jane's beautiful eyes dilated with horror. 'But of course . . . I should have realised. Lucy couldn't have killed herself without help. You mean Mrs Baston helped her to commit suicide and then took her own life?'

He let go her hands and slipped his arms gently round her, pulling her against him. 'No, it wasn't quite like that. As I told you a minute ago they seem to have had a quarrel. Mrs Baston lost her temper . . . went for the girl with a knife. Perhaps she didn't mean to kill her, but she did. When she realised what she'd done, she swallowed a bottle of pills and a lot of whisky. By the time Vibrac found them, she was dead, too.'

Jane gave a little moan and buried her face in his shoulder. But only for a few moments. Then she drew back and looked up at him.

'It's all right . . . I'm not going to make matters worse by having hysterics. How is Joël? Is he all to pieces? No, he can't be or he wouldn't have worried about it upsetting me. That was incredibly thoughtful of him in the circumstances.'

'Yes, it was,' North agreed. 'If you're sure you're all right, I'm going to get Allegra to come and sit with you while I go and support him through the police questioning.'

'Of course – don't worry about me. It's Joël who needs you right now. Go back to him quickly, North.'

'Flitton will let me know as soon as the police arrive. I didn't ring Longwarden Police Station. It seemed advisable to have a word with the Chief Constable first. Luckily he was at home tonight. I explained what had happened – or what appears to have happened – and left it to him to put the wheels in motion. He may come over himself in which case you'll have to make some civil noises to him, darling. Can you bear it?'

'Certainly I can. He's rather a nice man. I danced with him last December.'

Presently, after Allegra had come downstairs and had the news broken to her, and her brother had gone to receive the police, Jane said, 'What kind of row would drive a woman to an act of violence against her own daughter?'

'God knows. But there are undercurrents of tension in a lot of mother-daughter relationships. Also Mrs Baston may have been menopausal,' said Allegra. 'Quite a lot of women feel like killing their husbands then, so I've heard. A murderous impulse towards an invalid daughter who needs ... needed constant attention doesn't surprise me particularly. I only saw the woman once. We passed in the drive and said good morning. Didn't much like the look of her. She had piggy eyes.'

'I didn't like her either, but she seemed devoted to her daughter. Oh dear, I suppose this means we shall have all those vultures from the tabloids swarming round us again.'

''Fraid so,' Allegra agreed. 'I'd better let Mother know ... break it to her gently. Blowflies like Ronnie Wirral are quite capable of ringing her up in the middle of the night and making her think it's one of us who's been murdered.'

Late the next day the Chief Constable let North know the results of the autopsies.

512

Among the numerous stab wounds inflicted on Lucy Baston, the one which had caused her death had been the blow which had slashed two of the three large veins in her neck.

Neither the pills nor the liquor she had swallowed had killed Mrs Baston. She had died from inhaling vomit while lying on her back in an alcoholic stupor. Bruises on one of her wrists showed that not long before she died someone had gripped her arm with abnormal force.

The size and position of the marks indicated that the person had been her daughter. This fact, combined with the pathologist's report that the first wound had been inflicted on the daughter's arm, led the police to conclude that the attack had begun from a wish to break free which had developed into a murderous frenzy.

The murder weapon had not been, as North had assumed, a knife. It had been a pair of dressmaking shears.

---

## December

'That was an appalling business at Longwarden last month,' said Piers Ashford, throwing another olive log on the fire.

'Yes, very grim,' North agreed, reaching for the glass which his host had recently replenished with Spanish brandy.

He and his party had landed at Alicante early that afternoon. Now the women had all gone to bed, leaving the two men to talk.

'The inquest didn't throw much light on what might have been behind it. What's your theory?' Piers asked.

'God alone knows why she did it. We can only speculate. But Vibrac did tell me something which the police don't know and I didn't see fit to tell them.' North uncrossed and stretched his long legs. 'Lucy Vibrac should never have married. She was revolted by sex. Most men would have recognised that something was wrong from the start, but the penny didn't drop with her husband until they were on their honeymoon.'

'Are you suggesting that Vibrac went mad with frustration, killed his wife and made it look as if his mother-in-law had done it? That he's got away with a double murder?' Piers asked, raising his eyebrows.

'No, no . . . the police are satisfied he had nothing to do with it. So am I. I think he's a nice guy who had the bad luck to get involved with two warped and difficult women. Actually it's Allegra who's worked out a possible explanation, one which I find quite plausible. See what you think of it. Allegra says that a normal healthy woman – which Lucy Vibrac appears to have been before her riding accident – is only repelled by sex if she's been raped or forced into sexual relations which our culture prohibits.'

'You mean incest?'

'Exactly. You probably didn't see much of Mrs Baston when you were over this summer. Nor did I. But Jane spent quite a lot of time with the two of them. She was never able to overcome her instinctive dislike of the mother, and there was something about the daughter which worried her. From various remarks she's made about them, and from what little I saw of Mrs Baston, it's clear that the late Mr Baston was very unlikely to have had a good time in bed. He wouldn't be the first sex-starved husband to use his daughter as a substitute.'

'But this Baston woman was a widow. One could understand her going berserk if she'd caught him molesting the daughter during her teens. But in that case wouldn't it be the father she would attack? Not the girl?' Piers suggested.

'Not necessarily. Years ago, when Allegra and I were

children, there was a case in the village which became a big story in the *News of the World*. The mother of a large family – all of them rather dim-witted – was had up for wounding her teenage daughter. It turned out the girl had complained to her that the father was interfering with her, and had been for some time. The mother was a violent woman who'd already been in trouble for screaming abuse at her neighbours and even coming to blows with them. Instead of raising hell with her husband, as one would have expected, she went for the daughter . . . damn nearly killed her. I forget all the details – it was a long time ago – but the gist of it was that, even though all the evidence showed the reverse to be true, in that woman's not very bright mind it was better for the girl to be to blame.'

He paused to glance at the fire where the log had shifted, sending a flight of red sparks up the chimney.

'Allegra, who remembers the case better than I do, says a psychologist was brought in to explain the convoluted reasoning behind the attack on the daughter,' he continued. 'In the case of Mrs Baston's psyche, according to Jane, she was pathologically genteel . . . there were covers on everything which could be covered from the telephone book to the spare roll of lavatory paper. Jane feels she was a woman who might take a prurient interest in other people's perversions but would do her best to ignore any signs of them in her own family.'

'The sort of woman who pretends not to know her son is homosexual or her husband a lecher.'

'Precisely. Now let's suppose that Mrs Baston either genuinely didn't know or had closed her mind to the possibility that her husband had been having sex with the daughter. The weather is lousy, she and the girl are stuck indoors, getting on each other's nerves even more than usual. Suddenly the daughter breaks it to her . . . forces her to listen. That would explain the pathologist's evidence that Lucy had been holding her mother's wrists, her grip being more powerful than normal from turning the wheels of her chair. Don't you think it's possible that a woman with a bad temper might, under that provocation, go to any lengths to shut the girl up? I do. I think it's entirely possible that for a few minutes the mother went mad with rage, snatched up the nearest weapon – her dressmaking scissors – and struck the girl.'

Piers stroked the bridge of his nose with his finger and thumb, a habit of his when considering a premise.

'Then came to her senses, realised what she'd done and saw no way out but to do herself in,' he said. 'Yes, you may be right. Possibly that is what happened. No one will ever know for certain, but it's a feasible theory. What about Vibrac? How did he take it, once the first shock had worn off?'

'I think he was relieved. As soon as the inquest was over, we pushed him off to France to his family. Two weeks later he came back and insisted on carrying on as if nothing had happened. He seems to feel that to leave would be to let Jane down and also he wants time to think out his future. If he decides to go back to London or France, he'll stay with us till we've found a satisfactory replacement. In the circumstances I consider that's very decent of him. Naturally we've given him different accommodation. Jane thinks we should have the scene of the murder demolished. What's your view on that?'

'For all we know something equally gruesome may have happened here in the past,' said Piers, looking round his firelit and peaceful living room furnished with an eclectic mixture of cane and basketwork from the nearby town of Gata, furniture brought by Pickfords from Longwarden and pieces picked up in France where the sign *Brocante* had made them pause on their journey south in September.

'I don't myself believe in ghosts, poltergeists or any of that supernatural stuff,' he went on. 'At the same time I think most people – particularly women – aren't going to be happy living in a place when a violent crime has occurred in the recent past.'

He changed the subject. 'D'you fancy a swim tomorrow? Pen and I have been going in every day since we came back, but I have to admit it's a bit of a shock to the system for the first minute or two. It's quite amusing to watch the expressions of tourists who've been misled by the brochures into expecting the sea here to be tepid all year round.'

In a small room where exposed beams slanted from less than six feet where they rested on the window wall to twice that height on the wall at the back of the bed, Allegra was turning the pages of a Spanish magazine called *Hola!*, part of a selection of reading matter put out for her by her mother.

Sitting on the sunny terrace, soon after their arrival this afternoon, had evoked painful memories of the heat and bright light in Barbados where she and Andro had spent their last weeks together.

Yet, in spite of the many similarities between *Las Golondrinas* and the beautiful Caribbean house called *Paradise*, she was glad she had come here. She needed a change of scene and to meet some new people; and here in this charming house where Mother and Piers had made a new life for themselves, there was less anguish for her than there would have been at Longwarden at Christmas.

While the Carlyons were flying to Spain, Laura was on her way to an hotel in Devon which had advertised Christmas breaks. She was staying there till after the New Year.

She had told everyone who asked, including James, that she would be staying with friends. Had they known the truth they might have worried about her being on her own among strangers.

Now, as she settled herself in a comfortable bed in a room with a view of the south coast, she felt that if the rest of her stay was as pleasant as the first evening she would have nothing to complain about.

In the lounge before dinner she had got into conversation with an elderly couple who had invited her to eat with them. After dinner another couple had joined them for coffee. She had the impression that everyone staying at the hotel, a family-run establishment, was determined to be friendly and create a house party atmosphere. That she was ten years younger than any of the other guests – but not everyone had arrived yet – didn't depress her. It was what she had anticipated.

'I expected a bloodshot-eyed tyrant, snapping and snarling if we didn't all jump to his bidding, but he seems just a fretful old man,' said Damaris, as they undressed in a bedroom at Sam's family manor on Christmas Eve.

'Yes, he's changed . . . shrunk . . . diminished,' said Sam. 'It's hard to believe he was ever a terrifying bully. I feel almost sorry for him. But if anyone deserves an unpleasant end, he does. He's made life hell for a lot of people.'

The cause of his grandfather's recent chest troubles had been diagnosed as cancer. He was not expected to live long.

They had arrived too late for Damaris to see the garden but the house, as Polly had warned her, was a gloomy, comfortless place. Up to now the Warstocks and their wives had not been people of discerning taste. The house was full of her least liked colours; oxblood, magenta and rust. There was a great deal of dark panelling and seventeenth century oak furniture which had never appealed to her as much as the lighter more elegant forms made at the end of the following century.

But whether, when the old man died, Sam would decide to come back here was not the main thing on her mind. Now that her cousin Gary had ceased to worry her, what overshadowed her days and gave her restless nights – even after Sam had made long love to her – was the unresolved possibility that he was the arsonist.

No further fires had occurred while they were in America, but one night since their return she had again woken up to find him missing. Returning, he had told her he quite often went for walks at night if he couldn't sleep. He liked prowling about in the moonlight even in winter. Damaris had pretended to accept his explanation, but had suffered agonies of apprehension until late the next day by which time news of a fire in the vicinity would have been sure to reach Longwarden.


James spent Christmas Eve with his sisters who, each year, took it in turns to host a large family party. During the day, surrounded by nephews and nieces, he had little time to regret that these annual festivities would never include his children.

But at night, unable to read because he was sharing a room with two of his nephews, it was difficult to sleep for remembering Christmases past and wishing that future Christmases could be spent with Laura.


At *Las Golondrinas* Jane was the first to get up on Christmas morning.

With her two months old son snugly wrapped in a quilted baby bag given her by Alison Blakewell, she padded quietly down the stairs with their clay-tiled treads and ceramic risers patterned with blue and yellow flowers.

519

The sun was rising in fiery splendour when she opened the living room curtains made from old Paisley shawls hung from wooden rings on long poles.

She wondered if *Red in the morning, shepherd's warning* applied in this country. Perhaps not. Most of the sky was clear of cloud and those which were gilded and rouged by the sunrise were feathery streaks not rain clouds.

Leaving Simon on the sofa, surrounded by cushions, still asleep although she expected him to wake and demand his breakfast at any moment, she went to the kitchen to make tea. The walls between the worktops and the cupboards were clad with tiles like the risers; old tiles painted by hand and fired a long time ago. Through the window, as she filled the kettle with water which no longer came from a *cisterna* under the house but from a high tank supplied by the Ashfords' new bore-hole, she could see part of the garden and beyond it the unfamiliar landscape of low hills patterned with ancient terraces and drystone retaining walls.

She remembered Nick Dean talking to her about Spain, a land with which he seemed to feel a strong affinity. Had he returned here? Was he somewhere in this vast country whose crinkled rows of *sierras*, stretching as far as the eye could see, they had gazed at from the air yesterday? She remembered her last sight of Sarah, waving goodbye, smiling as if she didn't mind being left behind. Poor Sarah: it couldn't be a truly happy Christmas for her this year, even with Thomas to comfort her, Jane thought with a pang of pity.

With a mug of tea in her hand, she returned to the living room to drink it before feeding Simon. By next Christmas he would be old enough to enjoy the baubles she had brought with her to decorate the tree which Piers had bought in the market of their nearest town. The year after that he would be ready for his first Christmas stocking.

Thoughts of the Christmases to come, and images of her son growing from babyhood to boyhood, made Jane smile to herself.

He was leaning against her shoulder, having his back rubbed, when North came downstairs, wearing the Paisley silk dressing gown she had given him for Christmas last year.

'Happy Christmas, sweetie.' He sat down beside her, kissing her and then the baby.

'Happy Christmas.' For a minute she snuggled against him, her thoughts about Sarah making her doubly conscious of her own good fortune. Then, passing Thomas to him, she said 'If you'll carry on rubbing his back, I'll make you a cup of tea.'

'Don't dash off for a minute. I've got something for you.' With his son supported by one hand, North felt in the pocket of his robe and produced a small parcel.

'Something to wear on your red outfit tonight.' He had seen the dress Jane had bought to wear at his mother's Christmas dinner party to which, as she always had in England, she had invited two or three lonely people who would otherwise be on their own.

As Jane started to open the parcel, he said, 'Last year the brooch I gave you was one of Granny Flora's jewels, but this is something I chose and paid for myself.'

The wrappings contained a leather box which, opened, revealed an Art Nouveau brooch; a girl's head, in profile, in gold, with three strange, Egyptian-style flowers in dark blue and red enamel, their stalks emerging from leaves like water-lily pads.

Jane had a lot of deep, blue-reds in her wardrobe and the brooch would look good on those and on black and grey.

'Thank      you,      darling . . . for      this . . . and      for everything. '

*

At Longwarden, Sarah was tucking Thomas into the old-fashioned perambulator.

'Now you lie there, my angel, while Kate and I do our work and later on we'll open all the lovely presents you've been given.'

She found she was looking forward to seeing what everyone had chosen for him as much as to opening her own parcels.

For a few moments, when he was settled, she continued to hang over the pram, loving his button of a nose and even his funny little ears which were still a bit crumpled. Would they straighten out later?

As she thought of him getting bigger, starting to talk, running about, her expression clouded. When he began to ask questions, what was she going to tell him?

'Is Simon's daddy my daddy?'

'No, darling.'

'Why haven't I got a daddy?'

'Everyone has one, but not everyone's daddy lives with them.'

'Why not? Where is my daddy?'

'I don't know, Thomas.'


On New Year's Eve the Ashfords and their house guests went to a party given by Robin and Lucilla Bolton, a hospitable couple with whom Pen had made friends the previous winter when she was staying in a Spanish village house lent to her by a schoolfriend.

Although the Carlyons' nanny had chosen to come to Spain rather than go home for Christmas – her mother had recently re-married and Morag wasn't taken with her step-father – understandably she wasn't keen on being left on her own at night in an isolated house in a country where she didn't speak the language.

It had therefore been arranged that she should accompany the others to the party while Simon was left in the care of Maria, the Spanish woman who looked after the house in which Pen had stayed.

After the sequestered existence she had led for the past nine months, Allegra found it very strange to be in a large group of people. It was an effort to sparkle, a duty her mother fulfilled as if she had been doing it all her life, she noticed with wry amusement. Allegra would never be shy, as Pen had once been, but she would have been happy to sit in a corner and watch instead of being obliged to talk.

'It's so mild they're dancing on the terraces. Would you care for a whirl, Allegra?'

It was Piers, offering her an escape from the war-time reminiscences of two elderly men, one of whom, ten minutes earlier, had been trying to flirt with her.

'Are you bored?' he asked, as they walked through the French windows onto the fairy-lit terrace surrounding the swimming pool.

'Did I look it?'

'No, but I felt you might be. I've bitten back yawns with those two and I'm nearer their age than you are.'

'I don't think age has too much bearing on boring. I've known some men in their twenties who were crashing bores.'

They started to dance. For a man not far from sixty, he was still lean and fit. He didn't hold her as close, but the solid breadth of his shoulder reminded her of Risconti. It seemed ironic that her mother, for so long immured in widowhood, should now be sharing a bed with this virile charmer while Allegra herself – a veteran of countless affairs before she met Andro – felt sexual love was over for her. Would she ever again feel the stirring of erotic excitement? It seemed unlikely.


In Devon, Laura was dancing with a doctor from Dorset. A widower, he was staying at the hotel with his sister and brother-in-law. His two children and their three being scattered in other parts of the world, his sister had declared that the time had come for her to spend Christmas with her feet up while someone else did the work. She and her husband liked bridge but the doctor didn't and he and Laura had been for one or two walks while the others were in the card room.

'There's a National Trust garden not far from here which is open all the year round. I was thinking of going there tomorrow. Would it interest you?' he asked.

'Very much. Longwarden is the only large garden I've seen. It would interest me to compare them.'

'Good. Will ten o'clock be too early for you? I suppose it depends what time we all get to bed.'

Shortly before midnight, Lucilla Bolton distributed bags of grapes to all the guests at her party.

'Old Spanish custom: when it starts striking midnight, you eat a grape at each stroke and make a wish,' said Morag's dancing partner who was spending a week with his expatriate grandparents.

Ten minutes later, as the old year ended and the new one began, he put his arms round her and kissed her.

'Happy New Year. *Feliz año nuevo*,' he added, to impress her with his Spanish.

In Longwarden village, at the Warehams' party, Sarah had just been hugged and kissed by a friend of Rob's who had turned up late and couldn't believe his luck in finding a beautiful girl without a partner.

To his surprise and discomfiture, he drew back to find her big blue eyes filled with tears. He wasn't to know that, this time last year, she had just kissed Nick Dean.

# January 1987

In January, gardeners from all over Britain and beyond flocked to Sotheby's galleries in Bond Street to see 'The Glory of the Garden' – an exhibition covering five hundred years of English gardening.

Most of England's great houses were represented. North and Jane had lent the Longwarden Red Book, the portrait of Caspar Carlyon painted by John Singer Sargent and six studies of fruit and vegetables painted on rice paper which North's great-grandfather had found on one of his expeditions to China.

The Carlyons and Pen were still in Spain when Sotheby's and the Royal Horticultural Society gave a glittering party to launch the exhibition, but Piers knew his wife longed to see it and arranged for them to fly back with the others. The last thing he wanted to do was to visit London in January, but Pen's exclamation of delight as she gazed at an exquisite Fantin-Latour oil painting of azaleas and pansies, and hung over the glass case in which were displayed a pair of Chelsea porcelain pea-pods, also lent by the Queen Mother, made him glad he had brought her.

When their Christmas holiday in the sun was followed by a fortnight of English rain, Allegra said to her brother, 'I can't stand this hellish weather. I must get away. You've been more or less everywhere. Where would you recommend?'

North considered the question. It was no use suggesting a place where there was nothing to do but swim and lie in the sun. Allegra enjoyed doing both, but not all the time and certainly not in her present state of restless unhappiness. Any of the winter-sun places was bound to remind her of last year's trip to Barbados with Andro Risconti. All had certain things in common; things which would call up memories of her dead lover. She needed a place which offered distractions from those memories.

'What about Bali?' he suggested.

Allegra's geographic knowledge was confined to the countries where her great-grandfather had travelled in search of plants and the places she had been to herself. She had only a hazy idea of Bali's location somewhere in the scattering of large and small islands lying north of Australia, between the Indian Ocean and the Pacific. It seemed a long way to go.

'Why Bali?' she asked.

'It hasn't been spoilt by high-rise. They built one monstrous hotel a few years ago and afterwards made a law that no buildings were to be taller than the height of a palm tree. In the high season – July and August – it can be overrun with Aussies, but it won't be at this time of year. Bali's not only one of the most beautiful islands in the world, but the people are nice. Good-looking . . . friendly . . . happy. How long that will last, God knows. But that's the way it is now . . . or was the last time I was there.'

He went off to fetch his photographic file on Bali.


Two days later, with very little luggage, she took the train from Victoria to Gatwick, trying not to remember, when she arrived at the airport, that in January last year she had come here with Andro on a journey from which he had known he would never return.

'No suitcase?' The girl at the check-in desk for flight GA109 from London to Sydney, with seven intermediate stops, looked surprised when the tall striking woman listed as Miss A. Lomax failed to place a case on the conveyor.

'Only hand luggage.'

Knowing that, as she had in the Caribbean, she would be able to buy any more clothes she needed on arrival, Allegra was travelling with two roll-bags, one packed inside the other with the zip-bag containing her washing things and cosmetics, two changes of clothes and a few other necessities. The second roll-bag was for the things which, Jane assured her, she would want to bring back from South East Asia.


When, before the aircraft left Amsterdam, no one came to occupy the place next to hers, at first Allegra was relieved. On such a long flight a garrulous neighbour would be unbearable.

After the short hop to Paris, when they had begun the long haul across Europe and the Persian Gulf to the next stop at Abu Dhabi, she began to realise the empty seat was a mixed blessing. It gave her more elbow room, but it also made her more conscious of being on her own. With no one beside her, it was easier to imagine Andro sitting there.

Next month it would be a year since his death.


She first saw the tall Thai in the house of the legendary Jim Thompson, the American who had made Thai silk world famous and then disappeared in mysterious circumstances.

She was going round the house in a group led by a guide. The tall Thai was escorting an elderly European woman with whom he was speaking French.

Had he been an average-sized Thai, Allegra might scarcely have noticed him for the house was a fascinating place constructed, so they had been told, from six separate traditional Thai houses which Thompson had found in and outside Bangkok and transported to this site on the bank of a *klong* – the Thai name for a canal – opposite the homes of some of his silk weavers.

But not only was the Thai tall, he was exceptionally handsome, one of the best-looking men she had ever seen. Also, being by nature curious, she would have liked to know why the chic old lady was receiving special treatment. Was she someone important, or the wife of someone important? Was the tall Thai an official of the foundation which now owned and administered the Thompson house?

'It's beautiful, but I wouldn't want to live here,' Allegra heard an American tourist murmur to her husband, as the guide led them through rooms filled with richly carved furniture, statues and porcelains which Thompson had found in the antique shops of the Chinese quarter of the city thirty years ago.

Allegra didn't second the American's reservation. She found the house with its waxed teak walls and polished floorboards – they had been requested to leave their shoes in the hall – very much to her taste and would have been delighted to be offered the use of it for some weeks.

Here was a glimpse of old Bangkok before most of the *klongs* had been filled in to make way for roads to carry the teeming traffic; killing a lot of the magic which had enchanted Jim Thompson at the end of World War Two.

'The prefabrication of houses was invented in Thailand long ago,' said the slight, clear-voiced Thai girl who was their guide. 'The walls of old Thai houses such as these were attached to a frame of wooden pillars, without using nails, so they could easily be taken apart and rebuilt elsewhere when their owners wished to move. This room – now the drawing room – was originally built early in the last century by a family of weavers. When Mr Thompson bought it from their descendants, he removed the internal partitions and reversed the outer walls so that, as you see, the carving is on the inside.'

She waved a small hand at the massive posts at each corner of the lofty room and between the tall windows, their shutters open to give glimpses of the small but verdant tropical garden outside.

Allegra lingered in the drawing room after the others had moved on. She had never liked guided tours and this was not a large house where people could spread out. Even the drawing room wasn't as large as her bedroom at Longwarden.

She was admiring the vibrant colours of the Thai silk cushions on a sofa when the Frenchwoman and her tall companion arrived at the doorway at the far end of the room. He looked at Allegra and she at him.

Earlier, although he had glanced up from the hall at the foreigners on the landing, he hadn't noticed Allegra. Now he was sending a clear signal that, having seen her, he liked what he saw. It wasn't the impersonal appraisal she had given him. She had seen that look in men's eyes too often not to know what it meant. He was thinking he would like to have her on the coral silk covered Thai bed which served as an outsize stool in the centre of the room. Not that it would accommodate either of them comfortably, being made for much shorter occupants.

At one time she would have been amused by that unequivocal look of admiration and desire. Now her reaction was different. Wasn't it?

Was there perhaps just the smallest, almost imperceptible quickening of interest deep inside her as she met that bold, amorous look and held it for a few seconds before turning away.

The tour finished on the terrace, paved with seventeenth century bricks, where at Thompson's housewarming party in the spring of 1959 dancers in jewelled costumes had performed classical dances by the light of the moon and coconut oil torches.

529

As Allegra looked up at the exterior of the house, painted with a traditional dull red preservative which was striking by day and would look even more spectacular by torchlight, the Frenchwoman suddenly appeared at one of the first-floor windows and, behind her, the tall Thai.

This time he smiled at Allegra, showing that his teeth matched the rest of his features. She pretended not to notice and looked up at the steeply-pitched roofs ornamented at each end of the eaves with a shape representing a *naga* or serpent.

The outline of Jim Thompson's story, as told by the guide, made her long to have lived in an age when the East was less like the West and far fewer people travelled. She would have liked to see Bangkok at the time Thompson had discovered it.

After buying a few postcards and having another look at the spirit house which seemed an essential feature of all Thai gardens, Allegra strolled back to the lane where a taxi had dropped her at the gate.

The tall Thai was waiting while the Frenchwoman climbed stiffly into the back of a large car with a pennant on its bonnet and a uniformed driver holding the door.

Allegra didn't pause to see if the tall man also got in or if he remained in the lane when the car moved away. She turned in the opposite direction from the way it was facing and walked towards the main road.

Presently a youth who had been hanging about near the gateway caught up with her. 'You are American?' he asked.

She shook her head. 'English.'

He smiled at her. 'I am learning to speak your language but my English is not very good yet.'

She guessed where this overture would lead. In her short time in the city she had twice been picked up by touts offering to take her to factories where precious stones could be bought more cheaply than in the shops.

As she expected the youth made some polite small-talk before coming to the point.

Smiling, she said, 'Thank you, but I have no money for anything but my hotel. I can't afford presents or souvenirs. I'm going to Australia . . . to work there.'

'Australia is a very good country. I should like to go there. Where you stay in Bangkok?'

If she told him, he wouldn't believe she had no money.

'At Mrs Prathom's guest-house,' said Allegra, borrowing a name she had noticed in the *Bangkok Post* while having her breakfast.

'I don't know this place. You are going there now?'

'No, I'm going to do some more sightseeing. Goodbye.'

At her wave, a three-wheeled *tuk tuk* swerved out of the main stream of traffic and pulled alongside the kerb.

Before leaving the hotel she had asked at the desk how to pronounce the Thai name of the Temple of the Golden Buddha, and had also written it down on a piece of paper in case she got it wrong.

'How much to Wat Traimitr?'

The *tuk tuk* driver understood and held up four fingers. Guessing that forty *baht* was twice, if not more, what he would charge local people, Allegra looked pained and held up three fingers. He scowled and shook his head. She shrugged and turned away. He called her back with a resigned, 'Okay . . . okay' and a jerk of the head to indicate she should climb in.


Bien, the youth who had spoken to Allegra in Soi Kasemsam, worked as a desk clerk in a third grade hotel and used his off-duty hours to augment his pay by bringing bargain-hunting tourists to his cousin's jewellery factory.

Bien was waiting for the fiery-haired *farang* when she came out of the temple and headed for the nearby

Chinese quarter. It was easy to keep track of her. She was more than a head and shoulders taller than most other pedestrians and even if she had been the normal height for a woman her strange hair would have signalled her presence among the throng of glossy black heads bobbing along the narrow sidewalk.

Unaware that she was being tailed, Allegra was on her way to find the Chinese-owned antique shops where Jim Thompson had unearthed much of his unique collection including, no doubt, that delightful Chinese mouse house with two ivory rats inside it. Since then the shops would have changed hands, prices would have soared, good things become scarce and fakes and rubbish more plentiful, but it would be interesting to look.

Before reaching her objective, she made a detour to look round a busy market glimpsed at the end of an alleyway.

The labyrinth of narrow streets, their open-fronted shops displaying unfamiliar groceries, masses of vivid paper flowers, cheap shoes and many other wares, delighted Allegra and she took lots of photographs.

Everywhere food was on sale and people were snacking.

'Pardon me, but is it safe to eat those things?' asked an American matron, while Allegra was eating cubes of fried pork from a wooden skewer.

'Any germ which can survive boiling fat is welcome to have a crack at me,' she answered, grinning.

Ten minutes later Bien watched her buy a bag of fritters from another food stall.

Fortunately he wasn't on duty until six, by which time she would have grown weary of walking about and returned to her guest-house. Although from November to February the weather was relatively cool, foreigners still found the heat in Bangkok very tiring. Meanwhile he had nothing better to do and was confident that his client – whose card was tucked in the pocket of his crisply laundered white shirt – would pay well for the information he had ordered Bien to get for him.

Presently Allegra's meanderings led her into a Chinese department store. On the top floor was a cafeteria where she had a long iced drink and wrote a couple of postcards.

To her American publisher, Elliott Lincoln, she wrote: *Have been paying my respects to a golden Buddha who, so they say, was covered with stucco to save him from the Burmese in the 18th c. and remained in disguise until, moved from a ruined temple, he was dropped by the crane which was lifting him and the stucco cracked. Enjoying my stopover here. Allegra.*

The second card she addressed to her sister-in-law.

*You were right about J.T.'s house. An oasis of serenity in this traffic-tortured city. But the people make up for the noise and the fumes. They are so polite and friendly. How ugly Westerners are compared with these golden-skinned Asians. Will write from Sydney. Much love. A.*

The visit to Sydney had been mooted by Claudia Dunbar when Allegra had rung up to tell her she was going to Bali and, if the island appealed to her, might be away for some time.

'If you're going all that way, you might as well go on to Sydney and do some author promo for *Travels* there,' Claudia had suggested.

Reluctantly, aware that her publishers had been very patient with her and she ought to start pulling her weight again, Allegra had agreed to let Claudia arrange a publicity trip to Australia.

Several hours later Bien was watching the entrance to

Jim Thompson's Thai Silk Shop on Suriwongse Road when his friend Harin came by.

'On the lookout for suckers?' asked Harin, with a knowing glance at the shop which few rich female tourists failed to visit during their time in Bangkok.

Bien shook his head. 'I'm doing some detective work for a very important man.' He produced the card from his pocket.

Harin read it and was impressed. The name on the card had the prefix M.C. standing for Mom Chao, a title signifying descent from a king.

'What sort of detective work?' he asked.

'Following someone . . . she's in there. She told me she hadn't any money and I thought it was true. She doesn't dress like a person with money and she ate her dinner from street stalls.'

'Why does the Prince want her followed?'

'He didn't say. I suppose it's the usual reason. There's no accounting for tastes. She's no beauty, I can tell you. More like a giraffe than a woman. Ah, here she comes now . . . lying bitch,' added Bien, as he saw that Allegra was carrying not one but two of the shop's distinctive carriers.

'I'll keep you company,' said Harin. 'How come you've spoken to her?'

Bien explained. 'The Prince came away from the house a few minutes before this woman appeared. He was there with an old *farang*. I thought if I could get this giantess to spend some money at my cousin's place it would be a bonus for me, but she claimed to be short of money. She won't have got out of that shop without spending a few thousand *baht*. It's the dearest place for silk in the city.'

'What's the Prince like?' asked Harin. 'An old man, is he? Old men get peculiar fancies. Maybe he wants her to beat him. Someone who's worked in Europe tells

534

me it's popular there. A lot of older men like being beaten by a big strong girl.'

'He's not old. He's quite young and handsome, but he's another giraffe so it must be her size which attracts him. I wonder if she's really staying at a guest-house or if that was another lie. She looks as if she might be heading for the hotels by the river' – meaning the Oriental, the Shangri-La and the Royal Orchid Sheraton.

Refreshed by the air-conditioning in the silk shop, its walls ranged with lustrous silks not only in single colours but in vibrant combinations of colour, sophisticated plaids and subtle stripes, Allegra had temporarily forgotten that here it was necessary to stroll.

Shod in comfortable flat-heeled sandals, she walked at her usual brisk pace, making the young men trailing her quicken their steps as she cut through a side street connecting Suriwongse with Silom Road, another of the city's major thoroughfares.

Thinking about Sarah, for whom she had bought a length of blue silk threaded with silver, she suddenly realised she was starting to sweat and that it must be two hours since she had had a cold drink. Knowing she was going in the right direction, but not sure how much further it was to the Oriental, she slowed down and kept a lookout for somewhere to quench her thirst.

When he saw her go through the gateway of the Silom Village Trade Centre, a complex of shops and cafés built in the style of the wooden houses of his grandfather's time, Bien cursed impatiently.

'*Mai pen rai*. (Not to worry.) If you have to go to work before she's finished her shopping, I'll take over for you.' Harin worked in an all-night disco which didn't open till ten.

'If women were as keen on fucking as they are on shopping, the world would be a better place,' Bien said crossly. He didn't want to share his pay for the job with Harin.

Allegra made two more stops. She looked round a cool spacious shop called Design Thai which Jane had recommended, and she browsed in Thai Home Industries on Oriental Avenue where she couldn't resist a small lidded basket finely woven by the hill people in the north of Thailand. There were other things which tempted her, but she didn't want to buy much at this early stage of her trip.

By this time she was tired and with fatigue came depression. Throughout the day there had been moments she had wanted to share with someone else. Not anyone. Only one person. Andro Risconti.

Now, approaching her hotel, she felt a great wave of longing to find him waiting for her. Almost a year on her own had dulled if not deadened the pain. But there were times, and this was one, when it brought tears to her eyes to think how different the day would have been had they shared it, enjoyed it together.

'She may only be going in there for a drink,' said Harin, as they watched her enter the building. 'She may not be staying there. You'd better speak to the doorman. He'll know if she has a room.'

'You wait here while I ask him,' said Bien.

The good-looking young Thais selected to be the first staff to welcome visitors to the Oriental wore the traditional *panung*, a length of cloth wrapped round the hips like a sarong and drawn up between the legs to form knickerbockers. This garment had been widely worn until 1941 when it had been banned in the belief that it made the Thai appear primitive to the Japanese occupation force. Nowadays the *panung* was seen only on ceremonial occasions and as part of the uniform of people catering to tourists. Those worn by the doormen and bellboys at the Oriental were dark blue, with white tunics and white stockings.

The man to whom Bien spoke had opened the plate glass doors for many people in the past hour. Some he remembered, some hadn't registered with him. It happened that he had been on duty when Allegra arrived from the airport and had seen her several times since then. She had very strange coloured eyes. Also she was one of a diminishing number of guests who, when he opened the door for them, looked at him and thanked him.

'Why do you want to know?' was his response to Bien's enquiry.

Foreseeing that it might take more than a tip to get the information he needed, Bien produced the card.

'His Highness wishes to send flowers to the lady but forgot to ask where she was staying when he made her acquaintance in town today.' He hoped the doorman might think he was one of the Prince's staff.

'I could try to find out for you, but it won't be easy. We all have orders to guard the guests' privacy. Many are important people who don't want everyone knowing where they are staying.'

'The Prince is also important. Most ladies would be disappointed if he didn't find out where they were,' Bien pointed out, dextrously slipping some notes into the other man's hand.

Having beckoned a colleague from the baggage room to take his place, the doorman went off to make enquiries.


When Allegra stepped out of the lift on the seventh

floor of the River Wing, a couple in the pale blue robes provided by the hotel took her place on their way down to the pool.

The man had his arm round the girl's waist. She was laughing at something he had said just before the lift opened. After it closed, an emanation of happy companionship remained in the corridor, stronger and more evocative than the faint drift of scent the girl had left on the air.

Pinched by loneliness, Allegra walked to her room.

I'm an unmarried widow, she thought bleakly, as she unlocked the door.

They had given her a double room with wide twin beds side by side from which could be seen a spectacular view of the Chao Phraya river. She tossed her shopping on one and flung herself down on the other, dreading the evening ahead when she had the choice of dining up here by herself or in the Normandie Grill at the top of the Tower Wing where she was likely to be the only person on her own.


'The lady is one of our guests,' the doorman confirmed when he came back. He gave Bien a slip of paper. 'That is her name and her room number.'

'Does she have a husband?' asked Bien. It seemed a detail the Prince might be interested in.

'She is here alone, but although she's registered as a Miss it has been found out that that is not correct.'

'I don't understand you.'

After a pregnant pause several more notes changed hands.

'Her correct name is Lady Lomax,' said the doorman. 'She is an important person who prefers not to let it be known when she is travelling. She's in Bangkok until Friday. That is all I can tell you.'

*

At Longwarden Jane was thinking about Charles Helford, the man who had been her first lover and who had tried to dissuade her from marrying North.

She hadn't seen him since the summer before her wedding and had seldom thought of him. But when Allegra announced that she was going to break her journey at Bangkok, where Charles lived and worked, it crossed Jane's mind that he could do much to make her sister-in-law's short stay there enjoyable.

On second thoughts she had dismissed the idea. After parting from Charles on bad terms, she could hardly ring up out of the blue and ask him to meet and show around the sister of a man he disliked and mistrusted.

She remembered Charles' angry warning, on the beach at Cape Cod, that North wouldn't be faithful to her if she were fool enough to marry him. At the time she had had an uneasy feeling that he might be right. Now she had total confidence that her husband would never look at another woman. Nor would he like to be reminded that she had once made love with another man.

Far from putting Allegra and Charles in touch with each other, she was a little worried they might meet by accident.

It wouldn't please North if, next week, they received a postcard from Bangkok with a message saying – *Met an old friend of Jane's – Charles Helford.* In fact it would seriously displease him.

Perhaps because of his own amorous past, he was a possessive husband, quick to notice if anyone tried to flirt with her and to put a stop to it.

'I can't stand other men leering at you – even old buffers of sixty,' he had admitted after the Boltons' party.

As long as it never developed into jealous suspicions of *her* conduct, Jane was amused and warmed by his possessiveness. She wished there had never been anyone else in her life; that, like Countess Flora, she had met her husband when she was sixteen and had had her first lessons in love from him.

She felt sure he had forgotten his encounter with Charles in New York, and she didn't want anyone to jog his memory.


That evening, during a telephone call from Bangkok to London, someone who knew everyone who was anyone was asked to identify a tall, auburn-haired girl with eyes the colour of lilac who was thought to be on her way to Australia. Surname, Lomax. First name, not known. Title, Lady.

'Oh, that will be Allegra Lomax, Carlyon's sister,' said the woman in London.

The man in Bangkok said, 'Tell me everything you know about her.'


'One of our other guests has told me that you are a famous author and I should really address you as Lady Allegra,' said the assistant manager of the Oriental.

While Allegra was having breakfast, he had telephoned her room to ask if she had time to come to his office before going on the river trip to the old capital of Ayathuya.

'I prefer to travel incognito,' she told him. 'I was surprised to be recognised in the lobby yesterday morning. Apparently Mrs Bradenton had seen me on TV in Texas. She must have an excellent memory for faces. It's nearly two years since my tour of America.'

'Meeting you has added greatly to Mrs Bradenton's enjoyment of her stay here,' he told her. 'She and her husband are in the Joseph Conrad suite in the Authors' Wing. As you may know he was the first of many distinguished writers who have stayed at the Oriental. It

540

was a great thrill for Mrs Bradenton to meet one of today's well-known writers here. I respect your desire for privacy, Lady Allegra, but now that we know who you are would you permit me to give a small party for you? There are people in Bangkok who would very much like to meet you, and whom I'm sure you would find interesting.'

'It's kind of you to suggest it, but I'm leaving the day after tomorrow and when I arrive in Australia I'm going to be meeting people non-stop for two weeks,' said Allegra. 'I'd rather avoid any social life while I'm here. There's so much to see and unfortunately so little time. I may stay in Bangkok again on my way back to England.'

'In that case you must allow us to put you in one of the Authors' Suites. There are four in the Authors' Wing; the one which I've mentioned which commemorates the visits of Joseph Conrad, and also the Somerset Maugham, the James Michener and the Noël Coward suites. We also have suites named after Graham Greene, Barbara Cartland and John le Carré. Meanwhile, until we have the pleasure of welcoming you to the Oriental again, may we take a photograph of you to add to our gallery of famous visitors? It won't delay you more than a few minutes. I have a photographer on call.'

She felt it would be ungracious not to agree and the photographer was summoned. But before he arrived a bellboy brought in an envelope.

'This arrived at the desk a few moments ago,' said the assistant manager, handing it to her.

'For me?' said Allegra, mystified. She knew no one in Bangkok. How could there be a message for her? Even more puzzling, the envelope was addressed to *Lady Allegra Lomax* and at the bottom the same fluent pen had written *By hand – urgent*.

'Excuse me a moment,' she said. 'Oh, thank you' – this as he offered her a letter-opener.

Turning the envelope over, she found that the flap

bore an imposing insignia which was repeated at the top of the small sheet of expensive writing paper.

The die-stamped address below it consisted of two words. One was a long and at first glance unpronounceable Thai name. The other was the English word *Palace*.

*Dear Lady Allegra,* she read
*Her Highness the Princess Sirindra has heard that you are visiting Bangkok and, having enjoyed your book* The Travels of an Edwardian Naturalist, *would very much like to meet you. The Princess recalls meeting your great-grandparents, the seventh Earl and Countess of Carlyon, when they visited Thailand in 1937 and were received by His Majesty King Ananta Mahidol.*

*A car will be waiting to bring you to the palace at four o'clock this afternoon.*

'Is anything wrong, Lady Allegra?' the assistant manager asked, seeing her frown.

For answer she handed him the letter. When he had had time to scan it, she asked, 'Do you know the Princess?'

'Princess Sirindra is a descendant of King Mongkut who reigned from 1851 to 1868 and from whom the present King is also descended,' he told her. 'However, King Mongkut had many descendants and her connection with the Royal Family isn't close. She lives in seclusion in one of the smaller palaces. I believe she travels a great deal, although she must be in her late sixties now. You'll find it an interesting experience, having tea with her.'

'Probably, but I had other plans for this afternoon. One would think she would have asked her secretary to ring up and find out if today was convenient.'

He smiled slightly. 'Most people don't find invitations from royalty inconvenient,' he said dryly.

She laughed. 'You're right . . . I should feel honoured. What would you advise me to wear? Will it be terribly

542

formal? Must I rush out and find myself gloves and a hat?'

'I hardly think that will be necessary.' He glanced at the cool cotton shirt and trousers she was wearing. 'A dress is the only formality the Princess will expect. I'm sure you have something suitable.'


At two minutes to four Allegra put on her earrings and was ready to go to the palace.

Having cancelled the trip she had planned, she spent most of the morning going to see some more temples and a flower market where great bunches of exquisite orchids could be bought for the price of one carnation in London.

She had liked going up and down the broad river on boats which took the place of buses, ferrying people from one little pier to another, the passengers on them including many saffron-robed Buddhist novices.

After another lunch of delicious hot titbits from cooking stalls, she pottered about at random, reserving Bangkok's *pièce de résistance*, the Grand Palace, for her last day in Thailand.

Now, refreshed by a shower, she had on her favourite summer dress of mist grey voile, hand-smocked from waist to hipbone so that only someone with slim hips could wear it successfully. As a concession to the views of the Princess' age group, she had also put on sheer grey tights which no doubt would become extremely uncomfortable if the palace wasn't air-conditioned.

At precisely four o'clock she had a call from the desk to say a car had arrived for her. A few minutes later she was settling herself in the back of a large car which, as it began to glide forward, reminded her of the Rolls-Royce which Andro had sent to fetch her from Carlyon House to the Ritz Hotel on the night he re-entered her life and became her lover.

543

Closing her mind to that bitter-sweet memory, she looked out of the window and found herself the cynosure of curious looks from some passing tourists and the collection of touts, taxi drivers and bystanders who hung about all the big hotels.

The Princess' car *was* air-conditioned and Allegra remained cool and comfortable as it moved at a stately speed through the busy streets. But whenever it stopped at an intersection she wished it also had smoked glass windows for she found the hypnotised stares of people in surrounding vehicles rather an embarrassment. Presumably they were wondering what a *farang* was doing in a car flying a pennant with a cipher which perhaps they recognised as belonging to someone on the fringes of their Royal family.

Presently the shops, offices and congested streets gave place to wider roads with more trees and flowering hedges and large buildings in their own grounds, some of them embassies.

If her sense of direction was correct, she thought they were now on the northern side of the city, somewhere near Chitrlada Palace, the private palace of King Bhumiphol and his beautiful wife, Queen Sirikit.

Beside a high wall the car slowed and turned in through large gates which evidently had been opened for it by a man in uniform. Glancing over her shoulder, not sure if he were a policeman, a soldier or a private guard, Allegra saw him starting to close them.

The garden surrounding the straight tree-shaded drive would have been thought rather bare by her mother and Damaris. It was mainly lawn with shrubs and groups of small palms planted alongside paths.

At the end of the drive she could see a wide flight of steps leading up to an ornate porch, built of wood but in the grand manner. A servant in a white tunic and a dark brown silk *panung*, holding a large parasol, was waiting to open the door the moment the car drew up.

As she stepped out, the moist heat of the natural air enfolded her like a damp blanket. Raising the parasol to a great height when he saw how tall she was, the servant held it above her, shading her from the hot sun, as they mounted the steps.

He was barefoot, she noticed. Being unsure of the form in the house of a Thai princess, Allegra thought it best, on reaching the porch, quickly to slip off her shoes.

'That isn't necessary, Lady Allegra.'

With her eyes on her Jourdan pumps of grey glacé kid and lizardskin, she heard the voice before she looked up and saw the speaker.

The voice was, like her brother's, that of an upper class Englishman. But the man coming from the dimness of the inner hall into the dappled light of the porch wasn't English. She had seen him before. He was the tall Thai.

'You may keep your shoes on . . . unless they have stiletto heels, which I see they haven't. How do you do? I am Kit.'

He offered a long golden hand which felt cool and dry as it took hers in a firm clasp.

'In this country everyone uses first names immediately, as you may have discovered. In fact surnames are a comparatively recent innovation. They were made a legal requirement in 1916. Before that we managed without them.'

'How do you do? Are you the Princess' secretary?' Allegra asked.

'I'm her grandson. My surname is Kitayalongkorn . . . rather a mouthful for anyone but a Thai so it was shortened to Kit when I was at Harrow. Most of the men of the Chakri dynasty and its satellite families have been educated in England, either at Eton or Harrow. Later on I was at Harvard at the same time as your brother. But we moved in different circles. I doubt if he would remember me.'

'Do you remember him? He was only there a short time.'

'To be honest, I don't. But in more recent times I've admired his photographic work and was asked by a mutual friend if we met at Harvard. I'm sorry we didn't. Had we done so, I might have met you a long time ago. Still, better late than never.'

Smiling into her eyes, he slipped a hand under her elbow and conducted her into the house.

'We were both at Jim Thompson's house yesterday morning, if you remember?' he went on. 'I was doing my grand-filial duty with an old lady who first came to Thailand when it was still called Siam and her father was the French ambassador. She and my grandmother became friends but Madame la Comtesse hasn't been back to this country since the end of World War Two. She finds Bangkok unrecognisable, but then so is most of Europe to my grandmother. Is this your first visit here?'

'Yes, I've never been east of Greece before. How did the Princess find out I was in Bangkok?' asked Allegra, as he led her through a large room where her slim stockinged feet – despite his assurances she hadn't replaced her shoes – sank into the thick soft pile of a pale green silk carpet.

Between tall wooden pilasters, painted the colour her own grandmother would have called *eau de Nil*, several doorways opened onto a broad verandah on the other side of the house.

'The Princess knows everything. When I was a small boy her omniscience was alarming. I never got away with anything and sometimes she stopped my misdeeds at the planning stage. Very unnerving!'

He laughed, giving her a brief close-up of the attractive teeth she had glimpsed the day before. His skin was the most beautiful colour she had ever seen on a human being, reminding her of a tale heard as a child about God baking people like cakes; burning the first batch, undercooking the second but achieving perfection with His third batch – the Asiatic races. She found herself wanting to gaze at him as, long ago, she used to gaze at Flora Carlyon, mesmerised by a face which was different and far more interesting than the faces of other grown-ups.

Like Flora's, Prince Kitayalongkorn's eyelids covered the canthus, the pink inner corner visible in westerners' eyes. This too Allegra saw as an improvement on the design of other races. It appalled her to hear of Asian girls having surgery to remove the epicanthus. She knew that when her great-grandmother had arrived in England in 1903, she had worried about the shape of her eyes until her husband had convinced her that it was an essential part of her great beauty.

Not wishing the Prince to guess how fascinating she found him, Allegra turned her attention to the palace.

All along the outer side of the verandah, close to the carved balustrade, stood tall blue and white jardinières containing resplendent ferns. Further along was another projecting porch, like the one where she had left her shoes, but from this one steps led down to the surface of a lake. Or was it a *klong*?

'It's a canal,' said the Prince, when she asked. 'But kept rather cleaner than those in the centre of the city . . . the few that are left. When this house was built in the last century, everything was transported by water. Would you care to look round? A tour before tea is the usual form.'

'I'd love to.'

'Although we call it a palace, I doubt if it's half the size of your brother's place . . . or even a quarter. But it's an interesting example of the Siamese architecture of the period, and like most old family houses it's stuffed with an amazing assortment of bits and pieces collected on the family's travels.'

'Did you mind being sent to school in England . . . so far away and so cold most of the year?' Allegra asked, as they entered another large room with a dining table capable of seating at least thirty people.

'I didn't much care for the cold, but I already spoke English and I wasn't small like most of my cousins. I wasn't afraid of being bullied,' he said, with a grin. 'As far as I can remember I accepted being sent abroad as the natural order of things. It was my grandmother and my nurse who were upset.'

'I should think you must be one of the tallest men in Thailand, aren't you?'

'That's because my grandfather's first wife was an American from a very tall family. My father took after them in height and I am taller than he was. My real grandmother died soon after he was born. The Princess is my grandfather's second wife by whom he had only daughters, much to her disappointment. But she loved my father as if he were her own son, and she and I have always been very fond of each other. This is a portrait of her when she was younger.'

He pointed out an oil painting of a small, elegant woman dressed in dark amber silk and wearing a great many diamonds.

'Is that why you went to Harvard . . . because of your American connections?' Allegra asked.

'I should have wanted to spend time in America in any case. It has such an important influence on the rest of the world that one wants to see for oneself the source of those influences and what new ones are brewing. I like America very much but I don't feel myself to be even one quarter American. I'm a hundred per cent Thai in a cosmopolitan wrapping.'

Intrigued by this statement, she said, 'In what way is being Thai different from being, for example, French? I can see that the peasants of the two countries are different, but is a cultivated Thai very different from a cultivated Frenchman? It's always been my theory that educated people are pretty much alike everywhere. Am I wrong?'

'That's the view of an idealist. I am a cynic,' he answered, as they left the room. 'Historically, the difference between the Thais and the French is that they had to have a bloody revolution to start making life more tolerable for the masses while our social revolution was actually launched from the throne. Don't worry: I'm not going to lecture you on our history, but the only thing most people know about this country's past is the rubbish in *The King and I*. The reason that show is banned here is because it's not only rubbish, but pernicious rubbish. The real King Mongkut was nothing like the character played by Yul Brynner. Have you seen the show?'

She nodded. 'I saw it in London with Virginia McKenna in the part of the English governess.'

'Then at least let me disabuse you of the idea that Anna Leonowens taught the King to speak English and was a civilising influence on him. He learnt English while he was a monk, long before he came to the throne, and the reforms he inaugurated were *his* ideas. She didn't arrive until he'd been King for eleven years and she left a year before he died. I'm afraid Mrs Leonowens had an overactive imagination and made herself out to be far more important than she was.'

'How did a monk come to be king?' asked Allegra, as they mounted a staircase to the next floor.

'Not only a king but the husband of thirty-five wives by whom he had eighty-two children. As the son who became the next king had seventy-seven children, you can see why it used to be said that a stone thrown in Bangkok was sure to hit either a monk, a dog or a prince.'

'What one might call a plethora of princes. Was polygamy still being practised when your grandfather married his first wife?'

'It was, but I don't think he would have taken a second wife had the first one lived. Polygamy for the kings was largely a matter of statecraft. They were offered the daughters of important men who wanted a connection with the throne. The kings didn't wish to offend them. Chulalongkorn had ninety-two wives but only thirty-six of them had children. Probably most of the others never had sexual relations with him. This will amuse you. It's one of the original bathrooms.'

As he spoke, he opened the door and ushered her into a room which was in effect a huge shower stall with a marble floor and a marble dado. A brass pipe serving an extra large rose jutted from the outside wall and there was also a huge metal bath in which even a man of the Prince's height could submerge, but it had no taps.

'I suppose in this climate, before air conditioning, nobody wanted hot baths,' she said.

'If they did, the water arrived by the same system as in England . . . it was carried up by servants.' He led her into the next room. 'This was my grandfather's dressing room which is kept as it was in his lifetime . . . that's his mother as a young girl.'

At first glance, Allegra had thought the large portrait was his grandfather as a youth for the subject was wearing the traditional silk knickerbockers and 'his' hair was mannishly short.

'Siamese women used to wear the *panung* and crop their hair in those days,' he explained. 'It was King Vajiravudh, who came to the throne in 1910, who persuaded them to change to long hair and skirts.'

'This can't have been too becoming to large women, but it looks stunning on this girl.' Allegra moved closer to study the portrait in detail.

The girl was slight with no visible breasts under the

pearl-crusted silk of a high-necked, close-fitting top, but her slim calves and delicate ankles in white silk stockings and satin shoes with Louis heels were unmistakably feminine.

Turning, Allegra found the Prince studying her legs. He said, 'It would have suited you, that costume. Would you like me to show you how the *panung* is tied?'

She ignored the glint in his dark eyes. 'Yes, I should. Clothes are a serious interest with me.'

'And you choose your own well,' he said smoothly. 'That's a lovely dress and I noticed yesterday, at the Thompson house, you were much better dressed for sight-seeing than any of the other tourists. The so-called sun dress, especially on large pink-fleshed women, is not a pretty sight.'

'Your English is so up to date that you must spend a lot of time speaking and reading it. Are you a diplomat?'

In a country abundant with princes it seemed unlikely that they were all on a Civil List.

'I'm a climber,' he said. 'That's my favourite thing . . . climbing mountains. But I also enjoy scuba diving and flying and racing fast cars. One of my kinsmen, Prince Birabongse, was a successful racing driver in Europe in the Thirties.'

Obviously very rich with no need to work for his living, thought Allegra, as they passed into the next room. Here a curtained four-poster stood in the centre of the room on another sumptuous silk carpet, this one specially designed to fit the octagonal floor, its polished boards showing round the edge of the carpet's elaborate border.

The Prince touched a switch and three fans hanging from the high ceiling began to stir the warm air. Through several curtain-draped openings could be seen an adjoining large room furnished as a sitting room-cum-study.

He strolled to the bed and sat down on the edge of it.

551

'These rooms are kept open because in this climate closed rooms quickly deteriorate and also it keeps the servants busy. We still have quite a large staff who aren't really needed but can't be dismissed after years in our service. Does your brother have the same problem or does the Welfare State now take care of his pensioners?'

The look in his eyes didn't match the impersonal question. She sensed, as she had yesterday, that the thought in his mind as he watched her strolling round the room was of making love to her.

Obviously he was extremely fit. There was no spare flesh round his waist. His forearms, revealed by the short sleeves of his coral-coloured linen sports shirt, were as muscular as a labourer's. With that body and without the longueurs and pressures of a career, he was bound to need a lot of sex.

'I think North has a few people he helps,' she said vaguely. 'But it's years since there was a large staff at Longwarden. It's enlarging again now that my brother is married, but in England, where wages are high, machines do a lot of the work. Isn't that happening here?'

'Not to the same extent yet.'

With a supple and leisurely movement which reminded her of the big cats, the Prince uncrossed his long legs and rose from the silk-encased mattress which had a cylindrical bolster at its head.

As he came towards her, smiling slightly, she felt sure that in a few moments she would be in his arms. She didn't know what to do about it.


'Your eyes are the most extraordinary colour,' said the Prince, stopping about a yard away from her. 'I suppose dozens of men have told you that. Do they run in your family, these pupils like amethysts?'

'Not really.'

For the first time in her life Allegra felt paralysed with nerves at the prospect of being embraced.

'Won't the Princess be wondering where we are?' she asked tensely.

It seemed to her that the pause which followed her question went on forever.

But perhaps it was only a few seconds before he said cryptically, 'Your eyes are not the only unusual thing about you, are they? We'll go down now. I expect you are thirsty.'

On the way to meet the Princess they passed through a Music Room with a full size grand piano, and another room furnished with vitrines containing collections of ivory, gold boxes and, to her surprise, a menagerie of Fabergé animals.

'They may have been bought in Europe or possibly here,' said the Prince. 'Fabergé came to Bangkok for King Vajiravudh's coronation celebrations. He took a couple of rooms at the Oriental to display his stuff – a shrewd move considering that just about every royal family in the world sent representatives. I'm not mad about Fabergé's things myself. The craftsmanship is superb, of course, but I prefer jewels to these toys.'

'I agree . . . oh, but *that* is superb!' Allegra exclaimed, catching sight of a clock which made her long to possess it.

Seated on top of the clock's face was a tall, slim black girl, a huntress wearing a short skirt of golden feathers with a quiver of arrows slung behind her and a bow in her hand. Her left foot was resting on the top of a large tortoise. On the other side of the clock sat a gilded leopard with a collar round his neck.

'What a strange thing for you to like,' said the Prince, as she admired it.

'Not strange at all. You don't know me, Prince Kitay-alongkorn. You have no idea what sort of things I like.'

'Not yet, but I hope to find out . . . and although I'm

impressed that you remembered my full name, I'd rather you called me Kit.'

'Very well . . . Kit. Do you know how this clock came to be here?'

'Sorry . . . no idea.'

'Could I ask the Princess about it? Or would that be a gaffe?'

'I'm sure she wouldn't mind in the least. Come . . .'

The room to which they came next was both more modern and more comfortable than the formal apartments he had shown her. Here large sofas and armchairs covered in pastel silks invited relaxation. But of her hostess, the Princess, there was no sign.

'I have a confession to make.' He rang a small handbell. 'The Princess isn't here today. She's on a visit to Singapore where she has a close friend who is ill.'

She said nothing for a few moments. Then, '*You* invited me here?'

'Yes.'

'How . . . why . . . I don't understand?'

He said blandly, 'I saw you, wanted to meet you, had you followed and made some enquiries about you. It wasn't difficult. Are you annoyed that I've misled you a little? I'm sure, if she had been in Bangkok, my grandmother would have wanted to meet you. I've ordered a copy of your book for her . . . a dozen copies in fact. I know a number of people who will enjoy reading it.'

Before Allegra could reply, a man and two women entered and quickly and deftly arranged an English-style tea on a table in front of the sofa Kit indicated.

When they had gone, she said, 'If you haven't read the book, how did you know my great-grandparents came here in 1937?'

'I called my grandmother early this morning and asked her if she had met them. She has an excellent memory and the fact that the seventh Countess of Carlyon was partly Chinese made a lasting impression on her. Mixed marriages were less common then, particularly among the aristocracy. When Prince Chakrabongse married a Russian girl in 1906, it was four years before his marriage was officially recognised.'

'I see,' said Allegra. She supposed that she ought to be flattered he had gone to such lengths to meet her, but in fact she found it disturbing.

Clearly he was attracted by her, was determined to have her and would use every means at his command to achieve his objective. It wasn't that which worried her. Men had wanted her before and she had said yes or no, according to whim. But that had been long ago – before Andro. Now her heart and mind told her she didn't want an affair with this confident Thai, but her body said something else. It was so many weary months since she had felt strong arms round her. Could she resist him if he made a determined pass at her? If she didn't, could she live with herself? For she knew now, before he had touched her, that afterwards she would regret it.

It was only her flesh which wanted him. Her soul, all that was best in her, was still committed to Andro and always would be.

For a moment she toyed with walking out on him now; saying, 'I'm sorry, Your Highness, but what you weren't told about me is that I'm an unmarried widow, still mourning the man I loved. What you have in mind is not on. Good afternoon.'

But then he said, 'There's tea or iced coffee. Which would you prefer?' and that made it seem absurd to behave like a nervous girl when she was an experienced woman, well able to deal with the situation more adroitly.

'Iced coffee, please. Do you always have this sort of tea or is it only for my benefit?' she asked, looking at the sandwiches and cakes.

'My grandmother's chef spent several years in Europe,

mainly in Paris. He can cook virtually anything. I don't eat these things every day, but when we have English visitors I like to be reminded of the pleasures of my schooldays. Have you tried any Thai food yet?'

'Yesterday and today I lunched on things cooked at street stalls. That's one pleasure you can't indulge in.'

'Not in Bangkok – no. In other places I have. Where did you dine last night?'

'I was tired. I ate in my room. I'm on my way to Sydney. Have you been to Australia?'

'Once only . . . once was enough.' He poured thick creamy coffee from a silver vacuum flask.

'You didn't like it? Why not?'

His broad shoulders shrugged. 'It has no history to speak of. You're taken to see an "old" house and it turns out to be what in England is called Victorian. The people are not attractive. One expects Crocodile Dundee but in fact the majority of Aussies live in surburban bungalows and wouldn't survive for twenty-four hours in the Outback. The ones who've done well for themselves are obsessed with money. If you meet any of the graziers you'll find them fairly civilised, but I don't think you'll want to prolong your visit.'

Allegra wondered how much of his harsh views were affected by the fact that Australia had once been a No Entry country for other races. For all she knew it might still refuse non-white immigrants. Down Under wasn't a part of the globe in which she had taken much interest until very recently.

'If you've seen the work of their leading artist, Sidney Nolan, that should tell you something about them,' Kit said derisively. 'It's a pity that one of the most beautiful places in the world – Bali – is near enough to Australia to have become a playground for them. I have a house in the interior of Bali. Fortunately not many Aussies go beyond Kuta which is the Mecca for surfers.'

'I'm going to Bali on my way back from Australia.

My brother has been there and loved it. He advised me to stay at Candidasa. Do you know it?'

'It's a place where the backpackers go. Very cheap but extremely primitive. Why don't you use my house? I'll show you some photographs of it.'

He rose and went to a bookcase, leaving Allegra to sip her coffee – liberally laced with brandy, she noticed – and to wish she hadn't mentioned her return stopover to him.

When Kit returned to the sofa with a large leather-bound album, he sat down on the centre cushion, much closer to her than before. Placing the album on his left thigh, he opened the cover and rested it on her lap. Their legs were only inches apart. A slight movement of his would bring their knees into contact.

Except when she had wept in Elliott's arms and danced at the Bolton's party, this was the closest she had been to a man since that nightmare morning in Barbados when Andro had kissed her goodbye and gone to his death.

As she looked at the first photograph taken from a verandah with a view of the patterns formed by terraced rice fields, she was both intensely aware of the man sitting close beside her and painfully reminded of the man she had loved.

North's photographs of Bali had prepared her for the brilliantly lush green of the island's vegetation.

'How long have you had a house there?' she asked.

There was only one large print on the first page. Kit turned to the second and third pages with aerial views of the house and its surroundings; one showing that it wasn't far from a Balinese village and the second, nearer view that it had a thatched roof and a pool.

'I built it five years ago, calling myself Mr Korn to ensure complete privacy. The pool is for swimming but I didn't want it to be a blot on the landscape, as most pools are, so I had it lined with dark green mosaic.'

557

As he spoke, he slid his left arm along the back of the sofa, behind her shoulders, and leaned closer. She knew that he wasn't looking at the album but at her. She took another sip of coffee, knowing that he wouldn't kiss her while she was holding the glass. When he removed it from her hand she would make it clear he was wasting his time on her.

'I go there quite often and when I'm not using the place I lend it to friends. As it happens it's going to be empty for several months. I'd be delighted for you to make use of it. It's the ideal place to recover from a strenuous tour.'

'It's very kind of you to suggest it, but I don't suppose I'll need more than a couple of days' rest to restore me and I want to repeat my brother's tour of the island. Besides, you might suddenly find you wanted to use the house yourself.'

She hoped from this last remark he would get the message. If he did, he chose to ignore it. 'That wouldn't matter. It's designed so that up to four single people or four couples can stay there without tripping over each other. Being more or less in the centre of the island, it's an excellent base for excursions to places of interest. There's also a car you can use, and the house is kept clean by a woman from the village who will see to your breakfast, and other meals too if you wish.'

Taken at its face value, the offer was generous, but Allegra felt sure there were strings attached. Men did not, in her experience, lend their holiday houses to women out of disinterested kindness. Some return would be expected. As he continued to turn the pages, showing her views of the interior, she felt the best thing to do was to tell him the truth.

'Did your enquiries about me elicit the details of my private life?' she asked.

'Only that you're not married . . . have never been married.'

'The man I was in love with died . . . not quite a year ago,' she said quietly. 'Otherwise I should be married. Had he been with me, we'd have been delighted to take up your invitation. but, on my own, I think I'd miss him even more there. At present I'm better among other people. Talking to the backpackers will be a distraction. I hope you understand?'

He said smoothly, 'Of course: I shouldn't have suggested your staying there had I realised. I expect you are right . . . seclusion is better avoided at present, and obviously your brother will have warned you that the accommodation at Candidasa is very basic.'

Closing the album, he rose to return it to its place.

When he came back to the sofa, it was to where he had sat earlier. He said, 'Shall we have something to eat? What would you like? A sandwich? Some cake? This one, with dates and walnuts, made by an aunt of the boy who shared my study, was my favourite at school.'

'It's one my brother likes too. Obviously you weren't at Eton or you would have known him there.'

'No, I went to Harrow like Prince Mahidol, the father of our present King. And you? Cheltenham?'

She shook her head. 'I detested school and would have done badly anywhere. It's better to draw a veil over my school career. I've known quite a lot of Harrovians. Were you a contemporary of Giles Worlingham?'

'He was in my house but a couple of years younger. I'm thirty-five.'

Their conversation flowed as easily as if he were an Englishman not an Eastern prince, part of a court whose kings, he told her, had had absolute power until as late as 1932.

His manners were far too good for Allegra to feel that now he knew she was not a plum ripe for picking he had lost interest in her. So good in fact that when he discovered she had reserved the Grand Palace for her last day, he offered himself as her guide. When she demurred, thinking he was merely being polite, he insisted she would enjoy it far more with him.

Later, while she was being driven back to the hotel, Allegra was guiltily conscious that, having behaved sensibly earlier, now she was glad that they had said only au revoir, not goodbye.

She could have made the excuse that Kit could give her insights into Thai life and customs which she wouldn't have otherwise. But self-delusion had never been one of her failings and she knew that was only part of the reason she was glad they were meeting tomorrow. The main reason was that she wanted to see him again. She knew that, had they met a few years ago, she *would* have had an affair with him. Those casual relationships had finished forever when she met Andro. No matter how lonely she was, how desperate for the release and comfort of a shared bed, she could never resume the erratic relationships of her early twenties.

At the same time there was something about him which fascinated her; not only the physical appeal of his black hair, amused dark eyes and golden skin, but also the feeling that under a veneer of cosmopolitan sophistication he was different from anyone she had known.


Jane had always known that, sooner or later, she was bound to meet one of the women North had loved and left before he married her. She hadn't expected it to happen at the tiny airport on Mustique, one of the smaller islands in the chain known as the Grenadines.

Taking Simon, but leaving Morag behind because they'd been told that babysitters were no problem and they were only going for a week fitted in, on the spur of the moment, between other commitments, they had flown by Concorde to Barbados.

There, for the flight to Mustique, they had boarded a small LIAT aircraft with pairs of seats on one side of the aisle, single seats on the other and an uncurtained cockpit through which the procedures of take-off and landing could be seen by anyone interested.

Coming across the Atlantic, while Simon napped Jane had read a classic among travel books, *The Traveller's Tree*, in which the islands were described as 'hanging mysteriously in a blue dimensionless dream'. When Mustique came into view it did look a magical place to escape from the grey skies and falling temperatures of northern Europe.

Although it seemed short from the air, the island's frying pan runway proved to be more than long enough for their plane which made a light landing and then turned off halfway along to come to a standstill in front of a palm-thatched terminal building with a row of flag-poles in front of it and an open-fronted bar at one end.

Jane was holding Simon in her arms, enjoying the brilliant sunshine while her husband attended to the baggage, when she heard a loud exclamation of surprise and pleasure.

'North! What are you doing here?'

'Oh . . . hello Cressida.' He offered his hand to a woman in shorts and a sun top who had obviously been here for some time, judging by her tan.

But Cressida was not to be fobbed off with a hand-clasp. She lifted her cheek and as, having no choice, North bent to do what was expected, she managed to turn her head so that his lips brushed hers. It was adroitly done and, to any other observer, would have seemed casual and natural. But now Jane knew North well enough to see that he wasn't pleased. The only reason she could think of for him to be displeased was because he and this woman had once had an affair.

'This is marvellous luck,' Jane heard her say enthusiastically. 'The friends we've been sharing a house with have to leave sooner than planned, which leaves me with

561

no one to be energetic with. All Kyle wants to do is relax. Kyle . . . come and meet a very old friend of mine.'

Although Cressida was English, Kyle, as his name suggested and his appearance confirmed, was an American.

With a final word of farewell to the friends he was seeing off – in whom Cressida was clearly no longer interested – he came to be introduced; a thickset man in his forties with signs of rich living round his jaw and waistline and hair already going grey.

North glanced over his shoulder at Jane, beckoning her to join them with a glance which also signalled that he didn't want this delay but could see no way to avoid it.

'This is Jane, my wife,' he told Cressida.

'Oh yes . . . of course . . . you're married now.' Her tone suggested she had heard he was married but since then had forgotten that fact. 'And a father, too, I see. How d'you do, Lady Carlyon. I used to be Cressida Stevenage and now I'm Cressida Rainert and this is my husband Kyle.'

Having told him who they were, she said to North, 'You're borrowing a house, I expect. At Kyle's friends' insistence we're renting Les Jolies Eaux. It's charming . . . you must come and see it,' she added, with a smile at Jane. 'Whose house are you staying in?'

'We're at the hotel . . . The Cotton House,' Jane replied. She hoped they wouldn't be forced to socialise with these people. Kyle looked harmless but there was something about Cressida which made her hope this would be their only meeting.

'What's this little guy's name?' asked Kyle, smiling at the baby.

Cressida made no pretence of being interested in Simon. She left Kyle to ask the polite questions while she talked to North. But her animated chatter was soon interrupted by the driver who had come to transport the Carlyons to their hotel.

Much to Jane's relief, they and the Rainerts parted without any further mention of a visit to the house they had taken.


'Did you have an enjoyable evening?' asked Kit, when he met Allegra the next day.

'I went across the river to dine and watch the classical dancing at the Sala Rim Naam. I don't know how you would have rated it, but all the foreigners enjoyed it.'

'I've seen the show they put on there . . . not bad, if it isn't spoiled by people taking photos without consideration for the rest of the audience.'

'There were one or two camera hogs last night. I've brought my camera today but I'm not a fanatical snapper. Am I suitably dressed?'

She was wearing a navy blue shirt with white cotton culottes and had brushed her hair up from her neck and fixed it with two tortoiseshell spring clips.

'Admirably dressed: cool, comfortable and modest – all that the good tourist should be,' said Kit, with a smile.

She noticed that the way he looked at her was quite different from yesterday. Today she might have been a contemporary of Madame la Comtesse, not a young woman he wanted to take to bed.

'The Grand Palace is actually a city within a city,' he explained, as the Princess' driver took them there. 'If you've been disappointed by modern Bangkok – the noise, the fumes, the terrible traffic jams – wait till you see the old city.'

She understood what he meant when the car stopped outside a high white wall with a crenellated top above which rose fantastic spires and roofs clad with glittering tiles, the peak of each gable adorned with a gilded *naga*.

One spire, like a giant handbell, was completely covered with bright yellow gold burnished to a dazzling brilliance by the hot morning sun.

'Oh . . . magical!' murmured Allegra, feasting her eyes on the strange shapes, intrigued by this glimpse of an enclave surrounded yet set apart from the bustling street life.

Glancing at Kit she saw that, although he must have seen this view of it many times, the magic still worked for him.

The wall continued a long way, eventually broken by a gateway where uniformed guards sprang to attention at the sight of the car's blue pennant. Inside the gate was a drive with buildings on one side and an expanse of grass on the other. Strolling tourists moved aside to let the car pass, staring at its occupants.

'If you had been staying longer, I could have arranged to show you round at a time when it's closed to the public, but there shouldn't be too many people around at this hour,' said Kit. 'In the time when the king lived here, his quarters and those of his wives were in what was known as the Inside, behind an inner wall. There was never a system of purdah in Siam, but no men were allowed in the Inside. When workmen had to be admitted, they went in under the guard of special female police.'

The car drew up near a ticket office. When the driver opened the rear door, Kit sprang out and turned to help Allegra. Various men whom she took to be guides saluted him with a respectful *wai*, the gesture of placing the hands together and bringing them to eye level while bowing.

She had been a little nervous that he might tell her too much, giving her mental indigestion with a surfeit of forgettable facts. But as they wandered through courtyards between astonishing buildings jewelled with millions of pieces of coloured glass and ceramic fragments, her companion said very little, except to offer to photograph her standing in a particularly richly ornamented doorway.

They were entering the forecourt of the temple of the Emerald Buddha when they met an old and frail monk supported by a younger one. Now it was Kit who joined his hands in a deep *wai* before addressing the old man. Allegra retreated a few yards, having been told by Jane that women should not come near monks or even hand offerings to them.

'Who was that venerable person?' she asked, when the old man had shuffled on, his body skeletally thin under his robe, his ears pointed with age.

'He's an abbot at the monastery where I took the saffron robe. He's expecting to die soon and wanted to come and pray to this most revered Buddha,' Kit explained.

'You were a monk?' she exclaimed.

Her surprise made his dark eyes gleam with amusement. 'Here most young men become monks – usually only for three months. If you don't believe me, I'll show you some pictures of myself in the robe with my head shaved.'

They took off their shoes and placed them on the racks provided before passing the snarling bronze lions which guarded the steps to the temple.

'If you sit down, it's important to keep the soles of your feet turned away from the altar,' Kit murmured.

The statue was small, placed high up on an elaborate altar. Not unexpectedly, Allegra found it disappointing. First with the *Mona Lisa* and later with *The Night Watch*, she had learned that world-famous paintings and objects usually left her unmoved and other less important things would be fixed in her mind forever. At the moment, while gazing with suitable reverence at the Buddha, she was much more interested by the discovery that the man beside her had, even for three months, submitted himself to a discipline of poverty and chastity.

'It's not actually made of emerald, as you could see,' he said, as they left the temple. 'They think it was carved from a large piece of jade in northern India, probably by Greeks left behind by Alexander the Great.'

It was late morning before she had seen everything.

'Now we'll go and have lunch by the river, but not too much lunch because tonight I want to introduce you to some authentic Thai food – unless you dislike hot food, hot in the sense of being highly-spiced.'

'I like curries and Mexican dishes, but Kit – '

'Good, then you'll like our cuisine.'

'I was going to say don't you think you've already done more than your share of entertaining me? I don't want to be a drag.'

'Would you rather not have dinner with me?'

'That's not what I meant. I suspect that, having got me to the Palace by false pretences yesterday, you feel rather shamefaced about it. But it really isn't necessary. To devote the whole of today to me is overdoing it.'

'Not the whole day. After we've lunched, I'll take you back to the hotel and we shan't meet again until eight. Now let me tell you what I suspect. Although you've made it clear that there's no place in your life for anything but friendship, you're wondering if, after dinner, I may forget that. Am I right?'

Before she could answer, he went on, 'I shan't forget it, Allegra. My only wish is that you should enjoy your last evening here. Do you believe me?'

She might not have believed him if she hadn't seen him receive an affectionate blessing from the old monk and, soon afterwards, make his reverence to the Buddha. Yesterday she had thought him a playboy. Today she wasn't so sure.

*

At five o'clock, after an hour at the pool, Allegra returned to her room and lathered the oil from her skin before washing her hair under the shower.

She was drying it when the telephone rang. She switched off the dryer. 'Hello?'

'Allegra? This is Elliott. How are you liking Bangkok?'

'Elliott! What a nice surprise. I'm liking it very much but I hear we shouldn't call it that. Only foreigners speak of Bangkok. The proper name is Krung Thep which means City of Angels.'

'City of go-go dancers and massage parlours was my impression in the short time I spent there. I thought I might catch you about now. I'm calling for two reasons. First to wish you well on your tour. I know it will be difficult to contact you once the wheels are in motion, so I'll say now good luck and bon voyage.'

'How kind and thoughtful of you, Elliott.' And so typically American, she thought. A nation of efficient perfectionists, God bless them.

'The second thing is that I have to visit hong Kong and Manila next month and from there it's not far to Bali. If you tell me the dates you'll be there, I'll try to join you for a day or two. We've come up with some more ideas for your next book which I'd like to discuss with you. Does that seem a good plan?'

'Very good – except for the one snag that apart from the night I arrive I haven't made any reservations in Bali, and some of the places I'll be staying at may not be on the telephone.'

'No problem: I shall know when and where I'll be staying before you leave Australia. Bali' – he pronounced it with a short a and emphasised the second syllable – 'isn't very large. If you're on the other side of the island when I arrive, you'll only be a couple of hours away. I'll send a car to collect you. All you have to do is to call my hotel the day before I fly in and let them know where you are.'

'Okay . . . fine . . . I'll look forward to it.'

There was nothing else she could say when he had it all neatly sewn up. But inwardly she was less enthused than she sounded.

Elliott, like everyone else, had the defects of his qualities. The reverse side of perfectionism was a tendency to over-organise. Did she really want to interrupt a lazy time in Bali with two days of serious discussions about what to work on next?

'Now tell me what you've been doing today,' said Elliott, with the publishing world's blithe disregard for the cost of long distance calls.

She told him, omitting to mention that she hadn't been on her own. She had an instinctive feeling that he, with his ultra-WASP background, would not think a Thai – even a prince – a suitable companion for her. She had always suspected that although her great-grandfather's romantic marriage had made a bestseller for his list, Elliott didn't approve of the seventh Earl's Eurasian bride. He would not have married her himself, no matter how beautiful and intelligent she was. Allegra sensed too that he hadn't approved of her own love for an Italian of humble origins. Elliott was a snob. It was all right to mix with non-WASPs and indeed to make use of them, but he would be deeply disturbed if, when his daughter was older, she wanted to marry or to live with one of them.

'And now I guess you're about to go for a sundowner on that fabulous terrace,' he said presently. 'I wish I were with you. I remember dining at one of the window tables in the Normandie restaurant on the top floor when there was a full moon over the river. I was there for Loy Krathong which is when they float little boats with lighted candles in them to carry away all their troubles. That's a delightful ceremony but it's in November. In Sydney you'll be at the Regent of course?'

'Of course,' she said, smiling to herself. Anywhere he

went Elliott would always have to stay at the most deluxe hotel or he wouldn't feel comfortable.

After he had rung off, she thought it was odd that she liked him so much when he had many traits she didn't like.

She wondered how he would react if she turned up at his hotel in Bali in a backpacker's outfit. He would certainly make darn sure everyone knew she was an earl's daughter, she thought grinning. She went back to drying her hair.


Guests at the Oriental were paged by a bellboy walking through the public rooms with a stick of wind-bells to which was attached the name of the person who was wanted.

Allegra was sitting in the lobby, listening to the gentle tinkling and thinking what a charming and practical idea it was – many of the guests had names the boys would find hard to pronounce – when Kit arrived to collect her.

Tonight it was not the Princess' Daimler which waited outside but an Italian-looking sports car which he was driving himself. Allegra was wearing a dress she had bought in Bangkok. It had a skirt which allowed her to slide into the passenger seat without giving Kit and the doormen an eyeful of thigh.

'I wasn't sure what kind of restaurant would serve the most authentic Thai food. In some cities it could be a neighbourhood café but I didn't think you could eat at a place like that so I erred on the side of formality,' she told him.

Kit himself was wearing a pale silk-tweed blazer and a tie.

'Tonight you look very much the successful authoress,' he said, with a knowledgeable glance at the dress.

She laughed. ' "Authoress" smacks of mink and dia-

monds and hype. I'm a writer . . . who isn't writing,'
she added wryly. 'I just had a call from my American
publisher who wants me to get back to work. A biography of Jim Thompson, the silk man, would have interested me, if it hadn't been done already. What's your
theory about his mysterious disappearance, Kit?'

They discussed this subject through two traffic jams
and a hold-up caused by the sudden collapse of a load
of rolled up rugs from the back of a motorbike.

'Only here would anyone *attempt* to carry that lot on
a pillion,' said Allegra, laughing.

When Kit turned the car down a canopied ramp and
stretched his arm to insert a plastic card in a machine
which opened the door to a basement garage, she didn't
immediately realise that a restaurant would have what
the Americans called valet parking. It was only when
she saw the numbered spaces that she grasped they were
in a private building.

'I have a *pied-à-terre* in the city for entertaining my
friends and for spending the night when going back to
the palace might disturb my grandmother,' he
explained, as the car stopped. 'We can dine here and
talk more peacefully than in a restaurant. As it happens
the best food in town is very near here. They will send
up the meal I have chosen for us.'

She was not sure what to make of this. Dinner *à deux*
at a bachelor flat usually had only one conclusion. Yet
this morning he had assured her that he had no ulterior
motive in asking her to dine with him.

Evidently reading her mind, he said, 'At ten o'clock,
no later, I'll return you to the Oriental to have a good
night's rest before your long flight tomorrow. But I
wanted you to see my own place before we say goodbye.'

Allegra was reassured, yet still a tiny doubt lingered.
She had always loathed underground car parks and felt
claustrophobic in them. Perhaps this had something to
do with her sense of being trapped in a situation which

570

had the potential to turn out unpleasantly. What, after all, did she know about him, except that he was well-connected – and *that* was no guarantee of civilised behaviour.

The lift had to be unlocked as a second security measure. Once inside it, with mirrored walls and a carpeted floor instead of the concrete gloom of the garage, she felt less edgy.

'My apartment is on the top floor,' he told her. 'Originally it had a garden but the noise and pollution from below made it rather unpleasant so I had it converted into a garden room.'

They passed at least a dozen floors before the lift stopped and again had to be unlocked.

'The lift from the lobby opens automatically because there's always a porter on duty,' he said, as they stepped into a hallway. 'When I unlock the penthouse lift from the garage, a bell rings in the apartment telling my servant I am on my way up.'

Before he had finished speaking a heavy teak door had been opened by a small stocky man wearing the *panung* with a tunic of black silk.

Kit introduced him as Theh and he bowed to her. 'Good evening, *madame*.'

She wondered how many women before her had received that deferential bow and whether his private opinion was less respectful.

Then Kit took her by the elbow and they passed through a dimly-lit hall into a large dark space where all that could be seen was the calm, enigmatic face of an ancient stone Buddha bathed in an upward glow of light.

'Every collector has his most precious object,' he said quietly. 'This is mine.'

Allegra looked at it in silence, seeing in her mind's eye her own most precious object. Her throat tightened as she thought of it and how like and yet unlike it was;

showing only the structure of bone and the texture of hair but lacking the steely brilliance of Andro's most striking feature, his grey eyes.

'This is Indochinese, carved from sandstone in the twelfth or thirteenth century,' said Kit, bringing her back from the swift mental flight to Longwarden. 'I find it very soothing sometimes to sit and study it.'

She swallowed the ache in her throat and made an effort to speak normally. 'I shouldn't have thought you were a meditative person.'

'Ah, but you don't know me yet ... nor I you. We know only each other's superficial personalities. It takes time to peel back the layers and discover the inner person. Let me show you another of my treasures.'

Again with a touch on her arm he turned her away from the Buddha and led her a little distance until suddenly light beamed down on a black plinth topped with a small vermilion object.

'This is a carved lacquer cupstand ... Chinese ... early fifteenth century. The design is a phoenix among lotus flowers.'

'It's the most wonderful colour.'

'Cinnabar red.'

He touched some more concealed switches and more shafts of light appeared, each one focused on a work of art, a painting, another sculpture, a group of jewel-bright Indian miniatures. When all were lit up a very large room came to life, some areas of it set apart by Oriental screens and banks of plants. At first it seemed to have no windows until he touched another switch and what she had thought were walls showed themselves to be sliding panels and areas of vertical blinds which, opened, revealed breathtaking views of the city by night and the broad expanse of the Chao Phraya visible both upstream and downstream.

Allegra could find no words to describe its impact on

her. She was struck dumb, both by the views and the extraordinary interior.

'And now for the best of all. Would you sit here, please.'

He indicated a chair covered in the black or very dark midnight blue which was used for all the room's surfaces. 'Don't be surprised when the chair moves. It works on the same principle as a dentist's chair, but with a more enjoyable purpose.'

Allegra sat down and felt the chair swing slowly backwards and a leg rest come into play. In a matter of moments she was facing the ceiling which, as the walls had earlier, slid open, leaving only an expanse of glass between her and the shimmering sky.

'While you contemplate the stars, let me fix you a drink. What would you like?'

'It seems mundane to ask for a gin and tonic . . .'

'Not at all. By the way, let me warn you to avoid the *arak* in Bali. It will take the top of your head off . . . the nearest thing to brain surgery without a scalpel, as Lloyd Grossman once said.'

'I'll bear that in mind.'

She heard ice cubes dropped into glasses, the splash of liquid.

Before handing the drink to her, Kit set the chair in motion. Evidently it was controlled by a pedal as he had a glass in each hand. She assumed they both contained gin. It wasn't until they were dining that she found out otherwise. Theh poured wine for her but only water for his master.

'My advice about *arak* wasn't from first-hand experience, although I drank most forms of alcohol in my youth,' said Kit, seeing that she had noticed he had no wine. 'But I had to give it up when I entered the monastery and that was one habit I never resumed. I found I functioned better without it.'

'Did you like being a monk?'

'Not enough to remain one, but it was a valuable experience. Up to that point in my life I'd had every privilege and comfort – apart from some minor privations at Harrow,' he added dryly. 'To live in relative poverty, eating nothing after midday, was a salutary discipline.'

'How old were you when you went in?'

'Twenty.'

'I can't imagine my brother at twenty spending three months in an English order. Does everyone do it here?'

'It isn't obligatory but many do. Most Thais are practising Buddhists. Their religion is an everyday part of their lives, whereas in the West even the clergy don't often practise what they preach. Western missionaries have never made any headway here, even though King Mongkut was so tolerant of other religions that he actually subscribed to the funds for building Catholic and Protestant churches, and even a mosque.'

From where she was sitting Allegra could see the sandstone image of The Enlightened One. Looking at it while Theh removed the first course, she saw that the carved features were very like Kit's.

Both had the same broad forehead; the same subtle modelling of eyebrows and eyelids; the same long straight nose, rounded at the tip with slightly splayed curling nostrils. But it was in the lines of the mouth that the resemblance was strongest. Both had a full lower lip, the upper one faintly smiling even in repose.

Around Kit's mouth and jaw his skin had the darker tinge which by morning would be stubble. But there was no hair on his hands and she remembered from yesterday that his powerful forearms were smooth. She found herself wondering if, as a lover, he would be utterly different from a European.

The thought made her guilty and angry, the more so when he picked up his glass and looked at her while he was drinking. She was afraid he might read what had been in her mind.

In a way he did. 'Tell me about the man you mentioned yesterday.'

In Europe if people knew someone was dead, they were careful to avoid mentioning him. She was startled and disturbed by his directness.

'Was he also a writer?' Kit prompted, when she didn't answer.

'No, an artist . . . a painter of portraits.' Her normal reserve began to crumble. She started to talk about Andro in a way she had never done before, except to Jane.

Even when Theh came back with the next course, she didn't break off. It was as if, having begun, she couldn't stop. She didn't say much about their personal relationship, but she told him what an extraordinary man Andro had been and what a great gift had been wasted by his death.

When, finally, she did stop, knowing she had told him far too much about someone who couldn't be of any real interest to him, Kit said nothing for a moment or two.

'You are still full of anger and bitterness. That's understandable, but the only way you will find peace is to accept the unfairness of life. It's easier for those who believe in a scheme of things but, even for people like you who have no religion, acceptance is possible.'

'How do you know I have no religion?'

'If you had, you wouldn't be in such despair,' he said, with gentle logic.

Suddenly Allegra laughed. 'I've never met a man like you, Prince Kitayalongkorn.' She gave him his title with a slightly mocking bow. 'Yesterday I took you for a playboy looking for a new diversion. Even tonight, coming up here, I wasn't sure of your intentions. Now you are talking to me for the good of my soul. Anyone who unpeels the layers of your personality is in for several surprises.'

He smiled. 'This morning, when we stopped outside the walls of the old city and you first saw the golden mount of Wat Phra Keo, your face lit up like a child's. For a moment you looked happy . . . and very beautiful. I'd like to see that look again. I don't think this is our last meeting, do you?'

'Perhaps not. Who knows? Anyway, if there are times when the tour gets me down, I'll think of this wonderful room and feel mentally refreshed.'


On the flight from Bangkok to Sydney she sat next to a young Australian who was going home after two years of seeing the world. He was flying Tourist but because of over-booking had had to be put in First. As friendly as a puppy, he was touchingly excited by this unexpected taste of luxury.


The Cotton House had been recommended to Jane by Alison and Marcus Blakewell who had spent a relaxing holiday there several years before.

Taking its name from the eighteenth century cotton warehouse which was now the nucleus of a small complex of cottages, it was close to the island's north and west beaches where most of the private holiday houses had been and still were being built. Those overlooking L'Ansecoy Bay had had their views somewhat marred by the rusting hulk of a French liner whose captain, in giving his passengers a close up view of the hideaways of the rich and famous, had been in collision with a reef.

The whole island had once belonged to two maiden ladies, descendants of an English family who for generations had lived on the nearby large island of St Vincent. In 1959 it had been bought by the Hon. Colin Tennant

– now Lord Glenconner – who had subsequently given a piece of it to Princess Margaret as a wedding present. Later she had commissioned a famous theatrical designer, the late Oliver Messel, who had moved to Barbados for his health's sake, to design a small house for her.

It was this house, Les Jolies Eaux, at the southern end of the island, which Kyle Rainert's friends had insisted on renting, Jane discovered. She didn't learn this from North who, having said goodbye to the Rainerts, hadn't referred to them again. The person who told her about it was another guest at the hotel, an American who had been hoping the Princess would be in residence.

For the first two days of their holiday, North snorkeled and photographed hummingbirds sipping nectar from hibiscus, and Jane swam and lazed in the sun or, when it was too hot for comfort, on the verandah outside their pretty bedroom.

She had almost forgotten Cressida when, on their third morning there, Mrs Rainert rang up and invited them to a luncheon party which she claimed to have arranged specially for them.

Jane, who took the call, found herself at a loss to invent a watertight excuse not to go. She passed the buck to North, hoping he would think of something. To her dismay, he didn't.

'All right, we'll be there at one, Cressy,' she heard him agree, at the end of their conversation.

That he let slip, no doubt unintentionally, the intimate diminutive of Cressida's name, seemed to confirm what Jane had suspected at the airport.

Although in theory it was foolish to mind about past amours which had nothing to do with her, now that one of his former girlfriends had materialised, she found it was much more difficult to take a detached view. She

577

wondered if Kyle felt the same way about North, or if his antennae were not as sensitive as hers.

Leaving Simon in the care of one of the hotel's baby-minders, they drove to the party in a Mini Moke which North had rented to allow them to visit some of the island's remote beaches.

While the northern end of Mustique had been cleared of scrub and now had shade trees and lotus pools set among closely-mown lawns, as they headed south the tarmacked roads to the airport, Lovell Village and Basil's Raft Restaurant gave place to an unmade track over which the moke bumped and bounced into wilder, hillier terrain.

Their host and hostess came out to greet them as they arrived, Cressida looking cool and elegant in wide-legged white linen slacks and handkerchief linen top, also white, with a belt the colour of lemon peel cinching her narrow waist.

Jane's figure, though North claimed to like it better now than before, was neither as slim nor as firm as it had been when they married. But she couldn't diet while she was nursing, and she hadn't minded carrying a few extra pounds until Cressida made her feel conscious of them.

The Princess' house *was* charming; its living room simply furnished under a white-boarded ceiling, with double doors, topped by a fanlight, folded back to reveal a spectacular view of blue sea and white foam washing the shores of the islands and islets to the south.

From the garden with its gazebo and swimming pool, Kyle showed her how the land fell steeply away from the headland on which the house was perched to the bays on either side of it. If he felt any unease at being told to look after Jane while his wife concentrated on North, he didn't show it.

Neither did Jane, but as she chatted to the other guests she was very much aware that Cressida was not dividing her attention among them. She was giving it all to North.

'Well . . . what did you think of them?' he asked, as they drove back to The Cotton House.

'The Rainerts or their guests?'

'All of them.'

'They've put me off the idea of us building a winter place here to share with Marcus and Alison.'

North glanced at her. 'How have they done that?'

'By making me feel that Mustique, although it's lovely in some ways, isn't a very happy place. I heard gossip I didn't like . . . not all of it true, perhaps, but some which sounded believable. People taking to drink and drugs . . . having disastrous affairs . . . corrupting the islanders . . . making some rude and resentful.'

'That's inevitable, sweetie. Those things go on everywhere. But I agree with you: the island is fine for a week but I shouldn't want to build a place here.'

When they were back on the smooth road, she said, 'What about a return match? Do you want to ask them to dine with us?'

To her surprise and relief, North said, 'Definitely not. When you write or ring up to thank her – I should think Cressida telephones – suggest that they let us know when they're next in England. Which I hope won't be for some time,' he added. 'I didn't enjoy their party any more than you did. It would have been a lot more fun to take a picnic to one of the beaches we haven't explored yet.' He took one hand off the wheel to reach for her hand and press a kiss on the back of it.

Jane knew then she had been a fool to let jealousy seep into her mind. She felt ashamed of herself for letting her trust in him weaken, even for an hour. Perhaps it wasn't her trust which had failed but rather her confidence in herself. Maybe she was suffering from a delayed and very mild dose of post-natal blues.

'Tomorrow let's do that,' she said. 'Take lunch boxes to that beach on the west of the island . . . Macaroni Bay.'

---

# February

'Where is Laura today?' James asked during lunch.

'She's having a day off,' said Jane. 'Someone she met when she was away for Christmas has taken her out for the day. Laura doesn't take enough time off. She would work all day, every day if I wanted her to. She's one of the most unselfish, conscientious people I have ever met.'

'Yes, she's a very nice person,' he agreed.

'She has not had a very nice life,' said Jane.

She and the architect were the only people at the lunch table, North being in London today and Sarah having left before the coffee.

'Not that Laura has ever complained, but it's what I've deduced from things she has said,' she added. 'Perhaps you know more than I do about her life before she came here?'

She was puzzled by the fact that the friendship between James and her secretary seemed to have petered out. Jane had no wish to lose Laura's excellent services. At the same time she felt it was a shame for such a likeable woman to wither on the vine. Even North had conceded last week that Laura was more attractive than he had realised. Her confidence in herself seemed to have increased since her Christmas holiday. This was the second time the doctor from Dorset had driven over to take her out to lunch. From where he lived to Longwarden was not a day's journey but it was far enough to suggest that he was seriously interested.

Jane had met him briefly, and liked him, but not as much as she liked their architect. The doctor was in his early fifties with grown up children. He might want another wife but he probablyy wouldn't want to have a second batch of children and it seemed a great pity for Laura to miss the experience of motherhood. There was still time – just! – for her to have one child, even two. But she would have to get a move on. What had gone wrong between her and James?

Jane was seriously tempted to ask him. But perhaps she should mind her own business. She had already made two mistakes in her judgements about other people. She should never have encouraged Sarah's romantic feelings about Nick, and if she had revealed to North that Joël Vibrac's wife was severely disabled he would probably have opposed engaging him and the ghastly murder and suicide would never have happened. Or not at Longwarden.

'Laura had told me a little about her past life,' said James. 'Like you, I have the impression it was very restricted when her step-mother was alive. I'm sure she's much happier and has a fuller life here.'

Jane felt there could be no harm in saying, 'But not as full as it should be. It will be a pity if she never marries. She would make such a good wife and mother.'

'I'm sure you are right. Is the friend who is taking her out today a man?'

'Yes.' Perhaps knowing that someone else was interested would reinvigorate his interest, she thought hopefully.

But he quashed that notion by saying, 'Perhaps their friendship will develop – although I shouldn't have thought you would want to lose her, Lady Carlyon.'

'No, of course I don't. But I should like her to be

happy, and most women's lives are incomplete without a partner and children.'

He put his napkin on the table and pushed back his chair. 'And most men's.' Rising, he said, 'Would you excuse me?'


Allegra woke up in the night and fumbled around in the dark, thinking she was still on tour.

Between her departure from England and arrival in Sydney the tour had been expanded to include visits to all the major cities in Australia, except Perth, with a quick flip across to 'Tassie' and three nights in New Zealand.

She found the switch and the light came on. Above her was what looked like the lid of a huge, intricately-woven basket. For a moment or two she blinked up at it, completely disorientated. Where was this?

Then she remembered. The tour was over. The merry-go-round had stopped. This was Bali.

She had arrived after dark, greeted by gusts of sweet scent from the frangipani trees at the airport. There must have been the usual formalities but she couldn't recall them. Tired out by the last of so many long flights and a lot of alcohol, she had fallen asleep in the taxi, only waking up with a start when the driver spoke to her and she realised they had reached Kuta.

It had seemed a rowdy, honky-tonk kind of town. Shops selling garish souvenirs. A blond youth with *Fuck off!* printed on his tee shirt drinking beer out of a can, his arm round a girl with big floppy breasts and bead-strung hair. Restaurant touts thrusting leaflets at tourists. A poster proclaiming *Start the day right with a bonzer brekky at Bali Aussie*.

In spite of the fact that North had advised her to come to Kuta for the first night or two, her spirits had sunk.

Then, instead of arriving at the small cottage colony

where her brother had told her to stay, the driver had stopped in a busy street, jumped out and removed her baggage from the boot.

'This not Poppies,' protested Allegra, not sure if he spoke English.

'Poppies this way.'

Her book-laden flight bag on his shoulder, her roll-bag in his hand, he had plunged down a dimly-lit alley, leaving her with no choice but to follow.

Allegra had wondered if she were being led to some unsavoury spot to be robbed. She felt too tired to care. All she longed for was to stretch out at full length and sleep for at least twelve hours.

By a row of small shops, boarded and barred for the night, the alley came to a T-junction with another. They turned left, passing a gateway in a high wall which seemed to be a garden restaurant. The hubbub of voices and laughter reassured her.

A bit further on was a second gateway which the man entered. Another garden, this one empty and quiet. Then lights and a desk and an amber-skinned clerk saying politely, 'Good evening. Welcome to Poppies. I will show you your room.'

Ten minutes later, too weary to unpack anything, Allegra had gulped down two tumblers of water from the vacuum jug left on the table then collapsed, as if pole-axed, onto the turned down twin bed.


Now, suddenly wide awake, she looked more closely at her surroundings and liked what she saw; not only the lofty ceiling made of woven grass and bound canes, but the plain white walls and the blue-on-white cotton curtains, the same leafy design being used, colours-reversed, on the beds.

Where was the bathroom? She sat up, flinching at the headache which lanced her temples as she swung her

583

feet to the floor. Definitely too much alcohol on the flight and indeed since the tour began. It was time to ease up.

Opening the door between the wardrobe and the dressing table, she stepped into an atmosphere which was startlingly warm and humid compared with the coolness of the bedroom. Obviously the bathroom wasn't air-conditioned and she found out why not a few moments later. On one side of the door, in a recess, was the lavatory; on the other, tiled with earth-brown mosaic, was a sunken bath and shower. Facing the door was the handbasin, mirror and cupboards, on either side of and behind which was a garden, most of it open to the sky. Between the plants was a gravelled space with a drying horse intended for bathing suits and beach towels. Whoever had designed the cottages had both sense and taste, thought Allegra.

After a cool-feeling shower, some more iced water and a couple of Panadols, she tackled her unpacking. By the time she had dressed it was growing light. What she needed next was some exercise.

As she stepped onto her verandah, a smiling Balinese girl with a flower in her hair arrived with another flask and a dish of fruit. This flask contained fragrant tea. Allegra drank two cups of it and ate a small sweet banana, enjoying her secluded corner of the tropical garden and the freedom of having no appointments, no schedule, nothing to do but relax.

When she had found her way back to the gateway which, like the cottages, had a thatched roof, she turned in the opposite direction from the way she had arrived.

Although by now the sun was shining, at this early hour of the day it was still possible to walk rather than stroll. As she followed the lane the number of houses dwindled and the trees increased until they also thinned out and she found herself near one end of a long wide beach.

This must be Kuta's famous surfing beach; a place

584

she had meant to avoid not only because it would be crowded but because of the images pounding waves conjured up for her.

At this hour the surfers were still sleeping off last night's booze up, the great stretch of sand was almost deserted and the tide was out. Even so it was a painful reminder of the east coast beach in Barbados where she and Andro had walked and, later, he had drowned.

For several long moments she stared at the almost quiescent ocean which in a few hours would be boiling with powerful currents and dangerous undertows. There had been a leaflet in her room she had glanced at quickly and then thrust back in the folder. But she remembered parts of it.

### PLEASE READ CAREFULLY — IT MAY SAVE YOUR LIFE

*Dear Visitor, Welcome to the waters and beaches of Bali. The Government and the Surf Life Saving Club have combined to try and ensure that your use of both will be enjoyable and SAFE. They suggest as follows . . . Observe these simple rules, enjoy your stay with us and ensure your safe return to your country.*

Now, staring at the sea which every year claimed several victims here, she felt a moan rising inside her. She wanted to cover her eyes, to run back the way she had come.

'. . . *even for those like you, who have no religion, acceptance is possible.*'

The quiet cultured English voice, with no hint of foreignness in it, echoed in her mind like one of the error messages which sometimes came up on the monitor of her computer.

Almost as if it were there on the screen in front of her, she saw the succinct warning: ERROR IN: *if you continue your life will be damaged.* Then the options. *Continue anyway. Retry. Cancel.*

She chose to retry; forcing herself to walk forward

onto the sand which was soft at the back of the beach but firmer nearer the water. She would walk to the far end and back. She would not spend the rest of her life unable to be near the sea without having waking nightmares. She would think of Kit's rooftop room, the calm face of the sandstone Buddha.

Halfway along the beach where there were gardens and buildings at the back of it, she was approached by a Balinese woman, not young, dressed in a sarong and a modest cotton jacket. On her head was a shallow basket with a towel and other things in it.

'You like massage, *madame*? Very good . . . very cheap.'

Smiling, Allegra shook her head.

The woman didn't persist. Perhaps she felt it was too early to press, or perhaps the Balinese didn't. Nor, evidently, did they still walk around with bare breasts.

Pretending that Kit was walking with her, Allegra said softly – although there was no one to hear her talking to herself – 'I wonder what it was like here when Vicki Baum came to Bali in 1935 and met the old Dutchman, Doctor Fabius, who left her his papers and the draft of a novel about the Puputan Massacre?'

In her mind she heard Kit reply, 'Have you read *A Tale From Bali*, the novel she based on his draft?'

'Not yet. Only the first two pages of the introduction. I started it on the plane but I had a very chatty neighbour whom I couldn't stop talking.'

'But you saw the epigraph on the title page? *The end of birth is death. The end of death is birth. Such is the law.*'

'Yes . . . from the Bhagavad-Vita. What *is* the Bhagavad-Vita?'

There, because he was not really with her, the conversation foundered. She felt sure he would know the answer. Would she see him again? It was up to her. She could break her return journey at Bangkok, ring him up and say, 'Have you a copy of the Bhagavad-Vita you can lend me?'

Thinking about him, the man of action with a mystic streak in him, occupied her mind until she found herself back at the mouth of the lane. The sun was now much hotter. She was starting to sweat. More slowly she returned to Poppies.

From there, after another shower in her garden-bathroom, she followed North's instructions and set out to have a Balinese breakfast at Made's Warung in a street called Jalan Pantai.

This turned out to be the street where the taxi had stopped the night before. The *warung* or eating place was close by and unmistakable. As North had warned her it was an open-fronted café which in Europe would seem pretty scruffy but in Kuta was the best place to watch the world go by.

'Until you've had breakfast at Made's, you've missed one of life's great experiences. In its own way it's on a par with going up from Grindelwald in the chair-lift during the hay-making season, and picnicking on cheese straight from the caves at Roquefort,' he had said to her, mentioning two experiences they had shared as children on trips to the Continent with Flora Carlyon.

Having seen his photographs of the passing scene seen from Made's, and of the *warung* packed with people, she was surprised to find most of the prime seats, the benches facing the street, unoccupied.

There were a couple of men drinking beer at a table on the *warung*'s inner, higher floor. They both stripped her with their eyes. Allegra returned a glance, perfected in her late teens, of total indifference. Someone she knew who had received it had told her later that it made him feel like the invisible man.

When she had chosen a seat a waiter brought her a menu. She ordered the special breakfast and tea. Waiting for it to arrive, she wondered if her brother had been here on his own or with one of the many girls who had preceded Jane in his life.

Presently, tucking into a generous helping of rice mixed with all kinds of delicious titbits, Allegra watched a Balinese girl, dressed like the woman on the beach but with the addition of a sash round her narrow waist, placing a woven-leaf dish filled with flowers and some grains of rice on the pavement outside the *warung*.

It must be, she knew, an offering to the spirits and she found it heartening that even in a town like Kuta, so changed by tourism, the Balinese still carried out their forefathers' customs.

After breakfast she wandered around, looking at the shops and smilingly refusing offers of sightseeing tours from taxi and minibus drivers.

Some of the shops confirmed last night's impression: there was a lot of tat on sale in Kuta. But she also saw beautiful baskets of a kind which would sell for three figures in Liberty's in London and amazingly cheap silver jewellery, some of it pretty. Having bought herself a moonstone ring for a few thousand *rupiahs* – the price of a sandwich in a South Molton Street café – she returned to Poppies to sit by the ornamental pool in the garden and scribble some postcards to her family and friends.


There were times when – never for long – the weight on Damaris' mind was lifted by coming upon a clump of *Iris stylosa*, the long grey-green tassels of *garrya elliptica*, the pale green flowers of the sprawling, glossy-leaved shrub *ribes laurifolium*.

The woods near the house were still full of late aconites, drifts of snowdrops and snowflakes, crocuses, early primroses and all kinds of beautiful hellebores.

Everywhere in the garden shoots were beginning to push up through the cold earth.

The days were still short but as dusk fell and she cleaned and put away her tools, there were the evenings with Sam to look forward to.

If only she were not afraid that somehow his wretched childhood had left a twist in his mind; a deep, hidden vein of revengeful destructiveness at odds with the rest of his kind, stable, trustworthy nature.


For the second time that morning, Allegra emerged from her two-room hut, literally a stone's throw from the beach at Candidasa, to drape her rinsed-out bathing suit over the wooden horse on her verandah.

She was wrapped in a *batik* sarong she had bought in Denpasar market and her hair was wet from her pre-breakfast swim in the sea after which she had rinsed it under the freshwater shower in the basic but adequate bathroom at the back of the bedroom.

She had been at Candidasa for four days. Each morning, when they saw she was ready, the two Balinese girls who cleaned the huts and prepared their occupants' breakfasts brought her a big flask of tea, a bowl of fruit, toast and an egg. With another large flask of tea in the afternoon, her accommodation and food cost her the equivalent of four pounds. But she had to provide her own towel, soap and lavatory paper and the bed had no top sheet, nor was there air-conditioning or even a fan in the bedroom.

Ratna Bungalows were designed to accommodate the young and hardy, not people who wanted all the comforts of home. Most of the other bungalows were occupied by couples; men with girls, pairs of girls, pairs of men. In the hut directly opposite Allegra's were a young man and a girl who were either on honeymoon or in the early stages of a passionate affair. Although how they managed to make love in a fan-less bedroom without either melting or sticking together like super-glue she couldn't imagine.

She had just sat down in a chair made of lengths of very thick bamboo when an Australian voice coming from the next hut – hers was the closest to the beach apart from the little cook-house – said, 'G'day, miss.'

The morning before, her neighbour had been a Canadian girl who was on her way round the world. She had said she was checking out, but up to the time she had gone to bed Allegra had seen no sign of a newcomer moving in.

She turned her head, her eyes widening at the sight of the man who was her new neighbour.

'*Kit!*' she exclaimed.

For in spite of the Aussie greeting which had made her look round, it was Prince Kitayalongkorn who stood on the next door verandah, wearing a pair of burnt orange boxer shorts with a beach towel slung over his shoulder.

'Good morning,' he said in his own voice, amused by her astonishment. 'I'm just going for a swim. Then, if I may, I'll join you for breakfast.'

Stepping into a pair of thongs he had left beside his verandah, he gave her a mischievous grin and walked past her towards the beach.

Allegra stared after him, dumbfounded. But not so taken aback that she failed to register the splendour of his tall muscular body. When he had disappeared down the steps which led first to a wide ledge where people sun-bathed and then to the beach below, she had to admit that the sight of him had pleased as well as astonished her.

She had been in Bali for eight days. At first it had been a joy to be on her own, not speaking, not having to sparkle. In the past forty-eight hours she had begun to feel lonely again.

Had she been less discriminating, it would have been

easy to let herself be picked up at the restaurants where she ate at night. But although some of the men who had looked hopefully at her, or made tentative overtures, had been attractive, Allegra was unlikely ever to repeat the casual affairs she had once had. Having experienced love at its best, she could never again settle for inferior substitutes.

Ordinary companionship was what she wanted more than anything; someone to share the beauty of the Candidasa dawns and sunsets, someone with whom to potter along the beach where tiny transparent crabs scuttled out of the way and at certain times of the day particles of mica in the sand glittered like diamonds.

Her breakfast tray had arrived when Kit reappeared, towelling his black hair, his wet cotton shorts sending rivulets down his long thighs.

'When did you arrive?' she asked.

'Late last night. I was beginning to think you weren't at Candidasa when the man at the office here said yes, there was a tall English-speaking woman on her own staying here. I'd tried five or six other places before this one.'

He disappeared into his hut, leaving Allegra uncertain how to react to the pains he had taken to find her. Should she show that she was pleased to see him? Or should she keep him guessing?

When he joined her on her verandah he was also wearing a sarong but his, wrapped round his hips, was of a quality far superior to hers.

'Howasya trip Down Under, Lidy Alligra?' he asked her.

She gave a gurgle of laughter. 'It was beaut, y'Highness.' Deciding against dissimulation, she jumped up, offering him both hands. 'I couldn't believe my eyes when that Aussie voice said G'day and I looked round and saw you, of all people.'

'I hope it was a pleasant surprise.' He squeezed her hands, then kissed them lightly on the knuckles.

'Of course . . . but I shouldn't think you spent a very pleasant night in your hot little hut. What possessed you to stay here? This isn't a place for princes accustomed to every luxury. Weren't you eaten alive by mosquitoes? I have to burn a green coil or I should be one mass of bites.'

'I'm one of the fortunate few they don't seem to find appetising. But in case you've forgotten, my public school-priesthood years were an excellent preparation for a holiday here.' His gesture encompassed the double row of huts and the strip of garden between them.

At this point one of the girls approached with his breakfast tray. Kit said something to her in what Allegra took to be Bahasa Indonesia, the lingua franca spoken from northern Sumatra to Irian Jaya at the other end of the huge archipelago. She was picking up a little herself but he spoke it fluently. The girl changed direction and came to Allegra's verandah, shedding, with a practised movement, her flip-flops before stepping onto it.

What would you have done if I hadn't been here?' Allegra asked presently.

By this time breakfast was being eaten on several of the verandahs opposite. She knew his presence on hers was being noticed with interest.

'Continued to look for you today.' His eyes shifted from her face to a very old soft-topped Volkswagen parked nearby under a palm tree. 'That isn't your car, is it?'

Her mouth full, she nodded.

'What possessed you to hire that old banger? It looks like the model German staff officers drove round Occupied France. You must have seen Volkwagens of that vintage in old World War Two movies, haven't you?'

'Yes, but so what?' she said cheerfully. 'It was dirt

cheap. It goes. I think it's fun. Where have you left your car?'

'When I'm here by myself, I buzz around on a motor-bike. It's parked on the other side of my bungalow. I thought you would probably be travelling around by bus. Girls on their own don't often seem to rent cars.'

'Don't they? I always do.'

'Perhaps you are better at coping with breakdowns than the average woman.'

'Not in the least. What I know about engines wouldn't cover the head of a pin. I rely on the mechanical sex to get me out of trouble. I was going to Tenganan this morning. Would you like to come, or have you been there too often to want to go again?'

'Not at all. With you, I'll enjoy it. While you look at the flaming cloth, I'll look at your flaming hair.'

'Wet rats'-tails at the moment,' Allegra said, with a grimace.

But although her face was more angular than the rounded features of Balinese women, hair sleeked back from forehead and temple in the way most of them wore it wasn't unflattering to her. She didn't feel she looked a mess.

'How do you like Bali so far? Where else have you been?' Kit asked.

'It's a heavenly island. I love it. I was at Poppies in Kuta for the first few nights and then I came here and have stayed put. But tomorrow I'm moving to Ubud which I'm told is an artists' colony.'

'Founded by Walter Spies, a German musician and painter who settled in Bali in 1927 and had a tremendous influence on Balinese art before the war took him away, never to come back. He introduced the Balinese to new painting materials and new concepts such as perspective. My house isn't far from Ubud.'

Kit didn't repeat his invitation to stay with him but

there seemed no doubt it was what he expected to happen. Why else would he be here?

That night they locked the doors of their huts and set out to go by the beach to a restaurant belonging to one of the other cottage colonies.

In Kuta, Allegra had found a shop called Studio Lala selling clothes made from second-hand sarongs in the subtle tones *batik* acquired after many washings. Liking the combination of sun-faded indigo blues with all the earth colours, she had bought a lot there including the outfit displayed on a model in the window. This she was wearing tonight; a top and trousers, not matching, with a wide navy belt, in places the surface of the leather cut away in a simple design.

Even with large silver ear-rings, the overall effect was casual; at the top, but within the range, of styles seen at Candidasa after dark. People might look but they weren't going to raise their eyebrows. Nevertheless she wouldn't have bothered to get the clothes out of her second roll-bag in the boot of the car if Kit hadn't pitched up. She hadn't dressed up at all before his arrival. Which meant – what? she asked herself.

Always what she put on her back had been a barometer of her feelings. For a long time after Andro's death she hadn't cared what she wore. She had had to dress up for the recent tour, but buying things at Studio Lala had been the first unnecessary shopping she had done for more than a year and, more significantly, tonight was the first time she had dressed for a man since her life had fallen apart.

It was still light when they walked past the antiquated VW which amused Kit whenever he looked at it.

They reached the steps to the restaurant just as the brief tropical twilight faded into night. Candles inside glass storm shades burned on the tables, some of them outside under the tall slender palms, some sheltered by a thatched roof.

Twice a week the place had a buffet dinner with roast sucking pig, roast duck and fish satay. Allegra had eaten here on the night of her arrival.

'I see they have Australian wine,' said Kit, looking at the drinks card. 'Did you try it when you came before?'

'Yes . . . also the local rice wine which turned out to be something like the lemon barley water our old nanny gave my brother and me when we had colds as children. I didn't care for either much, but the food was terrific – and so incredibly cheap. Tonight I'll emulate you and drink bottled water.'

'Are you sure? Don't let me inhibit you.'

'I have never let anyone do that,' she said dryly. 'I come from a long line of people who have always lived to please themselves. It's a family characteristic . . . not a very admirable one, perhaps, but it's the way we are and one can't fight one's genes.'

Kit gave her a thoughtful look. 'Have you enjoyed today?'

'Very much. Haven't you?'

He nodded. 'More than yesterday when you were on your own?' he persisted.

Allegra decided to be honest. 'Much more. I don't dislike my own company but there are times when one needs someone to talk to. Coming back from Tenganan was one of them . . . and again this afternoon.'

They had spent the afternoon alternately swimming and lying on the sand, talking.


The next day, and the next, they passed all their time together, and each night they dined at one of the several informal restaurants which served the cottage colonies, and afterwards they strolled in the moonlight discussing many different subjects until Kit said goodnight to her at her verandah before disappearing into his own hut.

On the third morning, at breakfast, he said, 'I've enjoyed it here but I think we would be more comfortable at my house and there are so many places I want to show you around Ubud. Will you come and stay there with me?'

Allegra looked at him for a long time and he returned her gaze steadily, with a faint smile on his lips.

At last, she said, 'Yes, I'll come.'

She had no idea whether to continue their present chaste relationship or to change it. She only knew that he was wise and good and she trusted him to lead her along any path he thought best for them.


In the garden of Kit's airy Balinese house there was a pool where lotus buds grew on long green stalks. That evening she sat by the pool while the last light of day changed suddenly into darkness.

On the way here from Candidasa they had stopped at the gallery one of the island's most famous wood carvers, Ida Bagus Tilem. Most of the carvings had been too elaborate for her taste but she had bought half a dozen beautiful stylised hands intended as stands for rings; one to keep for herself and the others to give as presents.

Later on, at another gallery, she had seen, pinned to the wall, a notice.

> *The time to be happy is now . . .*
> *The place to be happy is here . . .*
> *The way to be happy is to make others so . . .*


She didn't know where or by whom it had been written, but it seemed to express the mood and spirit of the island.

Kit came out of the house. 'You had better come in before the mosquitoes start feasting on you.'

He took her by the hand and led her inside, through the spacious living room to a door at the opposite end from the room where she had unpacked her roll-bags.

When he moved the door, she saw that this also was a bedroom. A fan with a moving head was blowing cool gusts of air across the wide bed made up with a taut white sheet and three pillows side by side.

'This is my room,' he said. 'Shall we lie down for an hour before dinner?'

Without waiting for a reply, he drew her inside and closed the door.


'Laura!'

As she had expected, James looked amazed to find her standing on his doorstep.

'Hello,' she said. 'May I come in?'

'Of course. What brings you to London?'

'Lady Carlyon is always urging me to take more time off so I thought I'd come up for some shopping and to see Sir John Soane's house. I'm trying to do some of the things I neglected to do when I lived here. It was you who put me on to the Soane museum.'

'Why didn't you let me know? I'd have come with you.'

'I thought you would probably be busy . . . as you may be this evening.'

'Not at all. Where are you staying?'

'Where I stayed last time. I haven't been to London since you took me to *Heat Wave*.'

They had mounted the stairs and were entering the drawing room.

'Let me take your coat,' said James.

'Thank you.' She undid the buttons. 'I'm glad I found you in. I have . . . a favour to ask.'

'You must know if I can help you in any way I shall be delighted,' he said. 'But first let me get you a drink. What would you like? Sherry? Wine? Something stronger?'

'Definitely something stronger. I think I need a stiff gin and tonic before I tell you how I want you to help me.'

'Really? That makes it sound as if I may have been reckless in promising to help you,' he said, smiling.

'Surely it's always reckless to agree to something before you know what it is.'

'With some people – yes, extremely. Not with you. You are eminently trustworthy, Laura.'

'Thank you. I hope so. I feel the same about you. In fact you're the only person in the world of whom I could ask this.'

'Really? How flattering.' He brought the gin and tonic to where she was standing by one of the windows overlooking Connaught Square. He had made another for himself. 'So what is it you want me to do?'

'Before I tell you, I'd like to explain something. It's been some time since we talked and I think I've changed a good deal since our last proper conversation. A year ago . . . even six months ago . . . I should never have dreamt of coming here, uninvited, to ask you to do . . . this thing for me. When I started working for Lady Carlyon, I was terribly lacking in self-confidence. I was more like a very young girl than a mature woman. I think I've matured a good deal since then. I certainly mean to live the second half of my life much more courageously than the first half.'

He smiled at her. 'I doubt if you ever lacked courage, Laura. Self-confidence – yes. But courage lies dormant in some very quiet, unassertive people. Sometimes, when the need arises, they acquit themselves a great deal better than the people who stride through life with no moments of self-doubt. Let's sit down, shall we?'

Taking her lightly by the elbow, he steered her to a three-seater sofa where Laura sat down at one end and James settled himself at the other, the width of the centre cushion between them.

'I don't suppose you've seen much of Lady Carlyon's baby or Sarah's, have you?' she said.

'I haven't seen much of the Carlyons' infant. Sarah's baby is often in the stableyard. It seems a good-tempered little thing. I've never heard it bawling,' he said.

'No, Thomas hardly ever cries. Simon is the noisy one. I never had anything to do with babies until they arrived. I find I like them very much. I'd like to have one of my own. But I haven't got very much time left. Possibly only a few years. That's what I've come to ask you. Would you . . . would you be willing to father a child for me?'

Rehearsing what to say beforehand, she had thought she might stutter or blush. But apart from one slight hesitation, she had felt surprisingly calm. It was James who looked startled and embarrassed.

After staring at her for some moments, a dark flush appearing on his cheekbones, he jumped to his feet and started to pace about the room.

'I don't think you've thought this out, Laura. What you suggest is . . . impossible.'

'I don't see why,' she said quietly. 'Unless you find me unattractive. I thought you were . . . rather fond of me.'

'I am . . . more than fond. I love you . . . too much to agree to this mad idea. I don't know what put it into your head, but – '

'Simon and Thomas put it into my head. I suddenly realised that even if marriage is out of the question for me, having a baby isn't.'

'Marriage isn't out of the question for you. What

about this man you met at Christmas? How do you know he won't ask you to marry him?'

'As it happens he already has and I've explained why I can't. I don't love him.' She rose and went to him. 'How can you suggest that I should marry someone else when the only man I care for is you? That would really be madness! James, don't shake your head and scowl. Listen to me. Had this happened twenty or thirty years ago, there would have been no hope for me. Respectable unmarried women didn't have babies in those days. But now they do – if they want to. People do whatever they like. Which can be a bad thing, of course, but not in this case. What harm can there be in having a child? Lady Carlyon won't throw up her hands in horror. I know there's a place for me at Longwarden as long as I want it.'

She was standing close to him, but not touching him. James has his hands in his pockets and she had the feeling they were tightly clenched. She felt his whole body was tense with resistance to what he saw as a totally insane proposition.

The strange thing was that all the last lingering doubts she had had about it had evaporated as soon as she put it to him. Now she felt certain this was the right, the only way out of the impasse.

Moving closer, putting her hands lightly on his chest, she said, 'It may make a difference if I tell you that you wouldn't be my first lover. You are the first man I've loved, but when I was in my twenties, I thought myself in love with someone else. In fact it was only a short-lived infatuation and, on his side, not even that. He was amusing himself. So you see you wouldn't be seducing me. That was done a long time ago.'

'Oh Laura . . . Laura . . .' He put his hands over hers, his eyes showing the strong emotions he was trying his best to repress. 'How *can* I do what you ask?' His voice had a desperate ring. 'To have a child with you but not

600

to marry you . . . it's unthinkable. What sort of rat do you take me for?'

She pulled her hands free and backed away. 'You think it's the thin end of the wedge . . . a scheme to make you change your mind . . . but it isn't. It isn't, James. Truly. I would never try to persuade you to go against your conscience. That would be cruel and wicked of me. Surely you know I wouldn't do that?'

'Yes,' he said, 'yes, of course I know it, Laura. You're honesty personified. But what would it do to my conscience to stand by while you had my child and not to acknowledge that it was mine . . . not to marry you. I couldn't do it.'

'But I should be the only person who knew it was yours. No one else would. You and I stopped seeing each other – except on your days at Longwarden – months ago. It would probably be thought that the father was the man I met at Christmas, and why I chose not to marry him would be my business.'

'Are you sure you were right to refuse him? A good marriage is basically a close friendship, Laura. I'm not the only man who could make you happy, my dear. There are dozens who could. You've met so few men.'

'I've met the only one I want to be the father of my child. If you really do love me, how can you refuse me the one thing which could make up for everything else I've missed in life?' She darted back to him and flung her arms round him. 'Please, James . . . *please* . . . there's only a little time left.'

At first he tried to thrust her off, but she clung to him, all pride abandoned. She knew that the rest of her life depended on this desperate bid to salvage something from the waste of her love for him.

For a moment or two they struggled; James unable to use real force against a woman and Laura sure that really, deep down, he wanted and needed her as much as she wanted him.

601

Then, all at once, he was no longer trying to put her away from him but was crushing her painfully close, kissing her with a famished urgency which once would have terrified her but to which, now, she responded with relief and joy.


In the early hours of the morning Allegra awoke and turned her head to look at the moonlit shape of the man lying motionless beside her.

Her reactions to what had occurred were not the remorse and disgust she had expected to experience when visualising this situation in Bangkok after first meeting Kit.

Instead she felt calm and at peace for the first time in almost a year. Making love with him had been quite different from making love with Andro; indeed different from anything in her previous experience.

Her only misgiving was the possibility that she might conceive. But it seemed extremely unlikely. She had always suspected that the abortion she had had years ago had damaged her insides, and the fact that she hadn't started a baby in Barbados, after stopping taking her contraceptive pills, had seemed to confirm that suspicion.

She thought Kit was asleep until he said quietly, 'When I was a monk we were woken by drums at four-thirty. When it was light enough for us to see the lines on the palms of our hands, we went out with our bowls to receive whatever food was given to us.'

'Did you have enough to eat?'

'Oh yes . . . people are generous with their alms.'

As he turned to her, raising himself on one elbow, she said, 'You never showed me the photograph of yourself in the saffron robe. I can't imagine you with a shaven head.'

She lifted her hand to stroke his thick silky black hair.

Kit leaned over her for a long time, gazing deeply into her eyes. Then he began again the slow subtle caresses, prolonging her pleasure and his for so long that when it was over the moonlight had gone and it was dawn.


Allegra stood on the verandah, wrapped in a sarong, watching a man crossing the field below the house.

He was carrying a long piece of bamboo with a rag of cloth tied to the end of it. Behind him waddled a flock of slim, long-necked ducks, some white and some brown and grey. At the far end of the field he stuck the long cane in the earth and went away, leaving the ducks behind.

'They will stay there all day, never straying far from the flag, until he or one of his children comes to fetch them home for the night,' said Kit, coming out of the room behind her.

He too was wearing a sarong wrapped round his hips. He put his arms round her.

'No regrets?'

'Regrets? For one of the most wonderful nights of my life?' She reached up to take his face between her hands and draw it down to hers.


Damaris woke and knew instantly that she was alone. Sam had gone out on one of his nocturnal prowls.

He was making an insomniac of her. It was becoming a habit for her to wake in the small hours and, even when he was beside her, to lie awake wondering and worrying.

Half the time she was ecstatically happy, finding in her marriage all the love and companionship she had always longed for. Sam had wiped out forever the remembered horror and degradation of Kevin's assault on her. It was as if it had happened to someone else, not to her.

But now a different and more terrifying nightmare had replaced the bad memory from her teens. This wasn't something which had happened, but something which might. The uncertainty was tearing her apart.

There being no possibility of going back to sleep while he was out, and probably not for a long time after he came back, she got up to make some tea.

She was waiting for the kettle to boil, when she heard a sound in the distance which made her hold her breath, petrified with dread.


'What the hell . . . ?'

North sat up in bed, roused by a noise which, in the confusion of a sudden awakening, he couldn't be sure he wasn't dreaming.

His movement and exclamation woke Jane, lying close beside him.

'What is it? What's the matter?' she asked drowsily.

'Can't you hear it? That's a police or fire siren . . . and it's coming up the drive.' As he spoke he switched on the light and she saw him spring out of bed and snatch at his trousers. He never wore pyjamas but always kept a pair of trousers close by, a habit formed on expeditions to wild parts of the world.

'What time is it?' Still half asleep and blinking, Jane couldn't see the clock.

'Just gone quarter past three,' said North, pulling up his zipper. 'I can't think of any reason why the police should come here with their siren blasting at this time of night. That means it's the fire brigade. Some part of the building is on fire. Put some shoes on and something warm. We may have to spend the rest of the night in the garden. Hurry it up, there's a good girl. I'm going to sound our alarm. I'll be right back.'

As Jane flung aside the bedclothes and scrambled out of bed, she saw him go to the door and test first the wood and then the handle before gripping it and opening the door a few inches.

No smoke or smell of smoke entered the bedroom from the landing. North reached for the light switch outside their door. After taking a look in both directions along the now illuminated corridor, he called to her, 'There's no sign of fire in this part of the house yet but let's not take any chances. Get dressed as fast as you can.'

Jane was scrambling into suitable clothes when the clangour of Longwarden's alarm bells began to resound from all parts of the house, waking everyone in it who had not been disturbed by the siren.

'But if someone here sent for the fire brigade, why didn't they also sound the alarm?' she exclaimed, when North, having been to his bedroom by way of the landing, came back to her room, fully dressed, through the ante-room.

By this time she was warmly wrapped and shod and was busy bundling up Simon who still slept in a cot on the far side of their room except if they went out at night expecting to come home late. Then he slept in the night nursery which adjoined Morag's room and, if he woke, his nanny attended to him.

Although given to bellowing during the day if his needs were not instantly supplied, he no longer needed to be fed during the night hours. Jane was still nursing him by day and intended to continue until late April when he would be six months old. Even now, if she wanted to go out for the day, he accepted being bottle fed by Morag. Although not as placid as Thomas, he wasn't a difficult baby. Wrapping him up had woken him but he didn't immediately start grizzling.

'God knows! We'll find that out later. Come on: we'll let the firemen in – if they haven't already broken their way in,' he said, taking the baby from her and hurrying into the corridor.

However when they got downstairs the great double doors which were the main entrance to the house were still intact and as North opened them the noise of the fire alarm, which had only just stopped, was replaced by another cacophony – the burglar alarm.

North swore at forgetting to turn it off before opening the doors. 'Take the baby outside and stay there,' he told her firmly. 'I'll go back and round up the others.'

As she hurried across the portico and down the steps it was soon clear why the firemen had not been pounding for admittance at the main door. Already, by the light of powerful spotlights, they had run a long ladder to the top floor. A fireman was breaking into a window which would give them much closer access to the flames burning fiercely inside one of the attics.

'*Oh no!*' Jane exclaimed in dismay, gazing appalled at the fire raging in a room she hadn't had time to go through yet.

The thought of all the priceless things – in historic terms, not in monetary value – which might already have burned and were being burned at this moment filled her with almost physical pain. At this point, perhaps affected by her distress, Simon began to howl. She was rocking him, murmuring words of reassurance, when a police car came streaking up the drive, its blue light flashing. As it stopped in a flurry of gravel, three policemen scrambled out, two in uniform, one in plain clothes.

The latter came over to her. 'Lady Carlyon? I'm Detective Inspector Gunton. Is your husband about?'

'He's gone back inside. He brought me out and went back to get everyone else out. My sister-in-law is abroad and my husband's cousin and her baby sleep in a room above the archway to the stables. Our baby's nanny and my secretary are the only people sleeping in our wing.

Here comes my secretary now. Inspector . . . who called you here? How did you know we were on fire?'

'There was a 999 call from an unidentified person to say there was someone up to no good in your attics. That's all we know at the moment. Would you like to sit in the car, Lady Carlyon? You and the baby will be warmer there.'

'Thank you, but I'm not cold at the moment.' As Laura joined them, Jane said, 'Did you see North on your way down? Where's Morag?'

'She'll be here very soon. Lord Carlyon was coming to bang on my door but I met him in the corridor. I shouldn't think anyone could sleep through the noise of the alarm. Would it be a good idea if I fetched Simon's pram from the cloakroom? With the firemen getting here so quickly, it's very unlikely the fire will spread beyond the attics, don't you think?' said Laura, addressing the Inspector.

'Yes, but I'd rather you stayed here, madam, for the moment. It isn't only the fire we have to worry about. There's a possibility that, if this is arson, the man we want is still in there. If he is, he'll be desperate to get out without being caught. It wouldn't do for you to run into him. Ah, there's Lord Carlyon now.'

He left them, taking the steps two at a time to meet North who had just appeared under the portico with Morag beside him.

She hurried down to join Jane. 'As soon as I was dressed, I went to your room but you had already gone. I thought you might need some more warm things so I brought these,' she said, indicating the rug, shawl and two thick sweaters over her arm.

'Take Simon and go and sit in the back of the police car, would you, Morag,' said Jane. 'Here comes another police car . . . heavens! Three of them. But how many men will they need to block every possible way out? A lot more than these reinforcements, I should have thought. Ah, here come Sarah and Kate...and Damaris, but not Sam. Where's he got to?'

Before the three girls were close enough for her to ask, another vehicle with flashing lights appeared in the wake of the fourth police car. Another fire engine was arriving and, behind it, a Range Rover with FIRE SERVICE in large black letters on a fluorescent orange stripe along its side.

By now the sweep in front of the house was ablaze with light and full of people, while high above them the fire still burned but seemed not to be spreading beyond the attic where it had started and the one next to it.

'Are you all right, darling? Warm enough?' North asked, coming back to Jane.

'Yes... fine. Where is Flitton? Have you seen him?'

'Not yet. But don't worry. They've got the fire under control. We're not going to go up in flames lock, stock and barrel. A couple of attics don't matter.'

'This unknown man who dialled 999... why didn't he give his name? Could it have been Flitton?'

'Could have been, I suppose. Not like Flitton to get flustered though, no matter what the emergency. They're still trying to trace where the call came from.'

'Lord Carlyon...'

It was a senior-looking officer from the fire service, Jane saw, who wanted to speak to her husband.

North turned to him. 'Yes?'

'It will be all right for Lady Carlyon and these other ladies to wait inside the main entrance. We can't let them go back to their rooms yet, but there's no need to keep them out of doors any longer. I expect they'd like to sit down.'

'I'm sure they would,' North agreed. 'All right everyone... you can go back to the hall but nowhere else in the house. As soon as we can we'll lay on some tea and brandy. Make sure no one goes wandering off, Jane. The police think they've finally got the arsonist

608

cornered. But in a house of this size it could take time to winkle him out of wherever he's hiding.'

In the white glare of the spotlights, everyone had looked pale-faced. In the warmer lights of the hall, faces resumed their normal colours. Only Damaris still looked ashen.

'Are you feeling all right?' Jane asked her.

With everyone else taking the situation in their stride, she was surprised that Damaris should look strained.

'Yes, thank you.'

Jane remembered that she hadn't seen Sam.

'Where's Sam?'

'Somewhere about . . . I'm not sure.'

Her tone made Jane wonder if they had had a row yesterday and gone to bed still on bad terms. But surely being woken up by the fire alarm would have put an end to any quarrel they had had.

She became aware that a hush had fallen and everyone was looking towards the staircase.

Coming down the stairs, surrounded by policemen, were Sam and her butler. Sam was bleeding from an ugly gash on his forehead. Flitton, although somewhat dishevelled, looked as composed as he always did.

A horrible possibility was beginning to dawn in Jane's mind when North and a grey-haired police officer came in from the portico and saw the group descending the staircase.

As they reached the foot of the staircase, the police sergeant next to Sam said, 'We've got him, sir.'

There was a moment of tense silence.

'Look out . . . she's going over.'

It was Sam who shouted, and Laura who managed to grab Damaris before she fell.


When Damaris opened her eyes, she was lying down in

609

an unfamiliar room with Jane and Laura leaning over her.

'Don't worry. . . you fainted,' said Jane. 'But it's all right . . . everything's fine. The fire is under control and Sam is a hero. But for him it might have been much worse. He'll be here as soon as he's had the cut on his face dressed.'

Damaris tried to sit up but was gently prevented.

'Sam is a hero? I – I don't understand.'

'He'll tell you what happened himself. We don't know the details,' said Jane. 'All we know is that Flitton started it and Sam caught him in the act.'

'*Flitton?* I can't believe it.'

'Nor can I, but it seems to be true. The police are questioning him now.' As the door opened, Jane glanced over her shoulder. 'Here's Sam.' She rose from her kneeling position beside the *duchesse brisée* where Damaris was lying.

As Sam took her place, the gash on his forehead taped and the blood on his cheek wiped away, he said, 'Are you all right, darling? You gave me a scare suddenly toppling over like that.'

'I'm fine. Are *you* all right? Is it true that Flitton – ?'

He nodded. 'Yes, it's true. He set the fire. I can't explain it all now. They want me to make a statement. I'm sorry I gave you a scare . . . not showing up when the fire alarm went. I was upstairs, getting my brains damn nearly bashed out by Flitton. That guy is a serious nut case.'

He bent over and kissed her. 'You just take it easy. I'll be back as soon as I can.'


It was half past five in the morning when North returned to Jane's bedroom. She had gone back to bed some time earlier but wasn't asleep.

As her husband looked towards the cot, she said, 'No

need to whisper. He's finishing what's left of the night in the nursery. Are you exhausted? I hope not. I can't wait to hear what's been going on downstairs.'

'It seems we've been harbouring a maniac – although he seems to see himself as the instrument of Divine wrath,' said North. 'Flitton denies being behind *all* the fires in this area during the time he's been with us, but he's admitted to burning the cottage owned by the two queers, and to destroying two large houses in other parts of the country. He's not only a fire freak but frighteningly expert. If Sam hadn't stopped him, Longwarden might be in cinders like the other houses.'

'How did Sam stop him?'

'He was walking about outside, grappling with some problem to do with his private life, when he happened to look up and notice a light in the attics. He guessed that it had to be either a burglar or the arsonist so he let himself into the house by the door Sarah would use if she needed to get in during the night, turned off the delayed-alarm which rings if someone unauthorised uses it, and made a 999 call. Then he belted upstairs and was just too late to stop Flitton starting a fire designed to incinerate the entire building.'

'Why? What was his motive? He might have killed us!'

'I don't think that was his object. It was punishment, not murder he had in mind. According to him, all the houses he's burned have been owned by sinners. He particularly loathes homosexuals. We haven't got any of them here as far as I know, but we have got an unmarried mother, two people of low moral fibre – myself and Allegra – and someone who spends her money on swimming pools and other self-indulgent extravagances rather than good works. Meaning you, my love. I was there while he justified himself and a pretty decadent lot he made us sound.'

'How unfair . . . and how creepy to realise that all this

611

time he's been hating and despising us, and planning to destroy all the things I thought he cared about and would guard with his life,' said Jane, with a shiver. 'He had impeccable references and I checked them all out.'

'Not all his previous employers were as sinful as us, I suppose. Anyway he'll end up in Broadmoor and his trial will give the tabloids their third major Longwarden scandal in twelve months. Let's hope our run of bad luck is over for a bit and we can now look forward to a period of peace and quiet,' North said, with feeling.

'*Ohmygod!*' Allegra jack-knifed into a sitting position. 'What date is it, Kit?' she asked urgently.

He stretched a long golden arm for the watch he had taken off before they lay down.

On hearing the date, she gave a deep sigh of relief. 'For a ghastly moment I visualised Elliott arriving, finding no message and flying into a panic that something bad must have happened to me.'

She sank back on the fitted and therefore still smooth percale sheet on which, until seconds ago, she had been in a peaceful torpor.

'Who is this Elliott? I don't like the sound of him,' said Kit.

'Elliott Lincoln, my American publisher. He's stopping off here for a night or two, on his way home from the Philippines, to talk about my next book.'

'Can't you telex him not to come . . . tell him you're busy researching?'

'Don't know where he is.'

'His office will know. American businessmen never travel without leaving copious instructions to cover all eventualities.'

'Mm . . . could do that, I suppose. But I don't think I should. He's been awfully sweet and "caring" since . . .'

Since what she left unspecified. 'It wouldn't be kind to upset his carefully planned schedule.'

'Where are you supposed to leave a message for him?' Kit asked, raising himself on one elbow and leaning over to tuck a stray strand of hair behind her ear.

'I've forgotten the name of the hotel. It's in my address book. It's at Nusa Dua . . . wherever that may be.'

'It's where he would stay,' said Kit, smiling.

'What do you mean?'

He traced the line of her cheekbone with the tip of his finger. 'Nusa Dua is Bali but not Bali. It's where all the fat cats stay.'

'Elliott isn't a fat cat. He's an interesting man . . . you'll like him.'

As she spoke, she knew it wasn't true. Kit and Elliott were not kindred spirits and her publisher might not approve of her new relationship. Even if he were no longer interested in her himself, as a woman, he might see Kit as a threat to her future as a writer. She did herself, but didn't care.

'I don't want to meet him,' said Kit. 'Those two vast hotels at Nusa Dua depress me. They're Hollywood's idea of luxury. One of them is built like a temple with a split gate. They both have enormous swimming pools with pool-bars and the grounds are full of overweight bodies, most of them long past the age for lying about half-naked.' His fingertip paused at the little dent in her chin before sliding down her long throat to the hollow at the base of it.

'If they're really horrible places, perhaps I should get him a cottage at Poppies.'

'I shouldn't do that. Poppies doesn't have a swimming pool yet. He won't be happy without a pool. He may like it at Nusa Dua. Some people do. But it's not my kind of place . . . or yours either.' His finger continued down the line of her sternum and detoured round her

613

left breast. 'I prefer a more intimate atmosphere. Both the hotels at Nusa Dua are basically five-star battery houses. There's also a vast Club Med down there on the Bukit peninsula. It was empty land, no good for agriculture. So they built a fast road from the airport and made it a tourist enclave named after two offshore islands . . . *nusa* island . . . *dua* two.' His lips made a figure of eight round her breasts.

She closed her eyes and, for the time being, forgot about her publisher.

'Elliott – how are you?'

Allegra offered him her cheek. Although until his flight landed his visit had seemed a nuisance, now he was here she was pleased to see him.

'I'm fine – and you look great. I can see that the tropics suit you. It's good to see you again. We've got a lot to talk about.'

'Good God! Is all this your luggage?' she asked, seeing his porter's laden trolley.

'Mostly stuff from Hong Kong which is a great place to shop. Is that a Balinese outfit you're wearing?'

'It is – put on specially for you. I've been living in shorts and sarongs most of the time.'

To meet him she had put on a full *batik* skirt from Studio Lala with a plain cream cotton-knit halter which showed off her tan.

Dropped at the airport twenty minutes earlier by Kit, she had expected to leave it in a taxi, but Elliott's hotel had sent a limousine to meet him. Had he reserved the presidential suite? she wondered, watching him supervise the stowage of his expensive luggage.

'No need for you to stand around in this heat, Allegra.' He took his eyes off his bags long enough to usher her into the back of the air-conditioned car.

'I'm acclimatised now . . . and you're wearing too many clothes,' she said, when he joined her, looking hot.

'You're right.' He took off the coat of his tropic-weight suit, but he didn't discard his tie or roll up his shirt sleeves. She couldn't imagine her brother travelling in formal clothes, but North put comfort above everything and travelled round the world with a minimum of baggage apart from essential photographic equipment.

'Who's that?' asked Elliott, seeing the statue outside the airport.

Earlier she had asked Kit the same question. Arriving in Bali after dark, she hadn't noticed the commanding figure of the young army officer the first time she passed it.

'It's Lieutenant-Colonel I Gusti Ngurah Rai, the leader of the people's army against the Japanese during the war and the Dutch when they tried to take over again after the war. His slogan was "freedom or death". He was killed in the battle of Marga in 1946 and every November they have a Hero's Day for him. All Balinese have a caste title. I Gusti means that he belonged to the warrior class. The airport is called Ngurah Rai after him.'

'I can see that you're going to be an excellent guide to the island in the short time I'm here,' said Elliott, smiling at her.

'I shouldn't think you're much interested in Balinese history, but after being in Thailand where they cleverly managed to avoid being conquered and ruled by the West, what happened here is fascinating to me.'

'What did happen here? Give me a résumé.'

As he had when they first met in New York, and later in London before he discovered she was in love with Andro, Elliott was looking at her with more than ordinary warmth. She had an uneasy feeling he thought the time had come to try to advance their relationship beyond its present publisher-author limit.

She said, 'The Rajas of Bali had always believed that a ship which was wrecked on the reefs was a gift from the gods. They took everything they could salvage, including the crew and any passengers. The Dutch didn't like it when one of their ships was plundered. They wanted to take over Bali. When persuasion failed, they sent an expeditionary force. Their campaigns to subdue the Balinese went on from 1846 to the beginning of this century. Then the whole thing came to a head in 1906 when the sixth Dutch military expedition landed at Sanur Beach which is now the main tourist resort.'

'I would have thought with their more modern arms the Dutch could have licked the natives in a week,' said Elliott.

'They did win most of the battles and the Balinese always suffered horrendous casualties. But what happened eventually was that, feeling their cause was lost, the Rajas and their courts decided on *puputan* – mass suicide. They dressed in white, as for a cremation, and put on their jewels and gold ornaments. Then, in front of the Dutch, they killed themselves. Husbands killed their wives, mothers their children. The ground was piled high with corpses. It must have been ghastly.' She shuddered.

'It's happened elsewhere,' said Elliott. 'The people of Masada threw themselves off a cliff rather than surrender to the Romans.'

She found his detachment irritating. 'At least it wasn't a useless sacrifice. It did make the Dutch government more considerate. They wouldn't let Big Business in, as they had in Java, and they actually encouraged Balinese customs and culture.'

Suddenly she regretted not leaving a message at Elliot's hotel to tell him she had left Bali. Already her pleasure at seeing him had evaporated. Everything about him seemed alien to the life she had been leading with Kit. She was more certain than ever that when they met, as they must, they wouldn't get on, might not even be civil to each other.

She wished that instead of being in this ridiculous car she was back at the house, sitting on a cushion, peacefully reading or meditating while Kit performed *t'ai chi ch'uan* the gracefully Chinese callisthenics which were more like the movements of a ballet than exercises.


Having discovered that Sam didn't know the real reason why she had fainted – he thought it had been from a combination of worry about where he was and the sight of the gash on his forehead – Damaris had decided to keep the truth to herself. She felt it might not be easy for him to forgive her for suspecting him of a crime which, she realised now, was completely foreign to his nature however strongly the evidence had seemed at one time to point to him.

Now that his grandfather's illness had confined him to bed, with a nurse in attendance, the problem of whether, when the old man died, Sam should continue the life he had made for himself or take over the reins for his grandmother had become more pressing.

It had been a letter from her, appealing to him to go back, which had been on his mind the night of the fire.

Damaris was trying not to influence him either way. She wasn't sure how much, if anything, his inheritance meant to him. For her own part she much preferred the west of England to the bleak flat landscapes of East Anglia even though they were said to have a charm all their own when one knew them well.

She hadn't liked his grandparents' house or their garden, exposed and on heavy clay soil. She would have liked to continue working at Longwarden, particularly if they could find a freehold cottage of their own somewhere near.

But for Sam to be happy was the most important

thing. She couldn't be happy if he wasn't. In the same way that he had helped her to come to terms with her past, she wanted to take the sting out of his memories and make them seem unimportant.

'The main snag is lack of money,' he said, not for the first time, when they were discussing the problem. 'A large house and garden without an income to match is no end of a headache. It appears that the old man has been cutting into his capital. There's precious little left. Which means that if we take over, we're going to have endless problems making ends meet. Here we have virtually no problems. Is it worth it, I ask myself?'

'I don't know. It's impossible for me to grasp what family roots mean to people who have them,' she answered. 'I have no idea who my father was. I wish I didn't know who my mother was. Until I fell in love with you, I had no roots or ties of any kind. You are my sheet anchor now and wherever you want to be is where I want to be.'

Sam glanced at the clock. 'I think we should both be in bed.'

An hour later they fell asleep in each other's arms, the question of their future still unsettled.


'Has he told you he's married?'

Allegra tried not to show how deeply Elliott's question had shaken her.

Not only had she *not* known that Kit was married; it hadn't even occurred to her that he might be. From the first she had thought he was single; as free from all ties as she had been before Andro and now was again.

'How come *you* know that, Elliott?' she asked, raising her eyebrows.

'I called my office and made some enquiries about him. He's been married ten years to a cousin. Her name is Laksami. They have two young sons and a daughter aged four. But perhaps you knew that?'

If he had leaned across the table and struck her she couldn't have been more shocked. Why hadn't Kit told her? How could he have kept it from her?

Anger boiled up inside her; anger at him for deceiving her, anger at herself for letting him. How could she have been so naïve?

Mingled with her anger was the humiliation of finding out in this manner.

'Do you always make "enquiries" about the people you meet?' she asked coldly.

'If they interest me – yes.' Elliott shrugged. 'Why not? In this case it crossed my mind that there might be a book to be written about the descendants of Anna's King of Siam. It's an idea which may not come to anything, but as you have a contact at the Thai Court it seemed something to think about.'

It was a plausible explanation but Allegra didn't believe it. She felt sure he had had Kit checked out for personal reasons and in the hope of finding something to his discredit. She had sensed Elliott's antipathy from the moment she introduced them.

'Pity you didn't check out Anna Leonowens,' she said tartly. 'She's persona non grata in Thailand. Any mention of *The King and I* will kill your idea stone dead.'

'I've upset you. I'm sorry. But it's better you find out now than later, Allegra. The Prince hadn't told you he was married, had he?'

Wanting to tell him sharply to mind his own business, she forced herself to say quietly, 'I value your advice about my professional life, Elliott, but I can manage my private life. I'm not twenty or even twenty-five. My experience of life is quite extensive.'

'I'm aware of that,' he said, nodding. 'I'm also aware of the pressures on you. You've been through a bad experience. You're hurt and you're lonely, my dear.

That makes you especially vulnerable. I don't want to see you involved in something you'll regret . . . which can only lead to more pain for you.'

She was tempted to say: It's too late. I'm involved already. All you've done, by interfering, is to spoil my fool's paradise sooner than if you hadn't come to Bali.

As he could only guess how far things had gone, she saw no reason to confirm his speculations.

'I appreciate your concern, but you really needn't worry about me, Elliott. As for your book idea, I'll ask Kit what he thinks, if you like? I do know that one of the present King's daughters, Princess Shulabhorn, is a scientist married to a military pilot.'

'That idea is not as important as finding you a subject which you can get fired up about. Why not return to Europe via New York so that we can talk again?'


'Is it true that you have a wife and three small children?' Allegra asked.

Because Kit was so unlike all the men she had known before, she hadn't been able to guess how he would react. How *did* most men react? With anger? With guilt? She had never before been involved with a married man whose relationship with his wife wasn't already irretrievably damaged, known to be on the rocks.

'Yes . . . it's true,' he said gravely.

There was neither anger nor guilt in his expression, only a look of sadness.

'Don't you think you should have told me?'

'If I had, we shouldn't have had this time of great happiness together.'

'Happiness for us . . . great unhappiness for your wife if she knew you had spent two weeks with another woman. Oh Kit . . . I thought you were such a wonderful man . . . wise . . . self-disciplined . . . good. I can't bear finding out that you aren't. Please don't trot out the tired old excuses ... that she's cold ... she doesn't understand you. That would be the last straw.'

'My wife isn't cold and we understand each other very well. But it may be difficult for you to understand the nature of our relationship. Ours is a marriage of mutual convenience. We didn't marry for love and as long as I am discreet and don't embarrass her, my wife has no objection to my having other relationships which supply needs she cannot satisfy.'

'How can you say that? What makes you think she doesn't mind? That's an excuse if ever I heard one,' she said angrily.

'No: it's the truth. Laksami knew before we married that I wasn't likely to be sexually faithful to her. Unlike English and American women she doesn't see sex as the most important aspect of a man and woman's relationship. To her it's only a small and relatively trivial side of marriage. Once they are used to each other, how much time do most husbands and wives spend making love? Comparatively little. They spend far more time eating together and talking about the upbringing of their children and other domestic matters. For a Thai woman of Laksami's class and temperament, her children are her greatest joy. As long as her husband is kind and generous, she doesn't demand that he never looks at another woman.'

'And are you equally unconcerned about her affairs with other men?' she asked sarcastically.

'I'm not sure how I should feel if she wanted another man, but I don't think it will ever happen. She's entirely contented with her life. She has many friends of her own sex. They spend hours gossiping and shopping. They don't suffer from the frustrations which plague women in the West.'

'I wonder?' Allegra said sceptically. 'I wonder if you really know what goes on in your wife's mind? Anyway,

I don't care for being a married man's mistress – not while his marriage still works.'

'But you aren't my mistress,' said Kit. 'That's a word which implies a permanent liaison with the man providing some return for favours received. Our relationship isn't like that. We are merely two people from different worlds whose paths have crossed and who have something to give each other. Is it wrong for us to enrich our lives for a short time? I don't believe it is. Giving love to another human being can never be wrong, Allegra. It's only when love is given and received at someone else's expense that it becomes immoral. We aren't hurting Laksami, I promise you.'

'I don't believe that,' she said. 'The fact that you're here with me instead of with her makes it wrong.'

'I'm often away. She accepts my absences without complaint. She knows I'm too restless to stay in Bangkok all the time. I've always spent weeks, sometimes even months away from her.'

'It's no use arguing about it, Kit. As far as I'm concerned our affair is over . . . finished. I'm leaving Bali as soon as I can get a flight out.'

'Very well . . . if that's how you feel, I won't try to persuade you to stay. Who told you I was married?'

'Elliott.'

'Ah . . . so I was right. He wants you for himself and will go to considerable lengths to discredit all his rivals. What is his marital status?'

'He's divorced.'

'Are there children?'

'Yes. His wife has custody, he has access. I don't know whose fault it was.'

'If, one day, you find out he was unfaithful to his wife, will you cut him out of your life?' Kit asked.

'That's entirely different. He's my publisher, not my lover.'

'He would like to be both . . . and your husband as

well. But he wouldn't suit you. I don't suppose he realises it, but he's written himself off by telling tales about me. The British can't stand a sneak. Also, subconsciously, you'll blame him for putting an end to our happiness here.'

'I blame you for that,' she said crisply. 'And myself, for being taken in by you. I'm old enough to have known better.'

'But you don't deny that we've been very happy together?'

'No, I can't deny that,' she agreed, in a low voice.

'Then you should thank me,' he said. 'When you came to Bangkok you were very unhappy. That first day at Jim Thompson's house, the Comtesse said to me, "It's curious to see a woman so young and beautiful with such despair in her face". I've cured that despair – admit it.'

'You may have made it worse. I shan't know till I've gone away . . . till I'm on my own again.'

'You'll be all right now,' he said confidently. 'It's a pity it has to end as suddenly and as soon as this, but we both knew it must end, didn't we?'

Did we? Did I? she wondered. It was hard to remember now what thoughts she had had at the beginning.

'Did it never occur to you that I might fall in love with you and be badly hurt?' she asked. 'Or refuse to accept my congé, when you tired of me, and make an embarrassing fuss?'

'I didn't consider either of those contingencies – or that I might fall in love with you,' he said, smiling faintly. 'That's what's happened, you know. I am in more pain than you are – and shall be for a long time. Perhaps for the rest of my life.'

'I don't believe it,' she said, startled and shaken. 'You're not in love with me.'

'I wish you were right, but I've known for some days my feelings about you are different from any previous experiences. *You* are different. I've never known a woman like you.'

Is he saying this to hold me until he's ready to end it? she wondered. Perhaps my chief difference from his other amours is that I'm walking out on him and he doesn't like it.

'I can see you think that's a line, but it isn't,' he told her. 'What began as an amusement has, for me, become serious. All the women in my life from now on will seem wanting compared with you. I didn't believe one woman could fulfil all a man's needs. I thought it an impossibility. I was wrong.'

'Those things are easy to say when you've already made it clear that you would never leave your wife for me,' she said dryly. 'Not that I want you to, but it would make no difference if I did, would it?'

'No, I shall never desert Laksami,' he agreed gravely.

'At least you're honest about that, but it wasn't honest to keep your mouth shut about her existence.'

'You could easily have found out about her. You chose not to enquire about my private life – either by asking me or someone else. Was that being honest?' he asked. 'We wanted each other and we were both prepared to suppress some scruples which might have got in the way. But it was more than simple lust which brought us together. There's been a communion of minds as well as a coupling of bodies. Isn't that true for you? It is for me.'

When she didn't answer, he stepped forward and took her by the shoulders. She tried to shake his hands off but his fingers tightened and he wouldn't let her go.

'I love you, Allegra. I mean it. Life is going to be difficult without you, but I don't regret the short time we've had together. Nor should you. In a world full of misery, all happiness must be good. Let's go our separate ways glad that we had this time together. Don't spoil it by parting angrily.'

'Oh Kit –' she said helplessly, unable to resist the appeal in his dark eyes.


'Laura seems on cloud nine at the moment,' Jane said to North.

'Perhaps a romance is blossoming between her and the doctor from Dorset. I hope I'm not going to have to find a replacement for her as well as for Flitton and, possibly, Joël Vibrac. Although he's still here, I think he's very unsettled and hankering for France.'

She had just returned to her bedroom after going downstairs in her dressing gown to fetch the mail and finding her secretary humming one of the hits from *Heat Wave*.

'Oh good, a letter from Allegra,' she said, spotting an airmail envelope with Indonesian stamps among the envelopes which Laura had already sorted into two baskets; one for letters from friends and relations and the other for advertising bumph, appeals from charities, private begging letters and anything else which looked unlikely to be urgent or interesting.

Normally early risers, today she and North were having a late breakfast together after an exceptionally enjoyable and prolonged dinner party in a village a few miles away.

'Would you like to read it first?' she asked, offering his sister's letter to him.

But he was already engrossed in *The Times*. 'No, no . . . go ahead.' It wasn't until he had finished reading the leaders that he looked across the table and asked, 'Does she say when she's coming back?'

'Not for a long time by the sound of it.' Jane had reached the letter's last paragraph. 'She says: *I want to see more of this part of the world. I may spend the rest of the year here. There is so much to see and to learn. Europe, from where I'm sitting – on a balcony overlooking a tropical garden and a calm blue sea – isn't alluring. So expect me when you see me, my dears, which may even be this time next year.'*

'I shouldn't mind being there myself,' said North, glancing out of the window at the steady drizzle which had been falling since they got up. 'It will do her good to wander around the Far East for a while.'

'I guess so, but we shall miss her.'

Sarah was in the stables, grooming Beddo after exercising him. It had taken almost five months for the scar tissue from the episiotomy to heal completely. But now she was once more comfortable in the saddle. She and the horses were in training for Badminton in April and her life had resumed the pattern interrupted by having Thomas.

He was starting to bear a marked resemblance to his father, his second growth of hair being brown like Nick's. Thomas was a constant reminder of her lost love. But never for a moment did she regret her decision to have him. Even North seemed fond of him now, and played with and cuddled him when she took Thomas into the house.

But most of his life was spent in the yard with her and the horses. Tatty seemed a bit jealous of him. When Sarah had introduced him to her, she had tossed up her head and snorted. Most babies would have been alarmed. Not Thomas. He had goggled at her with big long-lashed fascinated eyes. Predictably, Beddo's reaction had been gentler. Sarah had already got Kate to hand the baby up to her while she was riding Beddo and had taken him for his first short ride round the indoor school. She was looking forward to finding a suitable pony for him and teaching him to ride.

Allegra sat on a crate under an awning on the deck of a small cargo boat.

Some time later in the day – depending on the wind – the boat would arrive at a nameless speck on the map of the Flores Sea where she might or might not disembark.

She wasn't the only European on board. Two young bearded backpackers in tattered but clean jeans were also island-hopping. Later she would probably join in their exchange of travellers' tales, but for the moment she wanted to sit by herself and think about the man who had changed her ideas about life and death.

She was on the brink of believing that Andro Risconti hadn't perished forever in the wild waves off Bathsheba Beach but had merely, as Buddhists believed, entered a new phase of existence in the long progression towards enlightenment. Perhaps if she stayed in the East long enough, she would believe it without question, as Kit did.

Kit. Prince Kitayalongkorn.

Had he loved her? Perhaps. Had she loved him? She wasn't sure. Would they ever meet again? It seemed unlikely.

The only certainties were that, for a little while, they had been happy together and she would never forget him. Not only because he was a remarkable man but because, before the year ended, she would have a living reminder of their brief idyll.

Allegra thought of her much-travelled great-grand-father, Caspar Carlyon, and the letter, preserved in the archives at Longwarden, he had sent to Mrs St Leger, his widowed aunt, before returning to England with a bride who was barely seventeen and, on her mother's side, Chinese.

*I am bringing home someone who, at first, will need all your good will and forbearance*, he had written. *I know I can rely on your support not only in teaching her the ways of a world with which she is unfamiliar, but in defending her from the cattishness of that world. It may, indeed will be thought by many*

*people that I have acted rashly. Time will, I am confident,*
*disprove that view. In the meantime I ask you to suspend your*
*own judgement of my action and welcome her with the kindness*
*you have always shown to me.*

That letter would serve as a model for the one she
would write to North and Jane – if all went well, thought
Allegra.

The realisation that she had missed her period and
was almost certainly pregnant had not changed her mind
about continuing to travel. Somewhere, when the time
came, she would find a tranquil place where she could
have the child she had longed for so intensely at the
beginning of the year.

Well, her wish had been granted. Not in its original
form, but in a way which was not unacceptable. There
was already one exotic thread in the tangled skein of her
family's history. Why not another?

A stronger breeze had sprung up and the boat had
begun to move faster over the shimmering sea. One of
the two young men standing in the bows turned and
beckoned to her. When Allegra joined them she saw
that a small school of flying fish was alongside, some
skimming under the surface, some flashing through the
bright air.

The taller young man said, 'Amazing, aren't they?'
and then, 'Maybe we should introduce ourselves. I'm
Dick from Toronto and this is Mike from Christchurch,
New Zealand.'

'I'm Allegra from England.'

They shook hands.

'Where are you heading?' asked Mike.

She smiled and shrugged. 'I'll only know that when
I get there.'

# *EPILOGUE*

A report in *The Daily Telegraph*, August 1987.

## STATELY HOME ARSONIST JAILED FOR LIFE

A butler who destroyed two country houses and the weekend cottage of a television star, and attempted to burn down Longwarden, home of the Earl and Countess of Carlyon, was given a life sentence at Melchester Crown Court yesterday.

Alfred Ernest Flitton, 50, was convicted by a jury on three counts of arson and one of attempted arson between June 1981 and February 1987.

On the first charge, the court heard how Flitton set fire to and destroyed Thickthorn Manor following the death of its owner, Lady Boxgrove, widow of the late Sir Giles Boxgrove, because it was to have been inherited by her husband's nephew of whom the defendant disapproved.

Mr John Thetford, defending, told the jury that Flitton had been upset when a youth employed by Lady Boxgrove, whom the butler had been training, was persuaded to go to London by Mr Theo Boxgrove.

It was to the defendant's credit, said Mr Thetford, that while the manor was burning, at great personal risk he removed Lady Boxgrove's body and saved a number of valuable objects and paintings.

On the strength of his impeccable references, Flitton was then engaged by the 75 year old Dowager Marchioness of Wisbech, to whom he gave excellent service up to her death in 1986. She had left all her property to her grandson whom Flitton considered unworthy of her regard. That was his motive for burning down the Marchioness' house.

In 1986 he was engaged by the Earl and Countess of Carlyon to replace their former butler, at one time a colonel in the Army, after his marriage to the Earl's widowed mother. Although outbreaks of arson in Longwarden village and its environs began shortly after Flitton's arrival, most of these were relatively trivial and had been committed by a local youth who had been tried and found guilty in another court.

Mr Alan Devon, for the prosecution, said Flitton could not escape the consequence of his crimes by claiming diminished responsibility. He had been interviewed by two psychologists, both of whom considered him to be exceptionally intelligent. He was a disturbed personality but far from being insane. His motive for burning Longwarden was that, in his estimation, certain members of the Earl's family were unworthy of their privileged position. It was purely by chance that another of Lord Carlyon's employees had had his suspicions aroused and called the police and the fire brigade before Flitton could carry out his plan to burn Longwarden to the ground.

On being caught in the act of setting fire to the attics, he admitted his intention and told the police it was he who, a few months earlier, had caused the destruction of a cottage, formerly the property of the present Earl's father, then owned by a well-known television actor and his companion.

Flitton, said Mr Devon, showed no remorse for his crimes, the last of which, had it succeeded, would have destroyed one of England's finest historic houses and many priceless contents, and might have led to loss of life.

# AN INTERVIEW WITH ANNE WEALE

**Time and Chance is your third novel about an English stately home called Longwarden. Is there going to be a fourth book?**

I'm at work on it now. I hope there are going to be *many* more novels about Longwarden. A great country house is a microcosm of the world; all kinds of people live and work there and almost anything can happen. It gives me tremendous scope for exciting plots and interesting characters.

**Your novel *All My Worldly Goods* covered the dramatic events of one year at Longwarden from May 1985 to the spring of the following year?**

Yes, and *Time and Chance* continues the story for a further twelve months, but with the emphasis on a new cast of leading characters, so that it can be enjoyed by readers who haven't read *All My Worldly Goods*.

**But *Flora*, your first book about Longwarden, was a period piece, wasn't it?**

Yes, *Flora* opened in China in 1903 and then moved to Longwarden as it was in the so-called 'golden afternoon' of the Edwardian era.

**What is the title and the time span of the next book?**

*Past Forgetting*, and it covers twenty years from 1925 to the end of World War II. I want to recapture the mood of the Twenties and Thirties. My godmother was a débutante in the Twenties and some of my earliest memories are of the wonderful clothes she and my mother wore in the late Thirties. My teens coincided with the 'austerity clothing' and 'make do and mend' of the war and post-war years. Perhaps that's why I have a passion for lovely clothes now.

**Is Longwarden based on a real stately home?**

No, but it has features borrowed from several real houses. After *All My Worldly Goods* was published, the owner of a great house in Scotland wrote to tell me that he and his wife had enjoyed the book and they had a silver staircase like the one at Longwarden. He was most amused when I told him I'd heard of his staircase years before and 'borrowed' it for Longwarden.

**If it wasn't inspired by a real house, what was the genesis of Longwarden?**

I think it grew out of the years when, after I'd followed my husband to the Far East as a bride, we moved house seventeen times. Even now our life is split between winters in a valley in Spain and summers in the Channel Islands – as well as a lot of travelling because my characters don't spend *all* their time at Longwarden. I like to contrast the Englishness of Longwarden with more exotic settings. Part of me loves my rather nomadic life, and part of me longs for the sense of permanence one gets in a very old house where the attics are stuffed with the junk of many generations.

## I'm told you're a very disciplined person?

Not really. That's an impression given by the fact that when I'm writing I get up at 5.45 every morning, including Sunday, and write for at least an hour. Then I go for a brisk two mile walk before having breakfast and returning to my workroom. It sounds more disciplined than it is. I enjoy early rising. It suits me better than late nights. And I love writing. My workroom is a bit like a private cinema. First I switch on the computer, then I switch on my imagination and the story I'm writing continues like a very long movie being screened in my head. The tricky part is finding the right words to convey what I'm seeing with my mind's eye. That can be difficult.

## You don't agree with the authors who say writing is a lonely way of life?

How can it be lonely spending one's time with characters who are interesting people doing exciting things? In real life one sometimes has to suffer bores patiently, but not in fiction. Some of my characters are as dear to me as my close friends. Flora, who gave her name to the first Longwarden book, is one of them. I know a lot of readers liked her and will be pleased to see her re-appear in my next book *Past Forgetting* although it's really the story of Flora's daughter-in-law, Diana, and four other women who lived and loved between the wars.

# A Selection of Arrow Books

# Bestselling Fiction

| | | | |
|---|---|---|---|
| ☐ | No Enemy But Time | Evelyn Anthony | £2.95 |
| ☐ | The Lilac Bus | Maeve Binchy | £2.99 |
| ☐ | Prime Time | Joan Collins | £3.50 |
| ☐ | A World Apart | Marie Joseph | £3.50 |
| ☐ | Erin's Child | Sheelagh Kelly | £3.99 |
| ☐ | Colours Aloft | Alexander Kent | £2.99 |
| ☐ | Gondar | Nicholas Luard | £4.50 |
| ☐ | The Ladies of Missalonghi | Colleen McCullough | £2.50 |
| ☐ | Lily Golightly | Pamela Oldfield | £3.50 |
| ☐ | Talking to Strange Men | Ruth Rendell | £2.99 |
| ☐ | The Veiled One | Ruth Rendell | £3.50 |
| ☐ | Sarum | Edward Rutherfurd | £4.99 |
| ☐ | The Heart of the Country | Fay Weldon | £2.50 |

Prices and other details are liable to change

---

ARROW BOOKS, BOOKSERVICE BY POST, PO BOX 29, DOUGLAS, ISLE
OF MAN, BRITISH ISLES

NAME..................................................................................................

ADDRESS ............................................................................................

.............................................................................................................

.............................................................................................................

Please enclose a cheque or postal order made out to Arrow Books Ltd. for the amount
due and allow the following for postage and packing.

U.K. CUSTOMERS: Please allow 22p per book to a maximum of £3.00.

B.F.P.O. & EIRE: Please allow 22p per book to a maximum of £3.00.

OVERSEAS CUSTOMERS: Please allow 22p per book.

Whilst every effort is made to keep prices low it is sometimes necessary to increase cover
prices at short notice. Arrow Books reserve the right to show new retail prices on covers
which may differ from those previously advertised in the text or elsewhere.

# Bestselling General Fiction

| | | | |
|---|---|---|---|
| ☐ | No Enemy But Time | Evelyn Anthony | £2.95 |
| ☐ | Skydancer | Geoffrey Archer | £3.50 |
| ☐ | The Sisters | Pat Booth | £3.50 |
| ☐ | Captives of Time | Malcolm Bosse | £2.99 |
| ☐ | Saudi | Laurie Devine | £2.95 |
| ☐ | Duncton Wood | William Horwood | £4.50 |
| ☐ | Aztec | Gary Jennings | £3.95 |
| ☐ | A World Apart | Marie Joseph | £3.50 |
| ☐ | The Ladies of Missalonghi | Colleen McCullough | £2.50 |
| ☐ | Lily Golightly | Pamela Oldfield | £3.50 |
| ☐ | Sarum | Edward Rutherfurd | £4.99 |
| ☐ | Communion | Whitley Strieber | £3.99 |

Prices and other details are liable to change

---

ARROW BOOKS, BOOKSERVICE BY POST, PO BOX 29, DOUGLAS, ISLE
OF MAN, BRITISH ISLES

NAME.............................................................................................................

ADDRESS........................................................................................................

.......................................................................................................................

.......................................................................................................................

Please enclose a cheque or postal order made out to Arrow Books Ltd. for the amount
due and allow the following for postage and packing.

U.K. CUSTOMERS: Please allow 22p per book to a maximum of £3.00.

B.F.P.O. & EIRE: Please allow 22p per book to a maximum of £3.00.

OVERSEAS CUSTOMERS: Please allow 22p per book.

Whilst every effort is made to keep prices low it is sometimes necessary to increase cover
prices at short notice. Arrow Books reserve the right to show new retail prices on covers
which may differ from those previously advertised in the text or elsewhere.

# Bestselling Romantic Fiction

| | | |
|---|---|---|
| ☐ The Lilac Bus | Maeve Binchy | £2.99 |
| ☐ The Sisters | Pat Booth | £3.50 |
| ☐ The Princess | Jude Deveraux | £3.50 |
| ☐ A World Apart | Marie Joseph | £3.50 |
| ☐ Erin's Child | Sheelagh Kelly | £3.99 |
| ☐ Satisfaction | Rae Lawrence | £3.50 |
| ☐ The Ladies of Missalonghi | Colleen McCullough | £2.50 |
| ☐ Lily Golightly | Pamela Oldfield | £3.50 |
| ☐ Women & War | Janet Tanner | £3.50 |

Prices and other details are liable to change

---

ARROW BOOKS, BOOKSERVICE BY POST, PO BOX 29, DOUGLAS, ISLE OF MAN, BRITISH ISLES

NAME................................................................................................

ADDRESS ...........................................................................................

.........................................................................................................

.........................................................................................................

Please enclose a cheque or postal order made out to Arrow Books Ltd. for the amount due and allow the following for postage and packing.

U.K. CUSTOMERS: Please allow 22p per book to a maximum of £3.00.

B.F.P.O. & EIRE: Please allow 22p per book to a maximum of £3.00.

OVERSEAS CUSTOMERS: Please allow 22p per book.

Whilst every effort is made to keep prices low it is sometimes necessary to increase cover prices at short notice. Arrow Books reserve the right to show new retail prices on covers which may differ from those previously advertised in the text or elsewhere.